D1338097

DICK FRANCIS
Straight
Banker

GUILD PUBLISHING
LONDON · NEW YORK · SYDNEY · TORONTO

This OMNIBUS edition published 1990 by
Guild Publishing
by arrangement with Michael Joseph Ltd

Straight Copyright © 1989 by Dick Francis
Banker Copyright © 1982 by Dick Francis

Typeset by The Design Team, Ascot, Berks
Printed in Great Britain by
Mackays of Chatham PLC, Chatham, Kent

CONTENTS

Straight

My thanks especially to

JOSEPH and DANIELLE ZERGER
of ZARLENE IMPORTS
Dealers in semi-precious stones
and also to
MARY BROMILEY – ankle specialist
BARRY PARK – veterinary surgeon
JEREMY THOMPSON – doctor, pharmacologist
ANDREW HEWSON – literary agent

and as always to
MERRICK and FELIX our sons

All the people in this story are imaginary.
All the gadgets exist.

CHAPTER 1

I inherited my brother's life. Inherited his desk, his business, his gadgets, his enemies, his horses and his mistress. I inherited my brother's life, and it nearly killed me.

I was thirty-four at the time and walking about on elbow crutches owing to a serious disagreement with the last fence in a steeplechase at Cheltenham. If you've never felt your ankle explode, don't try it. As usual it hadn't been the high-speed tumble that had done the damage but the half-ton of one of the other runners coming over the fence after me, his forefoot landing squarely on my boot on the baked earth of an Indian summer. The hoof mark was imprinted on the leather. The doctor who cut the boot off handed it to me as a souvenir. Medical minds have a macabre sense of humour.

Two days after this occurrence, while I was reluctantly coming to terms with the fact that I was going to miss at least six weeks of the steeplechasing season and with them possibly my last chance of making it to champion again (the middle thirties being the beginning of the end for jump jockeys), I answered the telephone for about the tenth time that morning and found it was not another friend ringing to commiserate.

'Could I speak,' a female voice asked, 'to Derek Franklin?'

'I'm Derek Franklin,' I said.

'Right.' She was both brisk and hesitant, and one could understand why. 'We have you listed,' she said, 'as your brother Greville's next of kin.'

1

Those three words, I thought with an accelerating heart, must be among the most ominous in the language.

I said slowly, not wanting to know, 'What's happened?'

'I'm speaking from St Catherine's Hospital, Ipswich. Your brother is here, in the intensive care unit...'

At least he was alive, I thought numbly.

'...and the doctors think you should be told.'

'How is he?'

'I'm sorry. I haven't seen him. This is the almoner's office. But I understand that his condition is very serious.'

'What's the matter with him?'

'He was involved in an accident,' she said. 'He has multiple injuries and is on life support.'

'I'll come,' I said.

'Yes. It might be best.'

I thanked her, not knowing exactly what for, and put down the receiver, taking the shock physically in light-headedness and a constricted throat.

He would be all right, I told myself. Intensive care meant simply that he was being carefully looked after. He would recover, of course.

I shut out the anxiety to work prosaically instead on the practicalities of getting from Hungerford in Berkshire, where I lived, to Ipswich in Suffolk, about a hundred and fifty miles across country, with a crunched ankle. It was fortunately the left ankle, which meant I would soon be able to drive my automatic gears without trouble, but it was on that particular day at peak discomfort and even with painkillers and icepacks was hot, swollen and throbbing. I couldn't move it without holding my breath, and that was partly my own fault.

Owing to my hatred – not to say phobia – about the damaging immobility of plaster of Paris I had spent a good deal of the previous day persuading a long-suffering orthopaedic surgeon to give me the support of a plain crêpe bandage instead of imprisonment in a cast. He was himself a plate-and-screw man by preference and had grumbled as usual at my request. Such a bandage as I was demanding might be better in the end for one's muscles, but it gave no protection against knocks, as he had reminded me on other occasions, and it would be more painful, he said.

2

'I'll be racing much quicker with a bandage.'

'It's time you stopped breaking your bones,' he said, giving in with a shrug and a sigh and obligingly winding the crêpe on tightly. 'One of these days you'll crack something serious.'

'I don't actually like breaking them.'

'At least I haven't had to pin anything this time,' he said. 'And you're mad.'

'Yes. Thanks very much.'

'Go home and rest it. Give those ligaments a chance.'

The ligaments took their chance along the back seat of my car while Brad, an unemployed welder, drove it to Ipswich. Brad, taciturn and obstinate, was unemployed by habit and choice but made a scratchy living doing odd jobs in the neighbourhood for anyone willing to endure his moods. As I much preferred his long silences to his infrequent conversation, we got along fine. He looked forty, hadn't reached thirty, and lived with his mother.

He found St Catherine's Hospital without much trouble and at the door helped me out and handed me the crutches, saying he would park and wait inside in the reception area and I could take my time. He had waited for me similarly for hours the day before, expressing neither impatience nor sympathy but simply being restfully and neutrally morose.

The intensive care unit proved to be guarded by brisk nurses who looked at the crutches and said I'd come to the wrong department, but once I'd persuaded them of my identity they kitted me sympathetically with a mask and gown and let me in to see Greville.

I had vaguely expected Intensive Care to involve a lot of bright lights and clanging bustle, but I found that it didn't, or at least not in that room in that hospital. The light was dim, the atmosphere peaceful, the noise level, once my ears adjusted to it, just above silence but lower than identification.

Greville lay alone in the room on a high bed with wires and tubes all over the place. He was naked except for a strip of sheeting lying loosely across his loins and they had shaved half the hair off his head. Other evidences of surgery marched like centipede tracks across his abdomen and down one thigh, and there were darkening bruises everywhere.

Behind his bed a bank of screens showed blank rectangular

3

faces, as the information from the electrodes fed into other screens in a room directly outside. He didn't need, they said, an attendant constantly beside him, but they kept an eye on his reactions all the time.

He was unconscious, his face pale and calm, his head turned slightly towards the door as if expecting visitors. Decompression procedures had been performed on his skull, and the wound was covered by a large padded dressing which seemed more like a pillow to support him.

Greville Saxony Franklin, my brother. Nineteen years my senior: not expected to live. It had to be faced. To be accepted.

'Hi, guy,' I said.

It was an Americanism he himself used often, but it produced no response. I touched his hand, which was warm and relaxed, the nails, as always, clean and cared for. He had a pulse, he had circulation: his heart beat by electrical stimulus. Air went in and out of his lungs mechanically through a tube in his throat. Inside his head the synapses were shutting down. Where was his soul, I wondered: where was the intelligent, persistent, energetic spirit? Did he known that he was dying?

I didn't want just to leave him. No one should die alone. I went outside and said so.

A doctor in a green overall replied that when all remaining brain activity had ceased, they would ask my consent before switching off the machines. I was welcome to be with my brother at that crisis point as well as before. 'But death,' he said austerely, 'will be for him an infinitesimal process, not a definitive moment.' He paused. 'There is a waiting room along the hall, with coffee and things.'

Bathos and drama, I thought: his everday life. I crutched all the way down to the general reception area, found Brad, gave him an update and told him I might be a long time. All night, perhaps.

He waved a permissive hand. He would be around, he said, or he would leave a message at the desk. Either way, I could reach him. I nodded and went back upstairs, and found the waiting room already occupied by a very young couple engulfed in grief, whose baby was hanging onto life by threads not much stronger than Greville's.

The room itself was bright, comfortable and impersonal, and

4

I listened to the mother's slow sobs and thought of the misery that soaked daily into those walls. Life has a way of kicking one along like a football, or so I've found. Fate had never dealt me personally a particularly easy time, but that was OK, that was normal. Most people, it seemed to me, took their turn to be football. Most survived. Some didn't.

Greville had simply been in the wrong place at the wrong time. From the scrappy information known to the hospital, I gleaned that he had been walking down Ipswich High Street when some scaffolding that was being dismantled had fallen on him from a considerable height. One of the construction workers had been killed, and a second had been taken to hospital with a broken hip.

I had been given my brother's clinical details. One metal bar had pierced his stomach, another had torn into his leg; something heavy had fallen on his head and caused brain damage with massive cerebral bleeding. It had happened late the previous afternoon, he had been deeply unconscious from the moment of impact and he hadn't been identified until workmen dealing with the rubble in the morning had found his diary and given it to the police.

'Wallet?' I asked.

No, no wallet. Just the diary with, neatly filled in on the first page, next of kin, Derek Franklin, brother; telephone number supplied. Before that, they had had no clue except the initials G.S.F. embroidered above the pocket of his torn and blood-stained shirt.

'A *silk* shirt,' a nurse added disapprovingly, as if monogram-med silk shirts were somehow immoral.

'Nothing else in his pockets?' I asked.

'A bunch of keys and a handkerchief. That was all. You'll be given them, of course, along with the diary and his watch and signet ring.'

I nodded. No need to ask when.

The afternoon stretched out, strange and unreal, a time-warped limbo. I went in again to spend some time with Greville, but he lay unmoving, oblivious in his dwindling twilight, already subtly not himself. If Wordsworth were right about immortality, it was the sleep and the forgetting that were slipping away and reawakening that lay ahead, and maybe I

5

should be glad for him, not grieve.

I thought of him as he had been, and of our lives as brothers.

We had never lived together in a family unit because, by the time I was born, he was away at university, building a life of his own. By the time I was six, he had married, by the time I was ten, he'd divorced. For years he was a semi-stranger whom I met briefly at family gatherings, celebrations which grew less and less frequent as our parents aged and died, and which stopped altogether when the two sisters who bridged the gap between Greville and me both emigrated, one to Australia and one to Japan.

It wasn't until I'd reached twenty-eight myself that after a long Christmas-and-birthday-card politeness we'd met unexpectedly on a railway platform and during the journey ahead had become friends. Not close time-sharing friends even then, but positive enough for telephoning each other sporadically and exchanging restaurant dinners and feeling good about it.

We had been brought up in different environments, Greville in the Regency London house which went with our father's job as manager of one of the great landowning estates, I in the comfortable country cottage of his retirement. Greville had been taken by our mother to museums, art galleries and the theatre: I had been given ponies.

We didn't even look much alike. Greville, like our father, was six feet tall, I three inches shorter. Greville's hair, now greying, had been light brown and straight, mine darker brown and curly. We had both inherited amber eyes and good teeth from our mother and a tendency to leanness from our father, but our faces, though both tidy enough, were quite different.

Greville best remembered our parents' vigorous years; I'd been with them through their illnesses and deaths. Our father had himself been twenty years older than our mother, and she had died first, which had seemed monstrously unfair. The old man and I had lived briefly together after that in tolerant mutual non-comprehension, though I had no doubt that he'd loved me, in his way. He had been sixty-two when I was born and he died on my eighteenth birthday, leaving me a fund for my continued education and a letter of admonitions and instructions, some of which I'd carried out.

Greville's stillness was absolute. I shifted uncomfortably on the crutches and thought of asking for a chair. I wouldn't see him smile again, I thought: not the lightening of the eyes and the gleam of teeth, the quick appreciation of the black humour of life, the awareness of his own power.

He was a magistrate, a justice of the peace, and he imported and sold semi-precious stones. Beyond these bare facts I knew few details of his day-to-day existence, as whenever we met it seemed that he was always more interested in my doings than his own. He had himself owned horses from the day he telephoned to ask my opinion: someone who owed him money had offered his racehorse to settle the debt. What did I think? I told him I'd phone back, looked up the horse, thought it was a bargain and told Greville to go right ahead if he felt like it.

'Don't see why not,' he'd said. 'Will you fix the paperwork?'

I'd said yes, of course. It wasn't hard for anyone to say yes to my brother Greville: much harder to say no.

The horse had won handsomely and given him a taste for future ownership, though he seldom went to see his horses run, which wasn't particularly unusual in an owner but always to me mystifying. He refused absolutely to own jumpers on the grounds that he might buy something that would kill me. I was too big for Flat races; he'd felt safe with those. I couldn't persuade him that I would like to ride for him and in the end I stopped trying. When Greville made up his mind he was unshakeable.

Every ten minutes or so a nurse would come quietly into the room to stand for a short while beside the bed, checking that all the electrodes and tubes were still in order. She gave me brief smiles and commented once that my brother was unaware of my presence and could not be comforted by my being there.

'It's as much for me as for him,' I said.

She nodded and went away, and I stayed for a couple more hours, leaning against a wall and relecting that it was ironic that it was he who should meet death by chance when it was I who actively risked it half the days of the year.

Strange to relect also, looking back now to that lengthening evening, that I gave no thought to the consequences of his death. The present was vividly alive still in the silent diminishing hours, and all I saw in the future was a pretty dreary programme of form-filling and funeral arrangements, which I didn't bother to think about in any detail. I would have to telephone the sisters, I vaguely supposed, and there might be a little long-distance grief, but I knew they would say, 'You can see to it, can't you? Whatever you decide will be all right with us,' and they wouldn't come back half way round the world to stand in mournful drizzle at the graveside of a brother they'd seen perhaps twice in ten years.

Beyond that, I considered nothing. The tie of common blood was all that truely linked Greville and me, and once it was undone there would be nothing left of him but memory. With regret I watched the pulse that flickered in his throat. When it was gone I would go back to my own life and think of him warmly sometimes, and remember this night with overall sorrow, but no more.

I went along to the waiting room for a while to rest my legs. The desperate young parents were still there, hollow-eyed and entwined, but presently a sombre nurse came to fetch them, and in the distance, shortly after, I heard the rising wail of the mother's agonised loss. I felt my own tears prickle for her, a stranger. A dead baby, a dying brother, a universal uniting misery. I grieved for Greville more intensely then because of the death of the child, and realised I had been wrong about the sorrow level. I would miss him very much.

I put my ankle up on a chair and fitfully dozed, and sometime before daybreak the same nurse with the same expression came to fetch me in my turn.

I followed her along the passage and into Greville's room. There was much more light in there this time, and more people, and the bank of monitoring screens behind the bed had been switched on. Pale greenish lines moved across them, some in regular spasms, some uncompromisingly straight.

I didn't need to be told, but they explained all the same. The straight lines were the sum of the activity in Greville's brain. None at all.

There was no private goodbye. There was no point. I was there, and that was enough. They asked for, and received, my agreement to the disconnection of the machines, and presently the pulsing lines straightened out also, and whatever had been in the quiet body was there no longer.

*

8

It took a long time to get anything done in the morning because it turned out to be Sunday.

I thought back, having lost count of time. Thursday when I broke my ankle, Friday when the scaffolding fell on Greville, Saturday when Brad drove me to Ipswich. It all seemed a cosmos away: relativity in action.

There was the possibility, it seemed, of the scaffolding constructors being liable for damages. It was suggested that I should consult a solicitor.

Plodding through the paperwork, trying to make decisions, I realised that I didn't know what Greville would want. If he'd left a will somewhere, maybe he had given instructions that I ought to carry out. Maybe no one but I, I thought with a jolt, actually knew he was dead. There had to be people I should notify, and I didn't know who.

I asked if I could have the diary the police had found in the rubble, and presently I was given not only the diary but everything else my brother had with him: keys, watch, handkerchief, signet ring, a small amount of change, shoes, socks, jacket. The rest of his clothes, torn and drenched with blood, had been incinerated, it appeared. I was required to sign for what I was taking, putting a tick against each item.

Everything had been tipped out of the large brown plastic bag in which they had been stored. The bag said 'St Catherine's Hospital' in white on the sides. I put the shoes, socks, handkerchief and jacket back into the bag and pulled the strings tight again, then I shovelled the large bunch of keys into my own trouser pocket, along with the watch, the ring and the money, and finally consulted the diary.

On the front page he had entered his name, his London home telephone number and his office number, but no addresses. It was near the bottom, where there was a space headed 'In case of accident please notify' that he had written 'Derek Franklin, brother, next of kin.'

The diary itself was one I had sent him at Christmas: the racing diary put out by the Jockeys' Association and the Injured Jockeys' Fund. That he should have chosen to use that particular diary when he must have been given several others I found unexpectedly moving. That he had put my name in it made me wonder what he had really thought of me; whether

9

there was much we might have been to each other, and had missed.

With regret I put the diary into my other trouser pocket. The next morning, I supposed, I would have to telephone his office with the dire news. I couldn't forewarn anyone as I didn't know the names, let alone the phone numbers, of the people who worked for him. I knew only that he had no partners, as he had said several times that the only way he could run his business was by himself. Partners too often came to blows, he said, and he would have none of it.

When all the signing was completed, I looped the strings of the plastic bag a couple of times round my wrist and took it and myself on the crutches down to the reception area, which was more or less deserted on that early Sunday morning. Brad wasn't there, nor was there any message from him at the desk, so I simply sat down and waited. I had no doubt he would come back in his own good time, glowering as usual, and eventually he did, slouching in through the door with no sign of haste.

He saw me across the acreage, came to within ten feet, and said, 'Shall I fetch the car, then?' and when I nodded, wheeled away and departed. A man of very few words, Brad. I followed slowly in his wake, the plastic bag bumping against the crutch. If I'd thought faster I would have given it to Brad to carry, but I didn't seem to be thinking fast in any way.

Outside, the October sun was bright and warm. I breathed the sweet air, took a few steps away from the door and patiently waited some more, and was totally unprepared to be savagely mugged.

I scarcely saw who did it. One moment I was upright, leaning without concentration on the crutches, the next I'd received a battering-ram shove in the back and was sprawling face forward onto the hard black surface of the entrance drive. To try to save myself, I put my left foot down instinctively and it twisted beneath me which was excruciating and useless. I fell flat down on my stomach in a haze and I hardly cared when someone kicked one of the fallen crutches away along the ground and tugged at the bag round my wrist.

He...it had to be a he, I thought, from the speed and strength...thumped a foot down on my back and put his weight on it. He yanked my arm up and back roughly, and cut through the plastic with a slash that took some of my skin with it. I scarcely felt it. The messages from my ankle obliterated all else.

A voice approached saying, 'Hey! Hey!' urgently, and my attacker lifted himself off me as fast as he'd arrived and sped away.

It was Brad who had come to my rescue. On any other day there might have been people constantly coming and going, but not on Sunday morning. No one else seemed to be around to notice a thing. No one but Brad had come running.

'Friggin' hell,' Brad said from above me. 'Are you all right?'

Far from it, I thought.

He went to fetch the scattered crutch and brought it back. 'Your hand's bleeding,' he said with disbelief. 'Don't you want to stand up?'

I wasn't too sure that I did, but it seemed the only thing to do. When I'd made it to a moderately vertical position he looked impassively at my face and gave it as his opinion that we ought to go back into the hospital. As I didn't feel like arguing, that's what we did.

I sat on the end of one of the empty rows of seats and waited for the tide of woe to recede, and when I had more command of things I went across to the desk and explained what had happened.

The woman behind the reception window was horrified.

'Someone stole your plastic bag!' she said, round-eyed. 'I mean, everyone around here knows what those bags signify, they're always used for the belongings of people who've died or come here after accidents. I mean, everyone knows they can contain wallets and jewellery and so on, but I've never heard of one being snatched. How awful! How much did you lose? You'd better report it to the police.'

The futility of it shook me with weariness. Some punk had taken a chance that the dead man's effects would be worth the risk, and the police would take notes and chalk it up among the majority of unsolved muggings. I reckoned I'd fallen into the ultra-vulnerable bracket which included little old ladies, and however much I might wince at the thought, I on my crutches had looked and been a pushover, literally.

I shuffled painfully into the washroom and ran cold water over my slowly bleeding hand, and found that the cut was more

11

extensive than deep and could sensibly be classified as a scratch. With a sigh, I dabbed a paper towel on the scarletly oozing spots and unwound the cut-off pieces of white and brown plastic which were still wrapped tightly round my wrist, throwing them in the bin. What a bloody stupid anti-climactic post-script, I thought tiredly, to the accident that had taken my brother.

When I went outside Brad said with a certain amount of anxiety, 'You going to the police, then?' and he relaxed visibly when I shook my head and said, 'Not unless you can give them a detailed description of whoever attacked me.'

I couldn't tell from his expression whether he could or not. I thought I might ask him later, on the way home, but when I did, all that he said was, 'He had jeans on, and one of them woolly hats. And he had a knife. I didn't see his face, he sort of had his back turned my way, but the sun flashed on the knife, see? It all went down so fast. I did think you were a goner. Then he ran off with the bag. You were dead lucky, I'd say.'

I didn't feel lucky, but all things were relative.

Brad, having contributed what was for him a long speech, relapsed into his more normal silence, and I wondered what the mugger would think of the worthless haul of shoes, socks, handkerchief and jacket whose loss hadn't been realistically worth reporting. Whatever of value Greville had set out with would have been in his wallet, which had fallen to an earlier predator.

I had been wearing, was still wearing, a shirt, tie and sweater, but no jacket. A sweater was better with the crutches than a jacket. It was pointless to wonder whether the thief would have dipped into my trouser pockets if Brad hadn't shouted. Pointless to wonder if he would have put his blade through my ribs. There was no way of knowing. I did know I couldn't have stopped him, but his prize in any case would have been meagre. Apart from Greville's things I was carrying only a credit card and a few notes in a small folder, from a habit of travelling light.

I stopped thinking about it and instead, to take my mind off the ankle, wondered what Greville had been doing in Ipswich. Wondered if, ever since Friday, anyone had been waiting for him to arrive. Wondered how he had got there. Wondered if he had parked his car somewhere there and, if so, how I would find it, considering I didn't know its number and wasn't even sure if he still had a Porsche. Someone else would know, I thought easily. His office, his local garage, a friend. It wasn't really my worry.

By the time we reached Hungerford three hours later, Brad had said, in addition, only that the car was running out of juice (which we remedied) and, half an hour from home, that if I wanted him to go on driving me during the following week, he would be willing.

'Seven-thirty tomorrow morning?' I suggested, reflecting, and he said 'Yerss' on a growl which I took to mean assent.

He drove me to my door, helped me out as before, handed me the crutches, locked the car and put the keys into my hand, all without speaking.

'Thanks,' I said.

He ducked his head, not meeting my eyes, and turned and shambled off on foot towards him mother's house. I watched him go; a shy difficult man with no social skills who had possibly that morning saved my life.

CHAPTER 2

I had for three years rented the ground floor of an old house in a turning off the main road running through the ancient country town. There was a bedroom and bathroom facing the street and the sunrise, and a large all-purpose room to the rear into which the sunset flooded. Beyond that, a small stream-bordered garden which I shared with the owners of the house, an elderly couple upstairs.

Brad's mother had cooked and cleaned for them for years; Brad mended, painted and chopped when he felt like it. Soon after I'd moved in, mother and son had casually extended their services to me, which suited me well. It was all in all an easy uncluttered existence, but if home was where the heart was, I really lived out on the windy Downs and in stable yards and on the raucous racetracks where I worked.

I let myself into the quiet rooms and sat with icepacks along a sofa, watching the sun go down on the far side of the stream and thinking I might have done better to stay in the Ipswich hospital. From the knee down my left leg was hurting abominably, and it was still getting clearer by the minute that falling had intensified Thursday's damage disastrously. My own surgeon had been going off to Wales for the weekend, but I doubted that he would have done very much except say 'I told you so', so in the end I simply took another Distalgesic and changed the icepacks and worked out the time zones in Tokyo and Sydney.

At midnight I telephoned to those cities where it was already morning and by good luck reached both of the sisters. 'Poor Greville,' they said sadly, and, 'Do whatever you think best.' 'Send some flowers for us.' 'Let us know how it goes.'

I would, I said. Poor Greville, they repeated, meaning it, and said they would love to see me in Tokyo, in Sydney, whenever. Their children, they said, were all fine. Their husbands were fine. Was I fine? Poor, poor Greveille.

I put the receiver down ruefully. Families did scatter, and some scattered more than most. I knew the sisters by that time only through the photographs they sometimes sent at Christmas. They hadn't recognised my voice.

Taking things slowly in the morning, as nothing was much better, I dressed for the day in shirt, tie and sweater as before, with a shoe on the right foot, sock alone on the left, and was ready when Brad arrived five minutes early.

'We're going to London,' I said. 'Here's a map with the place marked. Do you think you can find it?'

'Got a tongue in my head,' he said, peering at the maze of roads. 'Reckon so.'

'Give it a go, then.'

He nodded, helped me inch onto the back seat, and drove seventy miles through the heavy morning traffic in silence. Then, by dint of shouting at street vendors via the driver's window, he zig-zagged across Holborn, took a couple of wrong turns, righted himself, and drew up with a jerk in a busy street round the corner from Hatton Garden.

'That's it,' he said, pointing. 'Number fifty-six. That office block.'

'Brilliant.'

He helped me out, gave me the crutches, and came with me to hold open the heavy glass entrace door. Inside, behind a desk, was a man in a peaked cap personifying security who asked me forbiddingly what floor I wanted.

'Saxony Franklin,' I said.

'Name?' he asked, consulting a list.

'Franklin.'

'Your name, I mean.'

I explained who I was. He raised his eyebrows, picked up a

15

telephone, pressed a button and said 'A Mr Franklin is on his way up.'

Brad asked where he could park the car and was told there was a yard round the back. He would wait for me, he said. No hurry. No problem.

The office building, which was modern, had been built rubbing shoulders to the sixth floor with Victorian curlicued neighbours, soaring free to the tenth with a severe lot of glass.

Saxony Franklin was on the eighth floor, it appeared. I went up in a smooth lift and elbowed my way through some heavy double doors into a lobby furnished with a reception desk, several armchairs for waiting in and two policemen.

Behind the policemen was a middle-aged woman who looked definitely flustered.

I thought immediately that news of Greville's death had already arrived and that I probably hadn't needed to come, but it seemed the Force was there for a different reason entirely.

The flustered lady gave me a blank stare and said, 'That's not Mr Franklin. The guard said Mr Franklin was on his way up.'

I allayed the police suspicions a little by saying again that I was Greville Franklin's brother.

'Oh,' said the woman. 'Yes, he does have a brother.'

They all swept their gaze over my comparative immobility.

'Mr Franklin isn't here yet,' the woman told me.

'Er...' I said, 'what's going on?'

They all looked disinclined to explain. I said to her, 'I'm afraid I don't know your name.'

'Adams,' she said distractedly. 'Annette Adams. I'm your brother's personal assistant.'

'I'm sorry,' I said slowly, 'but my brother won't be coming at all today. He was involved in an accident.'

Annette Adams heard the bad news in my voice. She put a hand over her heart in the classic gesture as if to hold it still in her chest and with anxiety said, 'What sort of accident? A car crash? Is he hurt?'

She saw the answer clearly in my expression and with her free hand felt for one of the armchairs, buckling into it with shock.

'He died in hospital yesterday morning,' I said to her and to the policemen, 'after some scaffolding fell on him last Friday. I was with him in the hospital.'

16

One of the policemen pointed at my dangling foot. 'You were injured at the same time, sir?'

'No. This was different. I didn't see his accident. I meant, I was there when he died. The hospital sent for me.'

The two policemen consulted each other's eyes and decided after all to say why they were there.

'These offices were broken into during the weekend, sir. Mrs Adams here discovered it when she arrived early for work, and she called us in.'

'What does it matter? It doesn't matter now,' the lady said, growing paler.

'There''s a good deal of mess,' the policeman went on, 'and Mrs Adams doesn't know what's been stolen. We were waiting for your brother to tell us.'

'Oh dear, oh dear,' said Annette, gulping.

'Is there anyone else here?' I asked her. 'Someone who could get you a cup of tea?' Before you faint, I thought, but didn't say it.

She nodded a fraction, glancing at a door behind the desk, and I swung over there and tried to open it. It wouldn't open: the knob wouldn't turn.

'It's electronic,' Annette said weakly. 'You have to put in the right numbers...' She flopped her head back against the chair and said she couldn't remember what today's number was; it was changed often. She and the policemen had come through it, it seemed, and let it swing shut behind them.

One of the policemen came over and pounded on the door with his fist, shouting 'Police' very positively which had the desired effect like a reflex. Without finesse he told the much younger woman who stood there framed in the doorway that her boss was dead and that Mrs Adams was about to pass out and was needing some strong hot sweet tea, love, like five minutes ago.

Wild-eyed, the young woman retreated to spread more consternation behind the scenes and the policeman nullified the firm's defences by wedging the electronic door open, using the chair from behind the reception desk.

I took in a few more details of the surroundings, beyond my first impression of grey. On the light greenish-grey of the carpet stood the armchairs in charcoal and the desk in matt black

17

unpainted and unpolished wood. The walls, palest grey, were hung with a series of framed geological maps, the frames black and narrow and uniform in size. The propped-open door, and another similar door to one side, still closed, were painted the same colour as the walls. The total effect, lit by recessed spotlights in the ceiling, looked both straightforward and immensely sophisticated, a true representation of my brother.

Mrs Annette Adams, still flaccid from too many unpleasant surprises on a Monday morning, wore a cream shirt, a charcoal grey skirt and a string of knobbly pearls. She was dark haired, in her late forties, perhaps, and from the starkness in her eyes, just beginning to realise, I guessed, that the unheaval of the present would be permanent.

The younger woman returned effectively with a scarlet steaming mug and Annette Adams sipped from it obediently for a while, listening to the policemen telling me that the intruder had not come in this way up the front lift, which was for visitors, but up another lift at the rear of the building which was used by the staff of all floors of offices, and for freight. That lift went down into a rear lobby which, in its turn, led out to the yard where cars and vans were parked: where Brad was presumably waiting at that moment.

The intruder had apparently ridden to the tenth floor, climbed some service stairs to the roof, and by some means had come down outside the building to the eighth floor, where he had smashed a window to let himself in.

'What sort of means?' I asked.

'We don't know, sir. Whatever it was, he took it with him. Maybe a rope.' He shrugged. 'We've had only a quick preliminary look around up there. We wanted to know what's been stolen before we...er...See, we don't want to waste our time for nothing.'

I nodded. Like Greville's stolen shoes, I thought.

'This whole area round Hatton Garden is packed with the jewel trade. We get break-ins, or attempted break-ins, all the time.'

The other policeman said, 'This place here is loaded with stones, of course, but the vault's still shut and Mrs Adams says nothing seems to be missing from the other stockrooms. Only Mr Franklin has a key to the vault which is where their more valuable facetted stones are kept.'

Mr Franklin had no keys at all. Mr Franklin's keys were in my own pocket. There was no harm, I supposed, in producing them.

The sight of what must have been a familiar bunch brought tears to Annette Adams's eyes. She put down the mug, searched around for a tissue and cried, 'He really is dead, then,' as if she hadn't thoroughly believed it before.

When she'd recovered a little I asked her to point out the vault key, which proved to be the longest and slenderest of the lot, and shortly afterwards we were all walking through the propped-open door and down a central corridor with spacious offices opening to either side. Faces showing shock looked out at our passing. We stopped at an ordinary-looking door which might have been mistaken for a cupboard and certainly looked nothing like a vault.

'That's it,' Annette Adams insisted, nodding; so I slid the narrow key into the small ordinary keyhole, and found that it turned unexpectedly anti-clockwise. The thick and heavy door swung inwards to the right under pressure and a light came on automatically, shining in what did indeed seem exactly like a large walk-in cupboard, with rows of white cardboard boxes on several plain white-painted shelves stretching away along the left-hand wall.

Everyone looked in silence. Nothing seemed to have been disturbed.

'Who knows what should be in the boxes?' I asked, and got the expected answer: my brother.

I took a step into the vault and took the lid off one of the nearest boxes which bore a sticky label saying $MgAl_2O_4$, Burma. Inside the box there were about a dozen glossy white envelopes, each taking up the whole width. I lifted one out to open it.

'Be careful!' Annette Adams exclaimed, fearful of my clumsiness as I balanced on the crutches. 'The packets unfold.'

I handed to her the one I held, and she unfolded it carefully on the palm of her hand. Inside, cushioned by white tissue, lay two large red translucent stones, cut and polished, oblong in shape, almost pulsing with intense colour under the lights.

'Are they rubies?' I asked, impressed.

19

Annette Adams smiled indulgently. 'No, they're spinel. Very fine specimens. We rarely deal in rubies.'

'Are there any diamonds in here?' one of the policemen asked.

'No we don't deal in diamonds. Almost never.'

I asked her to look into some of the other boxes, which she did, first carefully folding the two red stones into their packet and restoring them to their right place. We watched her stretch and bend, tipping up random lids on several shelves to take out a white packet here and there for inspection, but there were clearly no dismaying surprises, and in the end she shook her head and said that nothing at all was missing, as far as she could see.

'The real value of these stones is in quantity,' she said. 'Each individual stone isn't worth a fortune. We sell stones in tens and hundreds...' Her voiced trailed off into a sort of forlornness. 'I don't know what to do,' she said, 'about the orders.'

The policemen weren't affected by the problem. If nothing was missing, they had other burglaries to look into, and they would put in a report, but goodbye for now, or words to that effect.

When they'd gone, Annette Adams and I stood in the passage and looked at each other.

'What do I do?' she said. 'Are we still in business?'

I didn't like to tell her that I hadn't the foggiest notion. I said, 'Did Greville have an office?'

'That's where most of the mess is,' she said, turning away and retracing her steps to a large corner room near the entrance lobby. 'In here.'

I followed her and saw what she meant about mess. The contents of every wide-open drawer seemed to be out on the floor, most of it paper. Pictures had been removed from the walls and dropped. One filing cabinet lay on its side like a fallen soldier. The desk top was a shambles.

'The police said the burglar was looking behind the pictures for a safe. But there isn't one...just the vault.' She signed unhappily. 'It's all so pointless.'

I looked around. 'How many people work here altogether?' I said.

'Six of us. And Mr Franklin, of course.' She swallowed. 'Oh

dear.'

'Mm,' I agreed. 'Is there anywhere I can meet everyone?'

She nodded mutely and led the way into another large office where three of the others were already gathered, wide-eyed and rudderless. Another two came when called; four women and two men, all worried and uncertain and looking to me for decisions.

Greville, I perceived, hadn't chosen potential leaders to work around him. Annette Adams herself was no aggressive waiting-in-the-wings manager but a true second-in-command, skilled at carrying out orders, incapable of initiating them. Not so good, all things considered.

I introduced myself and described what had happened to Greville.

They had liked him, I was glad to see. There were tears on his behalf. I said that I needed their help because there were people I ought to notify about his death, like his solicitor and his accountant, for instance, and his closest friends, and I didn't know who they were. I would like, I said, to make a list, and sat beside one of the desks, arming myself with paper and pen.

Annette said she would fetch Greville's address book from his office but after a while returned in frustration: in all the mess she couldn't find it.

'There must be other records,' I said. 'What about the computer?' I pointed across the room. 'Do you have addresses in that?'

The girl who had brought the tea brightened a good deal and informed me that this was the stock control room, and the computer in question was programmed to record 'stock in', 'stock out', statements, invoices and accounts. But, she said encouragingly, in her other domain across the corridor there was another computer which she used for letters. She was out of the door by the end of the sentence and Annette remarked that June was a whirlwind always.

June, blonde, long-legged, flat-chested, came back with a fast print-out of Greville's ten most frequent correspondents (ignoring customers) which included not only the lawyers and the accountants but also the bank, a stockbroker and an insurance company.

'Terrific,' I said. 'And could one of you get through to the big credit card companies, and see if Greville was a customer of theirs and say his cards have been stolen, and he's dead.' Annette agreed mournfully that she would do it at once.

I then asked if any of them knew the make and number of Greville's car. They all did. It seemed they saw it every day in the yard. He came to work in a ten-year-old Rover 3500 without radio or cassette player because the Porsche he'd owned before had been broken into twice and finally stolen altogether.

'That old car's still bursting with gadgets, though,' the younger of the two men said, 'but he keeps them all locked in the boot.'

Greville had always been a sucker for gadgets, full of enthusiasm for the latest fidgety way of performing an ordinary task. He'd told me more about those toys of his, when we'd met, than ever about his own human relationships.

'Why did you ask about his car?' the young man said. He had rows of badges attached to a black leather jacket and orange spiky hair set with gel. A need to prove he existed, I supposed.

'It may be outside his front door,' I said. 'Or it may be parked somewhere in Ipswich.'

'Yeah,' he said thoughtfully. 'See what you mean.'

The telephone rang on the desk beside me, and Annette after a moment's hesitation came and picked up the receiver. She listened with a worried expression and then, covering the mouthpiece, asked me, 'What shall I do? It's a customer who wants to give an order.'

'Have you got what he wants?' I asked.

'Yes, we're sure to have.'

'Then say it's OK.'

'But do I tell him about Mr Franklin?'

'No,' I said instinctively, 'just take the order.'

She seemed glad of the direction and wrote down the list, and when she'd disconnected I suggested to them all that for that day at least they should take and send out orders in the normal way, and just say if asked that Mr Franklin was out of the office and couldn't be reached. We wouldn't start telling people he was dead until after I'd talked to his lawyers, accountants, bank and the rest, and found out our legal position. They were relieved and agreed without demur, and the older man asked if I would soon get the broken window fixed, as it was in the

22

packing and despatch room, where he worked.

With a feeling of being sucked feet first into quicksand I said I would try. I felt I didn't belong in that place or in those people's lives, and all I knew of the jewellery business was where to find two red stones in a box marked $MgAl_2O_4$, Burma.

At the fourth try among the Yellow Pages I got a promise of instant action on the window and after that, with office procedure beginning to tick over again all around me, I put a call through to the lawyers.

They were grave, they were sympathetic, they were at my service. I asked if by any chance Greville had made a will, as specifically I wanted to know if he had left any instructions about cremation or burial, and if he hadn't, did they know of anyone I should consult, or should I make whatever arrangements I thought best.

There was a certain amount of clearing of throats and a promise to look up files and call back, and they kept their word almost immediately, to my surprise.

My brother had indeed left a will: they had drawn it up for him themselves three years earlier. They couldn't swear it was his *last* will, but it was the only one they had. They had consulted it. Greville, they said, pedantically, had expressed no preference as to the disposal of his remains.

'Shall I just...go ahead, then?'

'Certainly,' they said. 'You are in fact named as your brother's sole executor. It is your duty to make the decisions.'

Hell, I thought, and I asked for a list of the beneficiaries so I could notify them of the death and invite them to the funeral.

After a pause they said they didn't normally give out that information on the telephone. Could I not come to their office? It was just across the City, at Temple.

'I've broken an ankle,' I said, apologetically. 'It takes me all my time to cross the room.'

Dear, dear, they said. They consulted among themselves in guarded whispers and finally said they supposed there was no harm in my knowing. Greville's will was extremely simple; he had left everything he possessed to Derek Saxony Franklin, his brother. To my good self, in fact.

'What?' I said stupidly. 'He can't have.'

He had written his will in a hurry, they said, because he had been flying off to a dangerous country to buy stones. He had been persuaded by the lawyers not to go intestate, and he had given in to them, and as far as they knew, that was the only will he had ever made.

'He can't have meant it to be his last,' I said blankly.

Perhaps not, they agreed: few men in good health expected to die at fifty-three. They then discussed probate procedures discreetly and asked for my instructions, and I felt the quicksands rising above my knees.

'Is it legal,' I asked, 'for this business to go on running, for the time being?'

They saw no impediment in law. Subject to probate, and in the absence of any later will, the business would be mine. If I wanted to sell it in due course, it would be in my own interest to keep it running. As my brother's executor it would also be my duty to do my best for the estate. An interesting situation, they said with humour.

Not wholeheartedly appreciating the subtlety, I asked how long probate would take.

Always difficult to forecast was the answer. Anything between six months or two years, depending on the complexity of Greville's affairs.

'Two years!'

More probably six months, they murmured soothingly. The speed would depend on the accountants and the Inland Revenue, who could seldom be hurried. It was in the lap of the gods.

I mentioned that there might be work to do over claiming damages for the accident. Happy to see to it, they said, and promised to contact the Ipswich police. Meanwhile, good luck.

I put the receiver down in sinking dismay. This business, like any other, might run on its own impetus for two weeks, maybe even for four, but after that...After that I would be back on horses, trying to get fit again to race.

I would have to get a manager, I thought vaguely, and had no idea where to start looking. Anette Adams with furrows of anxiety across her forehead asked if it would be all right to begin clearing up Mr Franklin's office, and I said yes, and thought that her lack of drive could sink the ship.

Please would someone, I asked the world in general, mind

going down to the yard and telling the man in my car that I wouldn't be leaving for two or three hours; and June with her bright face whisked out of the door again and soon returned to relate that my man would lock the car, go on foot for lunch, and be back in good time to wait for me.

'Did he say all that?' I asked curiously.

June laughed. 'Actually he said, "Right. Bite to eat," and off he stomped.'

She asked if I would like her to bring me a sandwich when she went out for her own lunch and, surprised and grateful, I accepted.

'You foot hurts, doesn't it?' she said judiciously.

'Mm.'

'You should put it up on a chair.'

She fetched one without ado and placed it in front of me, watching with a motherly air of approval as I lifted my leg into place. She must have been all of twenty, I thought.

A telephone rang beside the computer on the far side of the room and she went to answer it.

'Yes, sir, we have everything in stock. Yes, sir, what size and how many? A hundred twelve-by-ten-millimetre ovals... yes...yes...yes.'

She tapped the lengthy order rapidly straight on to the computer, not writing in longhand as Annette had done.

'Yes, sir, they will go off today. Usual terms, sir, of course.' She put the phone down, printed a copy of the order and laid it in a shallow wire tray. A fax machine simultaneously clicked on and whined away and switched off with little shrieks, and she tore off the emergent sheet and tapped its information also into the computer, making a print-out and putting it into the tray.

'Do you fill all the orders the day they come in?' I asked.

'Oh, sure, if we can. Within twenty-four hours without fail. Mr Franklin says speed is the essence of good business. I've known him stay here all evening by himself packing parcels when we're swamped.'

She remembered with a rush that he would never come back. It did take a bit of getting used to. Tears welled in her uncontrollably as they had earlier, and she stared at me through them, which made her blue eyes look huge.

'You couldn't help liking him,' she said. 'Working with him, I

25

mean.'

I felt almost jealous that she'd known Greville better than I had; yet I could have known him better if I'd tried. Regret stabbed in again, a needle of grief.

Annette came to announce that Mr Franklin's room was at least partially clear so I transferred myself into there to make more phone calls in comparative privacy. I sat in Greville's black leather swivelling chunk of luxury and put my foot on the typist's chair June carried in after me, and I surveyed the opulent carpet, deep armchairs and framed maps as in the lobby, and smoothed a hand over the grainy black expanse of the oversized desk, and felt like a jockey, not a tycoon.

Annette had picked up from the floor and assembled at one end of the desk some of the army of gadgets, most of them matt black and small, as if miniaturisation were part of the attraction. Easily identifiable at a glance were battery-operated things like pencil sharpener, hand-help copier, printing calculator, dictionary-thesaurus, but most needed investigation. I stretched out a hand to the nearest and found that it was a casing with a dial face, plus a head like a microphone on a lead.

'What's this?' I asked Annette who was picking up a stack of paper from the far reaches of the floor. 'Some sort of meter?'

She flashed a look at it. 'A Geiger counter,' she said matter-of-factly, as if everyone kept a Geiger counter routinely among their pens and pencils.

I flipped the switch from off to on, but apart from a couple of clicks, nothing happened.

Annette paused, sitting back on her heels as she knelt among the remaining clutter.

'A lot of stones change colour for the better under gamma radiation,' she said. 'They're not radioactive afterwards, but Mr Franklin was accidentally sent a batch of topaz from Brazil that had been irradiated in a nuclear reactor and the stones were bordering on dangerous. A hundred of them. There was a terrible lot of trouble because, apart from being unsaleable, they had come in without a radioactivity import licence, or something like that, but it wasn't Mr Franklin's fault, of course. But he got the Geiger counter then.' She paused. 'He has an amazing flair for stones, you know. He just felt there was something wrong with that topaz. Such a beautiful deep blue

26

they'd made it, when it must have been almost colourless to begin with. So he sent a few of them to a lab for testing.' She paused again. 'He'd just been reading about some old diamonds that had been exposed to radium and turned green, and were as radioactive as anything...'

Her face crumpled and she blinked her eyes rapidly, turning away from me and looking down to the floor so that I shouldn't see her distress. She made a great fuss among the papers and finally, with a sniff or two, said indistinctly, 'Here's his desk diary,' and then, more slowly, 'That's odd.'

'What's odd?'

'October's missing.'

She stood up and brought me the desk diary, which proved to be a largish appointments calendar showing a week at a glance. The month on current display was November, with a few of the daily spaces filled in but most of them empty. I flipped back the page and came next to September.

'I expect October's still on the floor, torn off,' I said.

She shook her head doubtfully, and in fact couldn't find it.

'Has the address book turned up?' I asked.

'No.' She was puzzled. 'It hasn't'.

'Is anything else missing?'

'I'm not really sure.'

It seemed bizarre that anyone should risk breaking in via the roof simply to steal an address book and some pages from a desk diary. Something else had to be missing.

The Yellow-Pages glaziers arrived at that point, putting a stop to my speculation. I went along with them to the packing room and saw the efficient hole that had been smashed in the six-by-four-foot window. All the glass that must have been scattered over every surface had been collected and swept into a pile of dagger-sharp glittering triangles, and a chill little breeze ruffled papers in clipboards.

'You don't break glass this quality by tapping it with a fingernail,' one of the workmen said knowledgeably, picking up a piece. 'They must have swung a weight against it, like a wrecking ball.'

27

CHAPTER 3

While the workmen measured the window frame, I watched the oldest of Greville's employees take transparent bags of beads from one cardboard box, insert them into bubble-plastic sleeves and stack them in another brown cardboard box. When all was transferred he put a list of contents on top, crossed the flaps and stuck the whole box around with wide reinforced tape.

'Where do the beads come from?' I asked.

'Taiwan, I dare say,' he said briefly, fixing a large address label on the top.

'No...I meant, where do you keep them here?'

He looked at me in pitying astonishment, a white-haired grandfatherly figure in storemen's brown overalls. 'In the stockrooms, of course.'

'Of course.'

'Down the hall,' he said.

I went back to Greville's office and in the interests of good public relations asked Annette if she would show me the stockrooms. Her heavyish face lightened with pleasure and she led the way to the far end of the corridor.

'In here,' she said with obvious pride, passing through a central doorway into a small inner lobby, 'there are four rooms.' She pointed through open doorways. 'In there, mineral cabochons, oval and round; in there, beads,; in there, oddities, and in there, organics.'

'What are organics?' I asked.

She beckoned me forward into the room in question, and I walked into a windowless space lined from floor to shoulder height with column after column of narrow grey metal drawers each presenting a face to the world of about the size of a side of a shoe box. Each drawer, above a handle, bore a label identifying what it contained.

'Organics are things that grow,' Annette said patiently, and I reflected I should have worked that out for myself. 'Coral, for instance.' She pulled open a nearby drawer which proved to extend lengthily backwards, and showed me the contents: clear plastic bags, each packed with many strings of bright red twiglets. 'Italian,' she said. 'The best coral comes from the Mediterranean.' She closed that drawer, walked a few paces, pulled open another. 'Abalone, from abalone shells.' Another: 'Ivory. We still have a little, but we can't sell it now.' Another: 'Mother of pearl. We sell tons of it.' 'Pink mussel.' 'Freshwater pearls.' Finally, 'Imitation pearls. Cultured pearls are in the vault.'

Everything, it seemed, came in dozens of shapes and sizes. Annette smiled at my bemused expression and invited me into the room next door.

Floor to shoulder height metal drawers, as before, not only lining the walls this time but filling the centre space with aisles, as in a supermarket.

'Cabochons, for setting into rings, and so on,' Annette said. 'They're in alphabetical order.'

Amethyst to turquoise via garnet, jade, lapis lazuli and onyx, with dozens of others I'd only half heard of. 'Semi-precious,' Annette said briefly. 'All genuine stones. Mr Franklin doesn't touch glass or plastic.' She stopped abruptly. Let five seconds lengthen. 'He didn't touch them,' she said lamely.

His presence was there strongly, I felt. It was almost as if he would walk through the door, all energy, saying 'Hello, Derek, what brings you here?' and if he seemed alive to me, who had seen him dead, how much more physical he must still be to Annette and June.

And to Lily too, I supposed. Lily was in the third stockroom pushing a brown cardboard box around on a thing like a tea-trolley, collecting bags of strings of beads and checking them against a list. With her centre-parted hair drawn back into

29

a slide at her neck, with her small pale mouth and rounded cheeks, Lily looked like a Charlotte Brontë governess and dressed as if immolation were her personal choice. The sort to love the master in painful silence, I thought, and wondered what she'd felt for Greville.

Whatever it was, she wasn't letting it show. She raised downcast eyes briefly to my face and at Annette's prompting told me she was putting together a consignment of rhodonite, jasper, aventurine and tiger eye, for one of the largest firms of jewellery manufacturers.

'We import the stones,' Annette said. 'We're wholesalers. We sell to about three thousand jewellers, maybe more. Some are big businesses. Many are small ones. We're at the top of the semi-precious trade. Highly regarded.' She swallowed. 'People trust us.'

Greville, I knew, had travelled the world to buy the stones. When we'd met he'd often been on the point of departing for Arizona or Hong Kong or had just returned from Israel, but he'd never told me more than the destinations. I at last understood what he'd been doing, and realised he couldn't easily be replaced.

Depressed, I went back to his office and telephoned to his accountant and his bank.

They were shocked and they were helpful, impressively so. The bank manager said I would need to call on him in the morning, but Saxony Franklin, as a limited company, could go straight on functioning. I could take over without trouble. All he would want was confirmation from my brother's lawyers that his will was as I said.

'Thank you very much,' I said, slightly surprised, and he told me warmly he was glad to be of service. Greville's affairs, I thought with a smile, must be amazingly healthy.

To the insurance company, also, my brother's death seemed scarcely a hiccup. A limited company's insurance went marching steadily on, it seemed: it was the company that was insured, not my brother. I said I would like to claim for a smashed window. No problem. They would send a form.

After that I telephoned to the Ispwich undertakers who had been engaged to remove Greville's body from the hospital, and arranged that he should be cremated. They said they had 'a slot' at two o'clock on Friday: would that do? 'Yes,' I said, sighing, 'I'll be there.' They gave me the address of the crematorium in a hushed obsequious voice, and I wondered what it must be like to do business always with the bereaved. Happier by far to sell glittering baubles to the living or to ride jump-racing horses at thirty miles an hour, win, lose or break your bones.

I made yet another phone call, this time to the orthopaedic surgeon, and as usual came up against the barrier of his receptionist. He wasn't in his own private consulting rooms, she announced, but at the hospital.

I said, 'Could you ask him to leave me a prescription somewhere, because I've fallen on my ankle and twisted it, and I'm running out of Distalgesic.'

'Hold on,' she said, and I held until she returned. 'I've spoken to him,' she said. 'He'll be back here later. He says can you be here at five?'

I said gratefully that I could, and reckoned that I'd have to leave soon after two-thirty to be sure of making it. I told Annette, and asked what they did about locking up.

'Mr Franklin usually gets here first and leaves last.' She stopped, confused. 'I mean...'

'I know,' I said. 'It's all right. I think of him in the present tense too. So go on'.

'Well, the double front doors bolt on the inside. Then the door from the lobby to the offices has an electronic bolt, as you know. So does the door from the corridor to the stockrooms. So does the rear door, where we all come in and out. Mr Franklin changes...changed...the numbers at least every week. And there's another electronic lock, of course, on the door from the lobby to the showroom, and from the corridor into the showroom...' She paused. 'It does seem a lot, I know, but the electronic locks are very simple, really. You only have to remember three digits. Last Friday they were five, three, two. They're easy to work. Mr Franklin installed them so that we shouldn't have too many keys lying around. He and I both have a key, though, that will unlock all the electronic locks manually, if we need to.'

'So you've remembered the numbers?' I asked.

'Oh, yes. It was just, this morning, with everything...they went out of my head'.

31

'And the vault,' I said. 'Does that have any electronics?'

'No, but it has an intricate locking system in that heavy door, though it looks so simple from the outside. Mr Franklin always locks...locked...the vault before he left. When he went away on long trips, he made the key available to me.'

I wondered fleetingly about the awkward phrase, but didn't pursue it. I asked her instead about the showroom, which I hadn't seen and, again with pride, she went into the corridor, programmed a shining brass doorknob with the open sesame numbers, and ushered me into a windowed room that looked much like a shop, with glass-topped display counters and the firm's overall ambience of wealth.

Annette switched on powerful lights and the place came to life. She moved contentedly behind the counters, pointing out to me the contents now bright with illumination.

'In here are examples of everything we stock, except not all the sizes, of course, and not the facetted stones in the vault. We don't really use the showroom a great deal, only for new customers mostly, but I like being in here. I love the stones. They're fascinating. Mr Franklin says stones are the only things the human race takes from the earth and makes more beautiful.' She lifted a face heavy with loss. 'What will happen without him:'

'I don't know yet,' I said, 'but in the short term we fill the orders and despatch them, and order more stock from where you usually get it. We keep to all the old routines and practices. OK?'

She nodded, relieved at least for the present.

'Except,' I added, 'that it will be you who arrives first and leaves last, if you don't mind.'

'That's all right. I always do when Mr Franklin's away.'

We stared briefly at each other, not putting words to the obvious, then she switched off the showroom lights almost as if it were a symbolic act, and as we left pulled the self-locking door shut behind us.

Back in Greville's office I wrote down for her my own address and telephone number and said that if she felt insecure, or wanted to talk, I would be at home all evening.

'I'll come back here tomorrow morning, after I've seen the bank manager,' I said. 'Will you be all right until then?'

She nodded shakily. 'What do we call you? We can't call you Mr Franklin, it wouldn't seem right.'

'How about Derek?'

'Oh no.' She was instinctively against it. 'Would you mind, say...Mr Derek?'

'If you prefer it.' It sounded quaintly old-fashioned to me, but she was happy with it and said she would tell the others.

'About the others,' I said, 'sort everyone out for me, with their jobs. There's you, June, Lily...'

'June works the computers and the stock control,' she said. 'Lily fills the orders. Tina, she's a general assistant, she helps Lily and does some of the secretarial work. So does June. So do I, actually. We all do what's needed, really. There are few hard and fast divisions. Except that Alfie doesn't do much except pack up the orders. It takes him all his time.'

'And that younger guy with the spiky orange halo?'

'Jason? Don't worry about the hair, he's harmless. He's our muscles. The stones are very heavy in bulk, you know. Jason shifts boxes, fills the stockrooms, does odd jobs and hoovers the carpets. He helps Alfie sometimes, or Lily, if we're busy. Like I said, we all do anything, whatever's needed. Mr Franklin has never let anyone mark out a territory.'

'His words?'

'Yes, of course.'

Collective responsibility, I thought. I bowed to my brother's wisdom. If it worked, it worked. And from the look of everything in the place, it did indeed work, and I wouldn't disturb it.

I closed and locked the vault door with Greville's key and asked Annette which of his large bunch overrode the electronic locks. That one, she said, pointing, separating it.

'What are all the others, do you know?'

She looked blank. 'I've no idea.'

Car, house, whatever. I supposed I might eventually sort them out. I gave her what I hoped was a reassuring smile, sketched a goodbye to some of the others and rode down in the service lift to find Brad out in the yard.

'Swindon,' I said. 'The medical centre where we were on Friday. Would you mind?'

'Course not.' Positively radiant, I thought.

33

It was an eighty-mile journey, ten miles beyond home. Brad managed it without further communication and I spent the time thinking of all the things I hadn't yet done, like seeing to Greville's house and stopping delivery of his daily paper, wherever it might come from, and telling the post office to divert his letters... To hell with it, I thought wearily, why did the damned man have to die.

The orthopod X-rayed and unwrapped my ankle and tutt-tutted. From toes to shin it looked hard, black and swollen, the skin almost shiny from the stretching.

'I advised you to rest it,' he said, a touch crossly.

'My brother died...' and I explained about the mugging, and also about having to see to Greville's affairs.

He listened carefully, a strong sensible man with prematurely white hair. I didn't know a jockey who didn't trust him. He understood our needs and our imperatives, because he treated a good many of us who lived in or near the training centre of Lambourn.

'As I told you the other day,' he said when I'd finished, 'you've fractured the lower end of the fibula, and where the tibia and fibula should be joined, they've sprung apart. Today, they are further apart. They're now providing no support at all for the talus, the heel bone. You've now completely ripped the lateral ligament which normally binds the ankle together. The whole joint is insecure and coming apart inside, like a mortise joint in a piece of furniture when the glue's given way.'

'So how long will it take?' I asked.

He smiled briefly. 'In a crêpe bandage it will hurt for about another ten days, and after that you can walk on it. You could be back on a horse in three weeks from now, if you don't mind the stirrup hurting you, which it will About another three weeks after that, the ankle might be strong enough for racing.'

'Good,' I said, relieved. 'Not much worse than before, then.'

'It's worse, but it won't take much longer to mend.'

'Fine.'

He looked down at the depressing sight. 'If you're going to be doing all this travelling about, you'd be much more comfortable in a rigid cast. You could put your weight on it in a couple of days. You'd have almost no pain.'

34

'And wear it for six weeks? And get atrophied muscles?'

'Atrophy is a strong word.' He knew all the same that jump jockeys needed strong leg muscles above all else, and the way to keep them strong was to keep them moving. Inside plaster they couldn't move at all and weakened rapidly. If movement cost a few twinges, it was worth it.

'Delta-cast is lightweight,' he said persuasively. 'It's a polymer, not like the old plaster of Paris. It's porous, so air circulates, and you don't get skin problems. It's good. And I could make you a cast with a zip in it so you could take it off for physiotheraphy.'

'How long before I was racing?'

'Nine or ten weeks.'

I didn't say anything for a moment or two he looked up fast, his eyes bright and quizzical.

'A cast, then?' he said.

'No.'

He smiled and picked up a roll of crêpe bandage. 'Don't fall on it again in the next month, or you'll be back to square one.'

'I'll try not to.'

He bandaged it all tight again from just below the knee down to my toes and back, and gave me another prescription for Distalgesic. 'No more than eight tablets in twenty-four hours and not with alcohol.' He said it every time.

'Right.'

He considered me thoughtfully for a moment and then rose and went over to a cabinet where he kept packets and bottles of drugs. He came back tucking a small plastic bag into an envelope which he held out to me.

'I'm giving you something known as DF I-I-8s. Rather appropriate, as they're your own initials! I've given you three of them. They are serious painkillers, and I don't want you to use them unless something like yesterday happens again.'

'OK,' I said, putting the envelope in my pocket. 'Thanks.'

'If you take one, you won't feel a thing.' He smiled. 'If you take two at once, you'll be spaced out, high as a kite. If you take all three at once, you'll be unconscious. So be warned.' He paused. 'They are a last resort.'

'I won't forget,' I said, 'and I truly am grateful.'

*

35

Brad drove to a chemist's, took my prescription in, waited for it to be dispensed, and finished the ten miles home, parking outside my door.

'Same time tomorrow morning?' I asked. 'Back to London?'

'Yerss.'

'I'd be in trouble without you,' I said, climbing out with his help. He gave me a brief haunted glance and handed me the crutches. 'You drive great,' I said.

He was embarrassed, but also pleased. Nowhere near a smile, of course, but a definite twitch in the cheeks. He turned away, ducking my gaze, and set off doggedly towards his mother.

I let myself into the house and regretted the embargo on a large scotch. Instead, with June's lunchtime sandwich a distant memory, I refuelled with sardines on toast and ice cream after, which more or less reflected my habitual laziness about cooking.

Then, aligned with icepacks along the sofa, I telephoned the man in Newmarket who trained Greville's two racehorses.

He picked up the receiver as if he'd been waiting for it to ring.

'Yes?' he said. 'What are they offering?'

'I've no idea,' I said. 'Is that Nicholas Loder?'

'What? Who are you?' He was brusque and impatient, then took a second look at things and with more honey said, 'I beg your pardon, I was expecting someone else. I'm Loder, yes, who am I talking to?'

'Greville Franklin's brother.'

'Oh yes?'

It meant nothing to him immediately. I pictured him as I knew him, more by sight than face to face, a big light-haired man in his forties with enormous presence and self-esteem to match. Undoubtedly a good-to-great trainer, but in television interviews occasionally overbearing and condescending to the interviewer, as I'd heard he could be also to his owners. Greville kept his horses with him because the original horse he'd taken as a bad debt had been in that stable. Nicholas Loder had bought Greville all his subsequent horses and done notably well with them, and Greville had assured me that he got on well with the man by telephone, and that he was perfectly friendly.

The last time I'd spoken to Greville myself on the telephone he'd been talking of buying another two-year-old, saying that Loder would get him one at the October sales, perhaps.

I explained to Loder that Greville had died and after the first sympathetic exclamations of dismay he reacted as I would have expected, not as if missing a close friend but on a practical business level.

'It won't effect the running of his horses,' he said. 'They're owned in any case by the Saxony Franklin company, not by Greville himself. I can run the horses still in the company name. I have the company's Authority to Act. There should be no problem.'

'I'm afraid there may be,' I began.

'No, no. Dozen Roses runs on Saturday at York. In with a great chance. I informed Greville of it only a few days ago. He always wanted to know when they were running, though he never went to see them.'

'The problem is,' I said, 'about my being his brother. He has left the Saxony Franklin company to me.'

The size of the problem suddenly revealed itself to him forcibly. 'You're not his brother *Derek* Franklin? That brother? The jockey?'

'Yes. So...could you find out from Weatherby's whether the horses can still run while the estate is subject to probate?'

'My God,' he said weakly.

Professional jockeys, as we both knew well, were not allowed to own runners in races. They could own other horses such as brood mares, foals, stallions, hacks, hunters, show-jumpers, anything in horseshoes; they could even own racehorses, but they couldn't run them.

'Can you find out?' I asked again.

'I will.' He sounded exasperated. 'Dozen Roses should trot up on Saturday.'

Dozen Roses was currently the better of Greville's two horses whose fortunes I followed regularly in the newspapers and on television. A triple winner as a three-year-old he had been disappointing at four, but in the current year, as a five-year-old, he had regained all his old form and had scored three times in the past few weeks. A 'trot-up' on Saturday was a reasonable expectation.

37

Loder said, 'If Weatherby's give the thumbs down to the horse running, will you sell it? I'll find a buyer by Saturday, among my owners.'

I listened to the urgency in his voice and wondered whether Dozen Roses was more than just another trot-up, of which season by season he had many. He sounded a lot more fussed than seemed normal.

'I don't know whether I can sell before probate,' I said. 'You'd better find that out, too.'

'But if you can, will you?'

'I don't know,' I said, puzzled. 'Let's wait and see, first.'

'You won't be able to hang on to him, you know.' he said, forcefully. 'He's got another season in him. He's still worth a good bit. But unless you do something like turn in your licence, you won't be able to run him, and he's not worth turning in your licence for. It's not as if he were favourite for the Derby.'

'I'll decide during the week.'

'But you're not thinking of turning in your licence, are you?' He sounded almost alarmed. 'Didn't I read in the paper that you're on the injured list but hope to be back racing well before Christmas?'

'You did read that, yes.'

'Well, then.' The relief was a indefinable as the alarm, but came clear down the wires. I didn't understand any of it. He shouldn't have been so worried.

'Perhaps Saxony Franklin could lease the horse to someone,' I said.

'Oh. Ah. To me?' He sounded as if it were the perfect solution.

'I don't know,' I said cautiously. 'We'll have to find out.'

I realised that I didn't totally trust him, and it wasn't a doubt I'd have felt before the phone call. He was one of the top five Flat race trainers in the country, automatically held to be reliable because of his rock-solid success.

'When Greville came to see his horses,' I asked, 'did he ever bring anyone with him? I'm trying to reach people he knew, to tell them of his death.'

'He never came here to see his horses. I hardly knew him personally myself, except on the telephone.'

'Well, his funeral is on Friday at Ipswich,' I said. 'What if I called in at Newmarket that day, as I'll be over your way, to see you and the horses and complete any paperwork that's necessary?'

'No,' he said instantly. Then, softening it, 'I always discourage owners from visiting. They disrupt the stable routine. I can't make any exceptions. If I need you to sign anything I'll arrange it another way.'

'All right,' I agreed mildly, not crowding him into corners. 'I'll wait to hear from you about what Weatherby's decide.'

He said he would get in touch and abruptly disconnected, leaving me thinking that on the subject of his behaviour I didn't know the questions let alone the answers.

Perhaps I had been imagining things: but I knew I hadn't. One could often hear more nuances in someone's voice on the telphone than one could face to face. When people were relaxed, the lower vibrations of their voices came over the wires undisturbed; under stress, the lower vibrations disappeared because the vocal cords involuntarily tightened. After Loder had discovered I would be inheriting Dozen Roses, there had been no lower vibrations at all.

Shelving the enigma I pondered the persisting difficulty of informing Greville's friends. They had to exist, no one lived in a vacuum; but if it had been the other way round, I supposed that Greville would have had the same trouble. He hadn't known my friends either. Our worlds had scarcely touched except briefly when we met, and then we had talked a bit about horses, a bit about gadgets, a bit about the world in general and any interesting current events.

He'd lived alone, as I did. He'd told me nothing about any love life. He'd said merely, 'Bad luck' when three years earlier I'd remarked that my live-in girl friend had gone to live-in somewhere else. It didn't matter, I said. It had been a mutual agreement, a natural ending. I'd asked him once about his long-ago divorced wife. 'She remarried. Haven't seen her since,' was all he'd said.

If it had been I that had died, I thought, he would have told the world I worked in: he'd have told, perhaps, the trainer I mostly rode for and maybe the racing papers. So I should tell his world: tell the semi-precious stone fraternity. Annette could

39

do it, regardless of the absence of Greville's address book, because of June's computer. The computer made more and more nonsense of the break-in. I came back to the same conviction: something else had been stolen, and I didn't know what.

I remembered at about that point that I did have Greville's pocket diary, even if his desk diary had lost October, so I went and fetched it from the bedroom where I'd left it the night before. I though I might find friends' names and phone numbers in the addresses section at the back, but he had been frugal in that department as everywhere else in the slim brown book. I turned the pages, which were most unuseu, seeing only short entries like 'R arrives from Brazil' and 'B in Paris' and 'Buy citrine for P'.

In March I was brought up short. Because it was a racing diary, the race-meetings to be held on each day of the year were listed under the day's date. I came to Thursday 16 March which listed 'Cheltenham'. The word Cheltenham had been ringed in ball-point pen, and Greville had written 'Gold Cup' in the day's space; and then, with a different pen, he had added the words 'Derek won it!!'

It brought me to sudden tears. I couldn't help it.

I longed for him to be alive so I could get to know him better. I wept for the lost opportunities, the time wasted. I longed to know the brother who had cared what I did, who had noted in his almost empty diary that I'd won one of the top races of the year.

CHAPTER 4

There were only three telephone numbers in the addresses section at the back, all identified merely by initials. One, NL, was Nicholas Loder's. I tried the other two, which were London numbers, and got no reply.

Scattered through the rest of the diary were three more numbers. Two of them proved to be restaurants in full evening flood, and I wrote down their names, recognising one of them as the place I'd last dined with Grevelle, two or three months back. On 25 July, presumably, as that was the date on which he'd written the number. It had been an Indian restaurant, I remembered, and we had eaten ultra-hot curry.

Sighing, I turned the pages and tried a number occurring on 2 September, about five weeks earlier. It wasn't a London number, but I didn't recognise the code. I listened to the bell ringing continuously at the other end and had resigned myself to another blank when someone lifted the distant receiver and in a low breathy voice said, 'Hello?'

'Hello,' I replied. 'I'm ringing on behalf of Greville Franklin.'

'Who?'

'Greville Franklin.' I spoke the words slowly and clearly.

'Just a moment.'

There was a long uninformative silence and then someone else clattered on sharp heels up to the receiver and decisively spoke, her voice high and angry.

'How dare you!' she said. 'Don't ever do this again. I will not have your name spoken in this house.'

She put the receiver down with a crash before I could utter a word, and I sat bemusedly looking at my own telephone and feeling as if I'd swallowed a wasp.

Whoever she was, I thought wryly, she wouldn't want to send flowers to the funeral, though she might have been gladdened by the death. I wondered what on earth Greville could have done to raise such a storm, but that was the trouble, I didn't know him well enough to make a good guess.

Thankful on the whole that there weren't any more numbers to be tried I looked again at what few entries he had made, more out of curiosity than looking for helpful facts.

He had noted the days on which his horses had run, again only with initials. DR, Dozen Roses, appeared most, each time with a number following, like 300 at 8s, which I took to mean the amounts he'd wagered at what odds. Below the numbers he had put each time another number inside a circle which, when I compared them with the form book, were revealed as the placings of the horse at the finish. Its last three appearances, all with 1 in the circle, seemed to have netted Greville respectively 500 at 14s, 500 at 5s, 1000 at 6/4. The trot-up scheduled for Saturday, I thought, would be likely to be at odds-on.

Greville's second horse, Gemstones appearing simply as G, had run six times, winning only once but profitably; 500 at 100/6.

All in all, I thought, a moderate betting pattern for an owner. He had made, I calculated, a useful profit overall, more than most owners achieved. With his prize money in addition to offset both the training fees and the capital cost of buying the horses in the first place, I guessed that he had come out comfortably ahead, and it was in the business sense, I supposed, that owning horses had chiefly pleased him.

I flicked casually forward to the end of the book and in the last few pages headed 'NOTES' came across a lot of doodling and then a list of numbers.

The doodling was the sort one does while listening on the telephone, a lot of boxes and zig-zags, haphazard and criss-crossed with lines of shading. On the page facing, there was an equation: $CZ = C \times 1.7$. I supposed it had been of sparkling clarity to Greville, but of no use to me.

Overleaf I found the sort of numbers list I kept in my own diary: passport, bank account, national insurance. After those, in small capital letters further down the page, was a single word DEREK. Another jolt, seeing it again in his writing.

I wondered briefly whether, from its placing, Greville had used my name as some sort of mnemonic, or whether it was just another doodle: there was no way of telling. With a sigh I riffled back through the pages and came to something I'd looked at before, a lightly-pencilled entry for the day before his death. Second time around, it meant just as little.

Koningin Beatrix? he had written. Just the two words and the question mark. I wondered idly if it were the name of a horse, if he'd been considering buying it; my mind tended to work that way. Then I thought that perhaps he'd written the last name first, such as Smith, Jane, and that maybe he'd been going to Ipswich to meet a Beatrix Koningin.

I returned to the horse theory and got through to the trainer I rode for, Milo Shandy, who enquired breezily about the ankle and said would I please waste no time in coming back.

'I could ride out in a couple of weeks,' I said.

'At least that's something, I suppose. Get some massage.'

The mere thought of it was painful. I said I would, not meaning it, and asked about Koningin Beatrix, spelling it out.

'Don't know of any horse called that, but I can find out for you in the morning. I'll ask Weatherby's if the name's available, and if they say yes, it means there isn't a horse called that registered for racing.'

'Thanks a lot.'

'Think nothing of it. I heard your bother died. Bad luck.'

'Yes... How did you know?'

'Nicholas Loder rang me just now, explaining your dilemma and wanting me to persuade you to lease him Dozen Roses.'

'But that's crazy. His ringing you, I mean.'

He chuckled. 'I told him so. I told him I could bend you like a block of teak. He didn't seem to take it in. Anyway, I don't think leasing would solve anything. Jockeys aren't allowed to own racing horses, period. If you lease a horse, you still own it.'

'I'm sure you're right.'

'Put your shirt on it.'

'Loder bets, doesn't he?' I asked. 'In large amounts?'

'So I've heard.'

He said Dozen Roses would trot up at York on Saturday.'

'In that case, do you want me to put a bit on for you?'

Besides not being allowed to run horses in races, jockeys also were banned from betting, but there were always ways round that, like helpful friends.

'I don't think so, not this time,' I said, 'but thanks anyway.'

'You won't mind if I do?'

'Be my guest. If Weatherby's let it run, that is.'

'A nice litte puzzle.' he said appreciatively. 'Come over soon for a drink. Come for evening stables.'

I would, I said.

'Take care.'

I put down the phone, smiling at his easy farewell colloquialism. Jump jockeys were paid not to take care, on the whole. Not too much care.

Milo would be horrified if I obeyed him.

In the morning, Brad drove me to Saxony Franklin's bank to see the manager who was young and bright and spoke with deliberate slowness, as if waiting for his clients' intelligence to catch up. Was there something about crutches, I wondered, that intensified the habit? It took him five minutes to suspect that I wasn't a moron. After that he told me Greville had borrowed a sizeable chunk of the bank's money, and he would be looking to me to repay it. 'One point five million United States dollars in cash, as a matter of fact.'

'One point five million dollars,' I repeated, trying not to show that he had punched most of the breath out of me. '*What for?*'

'For buying diamonds. Diamonds from the DTC of the CSO are, of course, normally paid for in cash, in dollars.'

Bank managers around Hatton Garden, it seemed, saw nothing extraordinary in such an exercise.

'He doesn't ... didn't deal in diamonds,' I protested.

'He had decided to expand and, of course, we made the funds available. Your brother dealt with us for many years and as you'll know was a careful and conscientious businessman. A valued client. We have several times advanced him money for expansion and each time we have been repaid without difficulty. Punctiliously, in fact.' He cleared his throat. 'The present loan, taken out three months ago, is due for repayment progressively over a period of five years, and of course as the loan was made to the company, not to your brother personally, the terms of the loan will be unchanged by his death.'

'Yes,' I said.

'I understood from what you said yesterday that you propose to run the business yourself?' He seemed happy enough where I might have expected a shade of anxiety. So why no anxiety? What wasn't I grasping?

'Do you hold security for the loan?' I asked.

'An agreement. We lent the money against the stock of Saxony Franklin.'

'All the stones?'

'As many as would satisfy the debt. But our best security has always been your brother's integrity and his business ability.'

I said, 'I'm not a gemmologist. I'll probably sell the business after probate.'

He nodded comfortably. 'That might be the best course. We would expect the Saxony Franklin loan to be repaid on schedule, but we would welcome a dialogue with the purchasers.'

He produced papers for me to sign and asked for extra specimen signatures so that I could put my name to Saxony Franklin cheques. He didn't ask what experience I'd had in running a business. Instead, he wished me luck.

I rose to my crutches and shook his hand, thinking of the things I hadn't said.

I hadn't told him I was a jockey, which might have caused a panic in Hatton Garden. And I hadn't told him that, if Greville had bought one and a half million dollars' worth of diamonds, I didn't know where they were.

'Diamonds?' Annette said. 'No. I told you. We never deal in diamonds.'

'The bank manager believes that Greville bought some recently. From something called the DTC of the CSO.'

'The Central Selling Organisation? That's De Beers. The

45

DTC is their diamond trading company. No, no.' She looked anxiously at my face. 'He can't have done. He never said anything about it.'

'Well, has the stock-buying here increased over the past three months?'

'It usually does,' she said, nodding. 'The business always grows. Mr Franklin comes back from world trips with new stones all the time. Beautiful stones. He can't resist them. He sells most of the special ones to a jewellery designer who has several boutiques in places like Knightsbridge and Bond Street. Gorgeous costume jewellry, but with real stones. Many of his pieces are one-offs, designed for a single stone. He has a great name. People prize some of his pieces like Fabergé's.'

'Who is he?'

'Prospero Jenks,' she said, expecting my awe at least.

I hadn't heard of him, but I nodded all the same.

'Does he set the stones with diamonds?' I asked.

'Yes, sometimes. But he doesn't buy those from Saxony Franklin.'

We were in Greville's office, I sitting in his swivel chair behind the vast expanse of desk, Annette sorting yesterday's roughly heaped higgledy-piggledy papers back into the drawers and files that had earlier contained them.

'You don't think Greville would ever have kept diamonds in this actual office, do you?' I asked.

'Certainly not.' The idea shocked her. 'He was always very careful about security.'

'So no one who broke in here would expect to find anything valuable lying about?'

She paused with a sheaf of papers in one hand, her brow wrinkling.

'It's odd, isn't it? They wouldn't expect to find anything valuable lying about in an office if they knew anything about the jewellery trade. And if they didn't know anything about the jewellery trade, why pick this office?'

The same old unanswerable question.

June with her incongruous motherliness brought in the typist's chair again for me to put my foot on. I thanked her and asked if her stock control computer kept day-to-day tabs on the number and value of all the polished pebbles in the place.

'Goodness, yes,' she said with amusement. 'Dates and amounts in, dates and amounts out. Prices in, prices out, profit margin, VAT, tax, you name it, the computer will tell you what we've got, what it's worth, what sells slowly, what sells fast, what's been hanging around here wasting space for two years or more, which isn't much.'

'The stones in the vault as well?'

'Sure.'

'But no diamonds?'

'No, we don't deal in them.' She gave me a bright incurious smile and swiftly departed, saying over her shoulder that the Christmas rush was still going strong and they'd been bombarded by fax orders overnight.

'Who reorders what you sell?' I asked Annette.

'I do for ordinary stock. June tells me what we need. Mr Franklin himself ordered the facetted stones and anything unusual.'

She went on sorting the papers, basically unconcerned because her responsibility ended on her way home. She was wearing that day the charcoal skirt of the day before but topped with a black sweater, perhaps out of respect for Greville. Solid in body, but not large, she had good legs in black tights and a settled, well-groomed, middle-aged air. I couldn't imagine her being as buoyant as June even in her youth.

I asked her if she could lay her hands on the company's insurance policy and she said as it happened she had just re-filed it. I read its terms with misgivings and then telephoned the insurance company. Had my brother, I asked, recently increased the insurance? Had he increased it to cover diamonds to the value of one point five million dollars? He had not. It had been discussed only. My brother had said the premium asked was too high, and he had decided against it. The voice explained that the premium had been high because the stones would be often in transit, which made them vulnerable. He didn't know if Mr Franklin had gone ahead with buying the diamonds. It had been an enquiry only, he thought, three or four months ago. I thanked him numbly and put down the receiver.

The telephone rang again immediately and as Annette seemed to be waiting for me to do so, I answered it.

'Hello?' I said.

A male voice said, 'Is that Mr Franklin? I want to speak to Mr Franklin, please.'

'Er...could I help? I'm his brother.'

'Perhaps you can,' he said. 'This is the clerk of the West London Magistrates Court. Your brother was due here twenty minutes ago and it is unlike him to be late. Could you tell me when to expect him?'

'Just a minute.' I put my hand over the mouthpiece and told Annette what I'd just heard. Her eyes widened and she showed signs of horrified memory.

'It's his day for the Bench! Alternate Tuesdays. I'd clean forgotten.'

I returned to the phone and explained the situation.

'Oh. Oh. How dreadfully upsetting.' He did indeed sound upset, but also a shade impatient. 'It really would have been more helpful if you could have alerted me in advance. It's very short notice to have to find a replacement.'

'Yes,' I agreed, 'but his office was broken into during the weekend. My brother's appointments diary was stolen, and in fact we cannot alert anybody not to expect him.'

'How extremely inconvenient.' It didn't seem an inappropriate statement to him. I thought Greville might find it inconvenient to be dead. Maybe it wasn't the best time for black humour.

'If my brother had personal friends among the magistrates,' I said, 'I would be happy for them to get in touch with me here. If you wouldn't mind telling them.'

'I'll do that, certainly.' He hesitated. 'Mr Franklin sits on the licensing committee. Do you want me to inform the chairman?'

'Yes, please. Tell anyone you can.'

He said goodbye with all the cares of the world on his shoulders and I sighed to Annette that we had better begin telling everyone else as soon as possible, but the trade was to expect business as usual.

'What about the papers?' she asked. 'Shall we put it in *The Times* and so on?'

'Good idea. Can you do it?'

She said she could, but in fact showed me the paragraph she'd written before phoning the papers. 'Suddenly, as the result of an accident, Greville Saxony Franklin JP, son...' She'd left a space after 'son of' which I filled in for her' the late Lt Col and Mrs Miles Franklin'. I changed 'brother of Derek' to 'brother of Susan, Miranda and Derek', and I added a few final words, 'Cremation, Ipswich, Friday.'

'Have you any idea' I asked Annette, 'what he could have been doing in Ipswich?'

She shook her head. 'I've never heard him mention the place. But then he didn't ever tell me very much that wasn't business.' She paused. 'He wasn't exactly secretive, but he never chatted about his private life.' She hesitated. 'He never talked about you.'

I thought of all the times he'd been good company and told me virtually nothing, and I understood very well what she meant.

'He used to say that the best security was a still tongue,' she said. 'He asked us not to talk too much about our jobs to total strangers, and we all know it's safer not to, even though we don't have precious stones here. All the people in the trade are security mad and the diamantaires can be paranoid.'

'What,' I said, 'are diamantaires?'

'Not what, who,' she said. 'They're dealers in rough diamonds. They get the stones cut and polished and sell them to manufacturing jewellers. Mr Franklin always said diamonds were a world of their own, quite separate from other gemstones. There was a ridiculous boom and a terrible crash in world diamond prices during the eighties and a lot of the diamantaires lost fortunes and went bankrupt and Mr Franklin was often saying that they must have been mad to over-extend the way they had.' She paused. 'You couldn't help but know what was happening all around us in this area, where every second business is in gemstones. No one in the pubs and restaurants talked of much else. So you see, I'm sure the bank manager must be wrong. Mr Franklin would never buy diamonds.'

If he hadn't bought diamonds, I thought, what the hell had he done with one point five million dollars in cash.

Bought diamonds. He had to have done. Either that or the money was still lying around somewhere, undoubtedly carefully hidden. Either the money or diamonds to the value were lying

49

around uninsured, and if my semi-secretive ultra-security-conscious brother had left a treasure-island map with X marking the precious spot, I hadn't yet found it. Much more likely, I feared, that the knowledge had died under the scaffolding. If it had, the firm would be forfeited to the bank, the last thing Greville would have wanted.

If it had, a major part of the inheritance he'd left me had vanished like morning mist.

He should have stuck to his old beliefs, I thought gloomily, and let diamonds strictly alone.

The telephone on the desk rang again and this time Annette answered it, as she was beside it.

'Saxony Franklin, can I help you?' she said, and listened. 'No, I'm very sorry, you won't be able to talk to Mr Franklin personally...Could I have your name, please?' She listened. 'Well, Mrs Williams, we must most unhappily inform you that Mr Franklin died as a result of an accident over the weekend. We are however continuing in business. Can I help you at all?'

She listened for a moment or two in increasing puzzlement, then said, 'Are you there? Mrs Williams, can you hear me?' But it seemed as though there was no reply, and in a while she put the receiver down, frowning. 'Whoever it was hung up.'

'Do I gather you don't know Mrs Williams?'

'No, I don't.' She hesitated. 'But I think she rang yesterday, too. I think I told her yesterday that Mr Franklin wasn't expected in the office all day, like I told everyone. I didn't ask for her name yesterday. But she has a voice you don't forget.'

'Why not?'

'Cut glass,' she said succinctly. 'Like Mr Franklin, but more so. Like you too, a bit.'

I was amused. She herself spoke what I thought of as unaccented English, though I supposed any way of speaking sounded like an accent to someone else. I wondered briefly about the cut-glass Mrs Williams who had received the news of the accident in silence and hadn't asked where, or how, or when.

Annette went off to her own office to get through to the newspapers and I picked Greville's diary out of my trouser pocket and tried the numbers that had been unreachable the night before. The two at the back of the book turned out to be first his bookmaker and second his barber, both of whom sounded sorry to be losing his custom, though the bookmaker less so because of Greville's habit of winning.

My ankle heavily ached; the result, I dared say, of general depression as much as aggrieved bones and muscle. Depression because whatever decisions I'd made to that point had been merely commonsense, but there would come a stage ahead when I could make awful mistakes through ignorance. I'd never before handled finances bigger than my own bank balance and the only business I knew anything about was the training of racehorses, and that only from observation, not from hands-on experience. I knew what I was doing around horses: I could tell the spinel from the ruby. In Greville's world, I could be taken for a ride and never know it. I could lose badly before I'd learned even the elementary rules of the game.

Greville's great black desk stretched away to each side of me, the wide knee-hole flanked to right and left by twin stacks of drawers, four stacks in all. Most of them now contained what they had before the break-in, and I began desultorily to investigate the nearest on the left, looking vaguely for anything that would prompt me as to what I'd overlooked or hadn't known was necessary to be done.

I first found not tasks but the toys: the small black gadgets now tidied away into serried ranks. The Geiger counter was there, also the hand-held copier and a variety of calculators, and I picked out a small black contraption about the size of a paperback book and, turning it over curiously, couldn't think what it could be used for.

'That's an electric measurer,' June said, coming breezily into the office with her hands full of paper. 'Want to see how it works?'

I nodded and she put it flat on its back on the desk. 'It'll tell you how far it is from the desk to the ceiling,' she said, pressing knobs. 'There you are, seven feet five and a half inches. In metres,' she pressed another knob, 'two metres twenty-six centimetres.'

'I don't really need to know how far it is to the ceiling,' I said.

She laughed. 'If you hold it flat against a wall, it measures how far it is to the opposite wall. Does it in a flash, as you saw. You don't need to mess around with tape measures. Mr Franklin got it when he was redesigning the stockrooms. And he worked out how much carpet we'd need, and how much paint for the wall. This gadget tells you all that.'

'You like computers, don't you?' I said.

'Love them. All shapes, all sizes.' She peered into the open drawer. 'Mr Franklin was always buying the tiny ones.' She picked out a small grey leather slip-cover the size of a pack of cards and slid the contents onto her palm. 'This little dilly is a travel guide. It tells you things like phone numbers for taxis, airlines, tourist information, the weather, embassies, American Express.' She demonstrated, pushing buttons happily. 'It's an American gadget, it even tells you the TV channels and radio frequencies for about a hundred cities in the US, including Tucson, Arizona, where they hold the biggest gem fair every February. It helps you with fifty other cities round the world, places like Tel Aviv and Hong Kong and Taipei where Mr Greville was always going.'

She put the travel guide down and picked up something else. 'This little round number is a sort of telescope, but it also tells you how far you are away from things. It's for golfers. It tells you how far you are away from the flag on the green, Mr Franklin said, so that you know which club to use.'

'How often did he play golf?' I said, looking through the less than four-inch-long telescope and seeing inside a scale marked GREEN on the lowest line with diminishing numbers above, from 200 yards at the bottom to 40 yards at the top. 'He never talked about it much.'

'He sometimes played at weekends, I think,' June said doubtfully. 'You line up the word GREEN with the actual green, and then the flag stick is always eight feet high, I think, so wherever the top of the stick is on the scale, that's how far away you are. He said it was a good gadget for amateurs like him. He said never to be ashamed of landing in life's bunkers if you'd tried your best shot.' She blinked a bit. 'He always used to show these things to me when he bought them. He knew I liked them too.' She fished for a tissue and without apology wiped her eyes.

'Where did he get them all from?' I asked.

'Mail order catalogues, mostly.'

I was faintly surprised. Mail order and Greville didn't seem to go together, somehow, but I was wrong about that, as I promptly found out.

'Would you like to see our own new catalogue?' June asked, and was out of the door and back again before I could remember if I'd ever seen an old one and decide I hadn't. 'Fresh from the printers,' she said. 'I was just unpacking them.'

I turned the glossy pages of the 50-page booklet, seeing in faithful colours all the polished goodies I'd met in the stockrooms and also a great many of lesser breeding. Amulets, heart shapes, hoops and butterflies: there seemed to be no end to the possibilities of adornment. When I murmured derogatorily that they were a load of junk, June came fast and strongly to their defence, a mother-hen whose chicks had been snubbed.

'Not everyone can afford diamonds,' she said sharply, 'and, anyway, these things are pretty and we sell them in thousands, and they wind up in hundreds of High Street shops and department stores and I often see people buying the odd shapes we've had through here. People do like them, even if they're not your taste.'

'Sorry,' I said.

Some of her fire subsided. 'I suppose I shouldn't speak to you like that,' she said uncertainly, 'but you're not Mr Franklin...' She stopped with a frown.

'It's OK,' I said. 'I am, but I'm not. I know what you mean.'

'Alfie says,' she said slowly, 'that there's a steeplechase jockey called Derek Franklin.' She looked at my foot as if with new understanding. 'Champion jockey one year, he said. Always in the top ten. Is that...you?'

I said neutrally, 'Yes'

'I *had* to ask you,' she said. 'The others didn't want to.'

'Why not?'

'Annette didn't think you could be a jockey. You're too tall. She said Mr Franklin never said anything about you being one. All she knew was that he had a brother he saw a few times a year. She said she was going to ignore what Alfie thought, because it was most unlikely.' She paused. 'Alfie mentioned it yesterday, after you'd gone. Then he said ... they all said ... they didn't see how a jockey could run a business of this sort. If you were one, that is. They didn't want it to be true, so they didn't want to ask.'

'You tell Alfie and the others that if the jockey doesn't run the business their jobs will be down the tubes and they'll be out in the cold before the week's over.'

Her blue eyes widened. 'You sound just like Mr Franklin!'

'And you don't need to mention my profession to the customers, in case I get the same vote of no confidence I've got from the staff.'

Her lips shaped the word 'Wow' but she didn't quite say it. She disappeared fast from the room and presently returned, followed by all the others who were only too clearly in a renewed state of anxiety.

Not one of them a leader. What a pity.

I said, 'You all look as if the ship's been wrecked and the lifeboat's leaking. Well, we've lost the captain, and I agree we're in trouble. My job is with horses and not in an office. But, like I said yesterday, this business is going to stay open and thrive. One way or another, I'll see that it does. So if you'll all go on working normally and keep the customers happy, you'll be doing yourselves a favour because if we get through safely you'll all be due for a bonus. I'm not my brother, but I'm not a fool either, and I'm a pretty fast learner. So just let's get on with the orders, and, er, cheer up.'

Lily, the Charlotte Brontë lookalike, said meekly, 'We don't really doubt your ability ...'

'Of course we do,' interrupted Jason. He stared at me with half a snigger, with a suggestion of curling lip. 'Give us a tip for the three-thirty, then.'

I listened to the street-smart bravado which went with the spiky orange hair. He thought me easy game.

I said, 'When you are personally able to ride the winner of any three-thirty, you'll be entitled to your jeer. Until then, work or leave, it's up to you.'

There was a resounding silence. Alfie almost smiled. Jason looked merely sullen. Annette took a deep breath, and June's eyes were shining with laughter.

They all drifted away still wordless and I couldn't tell to what extent they'd been reassured, if at all. I listened to the echo of my own voice saying I wasn't a fool, and wondering ruefully if it were true: but until the diamonds were found or I'd lost all hope of finding them, I thought it more essential than ever that Saxony Franklin Ltd should stay shakily afloat. All hands, I thought, to the pumps.

June came back and said tentatively, 'The pep talk seems to be working.'

'Good.'

'Alfie gave Jason a proper ticking off, and Jason's staying.'

'Right.'

'What can I do to help?'

I looked at her thin alert face with its fair eylashes and blonde-to-invisible eyebrows and realised that without her the save-the-firm enterprise would be a non-starter. She, more than her computer, was at the heart of things. She more than Annette, I thought.

'How long have you worked her?' I asked.

'Three years. Since I left school. Don't ask if I like the job, I love it. What can I do?'

Look up in your computer's memory any reference to diamonds,' I said.

She was briefly impatient. 'I told you, we don't deal in diamonds.'

'All the same, would you?'

She shrugged and was gone. I got to my feet — foot — and followed her, and watched while she expertly tapped her keys.

'Nothing at all under diamonds,' she said finally. 'Nothing. I told you.'

'Yes.' I thought about the boxes in the vault with the mineral information on the labels. 'Do you happen to know the chemical formula for diamonds?'

'Yes, I do,' she said instantly. 'It's C. Diamonds are pure carbon.'

'Could you try again, then, under C?'

She tried. There was no file for C.

'Did my brother know how to use this computer?' I asked.

'He knew how to work all computers. Given five minutes or so to read the instructions.'

I pondered, staring at the blank unhelpful screen.

'Are there,' I asked eventually, 'any secret files in this?'

She stared. 'We never use secret files.'

'But you could do?'

'Of course. Yes. But we don't need to.'

'If,' I said, 'there were any secret files, would you know that they were there?'

She nodded briefly. 'I wouldn't know, but I could find out.'

'How?' I asked. 'I mean, please would you?'

'What am I looking for? I don't understand.'

'Diamonds.'

'But I told you, we don't ...'

'I know,' I said 'but my brother said he was going to buy diamonds, and I need to know if he did. If there's any chance he made a private entry on this computer some day when he was first or last in this office, I need to find it.'

She shook her head but tapped away obligingly, bringing what she called menus to the screen. It seemed a fairly lengthy business but finally, frowning, she found something that gave her pause. Then her concentration increased abruptly until the screen was showing the word 'Password?' as before.

'I don't understand,' she said. 'We gave this computer a general password which is Saxony, though we almost never use it. But you can put in any password you like on any particular document to supersede Saxony. This entry was made only a month ago. The date is on the menu. But whoever made it didn't use Saxony as the password. So the password could be anything, literally any word in the world.'

I said, 'By document you mean file?'

'Yes, file. Every entry has a document name, like, say, "oriental cultured pearls". If I load "oriental cultured pearls" onto the screen I can review our whole stock. I do it all the time. But this document with an unknown password is listed under pearl in the singular, not pearls in the plural, and I don't understand it. I didn't put it there.' She glanced at me. 'At any rate, it doesn't say diamonds.'

'Have another try to guess the password.'

She tried Franklin and Greville without result. 'It could be *anything*,' she said helplessly.

'Try Dozen Roses.'

'Why Dozen Roses?' She thought it extraordinary.

'Greville owned a horse — a racehorse — with that name.'

'Really? He never said. He was so nice, and awfully private.'

'He owned another horse called Gemstones.'

With visible doubt she tried 'Dozen Roses' and then 'Gemstones'. Nothing happened except another insistent demand for the password.

'Try "diamonds", then,' I said.

She tried 'diamonds'. Nothing changed.

'You knew him,' I said. 'Why would he enter something under "pearl?'

'No idea.' She sat hunched over the keys, drumming her fingers on her mouth. 'Pearl. Pearl. Why pearl?'

'What is a pearl?' I said. 'Does it have a formula?'

'Oh.' She suddenly sat up straight. 'It's a birthstone.'

She typed in 'birthstone', and nothing happened.

Then she blushed slightly.

'It's one of the birthstones for the month of June,' she said. 'I could try it, anyway.'

She typed 'June', and the screen flashed and gave up its secrets.

CHAPTER 5

We hadn't found the diamonds.
The screen said:

> June, if you are reading this, come straight into my office
> for a raise. You are worth you weight in your birthstone, but
> I'm only offering to increase your salary by twenty per cent.
> Regards, Greville Franklin.

'Oh!' She sat transfixed. 'So that's what he meant.'
'Explain,' I said.
'One morning...' She stopped, her mouth screwing up in an
effort not to cry. It took her a while to be able to continue, then
she said, 'One morning he told me he'd invented a little puzzle
for me and he would give me six months to solve it. After six
months it would self-destruct. He was smiling so much.' She
swallowed. 'I asked him what sort of puzzle and he wouldn't tell
me. He just said he hoped I would find it.'
'Did you look?' I asked.
'Of course I did. I looked everywhere in the office, though I
didn't know what I was looking for. I even looked for a new
document in the computer, but I just never gave a thought to its
being filed as a secret and my eyes just slid over the word
'pearl', as I see it so often. Silly of me. Stupid.'
I said 'I don't think you're stupid, and I'll honour my
brother's promise.'

She gave me a swift look of pleasure but shook her head a little and said, 'I didn't find it. I'd never have solved it except for you.' She hesitated. 'How about ten per cent?'

'Twenty,' I said firmly. 'I'm going to need your help and your knowledge, and if Annette is Personal Assistant, as it says on the door of her office, you can be Deputy Personal Assistant, with the new salary to go with the job.'

She turned a deeper shade of rose and busied herself with making a print-out of Greville's instruction, which she folded and put in her handbag.

'I'll leave the secret in the computer,' she said with misty fondness. 'No one else will ever find it.' She pressed a few buttons and the screen went blank, and I wondered how many times in private she would call up the magic words that Greville had left her.

I wondered if they would really self-destruct: if one could programme something on a computer to erase itself on a given date. I didn't see why not, but I thought Greville might have given her strong clues before the six months were out.

I asked her if she would print out first a list of everything currently in the vault and then as many things as she thought would help me understand the business better, like the volume and value of a day's, a week's, a month's sales; like which items were most popular, and which least.

'I can tell you that what's very popular just now is black onyx. Fifty years ago they say it was all amber, now no one buys it. Jewellery goes in and out of fashion like everything else.' She began tapping keys. 'Give me a little while and I'll print you a crash course.'

'Thanks,' I smiled, and waited while the printer spat out a gargantuan mouthful of glittering facets. Then I took the list in search of Annette, who was along in the stockrooms, and asked her to give me a quick canter round the vault.

'There aren't any diamonds there,' she said positively.

'I'd better learn what is.'

'You don't seem like a jockey,' she said.

'How many do you know?'

She stared. 'None, except you.'

'On the whole,' I said mildly, 'jockeys are like anyone else. Would you feel I was better able to manage here if I were, say,

59

a piano tuner? Or an actor? Or a clergyman?'

She said faintly, 'No.'

'OK, then. We're stuck with a jockey. Twist of fate. Do your best for the poor fellow.'

She involuntarily smiled a genuine smile which lightened her heavy face miraculously. 'All right.' She paused. 'You're really like Mr Franklin in some ways. The way you say things. Deal with honour, he said, and sleep at night.'

'You all remember what he said, don't you?'

'Of course.'

He would have been glad, I supposed, to have left so positive a legacy. So many precepts. So much wisdom. But so few sign-posts to his personal life. No visible sign-post to the diamonds.

In the vault Annette showed me that, besides its chemical formula, each label bore a number: if I looked at that number on the list June had printed, I would see the formula again, but also the normal names of the stones, with colours, shapes and sizes and country of origin.

'Why did he label them like this?' I asked. 'It just makes it difficult to find things.'

'I believe that was his purpose,' she answered. 'I told you, he was very security conscious. We had a secretary working here once who managed to steal a lot of our most valuable turquoise out of the vault. The labels read "turquoise" then, which made it easy, but now they don't.'

'What do they say?'

She smiled and pointed to a row of boxes. I looked at the labels and read $CuAl_6(PO_4)_4(OH)_8.4\text{-}5(H_2O)$ on each of them.

'Enough to put anyone off for life,' I said.

'Exactly. That's the point. Mr Franklin could read formulas as easily as words, and I've got used to them myself now. No one but he and I handle these stones in here. We pack them into boxes ourselves and seal them before they go to Alfie for despatch.' She looked along the rows of labels and did her best to educate me. 'We sell these stones at so much per carat. A carat weighs two hundred milligrams, which means five carats to a gram, a hundred and forty-two carats to an ounce and five thousand carats to the kilo.'

'Stop right there,' I begged.

'You said you learned fast.'

'Give me a day or two.'

She nodded and said if I didn't need her any more she had better get on with the ledgers.

Ledgers, I thought, wilting internally. I hadn't even started on those. I thought of the joy with which I'd left Lancaster University with a degree in Independent Studies, swearing never again to pore dutifully over books and heading straight (against my father's written wishes) to the steeplechase stable where I'd been spending truant days as an amateur. It was true that at college I'd learned fast, because I'd had to, and learned all night often enough, keeping faith with at least the first half of my father's letter. He'd hoped I would grow out of the lure he knew I felt for race-riding, but it was all I'd ever wanted and I couldn't have settled to anything else. There was no long-term future in it, he'd written, besides a complete lack of financial security along with a constant risk of disablement. I ask you to be sensible, he'd said, to think it through and decide against.

Fat chance.

I sighed for the simplicity of the certainty I'd felt in those days, yet, given a second beginning, I wouldn't have lived any differently. I had been deeply fulfilled in racing and grown old in spirit only because of the way life worked in general. Disappointments, injustices, small betrayals, they were everyone's lot. I no longer expected everything to go right, but enough had gone right to leave me at least in a balance of content.

With no feeling that the world owed me anything, I applied myself to the present boring task of opening every packet in every box in the quest for little bits of pure carbon. It wasn't that I expected to find the diamonds there: it was just that it would be so stupid not to look, in case they were.

I worked methodically, putting the boxes one at a time on the wide shelf which ran along the right-hand wall, unfolding the stiff white papers with the soft inner linings and looking at hundreds of thousands of peridots, chrysoberyls, garnets and aquamarines until my head spun. I stopped in fact when I'd done only a third of the stock because apart from the airlessness of the vault it was physically tiring standing on one leg all the time, and the crutches got in the way as much as they helped. I

61

refolded the last of the $XY_3Z_6[(O,OH,F)_4(BO_3)_3Si_6O_{18}]$ (tourmaline) and gave it best.

'What did you learn?' Annette asked when I reappeared in Greville's office. She was in there, replacing yet more papers in their proper files, a task apparently nearing completion.

'Enough to look at jewellery shops differently,' I said.

She smiled. 'When I read magazines I don't look at the clothes, I look at the jewellery.'

I could see that she would. I thought that I might also, despite myself, from then on. I might even develop an affinity with black onyx cufflinks.

It was by that time four o'clock in the afternoon of what seemed a very long day. I looked up the racing programme in Greville's diary, decided that Nicholas Loder might well have passed over going to Redcar, Warwick and Folkestone, and dialled his number. His secretary answered, and yes, Mr Loder was at home, and yes, he would speak to me.

He came on the line with almost none of the previous evening's agitation, bass resonances positively throbbing down the wire.

'I've been talking to Weatherby's and the Jockey Club,' he said easily, 'and there's fortunately no problem. They agree that before probate the horses belong to Saxony Franklin Limited and not to you, and they will not bar them from racing in that name.'

'Good,' I said, and was faintly surprised.

'They say of course that there has to be at least one registered agent appointed by the company to be responsible for the horses, such appointment to be sealed with the company's seal and registered at Weatherby's. Your brother appointed both himself and myself as registered agents, and although he has died I remain a registered agent as before and can act for the company on my own.'

'Ah,' I said.

'Which being so,' Loder said happily, 'Dozen Roses runs at York as planned.'

'And trots up?'

He chuckled. 'Let's hope so.'

That chuckle, I thought, was the ultimate in confidence.

I'd be grateful if you could let Saxony Franklin know

whenever the horses are due to run in the future,' I said.

'I used to speak to your brother personally at his home number. I can hardly do that with you, as you don't own the horses.'

'No,' I agreed. 'I meant, please will you tell the company? I'll give you the number. And would you ask for Mrs Annette Adams? She was Greville's second-in-command.'

He could hardly say he wouldn't, so I read the number and he repeated it as he wrote it down.

'Don't forget though that there's only a month left of the Flat season,' he said. 'They'll probably run only once more each. Two at the very most. Then I'll sell them for you, that would be best. No problem. Leave it to me.'

He was right, logically, but I still illogically disliked his haste.

'As executor, I'd have to approve any sale,' I said, hoping I was right. 'In advance.'

'Yes, yes, of course,' Reassuring heartiness. 'Your injury,' he said, 'what exactly is it?'

'Busted ankle.'

'Ah. Bad luck. Getting on well, I hope?' The sympathy sounded more like relief to me than anything else, and again I couldn't think why.

'Getting on,' I said.

'Good, good. Goodbye then. The York race should be on the television on Saturday. I expect you'll watch it?'

'I expect so.'

'Fine.' He put down the receiver in great good humour and left me wondering what I'd missed.

Greville's telephone rang again immediately, and it was Brad to tell me that he had returned from his day's visit to an obscure aunt in Walthamstow and was downstairs in the front hall: all he actually said was, 'I'm back.'

'Great I won't be long.'

I got a click in reply. End of conversation.

I did mean to leave almost at once but there were two more phone calls in fairly quick succession. The first was from a man introducing himself as Elliot Trelawney, a colleague of Greville's from the West London Magistrates Court. He was extremely sorry, he said, to hear about his death, and he truly sounded it. A positive voice, used to attention: a touch of plummy accent.

'Also,' he said, 'I'd like to talk to you about some projects Greville and I were working on. I'd like to have his notes.'

I said rather blankly, 'What projects? What notes?'

'I could explain better face to face,' he said. 'Could I ask you to meet me? Say tomorrow, early evening, over a drink? You know the pub just round the corner from Greville's house? The Rook and Castle? There. He and I often met there. Five-thirty, six, either of those suit you?'

'Five-thirty', I said obligingly.

'How shall I know you?'

'By my crutches.'

It silenced him momentarily. I let him off embarrassment.

'They're temporary,' I said'

'Er, fine, then. Until tomorrow.'

He cut himself off, and I asked Annette if she knew him, Elliot Trelawney? She shook her head. She couldn't honestly say she knew anyone outside the office who was known to Greville personally. Unless you counted Prospero Jenks, she said doubtfully. And even then, she herself had never really met him, only talked to him frequently on the telephone.

'Prospero Jenks...alias Fabergé?'

'That's the one.'

I thought a bit. 'Would you mind phoning him now?' I said. 'Tell him about Greville and ask if I can go to see him to discuss the future. Just say I'm Greville's brother, nothing else.'

'She grinned. 'No horses? Pas de gee-gees?'

Annette, I thought in amusement, was definitely loosening up.

'No horses,' I agreed.

She made the call but without results. Prospero Jenks wouldn't be reachable until morning. She would try then, she said.

I levered myself upright and said I'd see her tomorrow. She nodded, taking it for granted that I would be there. The quicksands were winning, I thought. I was less and less able to get out.

Going down the passage I stopped to look in on Alfie whose day's work stood in columns of loaded cardboard boxes waiting to be entrusted to the post.

'How many do you send out every day?' I asked, gesturing to

them.

He looked up briefly from stretching sticky tape round yet another parcel. 'About twenty, twenty-five regular, but more from August to Christmas.' He cut off the tape expertly and stuck an address label deftly on the box top. 'Twenty-eight so far today.'

'Do you bet, Alfie?' I asked. 'Read the racing papers?'

He glanced at me with a mixture of defensiveness and defiance, neither of which feeling was necessary. 'I *knew* you was him,' he said. 'The others said you couldn't be.'

'You know Dozen Roses too?'

A tinge of craftiness took over in expression. 'Started winning again, didn't he? I missed him the first time, but yes, I've had a little tickle since.'

'He runs on Saturday at York, but he'll be odds-on,' I said.

'Will he win, though? Will they be trying with him? I wouldn't put my shirt on that.'

'Nicholas Loder says he'll trot up.'

He knew who Nicholas Loder was: didn't need to ask. With cynicism, he put his just-finished box on some sturdy scales and wrote the result on the cardboard with a thick black pen. He must have been well into his sixties, I thought, with deep lines from his nose to the corners of his mouth and pale sagging skin everywhere from which most of the elasticity had vanished. His hands, with the veins of age beginning to show dark blue, were nimble and strong however, and he bent to pick up another heavy box with a supple back. A tough old customer, I thought, and essentially more in touch with street awareness than the exaggerated Jason.

'Mr Franklin's horses run in and out,' he said pointedly. 'And as a jock you'd know about that.'

Before I could decide whether or not he was intentionally insulting me, Annette came hurrying down the passage calling my name.

'Derek...Oh there you are. Still here, good. There's another phone call for you.' She about-turned and went back towards Greville's office, and I followed her, noticing with interest that she'd dropped the Mister from my name. Yesterday's unthinkable was today's natural, now that I was established as a jockey, which was OK as far as it went, as long as it didn't go too far.

I picked up the receiver which was lying on the black desk and said, 'Hello? Derek Franklin speaking.'

A familiar voice said, 'Thank God for that. I've been trying your Hungerford number all day. Then I remembered about your brother...' He spoke loudly, driven by urgency.

Milo Shandy, the trainer I'd ridden most for during the past three seasons: a perpetual optimist in the face of world evidence of corruption, greed and lies.

'I've a crisis on my hands,' he bellowed, 'and can you come over? Will you pull out all stops to come over first thing in the morning?'

'Er, what for?'

'You know the Ostermeyers? They've flown over from Pittsburgh for some affair in London and they phoned me and I told them Datepalm is for sale. And you know that if they buy him I can keep him here, otherwise I'll lose him because he'll have to go to auction. And they want you here when they see him work on the Downs and they can only manage first lot tomorrow, and they think the sun twinkles out of your backside, so for God's sake *come*.'

Interpreting the agitation was easy. Datepalm was the horse on which I'd won the Gold Cup: a seven-year-old gelding still near the beginning of what with luck would be a notable jumping career. Its owner had recently dropped the bombshell of telling Milo she was leaving England to marry an Australian, and if he could sell Datepalm to one of his other owners for the astronomical figure she named, she wouldn't send it to public auction and out of his yard.

Milo had been in a panic most of the time since then because none of his other owners had so far thought the horse worth the price, his Gold Cup success having been judged lucky in the absence through coughing of a couple of more established stars. Both Milo and I thought Datepalm better than his press, and I had as strong a motive as Milo for wanting him to stay in the stable.

'Calm down,' I assured him. 'I'll be there.'

He let out a lot of breath in a rush. 'Tell the Ostermeyers he's a really good horse.'

'He is,' I said, 'and I will.'

'Thanks, Derek.' His voice dropped to normal decibels. 'Oh

66

and by the way, there's no horse called Koningin Beatrix, and not likely to be. Weatherby's say Konignin Beatrix means Queen Beatrix, as In Queen Beatrix of the Netherlands, and they frown on people naming racehorses after royal persons.'

'Oh,' I said. 'Well, thanks for finding out.'

'Any time. See you in the morning. For God's sake don't be late. You know the Ostermeyers get up before larks.'

'What I need,' I said to Annette, putting down the receiver, 'is an appointments book, so as not to forget where I've said I'll be.'

She began looking in the drawerful of gadgets.

'Mr Franklin had an electric memory thing he used to put appointments in. You could use that for now.' She sorted through the black collection, but without result. 'Stay here a minute,' she said, closing the drawer, 'while I ask June if she knows where it is.'

She went away busily and I thought about how to convince the Ostermeyers, who could afford anything they set their hearts on, that Datepalm would bring them glory if not necessarily repay their bucks. They had had steeplechasers with Milo from time to time, but not for almost a year at the moment. I'd do a great deal, I thought, to persuade them it was time to come back.

An alarm like a digital watch alarm sounded faintly, muffled, and to begin with I paid it no attention, but as it persisted I opened the gadget drawer to investigate and, of course, as I did so it immediately stopped. Shrugging, I closed the drawer again, and Annette came back bearing a sheet of paper but no gadget.

'June doesn't know where the Wizard is, so I'll make out a rough calendar on plain paper.'

'What's the Wizard?' I asked.

'The calculator. Baby computer. June says it does everything but boil eggs.'

Why do you call it the Wizard?' I asked.

'It has that name on it. It's about the size of a paperback book and it was Mr Franklin's favourite object. He took it every-where.' She frowned. 'Maybe it's in his car, wherever that is.'

The car. Another problem. 'I'll find the car,' I said, with more confidence than I felt. Somehow or other I would have to find the car. 'Maybe the Wizard was stolen out of this office in the break-in,' I said.

She stared at me with widely opening eyes. 'The thief would have to have known what it was. It folds up flat. You can't see any buttons.'

'All the gadgets were out on the floor, weren't they?'

'Yes.' It troubled her. 'Why the address book? Why the engagements for October? Why the Wizard?'

Because of diamonds, I thought instinctively, but couldn't rationalise it. Someone had perhaps been looking, as I was, for the treasure map marked X. Perhaps they'd known it existed. Perhaps they'd found it.

'I'll get here a couple of hours later tomorrow,' I said to Annette. 'And I must leave by five to meet Elliot Trelawney at five-thirty. So if you reach Prospero Jenks, ask him if I could go to see him in between. Or failing that, any time Thursday. Write off Friday because of the funeral.'

Greville died only the day before yesterday, I thought. It already seemed half a lifetime.

Annette said, 'Yes, Mr Franklin,' and bit her lip in dismay.

I half smiled at her. 'Call me Derek. Just plain Derek. And invest it with whatever you feel.'

'It's confusing,' she said weakly, 'from minute to minute.'

'Yes, I know.'

With a certain relief I rode down in the service lift and swung across to Brad in the car. He hopped out of the front seat and shovelled me into the back, tucking the crutches in beside me and waiting while I lifted my leg along the padded leather and wedged myself into the corner for the most comfortable angle of ride.

'Home?' he said.

'No. Like I told you on the way up, we'll stop in Kensington for a while, if you don't mind.'

He gave the tiniest of nods. I'd provided him in the morning with a detailed large-scale map of West London, asking him to work out how to get to the road where Greville had lived, and I hoped to hell he had done it, because I was feeling more drained than I cared to admit and not ready to ride in irritating traffic-clogged circles.

'Look out for a pub called The Rook and Castle, would you?'

68

I asked, as we neared the area. 'Tomorrow at five-thirty I have to meet someone there.'

Brad nodded and with the unerring instinct of the beer drinker quickly found it, merely pointing vigorously to tell me.

'Great,' I said, and he acknowledged that with a wiggle of the shoulders.

He drew up so confidently outside Greville's address that I wondered if he had reconnoitred earlier in the day, except that his aunt lived theoretically in the opposite direction. In any case, he handed me the crutches, opened the gate of the small front garden and said loquaciously, 'I'll wait in the car.'

'I might be an hour or more. Would you mind having a quick recce up and down this street and those nearby to see if you can find an old Rover with this number?' I gave him a card with it on. 'My brother's car,' I said.

He gave me a brief nod and turned away, and I looked up at the tall townhouse that Greville had moved into about three months previously, and which I'd never visited. It was creamy-grey, gracefully proportioned, with balustraded steps leading up to the black front door, and businesslike but decorative metal grilles showing behind the glass in every window from semi-basement to roof.

I crossed the grassy front garden and went up the steps, and found there were three locks on the front door. Cursing slightly I yanked out Greville's half-ton of keys and by trial and error found the way into his fortress.

Late afternoon sun slanted yellowly into a long main drawing room which was on the left of the entrance hall, throwing the pattern of the grilles in shadows on the greyish-brown carpet. The walls, pale salmon, were adorned with vivid paintings of stained-glass cathedral windows, and the fabric covering sofa and armchairs was of a large broken herringbone pattern in dark brown and white, confusing to the eye. I reflected ruefully that I didn't know whether it all represented Greville's own taste or whether he'd taken it over from the past owner. I knew only his taste in clothes, food, gadgets and horses. Not very much. Not enough.

The drawing room was dustless and tidy; unlived in. I returned to the front hall from where stairs led up and down, but before tackling those I went through a door at the rear which opened into a much smaller room filled with a homely clutter of books, newspapers, magazines, black leather chairs, clocks, chrysanthemums in pots, a tray of booze and framed medieval brass rubbings on deep green walls. This was all Greville, I thought. This was home.

I left it for the moment and hopped down the stairs to the semi-basement, where there was a bedroom, unused, a small bathroom and decorator-style dining room looking out through grilles to a rear garden, with a narrow spotless kitchen alongside.

Fixed to the fridge by a magnetic strawberry was a note.

Dear Mr Franklin,
    I didn't know you'd be away this weekend. I brought in all the papers, they're in the back room. You didn't leave your laundry out, so I haven't taken it. Thanks for the money. I'll be back next Tuesday as usual.

Mrs P

I looked around for a pencil, found a ball-point, pulled the note from its clip and wrote on the back, asking Mrs P to call the following number (Saxony Franklin's) and speak to Derek or Annette. I didn't sign it, but put it back under the strawberry where I supposed it would stay for another week, a sorry message in waiting.

I looked in the fridge which contained little but milk, butter, grapes, a pork pie and two bottles of champagne.

Diamonds in the ice cubes? I didn't think he would have put them anywhere so chancy: besides, he was security conscious, not paranoid.

I hauled myself upstairs to the hall again and then went on up to the next floor where there was a bedroom and bathroom suite in self-conscious black and white. Greville had slept there: the built-in cupboards and drawers held his clothes, the bathroom closet his privacy. He had been sparing in his possessions, leaving a single row of shoes, several white shirts on hangers, six assorted suits and a rack of silk ties. The drawers were tidy with sweaters, sports shirts, underclothes, socks. Our mother, I thought with a smile, would have been proud of him. She'd tried hard and unsuccessfully to instil tidiness into both of us as children, and it looked as if we'd both got better with age.

There was little else to see. The drawer in the bedside table revealed indigestion tablets, a torch and a paperback, John D. MacDonald. No gadgets and no treasure maps.

With a sigh I went into the only other room on that floor and found it unfurnished and papered with garish metallic silvery roses which had been half ripped off at one point. So much for the decorator.

There was another flight of stairs going upwards, but I didn't climb them. There would only be, by the looks of things, unused rooms to find there, and I thought I would go and look later when stairs weren't such a sweat. Anything deeply interesting in that house seemed likely to be found in the small back sitting room, so it was to there that I returned.

I sat for a while in the chair that was clearly Greville's favourite, from where he could see the television and the view over the garden. Places that people had left for ever should be seen through their eyes, I thought. His presence was strong in that room, and in me.

Beside his chair there was a small antique table with, on its polished top, a telephone and an answering machine. A red light for messages received was shining on the machine, so after a while I pressed a button marked 'rewind', followed by another marked 'play'.

A woman's voice spoke without preamble.

'Darling, where are you? Do ring me.'

There was a series of between-message clicks, then the same voice again, this time packed with anxiety.

'Darling, please please ring. I'm very worried. Where are you, darling? *Please* ring. I love you.'

Again the clicks, but no more messages.

Poor lady, I thought. Grief and tears waiting in the wings.

I got up and explored the room more fully, pausing by two drawers in a table beside the window. They contained two small black unidentified gadgets which baffled me and which I stowed in my pockets, and also a slotted tray containing a rather nice collection of small bears, polished and carved from shaded pink, brown and charcoal stone. I laid the tray on top of the table beside some chrysanthemums and came next to a box

71

made of greenish stone, also polished and which, true to Greville's habit, was firmly locked. Thinking perhaps that one of the keys fitted it I brought out the bunch again and began to try the smallest.

I was facing the window with my back to the room, balancing on one foot and leaning a thigh against the table, my arms out of the crutches, intent on what I was doing and disastrously unheeding. The first I knew of anyone else in the house was a muffled exclamation behind me, and I turned to see a dark-haired woman coming through the doorway, her wild glance rigidly fixed on the green stone box. Without pause she came fast towards me, pulling out of a pocket a black object like a long fat cigar.

I opened my mouth to speak but she brought her hand round in a strong swinging arc, and in that travel the short black cylinder more than doubled its length into a thick silvery flexible stick which crashed with shattering force against my left upper arm, enough to stop a heavyweight in round one.

CHAPTER 6

My fingers went numb and dropped the box. I swayed and spun from the force of the impact and overbalanced, toppling, thinking sharply that I mustn't this time put my foot on the ground. I dropped the bunch of keys and grabbed at the back of an upright black leather chair with my right hand to save myself, but it turned over under my weight and came down on top of me onto the carpet in a tangle of chair legs, table legs and crutches, the green box underneath and digging into my back.

In a spitting fury I tried to orientate myself and finally got enough breath for one single choice, charming and heartfelt worl.

'*Bitch*.'

She gave me a baleful glare and picked up the telephone, pressing three fast buttons.

'Police,' she said, and in as short a time as it took the emergency service to connect her, 'Police, I want to report a burglary. I've caught a burglar.'

'I'm Greville's brother,' I said thickly, from the floor.

For a moment it didn't seem to reach her. I said again, more loudly, 'I'm Greville's brother'.

'What?' she said vaguely.

'For Christ's sake, are you deaf? I'm not a burglar, I'm Greville Franklin's brother.' I gingerly sat up into an L-shape and found no strength anywhere.

She put the phone down. 'Why didn't you say so?' she demanded.

73

'What chance did you give me? And who the hell are you, walking into my brother's house and belting people?'

She held at the ready the fearsome thing she'd hit me with, looking as if she thought I'd attack her in my turn, which I certainly felt like. In the last six days I'd been crunched by a horse, a mugger and a woman. All I needed was a toddler to amble up with a coup de grâce. I pressed the fingers of my right hand on my forehead and the palm against my mouth and considered the blackness of life in general.

'What's the matter with you?' she said after a pause.

I slid the hand away and drawled, 'Absolutely bloody nothing.'

'I only tapped you,' she said with criticism.

'Shall I give you a hefty clip with that thing so you can feel what it's like?'

'You're angry.' She sounded surprised.

'Dead right.'

I struggled up off the floor, straightened the fallen chair and sat on it. 'Who are you?' I repeated. But I knew who she was: the woman on the answering machine. The same voice. The cut-crystal accent. Darling, where are you? I love you.

'Did you ring his office?' I said. 'Are you Mrs Williams?'

She seemed to tremble and crumple inwardly and she walked past me to the window to stare out into the garden.

'Is he really dead?' she said.

'Yes.'

She was forty, I thought. Perhaps more. Nearly my height. In no way tiny or delicate. A woman of decision and power, sorely troubled.

She wore a leather-belted raincoat, though it hadn't rained for weeks, and plain black businesslike court shoes. Her hair thick and dark, was combed smoothly back from her forehead to curl under on her collar, a cool groomed look achieved only by expert cutting. There was no visible jewellery, little remaining lipstick, no trace of scent.

'How?' she said eventually.

I had a strong impulse to deny her the information, to punish her for her precipitous attack, to hurt her and get even. But there was no point in it, and I knew I would end up with more shame than satisfaction, so after a struggle I explained briefly

74

about the scaffolding.

'Friday afternoon,' I said. 'He was unconscious at once. He died early on Sunday.'

She turned her head slowly to look at me directly. 'Are you Derek?' she said.

'Yes.'

'I'm Clarissa Williams.'

Neither of us made any attempt to shake hands. It would have been incongruous, I thought.

'I came to fetch some things of mine,' she said. 'I didn't expect anyone to be here.'

It was an apology of sorts, I supposed: and if I had indeed been a burglar she would have saved the bric-à-brac.

'What things?' I asked.

She hesitated, but in the end said, 'A few letters, that's all.' Her gaze strayed to the answering machine and there was a definite tightening of muscles round her eyes.

'I played the messages,' I said.

'Oh God.'

'Why should it worry you?'

She had her reasons, it seemed, but she wasn't going to tell me what they were: or not then, at any rate.

'I want to wipe them off,' she said. 'it was one of the purposes of coming.'

She glanced at me, but I couldn't think of any urgent reason why she shouldn't so I didn't say anything. Tentatively, as if asking my forbearance every step of the way, she walked jerkily to the machine, rewound the tape and pressed the record button, recording silence over what had gone before. After a while she rewound the tape again and played it, and there were no desperate appeals any more.

'Did anyone else hear...?'

'I don't think so. Not unless the cleaner was in the habit of listening. She came today, I think.'

'Oh God.'

'You left no name.' Why the hell was I reassuring her, I wondered. I still had no strength in my fingers. I could still feel that awful blow like a shudder.

'Do you want a drink?' she said abruptly. 'I've had a dreadful day.' She went over to the tray of bottles and poured vodka into a heavy tumbler. 'What do you want?'

'Water,' I said. 'Make it a double.'

She tightened her mouth and put down the vodka bottle with a clink. 'Soda or tonic?' she asked starchily.

'Soda.'

She poured soda into a glass for me and tonic into her own, diluting the spirit by not very much. Ice was downstairs in the kitchen. No one mentioned it.

I noticed she'd left her lethal weapon lying harmlessly beside the answering machine. Presumably I no longer represented any threat. As if avoiding personal contact, she set my soda water formally on the table beside me between the little stone bears and the chrysanthemums and drank deply from her own glass. Better than tranquillisers, I thought. Alcohol loosened the stress, calmed the mental pain. The world's first anaesthetic. I could have done with some myself.

'Where are your letters?' I asked.

She switched on a table light. The on-creeping dusk in the garden deepened abruptly towards night and I wished whe would hurry up because I wanted to go home.

She looked at a bookcase which covered a good deal of one wall.

'In there, I think. In a book.'

'Do start looking, then. It could take all night.'

'You don't need to wait.'

'I think I will,' I said.

'Don't you trust me?' she demanded.

'No.'

She stared at me hard. 'Why not?'

I didn't say that because of the diamonds I didn't trust anyone. I didn't know who I could safely ask to look out for them, or who would search to steal them, if they knew they might be found.

'I don't know you,' I said neutrally.

'But I...' She stopped and shrugged. 'I suppose I don't know you either.' She went over to the bookshelves. 'Some of these books are hollow,' she said.

Oh Greville, I thought. How would I ever find anything he had hidden? I liked straight paths. He'd had a mind like a labyrinth.

She began pulling out books from the lower shelves and opening the front covers. Not methodically book by book along any row but always, it seemed to me, those with predominantly blue spines. After a while, on her knees, she found a hollow one which she laid open on the floor with careful sarcasm, so that I could see she wasn't concealing anything.

The interior of the book was in effect a blue velvet box with a close-fitting lid that could be pulled out by a tab. When she pulled the lid out, the shallow blue velvet-lined space beneath was revealed as being entirely empty.

Shrugging, she replaced the lid and closed the book, which immediately looked like any other book, and returned it to the shelves: and a few seconds later found another hollow one, this time with red velvet interiors. Inside this one lay an envelope.

She looked at it without touching it, and then at me.

'It's not my letters,' she said. 'Not my writing paper.'

I said, 'Greville made a will leaving everything he possessed to me.'

She didn't seem to find it extraordinary, although I did: he had done it that way for simplicity when he was in a hurry, and he would certainly have changed it, given time.

'You'd better see what's in here, then,' she said calmly, and she picked the envelope out and stretched across to hand it to me.

The envelope, which hadn't been stuck down, contained a single ornate key, about four inches long, the top flattened and pierced like metal lace, the business end narrow with small but intricate teeth. I laid it on my palm and showed it to her, asking her if she knew what it unlocked.

She shook her head. 'I haven't seen it before.' She paused. 'He was a man of secrets,' she said.

I listened to the wistfulness in her voice. She might be strongly controlled at that moment, but she hadn't been before Annette told her Greville was dead. There had been raw panicky emotion on the tape. Annette had simply confirmed her frightful fears and put what I imagined was a false calmness in place of escalating despair. A man of secrets ... Greville had apparently not opened his mind to her much more than he had to me.

I put the key back in its envelope and handed it across.

77

'It had better stay in the book for now,' I said, 'until I find a keyhole it fits.'

She put the key in the book and returned it to the shelves, and shortly afterwards found her letters. They were fastened not with romantic ribbons but held together by a prosaic rubber band; not a great many of them by the look of things but carefully kept.

She stared at me from her knees. 'I don't want you to read them,' she said. 'Whatever Greville left you, they're mine, not yours.'

I wondered why she needed so urgently to remove all traces of herself from the house. Out of curiosity I'd have read the letters with interest if I'd found them myself, but I could hardly demand now to see her love letters ... if they were love letters.

'Show me just a short page,' I said.

She looked bitter. 'You really don't trust me, do you? I'd like to know why.'

'Someone broke into Greville's office over the weekend,' I said, 'and I'm not sure what they were looking for.'

'Not my letters,' she said positively.

'Show me just a page,' I said, 'so I know they're what you say.'

I thought she would refuse altogether, but after a moment's thought she slid the rubber band off the letters and fingered through them, finally, with all expression repressed, handing me one small sheet.

It said:

...and until next Monday my life will be a desert. What am I to do? After your touch I shrink from him. It's dreadful. I am running out of headaches. I adore you.

C.

I handed the page back in silence, embarrassed at having intruded.

'Take them,' I said.

She blinked a few times, snapped the rubber band back round the small collection, and put them into a plain black leather handbag which lay beside her on the carpet.

I felt down onto the floor, collected the crutches and stood up, concentrating on at least holding the hand support of the left one, even if not putting much weight on it. Clarissa Williams watched me go over towards Greville's chair with a touch of awkwardness.

'Look,' she said. 'I didn't realise ... I mean, when I came in here and saw you stealing things ... I thought you were stealing things ... I didn't notice the crutches.'

I supposed that was the truth. Bona fide burglars didn't go around peg-legged, and I'd laid the supports aside at the time she'd come storming in. She'd been too fired up to ask questions: propelled no doubt by grief, anxiety and fear of the intruder. None of which lessened my contrary feeling that she damned well *ought* to have asked questions before waging war.

I wondered how she would have explained her presence to the police, if they had arrived, when she was urgent to remove all traces of herself from the house. Perhaps she would have realised her mistake and simply departed, leaving the incapacitated burglar on the floor.

I went over to the telephone table and picked up the brutal little man-tamer. The heavy handle, a black cigar-shaped cylinder, knurled for a good grip, was under an inch in diameter and about seven inches long. Protruding beyond that was a short length of solidly thick chromium-plated closely-coiled spring, with a similar but narrower spring extending beyond that, the whole tipped with a black metal knob, fifteen or sixteen inches overall. A kick as hard as a horse.

'What is this?' I said, holding it, feeling its weight.

'Greville gave it to me. He said the streets aren't safe. He wanted me to carry it always ready. He said all women should carry them because of muggers and rapists ... as a magistrate he heard so much about women being attacked ... he said one blow would render the toughest man helpless and give me time to escape.'

I hadn't much difficulty in believing it. I bent the black knob to one side and watched the close heavy spring flex and straighten fast when I let it go. She got to her feet and said, 'I'm sorry. I've never used it before, not in anger. Greville showed me how ... he just said to swing as hard as I could so that the springs would shoot out and do the maximum damage.'

My dear brother, I thought. Thank you very much.

'Does it go back into its shell?' I asked.

She nodded. 'Twist the bigger spring clockwise ... it'll come loose and slide into the casing.' I did that, but the smaller spring with the black knob still stuck out. 'You have to give the knob a bang against something, then it will slide in.'

I banged the knob against the wall, and like a meek lamb the narrower spring slid smoothly into the wider, and the end of the knob became the harmless-looking end of yet another gadget.

'What makes it work?' I asked, but she didn't know.

I found that the end opposite the knob unscrewed if one tried, so I unscrewed it about twenty turns until the inch-long piece came off, and I discovered that the whole end section was a very strong magnet.

Simple, I thought. Ordinarily the magnet held the heavy springs inside the cylinder. Make a strong flicking arc, in effect throw the springs out, and the magnet couldn't hold them, but let them go, letting loose the full whipping strength of the thing.

I screwed back the cap, held the cylinder, swung it hard. The springs shot out, flexible, shining, horrific.

Wordlessly, I closed the thing up again and offered it to her.

'It's called a kiyoga,' she said.

I didn't care what it was called. I didn't care if I never saw it again. She put it familiarly into her raincoat pocket, every woman's ultimate reply to footpads, maniacs and assorted misogynists.

She looked unhappily and uncertainly at my face.

'I suppose I can't ask you to forget I came here?' she said.

'It would be impossible.'

'Could you just ... not speak of it?'

If I'd met her in another way I suppose I might have liked her. She had generous eyes that would have looked better smiling, and an air of basic good humour which persisted despite her jumbling emotions.

With an effort she said, 'Please.'

'Don't beg,' I said sharply. It made me uncomfortable and it didn't suit her.

She swallowed. 'Greville told me about you. I guess ... I'll have to trust to his judgment.'

She felt in the opposite pocket to the one with the kiyoga and brought out a plain keyring with three keys on it.

'You'd better have these,' she said. 'I won't be using them any more.' She put them down by the answering machine and in her eyes I saw the shininess of sudden tears.

'He died in Ipswich,' I said. 'He'll be cremated there on Friday afternoon. Two o'clock.'

She nodded speechlessly in acknowledgment, not looking at me, and went past me, through the doorway and down the hall and out of the front door, closing it with a quiet finality behind her.

With a sigh, I looked round the room. The book-box that had contained her letters still lay open on the floor and I bent down, picked it up, and restored it to the shelves. I wondered just how many books were hollow. Tomorrow evening, I thought, after Elliot Trelawney, I would come and look.

Meanwhile I picked up the fallen green stone box and put it on the table by the chrysanthemums, reflecting that the ornate key in the red-lined box was far too large to fit its tiny lock. Greville's bunch of keys was down on the carpet also. I returned to what I'd been doing before being so violently interrupted, but found that the smallest of the bunch was still too big for the green stone.

A whole load of no progress, I thought moodily.

I drank the soda water, which had lost its fizz.

I rubbed my arm, which didn't make it much better.

I wondered what judgment Greville had passed on me, that could be trusted.

There was a polished cupboard that I hadn't investigated underneath the television set and, not expecting much, I bent down and pulled one of the doors open by its brass ring handle. The other door opened of its own accord and the contents of the cupboard slid outwards as a unit; a video machine on top with, on two shelves below, rows of black boxes holding recording tapes. There were small uniform labels on the boxes bearing, not formulas this time, but dates.

I pulled one of the boxes out at random and was stunned to see the larger label stuck to its front: 'Race Video Club', it said in heavy print, and underneath, in typing, 'July 7th Sandown Park, Dozen Roses.'

The Race Video Club, as I knew well, sold tapes of races to owners, trainers and anyone else interested. Greville, I thought in growing amazement as I looked further, must have given them a standing order: every race his horses had run in for the past two years, I judged, was there on his shelves to be watched.

He'd told me once, when I asked whey he didn't go to see his runners, that he saw them enough on television; and I'd thought he meant on the ordinary scheduled programmes, live from the racetracks in the afternoons.

The front doorbell rang, jarring and unexpected. I went along and looked through a small peephole and found Brad standing on the doorstep, blinking and blinded by two spotlights shining on his face. The lights came from above the door and lit up the whole path and the gate. I opened the door as he shielded his eyes with his arm.

'Hello,' I said. 'Are you all right?'

'Turn the lights off. Can't see.'

I looked for a switch beside the front door, found several, and by pressing them all upwards indiscriminately, put out the blaze.

'Came to see you were OK,' Brad explained. 'Those lights just went on.'

Of their own accord, I realised. Another manifestation of Greville's security, no doubt. Anyone who came up the path after dark would get illuminated for his pains.

'Sorry I've been so long,' I said. 'Now you're here, would you carry a few things?'

He nodded as if he'd let out enough words already to last the evening, and followed me silently, when I beckoned him, towards the small sitting room.

'I'm taking that green stone box and as many of those video tapes as you can carry, starting from that end,' I said, and he obligingly picked up about ten recent tapes, balancing the box on top.

I found a hall light, switched that on, and turned off the lamp in the sitting room. It promptly turned itself on again, unasked.

'Cor,' Brad said.

I thought that maybe it was time to leave before I tripped any other alarms wired direct after dark to the local constabulary. I closed the sitting-room door and we went along the hall to the outer world. Before leaving I pressed all the switches beside the front door downwards, and maybe I turned more on than I'd turned off: the spotlights didn't go on, but a dog started barking noisily behind us.

'Strewth,' Brad said, whirling round and clutching the video tapes to his chest as if they would defend him.

There was no dog. There was a loudspeaker like a bull horn on a low hall table emitting the deep-throated growls and barks of a determined Alsatian.

'Bleeding hell,' Brad said.

'Let's go,' I said in amusement, and he could hardly wait.

The barking stopped of its own accord as we stepped out into the air. I pulled the door shut, and we set off to go down the steps and along the path, and we'd gone barely three paces when the spotlights blazed on again.

'Keep going,' I said to Brad. 'I daresay they'll turn themselves off in time.'

It was fine by him. He'd parked the car round the corner, and I spent the swift journey to Hungerford wondering about Clarissa Williams; her life, love and adultery.

During the evening I failed both to open the green stone box and to understand the gadgets.

Shaking the box gave me no impression of contents and I supposed it could well be empty. A cigarette box, I thought, though I couldn't remember ever seeing Greville smoking. Perhaps a box to hold twin packs of cards. Perhaps a box for jewellery. Its tiny keyhole remained impervious to probes from nail scissors, suitcase keys and a piece of wire, and in the end I surrendered and laid it aside.

Neither of the gadgets opened or shut. One was a small black cylindrical object about the size of a thumb with one end narrowly ridged, like a coin. Turning the ridged end a quarter-turn clockwise, its full extent of travel, produced a thin faint high-pitched whine which proved to be the unexciting sum of the thing's activity. Shrugging, I switched the whine off again and stood the small tube upright on the green box.

The second gadget didn't even produce a whine. It was a flat black plastic container about the size of a pack of cards with a single square red button placed centrally on the front. I pressed the button: no results. A round chromiumed knob set into one of the sides of the cover revealed itself on further inspection as the end of a telescopic aerial. I pulled it out as far as it would go, about ten inches, and was rewarded with what I presumed was a small transmitter which transmitted I didn't know what to I didn't know where.

Sighing, I pushed the aerial back into its socket and added the transmitter to the top of the green box, and after that I fed Greville's tapes one by one into my video machine and watched the races.

Alfie's comment about in-and-out running had interested me more than I would have wanted him to know. Dozen Roses, from my own reading of the results, had had a long doldrum period followed by a burst of success, suggestive of the classic 'cheating' pattern of running a horse to lose and go on losing until he was low in the handicap and unbacked, then setting him off to win at long odds in a race below his latent abilities and wheeling away the winnings in a barrow.

All trainers did that in a mild way sometimes, whatever the rules might say about always running flat out. Young and inexperienced horses could be ruined by being pressed too hard too soon: one had to give them a chance to enjoy themselves, to let their racing instinct develop fully.

That said, there was a point beyond which no modern trainer dared go. In the bad old days before universal camera coverage, it had been harder to prove a horse hadn't been trying: many jockeys had been artists at waving their whips while hauling on the reins. Under the eagle lenses and fierce discipline of the current scene, even natural and unforeseen fluctuations in a horse's form could find the trainer yanked in before the Stewards for an explanation, and if the trainer couldn't explain why his short-priced favourite had turned leaden footed it could cost him a depressing fine.

No trainer, however industrious, was safe from suspicion, yet I'd never read or heard of Nicholas Loder getting himself into that sort of trouble. Maybe Alfie, I thought dryly, knew something the Stewards didn't. Maybe Alfie could tell me why Loder had all but panicked when he'd feared Dozen Roses might not run on Saturday next.

Brad had picked up the six most recent outings of Dozen

Roses, interspersed by four of Gemstones's. I played all six of Dozen Roses's first, starting with the earliest, back in May, checking the details with what Greville had written in his diary.

On the screen there were shots of the runners walking round the parade ring and going down to the start, with Greville's pink and orange colours bright and easy to see. The May race was a ten-furlong handicap for three-year-olds and upwards, run at Newmarket on a Friday. Eighteen runners. Dozen Roses ridden by a second-string jockey because Loder's chief retained jockey was riding the stable's other runner which started favourite.

Down at the start there was some sort of fracas involving Dozen Roses. I rewound the tape and played it through in slow motion and couldn't help laughing. Dozen Roses, his mind far from racing, had been showing unseemly interest in a mare.

I remembered Greville saying once that he thought it a shame and unfair to curb a colt's enthusiasm: no horse of his would ever be gelded. I remembered him vividly, leaning across a small table and saying it over a glass of brandy with a gleam in which I'd seen his own enjoyment of sex. So many glimpses of him in my mind, I thought. Too few, also. I couldn't really believe I would never eat with him again, whatever my senses said.

Trainers didn't normally run mares that had come into season, but sometimes one couldn't tell early on. Horses knew, though. Dozen Roses had been aroused. The mare was loaded into the stalls in a hurry and Dozen Roses had been walked around until the last minute to cool his ardour. After that, he had run without sparkle and finished mid-field, the mare to the rear of him trailing in last. Loder's other runner, the favourite, had won by a length.

Too bad, I thought, smiling, and watched Dozen Roses's next attempt three weeks later.

No distracting attractions this time. The horse had behaved quietly, sleepily almost, and had turned in the sort of moderate performance which set owners wondering if the game was worth it. The next race was much the same, and if I'd been Greville I would have decided it was time to sell.

Greville, it seemed, had had more faith. After seven weeks' rest Dozen Roses had gone bouncing down to the start, raced full of zest and zoomed over the finishing line in front, netting 14/1 for anyone ignorant enough to have backed him. Like Greville, of course.

Watching the sequence of tapes I did indeed wonder why the Stewards hadn't made a fuss, but Greville hadn't mentioned anything except his pleasure in the horse's return to his three-year-old form.

Dozen Roses had next produced two further copybook performances of stamina and determination, which brought us up to date. I rewound and removed the last tape and could see why Loder thought it would be another trot-up on Saturday.

Gemstones's tapes weren't as interesting. Despite his name he wasn't of much value and the one race he'd won looked more like a fluke than constructive engineering. I would sell them both, I decided, as Loder wanted.

CHAPTER 7

Brad came early on Wednesday and drove me to Lambourn. The ankle was sore in spite of Distalgesics but less of a constant drag that morning and I could have driven the car myself if I'd put my mind to it. Having Brad around, I reflected on the way, was a luxury I was all too easily getting used to.

Clarissa Williams's attentions had worn off completely except for a little stiffness and a blackening bruise like a bar midway between shoulder and elbow. That didn't matter. For much of the year I had bruises somewhere or other, result of the law of averages operating in steeplechasing. Falls occurred about once every fourteen races, sometimes oftener, and while a few of the jockeys had bodies that hardly seemed to bruise at all, mine always did. On the other hand I healed everywhere fast, bones, skin and optimism.

Milo Shandy, striding about in his stable yard as if incapable of standing still, came over to my car as it rolled to a stop and yanked open the driver's door. The words he was about to say didn't come out as he stared first at Brad, then at me on the back seat, and what he eventually said was, 'A chauffeur, by God. Coddling yourself, aren't you?'

Brad got me out of the car, gave Milo a neanderthal look and handed me the crutches as usual.

Milo, dark, short and squarely built, watched the proceedings with disgust.

'I want you to ride Datepalm.' he said.

'Well, I can't.'

'The Ostermeyers will want it. I told them you'd be here.'

'Gerry rides Datepalm perfectly well,' I said, Gerry being the lad who rode the horse at exercise as a matter of course most days of the week.

'Gerry isn't you.'

'He's better than me with a groggy ankle.'

Milo glared. 'Do you want to keep the horse here or don't you?'

I did.

Milo and I spent a fair amount of time arguing at the best of times. He was pugnacious by nature, mercurial by temperament, full of instant opinions that could be reversed the next day, didactic, dynamic and outspoken. He believed absolutely in his own judgement and was sure that everything would turn out right in the end. He was moderately tactful to the owners, hard on his workforce and full of swearwords for his horses, which he produced as winners by the dozen.

I'd been outraged by the way he'd often spoken to me when I first started to ride for him three years earlier, but one day I lost my temper and yelled back at him, and he burst out laughing and told me we would get along just fine, which in fact we did, though seldom on the surface.

I knew people thought ours an unlikely alliance, I neat and quiet, he restless and flamboyant, but in fact I liked the way he trained horses and they seemed to run well for him, and we had both prospered.

The Ostermeyers arrived at that point and they too had a chauffeur, which Milo took for granted. The bullishness at once disappeared from his manner to be replaced by the jocular charm that had owners regularly mesmerised, that morning being no exception. The Ostermeyers responded immediately, she with a roguish wiggle of the hips, he with a big handshake and a wide smile.

They were not so delighted about my crutches.

'Oh dear,' Martha Ostermeyer exclaimed in dismay. 'What have you done? Don't say you can't ride Datepalm. We only came, you know, because dear Milo said you'd be here to ride it.'

'He'll ride it,' Milo said before I had a chance of answering, and Martha Ostermeyer clapped her small gloved hands with relief.

'If we're going to buy him,' she said, smiling, 'we want to see him with his real jockey up, not some exercise rider.'

Harley Ostermeyer nodded in agreement, benignly.

Not really my week, I thought.

The Ostermeyers were all sweetness and light while people were pleasing them, and I'd never had any trouble liking them, but I'd also seen Harley Ostermeyer's underlying streak of ruthless viciousness once in a racecourse car-park where he'd verbally reduced to rubble an attendant who had allowed someone to park behind him, closing him in. He had had to wait half an hour. The attendant had looked genuinely scared. 'Goodnight, Derek,' he'd croaked as I went past, and Ostermeyer had whirled round and cooled his temper fifty per cent, inviting my sympathy in his trouble. Harley Ostermeyer liked to be thought a good guy, most of the time. He was the boss, as I understood it, of a giant supermarket chain. Martha Ostermeyer was also rich, a fourth generation multi-millionaire in banking. I'd ridden for them often in the past years and been rewarded, because generosity was one of their pleasures.

Milo drove them and me up to the Downs where Datepalm and the other horses were already circling, having walked up earlier. The day was bright and chilly, the Downs rolling away to the horizon, the sky clear, the horses' coats glossy in the sun. A perfect day for buying a champion chaser.

Milo sent three other horses down to the bottom of the gallop to work fast so that the Ostermeyers would know where to look and what to expect when Datepalm came up and passed them. They stood out on the grass, looking where Milo pointed, intent and happy.

Milo had brought a spare helmet with us in the big-wheeled vehicle that rolled over the mud and ruts on the Downs, and with an inward sign I put it on. The enterprise was stupid really, as my leg wasn't strong enough and if anything wild happened to upset Datepalm, he might get loose and injure himself and we'd lose him surely one way or another.

On the other hand, I'd ridden races now and then with cracked bones, not just exercise gallops, and I knew one jockey who in the past had broken three bones in his foot and won

89

races with it, sitting with it in an ice bucket in the changing room between times and literally hopping out to the parade ring, supported by friends. The authorities had later brought in strict medical rules to stop that sort of thing as being unfair to the betting public, but one could still get away with it sometimes.

Milo saw me slide out of the vehicle with the helmet on and came over happily and said, 'I knew you would.'

'Mm,' I said. 'When you give me a leg up, put both hands round my knee and be careful, because if you twist my foot there'll be no sale.'

'You're such a wimp,' he said.

Nevertheless, he was circumspect and I landed in the saddle with little trouble. I was wearing jeans, and that morning for the first time I'd managed to get a shoe on, or rather one of the wide soft black leather moccasins I used as bedroom slippers. Milo threaded the stirrup over the moccasin with unexpected gentleness and I wondered if he were having last-minute doubts about the wisdom of all this.

One look at the Ostermeyers' faces dispelled both his doubts and mine. They were beaming at Datepalm already with proprietary pride.

Certainly he looked good. He filled the eye, as they say. A bay with black points, excellent head, short sturdy legs with plenty of bone. The Ostermeyers always preferred handsome animals, perhaps because they were handsome themselves, and Datepalm was well-mannered besides, which made him a peach of a ride.

He and I and two others from the rest of the string set off at a walk towards the far end of the gallop but were presently trotting, which I achieved by standing in the stirrups with all my weight on my right foot while cursing Milo imaginatively for the sensations in my left. Datepalm, who knew how horses should be ridden, which was not lopsided like this, did a good deal of head and tail shaking but otherwise seemed willing to trust me. He and I knew each other well as I'd ridden him in all his races for the past three years. Horses had no direct way of expressing recognition, but occasionally he would turn his head to look at me when he heard my voice, and I also thought he might know me by scent as he would put his muzzle against my neck sometimes and make small whiffling movements of his nostrils. In any case we did have a definite rapport and that morning it stood us in good stead.

At the far end the two lads and I sorted out our three horses ready to set off at a working gallop back towards Milo and the Ostermeyers, a pace fast enough to be interesting but not flat out like racing.

There wasn't much finess in riding a gallop to please customers, one simply saw to it that one was on their side of the accompanying horses, to give them a clear view of the merchandise, and that one finished in front to persuade them that that's what would happen in future.

Walking him around to get in position I chatted quietly as I often did to Datepalm, because in common with many racehorses he was always reassured by a calm human voice, sensing from one's tone that all was well. Maybe horses heard the lower resonances: one never knew.

'Just go up there like a pro,' I told him, 'because I don't want to lose you, you old bugger. I want us to win the National one day, so shine, boy. Dazzle. Do your bloody best.'

I shook up the reins as we got the horses going, and in fact Datepalm put up one of his smoothest performances, staying with his companions for most of the journey, lengthening his stride when I gave him the signal, coming away alone and then sweeping collectedly past the Ostermeyers with fluid power; and if the jockey found it an acutely stabbing discomfort all the way, it was a fair price for the result. Even before I'd pulled up, the Ostermeyers had bought the horse and shaken hands on the deal.

'Subject to a veterinarian's report, of course,' Harley was saying as I walked Datepalm back to join them. 'Otherwise he's superb.'

Milo's smile looked as if it would split his face. He held the reins while Martha excitedly patted the new acquisition, and went on holding them while I took my feet out of the stirrups and lowered myself very carefully to the ground, hopping a couple of steps to where the crutches lay on the grass.

'What did you do to your foot?' Martha asked unworriedly.

'Wrenched it,' I said, slipping the arm cuffs on with relief. 'Very boring.'

She smiled, nodded and patted my arm. 'Milo said it was nothing much.'

Milo gave me a gruesome look, handed Datepalm back to his lad, Gerry, and helped the Ostermeyers into the big-wheeled vehicle for the drive home. We bumped down the tracks and I took off the helment and ran my fingers through my hair, reflecting that although I wouldn't care to ride gallops like that every day of the week, I would do it again for as good an outcome.

We all went into Milo's house for breakfast, a ritual there as in many other racing stables, and over coffee, toast and scrambled eggs Milo and the Ostermeyers planned Datepalm's future programme, including all the top races with of course another crack at the Gold Cup.

'What about the Grand National?' Martha said, her eyes like stars.

'Well, now, we'll have to see,' Milo said, but his dreams too were as visible as searchlights. First thing on our return, he'd telephoned to Datepalm's former owner and got confirmation that she agreed to the sale and was pleased by it, and since then one had almost needed to pull him down from the ceiling with a string like a helium-filled balloon. My own feelings weren't actually much lower. Datepalm really was a horse to build dreams on.

After the food and a dozen repetitions of the horse's virtues, Milo told the Ostermeyers about my inheriting Dozen Roses and about the probate saga, which seemed to fascinate them. Martha sat up straighter and exclaimed, 'Did you say York?'

Milo nodded.

'Do you mean this Saturday? Why, Harley and I are going to York races on Saturday, aren't we Harley?'

Harley agreed that they were. 'Our dear friends Lord and Lady Knightwood have asked us to lunch.'

Martha said, 'Why don't we give Derek a ride up there to see his horse run? What do you say, Harley?'

'Be glad to have you along,' Harley said to me genuinely. 'Don't give us no for an answer.'

I looked at their kind insistent faces and said lamely, 'I thought of going by train, if I went at all.'

'No, no,' Martha said. 'Come to London by train and we'll go

92

up together. Do say you will.'

Milo was looking at me anxiously: pleasing the Ostermeyers was still an absolute priority. I said I'd be glad to accept their kindness and Martha, mixing gratification with sudden alarm, said she hoped the inheritance wouldn't persuade me to stop riding races.

'No,' I said.

'That's positive enough.' Harley was pleased. 'You're part of the package, fella. You and Datepalm together.'

Brad and I went on to London, and I was glad to have him drive.

'Office?' he asked, and I said, 'Yes' and we travelled there in silent harmony.

He'd told me the evening before that Greville's car wasn't parked anywhere near Greville's house: or rather he'd handed me back the piece of paper with the car's number on it and said, 'Couldn't find it.' I thought I'd better get on to the police and other towers-away in Ipswich, and I'd better start learning the company's finances and Greville's as well, and I had two-thirds of the vault still to check and I could feel the suction of the quicksands inexorably.

I took the two baffling little gadgets from Greville's sitting room upstairs to Greville's office and showed them to June.

'That one,' she said immediately, pointing to the thumb-sized tube with the whine, 'is a device to discourage mosquitos. Mr Franklin said it's the noise of the male mosquito, and it frightens the blood-sucking females away.' She laughed. 'He said every man should have one.'

She picked up the other gadget and frowned at it, pressing the red button with no results.

'It has an aerial,' I said.

'Oh yes.' She pulled it out to its full extent. 'I think ...' She paused. 'He used to have a transmitter which started his car from a distance, so he could warm the engine up in cold weather before he left his house, but the receiver bit got stolen with his Porsche. Then he bought the old Rover, and he said a car-starter wouldn't work on it because it only worked with direct transmission or fuel injection, or something, which the

93

Rover doesn't have.'

'So this is the car-starter?'

'Well ... no. This one doesn't do so much. The car-starter had buttons that would also switch on the headlights so that you could see where your car was, if you'd left it in a dark car-park.' She pushed the aerial down again. 'I think this one only switches the lights on, or makes the car whistle, if I remember right. He was awfully pleased with it when he got it, but I haven't seen it for ages. He had so many gadgets, he couldn't take them all in his pockets and I think he'd got a bit tired of carrying them about. He used to leave them in this desk, mostly.'

'You just earned your twenty per cent all over again,' I said.

'What?'

'Let's just check that the batteries work,' I said.

She opened the battery compartment and discovered it was empty. As if it were routine, she then pulled open a drawer in one of the other tiers of the desk and revealed a large open box containing packet after packet of new batteries in every possible size. She pulled out a packet, opened it and fed the necessary power packs into the slots, and although pressing the red button still provided no visible results, I was pretty confident we were in business.

June said suddenly, 'You're going to take this to Ipswich, aren't you? To find his car? Isn't that what you mean?'

I nodded. 'Let's hope it works.'

'Oh, it must.'

'It's quite a big town, and the car could be anywhere.'

'Yes,' she said, 'but it must be *somewhere*. I'm sure you'll find it.'

'Mm.' I looked at her bright intelligent face. 'June,' I said slowly, 'Don't tell anyone else about this gadget.'

'Why ever not?'

'Because,' I said, 'someone broke into this office looking for something and we don't know if they found it. If they didn't, and it is by any chance in the car, I don't want anyone to realise that the car is still lost.' I paused. 'I'd much rather you said nothing.'

'Not even to Annette?'

'Not to anyone.'

'But that means you think ... you think ...'

'I don't really think anything. It's just for security.'

Security was all right with her. She looked less troubled and agreed to keep quiet about the car-finder; and I hadn't needed to tell her about the mugger who had knocked me down to steal Greville's bag of clothes, which to me, in hindsight, was looking less and less a random hit and more and more a shot at a target.

Someone must have known Greville was dying, I thought. Someone who had organised or executed a mugging. I hadn't the faintest idea who could have done either, but it did seem to me possible that one of Greville's staff might have unwittingly chattered within earshot of receptive ears. Yet what could they have said? Greville hadn't told any of them he was buying diamonds. And why hadn't he? Secretive as he was, gems were his business.

The useless thoughts squirrelled around and got me nowhere. The gloomiest of them was that someone could have gone looking for Greville's car any time since the scaffolding fell, and although I might find the engine and the wheels, the essential cupboard would be bare.

Annette came into the office carrying a fistful of papers which she said had come in the morning post and needed to be dealt with — by me, her manner inferred.

'Sit down, then,' I said, 'and tell me what they all mean.'

There were letters from insurance people, fund raisers, dissatisfied customers, gemmology forecasters, and a cable from a supplier in Hong Kong saying he didn't have enough African 12 mm amethyst AA quality beads to fill our order and would we take Brazilian amethyst to make it up.

'What's the difference?' I asked. 'Does it matter?'

Annette developed worry lines over my ignorance. 'The best amethyst is found in Africa,' she said. 'Then it goes to Hong Kong or Taiwan for cutting and polishing into beads, then comes here. The amethyst from Brazil isn't such a good deep colour. Do you want me to order the Brazilian amethyst or wait until he has more of the African?'

'What do you think?' I said.

'Mr Franklin always decided.'

She looked at me anxiously. Its hopeless, I thought. The simplest decision was impossible without knowledge.

'Would the customers take the Brazilian instead?' I asked.

95

'Some would, some wouldn't. It's much cheaper. We sell a lot of the Brazilian anyway, in all sizes.'

'Well,' I said, 'if we run out of the African beads, offer the customers Brazilian. Or offer a different size of African. Cable the Chinese supplier to send just the African AA 12 mm he's got now and the rest as soon as he can.'

She looked relieved. 'That's what I'd have said.'

Then why didn't you, I thought, but it was no use being angry. If she gave me bad advice I'd probably blame her for it: it was safer from her viewpoint, I supposed, not to stick her neck out.

'Incidentally,' she said, 'I did reach Prospero Jenks. He said he'd be in his Knightsbridge shop at two-thirty today, if you wanted to see him.'

'Great.'

She smiled. 'I didn't mention horses.'

I smiled back. 'Fine.'

She took the letters off to her own office to answer them, and I went from department to department on a round trip to the vault, watching everyone at work, all of them capable, willing and beginning to settle obligingly into the change of regime, keeping their inner reservations to themselves. I asked if one of them would go down and tell Brad I'd need him at two, not before: June went and returned like a boomerang.

I unlocked the vault and started on topaz: thousands of brilliant translucent slippery stones in a rainbow of colours, some bigger than acorns, some like peas.

No diamonds.

After that, every imaginable shape and size of garnet which could be yellow and green, I found, as well as red, and boxes of citrine.

Two and a half hours of unfolding and folding glossy white packets, and no diamonds.

June swirled in and out at one point with a long order for facetted stones which she handed to me without comment, and I remembered that only Greville and Annette packed orders from the vault. I went in search of Annette and asked if I might watch while she worked down the list, found what was needed from twenty or more boxes and assembled the total on the shelf. She was quick and sure, knowing exactly where to find everything. It was quite easy, she said, reassuring me. I would soon get the hang of it. God help me, I thought.

At two, after another of June's sandwich lunches, I went down to the car and gave Prospero Jenks's address to Brad. 'It's a shop somewhere near Harrods,' I said, climbing in.

He nodded, drove through the traffic, found the shop.

'Great,' I said. 'Now this time you'll have to answer the car phone whether you like it or not, because there's nowhere here to park.'

He shook his head. He'd resisted the suggestion several times before.

'Yes,' I said. 'It's very easy. I'll switch it on for you now. When it rings pick it up and press this button, SND, and you'll be able to hear me. OK? I'll ring when I'm ready to leave, then you just come back here and pick me up.'

He looked at the telephone as if it were contaminated.

It was a totally portable phone, not a fixture in the car, and it didn't receive calls unless one switched it on, which I quite often forgot to do and sometimes didn't do on purpose. I put the phone ready on the passenger seat beside him, to make it easy, and hoped for the best.

Prospero Jenks's shop window glittered with the sort of intense lighting that makes jewellery sparkle, but the lettering of his name over the window was neat and plain, as if ostentation there would have been superfluous.

I looked at the window with a curiosity I would never have felt a week earlier and found it filled not with conventional displays of rings and wristwatches but with joyous toys: model cars, aeroplanes, skiing figures, racing yachts, pheasants and horses, all gold and enamel and shining with gems. Almost every passer-by, I noticed, paused to look.

Pushing awkwardly through the heavy glass front door I stepped into a deep-carpeted area with chairs at the ready before every counter. Apart from the plushness, it was basically an ordinary shop, not very big, quiet in decor, all the excitement in the baubles.

There was no one but me in there and I swung over to one of the counters to see what was on display. Rings, I found, but not simple little circles. These were huge, often asymmetric, all colourful eyecatchers supreme.

'Can I help you?' a voice said.

A neutral man, middle-aged, in a black suit, coming from a doorway at the rear.

'My name's Franklin,' I said. 'Came to see Prospero Jenks.'

'A minute.'

He retreated, returned with a half-smile and invited me through the doorway to the privacies beyond. Shielded from customers' view by a screening partition lay a much longer space which doubled as office and workroom and contained a fearsome-looking safe and several tiers of little drawers like the ones in Saxony Franklin. On one wall a large framed sign read: 'NEVER TURN YOUR BACK TO CUSTOMERS. ALWAYS WATCH THEIR HANDS.' A fine statement of no trust, I thought in amusement.

Sitting on a stool by a workbench, a jeweller's lens screwed into one eye, was a hunched man in pale pink and white striped shirtsleeves, fiddling intently with a small gold object fixed into a vice. Patience and expert workmanship were much on view, all of it calm and painstaking.

He removed the lens with a sigh and rose to his feet, turning to inspect me from crown to crutches to toecaps with growing surprise. Whatever he'd been expecting, I was not it.

The feeling, I supposed, was mutual. He was maybe fifty but looked younger in a Peter Pan sort of way; a boyish face with intense bright blue eyes and a lot of lines developing across the forehead. Fairish hair, no beard, no moustache, no personal display. I had expected someone fancier, more extravagant, temperamental.

'Grev's brother?' he said. 'What a turn-up. There I was thinking you'd be his age, his height.' He narrowed his eyes. 'He never said he had a brother. How do I know you're legit?'

'His assistant, Annette Adams, made the appointment.'

'Yes, so she did. Fair enough. Told me Grev was dead, long live the King. Said his brother was running the shop, life would go on. But I'll tell you, unless you know as much as Grev, I'm in trouble.'

'I came to talk to you about that.'

'It don't look like tidings of great joy,' he said, watching me judiciously. 'Want a seat?' He pointed at an office chair for me and took his place on the stool. His voice was a long way from cut-glass. More like East End London tidied up for West; the sort that came from nowhere with no privileges and made it to the top from sheer undeniable talent. He had the confident manner of long success, a creative spirit who was also a tradesman, an original artist without airs.

'I'm just learning the business,' I said cautiously. 'I'll do what I can.'

'Grev was a genius,' he said explosively. 'No one like him with stones. He'd bring me oddities, one-offs from all over the world, and I've made pieces ...' He stopped and spread his arms out. 'They're in palaces,' he said, 'and museums and mansions in Palm Beach. Well, I'm in business. I sell them to wherever the money's coming from. I've got my pride, but it's in the pieces. They're good, I'm expensive, it works a treat.'

'Do you make everything you sell?' I asked.

He laughed. 'No, not myself personally, I couldn't. I design everything, don't get me wrong, but I have a workshop making them. I just make the special pieces myself, the unique ones. In between, I invent for the general market. Grev said he had some decent spinel, have you still got it?'

'Er,' I said, 'red?'

'Red,' he affirmed. 'Three, four or five carats. I'll take all you've got.'

'We'll send it tomorrow.'

'By messenger,' he said. 'Not post.'

'All right.'

'And a slab of rock crystal like the Eiger. Grev showed me a photo. I've got a commission for a fantasy ... Send the crystal too.'

'All right,' I said again, and hid my doubts. I hadn't seen any slab of rock crystal. Annette would know, I thought.

He said casually, 'What about the diamonds?'

I let the breath out and into my lungs with conscious control.

'What about them?' I said.

'Grev was getting me some. He'd got them, in fact. He told me. He'd sent a batch off to be cut. Are they back yet?'

'Not yet,' I said, hoping I wasn't croaking. 'Are those the diamonds he bought a couple of months ago from the Central Selling Organisation that you're talking about?'

'Sure. He bought a share in a sight from a sightholder. I

asked him to. I'm still running the big chunky rings and necklaces I made my name in, but I'm setting some of them now with bigger diamonds, making more profit per item since the market will stand it, and I wanted Grev to get them because I trust him. Trust is like gold dust in this business, even though diamonds weren't his thing really. You wouldn't want to buy two- to three-carat stones from just anyone, even if they're not D or E flawless, right?'

'Er, right.'

'So he bought the share of the sight and he's having them cut in Antwerp as I require them, as I expect you know.'

I nodded I did know, but only since he'd just told me.

'I'm going to make stars of some of them to shine from the rock crystal ...' He broke off, gave a self-deprecating shrug of his shoulders, and said, 'And I'm making a mobile, with diamonds on gold trembler wires that move in the lightest air. It's to hang by a window and flash fire in the sunlight.' Again the self-deprecation, this time in a smile. 'Diamonds are ravishing in sunlight, they're at their best in it, and all the social snobs in this city scream that it's so frightfully vulgar, darling, to wear diamond earrings or bracelets in the daytime. It makes me sick, to be honest. Such a waste.'

I had never thought about diamonds in sunlight before, though I suppose I would in future. Vistas opened could never be closed, as maybe Greville would have said.'

'I haven't caught up with everything yet,' I said, which was the understatement of the century. 'Have any of the diamonds been delivered to you so far?'

He shook his head. 'I haven't been in a hurry for them before.'

'And ... er ... how many are involved?'

'About a hundred. Like I said, not the very best colour in accepted way of things but they can look warmer with gold sometimes if they're not ultra blue-white. I work with gold mostly. I like the feel.'

'How much,' I said slowly, doing sums, 'will your rock crystal fantasy sell for?'

'Trade secret. But then, I guess you're trade. It's commissioned, I've got a contract for a quarter of a million if they like it. If they don't like it, I get it back, sell it somewhere else, dismantle it, whatever. In the worst event I'd lose nothing but my time in making it, but don't you worry, they'll like it.'

His certainty was absolute, built on experience.

I said, 'Do you happen to know the name of the Antwerp cutter Greville sent the diamonds to? I mean, it's bound to be on file in the office, but if I know who to look for ...' I paused. 'I could try to hurry him up for you, if you like.'

'I'd like you to, but I don't know who Grev knew there, exactly.'

I shrugged. 'I'll look it up, then.'

Exactly where was I going to look it up I wondered? Not in the missing address book for sure.

'Do you know the name of the sightholder?' I asked.

'Nope.'

'There's a ton of paper in the office,' I said in explanation. 'I'm going through it as fast as I can.'

'Grev never said a word he didn't have to,' Jenks said unexpectedly. 'I'd talk, he listened. We got on fine. He understood what I do better than anybody.'

The sadness of his voice was my brother's universal accolade, I thought. He'd been liked. He'd been trusted. He would be missed.

I stood up and said, 'Thank you, Mr Jenks.'

'Call me Pross,' he said easily. 'Everyone does.'

'My name's Derek.'

'Right,' he said, smiling. 'Now I'll keep on dealing with you, I won't say I won't, but I'm going to have to find me another traveller like Grev, with an eye like his ... He's been supplying me ever since I started on my own, he gave me credit when the banks wouldn't, he had faith in what I could do ... Near the beginning he brought me two rare sticks of watermelon tourmaline that were each over two inches long and were half pink, half green mixed all the way up and transparent with the light shining through them and changing while you watched. It would have been a sin to cut them for jewellery. I mounted them in gold and platinum to hang and twist in sunlight.' He smiled his deprecating smile. 'I like gemstones to have life. I didn't have to pay Grev for that tourmaline ever. It made my name for me, the piece was reviewed in the papers and won prizes, and he said the trade we'd do together would be his

101

reward.' He clicked his mouth. 'I do go on a bit.'

'I like to hear it,' I said. I looked down the room to his workbench and said, 'Where did you learn all this? How does one start?'

'I started in metalwork classes at the local comprehensive,' he said frankly. 'Then I stuck bits of glass in gold-plated wire to give to my mum. Then her friends wanted some. So when I left school I took some of those things to show to a jewellery manufacturer and asked for a job. Costume jewellery, they made. I was soon designing for them, and I never looked back.

CHAPTER 8

I borrowed Prospero's telephone to get Brad, but although I could hear the ringing tone in the car, he didn't answer. Cursing slightly, I asked Pross for a second call and got through to Annette.

'Please keep on trying this number,' I said, giving it to her. 'When Brad answers, tell him I'm ready to go.'

'Are you coming back here?' she asked.

I looked at my watch. It wasn't worth going back as I had to return to Kensington by five-thirty. I said no, I wasn't.

'Well, there are one or two things ...'

'I can't really tie this phone up,' I said. I'll go to my brother's house and ring you from there. Just keep trying Brad.'

I thanked Pross again for the calls. Any time, he said vaguely. He was sitting again in front of his vice, thinking and tinkering, producing his marvels.

There were customers in the shop being attended to by the black-suited salesman. He glanced up briefly in acknowledgement as I went through and immediately returned to watching the customers' hands. A business without trust; much worse than racing. But then, it was probably impossible to slip a racehorse into a pocket when the trainer wasn't looking.

I stood on the pavement and wondered pessimistically how long it would take Brad to answer the telephone but in the event he surprised me by arriving within a very few minutes. When I opened the car door, the phone was ringing.

'Why don't you answer it?' I asked, wriggling my way into the seat.

'Forgot which button.'

'But you came,' I said.

'Yerss.'

I picked up the phone myself and talked to Annette, 'Brad apparently reckoned that if the phone rang it meant I was ready, so he saw no need to answer it.'

Brad gave a silent nod.

'So now we're setting off to Kensington.' I paused. 'Annette, what's a sightholder, and what's a sight?'

'You're back to diamonds again!'

'Yes. Do you know?'

'Of course, I do. A sightholder is someone who is permitted to buy rough diamonds from the CSO. There aren't so many sightholders, only about a hundred and fifty world-wide, I think. They sell the diamonds then to other people. A sight is what they call the sales CSO hold every five weeks, and a sight-box is a packet of stones they sell, though that's often called a sight too.'

'Is a sightholder the same as a diamantaire?' I asked.

'All sightholders are diamantaires, but all diamantaires are not sightholders. Diamantaires buy from the sightholders, or share in a sight, or buy somewhere else, not from De Beers.'

Ask a simple question, I thought.

Annette said, 'A consignment of cultured pearls has come from Japan. Where shall I put them?'

'Um ... Do you mean where because the vault is locked?'

'Yes'

'Where did you put things when my brother was travelling?'

She said doubtfully, 'He always said to put them in the stockroom under "miscellaneous beads".'

'Put them in there, then.'

'But the drawer is full with some things that came last week. I wouldn't want the responsibility of putting the pearls anywhere Mr Franklin hadn't approved.' I couldn't believe she needed direction over the simplest thing, but apparently she did. 'The pearls are valuable,' she said. 'Mr Franklin would never leave them out in plain view.'

'Aren't there any empty drawers?'

'Well, I ...'

'Find an empty drawer or a nearly empty drawer and put them there. We'll see to them properly in the morning.'

'Yes, all right.'

She seemed happy with it and said everything else could wait until I came back. I switched off the telephone feeling absolutely swamped by the prospect she'd opened up: if Greville hid precious things under 'miscellaneous beads', where else might he not have hidden them? Would I find a hundred diamonds stuffed in at the back of rhodocrosite or jasper, if I looked?

The vault alone was taking too long. The four big stockrooms promised a nightmare.

Brad miraculously found a parking space right outside Greville's house, which seemed obscurely to disappoint him.

'Twenty past five,' he said, 'for the pub?'

'If you wouldn't mind. And ... er ... would you just stand there now while I take a look-see?' I had grown cautious, I found.

He ducked his head in assent and watched me manoeuvre the few steps up to the front door. No floodlights came on and no dog barked, presumably because it was daylight. I opened the three locks and pushed the door.

The house was still. No movements of air. I propped the door open with a bronze horse clearly lying around for the purpose and went down the passage to the small sitting room.

No intruders. No mess. No amazons waving riot sticks, no wrecking balls trying to get past the grilles on the windows. If anyone had attempted to penetrate Greville's fortress, they hadn't succeeded.

I returned to the front door. Brad was still standing beside the car, looking towards the house. I gave him a thumbs-up sign, and he climbed into the driver's seat while I closed the heavy door, and in the little sitting room, started taking all of the books off the shelves methodically, riffling the pages and putting each back where I found it.

There were ten hollow books altogether, mostly with titles like *Tales of the Outback* and *With a Mule in Patagonia*. Four were empty, including the one which had held Clarissa Williams's letters. One held the big ornate key. One held an expensive-looking gold watch, the hands pointing to the correct time.

The watch Greville had been wearing in Ipswich was one of those affairs with more knobs than instructions. It lay now beside my bed in Hungerford emitting bleeps at odd intervals and telling me which way was north. The slim gold elegance in the hollow box was for a different mood, a different man, and when I turned it over on my palm I found the inscription of the back: G my love C.

She couldn't have known it was there, I thought. She hadn't looked for it. She'd looked only for the letters, and by chance had come to them first. I put the watch back into the box and back on the shelf. There was no way I could return it to her and perhaps she wouldn't want it, not with that inscription.

Two of the remaining boxes contained large keys, again unspecified, and one contained a folded instruction leaflet detailing how to set a safe in a concrete nest. The last revealed two very small plastic cases containing baby recording tapes, each adorned with the printed legend 'microcassette'. The cassette cases were all of two inches long by one and a half wide, the featherweight tapes inside a fraction smaller.

I tossed one in my hand indecisively. Nowhere among Greville's tidy belongings had I so far found a microcassette player, which didn't mean I wouldn't in time. Sufficient to the day, I thought in the end, and left the tiny tapes in the book.

With the scintillating titles and their secrets all back on the shelves I stared at them gloomily. Not a diamond in the lot.

Instructions for concrete nests were all very well, but where was the safe? Tapes were OK, but where was the player? Keys were fine, but where were the keyholes? The most frustrating thing about it all was that Greville hadn't meant to leave such puzzles. For him, the answers were part of his fabric.

I'd noticed on my way in and out of the house that mail was accumulating in the wire container fixed inside the letter-box on the front door, so to fill in the time before I was due at the pub I took the letters along to the sitting room and began opening the envelopes.

It seemed all wrong. I kept telling myself it was necessary but I still felt as if I were trespassing on ground Greville had surrounded with keep-out fences. There were bills, requests from charities, a bank statement for his private account, a gemmology magazine and two invitations. No letters from sightholders, diamantaires or cutters in Antwerp. I put the letters into the gemmology magazine's large envelope and added to them some similar unfinished business that I'd found in the drawer under the telephone, and reflected ruefully, putting it all ready to take to Hungerford, that I loathed paperwork at the best of times. My own had a habit of mounting up into increasingly urgent heaps. Perhaps having to do Greville's would teach me some sense.

Brad whisked us round to The Rook and Castle at five-thirty and pointed to the phone to let me know how I could call him when I'd finished, and I saw from his twitch of a smile that he found it a satisfactory amusement.

The Rook and Castle was old fashioned inside as well as out, an oasis of drinking peace without a juke-box. There was a lot of dark wood and tiffany lampshades and small tables with beer mats. A clientele of mostly business-suited men was beginning to trickle in and I paused inside the door both to get accustomed to the comparative darkness and to give anyone who was interested a plain view of the crutches.

The interest level being nil, I judged Elliot Trelawney to be absent. I went over to the bar, ordered some Perrier and swallowed a Distalgesic, as it was time. The morning's gallop had done no good to the ankle department but it wasn't to be regretted.

A bulky man of about fifty came into the place as if familiar with his surroundings and looked purposefully around, sharpening his gaze on the crutches and coming without hesitation to the bar.

'Mr Franklin?'

I shook his offered hand.

'What are you drinking?' he said briskly, eying my glass.'

'Perrier. That's temporary also.'

He smiled swiftly, showing white teeth.'You won't mind if I have a double Glenlivet? Greville and I drank many of them together here. I'm going to miss him abominably. Tell me what happened.'

I told him. He listened intently, but at the end he said merely, 'You look very uncomfortable propped against that stool. Why don't we move to a table?' And without more ado he picked up my glass along with the one the bartender had fixed for him, and carried them over to two wooden armchairs under a multicoloured lampshade by the wall.

'That's better,' he said, taking a sip and eying me over the glass. 'So you're the brother he talked about. You're Derek.'

'I'm Derek. His only brother, actually. I didn't know he talked about me.'

'Oh, yes. Now and then.'

Elliot Trelawney was big, almost bald, with half-moon glasses and a face that was fleshy but healthy looking. He had thin lips but laugh lines around his eyes, and I'd have said on a snap judgment that he was a realist with a sense of humour.

'He was proud of you,' he said.

'Proud?' I was surprised.

He glimmered. 'We often played golf together on Saturday mornings and sometimes he would be wanting to finish before the two o'clock race at Sandown or somewhere, and it would be because you were riding and it was on the box. He liked to watch you. He liked you to win.'

'He never told me,' I said regretfully.

'He wouldn't, would he? I watched with him a couple of times and all he said after you'd won was, "That's all right then."'

'And when I lost?'

'When you lost?' He smiled. 'Nothing at all. Once you had a crashing fall and he said he'd be glad on the whole when you retired, as race-riding was so dangerous. Ironic, isn't it?'

'Yes.'

'By God, I'll miss him.' His voice was deep. 'We were friends for twenty years.'

I envied him. I wanted intolerably what it was too late to have, and the more I listened to people remembering Greville the worse it got.

'Are you a magistrate?' I asked.

He nodded. 'We often sat together. Greville introduced me to it, but I've never had quite his gift. He seemed to know the truth of things by instinct. He said goodness was visible, therefore in its absence one sought for answers.'

'What sort of cases did ... do you try?'

'All sorts.' He smiled again briefly. 'Shoplifters. Vagrants. Possession of drugs. TV licence fee evaders. Sex offenders ... that's prostitution, rape, sex with minors, kerb crawlers. Greville always seemed to know infallibly when those were lying.'

'Go on,' I said, when he stopped. 'Anything else?'

'Well, there are a lot of diplomats in West London, in all the embassies. You'd be astonished what they get away with by claiming diplomatic immunity. Greville hated diplomatic immunity, but we have to grant it. Then we have a lot of small businessmen who "forget" to pay the road tax on the company vehicles, and there are TDAs by the hundred — that's Taking and Driving Away cars. Other motoring offences, speeding and so on, are dealt with separately, like domestic offences and juveniles. And then occasionally we get the preliminary hearings in a murder case, but of course we have to refer those to the Crown Court.'

'Does it all ever depress you?' I said.

He took a sip and considered me. 'It makes you sad,' he said eventually. 'We see as much inadequacy and stupidity as downright villainy. Some of it makes you laugh. I wouldn't say it's depressing, but one learns to see the world from underneath, so to speak. To see the dirt and the delusions, to see through the offenders' eyes and understand their weird logic. But one's disillusion is sporadic because we don't have a bench every day. Twice a month, in Greville's and my cases, plus a little committee work. And that's what I really want from you: the notes Greville was making on the licensing of a new-style gaming club. He said he'd learned disturbing allegations against one of the organisers and he was going to advise turning down the application at the next committee meeting even though it was a project we'd formerly looked on favourably.'

'I'm afraid,' I said, 'that I haven't so far found any notes like that.'

'Damm ... Where would he have put them?'

'I don't know. I'll look for them, though.' No harm in keeping an eye open for notes while I searched for C.

Elliot Trelawney reached into an inner jacket pocket and brought out two flat black objects, one a notebook, the other a folded black case a bit like a cigarette case.

109

'These were Greville's,' he said. 'I brought them for you.' He put them on the small table and moved them towards me with plump and deliberate fingers. 'He lent me that one,' he pointed, 'and the notebook he left on the table after a committee meeting last week.'

'Thank you,' I said. I picked up the folded case and opened it and found inside a miniature electronic chess set, the sort that challenged a player to beat it. I looked up. Trelawney's expression, unguarded, was intensely sorrowful. 'Would you like it?' I said. 'I know it's not much, but would you like to keep it?'

'If you mean it.'

I nodded and he put the chess set back in his pocket. 'Greville and I used to play ... *dammit* ...' he finished explosively, 'Why should such a futile thing happen?'

No answer was possible. I regretfully picked up the black notebook and opened it at random.

'The bad scorn the good,' I read aloud, 'and the crooked despise the straight.'

'The thoughts of Chairman Mao,' Trelawney said dryly, recovering himself. 'I used to tease him ... he said it was a habit he'd had from university when he'd learned to clarify his thoughts by writing them down. When I knew he was dead I read that notebook from cover to cover. I've copied down some of the things in it, I hope you won't mind.' He smiled. 'You'll find parts of it especially interesting.'

'About his horses?'

'Those too.'

I stowed the notebook in a trouser pocket which was already pretty full and brought out from there the racing diary, struck by a thought, I explained what the diary was, showing it to Trelawney.

'I phoned that number,' I said, turning pages and pointing, 'and mentioned Greville's name, and a woman told me in no uncertain terms never to telephone again as she wouldn't have the name Greville Franklin spoken in her house.'

Elliot Trelawney blinked. 'Greville? Doesn't sound like Greville.'

'I didn't think so, either. So would it have had something to do with one of your cases? Someone he found guilty of

110

something?'

'Hah. Perhaps.' He considered. 'I could probably find out whose number it is, if you like. Strange he would have had it in his diary, though. Do you want to follow it up?'

'It just seemed so odd,' I said.

'Quite right.' He unclipped a gold pencil from another inner pocket and in a slim notebook of black leather with gold corners wrote down the number.

'Do you make enemies much, because of the court?' I asked.

He looked up and shrugged. 'We get cursed now and then. Screamed at, one might say. But usually not. Mostly they please guilty because it's so obvious they are. The only real enemy Greville might have had is the gambling club organiser who's not going to get his licence. A drugs baron is what Greville called him. A man suspected of murder but not tried through lack of evidence. He might have had very hard feelings.' He hesitated. 'When I heard Greville was dead, I even wondered about Vaccaro. But it seems clear the scaffolding was a sheer accident ... wasn't it?'

'Yes, it was. The scaffolding broke high up. One man working on it fell three storeys to his death. Pieces just rained down on Greville. A minute earlier, a minute later ...' I sighed. 'Is Vaccaro the gambling-licence man?'

'He is. He appeared before the committee and seemed perfectly straightforward. Subject to screening, we said. And then someone contacted Greville and uncovered the muck. But we don't ourselves have any details, so we need his notes.'

'I'll look for them,' I promised again. I turned more pages in the diary. 'Does Koningin Beatrix mean anything to you?' I showed him the entry. 'Or CZ = C x 1.7?'

'Nothing,' Elliot Trelawney said. 'But as you know, Greville could be as obscure as he was clear-headed. And those were private notes to himself, after all. Same as his notebook. It was never for public consumption.'

I nodded and put away the diary and paid for Elliot Trelawney's repeat Glenlivet but felt waterlogged myself. He stayed for a while, seeming to be glad to talk about Greville, as I was content to listen. We parted eventually on friendly terms, he giving me his card with his phone number for when I found Greville's notes.

If, I silently thought. If I find them.

When he'd gone I used the pub's telephone to ring the car and after five unanswered brr-brrs disconnected and went outside, and Brad with almost a grin reappeared to pick me up.

'Home,' I said, and he said, 'Yerss,' and that was that.

On the way I read bits of Greville's notebook, pausing often to digest the passing thoughts which had clearly been chiefly prompted by the flotsam drifting through the West London Magistrates Court.

'Goodness is sickening to the evil,' he wrote, 'as evil is sickening to the good. Both the evil and the good may be complacent.'

'In all income groups you find your average regulation slob who sniggers at anarchy but calls the police indignantly to his burglarised home, who is actively anti-authority until he needs to be saved from someone with a gun.'

'The palm outstretched for a hand-out can turn in a flash into a cursing fist. A nation's palm, a nation's fist.'

'Crime to many is not crime but simply a way of life. If laws are inconvenient, ignore them, they don't apply to you.'

'Infinite sadness is not to trust an old friend.'

'Historically, more people have died of religion than cancer.'

'I hate rapists. I imagine being anally assaulted myself, and the anger overwhelms me. It's essential to make my judgment cold.'

Further on I came unexpectedly to what Elliot Trelawney must have meant.

Greville had written, 'Derek came to dinner very stiff with broken ribs. I asked him how he managed to live with all those injuries. "Forget the pain and get on with the party," he said. So we drank fizz.'

I stopped reading and stared out at the autumn countryside which was darkening now, lights going on. I remembered that evening very well, up to a point. Greville had been good fun. I'd got pretty high on the cocktail of champagne and painkillers and I hadn't felt a thing until I'd woken in the morning. I'd driven myself seventy miles home and forgotten it, which frightening fact was roughly why I was currently and obediently sticking to water.

It was almost too dark to read more, but I flicked over one

more page and came to what amounted to a prayer, so private and impassioned that I felt my mouth go dry. Alone on the page were three brief lines:

> May I deal with honour.
> May I act with courage.
> May I achieve humility.

I felt as if I shouldn't have read it; knew he hadn't meant it to be read. May I achieve humility ... that prayer was for saints.

When we reached my house I told Brad I would go to London the next day by train, and he looked devastated.

'I'll drive you for nowt,' he said, hoarsely.

'It isn't the money.' I was surprised by the strength of his feelings. 'I just thought you'd be tired of all the waiting about.'

He shook his head vigorously, his eyes positively pleading.

'All right, then,' I said. 'London tomorrow, Ipswich on Friday. OK?'

'Yerss,' he said with obvious relief.

'And I'll pay you, of course.'

He looked at me dumbly for a moment, then ducked his head into the car to fetch the big brown envelope from Greville's house, and he waited while I unlocked my door and made sure that there were no unwelcome visitors lurking.

Everything was quiet, everything orderly. Brad nodded at my all-clear, gave me the envelope and loped off into the night more tongue-tied than ever. I'd never wondered very much about his thought during all the silent hours; had never tried, I supposed, to understand him. I wasn't sure I wanted to. It was restful the way things were.

I ate a micro-waved chicken pie from the freezer and made an unenthusiastic start on Greville's letters, paying his bills for him, closing his accounts, declining his invitations, saying sorry, sorry, very sorry.

After that, in spite of good resolutions, I did not attack my own backlog but read right through Greville's notebook looking for diamonds. Maybe there were some solid gold nuggets, maybe some pearls of wisdom, but no helpful instructions like

113

turn right at the fourth apple tree, walk five paces and dig.

I did however find the answer to one small mystery, which I read with wry amusement.

The green soapstone box pleases me as an exercise in misdirection and deviousness. The keyhole has no key because it has no lock. It's impossible to unlock men's minds with keys, but guile and pressure will do it, as with the box.

Even with the plain instruction to be guileful and devious it took me ages to find the secret. I tried pressing each of the two hinges, pressing the lock, twisting, pressing everything again with the box upside down. The green stone stayed stubbornly shut.

Misdirection, I thought. If the keyhole wasn't a lock, maybe the hinges weren't hinges. Maybe the lid wasn't a lid. Maybe the whole thing was solid.

I tried the box upside down again, put my thumb on its bottom surface with firm pressure and tried to push it out endways, like a slide. Nothing happened. I reversed it and pushed the other way and as if with a sigh for the length of my stupidity the bottom of the box slid out reluctantly to half way, and stopped.

It was beautifully made, I thought. When it was shut one couldn't see the bottom edges weren't solid stone, so closely did they fit. I looked with great curiosity to see what Greville had hidden in his ingenious hiding place, not really expecting diamonds, and brought out two well-worn chamois leather pouches with drawstrings, the sort jewellers use, with the name of the jeweller indistinctly stamped on the front.

Both of the pouches were empty, to my great disappointment. I stuffed them back into the hole and shut the box, and it sat on the table beside the telephone all evening, an enigma solved but useless.

It wasn't until I'd decided to go to bed that some switch or other clicked in my brain and a word half-seen became suddenly a conscious thought. Van Ekeren, stamped in gold. Perhaps the jeweller's name stamped on the chamois pouches was worth another look.

I opened the box and pulled the pouches out again and in the rubbed and faded lettering read the full name and address.

> Jacob van Ekeren
> Pelikanstraat 70
> Antwerp

There had to be, I thought, about ten thousand jewellers in Antwerp. The pouches were far from new, certainly not only a few weeks old. All the same ... better find out.

I took one and left one, closing the box again, and in the morning bore the crumpled trophy to London and through international telephone enquiries found Jacob van Ekeren's number.

The voice that answered from Antwerp spoke either Dutch or Flemish, so I tried in French, '*Je veux parler avec Monsieur Jacob van Ekeren, s'il vous plaît.*'

'*Ne quittez pas.*'

I held on as instructed until another voice spoke, this time in French, of which I knew far too litte.

'*Monsieur van Ekeren n'est pas ici maintenant, monsieur.*'

'*Parlez vous anglais?*' I asked. 'I'm speaking from England.'

'*Attendez.*'

I waited again and was rewarded with an extremely English voice asking if he could help.

I explained that I was speaking from Saxony Franklin Ltd, gemstone importers in London.

'How can I help you?' He was courteous and noncommittal.'

'Do you,' I said baldly, 'cut and polish rough diamonds?'

'Yes, of course,' he answered. 'But before we do business with any new client we need introductions and references.'

'Um,' I said. 'Wouldn't Saxony Franklin Ltd be a client of yours already? Or Greville Saxony Franklin, maybe? Or just Greville Franklin? It's really important.'

'May I have your name?'

'Derek Franklin. Greville's brother.'

'One moment.' He returned after a while and said he would call me back shortly with an answer.

'Thank you very much,' I said.

'*Pas du tout.*' Bilingual besides.

115

I put down the phone and asked both Annette and June, who were busily moving around, if they could find Jacob van Ekeren anywhere in Greville's files. 'See if you can find any mention of Antwerp in the computer,' I added to June.

'Diamonds again!'

'Yup. The van Ekeren address is 70 Pelikanstraat.'

Annette wrinkled her brow. 'That's the Belgian equivalent of Hatton Garden,' she said.

It disrupted their normal work and they weren't keen, but Annette was very soon able to say she had no record of any Jacob van Ekeren, but the files were kept in the office for only six years, and any contact before that would be in storage in the basement. June whisked in to confirm that she couldn't find van Ekeren or Pelikanstraat or Antwerp in the computer.

It wasn't exactly surprising. If Greville had wanted his diamond transaction to be common knowledge in the office he would have conducted it out in the open. Very odd, I thought, that he hadn't. If it had been anyone but Greville one would have suspected him of something underhand, but as far as I knew he always had dealt with honour, as he'd prayed.

The telephone rang and Annette answered it. 'Saxony Franklin, can I help you?' She listened. 'Derek Franklin? Yes, just a moment.' She handed me the receiver and I found it was the return of the smooth French-English voice from Belgium. I knew as well as he did that he had spent the time between the two calls getting our number from international enquiries so that he could check back and be sure I was who I'd said. Merely prudent. I'd have done the same.

'Mr Jacob van Ekeren has retired,' he said. 'I am his nephew Hans. I can tell you now after our researches that we have done no business with your firm within the past six or seven years, but I can't speak for the time before that, when my uncle was in charge.'

'I see,' I said. 'Could you, er, ask your uncle?'

'I will if you like,' he said civilly. 'I did telephone his house, but I understand that he and my aunt will be away from home until Monday, and their maid doesn't seem to know where they went.' He paused. 'Could I ask what all this is about?'

I explained that my brother had died suddenly, leaving a good deal of unfinished business which I was trying to sort out.

116

'I came across the name and address of your firm. I'm following up everything I can.'

'Ah,' he said sympathetically. 'I will certainly ask my uncle on Monday, and let you know.'

'I'm most grateful.'

'Not at all.'

The uncle, I thought morosely, was a dead-end.

I went along and opened the vault, telling Annette that Prospero Jenks wanted all the spinel. 'And he says we have a piece of rock crystal like the Eiger.'

'The What?'

'Sharp mountain. Like Mont Blanc.'

'Oh.' She moved down the rows of boxes and chose a heavy one from near the bottom at the far end. 'This is it,' she said, humping it on to the shelf and opening the lid. 'Beautiful.'

The Eiger, filling the box, was lying on its side and had a knobbly base so that it wouldn't stand up, but I supposed one could see in the lucent faces and angled planes that, studded with diamond stars and given the Jenks' sunlight treatment, it could make the basis of a fantasy worthy of the name.

'Do we have a price for it?' I asked.

'Double what it cost,' she said cheerfully. 'Plus VAT, plus packing and transport.'

'He wants everything sent by messenger.'

She nodded. 'He always does. Jason takes them in a taxi. Leave it to me, I'll see to it.'

'And we'd better put the pearls away that came yesterday.'

'Oh, yes.'

She went off to fetch them and I moved down to where I'd given up the day before, feeling certain that the search was futile but committed to it all the same. Annette returned with the pearls, which were at least in plastic bags on strings, not in the awkward open envelopes, so while she counted and stored the new intake, I checked my way through the old.

Boxes of pearls, all sizes. No diamonds.

'Does CZ mean anything to you?' I asked Annette idly.

'CZ is cubic zirconia,' she said promptly. 'We sell a fair amount of it.'

'Isn't that, um, imitation diamond?'

'It's a manufactured crystal very like diamond,' she said, 'but

117

about ten thousand times cheaper. If it's in a ring, you can't tell the difference.'

'Can't anyone?' I asked. 'They must do.'

'Mr Franklin said that most high street jewellers can't at a glance. The best way to tell the difference, he said, is to take the stones out of their setting and weigh them.'

'*Weigh* them?'

'Yes. Cubic zirconia's much heavier than diamond, so one carat of cubic zirconia is smaller than a one carat diamond.'

'CZ equals C times one point seven,' I said slowly.

'That's right,' she said, surprised. 'How did you know?'

CHAPTER 9

From noon on, when I closed the last box-lid unproductively on the softly changing colours of rainbow opal from Oregon, I sat in Greville's office reading June's print-out of a crash course in business studies, beginning to see the pattern of a cash flow that ended on the side of the angels. Annette, who as a matter of routine had been banking the receipts daily, produced a sheaf of cheques for me to sign, which I did, feeling that it was the wrong name on the line, and she brought the day's post for decisions, which I strugglingly made.

Several people in the jewellery business telephoned in response to the notices of Greville's death which had appeared in the papers that morning. Annette, reassuring them that the show would go on, sounded more confident than she looked. 'They all say Ipswich is too far, but they'll be there in spirit,' she reported.

At four there was a phone call from Elliot Trelawney, who said he'd cracked the number of the lady who didn't want Greville's name spoken in her house.

'It's sad, really,' he said with a chuckle. 'I suppose I shouldn't laugh. The lady can't and won't forgive Greville because he sent her upper-crust daughter to jail for three months for selling cocaine to a friend. The mother was in court, I remember her, and she talked to the press afterwards. She couldn't believe that selling cocaine to a friend was an offence. Drug peddlers were despicable, of course, but that wasn't the same as selling to a friend.'

'If a law is inconvenient, ignore it, it doesn't apply to you.'

'What?'

'Something Greville wrote in his notebook.'

'Oh yes. It seems Greville got the mother's phone number to suggest ways of rehabilitation for the daughter, but mother wouldn't listen. Look,' he hesitated. 'Keep in touch now and then, would you? Have a drink in The Rook and Castle occasionally?'

'All right.'

'And let me know as soon as you find those notes.'

'Sure,' I said.

'We want to stop Vaccaro, you know.'

'I'll look everywhere,' I promised.

When I put the phone down I asked Annette.

'Notes about his cases?' she said. 'Oh no, he never brought those to the office.'

Like he never bought diamonds, I thought dryly. And there wasn't a trace of them in the spreadsheets or the ledgers.

The small insistent alarm went off again, muffled inside the desk. Twenty past four, my watch said. I reached over and pulled open the drawer and the alarm stopped, as it had before.

'Looking for something?' June said, breezing in.

'Something with an alarm like a digital watch.'

'It's bound to be the world clock,' she said. 'Mr Franklin used to set it to remind himself to phone suppliers in Tokyo, and so on.'

I reflected that as I wouldn't know what to say to suppliers in Tokyo I hardly needed the alarm.

'Do you want me to send a fax to Tokyo to say the pearls arrived OK?' she said.

'Do you usually?'

She nodded. 'They worry.'

'Then please do.'

When she'd gone Jason with his orange hair appeared through the doorway and without any trace of insolence told me he'd taken the stuff to Prospero Jenks and brought back a cheque, which he'd given to Annette.

'Thank you,' I said neutrally.

He gave me an unreadable glance, said, 'Annette said to tell you,' and took himself off. An amazing improvement, I thought.

I stayed behind that evening after they'd all left and went slowly round Greville's domain looking for hiding places that were guileful and devious and full of misdirection.

It was impossible to search the hundreds of shallow drawers in the stockrooms and I concluded he wouldn't have used them because Lily or any of the others might easily have found what they weren't meant to. That was the trouble with the whole place, I decided in the end. Greville's own policy of not encouraging private territories had extended also to himself, as all of his staff seemed to pop in and out of his office familiarly whenever the need arose.

Hovering always was the uncomfortable thought that if any pointer to the diamonds' whereabouts had been left by Greville in his office, it could have vanished with the break-in artist, leaving nothing for me to find: and indeed I found nothing of any use. After a fruitless hour I locked everything that locked and went down to the yard to find Brad and go home.

The day of Greville's funeral dawned cold and clear and we were heading east when the sun came up. The run to Ipswich taking three hours altogether, we came into the town with generous time to search for Greville's car.

Enquiries from the police had been negative. They hadn't towed, clamped or ticketed any ancient Rover. They hadn't spotted its number in any public road or car-park, but that wasn't conclusive, they'd assured me. Finding the car had no priority with them as it hadn't been stolen but they would let me know if, if.

I explained the car-finder to Brad en route, producing a street map to go with it.

'Apparently when you press this red button the car's lights switch on and a whistle blows,' I said. 'So you drive and I'll press, OK?'

He nodded, seeming amused, and we began to search in this slightly bizarre fashion, starting in the town centre near to where Greville had died and very slowly rolling up and down the streets, first to the north, then to the south, checking them off on the map. In many of the residential streets there were cars parked nose to tail outside houses, but nowhere did we get a whistle. There were public car-parks and shop car-parks and the station car-park, but nowhere did we turn lights on. Rover 3500s in any case were sparse: when we saw one we stopped to look at the plates, even if the paint wasn't grey, but none of them was Greville's

Disappointment settled heavily. I'd seriously intended to find that car. As lunchtime dragged towards two o'clock I began to believe that I shouldn't have left it so long, that I should have started looking as soon as Greville died. But last Sunday, I thought, I hadn't been in any shape to, and anyway it wasn't until Tuesday that I knew there was anything valuable to look for. Even now I was sure that he wouldn't have left the diamonds themselves vulnerable, but some reason for being in Ipswich at all ... given luck, why not?

The crematorium was set in a garden with neatly-planted rose trees: Brad dropped me at the door and drove away to find some food. I was met by two black-suited men, both with suitable expressions, who introduced themselves as the under-taker I'd engaged and one of the crematorium's officials. A lot of flowers had arrived, they said, and which did I want on the coffin.

In some bemusement I let them show me where the flowers were, which was in a long covered cloister beside the building, where one or two weeping groups were looking at wreaths of their own.

'These are Mr Franklin's,' the official said, indicating two long rows of bright bouquets blazing with colourful life in that place of death.

'All of these?' I said, astonished.

'They've been arriving all morning. Which do you want inside, on the coffin?'

There were cards on the bunches, I saw.

'I sent some from myself and our sisters,' I said doubtfully. 'The card has Susan, Miranda and Derek on it. I'll have that.'

The official and the undertaker took pity on the crutches and helped me find the right flowers; and I came first not to the card I was looking for but to another that shortened my breath.

'I will think of you every day at four-twenty.

Love, C.'

The flowers that went with it were velvety red roses arranged with ferns in a dark green bowl. Twelve sweet-smelling blooms. Dozen Roses, I thought. Heavens above.

'I've found them,' the undertaker called, picking up a large display of pink and bronze chrysanthemums. 'Here you are.'

'Great. Well, we'll have these roses as well, and this wreath next to them, which is from the staff in his office. Is that all right?'

It appeared to be. Annette and June had decided on all-white flowers after agonising and phoning from the office, and they'd made me promise to notice and tell them that they were pretty. We had decided that all the staff should stay behind and keep the office open as trade was so heavy, though I'd thought from her downcast expression that June would have liked to have made the journey.

I asked the official where all the other flowers had come from: from businesses, he said, and he would collect all the cards afterwards and give them to me.

I supposed for the first time that perhaps I should have taken Greville back to London to be seen off by colleagues and friends, but during the very quiet half-hour that followed had no single regret. The clergyman engaged by the undertakers asked if I wanted the whole service read as I appeared to be the only mourner, and I said yes, go ahead, it was fitting.

His voice droned a bit. I half listened and half watched the way the sunshine fell onto the flowers on the coffin from the high windows along one wall and thought mostly not of Greville as he'd been alive but what he had become to me during the past week.

His life had settled on my shoulders like a mantle. Through Monday, Tuesday, Wednesday and Thursday I'd learned enough of his business never to forget it. People who'd relied on him had transferred their reliance onto me, including in a way his friend Elliot Trelawney who wanted me as a Greville substitute to drink with. Clarissa Williams had sent her flowers knowing I would see them, wanting me to be aware of her, as if I weren't already. Nicholas Loder aimed to manipulate me for his own stable's ends. Prospero Jenks would soon be pressing hard for the diamonds for his fantasy, and the bank loan hung like a thundercloud in my mind.

123

Greville, lying cold in the coffin, hadn't meant any of it to happen.

A man of honour, I thought. I mentally repeated his own prayer for him, as it seemed a good time for it. May I deal with honour. May I act with courage. May I achieve humility. I didn't know if he'd managed the last one; I knew that I couldn't

The clergyman droned to a halt. The official removed the three lots of flowers from the coffin to put them on the floor and, with a whirring and creaking of machinery that sounded loud in the silence, the coffin slid away forward, out of sight, heading for fire.

Goodbye pal, I said silently. Goodbye, except that you are with me now more than ever before.

I went outside into the cold fresh air and thanked everyone and paid them and arranged for all of the flowers to go to St Catherine's Hospital, which seemed to be no problem. The official gave me the severed cards and asked what I wanted to do with my brother's ashes, and I had a ridiculous urge to laugh, which I saw from his hushed face would be wildly inappropriate. The business of ashes had always seemed to me an embarrassment.

He waited patiently for a decision. 'If you have any tall red rose trees,' I said finally, 'I daresay that would do, if you plant one along there with the others. Put the ashes there.'

I paid for the rose tree and thanked him again, and waited for a while for Brad to return, which he did looking smug and sporting a definite grin.

'I found it,' he said.

'What?' I was still thinking of Greville.

'Your brother's wheels.'

'You didn't!'

He nodded, highly pleased with himself.

'Where?'

He wouldn't say. He waited for me to sit and drove off in triumph into the centre of town, drawing up barely three hundred yards from where the scaffolding had fallen. Then, with his normal economy, he pointed to the forecourt of a used car sales business where under strips of fluttering pennants rows of offerings stood with large white prices painted on their windscreens.

'One of those?' I asked in disbelief.

Brad gurgled; no other word for the delight in his throat. 'Round the back,' he said.

He drove into the forecourt, then along behind the cars, and turned a corner, and we found ourselves outside the wide-open doors of a garage advertising repairs, oil changes, MOT tests and Ladies and Gents. Brad held the car-finder out of his open window and pressed the red button, and somewhere in the shadowy depths of the garage a pair of headlights began flashing on and off and a piercing whistle shrieked.

A cross-looking mechanic in oily overalls came hurrying out. He told me he was the foreman in charge and he'd be glad to see the back of the Rover 3500, and I owed him a week's parking besides the cleaning of the sparking plugs of the V.8 engine, plus a surcharge for inconvenience.

'What inconvenience?'

'Taking up space for a week when it was meant to be for an hour, and having that whistle blast my eardrums three times today.'

'Three times?' I said, surprised.

'Once this morning, twice this afternoon. This man came here earlier, you know. He said he'd bring the Rover's new owner.'

Brad gave me a bright glance. The car-finder had done its best for us early on in the morning, it seemed: it was our own eyes and ears that had missed it, out of sight as the car had been.

I asked the foreman to make out a bill and, getting out of my own car, swung over to Greville's. The Rover's doors would open, I found, but the boot was locked.

'Here,' said the foreman, coming over with the account and the ignition keys. 'The boot won't open. Some sort of fancy lock. Custom made. It's been a bloody nuisance.'

I mollifyingly gave him a credit card in settlement and he took it off to his cubby hole of an office.

I looked at the Rover. 'Can you drive that?' I asked Brad.

'Yerss,' he said gloomily.

I smiled and pulled Greville's keys out of my pocket to see if any of them would unlock the boot; and one did, to my relief, though not a key one would normally have associated with cars.

More like the keys to a safe, I thought; and the lock revealed was intricate and steel. Its installation was typically Greville, ultra security-conscious after his experiences with the Porsche.

The treasure so well guarded included an expensive-looking set of golf clubs, with a trolley and a new box of golf balls, a large brown envelope, an overnight bag with pyjamas, clean shirt, toothbrush and a scarlet can of shaving cream, a portable telephone like my own, a personal computer, a portable Fax machine, an opened carton of spare fax paper, a polished wooden box containing a beautiful set of brass scales with featherlight weights, an anti-thief device for locking onto the steering wheel, a huge torch, and a heavy complicated-looking orange metal contraption that I recognised from Greville's enthusiastic description as a device for sliding under flat tyres so that one could drive to a garage on it instead of changing a wheel by the roadside.

'Cor,' Brad said, looking at the haul, and the foreman too, returning with the paperwork, was brought to an understanding of the need for the defences.

I shut the boot and locked it again, which seemed a very Greville-like thing to do, and took a quick look round inside the body of the car, seeing the sort of minor clutter which defies the tidiest habit: matchbooks, time-clock parking slips, blue sunglasses, and a cellophane packet of tissues. In the door pocket on the driver's side, jammed in untidily, a map.

I picked it out. It was a road map of East Anglia, the route from London to Ipswich drawn heavily in black with, written down one side, the numbers of the roads to be followed. The marked route, I saw with interest, didn't stop at Ipswich but went on beyond, to Harwich.

Harwich, on the North Sea, was a ferry port. Harwich to the Hook of Holland; the route of one of the historic crossings, like Dover to Calais, Folkestone to Ostend. I didn't know if the Harwich ferries still ran, and I thought that if Greville had been going to Holland he would certainly have gone by air. All the same he had, presumably, been going to Harwich.

I said abruptly to the foreman, who was showing impatience for our departure, 'Is there a travel agent near here?'

'Three doors along,' he said pointing, 'and you can't park here while you go there.'

I gave him a tip big enough to change his mind, and left Brad keeping watch over the cars while I peg-legged along the street. Right on schedule the travel agents came up, and I went in to enquire about ferries from the Hook of Holland.

'Sure,' said an obliging girl. 'They run every day and every night. Sealink operate them. When do you want to go?'

'I don't know, exactly.'

She thought me feeble. 'Well, the *St Nicholas* goes over to Holland every morning, and the *Koningin Beatrix* every night.'

I must have looked as stunned as I felt. I closed my open mouth.

'What's the matter?' she said.

'Nothing at all. Thank you very much.'

She shrugged as if the lunacies of the travelling public were past comprehension, and I shunted back to the garage with my chunk of new knowledge which had solved one little conundrum but posed another, such as what was Greville doing with Queen Beatrix, not a horse but a boat.

Brad drove the Rover to London and I drove my own car, the pace throughout enough to make a snail weep. Whatever the Ipswich garage had done to Greville's plugs hadn't cured any trouble, the V.8 running more like a V.4 or even a V.1½ as far as I could see. Brad stopped fairly soon after we'd left the town and, cursing, cleaned the plugs again himself, but to no avail.

'Needs new ones,' he said.

I used the time to search thoroughly through the golf bag, the box of golf balls, the overnight bag and all the gadgets.

No diamonds.

We set off again, the Rover going precariously slowly in very low gear up hills, with me staying on its tail in case it petered out altogether. I didn't much mind the slow progress except that resting my left foot on the floor sent frequent jabs up my leg and eventually reawoke the overall ache in the ankle, but in comparison with the ride home from Ipswich five days earlier it was chickenfeed. I still mended fast, I thought gratefully. By Tuesday at the latest I'd be walking. Well, limping, maybe, like Greville's car.

There was no joy in reflecting, as I did, that if the sparking plugs had been efficient he wouldn't have stopped to have them fixed and he wouldn't have been walking along a street in Ipswich at the wrong moment. If one could foresee the future, accidents wouldn't happen. 'If only' were wretched words.

We reached Greville's road eventually and found two spaces to park, though not outside the house. I'd told Brad in the morning that I would sleep in London that night to be handy for going to York with the Ostermeyers the next day. I'd planned originally that if we found the Rover he would take it on the orbital route direct to Hungerford and I would drive into London and go on home from there after I got back from York. The plugs having changed that plan near Ipswich, it was now Brad who would go to Hungerford in my car, and I would finish the journey by train. Greville's car, ruin that it was, could decorate the street.

We transferred all the gear from Greville's boot into the back of my car, or rather Brad did the transferring while I mostly watched. Then, Brad carrying the big brown envelope from the Rover and my own overnight grip, we went up the path to the house in the dark and set off the lights and the barking. No one in the houses around paid any attention. I undid the three locks and went in cautiously but, as before, once I'd switched the dog off the house was quiet and deserted. Brad, declining food and drink, went home to his mum, and I, sitting in Greville's chair, opened the big brown envelope and read all about Vaccaro who had been a very bad boy indeed.

Most of the envelope's contents were a copy of Vaccaro's detailed application, but on an attached sheet in abbreviated prose Greville had hand-written:

Ramon Vaccaro, wanted for drug-running, Florida, USA. Suspected of several murders, victims mostly pilots, wanting out from flying drug crates. Vaccaro leaves no mouths alive to chatter. My info from scared-to-death pilot's widow. She won't come to the committee meeting but gave enough insider details for me to believe her.

Vaccaro seduced private pilots with a big pay-off, then when they'd done one run to Colombia and got away with it, they'd be hooked and do it again and again until they finally got rich enough to have cold feet. Then the poor sods would die from being shot on their own doorsteps from passing cars, no sounds because of silencers, no witnesses and no clues. But all were pilots owning their own small planes, too many for coincidence. Widow says her husband scared stiff but left it too late. She's remarried, lives in London, always wanted revenge, couldn't believe it was the same man when she saw local newspaper snippet, Vaccaro's Family Gaming, with his photo. Family! She went to Town Hall anonymously, they put her on to me.

We don't have to find Vaccaro guilty. We just don't give him a gaming licence. Widow says not to let him know who turned his application down, he's dangerous and vengeful, but how can he silence a whole committee? The Florida police might like to know his whereabouts. Extradition?

I telephoned Elliot Trelawney at his weekend home, told him I'd found the red-hot notes and read them to him, which brought forth a whistle and a groan.

'But Vaccaro didn't kill Greville,' I said.

'No.' He sighed. 'How did the funeral go?'

'Fine. Thank you for your flowers.'

'Just sorry I couldn't get there — but on a working day, and so far ...'

'It was fine,' I said again, and it had been. I'd been relieved, on the whole, to be alone.

'Would you mind,' he said, diffidently, 'if I arranged a memorial service for him? Sometime soon. Within a month?'

'Go right ahead,' I said warmly. 'A great idea.'

He hoped I would send the Vaccaro notes by messenger on Monday to the Magistrates Court, and he asked if I played golf.

In the morning, after a dream-filled night in Greville's black and white bed, I took a taxi to the Ostermeyers' hotel, meeting them in the foyer as arranged on the telephone the evening before.

They were in good form, Martha resplendent in a red wool tailored dress with a mink jacket, Harley with a new English-looking hat over his easy grin, binoculars and racing paper ready. Both of them seemed determined to enjoy whatever the day brought forth and Harley's occasional ill-humour was far out of sight.

The driver, a different one from Wednesday, brought a huge super-comfortable Daimler to the front door exactly on time, and with all auspices pointing to felicity, the Ostermeyers arranged themselves on the rear seat, I sitting in front of them beside the chauffeur.

The chauffeur, who announced his name as Simms, kindly stowed my crutches in the boot and said it was no trouble at all, sir, when I thanked him. The crutches themselves seemed to be the only tiny cloud on Martha's horizon, bringing a brief frown to the proceedings.

'Is that foot still bothering you? Milo said it was nothing to worry about.'

'No, it isn't, and it's much better,' I said truthfully.

'Oh, good. Just as long as it doesn't stop you riding Datepalm.'

'Of course not,' I assured her.'

We're so pleased to have him. He's just darling.'

I made some nice noises about Datepalm, which wasn't very difficult, as we nosed through the traffic to go north on the M1.

Harley said, 'Milo says Datepalm might go for the Charisma 'Chase at Kempton next Saturday. What do you think?'

'A good race for him,' I said calmly. I would kill Milo, I thought. A dicey gallop was one thing, but no medic on earth was going to sign my card in one week to say I was fit; and I wouldn't be, because half a ton of horse over jumps at thirty-plus miles an hour was no puffball matter.

'Milo might prefer to save him for the Mackeson at Cheltenham next month,' I said judiciously, sowing the idea. 'Or of course for the Hennessy Cognac Gold Cup two weeks later.' I'd definitely be fit for the Hennessy, six weeks ahead. The Mackeson, at four weeks, was a toss-up.

'Then there's that big race the day after Christmas,' Martha signed happily. 'It's all so exciting. Harley promises we can come back to see him run.'

They talked about horses for another half hour and then asked if I knew anything about a Dick Turpin.

'Oh, sure.'

130

'Some guy said he was riding to York. I didn't understand any part of it.'

I laughed. 'It happened a couple of centuries ago. Dick Turpin was a highwayman, a real villain, who rode his mare Black Bess north to escape the law. They caught him in York and flung him in jail, and for a fortnight he held a sort of riotous court in his cell, making jokes and drinking with all the notables of the city who came to see the famous thief in his chains. Then they took him out and hanged him on a piece of land called the Knavesmire, which is now the racecourse.'

'Oh, my,' Martha said, ghoulishly diverted. 'How perfectly grisly.'

In time we left the M1 and travelled north-east to the difficult old A1, and I thought that no one in their senses would drive from London to York when they could go by train. The Ostermeyers, of course, weren't doing the driving.

Harley said as we neared the city, 'You're expected at lunch with us, Derek.'

Expected, in Ostermeyer speech, meant invited. I protested mildly that it wasn't so.

'It sure is. I talked with Lord Knightwood yesterday evening, told him we'd have you with us. He said right away to have you join us for lunch. They're giving their name to one of the races, it'll be a big party.'

'Which race?' I asked with curiosity. Knightwood wasn't a name I knew.

'Here it is.' Harley rustled the racing newspaper. 'The University of York Trophy. Lord Knightwood is the University's top man, president or governor, some kind of figurehead. A Yorkshire VIP. Anyway, you're expected.'

I thanked him. There wasn't much else to do, though a sponsor's lunch on top of no exercise could give me weight problems if I wasn't careful. However, I could almost hear Milo's agitated voice in my ear: 'Whatever the Ostermeyers want, for Christ's sake give it to them.'

'There's also the York Minster Cup, Harley said, reading his paper, 'and the Civic Pride Challenge. Your horse Dozen Roses is in the York Castle Champions.'

'My brother's horse,' I said.

Harley chuckled. 'We won't forget.'

131

Simms dropped us neatly at the Club entrance. One could get addicted to chauffeurs, I thought, accepting the crutches gravely offered. No parking problems. Someone to drive one home on crunch days. But no spontaneity, no real privacy ... No thanks, not even long-term Brad.

Back the first horse you see, they say. Or the first jockey. Or the first trainer.

The first trainer we saw was Nicholas Loder. He looked truly furious and, I thought in surprise, alarmed when I came face to face with him after he'd watched our emergence from the Daimler.

'What are *you* doing here?' he demanded brusquely. 'You've no business here.'

'Do you know Mr and Mrs Ostermeyer?' I asked politely, introducing them. 'They've just bought Datepalm. I'm their guest today.'

He glare; there wasn't any other word for it. He had been waiting for a man, perhaps one of his owners, to collect a Club badge from the allotted window and, the transaction achieved, the two of them marched off into the racecourse without another word.

'Well!' Martha said, outraged. 'If Milo ever behaved like that we'd whisk our horses out of his yard before he could say goodbye.'

'It isn't my horse,' I pointed out. 'Not yet.'

'When it is, what will you do?'

'The same as you, I think, though I didn't mean to.'

'Good,' Martha said emphatically.

I didn't really understand Loder's attitude or reaction. If he wanted a favour from me, which was that I'd let him sell Dozen Roses and Gemstones to others of his owners either for the commission or to keep them in his yard, he should at least have shown an echo of Milo's feelings for the Ostermeyers.

If Dozen Roses had been cleared by the authorities to run, why was Loder scared that I was there to watch it?

Crazy, I thought. The only thing I'd wholly learned was that Loder's ability to dissimulate was underdeveloped for a leading trainer.

Harley Ostermeyer said the York University's lunch was to be held at one end of the Club members' dining room in the

132

grandstand, so I showed the way there, reflecting that it was lucky I'd decided on a decent suit for that day, not just a sweater. I might have been a last-minute addition to the party but I was happy not to look it.

There was already a small crowd of people, glasses in hand, chatting away inside a temporary white-lattice-fenced area, a long buffet set out behind them with tables and chairs to sit at for eating.

'There are the Knightwoods,' said the Ostermeyers, clucking contentedly, and I found myself being introduced presently to a tall white-haired kindly-looking man who had benevolence shining from every perhaps seventy-year-old wrinkle. He shook my hand amicably as a friend of the Ostermeyers with whom, it seemed, he had dined on a reciprocal visit to Harley's alma mater, the University of Pennsylvania. Harley was endowing a Chair there. Harley was a VIP in Pittsburgh, Pennsylvania.

I made the right faces and listened to the way the world went round, and said I thought it was great of the city of York to support its industry on the turf.

'Have you met my wife?' Lord Knightwood said vaguely. 'My dear,' he touched the arm of a woman with her back to us, 'you remember Harley and Martha Ostermeyer? And this is their friend Derek Franklin that I told you about.'

She turned to the Ostermeyers smiling and greeting them readily, and she held out a hand for me to shake, saying, 'How do you do. So glad you could come.'

'How do you do, Lady Knightwood,' I said politely.

She gave me a very small smile, in command of herself.

Clarissa Williams was Lord Knightwood's wife.

CHAPTER 10

She had known I would be there, it was clear, and if she hadn't wanted me to find out who she was she could have developed a strategic illness in plenty of time.

She was saying graciously, 'Didn't I see you on television winning the Gold Cup?' and I thought of her speed with that frightful kiyoga and the tumult of her feelings on Tuesday, four days ago. She seemed to have no fear that I would give her away, and indeed, what could I say? Lord Knightwood, my brother was your wife's lover? Just the right sort of thing to get the happy party off to a good start.

The said Lord was introducing the Ostermeyers to a professor of physics who with twinkles said that as he was the only true aficionado of horse racing among the teaching academics he had been pressed into service to carry the flag, although there were about fifty undergraduates out on the course ready to bet their socks off in the cause.

'Derek has a degree,' Martha said brightly, making conversation.

The professorial eyeballs swivelled my way speculatively. 'What university?'

'Lancaster,' I said dryly, which raised a laugh. Lancaster and York had fought battles of the red and white roses for many a long year.

'And subject?'

'Independent Studies.'

His desultory attention sharpened abruptly.

'What are Independent Studies?' Harley asked, seeing his interest.

'The student designs his own course and invents his own final subject,' the professor said. 'Lancaster is the only university offering such a course and they let only about eight students a year do it. It's not for the weak-willed or the feeble-minded.'

The Knightwoods and the Ostermeyers listened in silence and I felt embarassed. I had been young then, I thought.

'What did you choose as your subject?' asked the professor, intent now on an answer. 'Horses, in some way?'

I shook my head. 'No ... er ... "Roots and Results of War"'

'My dear chap,' Lord Knightwood said heartily, 'sit next to the professor at lunch.' He moved away benignly, taking his wife and the Ostermeyers with him, and the professor, left behind, asked what I fancied for the races.

Clarissa, by accident or design, remained out of talking distance throughout the meal and I didn't try to approach her. The party broke up during and after the first race, although everyone was invited to return for tea, and I spent most of the afternoon, as I'd spent so many others, watching horses stretch and surge and run as their individual natures dictated. The will to win was born and bred in them all, but some cared more than others: it was those with the implacable impulse to lead a wild herd who fought hardest and oftenest won. Sports writers tended to call it courage but it went deeper than that, right down into the gene pool, into instinct, into the primordial soup on the same evolutionary level as the belligerence so easily aroused in Homo sapiens, that was the tap root of war.

I was no stranger to the thought that I sought battle on the turf because though the instinct to fight and conquer ran strong I was averse to guns. Sublimation, the pundits would no doubt call it. Datepalm and I both, on the same primitive plane, wanted to win.

'What are you thinking?' someone asked at my shoulder.

I would have known her voice anywhere, I thought. I turned to see her half-calm half-anxious expression, the Lady Knightwood social poise explicit in the smooth hair, the patrician bones and the tailoring of her clothes, the passionate woman merely a hint in the eyes.

135

'Thinking about horses.' I said.

'I suppose you're wondering why I came today, after I learned last night that you'd not only be at the races, which I expected you might be anyway because of Dozen Roses, but actually be coming to our lunch ...' She stopped, sounding uncertain.

'I'm not Greville,' I said. 'Don't think of me as Greville.'

Her eyelids flickered. 'You're too damned perceptive.' She did a bit of introspection. 'Yes, all right, I wanted to be near you. It's a sort of comfort.'

We were standing by the rails of the parade ring watching the runners for the next race walk round, led by their lads. It was the race before the University Trophy, two races before that of Dozen Roses, a period without urgency for either of us. There were crowd noises all around and the clip-clop of horses walking by, and we could speak quietly as in an oasis of private space without being overheard.

'Are you still angry with me for hitting you?' she said a shade bitterly, as I'd made no comment after her last remark.

I half smiled. 'No.'

'I did think you were a burglar.'

'And what would you have explained to the police, if they'd come?'

She said ruefully, 'I hope I would have come to my senses and done a bunk before they got there.' She sighed. 'Greville said if I ever had to use the kiyoga in earnest to escape at once and not worry what I'd done to my attacker, but he never thought of a burglar in his own house.'

'I'm surprised he gave you a weapon like that,' I said mildly. 'Aren't they illegal? And him a magistrate.'

'I'm a magistrate too,' she said unexpectedly. 'That's how we originally met, at a magistrates' conference. I've not enquired into the legality of kiyogas. If I were prosecuted for carrying and using an offensive weapon, well, that would be much preferable to being a victim of the appalling assaults that come before us every week.'

'Where did he get it?' I asked curiously.

'America.'

'Do you have it with you here?'

She nodded and touched her handbag. 'It's second nature, now.'

136

She must have been thirty years younger than her husband, I thought inconsequently, and I knew what she felt about him. I didn't know whether or not I liked her, but I did recognise there was a weird sort of intimacy between us and that I didn't resent it.

The jockeys came out and stood around the owners in little groups. Nicholas Loder was there with the man he'd come in with, a thickset powerful-looking man in a dark suit, the pink cardboard Club badge fluttering from his lapel.

'Dozen Roses,' I said, watching Loder talking to the owner and his jockey, 'was he named for you?'

'Oh, God,' she said, disconcerted. 'How ever ...?'

I said, 'I put your roses on the coffin for the service.'

'Oh ...' she murmured with difficulty, her throat closing, her mouth twisting, 'I ... I can't ...'

'Tell me how York University came to be putting its name to a race.' I made it sound conversational, to give her composure time.

She swallowed, fighting for control, steadying her breathing. 'I'm sorry. It's just that I can't even mourn for him except inside; can't let it show to anyone except you, and it sweeps over me, I can't help it.' She paused and answered my unimportant question. 'The Clerk of the Course wanted to involve the city. Some of the bigwigs of the University were against joining in, but Henry persuaded them. He and I have always come here to meetings now and then. We both like it, for a day out with friends.'

'Your husband doesn't actually lecture at the University, does he?'

'Oh no, he's just a figurehead. He's chairman of a fair number of things in York. A public figure here.'

Vulnerable to scandal, I thought: as she was herself, and Greville also. She and he must have been unwaveringly discreet.

'How long since you first met Greville?' I asked noncommittally.

'Four years.' She paused. 'Four marvellous years. Not enought.'

The jockeys swung up onto the horses and moved away to go out onto the course. Nicholas Loder and his owner, busily talking, went off to the stands.

'May I watch the race with you?' Clarissa said. 'Do you mind?'

'I was going to watch from the grass.' I glanced down apologetically at the crutches. 'It's easier.'

'I don't mind the grass.'

So we stood side by side on the grass in front of the grandstand and she said, 'Whenever we could be together, he bought twelve red roses. It just ... well ...' She stopped, swallowing again hard.

'Mm,' I said. I thought of the ashes and the red rose tree and decided to tell her about that another time. It had been for him, anyway, not for her.

Nicholas Loder's two-year-old won the sprint at a convincing clip and I caught a glimpse of the owner afterwards looking heavily satisfied but unsmiling. Hardly a jolly character, I thought.

Clarissa went off to join her husband for the University race and after that, during their speeches and presentations, I went in search of Dozen Roses who was being led round in the pre-parade ring before being taken into a box or a stall to have his saddle put on.

Dozen Roses looked docile to dozy, I thought. An unremarkable bay, he had none of the looks or presence of Datepalm, nor the chaser's alert interest in his surroundings. He was a good performer, of that there was no question, but he didn't at that moment give an impression of going to be a 'trot-up' within half an hour, and he was vaguely not what I'd expected. Was this the colt that on the video tapes had won his last three races full of verve? Was this the young buck who had tried to mount a filly at the starting gate at Newmarket?

No, I saw with a sense of shock, he was not. I peered under his belly more closely, as it was sometimes difficult to tell, but there seemed to be no doubt that he had lost the essential tackle; that he had in fact been gelded.

I was stunned, and I didn't know whether to laugh or be furious. It explained so much: the loss of form when he had his mind on procreation rather than racing, and the return to speed once the temptation was removed. It explained why the Stewards hadn't called Loder in to justify the difference in running: horses very often did better after the operation.

I unfolded my racecard at Dozen Roses's race, and there, sure enough, against his name stood not c for colt or h for horse, but g for gelding.

Nicholas Loder's voice, vibrating with fury, spoke from not far behind me, 'That horse is not your horse. Keep away from him.'

I turned. Loder was advancing fast with Dozen Roses's saddle over his arm and full-blown rage in his face. The heavily unjoyful owner, still for some reason in tow, was watching the proceedings with puzzlement.

'Mine or not, I'm entitled to look at him,' I said. 'And look at him I darned well have, and either he is not Dozen Roses or you have gelded him against my brother's express wishes.'

His mouth opened and snapped shut.

'What's the matter, Nick?' the owner said. 'Who is this?'

Loder failed to intoduce us. Instead he said to me vehemently, 'You can't do anything about it. I have an Authority to Act. I am the registered agent for this horse and what I decide is none of your business.'

'My brother refused to have any of his horses gelded. You knew it well. You disobeyed him because you were sure he wouldn't find out, as he never went to the races.'

He glared at me. He was aware that if I lodged a formal complaint he would be in a good deal of trouble, and I thought he was certainly afraid that as my brother's executor I could and quite likely would do just that. Even if I only talked about it to others, it could do him damage: it was the sort of titbit the hungry racing press would pounce on for a giggle, and the owners of all the princely colts in his prestigious stable would get cold feet that the same might happen to their own property without their knowledge or consent.

He had understood all that, I thought, in the moment I'd told him on the telephone that it was I who would be inheriting Dozen Roses. He'd known that if I ever saw the horse I would realise at once what had been done. No wonder he'd lost his lower resonances.

'Greville was a fool,' he said angrily. 'The horse has done much better since he was cut.'

'That's true,' I agree, 'but it's not the point.'

139

'How much do you want, then?' he demanded roughly.

My own turn, I thought, to gape like a fish. I said feebly, 'It's not a matter of money.'

'Everything is,' he declared. 'Name your price and get out of my way.'

I glanced at the attendant owner who looked more phlegmatic than rivetted, but might remember and repeat this conversation, and I said merely, 'We'll discuss it later, OK?' and hitched myself away from them without aggression.

Behind me the owner was saying, 'What was that all about, Nick?' and I heard Loder reply, 'Nothing, Rollo. Don't worry about it,' and when I looked back a few seconds later I saw both of them stalking off towards the saddling boxes followed by Dozen Roses in the grasp of his lad.

Despite Nicholas Loder's anxious rage, or maybe because of it, I came down on the side of amusement. I would myself have had the horse gelded several months before the trainer had done it out of no doubt unbearable frustration: Greville had been pigheaded on the subject from both misplaced sympathy and not knowing enough about horses. I thought I would make peace with Loder that evening on the telephone, whatever the outcome of the race, as I certainly didn't want a fight on my hands for so rocky a cause. Talk about the roots of war, I thought wryly: there had been sillier reasons for bloody strife in history than the castration of a thoroughbred.

At York some of the saddling boxes were open to public view, some were furnished with doors. Nicholas Loder seemed to favour the privacy and took Dozen Roses inside away from my eyes.

Harley and Martha Ostermeyer, coming to see the horses saddled, were full of beaming anticipation. They had backed the winner of the University Trophy and had wagered all the proceeds on my, that was to say, my *brother*'s horse.

'You won't get much return,' I warned them. 'It's favourite.'

'We know that, dear,' Martha said happily, looking around. 'Where is he? Which one?'

'He's inside that box,' I pointed, 'being saddled.'

'Harley and I have had a marvellous idea,' she said sweetly her eyes sparkling.

'Now, Martha,' Harley said. He sounded faintly alarmed as if

Martha's marvellous ideas weren't always the best possible news.

'We want you to dine with us when we get back to London,' she finished.

Harley relaxed, relieved. 'Yes. Hope you can.' He clearly meant that this particular marvellous idea was passable, even welcome. 'London at weekends is a graveyard.'

With a twitching of an inward grin I accepted my role as graveyard alleviator and, in the general good cause of cementing Ostermeyer-Shandy-Franklin relations, said I would be very pleased to stay to dinner. Martha and Harley expressed such gratification as to make me wonder whether when they were alone they bored each other to silence.

Dozen Roses emerged from his box with his saddle on and was led along towards the parade ring. He walked well, I thought, his good straight hocks encouraging lengthy strides, and he also seemed to have woken up a good deal, now that the excitement was at hand.

In the horse's wake hurried Nicholas Loder and his friend Rollo, and it was because they were crowding him, I thought, that Dozen Roses swung round on his leading rein and pulled backwards from his lad, and in straightening up again hit the Rollo man a hefty buffet with his rump and knocked him to his knees.

Martha with instinctive kindness rushed forward to help him, but he floundered to his feet with a curse that made her blink. All the same she bent and picked up a thing like a blue rubber ball which had fallen out of his jacket and held it towards him, saying, 'You dropped this, I think.'

He ungraciously snatched it from her, gave her an unnecessarily fierce stare as if she'd frightened the horse into knocking him over, which she certainly hadn't, and hurried into the parade ring after Nicholas Loder. He, looking back and seeing me still there, reacted with another show of fury.

'What perfectly horrid people,' Martha said, making a face. 'Did you hear what that man said? Disgusting! Fancy saying it aloud!'

Dear Martha, I thought, that word was everyday coinage on racecourses. The nicest people used it: it made no one a villain. She was brushing dust off her gloves fastidiously as if getting rid of contamination and I half expected her to go up to Rollo and

141

in the tradition of the indomitable American female to tell him to wah his mouth out with soap.

Harley had meanwhile picked something else up off the grass and was looking at it helplessly. 'He dropped this too,' he said. 'I think.'

Martha peered at his hands and took the object out of them.

'Oh, yes,' she said with recognition, 'that's the other half of the baster. You'd better have it Derek, then you can give it back to that obnoxious friend of your trainer, if you want to.'

I frowned at what she'd given me, which was a rigid plastic tube, semi-transparent, about an inch in diameter, nine inches long, open at one end and narrowing to half the width at the other.

'A baster,' Martha said again. 'For basting meat when it's roasting. You know them, don't you? You press the bulb thing and release it to suck up the juices which you then squirt over the meat.'

I nodded. I knew what a baster was.

'What an extraordinary thing to take to the races.' Martha said wonderingly.

'Mm,' I agreed. 'He seems an odd sort of man altogether.' I tucked the plastic tube into an inside jacket pocket, from which its nozzle end protruded a couple of inches, and we went first to see Dozen Roses joined with his jockey in the parade ring and then up onto the stands to watch him race.

The jockey was Loder's chief stable jockey, as able as any, as honest as most. The stable money was definitely on the horse, I thought, watching the forecast odds on the information board change from 2/1 on to 5/2 on. When a gambling stable didn't put its money up front, the whisper went round and the price eased dramatically. The whisper where it mattered that day had to be saying that Loder was in earnest about the 'trot-up' and Alfie's base imputation would have to wait for another occasion.

Perhaps as a result of his year-by-year successes, Loder's stable always, it was well-known in the racing world, attracted as owners serious gamblers whose satisfaction was more in winning money than in winning races: and that wasn't the truism it seemed, because in steeplechasing the owners tended to want to win the races more than the money. Steeplechasing owners only occasionally made a profit overall and realistically

142

expected to have to pay for their pleasure.

Wondering if the Rollo man was one of the big Loder gamblers, I flicked back the pages of the racecard and looked up his name beside the horse of his that had won the sprint. Owner,Mr T. Rollway, the card read. Rollo for short to his friends. Never heard of him, I thought, and wondered if Greville had.

Dozen Roses cantered down to the start with at least as much energy and enthusiasm as any of the seven other runners and was fed into the stalls without fuss. He'd been striding out well, I thought, and taking a good hold of the bit. An old hand at the game by now, of course, as I was also, I thought dryly.

I'd ridden in several Flat races in my teens as an amateur, learning that the hardest and most surprising thing about the unrelenting Flat race crouch over the withers was the way it cramped one's lungs and affected one's breathing. The first few times I'd almost fallen off at the finish from lack of oxygen. A long time ago, I thought, watching the gates fly open in the distance and the colours spill out, long ago when I was young and it all lay ahead.

If I could find Greville's diamonds, I thought, I would in due course be able to buy a good big yard in Lambourn and start training free of a mortgage and on a decent scale, providing of course I could get owners to send me horses, and I had no longer any doubt that one of these years, when my body packed up mending fast, as everyone's did in the end, I would be content with the new life, even though the consuming passion I still felt for race-riding couldn't be replaced by anything tamer.

Dozen Roses was running with the pack, all seven bunched after the first three furlongs, flying along the far side of the track at more than cruising speed but with acceleration still in reserve.

If I didn't find Greville's diamonds, I thought, I would just scrape together whatever I could and borrow the rest, and still buy a place and set my hand to the future. But not yet, not yet.

Dozen Roses and the other swung left-handed into the long bend round the far end of the track, the bunch coming apart as the curve element hit them. Turning into the staight five furlongs from the winning post Dozen Roses was in fourth place and making not much progress. I wanted him quite suddenly to

143

win and was surprised by the strength of the feeling; I wanted him to win for Greville, who wouldn't care anyway, and perhaps also for Clarissa, who would. Sentimental fool, I told myself. Anyway, when the crowd started yelling home their fancy I yelled for mine also, and I'd never done that before as far as I could remember.

There was not going to be a trot-up, whatever Nicholas Loder might have thought. Dozen Roses was visibly struggling as he took second place at a searing speed a furlong from home and he wouldn't have got the race at all if the horse half a length in front, equally extended and equally exhausted, hadn't veered from a straight line at the last moment and bumped into him.

'Oh dear,' Martha exclaimed sadly, as the two horses passed the winning post. 'Second. Oh well, never mind.'

'He'll get the race on an objection,' I said. 'Which I suppose is better than nothing. Your winnings are safe.'

'Are you sure?'

'Certain,' I said, and almost immediately the loudspeakers were announcing 'Stewards' enquiry'.

More slowly than I would have liked to be able to manage, the three of us descended to the area outside the weighing room where the horse that was not my horse stood in the place for the unsaddling of the second, a net rug over his back and steam flowing from his sweating skin. He was moving about restlessly, as horses often do after an all-out effort, and his lad was holding tight to the reins, trying to calm him.

'He ran a great race,' I said to Martha, and she said, 'Did he dear?'

'He didn't give up. That's really what matters.'

Of Nicholas Loder there was no sign: probably inside the Stewards' room putting forward his complaint. The Stewards would show themselves the views from the side camera and the head-on camera, and at any moment now ...

'Result of the Stewards' enquiry,' said the loudspeakers. 'Placing of first and second reversed.' Hardly justice, but inevitable: the faster horse had lost. Nicholas Loder came out of the weighing room and saw me standing with the Oster-meyers, but before I could utter even the first conciliatory words like, 'Well done,' he'd given me a sick look and hurried off in the opposite direction. No Rollo in his shadow, I noticed.

Martha, Harley and I returned to the luncheon room for the University's tea where the Knightwoods were being gracious hosts and Clarissa, at the sight of me, developed renewed trouble with the tear glands. I left the Ostermeyers taking cups and saucers from a waitress and drifted across to her side.

'So silly,' she said crossly, blinking hard as she offered me a sandwich. 'But wasn't he great?'

'He was.'

'I wish ...' She stopped. I wished it too. No need at all to put it into words. But Greville never went to the races.

'I go to London fairly often,' she said. 'May I phone you when I'm there?'

'Yes, if you like.' I wrote my home number on my racecard and handed it to her. 'I live in Berkshire,' I said, 'not in Greville's house.'

She met my eyes, hers full of confusion.

'I'm not Greville,' I said.

'My dear chap,' said her husband boomingly, coming to a halt beside us, 'delighted your horse finally won. Though, of course, not technically your horse, what?'

'No, sir.'

He was shrewd enough, I thought, looking at the intelligent eyes amid the bonhomie. Not easy to fool. I wondered fleetingly if he'd ever suspected his wife had a lover, even if he hadn't known who. I thought that if he had known who, he wouldn't have asked me to lunch.

He chuckled. 'The professor says you tipped him three winners.'

'A miracle.'

'He's very impressed.' He looked at me benignly. 'Join us at any time, my dear chap,' It was the sort of vague invitation, not meant to be accepted, that was a mild seal of approval, in its way.

'Thank you,' I said, and he nodded, knowing he'd been understood.

Martha Ostermeyer gushed up to say how marvellous the whole day had been, and gradually from then on, as such things always do, the University party evaporated.

I shook Clarissa's outstretched hand in farewell, and also her husband's who stood beside her. They looked good together,

145

and settled, a fine couple on the surface.

'We'll see you again,' she said to me, and I wondered if it were only I who could hear her smothered desperation.

'Yes,' I said positively. 'Of course.'

'My dear chap,' her husband said. 'Any time.'

Harley, Martha and I left the racecourse and climbed into the Daimler, Simms following Brad's routine of stowing the crutches.

Martha said reproachfully, 'Your ankle's broken, not twisted. One of the guests told us. I said you'd ridden a gallop for us on Wednesday and they couldn't believe it.'

'It's practically mended,' I said weakly.

'But you won't be able to ride Datepalm in that race next Saturday, will you?'

'Not really. No.'

She signed. 'You're very naughty. We'll simply have to wait until you're ready.'

I gave her a fast smile of intense gratitude. There weren't many owners who would have dreamed of waiting. No trainer would; they couldn't afford to. Milo was currently putting up one of my arch-rivals on the horses I usually rode, and I just hoped I would get all of them back once I was fit. That was the main trouble with injuries, not the injury itself but losing one's mounts to other jockeys. Permanently, sometimes, if they won.

'And now,' Martha said as we set off south towards London, 'I have had another simply marvellous idea, and Harley agrees with me.'

I glanced back to Harley who was sitting behind Simms. He was nodding indulgently. No anxiety this time.

'We think,' she said happily, 'that we'll buy Dozen Roses and send him to Milo to train for jumping. That is,' she laughed, 'if your brother's executor will sell him to us.'

'Martha!' I was dumbstruck and used her first name without thinking, though I'd called her Mrs Ostermeyer before, when I'd called her anything.

'There,' she said, gratified at my reaction, 'I told you it was a marvellous idea. What do you say?'

'My brother's executor is speechless.'

'But you will sell him?'

'I certainly will.'

'Then let's use the car phone to call Milo and tell him.' She was full of high good spirits and in no mood for waiting, but when she reached Milo he apparently didn't immediately catch fire. She handed the phone to me with a frown, saying, 'He wants to talk to you.'

'Milo,' I said, 'what's the trouble?'

'That horse is an entire. They don't jump well.'

'He's a gelding,' I assured him.

'You told me your brother wouldn't ever have it done.'

'Nicholas Loder did it without permission.'

'You're kidding!'

'No,' I said. 'Anyway the horse got the race today on a Stewards' enquiry but he ran gamely, and he's fit.'

'Has he ever jumped?'

'I shouldn't think so. But I'll teach him.'

'All right then. Put me back to Martha.'

'Don't go away when she's finished. I want another word.'

I handed the phone to Martha who listened and spoke with a return to enthusiasm, and eventually I talked to Milo again.

'Why,' I asked, 'would one of Nicholas Loder's owners carry a baster about at the races?'

'A what?'

'Baster. Thing that's really for cooking. You've got one. You use it as a nebuliser.'

'Simple and effective.'

He used it, I reflected, on the rare occasions when it was the best way to give some sort of medication to a horse. One dissolved or diluted the medicine in water and filled the rubber bulb of the baster with it. Then one fitted the tube onto that, slid the tube up the horse's nostril, and squeezed the bulb sharply. The liquid came out in a vigorous spray straight onto the mucous membranes and from there passed immediately into the blood stream. One could puff out dry powder with the same result. It was the fastest way of getting some drugs to act.

'At the races?' Milo was saying. 'An owner?'

'That's right. His horse won the five-furlong sprint.'

'He'd have to be mad. They dope test two horses in every race, as you know. Nearly always the winner, and another at random. No owner is going to pump drugs into his horse at the races.'

147

'I don't know that he did. He had a baster with him, that's all.'

'Did you tell the Stewards?'

'No, I didn't. Nicholas Loder was with his owner and he would have exploded as he was angry with me already for spotting Dozen Roses's alteration.'

Milo laughed. 'So that was what all the heat was about this past week?'

'You've got it.'

'Will you kick up a storm?'

'Probably not.'

'You're too soft,' he said, 'and oh yes, I almost forgot. There was a phone message for you. Wait a tick. I wrote it down.' He went away for a bit and returned. 'Here you are. Something about your brother's diamonds.' He sounded doubtful. 'Is that right?'

'Yes. What about them?'

He must have heard the urgency in my voice because he said, 'It's nothing much. Just that someone had been trying to ring you last night and all day today, but I said you'd slept in London and gone to York.'

'Who was it?'

'He didn't say. Just said that he had some info for you. Then he hummed and hahed and said if I talked to you would I tell you he would telephone your brother's house, in case you went there, at about ten tonight, or later. Or it might have been a she. Difficult to tell. One of those middle-range voices. I said I didn't know if you would be speaking to me, but I'd tell you if I could.'

'Well, thanks.'

'I'm not a message service,' he said testily. 'Why don't you switch on your answer phone like everyone else?'

'I do sometimes.'

'Not enough.'

I switched off the phone with a smile and wondered who'd been trying to reach me. It had to be someone who knew Greville had bought diamonds. It might even be Annette, I thought: her voice had a mid-range quality.

I would have liked to have gone to Greville's house as soon as we got back to London, but I couldn't really renege on the dinner after Martha's truly marvellous idea, so the three of us ate together as planned and I tried to please them as much as they'd pleased me.

Martha announced yet another marvellous idea during dinner. She and Harley would get Simms or another of the car firm's chauffeurs to drive us all down to Lambourn the next day to take Milo out to lunch, so that they could see Datepalm again before they went back to the States on Tuesday. They could drop me at my house afterwards, and then go to visit a castle in Dorset they'd missed last time around. Harley looked resigned. It was Martha, I saw, who always made the decisions, which was maybe why the repressed side of him needed to lash out sometimes at car-park attendants who boxed him in.

Milo, again on the telephone, told me he'd do practically anything to please the Ostermeyers, definitely including Sunday lunch. He also said that my informant had rung again and he had told him/her that I'd got the message.

'Thanks,' I said.

'See you tomorrow.'

I thanked the Ostermeyers inadequately for everything and went to Greville's house by taxi. I did think of asking the taxi driver to stay, like Brad, until I'd reconnoitred, but the house was quiet and dark behind the impregnable grilles, and I thought the taxi driver would think me a fool or a coward or both, so I paid him off and, fishing out the keys, opened the gate in the hedge and went up the path until the lights blazed on and the dog started barking.

Everyone can make mistakes.

CHAPTER 11

I didn't get as far as the steps up to the front door. A dark figure, dimly glimpsed in the floodlights' glare, came launching itself at me from behind in a cannonball rugger tackle and when I reached the ground something very hard hit my head.

I had no sensation of blacking out or of time passing. One moment I was awake, and the next moment I was awake also, or so it seemed, but I knew in a dim way that there had been an interval.

I didn't know where I was except that I was lying face down on grass. I'd woken up concussed on grass several times in my life, but never before in the dark. They couldn't have all gone home from the races, I thought, and left me alone out on the course all night.

The memory of where I was drifted back quietly. In Greville's front garden. Alive. Hooray for small mercies.

I knew from experience that the best way to deal with being knocked out was not to hurry. On the other hand, this time I hadn't come off a horse, not on Greville's pocket handkerchief turf. There might be urgent reasons for getting up quickly, if I could think of them.

I remembered a lot of things in a rush and groaned slightly, rolling up on to my knees, wincing and groping about for the crutches. I felt stupid and went on behaving stupidly, acting on fifty per cent brain power. Looking back afterwards, I thought that what I ought to have done was slither silently away through the gate to go to any neighbouring house and call the police. What I actually did was to start towards Greville's front door, and of course the lights flashed on again and the dog started barking and I stood rooted to the spot expecting another attack, swaying unsteadily on the crutches, absolutely dim and pathetic.

The door was ajar, I saw, with lights on in the hall, and while I stood dithering it was pulled wide open from inside and the cannonball figure shot out.

The cannonball was a motor-cycle helmet, shiny and black, its transparent visor pulled down over the face. Behind the visor the face also seemed to be black, but a black balaclava, I thought, not black skin. There was an impression of jeans, denim jacket, gloves, black running shoes, all moving fast. He turned his head a fraction and must have seen me standing there insecurely, but he didn't stop to give me another unbalancing shove. He vaulted the gate and set off at a run down the street and I simply stood where I was in the garden waiting for my head to clear a bit more and start working.

When that happened to some extent, I went up the short flight of steps and in through the front door. The keys, I found, were still in the lowest of the locks; the small bunch of three keys that Clarissa had had, which I'd been using instead of Greville's larger bunch as they were easier. I'd made things simple for the intruder, I thought, by having them ready in my hand.

With a spurt of alarm I felt my trouser pocket to find if Greville's main bunch had been stolen, but to my relief they were still there, clinking.

I switched off the floodlights and the dog and in the sudden silence closed the front door. Greville's small sitting room, when I reached it, looked like the path of a hurricane. I surveyed the mess in fury rather than horror and picked the tumbled phone off the floor to call the police. A burglary, I said. The burglar had gone.

Then I sat in Greville's chair with my head in my hands and said '*Shit*' aloud with heartfelt rage and gingerly felt the sore bump swelling on my scalp. A bloody pushover, I thought. Like last Sunday. Too like last Sunday to be a coincidence. The cannonball had known both times that I wouldn't be able to stand upright against a sudden unexpected rush. I supposed I should be grateful he hadn't smashed my head in altogether this time while he had the chance. No knife, this time, either.

After a bit I looked wearily round the room. The pictures were off the walls, most of the glass smashed. The drawers had been yanked out of the tables and the tables themselves overturned. The little pink and brown stone bears lay scattered on the floor, the chrysanthemum plant and its dirt were trampled into the carpet, the chrysanthemum pot itself was embedded in the smashed screen of the television, the video recorder had been torn from its unit and dropped, the video cassettes of the races lay pulled out in yards of ruined tape. The violence of it all angered me as much as my own sense of failure in letting it happen.

Many of the books were out of the bookshelves, but I saw with grim satisfaction that none of them lay open. Even if none of the hollow books had contained diamonds, at least the burglar hadn't known the books were hollow. A poor consolation, I thought.

The police arrived eventually, one in uniform, one not. I went along the hall when they rang the doorbell, checked through the peep-hole and let them in, explaining who I was and why I was there. They were both of about my own age and they'd seen a great many break-ins.

Looking without emotion at Greville's wrecked room, they produced notebooks and took down an account of the assault in the garden. (Did I want a doctor for the bump? No, I didn't.) They knew of this house, they said. The new owner, my brother, had installed all the window grilles and had them wired on a direct alarm to the police station so that if anyone tried to enter that way they would be nicked. Police specialists had given their advice over the defences and had considered the house as secure as was possible, up to now: but shouldn't there have been active floodlights and a dog alarm? They'd worked well, I said, but before they came I'd turned them off.

'Well, sir,' they said, not caring much, 'what's been stolen?'

I didn't know. Nothing large, I said, because the burglar had had both hands free, when he vaulted the gate.

Small enough to go in a pocket, they wrote.

What about the rest of the house? Was it in the same state?

I said I hadn't looked yet. Crutches. Bang on head. That sort of thing. They asked about the crutches. Broken ankle, I said. Paining me, perhaps? Just a bit.

I went with them on a tour of the house and found the tornado had blown through all of it. The long drawing room on the ground floor was missing all the pictures from the walls and all the drawers from chests and tables.

'Looking for a safe,' one of the policemen said, turning over a ruined picture. 'Did your brother have one here, do you know?'

'I haven't seen one', I said.

They nodded and we went upstairs. The black and white bedroom had been ransacked in the same fashion and the bathroom also. Clothes were scattered everywhere. In the bathroom, aspirins and other pills were scattered on the floor. A toothpaste tube had been sqeezed flat by a shoe. A can of shaving cream lay in the wash basin, with some of the contents squirted out in loops on the mirror. They commented that as there was no graffiti and no excrement smeared over everything, I had got off lightly.

'Looking for something small,' the non-uniformed man said. 'Your brother was a gem merchant, wasn't he?'

'Yes.'

'Have you found any jewels here yourself?'

'No, I haven't.'

They looked into the empty bedroom on that floor, still empty, and went up the stairs to look around above, but coming down reported nothing to see but space. It's one big attic room, they explained, when I said I hadn't been up there. Might have been a studio once, perhaps.

We all decended to the semi-basement where the mess in the kitchen was indescribable. Every packet of cereal had been poured out, sugar and flour had been emptied and apparently sieved in a strainer. The fridge's door hung open with the contents gutted. All liquids had been poured down the sinks, the cartons and bottles either standing empty or smashed by the draining boards. The ice cubes I'd wondered about were missing, presumably melted. Half of the floor of carpet tiles had been pulled up from the concrete beneath.

The policemen went phlegmatically round looking at things but touching little, leaving a few footprints in the floury dust.

I said uncertainly, 'How long was I unconscious? If he did all this ....'

'Twenty minutes, I'd say,' one said, and the other nodded. 'He was working fast, you can see. He was probably longest down here. I'd say he was pulling up these tiles looking for a floor safe when you set the alarms off again. I'd reckon he panicked then, he'd been here long enough. And also, if it's any use to you, I'd guess that if he was looking for anything particular, he didn't find it.'

'Good news, is that?' asked the other, shrewdly, watching me.

'Yes, of course.' I explained about the Saxony Franklin office being broken into the previous weekend. 'We weren't sure what had been stolen, apart from an address book. In view of this,' I gestured to the shambles, 'probably nothing was.'

'Reasonable assumption,' one said.

'When you come back here another time in the dark,' the other advised, 'shine a good big torch all around the garden before you come through the gate. Sounds as if he was waiting there for you, hiding in the shadow of the hedge, out of range of the body-heat detecting mechanism of the lights.'

'Thank you,' I said.

'And switch all the alarms on again, when we leave.'

'Yes.'

'And draw all the curtains. Burglars sometimes wait about outside, if they haven't found what they're after, hoping that the householders, when they come home, will go straight to the valuables to check if they're there. Then they come rampaging back to steal them.'

'I'll draw the curtains,' I said.

They looked around in the garden on the way out and found half a brick lying on the grass near where I'd woken up. They showed it to me. Robbery with violence, that made it.

'If you catch the robber,' I said.

They shrugged. They were unlikely to, as things stood. I thanked them for coming and they said they'd be putting in a report, which I could refer to for insurance purposes when I made a claim. Then they retreated to the police care double-parked outside the gate and presently drove away, and I shut the front door, switched on the alarms, and felt depressed and stupid and without energy, none of which states was normal.

The policemen had left lights on behind them everywhere. I went slowly down the stairs to the kitchen meaning merely to turn them off, but when I got there I stood for a while contemplating the mess and the reason for it.

Whoever had come had come because the diamonds were still somewhere to be found. I supposed I should be grateful at least for that information; and I was also inclined to believe the policeman who said the burglar hadn't found what he was looking for. But could I find it, if I looked harder?

I hadn't particularly noticed on my first trip downstairs that the kitchen's red carpet was in fact carpet tiles, washable squares that were silent and warmer underfoot than conventional tiles. I'd been brought up on such flooring in our parents' house.

The big tiles, lying flat and fitting snugly, weren't stuck to the hard surface beneath, and the intruder had had no trouble in pulling them up. The intruder hadn't been certain there was a safe, I thought, or he wouldn't have sieved the sugar. And if he'd been successful and found a safe, what then? He hadn't given himself time to do anything about it. He hadn't killed me. Hadn't tied me. Must have known I would wake up.

All it added up to, I thought, was a frantic and rather unintelligent search, which didn't make the bump on my head or my again knocked-about ankle any less sore. Mincing machines had no brains either. Nor, I thought dispiritedly, had the mince.

I drew the curtains as advised and bent down and pulled up another of the red tiles, thinking about Greville's security complex. It would be just like him to build a safe into the solid base of the house and cover it with something deceptive. Setting a safe in concrete, as the pamphlet had said. People tended to think of safes as being built into walls: floors were less obvious and more secure, but far less convenient. I pulled up a few more tiles, doubting my conclusions, doubting my sanity.

The same sort of feeling as in the vaults kept me going. I didnt expect to find anything but it would be stupid not to make sure, just in case. This time it took half an hour, not three days, and in the end the whole area was up except for a piece under a serving table on wheels. Under that carpet square, when I'd

155

moved the table, I found a flat circular piece of silvery metal flush with the hard base floor, with a recessed ring in it for lifting.

Amazed and suddenly unbearably hopeful I knelt and pulled the ring up and tugged, and the flat piece of metal came away and off like the lid of a biscuit tin, revealing another layer of metal beneath: an extremely solid-looking circular metal plate the size of a dinner plate in which there was a single keyhole and another handle for lifting.

I pulled the second handle. As well try to pull up the house by its roots. I tried all of Greville's bunch of keys in the keyhole but none of them came near to fitting.

Even Greville, I thought, must have kept the key reasonably handy, but the prospect of searching anew for anything at all filled me with weariness. Greville's affairs were a maze with more blind alleys than Hampton Court.

There were keys in the hollow books, I remembered. Might as well start with those. I shifted upstairs and dug out *With a Mule in Patagonia* and the others, rediscovering the two businesslike keys and also the decorative one which looked too flamboyant for sensible use. True to Greville's mind, however, it was that one whose wards slid easily into the keyhole of the safe and under pressure turned the mechanism inside.

Even then the circular lid wouldn't pull out. Seesawing between hope and frustration I found that, if one turned instead of pulling, the whole top of the safe went round like a wheel until it came against stops; and at that point it finally gave up the struggle and came up loose in my grasp.

The space below was big enough to hold a case of champagne but to my acute disappointment it contained no nest-egg, only a clutch of business-like brown envelopes. Sighing deeply I took out the top two and found the first contained the freehold deeds of the house and the second the paperwork involved in raising a mortgage to buy it. I read the latter with resignation: Greville's house belonged in essence to a finance company, not to me.

Another of the envelopes contained a copy of his will, which was as simple as the lawyers had said, and in another there was his birth certificate and our parents' birth and marriage certificates. Another yielded an endowment insurance policy taken out long ago to provide him with an income at sixty-five:

but inflation had eaten away its worth and he had apparently not bothered to increase it. Instead, I realised, remembering what I'd learned of his company's finances, he had ploughed back his profits into expanding his business which would itself ride on the tide of inflation and provide him with a munificent income when he retired and sold.

A good plan, I thought, until he'd knocked the props out by throwing one point five million dollars to the winds. Only he hadn't, of course. He'd had a sensible plan for a sober profit. Deal with honour ... He'd made a good income, lived a comfortable life and run his racehorses, but he had stacked away no great personal fortune. His wealth, whichever way one looked at it, was in the stones.

Hell and damnation, I thought. If I couldn't find the damned diamonds I'd be failing him as much as myself. He would long for me to find them, but where the bloody *hell* had he put them?

I stuffed most of the envelopes back into their private basement, keeping out only the insurance policy, and replaced the heavy circular lid. Turned it, turned the key, replaced the upper piece of metal and laid a carpet tile on top. Fireproof the hiding place undoubtedly was, and thiefproof it had proved, and I couldn't imagine why Greville hadn't used it for jewels.

Feeling defeated, I climbed at length to the bedroom where I found my own overnight bag had, along with everything else, been tipped up and empied. It hardly seemed to matter. I picked up my sleeping shorts and changed into them and went into the bathroom. The mirror was still half covered with shaving cream and by the time I'd wiped that off with a face cloth and swallowed a Distalgesic and brushed my teeth and swept and lot of the crunching underfoot junk to one side with a towel, I had used up that day's ration of stamina pretty thoroughly.

Even then, though it was long past midnight, I couldn't sleep. Bangs on the head were odd, I thought. There had been one time when I'd dozed for a week afterwards, going to sleep in mid-sentence as often as not. Another time I'd apparently walked and talked rationally to a doctor but hadn't any recollection of it half an hour later. This time, in Greville's bed, I felt shivery and unsettled, and thought that that had probably as much to do with being attacked as concussed.

I lay still and let the hours pass, thinking of bad and good and of why things happened, and by morning felt calm and much better. Sitting on the lid of the loo in the bathroom I unwrapped the crêpe bandage and by hopping and holding on to things took a long, luxurious and much needed shower, washing my hair, letting the dust and debris and the mental tensions of the week run away in the soft bombardment of water. After that, loin-clothed in a bath towel, I sat on the black and white bed and more closely surveyed the ankle scenery.

It was better than six days earlier, one could confidently say that. On the other hand, it was still black, still fairly swollen and still sore to the touch. Still vulnerable to knocks. I flexed my calf and foot muscles several times: the bones and ligaments still violently protested, but none of it could be helped. To stay strong, the muscles had to move, and that was that. I kneaded the calf muscle a bit to give it some encouragement and thought about borrowing an apparatus called Electrovet which Milo had tucked away somewhere, which he used on his horses' legs to give their muscles electrical stimuli to bring down swelling and get them fit again. What worked on horses should work on me, I reckoned.

Eventually I wound the bandage on again, not as neatly as the surgeon, but I hoped as effectively. Then I dressed, borrowing one of Greville's clean white shirts and, down in the forlorn little sitting room, telephoned to Nicholas Loder.

He didn't sound pleased to hear my voice.

'Well done with Dozen Roses,' I said.

He grunted.

'To solve the question of who owns him,' I continued, 'I've found a buyer for him.'

'Now look here!' he began angrily. 'I —'

'Yes, I know,' I interrupted, 'you'd ideally like to sell him to one of your owners and keep him in your yard, and I do sympathise with that, but Mr and Mrs Ostermeyer, the people I was with yesterday at York, they've told me they would like the horse themselves.'

'I stongly protest,' he said.

'They want to send him to Milo Shandy to be trained for jumping.'

'You owe it to me to leave him here,' he said obstinately.

'Four wins in a row … it's downright dishonourable to take him away.'

'He's suitable for jumping, now that he's been gelded.' I said it without threat, but he knew he was in an awkward position. He'd had no right to geld the horse. In addition, there was in fact nothing to stop Greville's executor selling the horse to whomever he pleased, as Milo had discovered for me, and which Nicholas Loder had no doubt discovered for himself, and in the racing world in general the sale to the Ostermeyers would make exquisite sense as I would get to ride the horse even if I couldn't own him.

Into Loder's continued silence I said, 'If you find a buyer for Gemstones, though, I'll give my approval.'

'He's not as good.'

'No, but not useless. No doubt you'd take a commission, I wouldn't object to that.'

He grunted again, which I took to mean assent, but he also said grittily, 'Don't expect any favours from me ever.'

'I've done one for you,' I pointed out, 'in not lodging a complaint. Anyway, I'm lunching with the Ostermeyers at Milo's today and we'll do the paperwork of the sale. So Milo should be sending a box to collect Dozen Roses sometime this week. No doubt he'll fix a day with you.'

'Rot you,' he said.

'I don't want to quarrel.'

'You're having a damn good try.' He slammed down his receiver and left me feeling perplexed as much as anything else by his constant rudeness. All trainers lost horses regularly when owners sold them and, as he'd said himself, it wasn't as if Dozen Roses were a Derby hope. Nicholas Loder's stable held far better prospects than a five-year-old gelding, prolific winner though he might be.

Shrugging, I picked up my overnight bag and felt vaguely guilty at turning my back on so much chaos in the house. I'd done minimum tidying upstairs, hanging up Greville's suits and shirts and so on, and I'd left my own suit and some other things with them because it seemed I might spend more nights there, but the rest was physically difficult and would have to wait for the anonymous Mrs P, poor woman, who was going to get an atrocious shock.

I went by taxi to the Ostermeyers' hotel and again found them in champagne spirits, and it was again Simms, fortyish, with a moustache, who turned up as chauffeur. When I commented on his working Sunday as well as Saturday he smiled faintly and said he was glad of the opportunity to earn extra; Monday to Friday he developed films in the dark.

'Films?' Martha asked. 'Do you mean movies?'

'Family snapshots, madam, in a one-hour photo shop.'

'Oh.' Martha sounded as if she couldn't envisage such a life. 'How interesting.'

'Not very, madam,' Simms said resignedly, and set off smoothly into the sparse Sunday traffic. He asked me for directions as we neared Lambourn and we arrived without delay at Milo's door, where Milo himself greeted me with the news that Nicholas Loder wanted me to phone him at once.

'It sounded to me.' Milo said, 'like a great deal of agitation pretending to be casual.'

'I don't understand him.'

'He doesn't want me to have Dozen Roses, for some reason.'

'Oh, but,' Martha said to him anxiously, overhearing, 'you are going to, aren't you?'

'Of course, yes, don't worry. Derek, get it over with while we go and look at Datepalm.' He bore the Ostermeyers away, dazzling them with twinkling charm, and I went into his kitchen and phoned Nicholas Loder, wondering why I was bothering.

'Look,' he said, sounding persuasive. 'I've an owner who's very interested in Dozen Roses. He says he'll top whatever your Ostermeyers are offering. What do you say?'

I didn't answer immediately, and he said forcefully, 'You'll make a good clear profit that way. There's no guarantee the horse will be able to jump. You can't ask a high price for him, because of that. My owner will top their offer and add a cash bonus for you personally. Name your figure.'

'Um,' I said slowly, 'this owner wouldn't be yourself, would it?'

He said sharply, 'No, certainly not.'

'The horse that ran at York yesterday,' I said even more slowly, 'does he fit Dozen Roses's passport?'

'That's slanderous!'

'It's a question.'

'The answer is yes. The horse is Dozen Roses. Is that good enough for you?'

'Yes.'

'Well, then,' he sounded relieved, 'name your figure.'

I hadn't yet discussed any figure at all with Martha and Harley and I'd been going to ask a bloodstock agent friend for a snap valuation. I said as much to Nicholas Loder who, sounding exasperated, repeated that his owner would offer more, plus a tax-free sweetener for myself.

I had every firm intention of selling Dozen Roses to the Ostermeyers and no so-called sweetener that I could think of would have persuaded me otherwise.

'Please tell your owner I'm sorry,' I said, 'but the Ostermeyers have bought Datepalm, as I told you, and I am obligated to them, and loyalty to them comes first. I'm sure you'll find your owner another horse as good as Dozen Roses.'

'What if he offered double what you'd take from the Ostermeyers?'

'It's not a matter of money.'

'Everyone can be bought,' he said.

'Well, no. I'm sorry, but no.'

'Think it over,' he said, and slammed the receiver down again. I wondered in amusement how often he broke them. But he hadn't in fact been amusing, and the situation as a whole held no joy. I was going to have to meet him on racecourses for ever once I was a trainer myself, and I had no appetite for chronic feuds.

I went out into the yard where, seeing me, Milo broke away from the Ostermeyers who were feasting their eyes as Datepalm was being led round on the gravel to delight them.

'What did Loder want?' Milo demanded, coming towards me.

'He offered double whatever I was asking the Ostermeyers to pay for Dozen Roses.'

Milo stared. 'Double! Without knowing what it was?'

'That's right.'

'What are you going to do?'

'What do you think?' I asked.

'If you've accepted, I'll flatten you.'

I laughed. Too many people that past week had flattened me

161

and no doubt Milo could do it with the best.

'Well?' he said belligerently.

'I told him to stuff it.'

'Good.'

'Mm, perhaps. But you'd better arrange to fetch the horse here at once. Like tomorrow morning, as we don't want him having a nasty accident and ending up at the knackers, do you think?'

'Christ!' He was appalled. 'He wouldn't! Not Nicholas Loder.'

'One wouldn't think so. But no harm in removing the temptation.'

'No.' He looked at me attentively. 'Are you all right?' he asked suddenly. 'You don't look too well.'

I told him briefly about being knocked out in Greville's garden. 'Those phone calls you took,' I said, 'were designed to make sure I turned up in the right place at the right time. So I walked straight into an ambush and, if you want to know, I feel a fool.'

'Derek!' He was dumbfounded, but also of course practical. 'It's not going to delay your getting back on a horse?'

'No, don't worry.'

'Did you tell the Ostermeyers?'

'No, don't bother them. They don't like me being unfit.'

He nodded in complete understanding. To Martha, and to Harley to a lesser but still considerable extent, it seemed that proprietorship in the jockey was as important as in the horse. I'd met that feeling a few times before and never undervalued it: they were the best owners to ride for, even if often the most demanding. The quasi-love relationship could however turn to dust and damaging rejection if one ever put them second, which was why I would never jeopardise my place on Datepalm for a profit on Dozen Roses. It was hard to explain to more rational people, but I rode races, as every jump jockey did, from a different impetus than making money, though the money was nice enough and thoroughly earned besides.

When Martha and Harley at length ran out of questions and admiration of Datepalm we all returned to the house, where over drinks in Milo's comfortable sitting room we telephoned to the bloodstock agent for an opinion and then agreed on a price which was less than he'd suggested. Milo beamed. Martha clapped her hands together with pleasure. Harley drew out his chequebook and wrote in it carefully, 'Saxony Franklin Ltd.'

'Subject to a vet's certificate,' I said.

'Oh yes, dear,' Martha agreed, smiling. 'As if you would ever sell us a lemon.'

Milo produced the 'Change of Ownership' forms which Martha and Harley and I all signed, and Milo said he would register the new arrangements with Weatherby's in the morning.

'Is Dozen Roses ours, now?' Martha asked, shiny-eyed.

'Indeed he is,' Milo said, 'subject to his being alive and in good condition when he arrives here. If he isn't the sale is void and he still belongs to Saxony Franklin.'

I wondered briefly if he were insured. Didn't want to find out the hard way.

With the business concluded, Milo drove us all out to lunch at a nearby restaurant which as usual was crammed with Lambourn people: Martha and Harley held splendid court as the new owners of Gold Cup winner Datepalm and were pink with gratification over the compliments to their purchase. I watched their stimulated faces, hers rounded and still pretty under the blonde-rinsed grey hair, his heavily handsome, the square jaw showing the beginning of jowls. Both now looking sixty, they still displayed enthusiasms and enjoyments that were almost childlike in their simplicity, which did no harm in the weary old world.

Milo drove us back to rejoin the Daimler and Simms, who'd eaten his lunch in a village pub, and Martha in farewell gave Milo a kiss with flirtation but also real affection. Milo had bound the Ostermeyers to his stable with hoops of charm and all we needed now was for the two horses to carry on winning.

Milo said 'Thanks' to me briefly as we got into the car, but in truth I wanted what he wanted, and securing the Ostermeyers had been a joint venture. We drove out of the yard with Martha waving and then settling back into her seat with murmurs and soft remarks of pleasure.

I told Simms the way to Hungerford so that he could drop me off there, and the big car purred along with Sunday afternoon somnolence.

163

Martha said something I didn't quite catch and I turned my face back between the headrests, looking towards her and asking her to say it again. I saw a flash of raw horror begin on Harley's face, and then with a crash and a bang the car rocketed out of control across the road towards a wall and there was blood and shredded glass everywhere and we careered off the wall back onto the road and into the path of a fifty-seater touring coach which had been behind us and was now bearing down on us like a runaway cliff.

CHAPTER 12

In the split second before the front of the bus hit the side of the car where I was sitting, in the freeze-frame awareness of the tons of bright metal thundering inexorably towards us, I totally believed I would be mangled to pulp within a breath.

There was no time for regrets or anger or any other emotion. The bus plunged into the Daimler and turned it again forwards and both vehicles screeched along the road together, monstrously joined wheel to wheel, the white front wing of the coach buried deep in the black Daimler's engine, the noise and buffeting too much for thinking, the speed of everything truly terrifying and the nearness of death an inevitability merely postponed.

Inertia dragged the two vehicles towards a halt, but they were blocking the whole width of the road. Towards us, round the bend, came a family car travelling too fast to stop in the space available. The driver in a frenzy braked so hard that his rear end swung round and hit the front of the Daimler broadside with a sickening jolt and a crunching bang and behind us, somewhere, another car ran into the back of the bus.

About that time I stopped being clear about the sequence of events. Against all catastrophe probability, I was still alive and that seemed enough. After the first stunned moments of silence when the tearing of metal had stopped, there were voices shouting everywhere, and people screaming and a sharp petrifying smell of raw petrol.

165

The whole thing was going to burn, I thought. Explode. Fireballs coming. Greville had burned two days ago. Greville had at least been dead at the time. Talk about delirious. I had half a car in my lap and in my head the warmed-up leftovers of yesterday's concussion.

The heat of the dead engine filled the cracked-open body of the car, forewarning of worse. There would be oil dripping out of it. There were electrical circuits ... sparks ... there was dread and despair and a vision of hell.

I couldn't escape. The glass had gone from the window beside me and from the windscreen, and what might have been part of the frame of the door had bent somehow across my chest, pinning me deep against the seat. What had been the fascia and the glove compartment seemed to be digging into my waist. What had been ample room for a dicky ankle was now as constricting as any cast. The car seemed to have wrapped itself around me in an iron-maiden embrace and the only parts free to move at all were my head and the arm nearest Simms. There was intense pressure rather than active agony, but what I felt most was fear.

Almost automatically, as if logic had gone on working on its own, I stretched as far as I could, got my fingers on the keys, twisted and pulled them out of the ignition. At least, no more sparks. At most, I was breathing.

Martha, too, was alive, her thoughts probably as abysmal as my own. I could hear her wimpering behind me, a small moaning without words. Simms and Harley were silent: and it was Simms's blood that had spurted over everything, scarlet and sticky. I could smell it under the smell of petrol; it was on my arm and face and clothes and in my hair.

The side of the car where I sat was jammed tight against the bus. People came in time to the opposite side and tried to open the doors, but they were immovably buckled. Dazed people emerged from the family car in front, the children weeping. People from the coach spread along the roadside, all of them elderly, most of them, it seemed to me, with their mouths open. I wanted to tell them all to keep away, to go further to safety, far from what was going to be a conflagration at any second, but I didn't seem to be able to shout, and the croak I achieved got no further than six inches.

Behind me Martha stopped moaning. I thought wretchedly that she was dying, but it seemed to be the opposite. In a quavery small voice she said, 'Derek?'

'Yes,' Another croak.'

I'm frightened.'

So was I, by God. I said futilely, hoarsely, 'Don't worry.'

She scarely listened. She was saying 'Harley? Harley, honey?' in alarm and awakening anguish. 'Oh, get us out, please, someone get us out.'

I turned my head as far as I could and looked back sideways at Harley. He was cold to the world but his eyes were closed, which was a hopeful sign on the whole.

Simms's eyes were half open and would never blink again. Simms, poor man, had developed his last one-hour photo. Simms wouldn't feel any flames.'

'Oh God, honey. Honey, wake up.' Her voice cracked, high with rising panic. 'Derek, get us out of here, can't you smell the gas?'

'People will come,' I said, knowing it was of little comfort. Comfort seemed impossible, out of reach.

People and comfort came, however, in the shape of a works foreman-type of man, used to getting things done. He peered through the window beside Harley and was presently yelling to Martha that he was going to break the rear window to get her out and she should cover her face in case of flying glass.

Martha hid her face against Harley's chest, calling to him and weeping, and the rear window gave way to determination and a metal bar.

'Come on, Missis,' encouraged the best of British workmen. 'Climb up on the seat, we'll have you out of there in no time.'

'My husband ...' she wailed.

'Him too. No trouble. Come on, now.'

It appeared that stong arms hauled Martha out bodily. Almost at once her rescuer was himself inside the car, lifting the still unconscious Harley far enough to be raised by other hands outside. Then he put his head forward near to mine, and took a look at me and Simms.

'Christ,' he said.

He was smallish, with a moustache and bright brown eyes. 'Can you slide out of there?' he asked.

167

'No.'

He tried to pull me, but we could both see it was hopeless. 'They'll have to cut you out,' he said, and I nodded. He wrinkled his nose. 'The smell of petrol's very strong in here. Much worse than outside.'

'It's vapour,' I said. 'It ignites.'

He knew that, but it hadn't seemed to worry him until then.

'Clear all those people further away,' I said. I raised perhaps a twitch of a smile. 'Ask them not to smoke.'

He gave me a sick look and retreated through the rear window, and soon I saw him outside delivering a warning which must have been the quickest crowd control measure on record.

Perhaps because with more of the glass missing there was a through current of air, the smell of petrol did begin to abate, but there was still, I imagined, a severed fuel line somewhere beneath me, with freshly-released vapour continually seeping through the cracks. How much liquid bonfire, I wondered numbly, did a Daimler's tank hold.

There were a great many more cars now ahead in the road, all stopped, their occupants out and crash-gazing. No doubt to the rear it would be the same thing. Sunday afternoon entertainment at its worst.

Simms and I sat on in our silent immobility and I thought of the old joke about worrying, that there was no point in it. If one worried that things would get bad and they didn't, there was not point in worrying. If they got bad and one worried they would get worse, and they didn't, there was no point in worrying. If they got worse and one worried that one might die, and one didn't, there was no point in worrying, and if one died one could no longer worry, so why worry.

For worry read fear, I thought; but the theory didn't work. I went straight on being scared silly.

It was odd, I thought, that for all the risks I took, I very seldom felt any fear of death. I thought about physical pain, as indeed one often had to in a trade like mine, and remembered things I'd endured, and I didn't know why the imagined pain of burning should fill me with a terror hard to control. I swallowed and felt lonely, and hoped that if it came it would be over quickly.

There were sirens at length in the distance and the best sight in the world, as far as I was concerned, was the red fire-engine which slowly forced its way forward, scattering spectator cars to either side of the road. There was room, just, for three cars abreast; a wall on one side of the road, a row of trees on the other. Behind the fire-engine I could see the flashing blue light of a police car and beyond that another flashing light which might betoken an ambulance.

Figures in authority uniforms appeared from the vehicles, the best being in flameproof suits lugging a hose. They stopped in front of the Daimler, seeing the bus wedged into one side of it and the family car on the other and one of them shouted to me through the space where the windscreen should have been.

'There's petrol running from these vehicles,' he said. 'Can't you get out?'

What a damn silly question, I thought. I said, 'No.'

'We're going to spray the road underneath you. Shut your eyes and hold something over your mouth and nose.'

I nodded and did as I was bid, managing to shield my face inside the neck of my jersey. I listened to the long whooshing of the spray and thought no sound could be sweeter. Incineration faded progressively from near certainty to diminishing probability to unlikely outcome, and the release from fear was almost as hard to manage as the fear itself. I wiped blood and sweat off my face and felt shaky.

After a while some of the firemen brought up metal-cutting gear and more or less tore out of its frame the buckled door next to where Harley had been sitting. Into this new entrance edged a policeman who took a preliminary look at Simms and me and then perched on the rear seat where he could see my head. I turned it far as I could towards him, seeing a serious face under the peaked cap: about my own age, I judged, and full of strain.

'A doctor's coming,' he said, offering crumbs. 'He'll deal with your wounds.'

'I don't think I'm bleeding,' I said. 'It's Simms's blood that's on me.'

'Ah.' He drew out a notebook and consulted it. 'Did you see what caused this ... all this?'

'No,' I said, thinking it faintly surprising that he should be asking at this point. 'I was looking back at Mr and Mrs

Ostermeyer, who were sitting where you are now. The car just seemed to go out of control.' I thought back, remembering. 'I think Harley ... Mr Ostermeyer ... may have seen something. For a second he looked horrified ... then we hit the wall and rebounded into the path of the bus.'

He nodded, making a note.

'Mr Ostermeyer is now conscious,' he said, sounding carefully noncommittal. 'He says you were shot.'

'We were *what*?'

'Shot. Not all of you. You, personally.'

'No.' I must have sounded as bewildered as I felt. 'Of course not.'

'Mr and Mrs Ostermeyer are very distressed but he is quite clear he saw a gun. He says the chauffeur had just pulled out to pass a car that had been in front of you for some way, and the driver of that car had the window down and was pointing a gun out of it. He says the gun was pointing at you, and you were shot. Twice at least, he says. He saw the spurts of flame.'

I looked from the policeman to Simms, and at the chauffeur's blood over everything and at the solidly scarlet congealed mess below his jaw.

'No,' I protested, not wanting to believe it. 'It can't be right.'

'Mrs Ostermeyer is intensely worried that you are sitting here bleeding to death.'

'I feel squeezed, not punctured.'

'Can you feel your feet?'

I moved my toes, one foot after another. There wasn't the slightest doubt, particularly about the left.

'Good,' he said. 'Well, sir, we are treating this from now on as a possible murder enquiry, and apart from that I'm afraid the firemen say it may be some time before they can get you loose. They need more gear. Can you be patient?' He didn't wait for a reply, but went on, 'As I said, a doctor is here and will come to you, but if you aren't in urgent need of him there are two other people back there in a very bad way, and I hope you can be patient about that also.'

I nodded slightly. I could be patient for hours if I wasn't going to burn.

'Why,' I asked, 'would anyone shoot at us?'

'Have you no idea?'

170

'None at all.'

'Unfortunately,' he said, 'there isn't always an understandable reason.'

I met his eyes. 'I live in Hungerford,' I said.

'Yes, sir, so I've been told.' He nodded and slithered out of the car, and left me thinking about the time in Hungerford when a berserk man had gunned down many innocent people, including some in cars, and turned the quiet country town into a place of horror. No one who lived in Hungerford would ever discount the possibility of being randomly slaughtered.

The bullet that had torn into Simms would have gone through my own neck or head, I thought, if I hadn't turned round to talk to Martha. I'd put my head between the headrests, the better to see her. I tried to sort out what had happened next, but I hadn't seen Simms hit. I'd heard only the bang and crash of the window breaking and felt the hot spray of the blood that had fountained out of his smashed main artery in the time it had taken him to die. He had been dead, I thought, before anyone had started screaming: the jet of blood had stopped by then.

The steering wheel was now rammed hard against his chest with the instrument panel slanting down across his knees, higher my end than his. The edge of it pressed uncomfortably into my stomach, and I could see that if it had travelled back another six inches, it would have cut me in half.

A good many people arrived looking official with measuring tapes and cameras, taking photographs of Simms particularly and consulting in low tones. A police surgeon solemnly put a stethoscope to Simms's chest and declared him dead, and without botherng with the stethoscope declared me alive.

How bad was the compression, he wanted to know. Uncomfortable, I said.

I know you, don't I?' he said, considering me. 'Aren't you one of the local jockeys? The jumping boys?'

'Mm.'

'Then you know enough about being injured to give me an assessment of your state.'

I said that my toes, fingers and lungs were OK and that I had cramp in my legs, the trapped arm was aching and the instrument panel was inhibiting the digestion of a good Sunday lunch.

'Do you want an injection?' he asked, listening.

'Not unless it gets worse.'

He nodded, allowed himself a small smile and wriggled his way out onto the road. It struck me that there was much less legroom for the back seat than there had been when we set out. A miracle Martha's and Harley's legs hadn't been broken. Three of us, I thought, had been incredibly lucky.

Simms and I went on sitting quietly side by side for what seemed several more ages but finally the extra gear to free us appeared in the form of winches, cranes and an acetylene torch, which I hope they would use around me with discretion.

Large mechanics scratched their heads over the problems. They couldn't get to me from my side of the car because it was tight against the bus. They decided that if they tried to cut through the support under the front seats and pull them backwards they might upset the tricky equilibrium of the engine and instead of freeing my trapped legs bring the whole weight of the front of the car down to crush them. I was against the idea, and said so.

In the end, working from inside the car in fireproof suits and with thick foam pumped all around, using a well-sheltered but still scorching hot acetylene flame, which roared and threw terrifying sparks around like matches, they cut away most of the driver's side, and after that, because he couldn't feel or protest, they forcefully pulled Simms's stiffening body out and laid it on a stretcher. I wondered greyly if he had a wife, who wouldn't know yet.

With Simms gone, the mechanics began fixing chains and operating jacks and I sat and waited without bothering them with questions. From time to time they said, 'You all right, mate?' and I answered 'Yes,' and was grateful to them.

After a while they fastened chains and a winch to the family car still impacted broadside on the Daimler's wing and with inching care began to pull it away. There was almost instantly a fearful shudder through the Daimler's crushed body and also through mine, and the pulling stopped immediately. A little more headscratching went on, and one of them explained to me that their crane couldn't get a good enough stabilising purchase on the Daimler because the family car was in the way, and they would have to try something else. Was I all right? Yes, I said.

172

One of them began calling me Derek. 'Seen you in Hungerford, haven't I,' he said, 'and on the telly?' He told the others who made jolly remarks like, 'Don't worry, we'll have you out in time for the three-thirty tomorrow. Sure to.' One of them seriously told me that it sometimes did take hours to free people because of the dangers of getting it wrong. Lucky, he said, that it was a Daimler I was in, with its tank-like strength. In anything less I would have been history.

They decided to rethink the rear approach. They wouldn't disturb the seat anchorages from their pushed-back position: the seats were off their runners, they said, and had dug into the floor. Also the recliner-mechanism had jammed and broken. However they were going to cut off the back of Simms's seat to give themselves more room to work. They were then going to extract the padding and springs from under my bottom and see if they could get rid of the back of my seat also, and draw me out backwards so that they wouldn't have to manoeuvre me out sideways past the steering column, which they didn't want to remove as it was the anchor for one of the chief stabilising chains. Did I understand? Yes, I did.

They more or less followed this plan, although they had to dismantle the back of my seat before the cushion, the lowering effect of having the first spring removed from under me having jammed me even tighter against the fascia and made breathing difficult. They yanked padding out from behind me to relieve that, and then with a hacksaw took the back of the seat off near the roots; and, finally, with one of them supporting my shoulders, another pulled out handfuls of springs and other seat innards, and the bear-hug pressure on my abdomen and arm and legs lessened and went away, and I had only blessed pins and needles instead.

Even then the big car was loath to let me go. With my top half free the two men began to pull me backwards, and I grunted and stiffened, and they stopped at once.

'What's the matter?' one asked anxiously.

'Well, nothing. Pull again.'

In truth, the pulling hurt the left ankle but I'd sat there long enough. It was at least an old, recognisable pain, nothing threateningly new. Reassured, my rescuers hooked their arms under my armpits and used a bit of strength, and at last

173

extracted me from the car's crushing embrace like a breeched calf from a cow.

Relief was an inadequate word. They gave me a minute's rest on the back seat, and sat each side of me, all three of us breathing deeply.

'Thanks,' I said briefly.

'Think nothing of it.'

I guessed they knew the depths of my gratitude, as I knew the thought and care they'd expended. Thanks, think nothing of it: it was enough.

One by one we edged out onto the road, and I was astonished to find that after all that time there was still a small crowd standing around waiting: policemen, firemen, mechanics, ambulance men and assorted civilians, many with cameras. There was a small cheer and applause as I stood up free, and I smiled and moved my head in a gesture of both embarrassment and thanksgiving.

I was offered a stretcher but said I'd much rather have the crutches that might still be in the boot, and that caused a bit of general consternation, but someone brought them out unharmed, about the only thing still unbent in the whole mess. I stood for a bit with their support simply looking at all the intertwined wreckage: at the bus and the family car and above all at the Daimler's buckled-up roof, at its sheared-off bonnet, its dislodged engine awry at a tilted angle, its gleaming black paintwork now unrecognisable scrap, its former shape mangled and compressed like a stamped-on toy. I thought it incredible that I'd sat where I'd sat and lived. I reckoned that I'd used up a lifetime's luck.

The Ostermeyers had been taken to Swindon Hospital and treated for shock, bruises and concussion. From there, recovering a little, they had telephoned Milo and told him what had happened and he, reacting I guessed with spontaneous generosity but also with strong business sense, had told them they must stay with him for the night and he would collect them. All three were on the point of leaving when I in my turn arrived.

There was a predictable amount of fussing from Martha over my rescue, but she herself looked as exhausted as I felt and she was pliably content to be supported on Harley's arm on their way to the door.

Milo, coming back a step, said, 'Come as well, if you like. There's always a bed.'

'Thanks, I'll let you know.'

He stared at me. 'Is it true Simms was shot?'

'Mm'

'It could have been you.'

'Nearly was.'

'The police took statements here from Martha and Harley, it seems.' He paused, looking towards them as they reached the door. 'I'll have to go. How's the ankle?'

'Be back racing as scheduled.'

'Good.'

He bustled off and I went through the paperwork routines, but there was nothing wrong with me that a small application of time wouldn't fix and I got myself discharged pretty fast as a patient and was invited instead to give a more detailed statement to the police. I couldn't add much more than I'd told them in the first place, but some of their questions were in the end disturbing.

Could we have been shot at for any purpose?

I knew of no purpose.

How long had the car driven by the man with the gun been in front of us?

I couldn't remember: hadn't noticed.

Could anyone have known we would be on that road at that time? I stared at the policeman. Anyone, perhaps, who had been in the restaurant for lunch. Anyone there could have followed us from there to Milo's house, perhaps, and waited for us to leave, and passed us, allowing us then to pass again. But why ever should they?

Who else might know?

Perhaps the car company who employed Simms.

Who else?

Milo Shandy, and he'd have been as likely to shoot himself as the Ostermeyers.

Mr Ostermeyer said the gun was pointing at you, sir.

With all due respect to Mr Ostermeyer, he was looking through the car and both cars were moving, and at different speeds presumably, and I didn't think one could be certain.

175

Could I think of any reason why anyone should want to kill me?

Me, personally? No ... I couldn't.

They pounced on the hesitation I could hear in my own voice, and I told them I'd been attacked and knocked out the previous evening. I explained about Greville's death. I told them he had been dealing in precious stones as he was a gem merchant and I thought my attacker had been trying to find and steal part of the stock. But I had no idea why the would-be thief should want to shoot me today when he could easily have bashed my head in yesterday.

They wrote it down without comment. Had I any idea who had attacked me the previous evening?

No, I hadn't.

They didn't say they didn't believe me, but something in their manner gave me the impression they thought anyone attacked twice in two days had to know who was after him.

I would have like very much to be able to tell them. It had just occurred to me, if not to them, that there might be more to come.

I'd better find out soon, I thought.

I'd better not find out too late.

CHAPTER 13

I didn't go to Milo's house nor to my own bed, but stayed in an anonymous hotel in Swindon where unknown enemies wouldn't find me.

The urge simply to go home was strong, as if one could retreat to safety into one's den, but I thought I would probably be alarmed and wakeful all night there, when what I most wanted was sleep. All in all it had been a rough ten days, and however easily my body usually shook off bumps and bangs, the accumulation was making an insistent demand for rest.

RICE, I thought wryly, RICE being the acronym of the best way to treat sports injuries: rest, ice, compression, elevation. I rarely seemed to be managing all of them at the same time, though all, in one way or another, separately. With elevation in place, I phoned Milo from the hotel to say I wouldn't be coming and asked how Martha and Harley were doing.

'They're quavery. It must have been some crash. Martha keeps crying. It seems a car ran into the back of the bus and two people in the car were terribly injured. She saw them, and it's upsetting her almost as much as knowing Simms was shot. Can't you come and comfort her?'

'You and Harley can do it better.'

'She thought you were dying too. She's badly shocked. You'd better come.'

'They gave her a sedative at the hospital, didn't they?'

'Yes,' he agreed grudgingly. 'Harley too.'

'Look ... persuade them to sleep. I'll come in the morning and pick them up and take them back to their hotel in London. Will that do?'

He said unwillingly that he supposed so.

'Say goodnight to them from me,' I said. 'Tell them I think they're terrific.'

'Do you?' He sounded surprised.

'It does no harm to say it.'

'Cynic.'

'Seriously,' I said, 'they'll feel better if you tell them.'

'All right then. See you at breakfast.'

I put down the receiver and on reflection a few minutes later got through to Brad.

'Cor,' he said, 'you were in that crash.'

'How did you hear about it?' I asked, surprised.

'Down the pub. Talk of Hungerford. Another madman. It's shook everyone up. My mum won't go out.'

It had shaken his tongue loose, I thought in amusement.

'Have you still got my car?' I said.

'Yerss.' He sounded anxious. 'You said keep it here.'

'Yes. I meant keep it there.'

'I walked down to your house earlier. There weren't no one there then.'

'I'm not there now,' I said. 'Do you still want to go on driving?'

'Yerss.' Very positive. 'Now?'

'In the morning.' I said I would meet him at eight outside the hotel near the railway station at Swindon, and we would be going to London. 'OK?'

'Yerss,' he said again, signing off, and it sounded like a cat purring over the resumption of milk.

Smiling and yawning, a jaw-cracking combination, I ran a bath took off my clothes and the bandage and lay gratefully in hot water, letting it soak away the fatigue along with Simms's blood. Then, my overnight bag having survived unharmed along with the crutches, I scrubbed my teeth, put on sleeping shorts, rewrapped the ankle, hung a 'Do not disturb' card outside my door and was in bed by nine and slept and dreamed of crashes and fire and hovering unidentified threats.

*

178

Brad came on the dot in the morning and we went first to my place in a necessary quest for clean clothes. His mum, Brad agreed, would wash the things I'd worn in the crash.

My rooms were still quiet and unransacked and no dangers lurked outside in daylight. I changed uneventfully and repacked the travelling bag and we drove in good order to Lambourn, I sitting beside Brad and thinking I could have done the driving myself, except that I found his presence reassuring and I'd come to grief on both of the days he hadn't been with me.

'If a car passes us and sits in front of us,' I said, 'don't pass it. Fall right back and turn up a side road.'

'Why?'

I told him that the police thought we'd been caught in a deliberate moving ambush. Neither the Ostermeyers nor I, I pointed out, would be happy to repeat the experience, and Brad wouldn't be wanting to double for Simms. He grinned, an unnerving sight, and gave me to understand with a nod that he would follow the instruction.

The usual road to Lambourn turned out to be still blocked off, and I wondered briefly, as we detoured, whether it was because of the murder enquiry or simply technical difficulties in disentangling the omelette.

Martha and Harley were still shaking over breakfast, the coffee cups trembling against their lips. Milo with relief shifted the burden of their reliance smartly from himself to me, telling them that now Derek was here, they'd be safe. I wasn't so sure about that, particularly if both Harley and the police were right about me personally being yesterday's target. Neither Martha nor Harley seemed to suffer such qualms and gave me the instant status of surrogate son/nephew, the one to be naturally leaned on, psychologically if not physically, for succour and support.

I looked at them with affection. Martha had retained enough spirit to put on lipstick. Harley was making light of a sticking plaster on his temple. They couldn't help their nervous systems' reaction to mental trauma, and I hoped it wouldn't be long before their habitual preference for enjoyment resurfaced.

'The only good thing about yesterday,' Martha said with a sigh, 'was buying Dozen Roses. Milo says he's already sent a van for him.'

I'd forgotten about Dozen Roses. Nicholas Loder and his tizzies seemed a long way off and unimportant. I said I was glad they were glad, and that in about a week or so, when he'd settled down in his new quarters, I would start teaching him to jump.

'I'm sure he'll be brilliant,' Martha said bravely, trying hard to make normal conversation. 'Won't he?'

'Some horses take to it better than others,' I said neutrally. 'Like humans.'

'I'll believe he'll be brilliant.'

Averagely good, I thought, would be good enough for me: but most racehorses could jump if started patiently over low obstacles like logs.

Milo offered fresh coffee and more toast, but they were ready to leave and in a short while we were on the road to London. No one passed us and slowed, no one ambushed or shot us, and Brad drew up with a flourish outside their hotel, at least the equal of Simms.

Martha with a shine of tears kissed my cheek in goodbye, and I hers: Harley gruffly shook my hand. They would come back soon, they said, but they were sure glad to be going home tomorrow. I watched them go shakily into the hotel and thought uncomplicated thoughts, like hoping Datepalm would cover himself with glory for them, and Dozen Roses also, once he could jump.

'Office?' I suggested to Brad, and he nodded, and made the now familiar turns towards the environs of Hatton Garden.

Little in Saxony Franklin appeared to have changed. It seemed extraordinary that it was only a week since I'd walked in there for the first time, so familiar did it feel on going back. The staff said, 'Good morning, Derek,' as if they'd been used to me for years, and Annette said there were letters left over from Friday which needed decisions.

'How was the funeral?' she asked sadly, laying out papers on the desk.

A thousand light years ago, I thought. 'Quiet,' I said. 'Good. Your flowers were good. They were on top of his coffin.'

She looked pleased and said she would tell the others, and received the news that there would be a memorial service with obvious satisfaction. 'It didn't seem right, not being at his funeral, not on Friday. We had a minute's silence here at two o'clock. I suppose you'll think us silly.'

'Far from it.' I was moved and let her see it. She smiled sweetly in her heavy way and went off to relay to the others and leave me floundering in the old treacle of deciding things on a basis of no knowledge.

June whisked in looking happy with a pink glow on both cheeks and told me we were low in blue lace agate chips and snowflake obsidian and amozonite beads.

'Order some more, same as before.'

'Yes, right.'

She turned and was on her way out again when I called her back and asked her if there was an alarm clock among all the gadgets. I pulled open the deep drawer and pointed downwards.

'An alarm clock?' She was doubtful and peered at the assorted black objects. 'Telescopes, dicitionaries, Geiger counter, calculators, spy juice ...'

'What's spy juice?' I asked, intrigued.

'Oh, this.' She reached in and extracted an aerosol can. 'That's just my name for it. You squirt this stuff on anyone's envelopes and it makes the paper transparent so you can read the private letters inside.' She looked at my face and laughed. 'Banks have got round it by printing patterns all over the insides of their envelopes. If you spray their envelopes, all you see is the pattern.'

'Whatever did Greville use it for?'

'Someone gave it to him, I think. He didn't use it much, just to check if it was worth opening things that looked like advertisements.'

She put a plain sheet of paper over one of the letters lying on the desk and squirted a little liquid over it. The plain paper immediately became transparent so that one could read the letter through it, and then slowly went opaque again as it dried.

'Sneaky,' she said, 'isn't it?'

'Very.'

She was about to replace the can in the drawer but I said to put it on top of the desk, and I bought out all the other gadgets and stood them around in plain sight. None of them, as far as I could see, had an alarm function.

'You mentioned something about a world clock,' I said, 'but there isn't one here.'

'I've a clock with an alarm in my room,' she said helpfully. 'Would you like me to bring that?'

'Um, yes, perhaps. Could you set it to four-fifteen?'

'Sure, anything you like.'

She vanished and returned fiddling with a tiny thing like a black credit card which turned out to be a highly versatile timepiece.

'There you are,' she said. 'Four-fifteen — pm, I suppose you mean.' She put the clock on the desk.

'This afternoon, yes. There's an alarm somewhere here that goes off every day at four-twenty. I thought I might find it.'

Her eyes widened. 'Oh, but that's Mr Franklin's watch.'

'Which one?' I asked.

'He only ever wore one. It's a computer itself, a calendar and a compass.'

That watch, I reflected, was beside my bed in Hungerford.

'I think,' I said, 'that he may have had more than one alarm set to four-twenty.'

The fair eybrows lifted. 'I did sometimes wonder why,' she said. 'I mean, why four-twenty? If he was in the stockroom and his watch alarm went off he would stop doing whatever it was for a few moments. I sort of asked him once, but he didn't really answer, he said it was a convenient time for communication, or something like that. I didn't understand what he meant, but that was all right, he didn't mean me to.'

She spoke without resentment and with regret. I thought that Greville must have enjoyed having June around him as much as I did. All that bright intelligence and unspoiled good humour and commonsense. He'd liked her enough to make puzzles for her and let her share his toys.

'What's this one?' I asked, picking up a small grey contraption with black ear sponges on a headband with a cord like a walkabout cassette player, but with no provision for cassettes in what might have been a holder.

'That's a sound-enhancer. It's for deaf people, really, but Mr Franklin took it away from someone who was using it to listen to a private conversation he was having with another gem merchant. In Tucson, it was. He said he was so furious at the

182

time that he just snatched the amplifier and headphones off the man who was listening and walked away with them uttering threats about commercial espionage, and he said the man hadn't even tried to get them back.' She paused. 'Put the earphones on. You can hear everything anyone's saying anywhere in the office. It' pretty powerful. Uncanny, really.'

I put on the ulta-light earphones and pressed the ON switch on the cigarette-packet-sized amplifier and sure enough I could staightaway hear Annette across the hallway talking to Lily about remembering to ask Derek for time off for the dentist.

I removed the earphones and looked at June.

'What did you hear?' she asked. 'Secrets?'

'Not that time, no.'

'Scary, thought?'

'As you say.'

The sound quality was in fact excellent, astonishingly sensitive for so small a microphone and amplifier. Some of Greville's toys, I thought, were decidedly unfriendly.

'Mr Franklin was telling me that there's a voice transformer that you can fix on the telephone that can change the pitch of your voice and make a woman sound like a man. He said he thought it was excellent for women living alone so that they wouldn't be bothered by obscene phone calls and no one would think they were alone and vulnerable.'

I smiled. 'It might disconcert a bona fide boy friend innocently ringing up.'

'Well, you'd have to warn them,' she agreed. 'Mr Franklin was very keen on women taking precautions.'

'Mm,' I said wryly.

'He said the jungle came into his court.'

'Did you get a voice changer?' I asked.

'No. We were only talking about it just before ...' She stopped. 'Well ... anyway, do you want a sandwich for lunch?'

'Yes, please.'

She nodded and was gone. I sighed and tried to apply myself to the tricky letters and was relieved at the interruption when the telephone rang.

It was Elliot Trelawney on the line, asking if I would messenger round the Vaccaro notes at once if I wouldn't mind as they had a committee meeting that afternoon.

'Vaccaro notes,' I repeated. I'd clean forgotten about them. I couldn't remember, for a moment, where they were.

'You said you would send them this morning,' Trelawney said with a tinge of civilised reproach. 'Do you remember?'

'Yes.' I did, vaguely.

Where the hell were they? Oh yes, in Greville's sitting room. Somewhere in all that mess. Somewhere there, unless the thief had taken them.

I apologised. I didn't actually say I'd come near to being killed twice since I'd last spoken to him and it was playing tricks with my concentration. I said things had cropped up. I was truly sorry. I would try to get them to the court by ... when?

'The committee meets at two and Vaccaro is first on the agenda,' he said.

'The notes are still in Greville's house,' I replied, 'but I'll get them to you.'

'Awfully good of you.' He was affable again. 'It's frightfully important we turn this application down.'

'Yes, I know.'

Vaccaro, I thought uncomfortably, replacing the receiver, was alleged to have had his wanting-out cocaine-smuggling pilots murdered by shots from moving cars.

I stared into space. There was no reason on earth for Vaccaro to shoot me, even supposing he knew I existed. I wasn't Greville, and I had no power to stand in the way of his plans. All I had, or probably had, were the notes on his transgressions, and how could he know that? And how could he know I would be in a car between Lambourn and Hungerford on Sunday afternoon? And couldn't the notes be gathered again by someone else besides Greville, even if they were now lost?

I shook myself out of the horrors and went down to the yard to see if Brad was sitting in the car, which he was, reading a magazine about fishing.

Fishing? 'I didn't know you fished,' I said.

'I don't.'

End of conversation.

Laughing inwardly I invited him to go on the journey. I gave him the simple keyring of three keys and explained about the upheaval he would find. I described the Vaccaro notes in and out of their envelope and wrote down Elliot Trelawney's name and address of the court.

'Can you do it?' I asked, a shade doubtfully.

'Yerss.' He seemed to be slighted by my tone and took the paper with the address with brusqueness.

'Sorry,' I said.

He nodded without looking at me and started the car, and by the time I'd reached the rear entrance to the offices he was driving out of the yard.

Upstairs, Annette said there had just been a phone call from Antwerp and she had written down the number for me to ring back.

Antwerp.

With an effort I thought back to Thursday's distant conversations. What was it I should remember about Antwerp?

Van Ekeren. Jacob. His nephew, Hans.

I got through to the Belgian town and was rewarded with the smooth bilingual voice telling me that he had been able now to speak to his uncle on my behalf.

You're very kind,' I said.

'I'm not sure that we will be of much help. My uncle says he knew your brother for a long time, but not very well. However about six months ago your brother telephoned my uncle for advice about a sightholder.' He paused. 'It seems your brother was considering buying diamonds and trusted my uncle's judgment.'

'Ah,' I said hopefully. 'Did your uncle recommend anyone?'

'Your brother suggested three or four possible names. My uncle said they were all trustworthy. He told your brother to go ahead with any of them.'

I sighed. 'Does he possibly remember who they were?'

Hans said, 'He knows one of them was Guy Servi here in Antwerp, because we ourselves do business with him often. He can't remember the others. He doesn't know which one your brother decided on, or if he did business at all.'

'Well, thank you, anyway.'

'My uncle wishes to express his condolences.'

'Very kind.'

He disconnected with politeness, having dictated to me carefully the name, address and telephone number of Guy Servi, the one sightholder Greville had asked about that his

185

uncle remembered.

I dialled the number immediately and again went through the rigmarole of being handed from voice to voice until I reached someone who had both the language and the information.

Mr Greville Saxony Franklin, now deceased, had been my brother? They would consult their files and call me back.

I waited without much patience while they went through whatever security checks they considered necessary but finally, after a long hour, they came back on the line.

What was my problem, they wanted to know.

'My problem is that our offices were ransacked and a lot of paperwork is missing. I've taken over since Greville's death, and I'm trying to sort out his affairs. Could you please tell me if it was your firm who bought diamonds for him?'

'Yes,' the voice said matter-of-factly. 'We did.'

Wow, I thought. I quietened my breath and tried not to sound eager.

'Could you, er, give me the details?' I asked.

'Certainly. Your brother wanted colour H diamonds of approximately three carats each. We buoght a normal sight-box of mixed diamonds at the July sight at the CSO in London and from it and our stocks chose one hundred colour H stones, total weight three hundred and twenty carats, which we delivered to your brother.'

'He ... er ... paid for them in advance, didn't he?'

'Certainly. One point five million United States dollars in cash. You don't need to worry about that.'

'Thank you,' I said, suppressing irony. 'Um, when you delivered them, did you send any sort of, er, packing note?'

It seemed he found the plebeian words 'packing note' faintly shocking.

'We sent the diamonds by personal messenger,' he said austerely. 'Our man took them to your brother at his private residence in London. As is our custom, your brother inspected the merchandise in our messenger's presence and weighed it, and when he was satisfied he signed a release certificate. He would have the carbon copy of that release. There was no other — uh — packing note.'

'Unfortunately I can't find the carbon copy.'

'I assure you, sir ...'

'I don't doubt you,' I said hastily. 'It's just that the tax people have a habit of wanting documentation.'

'Ah.' His hurt feelings subsided. 'Yes, of course.'

I thought a bit and asked, 'When you delivered the stones to him, were they rough or facetted?'

'Rough, of course. He was going to get them cut and polished over a few months, as he needed them, I believe, but it was more convenient for us and for him to buy them all at once.'

'You don't happen to know who he was getting to polish them?'

'I understood they were to be cut for one special client who had his own requirements, but no, he didn't say who would be cutting them.'

I sighed. 'Well, thank you anyway.'

'We'll be happy to send you copies of the paperwork of the transaction, if it would be of any use?'

'Yes, please,' I said. 'It would be most helpful.'

'We'll put them in the post this afternoon.'

I put the receiver down slowly. I might now know where the diamonds had come *from* but was no nearer knowing where they'd gone *to*. I began to hope that they were safely sitting somewhere with a cutter who would kindly write to tell me they were ready for delivery. Not an impossible dream, really. But if Greville had sent them to a cutter, why was there no record?

Perhaps there had been a record, now stolen. But if the record had been stolen the thief would know the diamonds were with a cutter,and there would be no point in searching Greville's house. Unprofitable thoughts, chasing their own tails.

I straightened my neck and back and eased a few of the muscles which had developed small aches since the crash.

June came in and said, 'You look fair knackered,' and then put her hand to her mouth in horror and said, 'I'd never have said that to Mr Franklin.'

'I'm not him.'

'No, but ... you're the boss.'

'Then think of someone who could supply a list of cutters and polishers of diamonds, particularly those specialising in unusual requirements, starting with Antwerp. What we want is a sort of Yellow Pages directory. After Antwerp, New York, Tel Aviv

187

and Bombay, isn't that right? Aren't those the four main centres?' I'd been reading his books.

'But we don't deal —'

'Don't say it,' I said. 'We do. Greville bought some for Prospero Jenks who wants them cut to suit his sculptures or fantasy pieces, or whatever one calls them.'

'Oh.' She looked first blank and then interested. 'Yes, all right, I'm sure I can do that. Do you want me to do it now?'

'Yes, please.'

She went as far as the door and looked back with a smile. 'You still look fair ...'

'Mm. Go and get on with it.'

I watched her back view disappear. Grey skirt, white shirt. Blonde hair held back with combs behind the ears. Long legs. Flat shoes. Exit June.

The day wore on. I assembled three orders in the vault by myself and got Annette to check they were all right, which it seemed they were. I made a slow tour of the whole place, calling in to see Alfie pack his parcels, watching Lily with her squashed governess air move endlessly from drawer to little drawer collecting orders, seeing Jason manhandle heavy boxes of newly arrived stock, stopping for a moment beside strong-looking Tina, whom I knew least, as she checked the new intake against the packing list and sorted it into trays.

None of them paid me great attention. I was already wallpaper. Alfie made no more innuendoes about Dozen Roses and Jason, though giving me a dark sideways look, again kept his cracks to himself. Lily said, 'Yes, Derek,' meekly, Annette looked anxious, June was busy. I returned to Greville's office and made another effort with the letters.

By four o'clock, in between her normal work with the stock movements on the computer, June had received answers to her 'feelers', as she described them, in the shape of a long list of Antwerp cutters and a shorter one so far for New York. Tel Aviv was 'coming' but had language difficulties and she had nothing for Bombay, though she didn't think Mr Franklin would have sent anything to Bombay because with Antwerp so close there was no point. She put the lists down and departed.

At the rate all the cautious diamond-dealers worked, I thought, picking up the roll call, it would take a week just to get yes or no answers from the Antwerp list. Maybe it would be worth trying. I was down to straws. One of the letters was from the bank, reminding me that interest on the loan was now due.

June's tiny alarm clock suddenly began bleeping. All the other mute gadgets on top of the desk remained unmoved. June returned through my doorway at high speed and paid them vivid attention.

'Five minutes to go,' I said calmingly. 'Is every single gadget in sight?'

She checked all the drawers swiftly and peered into filing cabinets, leaving everything wide open, as I asked.

'Can't find any more,' she said. 'Why does it matter?'

'I don't know,' I said. 'I try everything.'

She stared. I smiled lopsidedly.

'Greville left me a puzzle too,' I said. 'I try to solve it, though I don't know where to look.'

'Oh.' It made a sort of sense to her, even without more explanation. 'Like my raise?'

I nodded. 'Something like that.' But not so positive, I thought. Not so certain. He had at least assured her that the solution was there to find.

The minutes ticked away and at four-twenty by June's clock the little alarm duly sounded. Very distant, not at all loud. Insistent. June looked rather wildly at the assembled gadgets and put her ear down to them.

'I will think of you every day at four-twenty.'

Clarissa had written it on her card at the funeral. Greville had apparently done it every day in the office. It had been their own private language, a long way from diamonds. I acknowledged with regret that I would learn nothing from whatever he'd used to jog his awareness of loving and being loved.

The muffled alarm stopped. June raised her head, frowning.

'It wasn't any of these,' she said.

'No. It was still inside the desk.'

'But it can't have been.' She was mystified. 'I've taken everything out.'

'There must be another drawer.'

She shook her head, but it was the only reasonable explanation.

'Ask Annette,' I suggested.

Annette, consulted, said with a worried frown that she knew nothing at all about another drawer. The three of us looked at the uninformative three-inch-deep slab of black grainy wood that formed the enormous top surface. There was no way it could be a drawer, but there wasn't any other possibility.

I thought back to the green stone box. To the keyhole that wasn't a keyhole, to the sliding base.

To the astonishment of Annette and June I lowered myself to the floor and looked upwards at the desk from under the kneehole part. The wood from there looked just as solid, but in the centre, three inches in from the front, there was what looked like a sliding switch. With satisfaction I regained the black leather chair and felt under the desk top for the switch. It moved away from one under pressure, I found. I pressed it, and absolutely nothing happened.

Something had to have happened, I reasoned. The switch wasn't there for nothing. Nothing about Greville was for nothing. I pressed it back hard again and tried to raise, slide or otherwise move anything else I could reach. Nothing happened. I banged my fist with frustration down on the desk top, and a section of the front edge of the solid-looking slab fell off in my lap.

Annette and June gasped. The piece that had come off was like a strip of veneer furnished with metal clips for fastening it in place. Behind it was more wood, but this time with a keyhole in it. Watched breathlessly by Annette and June, I brought out Greville's bunch of keys and tried those that looked the right size: and one of them turned obligingly with hardly a click. I pulled the key, still in the hole, towards me, and like silk a wide shallow drawer slid out.

We all looked at the contents. Passport. Little flat black gadgets, four or five of them.

No diamonds.

June was delighted.'That's the Wizard,' she said.

CHAPTER 14

'Which is the Wizard?' I asked.

'That one.'

She pointed at a black rectangle a good deal smaller than a paperback, and when I picked it up and turned it over, sure enough, it had WIZARD written on it in gold. I handed it to June who opened it like a book, laying it flat on the desk. The right-hand panel was covered with buttons and looked like an ultra-versatile calculator. The left-hand side had a small screen at the top and a touch panel at the bottom with headings like 'expense record', 'time accounting', 'reports' and 'reference'.

'It does everything,' June said. 'It's a diary, a phone directory, a memo pad, an appointments calendar, an accounts keeper ... a world clock.'

'And does it have an alarm system set to four-twenty?'

She switched the thing on, pressed three keys and showed me the screen. Daily alarm, it announced. 4.20 pm, set.

'Fair enough.'

For Annette the excitement seemed to be over. There were things she needed to see to, she said, and went away. June suggested she should tidy away all the gadgets and close all the doors, and while she did that I investigated further the contents of the one drawer we left open.

I frowned a bit over the passport. I'd assumed that in going to Harwich, Greville had meant to catch the ferry. The *Koningin Beatrix* sailed every night ...

191

If one looked at it the other way round, the *Koningin Beatrix* must sail from Holland to Harwich every day. If he hadn't taken the passport with him, perhaps he'd been going to *meet* the *Koningin Beatrix*, not leave on her.

Meet *who*?

I looked at his photograph which, like all passport photographs, wasn't very good but good enough to bring him vividly into the office; his office, where I sat in his chair.

June looked over my shoulder and said, 'Oh,' in a small voice. 'I do miss him, you know.'

'Yes'

I put the passport with regret back into the drawer and took out a flat square object hardly larger than the Wizard, that had a narrow curl of paper coming out of it.

'That's the printer,' June said.

'A printer? So small?'

'It'll print everything stored in the Wizard.'

She plugged the printer's short cord into a slot in the side of the Wizard and dexterously pressed a few keys. With a whirr the tiny machine went into action and began printing out a strip of half the telephone directory, or so it seemed.

'Lovely, isn't it?' June said, pressing another button to stop it. 'When he was away on trips, Mr Franklin would enter all his expenses on here and we would print them out when he got home, or sometimes transfer them from the Wizard to our main computer through an interface ... oh, dear.' She smothered the uprush of emotion and with an attempt at controlling her voice said, 'He would note down in there a lot of things he wanted to remember when he got home. Things like who had offered him unusual stones. Then he'd tell Prospero Jenks, and quite often I'd be writing to the addresses to have the stones sent.'

I looked at the small black electronic marvel. So much information quiescent in its circuits.

'Is there an instruction manual?' I asked.

'Of course. All the instruction manuals for everything are in this drawer.' She opened one on the outer right-hand stack. 'So are the warranty cards, and everything.' She sorted through a rank of booklets. 'Here you are. One for the Wizard, one for the printer, one for the expenses organiser.'

'I'll borrow them,' I said.

'They're yours now,' she replied blankly. 'Aren't they?'

'I can't get used to it any more than you can.'

I laid the manuals on top of the desk next to the Wizard and the printer and took a third black object out of the secret drawer.

This one needed no explanation. This was the microcassette recorder that went with the tiny tapes I'd found in the hollowed-out books.

'That's voice activated,' June said, looking at it. 'It will sit quietly around doing nothing for hours, then when anyone speaks it will record what's said. Mr Franklin used it sometimes for dictating letters or notes because it let him say a bit, think a bit, and say a bit more, without using up masses of tape. I used to listen to the tapes and type straight onto the word processor.'

Worth her weight in pearls, Greville had judged. I wouldn't quarrel with that.

I put the microcassette player beside the other things and brought out the last two gadgets. One was a tiny Minolta camera which June said Greville used quite often for pictures of unusual stones for Prospero Jenks, and the last was a grey thing one could hold in one's hand that had an on/off switch but no obvious purpose.

'That's to frighten dogs away,' June said with a smile. 'Mr Franklin didn't like dogs, but I think he was ashamed of not liking them, because at first he didn't want to tell me what that was, when I asked him.'

I hadn't known Greville didn't like dogs. I fiercely wanted him back, if only to tease him about it. The real trouble with death was what it left unsaid: and knowing that that thought was a more or less universal regret made it no less sharp.

I put the dog frightener back beside the passport and also the baby camera, which had no film in it. Then I closed and locked the shallow drawer and fitted the piece of veneer back in place, pushing it home with a click. The vast top again looked wholly solid, and I wondered if Greville had bought that desk simply because of the drawer's existence, or whether he'd had the whole piece especially made.

'You'd never know that drawer was there,' June said. 'I wonder how many fortunes have been lost by people getting rid of hiding places they didn't suspect?'

'I read a story about that once. Something about money stuffed in an old armchair that was left to someone.' I couldn't remember the details: but Greville had left me more than an old armchair, and more than one place to look, and I too could get rid of the treasure from not suspecting the right hiding place, if there were one at all to find.

Meanwhile there was the problem of staying healthy while I searched. There was the worse problem of sorting out ways of taking the war to the enemy, if I could identify the enemy in the first place.

I asked June if she could find something I could carry the Wizard and the other things in and she was back in flash with a soft plastic bag with handles. It reminded me fleetingly of the bag I'd had snatched at Ipswich but this time, I thought, when I carried the booty to the car, I would take with me an invincible bodyguard, a long-legged flat-chested twenty-one-year-old blonde half in love with my brother.

The telephone rang. I picked up the receiver and said, 'Saxony Franklin' out of newly-acquired habit.

'Derek? Is that you?'

'Yes, Milo, it is.'

'I'm not satisfied with this horse.' He sounded aggressive, which wasn't unusual, and also apologetic, which was.

'Which horse?' I asked.

'Dozen Roses, of course. What else?'

'Oh.'

'What do you mean, oh? You knew damn well I was fetching it today. The damn thing's half asleep. I'm getting the vet round at once and I'll want urine and blood tests. The damn thing looks doped.'

'Maybe they gave him a tranquilliser for the journey.'

'They've no right to, you know that. If they have, I'll have Nicholas Loder's head on a platter, like you should, if you had any sense. The man does what he damn well likes. Anyway, if the horse doesn't pass my vet he's going straight back, Ostermeyers or no Ostermeyers. It's not fair on them if I accept shoddy goods.'

'Um,' I said calmingly, 'perhaps Nicholas Loder wants you to do just that.'

'What? What do you mean?'

'Wants you to send him straight back.'

'Oh.'

'And,' I said, 'Dozen Roses was the property of Saxony Franklin Ltd, not Nicholas Loder, and if you think it's fair to the Ostermeyers to void the sale, so be it, but my brother's executor will direct you to send the horse anywhere else but back to Loder.'

There was a silence. Then he said with a smothered laugh, 'You always were a bright tricky bastard.'

'Thanks.'

'But get down here, will you? Take a look at him. Talk to the vet. How soon can you get here?'

'Couple of hours. Maybe more.'

'No, come on, Derek.'

'It's a long way to Tipperary,' I said. 'It never gets any nearer.'

'You're delirious.'

'I shouldn't wonder.'

'Soon as you can, then,' he said. 'See you.'

I put down the receiver with an inward groan. I did not want to go belting down to Lambourn to a crisis, however easily resolved. I wanted to let my aches unwind.

I telephoned the car and heard the ringing tone, but Brad, wherever he was, didn't answer. Then, as the first step towards leaving, I went along and locked the vault. Alfie in the packing room was stretching his back, his day's load finished. Lily, standing idle, gave me a repressed look from under her lashes. Jason goosed Tina in the doorway to the stockrooms, which she didn't seem to mind. There was a feeling of afternoon ending, of abeyance in the offing, of corporate activity drifting to suspense. Like the last race on an October card.

Saying goodnights and collecting the plastic bag I went down to the yard and found Brad there waiting.

'Did you find those papers OK?' I asked him, climbing in beside him after storing the crutches on the back seat.

'Yerss,' he said.

'And delivered them?'

'Yerss.'

'Thanks. Great. How long have you been back?'

He shrugged. I left it. It wasn't important.

'Lambourn,' I said, as we turned out of the yard. 'But on the way, back to my brother's house to collect something else. OK?'

He nodded and drove to Greville's house skilfully, but slowed just before we reached it and pointed to Greville's car, still standing by the kerb.

'See?' he said. 'It's been broken into.'

He found a parking place and we went back to look. The heavily locked boot had been jemmied open and now wouldn't close again.

'Good job we took the things out,' I said. 'I suppose they are still in my car.'

He shook his head. 'In our house, under the stairs. Our mum said to do it, with your car outside our door all night. Dodgy neighbourhood, round our part.'

'Very thoughtful,' I said.

He nodded. 'Smart, our Mum.'

He came with me into Greville's garden, holding the gate open.

'They done this place over proper,' he said, producing the three keys from his pocket. 'Want me to?'

He didn't wait for particular assent but went up the steps and undid the locks. Daylight: no floods, no dog.

He waited in the hall while I went along to the little sitting room to collect the tapes. It all looked forlorn in there, a terrible mess made no better by time. I put the featherweight cassettes in my pocket and left again, thinking that tidying up was a long way down my urgency list. When the ankle had altogether stopped hurting; maybe then. When the insurance people had seen it, if they wanted to.

I had brought with me a note which I left prominently on the lowest step of the staircase, where anyone coming into the house would see it.

'Dear Mrs P. I'm afraid there is bad news for you. Don't clean the house. Telephone Saxony Franklin Ltd instead.'

I'd added the number in case she didn't know it by heart, and I'd warned Annette to go gently with anyone ringing. Nothing else I could do to cushion the shock.

Brad locked the front door and we set off again to Lambourn. He had done enough talking for the whole journey and we travelled in customary silence, easy if not comrades.

Milo was striding about in the yard, expending energy to no purpose. He yanked the passenger side door of my car open and scowled in at Brad, more as a reflection of his general state of mind, I gathered, than from any particular animosity.

I retrieved the crutches and stood up, and he told me it was high time I threw them away.

'Calm down,' I said.

'Don't patronise me.'

'Is Phil here?'

Phil was Phil Urquhart, veterinary surgeon, pill pusher to the stable.

'No, he isn't,' Milo said crossly, 'but he's coming back. The damned horse won't give a sample. And for a start, you can tell me whether it is or isn't Dozen Roses. His passport matches, but I'd like to be sure.'

He strode away towards a box in one corner of the yard and I followed and looked where he looked, over the bottom half of the door.

Inside the box were an obstinate-looking horse and a furious red-faced lad. The lad held a pole which had on one end of it an open plastic bag on a ring, like a shrimping net. The plastic bag was clean and empty.

I chuckled.

'It's all right for you,' Milo said sharply. 'You haven't been waiting for more than two hours for the damned animal to stale.'

'On Singapore racecourse, one time,' I said, 'they got a sample with nicotine in it. The horse didn't smoke, but the lad did. He got tired of waiting for the horse and just supplied the sample hmself.'

'Very funny,' Milo said repressively.

'This often takes hours, though, so why the rage?'

It sounded always so simple, of course, to take a regulation urine sample from two horses after every race, one nearly always from the winner. In practice, it meant waiting around for the horses to oblige. After two hours of non-performance, blood samples were taken instead, but blood wasn't as easy to come by. Many tempers were regularly lost while the horses made up their minds.

197

'Come away,' I said, 'he'll do it in the end. And he's definitely the horse that ran at York. Dozen Roses without doubt.'

He followed me away reluctantly and we went into the kitchen where Milo switched lights on and asked me if I'd like a drink.

'Wouldn't mind some tea,' I said.

'Tea? At this hour: Well, help yourself.' He watched me fill the kettle and set it to boil. 'Are you off booze for ever?'

'No.'

'Thank God.'

Phil Urquhart's car scrunched into the yard and pulled up outside the window, and he came breezing into the kitchen asking if there were any results. He read Milo's scowl aright and laughed.

'Do you think the horse is doped?' I asked him.

'Me? No, not really. Hard to tell. Milo thinks so.'

He was small and sandy-haired, and about thirty, the grandson of a three-generation family practice, and to my mind the best of them. I caught myself thinking that when I in the future trained here in Lambourn, I would want him for my horses. An odd thought. The future planning itself behind my back.

'I hear we're lucky you're still with us,' he said. 'An impressive crunch, so they say.' He looked at me assessingly with friendly professional eyes. 'You've a few rough edges, one can see.'

'Nothing that will stop him racing,' Milo said crisply.

Phil smiled. 'I detect more alarm than sympathy.

'Alarm?'

'You've trained more winners since he came here.'

'Rubbish,' Milo said.

He poured drinks for himself and Phil, and I made my tea; and Phil assured me that if the urine passed all tests he would give the thumbs up to Dozen Roses.

'He may just be showing the effects of the hard race he had at York,' he said. 'It might be that he's always like this. Some horses are, and we don't know how much weight he lost.'

'What will you get the urine tested for?' I asked.

He raised his eyebrows. 'Barbiturates, in this case.'

'At York,' I said thoughtfully, 'one of Nicholas Loder's owners was walking around with a nebuliser in his pocket. A kitchen baster, to be precise.'

'An owner?' Phil asked, surprised.

'Yes. He owned the winner of the five-furlong sprint. He was also in the saddling box with Dozen Roses.'

Phil frowned. 'What are you implying?'

'Nothing. Merely observing. I can't believe he interfered with the horse. Nicholas Loder wouldn't have let him. The stable money was definitely on. They wanted to win, and they knew if it won it would be tested. So the only question is, what could you give a horse that wouldn't disqualify it? Give it via a nebuliser just before a race?'

'Nothing that would make it go faster. They test for all stimulants.'

'What if you gave it, say, sugar? Glucose? OR Adrenalin?'

'You've a criminal mind!'

'I just wondered.'

'Glucose would give energy, as to human athletes. It wouldn't increase speed, though. Adrenalin is more tricky. If it's given by injection you can see it, because the hairs stand up all round the puncture. But straight into the mucous membranes ... well, I suppose it's possible.'

'And no trace.'

He agreed. 'Adrenalin pours into a horse's bloodstream naturally anyway, if he's excited. If he wants to win. If he feels the whip. Who's to say how much? If you suspected a booster, you'd have to take a blood sample in the winner's enclosure, practically, and even then you'd have a hard job proving any reading was excessive. Adrenalin levels vary too much. You'd even have a hard job proving extra adrenalin made any difference at all.' He paused and considered me soberly. 'You do realise that you're saying that if anything was done, Nicholas Loder condoned it?'

'Doesn't seem likely, does it?'

'No, it doesn't,' he said. 'If he were some tin-pot little crook, well then, maybe, but not Nicholas Loder with his Classic winners and everything to lose.'

'Mm.' I thought a bit. 'If I asked, I could get some of the urine sample that was taken from Dozen Roses at York. They always made it available to owners for private checks. To my brother's company, that is to say, in this instance.' I thought a bit more. 'When Nicholas Loder's friend dropped his baster, Martha Ostermeyer handed the bulb part back to him, but then Harley Ostermeyer picked up the tube part and gave it to me. But it was clean. No trace of liquid. No adrenalin. So I suppose i's possible he might have used it on his own horse and still had it in his pocket, but did nothing to Dozen Roses.'

They considered it.

'You could get into a lot of trouble making unfounded accusations,' Phil said.

'So Nicholas Loder told me.'

'Did he? I'd think twice, then, before I did. It wouldn't do you much good generally in the racing world, I shouldn't think.'

'Wisdom from babes,' I said, but he echoed my thoughts.

'Yes, old man.'

'I kept the baster tube,' I said, shrugging, 'but I guess I'll do just what I did at the races, which was nothing.'

'As long as Dozen Roses tests clean both at York and here, that's likely best,' Phil said, and Milo, for all his earlier pugnaciousness, agreed.

A commotion in the darkening yard heralded the success of the urine mission and Phil went outside to unclip the special bag and close its patented seal. He wrote and attached the label giving the horse's name, the location, date and time and signed his name.

'Right,' he said, 'I'll be off. Take care.' He loaded himself, the sample and his gear into his car and with economy of movement scrunched away. I followed soon after with Brad still driving, but decided again not to go home.

'You saw the mess in London,' I said. 'I got knocked out by whoever did that. I don't want to be in if they come to Hungerford. So let's go to Newbury instead, and try The Chequers.'

Brad slowed, his mouth open.

'A week ago yesterday,' I said, 'you saved me from a man with a knife. Yesterday someone shot at the car I was in and killed the chauffeur. It may not have been your regulation madman. So last night I slept in Swindon, tonight in Newbury.'

'Yerss,' he said, understanding.

'If you'd rather not drive me any more, I wouldn't blame you.'

After a pause, with a good deal of stalwart resolution, he made a statement, 'You need me.'

'Yes,' I said. 'Until I can walk properly, I do.'

'I'll drive you, then.'

'Thanks,' I said, and meant it wholeheartedly, and he could hear that, because he nodded twice to himself emphatically and seemed even pleased.

The Chequers Hotel having a room free, I booked in for the night. Brad took himself home in my car, and I spent most of the evening sitting in an armchair upstairs learning my way round the Wizard.

Computers weren't my natural habitat like they were Greville's and I hadn't the same appetite for them. The Wizard's instructions seemed to take it for granted that everyone reading them would be computer-literate, so it probably took me longer than it might have done to get results.

What was quite clear was that Greville had used the gadget extensively. There were three separate telephone and address lists, the world-time clock, a system for entering daily appointments, a prompt for anniversaries, a calendar flashing with the day's date, and provision for storing oddments of information. By plugging in the printer, and after a few false starts, I ended with long printed lists of everything held listed under all the headings, and read them with growing frustration.

None of the addresses or telephone numbers seemed to have anything to do with Antwerp or with diamonds, though the 'Business Overseas' list contained many gem merchants' names from all around the world. None of the appointments scheduled, which stretched back six weeks or more, seemed to be relevant, and there were no entries at all for the Friday he'd gone to Ipswich. There was no reference to *Koningin Beatrix*.

I thought of my question to June the day she'd found her way to 'pearl': what if it were all in there, but stored in secret?

The Wizard's instruction manual, two hundred pages long, certainly did give lessons in how to lock things away. Entries marked 'secret' could only be retrieved by knowing the password which could be any combination of numbers and letters up to seven in all. Forgetting the password meant

201

bidding farewell to the entries: they could never be seen again. They could be deleted unseen, but not printed or brought to the screen.

One could tell if secret files were present, the book said, by the small symbol s, which could be found on the lower righthand side of the screen. I consulted Greville's screen and found the s there, sure enough.

It would be, I thought. It would have been totally unlike him to have had the wherewithal for secrecy and not used it.

Any combination of numbers or letters up to seven ...

The book suggested 1 2 3 4, but once I'd sorted out the opening moves for unlocking and entered 1 2 3 4 in the space headed 'Secret Off', all I got was a quick dusty answer, 'Incorrect Password'.

Damn him, I thought, wearily defeated. Why couldn't he make any of it easy?

I tried every combination of letters and numbers I thought he might have used but got absolutely nowhere. Clarissa was too long, 12Roses should have been right but wasn't. To be right, the password had to be entered exactly as it had been set, whether in capital letters or lower case. It all took time. In the end I was ready to throw the confounded Wizard across the room, and stared at its perpetual 'Incorrect Password' with hatred.

I finally laid it aside and played the tiny tape recorder instead. There was a lot of office chat on the tapes and I couldn't think why Greville should have bothered to take them home and hide them. Long before I reached the end of the fourth side, I was asleep.

I woke stiffly after a while, unsure for a second where I was. I rubbed my face, looked at my watch, thought about all the constructive thinking I was supposed to be doing and wasn't, and rewound the second of the baby tapes to listen to what I'd missed. Greville's voice, talking business to Annette.

The most interesting thing, the only interesting thing about those tapes, I thought, was Greville's voice. The only way I would ever hear him again.

'... going out to lunch,' he was saying. 'I'll be back by two-thirty.'

Annette's voice said, 'Yes, Mr Franklin.'

A click sounded on the tape.

Almost immediately, because of the concertina-ing of time by the voice-activated mechanism, a different voice said, 'I'm in his office now and I can't find them. He hides everything, he's security mad, you know that.' Click. 'I can't ask. He'd never tell me, and I don't think he trusts me.' Click. 'Po-faced Annette doesn't sneeze unless he tells her to. She'd never tell me anything.' Click. 'I'll try. I'll have to go, he doesn't like me using this phone, he'll be back from lunch any second.' Click.

End of tape.

Bloody hell, I thought. I rewound the end of the tape and listened to it again. I knew the voice, as Greville must have done. He'd left the recorder on, I guessed by mistake, and he'd come back and listened, with I supposed sadness, to treachery. It opened up a whole new world of questions and I went slowly to bed groping towards answers.

I lay a long time awake. When I slept, I dreamed the usual surrealist muddle and found it no help, but around dawn, awake again and thinking of Greville, it occurred to me that there was one password I hadn't tried because I hadn't thought of his using it.

The Wizard was across the room by the armchair. Impelled by curiosity I turned on the light, rolled out of bed and hopped over to fetch it. Taking it back with me, I switched it on, pressed the buttons, found 'Secret Off' and into the offered space typed the word Greville had written on the last page of his racing diary, below the numbers of his passport and national insurance.

DEREK, all in capital letters.

I typed DEREK and pressed Enter, and the Wizard with resignation let me into its data.

CHAPTER 15

I began printing out everything in the secret files as it seemed from the manual that, particularly as regarded the expense organiser, it was the best way to get at the full information stored there.

Each category had to be printed separately, the baby printer clicking away line by line and not very fast. I watched its steady output with fascination, hoping the small roll of paper would last to the end, as I hadn't any more.

From the Memo section, which I printed first, came a terse note, 'Check, don't trust'.

Next came a long list of days and dates which seemed to bear no relation to anything. Monday, 30 January, Wednesday, 8 March ... Mystified I watched the sequence lengthen, noticing only that most of them were Mondays, Tuesdays or Wednesdays, five or six weeks apart, sometimes less, sometimes longer. The list ended five weeks before his death, and it began ... it began, I thought blankly, four years earlier. Four years ago; when he first met Clarissa.

I felt unbearable sadness for him. He'd fallen in love with a woman who wouldn't leave home for him, whom he hadn't wanted to compromise: he'd kept a record, I was certain, of every snatched day they'd spent together, and hidden it away as he had hidden so much else. A whole lot of roses, I thought.

The Schedule section, consulted next, contained appointments not hinted at earlier, including the delivery of the diamonds to his London house. For the day of his death there were two entries: the first, 'Ipswich. Orwell Hotel, P. 3.30 pm', and the second, 'Meet Koningin Beatrix 6.30 pm, Harwich.' For the following Monday he had noted, 'Meet C King's Cross 12.10 Lunch Luigi's.'

Meet C at King's Cross ... He hadn't turned up, and she'd telephoned his house, and left a message on his answering machine, and sometime in the afternoon she'd telephoned his office to ask for him. Poor Clarissa. By Monday night she'd left the ulta-anxious second message, and on Tuesday she had learned he was dead.

The printer whirred and produced another entry, for the Saturday after. 'C and Dozen Roses both at York! Could I go? Not wise. Check TV.'

The printer stopped, as Greville's life had done. No more appointments on record.

Next I printed the Telephone sections, Private, Business and Business Overseas. Private contained only Knightwood. Business was altogether empty, but from Business Overseas I watched with widening eyes the emergence of five numbers and addresses in Antwerp. One was van Ekeren, one was Guy Servi: three were so far unknown to me. I breathed almost painfully with exultation, unable to believe Greville had entered them there for no purpose.

I printed the Expense Manager's secret section last as it was the most complicated and looked the least promising, but the first item that emerged was galvanic.

> Antwerp says 5 of the first
> batch of rough are CZ.
> Don't want to believe it.
> Infinite sadness.
> Priority 1.
> Arrange meetings. Ipswich?
> Undecided. Damnation!

I wished he had been more explicit, more specific, but he'd seen no need to be. It was surprising he'd written so much. His feelings must have been strong to have been entered at all. No other entries afterwards held any comment but were short records of money spent on courier services with a firm called

Euro-Securo, telephone number supplied. In the middle of those the paper ran out. I brought the rest of the stored information up on to the screen and scrolled through it, but there was nothing else disturbing.

I switched off both baby machines and reread the long curling strip of printing from the beginning, afterwards flattening it out and folding it to fit a shirt pocket. Then I dressed, packed, breakfasted, waited for Brad and travelled to London hopefully.

The telephone calls to Antwerp had to be done from the Saxony Franklin premises because of the precautionary checking back. I would have preferred more privacy than Greville's office but couldn't achieve it, and one of the first things I asked Annette that morning was whether my brother had had one of those gadgets that warned you if someone was listening to your conversation on an extension. The office phones were all interlinked.

'No, he didn't,' she said, troubled.

'He could have done with one,' I said.

Are you implying that we listened when he didn't mean us to?'

'Not you,' I assured her, seeing her resentment of the suggestion. 'But yes, I'd think it happened. Anyway, at some point this morning, I want to make sure of not being overheard, so when that call comes through perhaps you'll all go into the stockroom and sing Rule Britannia.'

Annette never made jokes. I had to explain I didn't mean sing literally. She rather huffily agreed that when I wanted it, she would go round the extensions checking against eavesdroppers.

I asked her why Greville hadn't had a private line in any case, and she said he had had one earlier but they now used that for the Fax machine.

'If he wanted to be private,' she said, 'he went down to the yard and telephoned from his car.'

There, I supposed, he would have been safe also from people with sensitive listening devices, if he'd suspected their use. He had been conscious of betrayal, that was for sure.

I sat at Greville's desk with the door closed and matched the three unknown Antwerp names from the Wizard with the full list June had provided, and found that all three were there.

The first and second produced no results, but from the third, once I explained who I was, I got the customary response about checking the files and calling back. They did call back, but the amorphous voice on the far end was cautious to the point of repression.

'We at Maarten-Pagnier cannot discuss anything at all with you, monsieur,' he said. 'Monsieur Franklin gave express orders that we were not to communicate with anyone in his office except himself.'

'My brother is dead,' I said.

'So you say, monsieur. But he warned us to beware of any attempt to gain information about his affairs and we cannot discuss them.'

'Then please will you telephone to his lawyers and get their assurance that he's dead and that I am now managing his business?'

After a pause the voice said austerely, 'Very well, monsieur. Give us the name of his lawyers.'

I did that and waited for ages during which time three customers telephoned with long orders which I wrote down, trying not to get them wrong from lack of concentration.

Then there was a frantic call from a nearly incoherent woman who wanted to speak to Mr Franklin urgently.

'Mrs P?' I asked tentatively.

Mrs P it was. Mrs Patterson, she said. I gave her the abysmal news and listened to her telling me what a fine nice gentleman my brother had been, and oh dear, she felt faint, had I seen the mess in the sitting room?

I warned her that the whole house was the same. 'Just leave it,' I said. 'I'll clean it up later. Then if you could come after that to hoover and dust, I'd be very grateful.'

Calming a little, she gave me her phone number. 'Let me know, then,' she said. 'Oh dear, oh dear.'

Finally the Antwerp voice returned and, begging him to hold on, I hopped over to the door, called Annette, handed her the customers' orders and said this was the moment for securing the defences. She gave me a disapproving look as I again closed the door.

Back in Greville's chair I said to the voice, 'Please, monsieur,

207

tell me if my brother had any dealings with you. I am trying to sort out his office but he has left too few records.'

'He asked us particularly not to send any records of the work we were doing for him to his office.'

'He, er, what?' I said.

'He said he could not trust everyone in his office as he would like. Instead, he wished us to send anything necessary to the Fax machine in his car, but only when he telephoned from there to arrange it.'

'Um,' I said, blinking, 'I found the Fax machine in his car but there were no statements or invoices or anything from you.'

'I believe if you ask his accountants, you may find them there.'

'Good grief.'

'I beg your pardon, monsieur?'

'I didn't think of asking his accountants,' I said blankly.

'He said for tax purposes ...'

'Yes, I see.' I hesitated. 'What exactly were you doing for him?'

'Monsieur?'

'Did he,' I asked a shade breathlessly, 'send you a hundred diamonds, colour H, average uncut weight three point two carats, to be cut and polished?'

'No, monsieur.'

'Oh.' My disappointment must have been audible.

'He sent twenty-five stones, monsieur, but five of them were not diamonds.'

'Cubic zirconia,' I said, enlightened.

'Yes, monsieur. We told Monsieur Franklin as soon as we discovered it. He said we were wrong, but we were not, monsieur.'

'No,' I agreed. 'He did leave a note saying five of the first batch were CZ.'

'Yes, monsieur. He was extremely upset. We made several enquiries for him, but he had bought the stones from a sightholder of impeccable honour and he had himself measured and weighed the stones when they were delivered to his London house. He sent them to us in a sealed Euro-Securo courier package. We assured him that the mistake could not have been made here by us, and it was then, soon after that, that he asked us not to send or give any information to anyone in his ... your ... office.' He paused. 'He made arrangements to receive the finished stones from us, but he didn't meet our messenger.'

'Your messenger?'

'One of our partners, to be accurate. We wished to deliver the stones to him ourselves because of the five disputed items, and Monsieur Franklin thought it an excellent idea. Our partner dislikes flying, so it was agreed he should cross by boat and return the same way. When Monsieur Franklin failed to meet him he came back here. He is elderly and had made no provision to stay away. He was ... displeased ... at having made a tiring journey for nothing. He said we should wait to hear from Monsieur Franklin. Wait for fresh instructions. We have been waiting, but we've been puzzled. We didn't try to reach Monsieur Franklin at his office as he had forbidden us to do that, but we were considering asking someone else to try on our behalf. We are very sorry to hear of his death. It explains everything, of course.'

I said, 'Did your partner travel to Harwich on the *Koningin Beatrix*?'

'That's right, monsieur.'

'He brought the diamonds with him.'

'That's right, monsieur. And he brought them back. We will now wait your instructions instead.'

I took a deep breath. Twenty of the diamonds at least were safe. Five were missing. Seventy-five were ... *where*?

The Antwerp voice said, 'It's to be regretted that Monsieur Franklin didn't see the polished stones. They cut very well. Twelve tear drops of great brilliance, remarkable for that colour. Eight were not suitable for tear drops, as we told Monsieur Franklin, but they look handsome as stars. What shall we do with them, monsieur?'

'When I've talked to the jeweller they were cut for, I'll let you know.'

'Very good, monsieur. And our account? Where shall we send that?' He mentioned considerately how much it would be.

'To this office,' I said, sighing at the prospect. 'Send it to me marked "Personal".'

'Very good, monsieur.'

'And thank you,' I said. 'You've been very helpful.'

'At your service, monsieur.'

I put the receiver down slowly, richer by twelve glittering tear drops destined to hang and flash in sunlight, and by eight handsome stars that might twinkle in a fantasy of rock crystal. Better than nothing, but not enough to save the firm.

Using the crutches, I went in search of Annette and asked her if she would please find Prospero Jenks, wherever he was, and make another appointment for me, that afternoon if possible. Then I went down to the yard, taking a tip from Greville, and on the telephone in my car put a call through to his accountants.

Brad, reading a golfing magazine, paid no attention.

Did he play golf, I asked?

No, he didn't

The accountants helpfully confirmed that they had received envelopes both from my brother and from Antwerp, and were holding them unopened, as requested, pending further instructions.

'You'll need them for general accounts,' I said. 'So would you please just keep them?'

Absolutely no problem.

'On second thoughts,' I said, 'please open all the envelopes and tell me who all the letters from Antwerp have come from.'

Again no problem: but the letters were all either from Guy Servi, the sightholder, or from Maarten-Pagnier, the cutters. No other firms. No other safe havens for seventy-five rocks.

I thanked them, watched Brad embark on a learned comparison of Ballesteros and Faldo and thought about disloyalty and the decay of friendship.

It was restful in the car, I decided, Brad went on reading. I thought of robbery with violence and violence without robbery, of being laid out with a brick and watching Simms die of a bullet meant for me, and I wondered whether, if I were dead, anyone could find what I was looking for, or whether they reckoned they now couldn't find it if I were alive.

I stirred and fished in a pocket and give Brad a cheque I'd written out for him upstairs.

'What's this?' he said, peering at it.

I usually paid him in cash, but I explained I hadn't enough for what I owned him, and cash dispensers wouldn't disgorge enough all at once and we hadn't recently been in Hungerford when the banks were open, as he might have noticed.

'Give me cash later,' he said, holding the cheque out to me. 'And you paid me double.'

'For last week and this week,' I nodded. 'When we get to the bank I'll swap it for cash. Otherwise, you could bring it back here. It's a company cheque. They'd see you got cash for it.'

He gave me a long look.

'Is this because of guns and such? In case you never get to the bank?'

I shrugged. 'You might say so.'

He looked at the cheque, folded it deliberately and stowed it away. Then he picked up the magazine and stared blindly at a page he'd just read. I was grateful for the absence of comment or protest, and in a while said matter-of-factly that I was going upstairs for a bit, and why didn't he get some lunch.

He nodded.

'Have you got enough money for lunch?'

'Yerrs.'

'You might make a list of what you've spent. I've enough cash for that.'

He nodded again.

'OK, then,' I said. 'See you.'

Upstairs, Annette said she had opened the day's post and put it ready for my attention, and she'd found Prospero Jenks and he would be expecting me in the Knightsbridge shop any time between three and six.

'Great.'

She frowned. 'Mr Jenks wanted to know if you were taking him the goods Mr Franklin bought for him. Grev — he always calls Mr Franklin, Grev. I do wish he wouldn't — I asked what he meant about goods and he said you would know.'

'He's talking about diamonds,' I said.

'But we haven't ...' She stopped and then went on with a sort of desperate vehemence. 'I *wish* Mr Franklin was here. Nothing's the same without him.'

She gave me a look full of her insecurity and doubt of my ability and plodded off into her own domain and I thought that with what lay ahead I'd have preferred a vote of confidence: and I too, with all my heart, wished Greville back.

The police from Hungerford telephoned, given my number

211

by Milo's secretary. They wanted to know if I had remembered anything more about the car driven by the gunman. They had asked the family in the family car if they had noticed the make and colour of the last car they'd seen coming towards them before they rounded the bend and crashed into the Daimler, and one of the children, a boy, had given them a description. They had also, while the firemen and others were trying to free me, walked down the row of spectator cards asking them about the last car they'd seen coming towards them. Only the first two drivers had seen a car at all, that they could remember, and they had no helpful information. Had I any recollection, however vague, as they were trying to piece together all the impressions they'd been given.

'I wish I could help,' I said, 'but I was talking to Mr and Mrs Ostermeyer, not concentrating on the road. It winds a bit, as you know, and I think Simms had been waiting for a place where he could pass the car in front, but all I can tell you, as on Sunday, is that it was a greyish colour and fairly large. Maybe a Mercedes. It's only an impression.'

'The child in the family car says it was grey Volvo travelling fast. The bus driver says the car in question was travelling slowly before the Daimler tried to pass it, and he was aiming to pass also at that point, and was accelerating to do so, which was why he rammed the Daimler so hard. He says the car was silver grey and accelerated away at high speed, which matched what the child says.'

'Did the bus driver,' I asked, 'see the gun or the shots?'

'No, sir. He was looking at the road ahead and at the Daimler, not at the car he intended to pass. Then the Daimler veered sharply, and bounded off the wall straight into his path. He couldn't avoid hitting it, he said. Do you confirm that, sir?'

'Yes. It happened so fast. He hadn't a chance.'

'We are asking in the neighbourhood for anyone to come forward who saw a grey four-door saloon, possibly a Volvo, on that road on Sunday afternoon, but so far we have heard nothing new. If you remember anything else, however minor, let us know.'

I would, I said.

I put the phone down wondering if Vaccaro's shot-down pilots had seen the make of car from which their deaths had come spitting .Anyone seeing those murders would, I supposed, have been gazing with uncomprehending horror at the falling victims, not dashing into the road to peer at a fast disappearing number plate.

No one had heard any shots on Sunday. No one had heard the shots, the widow had told Greville, when her husband was killed. A silencer on a gun in a moving car ... a swift pfftt ...' curtains.

It couldn't have been Vaccaro who shot Simms. Vaccaro didn't make sense. Someone with the same anti-social habits, as in Northern Ireland and elsewhere. A copycat. Plenty of precedent.

Milo's secretary had been busy and given my London number also to Phil Urquhart who came on the line to tell me that Dozen Roses had tested clean for barbiturates and he would give a certificate of soundness for the sale.

'Fine,' I said.

'I've been to examine the horse again this morning. He's still very docile. It seems to be his natural state.'

'Mm.'

'Do I hear doubt?'

'He's excited enough every time cantering down to the start.'

'Natural adrenalin,' Phil said.

'If it was anyone but Nicholas Loder ...'

'He would never risk it,' Phil said, agreeing with me. 'But look ... there are things that potentiate adrenalin, like caffeine. Some of them are never tested for in racing, as they are not judged to be stimulants. It's your money that's being spent on the tests I've done for you. We have some more of that sample of urine. Do you want me to get different tests done, for things not usually looked for? I mean, do you really think Nicholas Loder gave the horse something, and if you do, do you want to know about it?'

'It was his owner, a man called Rollway, who had the baster, not Loder himself.'

'Same decision. Do you want to spend more, or not bother? It may be money down the drain, anyway. And if you get any results, what then? You don't want to get the horse disqualified, that wouldn't make sense.'

'No ... it wouldn't.'

'What's your problem?' he asked. 'I can hear it in your voice.'

'Fear,' I said. 'Nicholas Loder was afraid.'

'Oh.' He was briefly silent. 'I could get the tests done anonymously, of course.'

'Yes. Get them done, then. I particularly don't want to sell the Ostermeyers a lemon, as she would say. If Dozen Roses can't win on his own merits, I'll talk them out of the idea of owning him.'

'So you'll pray for negative results.'

'I will indeed.'

'While I was at Milo's this morning,' he said, 'he was talking to the Ostermeyers in London, asking how they were and wishing them a good journey. They were still a bit wobbly from the crash, it seems.'

'Surprising if they weren't.'

'They're coming back to England though to see Datepalm run in the Hennessy. How's your ankle?'

'Good as new by then.'

'Bye then.' I could hear his smile. 'Take care.'

He disconnected and left me thinking that there still were good things in the world, like the Ostermeyers' faith and riding Datepalm in the Hennessy, and I stood up and put my left foot flat on the floor for a progress report.

It wasn't so bad if I didn't lean any weight on it, but there were still jabbingly painful protests against attempts to walk. Oh well, I thought, sitting down again, give it another day or two. It hadn't exactly had a therapeutic week and no doubt doing its best against odds. On Thursday, I thought, I would get rid of the crutches. By Friday, definitely. Any day after that I'd be running. Ever optimistic. It was the belief that cured.

The ever-busy telephone rang again, and I answered it with 'Saxony Franklin?' as rountine.

'Derek?'

'Yes,' I said.

Clarissa's unmistakable voice said, 'I'm in London. Could we meet?'

I hadn't expected her so soon, I thought. I said, 'Yes, of course. Where?'

'I thought … perhaps … Luigi's. Do you know Luigi's bar and restaurant?'

'I don't,' I said slowly, 'but I can find it.'

'It's in Swallow Street near Picadilly Circus. Would you mind coming at seven, for a drink?'

'And dinner?'

'Well ...'

'And dinner,' I said

I heard her sigh, 'Yes. All right,' as she disconnected, and I was left with a vivid understanding both of her compulsion to put me where she had been going to meet Greville and of her awareness that perhaps she ought not to.

I could have said no, I thought. I could have, but hadn't. A little introspection revealed ambiguities in my response to her also, like did I want to give comfort, or to take it.

By three-thirty I'd finished the paperwork and filled an order for pearls and another for turquoise and relocked the vault and got Annette to smile again, even if faintly. At four, Brad pulled up outside Prospero Jenks's shop in Knightsbridge and I put the telephone ready to let him know when to collect me.

Prospero Jenks was where I'd found him before, sitting in shirtsleeves at his workbench. The discreet dark-suited man, serving customers in the shop, nodded me through.

'He's expecting you, Mr Franklin.'

Pross stood up with a smile on his young-old Peter Pan face and held out his hand, but let it fall again as I waggled a crutch handle at him instead.

'Glad to see you,' he said, offering a chair, waiting while I sat. 'Have you brought my diamonds?' He sat down again on his own stool.

'No. Afraid not.'

He was disappointed. 'I thought that was what you were coming for.'

'No, not really.'

I looked at his long efficient workroom with its little drawers full of unset stones and thought of the marvels he produced. The big notice on the wall still read. 'NEVER TURN YOUR BACK TO CUSTOMERS. ALWAYS WATCH THEIR HANDS.'

I said, 'Greville sent twenty-five rough stones to Antwerp to be cut for you.'

'That's right.'

215

'Five of them were cubic zirconia.'

'No, no.'

'Did you,' I asked neutrally, 'swap them over?'

The half-smile died out of his face, which grew stiff and expressionless. The bright blue eyes stared at me and the lines deepened across his forehead.

'That's rubbish,' he said. 'I'd never do anything stupid like that.'

I didn't say anything immediately and it seemed to give him force.

'You can't come in here making wild accusations. Go on, get out, you'd better leave.' He half-rose to his feet.

I said, not moving, 'When the cutters told Greville five of the stones were cubic zirconia, he was devastated. Very upset.'

I reached into my shirt pocket and drew out the print-out from the Wizard.

'Do you want to see?' I asked. 'Read there.'

After a hesitation he took the paper, sat back on the stool and read the entry:

> Antwerp say 5 of the first
> batch of rough are CZ.
> Don't want to believe it.
> Infinite sadness.
> Priority 1.
> Arrange meetings. Ipswich?
> Undecided. Damnation!

'Greville used to write his thoughts in a notebook,' I said. 'In there it says, "Infinite sadness is not to trust an old friend."'

'So what?'

'Since Greville died,' I said, 'someone has been trying to find his diamonds, to steal them from me. That someone had to be someone who knew they were there to be found. Greville kept the fact that he'd bought them very quiet for security reasons. He didn't tell even his staff. But of course you yourself knew, as it was for you he bought them.'

He said again, 'So what?'

'If you remember,' I said, still conversationally, 'someone broke into Greville's office after he died and stole things like an address book and an appointments diary. I began to think the thief had also stolen any other papers which might point to where the diamonds were, like letters or invoices. But I know now there weren't any such papers to be found there, because Greville was full of distrust. His distrust dated from the day the Antwerp cutters told him five of his stones were cubic zirconia, which was about three weeks before he died.'

Pross, Greville's friend, said nothing.

'Greville bought the diamonds,' I went on, 'from a sightholder based in Antwerp who sent them by messenger to his London house. There he measured them and weighed them and signed for them. Then it would be reasonable to suppose that he showed them to you, his customer. Or showed you twenty-five of them, perhaps. Then he sent that twenty-five back to Antwerp by the Euro-Securo couriers. Five diamonds had mysteriously become cubic zirconia, and yes, it was an entirely stupid thing to do, because the substitution was bound to be discovered almost at once, and you knew it would be. Had to be. I'd think you reckoned Greville would never believe it of you, but would swear the five stones had to have been swapped by someone in the couriers or the cutters in Antwerp, and he would collect the insurance in due course, and that would be that. You would be five diamonds to the good, and he would have lost nothing.'

'You can't prove it,' he said flatly.

'No, I can't prove it. But Greville was full of sorrow and distrust, and why should he be if he thought his stones had been taken by strangers?'

I looked with some of Greville's own sadness at Prospero Jenks. A likeable, entertaining genius whose feelings for my brother had been strong and long-lasting, whose regret at his death had been real.

'I'd think,' I said, 'that after your long friendship, after all the treasures he'd brought you, after the pink and green tourmaline, after your tremendous success, that he could hardly bear your treachery.'

'Stop it,' he said sharply. 'It's bad enough ...'

He shut his mouth tight and shook his head, and seemed to sag internally.

'He forgave me,' he said.

217

He must have thought I didn't believe him.

He said wretchedly, 'I wished I hadn't done it almost from the beginning, if you want to know. It was just an impulse. He left the diamonds here while he went off to do a bit of shopping, and I happened to have some rough CZ the right size in those drawers, as I often do, waiting for when I want special cutting, and I just ... exchanged them. Like you said. I didn't think he'd lose by it.'

'He knew, though,' I said. 'He knew you, and he knew a lot about thieves, being a magistrate. Another of the things he wrote was, "If laws are inconvenient, ignore them, they don't apply to you."'

'Stop it. Stop it. He forgave me.'

'When?'

'In Ipswich. I went to meet him there.'

I lifted my head. 'Ipswich. Orwell Hotel, P. 3.30 pm,' I said.

'What? Yes.' He seemed unsurprised that I should know. He seemed to be looking inwards to an unendurable landscape.

'I saw him die,' he said.

CHAPTER 16

'I saw the scaffolding fall on him,' he said.

He'd stunned me to silence.

'We talked in the hotel. In the lounge there. It was almost empty ... then we walked down the street to where I'd left my car. We said goodbye. He crossed the road and walked on, and I watched him. I wanted him to look back and wave ... but he didn't.'

Forgiveness was one thing, I thought, but friendship had gone. What did he expect? Absolution and comfort? Perhaps Greville in time would have given those too, but I couldn't.

Prospero Jenks with painful memory said, 'Grev never knew what happened ... There wasn't any warning. Just a clanging noise and metal falling and men with it. Crashing down fast. It buried him. I couldn't see him ... I ran across the road to pull him out and there were bodies ... and he ... he ... I thought he was dead already. His head was bleeding ... there was a metal bar in his stomach and another had ripped into his leg ... it was ... I can't ... I try to forget but I see it all the time.'

I waited and in a while he went on.

'I didn't move him. Couldn't. There was so much blood ... and a man lying over his legs ... and another man groaning. People came running ... then the police ... it was just chaos ...'

He stopped again, and I said, 'When the police came, why didn't you stay with Greville and help him? Why didn't you identify him to them, even?'

His genuine sorrow was flooded with a shaft of alarm. The dismay was momentary, and he shrugged it off.

'You know how it is.' He gave me a little-boy shamefaced look, much the same as when he'd admitted to changing the stones. 'Don't get involved. I didn't want to be dragged in ... I thought he was dead.'

Somewhere along the line, I thought, he was lying to me. Not about seeing the accident: his description of Greville's injuries had been piercingly accurate.

'Did you simply ... drive off?' I asked bleakly.

'No, I couldn't. Not for ages. The police cordoned off the street and took endless statements. Something about criminal responsibility and insurance claims. But I couldn't help them. I didn't see why the scaffolding fell. I felt sick because of the blood ... I sat in my car till they let us drive out. They'd taken Grev off in an ambulance before that ... and the bar was still sticking out of his stomach...'

The memory was powerfully reviving his nausea.

'You knew by then that he was still alive,' I said.

He was shocked, 'How? How could I have known?'

'They hadn't covered his face.'

'He was dying. Anyone could see. His head was dented ... and bleeding ...'

Dead men don't bleed, I thought, but didn't say it. Prospero Jenks already looked about to throw up, and I wondered how many times he actually had, in the past eleven days.

Instead, I said, 'What did you talk about in the Orwell Hotel?'

He blinked. 'You know what.'

'He accused you of changing the stones.'

'Yes.' He swallowed. 'Well, I apologised. Said I was sorry. Which I was. He could see that. He said why did I do it when I was bound to be found out, but when I did it, it was an impulse, and I didn't think I'd be found out, like I told you.'

'What did he say?'

'He shook his head as if I were a baby. He was sad more than angry. I said I would give the diamonds back, of course, and I begged him to forgive me.'

'Which he did?'

'Yes, I told you. I asked if we could go on trading together. I mean, no one was as good as Grev at finding marvellous stones, and he always loved the things I made. It was good for both of us. I wanted to go back to that.'

Going back was one of life's impossibilities, I thought. Nothing was ever the same.

'Did Greville agree?' I asked.

'Yes. He said he had the diamonds with him but he had arrangements to make. He didn't say what. He said he would come here to the shop at the beginning of the week and I would give him his five stones and pay for the tear drops and stars. He wanted cash for them, and he was giving me a day or two to find the money.'

'He didn't usually want cash for things, did he? You sent a cheque for the spinel and rock crystal.'

'Yes, well ...' Again the quick look of shame, 'He said cash in future, as he couldn't trust me. But you didn't know that.'

Greville certainly hadn't trusted him, and it sounded as if he'd said he had the diamonds with him when he knew they were at that moment on a boat crossing the North Sea. Had he said that, I wondered? Perhaps Prospero Jenks had misheard or misunderstood, but he'd definitely believed Greville had had the diamonds with him.

'If I give you those diamonds now, then that will be the end of it?' he said. 'I mean, as Grev had forgiven me, you won't go back on that and make a fuss, will you? Not the police ... Grev wouldn't have wanted that, you know he wouldn't.'

I didn't answer. Greville would have to have balanced his betrayed old friendship against his respect for the law, and I supposed he wouldn't have had Prospero prosecuted, not for a first offence, admitted and regretted.

Prospero Jenks gave my silence a hopeful look, rose from his stool and crossed to the ranks of little drawers. He pulled one open, took out several apparently unimportant packets and felt deep inside with a searching hand. He brought out a twist of white gauze fastened with a band of sticky tape and held it out to me.

'Five diamonds,' he said. 'Yours.'

I took the unimpressive little parcel which most resembled the muslin bag of herbs cooks put in stews, and weighed it in my hand. I certainly couldn't myself tell CZ from C and he could

221

see the doubt in my face.

'Have them appraised,' he said with unjustified bitterness, and I said we would weigh them right there and then and he would write out the weight and sign it.

'Grev didn't ...'

'More fool he. He should have done. But he trusted you. I don't.'

'Come on, Derek.' He was cajoling; but I was not Greville.

'No. Weigh them,' I said.

With a sigh and an exaggerated shrug he cut open the little bag when I handed it back to him, and on small fine scales weighed the contents.

It was the first time I'd actually seen what I'd been searching for, and they were unimposing, to say the least. Five dull-looking greyish pieces of crystal the size of large misshapen peas without a hint of the fire waiting within. I watched the weighing carefully and took them myself off the scales, wrapping them in a fresh square of gauze which Prospero handed me and fastening them safely with sticky tape.

'Satisfied?' he said with a touch of sarcasm, watching me stow the bouquet garni in my trouser pocket.

'No. Not really.'

'They're the genuine article,' he protested. He signed the paper on which he'd written their combined weight, and gave it to me. 'I wouldn't make that mistake again.' He studied me. 'You're much harder than Grev.'

'I've reason to be.'

'What reason?'

'Several attempts at theft. Sundry assaults.'

His mouth opened.

'Who else?' I said.

'But I've never ... I didn't ...' He wanted me to believe him. He leaned forward with earnestness. 'I don't know what you're talking about.'

I sighed slightly. 'Greville hid the letters and invoices dealing with the diamonds because he distrusted someone in his office. Someone that he guessed was running to you with little snippets of information. Someone who would spy for you.'

'Nonsense.' His mouth seemed dry, however.

I pulled out of a pocket the microcassette recorder and laid it on his workbench.

'This is voice activated,' I said. 'Greville left it switched on one day when he went to lunch, and this is what he found on the tape when he returned.' I pressed the switch and the voice that was familiar to both of us spoke revealing forth:

'I'm in his office now and I can't find them. He hides everything, he's security mad, you know that. I can't ask. He'd never tell me, and I don't think he trusts me. Po-faced Annette doesn't sneeze unless he tells her to ...'

Jason's voice, full of the cocky street-smart aggression that went with the orange spiky hair, clicked off eventually into silence. Prospero Jenks worked some saliva into his mouth and carefully made sure the recorder was not still alive and listening.

'Jason wasn't talking to me,' he said unconvincingly. 'He was talking to someone else.'

'Jason was the regular messenger between you and Greville,' I said. 'I sent him round here myself last week. Jason wouldn't take much seducing to bring you information along with the merchandise. But Greville found out. It compounded his sense of betrayal. So when you and he were talking in the Orwell at Ipswich, what was his opinion of Jason?'

He made a gesture of half-suppressed fury.

I don't know how you know all this,' he said.

It had taken nine days and a lot of searching and a good deal of guessing at possibilities and probabilities, but the pattern was now a reliable path through at least part of the maze, and no other interpretation that I could think of explained the facts.

I said again, 'What did he say about Jason?'

Prospero Jenks capitulated. 'He said he'd have to leave Saxony Franklin. He said it was a condition of us ever doing business again. He said I was to tell Jason not to turn up for work on the Monday.'

'But you didn't do that,' I said.

'Well, no.'

'Because when Greville died, you decided to try to steal not only five stones but the lot.'

The blue eyes almost smiled. 'Seemed logical, didn't it?' he said. 'Grev wouldn't know. The insurance would pay. No one would lose.'

Except the underwriters, I thought. But I said, 'The diamonds weren't insured. Are not now insured. You were stealing them directly from Greville.'

He was almost astounded, but not quite.

'Greville told you that, didn't he?' I guessed.

Again the little-boy shame. 'Well, yes, he did.'

'In the Orwell?'

'Yes.'

'Pross,' I said, 'did you ever grow up?'

'You don't know what growing up is. Growing up is being ahead of the game.'

'Stealing without being found out?'

'Of course. Everyone does it. You have to make what you can.'

'But you have this marvellous talent,' I said.

'Sure. But I make things for money. I make what people like. I take their bread, whatever they'll pay. Sure, I get a buzz when what I've made is brilliant, but I wouldn't starve in a garret for art's sake. Stones sing to me, I give them life. Gold is my paintbrush. All that, sure. But I'll laugh behind people's backs. They're gullible. The day I understood all customers are suckers is the day I grew up.'

I said, 'I'll bet you never said all that to Greville.'

'Do me a favour. Grev was a saint, near enough. The only truly good person through and through I've ever known. I wish I hadn't cheated him. I regret it something rotten.'

I listened to the sincerity in his voice and believed him, but his remorse had been barely skin deep, and nowhere had it altered his soul.

'Jason,' I said, 'knocked me down outside St Catherine's Hospital and stole the bag containing Greville's clothes.'

'No.' The Jenks' denial was automatic, but his eyes were full of shock.

I said, 'I thought at the time it was an ordinary mugging. The attacker was quick and strong. A friend who was with me said the mugger wore jeans and a woolly hat, but neither of us saw his face. I didn't bother to report it to the police because there was nothing of value in the bag.'

'So how can you say it was Jason?'

I answered his question obliquely.

'When I went to Greville's firm to tell them he was dead,' I said, 'I found his office had been ransacked. As you know. The next day I discovered that Greville had bought diamonds. I began looking for them, but there was no paperwork, no address book, no desk diary, no reference to or appointments with diamond dealers. I couldn't physically find the diamonds either. I spent three days searching the vault, with Annette and June, her assistant, telling me that there never were any diamonds in the office. Greville was far too security-conscious. You yourself told me the diamonds were intended for you, which I didn't know until I came here. Everyone in the office knew I was looking for diamonds, and at that point Jason must have told you I was looking for them, which informed you that I didn't know where they were.'

He watched my face with his mouth slightly open, no longer denying, showing only the stunned disbelief of the profoundly found out.

'The office staff grew to know I was a jockey,' I said, 'and Jason behaved to me with an insolence I thought inappropriate, but I now think his arrogance was the result of his having had me face down on the ground under his foot. He couldn't crow about that, but his belief in his superiority was stamped all over him. I asked the office staff not to unsettle the customers by telling them that they were now trading with a jockey not a gemmologist, but I think it's certain that Jason told *you*.'

'What makes you think that?' He didn't say it hadn't happened.

'You couldn't get into Greville's house to search it,' I said, 'because it's a fortress. You couldn't swing any sort of wrecking ball against the windows because the grilles inside made it pointless, and anyway they're wired on a direct alarm to the police station. The only way to get into that house is by key, and I had the keys. So you worked out how to get me there, and you set it up through the trainer I ride for, which is how I know you were aware I was a jockey. Apart from the staff, no one else who knew I was a jockey knew I was looking for diamonds, because I carefully didn't tell them. Come to the telephone in Greville's house for information about the diamonds, you said, and I obediently turned up, which was foolish.'

'But I never went to Greville's house ...' he said.

225

'No, not you, Jason. Strong and fast in the motor-cycle helmet which covered his orange hair, butting me over again just like old times. I saw him vault the gate on the way out. That couldn't have been you. He turned the house upside down but the police didn't think he found what he was looking for, and I'm sure he didn't.'

'Why not?' he asked, and then said, 'That's to say ...'

'Did you mean Jason to kill me?' I asked flatly.

'No! Of course not!' The idea seemed genuinely to shock him.

'He could have done,' I said.

'I'm not a murderer!' His indignation, as far as I could tell, was true and without reservation, quite different to his reaction to my calling him a thief.

'What were you doing two days ago, on Sunday afternoon?' I said.

'What?' He was bewildered by the question but not alarmed.

'Sunday afternoon,' I said.

'What about Sunday afternoon? What are you talking about?'

I frowned. 'Never mind. Go back to Saturday night. To Jason giving me concussion with half a brick.'

The knowledge of that was plain to read. We were again on familiar territory.

'You can kill people,' I said, 'hitting them with bricks.'

'But he said ...' He stopped dead.

'You might as well go on,' I said reasonably, 'we both know that what I've said is what happened.'

'Yes, but ... what are you going to do about it?'

'I don't know yet.'

'I'll deny everything.'

'What did Jason say about the brick?'

He gave a hopeless little sign. 'He said he knew how to knock people out for half an hour. He'd seen it done in street riots, he said, and he'd done it himself. He said it depended on where you hit.'

'You can't time it,' I objected.

'Well, that's what he said.'

He hadn't been so wrong, I supposed. I'd beaten his estimate by maybe ten minutes, not more.

'He said you'd be all right afterwards,' Pross said.

'He couldn't be sure of that.'

'But you are, aren't you?' There seemed to be a tinge of regret that I hadn't emerged punch drunk and unable to hold the present conversation. Callous and irresponsible, I thought, and unforgivable, really. Greville had forgiven treachery; and which was worse?

'Jason knew which office window to break,' I said, 'and he came down from the roof. The police found marks up there.' I paused. 'Did he do that alone, or were you with him?'

'Do you expect me to tell you?' he said incredulously.

'Yes, I do. Why not? You know what plea bargaining is, you just tried it with five diamonds.'

He gave me a shattered look and searched his commonsense; not that he had much of it, when one considered.

Eventually, without shame, he said, 'We both went.'

'When?'

'That Sunday. Late afternoon. After he brought Grev's things back from Ipswich and they were a waste of time.'

'You found out which hospital Greville was in,' I said, 'and you sent Jason to steal his things because you believed they would include the diamonds which Greville had told you he had with him, is that right?'

He rather miserably nodded. 'Jason phoned me from the hospital on the Saturday and said Grev wasn't dead yet but that his brother had turned up, some frail old creature on crutches, and it was good because he'd be an easy mark ... which you were.'

He looked at me and repeated, 'Frail old creature,' and faintly smiled, and I remembered his surprise at my physical appearance when I'd first come into this room. Jason, I supposed, had seen only my back view and mostly at a distance. I certainly hadn't noticed anyone lurking, but I probably wouldn't at the time have noticed half a ship's company standing at attention. Being with the dying, seeing the death, had made ordinary life seem unreal and unimportant, and it had taken me until hours after Jason's attack to lose that feeling altogether.

'All right,' I said, 'so Jason came back empty-handed. What then?'

He shrugged. 'I thought I'd probably got it wrong. Grev couldn't have meant he had the diamonds with him.' He frowned. 'I thought that was what he said, though.'

I enlightened him. 'Greville was on his way to Harwich to meet a diamond cutter coming from Antwerp by ferry, who was bringing your diamonds with him. Twelve tear drops and eight stars.'

'Oh.' His face cleared momentarily with pleasure but gloom soon returned. 'Well, I thought it was worth looking in his office, though Jason said he never kept anything valuable there. But for diamonds ... so many diamonds ... it was worth a chance. Jason didn't take much persuading. He's a violent young bugger ...'

I wondered fleetingly if that description mightn't be positively and scatologically accurate.

'So you went up to the roof in the service lift,' I said, 'and swung some sort of pendulum at the packing room window.'

He shook his head. 'Jason brought grappling irons and a rope ladder and climbed down that to the window, and broke the glass with a baseball bat. Then when he was inside I threw the hooks and ladder down into the yard, and went down in the lift to the eighth floor, and Jason let me in through the staff door. But we couldn't get into the stockrooms because of Grev's infernal electronic locks, or into the showroom, same reason. And that vault ... I wanted to try to beat it open with the bat but Jason said the door is six inches thick.' He shrugged. 'So we had to make do with papers ... and we couldn't find anything about diamonds. Jason got angry ... we made quite a mess.'

'Mm.'

'And it was all a waste of time. Jason said what we really needed was something called a Wizard, but we couldn't find that either. In the end we simply left. I gave up. Grev had been too careful. I got resigned to not having the diamonds unless I paid for them. Then Jason said you were hunting high and low for them, and I got interested again. Very. You can't blame me.'

I could and did, but I didn't want to switch off the fountain.

'And then,' he said, 'like you guessed, I inveigled you into Grev's garden, and Jason had been waiting ages there getting furious you took so long. He let his anger out on the house, he said.'

'He made a mess there too, yes.'

'Then you woke up and set the alarms off and Jason said he was getting right nervous by then and he wasn't going to wait around for the handcuffs. So Grev had beaten us again ... and he's beaten you too, hasn't he?' He looked at me shrewdly. 'You haven't found the diamonds either.'

I didn't answer him. I said, 'When did Jason break into Greville's car?'

'Well ... when he finally found it in Greville's road. I'd looked for it at the hotel and round about in Ipswich, but Grev must have hired a car to drive there because his own car won't start.'

'When did you discover that?'

'Saturday. If the diamonds had been in it, we wouldn't have needed to search the house.'

'He wouldn't have left a fortune in the street.' I said.

Pross shook his head resignedly. 'You'd already looked there, I suppose.'

'I had.' I considered him. 'Why Ipswich?' I said.

'What?'

'Why the Orwell Hotel at Ipswich, particularly? Why did he want you to go there?'

'No idea,' he said blankly. 'He didn't say. He'd often ask me to meet him in odd places. It was usually because he'd found some heirloom or other and wanted to know if the stones would be of use to me. An ugly old tiara once, with a boring yellow diamond centrepiece filthy from neglect. I had the stone recut and set it as the crest of a rock crystal bird and hung it in a golden cage ... it's in Florida, in the sun.'

I was shaken with the pity of it. So much soaring priceless imagination and such grubby, perfidious greed.

I said, 'Had he found you a stone in Ipswich?'

'No. He told me he'd asked me to come there because he didn't want to be interrupted. Somewhere quiet, he said. I suppose it was because he was going to Harwich.'

I nodded. I supposed so also, though it wasn't on the most direct route which was further south, through Colchester. But Ipswich was where Greville had chosen, by freak mischance.

I thought of all Pross had told me, and was struck by one

229

unexplored and dreadful possibility.

'When the scaffolding fell,' I said slowly, 'when you ran across the road and found Greville lethally injured ... when he was lying there bleeding with the metal bar in him ... did you steal his wallet?'

Pross's little-boy face crumpled and he put up his hands to cover it as if he would weep. I didn't believe in the tears and the remorse. I couldn't bear him any longer. I stood up to go.

'You thought he might have diamonds in his wallet,' I said bitterly. 'And then, even then, when he was dying, you were ready to rob him.'

He said nothing. He in no way denied it.

I felt such anger on Greville's behalf that I wanted suddenly to hurt and punish the man before me with a ferocity I wouldn't have expected in myself, and I stood there trembling with the self-knowledge and the essential restraint, and felt my throat close over any more words.

Without thinking, I put my left foot down to walk out and felt the pain as an irrelevance, but then after three steps used the crutches to make my way to his doorway and round the screen into the shop and through there out onto the pavement, and I wanted to yell and scream at the bloody injustice of Greville's death and the wickedness of the world and call down the rage of angels.

CHAPTER 17

I stood blindly on the pavement oblivious to the passers-by
finding me an obstacle in their way. The swamping tidal wave of
fury and desolation swelled and broke and gradually ebbed,
leaving me still shaking from its force, a tornado in the spirit.

I loosened a jaw I hadn't realised was clamped tight shut and
went on feeling wretched.

A grandmotherly woman touched my arm and said, 'Do you
need help?' and I shook my head at her kindness because the
help I needed wasn't anyone's to give. One had to heal from the
inside: to knit like bones.

'Are you all right?' she asked again, her eyes concerned.

'Yes.' I made an effort. 'Thank you.'

She looked at me uncertainly, but finally moved on, and I
took a few sketchy breaths and remembered with bathos that I
needed a telephone if I were ever to move from that spot.

A hairdressing salon having (for a consideration) let me use
their instrument, Brad came within five minutes to pick me up.
I shoved the crutches into the back and climbed wearily in
beside him, and he said, 'Where to?' giving me a repeat of the
grandmotherly solicitude in his face if not his words.

'Uh,' I said. 'I don't know.'

'Home?'

'No ...' I gave it a bit of thought. I had intended to go to
Greville's house to change into my suit that was hanging in his
wardrobe before meeting Clarissa at seven, and it still seemed

231

perhaps the best thing to do, even if my energy for the project had evaporated.

Accordingly we made our way there, which wasn't far, and when Brad stopped outside the door, I said, 'I think I'll sleep here tonight. This house is as safe as anywhere. So you can go on to Hungerford now, if you like.'

He didn't look as if he liked, but all he said was, 'I come back tomorrow:'

'Yes, please,' I agreed.

'Pick you up. Take you to the office?'

'Yes, please.'

He nodded, seemingly reassured that I still needed him. He got out of the car with me and opened the gate, brought my overnight bag and came in with me to see, upstairs and down, that the house was safely empty of murderers and thieves. When he'd departed I checked that all the alarms were switched on and went up to Greville's room to change.

I borrowed another of his shirts and a navy silk tie, and shaved with his electric razor which was among the things I'd picked up from the floor and had put on his white chest of drawers, and brushed my hair with his brushes for the same reason, and thought with an odd frisson that all of these things were mine now, that I was in his house, in his room, in his clothes ... in his life.

I put on my own suit, because his anyway were too long, and came across the tube of the baster, still there in an inner breast pocket. Removing it, I left it among the jumble on the dressing chest and checked in the looking glass on the wall that Franklin, Mark II, wouldn't entirely disgrace Franklin, Mark I. He had looked in that mirror every day for three months, I supposed. Now his reflection was my reflection and the man that was both of us had dark marks of tiredness under the eyes and a taut thinness in the cheeks, and looked as if he could do with a week's lying in the sun. I gave him a rueful smile and phoned for a taxi, which took me to Luigi's with ten minutes to spare.

She was there before me all the same, sitting at a small table in the bar area to one side of the restaurant, with an emptyish glass looking like vodka on a prim mat in front of her. She stood up when I went in and offered me a cool cheek for a polite social greeting, inviting me with a gesture to sit down.

'What will you drink' she asked formally, but battling, I thought, with an undercurrent of diffidence.

I said I would pay for our drinks and she said no, no, this was her suggestion. She called the waiter and said, 'Double water?' to me with a small smile and when I nodded ordered Perrier with ice and fresh lime juice for both of us.

I was down by then to only two or three Distalgesics a day and would soon have stopped taking them, though the one I'd just swallowed in Greville's house was still an inhibitor for the evening. I wondered too late which would have made me feel better, a damper for the ankle or a large scotch everywhere else.

Clarissa was wearing a blue silk dress with a double-strand pearl necklace, pearl, sapphire and diamond earrings and a sapphire and diamond ring. I doubted if I would have noticed those, in the simple old jockey days. Her hair, smooth as always, curved in the expensive cut and her shoes and handbag were quiet black calf. She looked as she was, a polished, well-bred woman of forty or so, nearly beautiful, slender, with generous eyes.

'What have you been doing since Saturday?' she asked, making conversation.

'Peering into the jaws of death. What have you?'

'We went to ...' She broke off. '*What* did you say?'

'Martha and Harley Ostermeyer and I were in a car crash on Sunday. They're OK, they went back to America today, I believe. And I, as you see, am here in one piece. Well ... almost one piece.'

She was predictably horrified and wanted to hear all the details, and the telling at least helped to evaporate any awkwardness either of us had been feeling at the meeting.

'Simms was *shot*?'

'Yes.'

'But ... do the police know who did it?'

I shook my head. 'Someone in a large grey Volvo, they think, and there are thousands of those.'

'Good heavens.' She paused. 'I didn't like to comment, but you look ...' She hesitated, searching for the word.

'Frazzled?' I suggested.

'Smooth.' She smiled. 'Frazzled underneath.'

233

'It'll pass.'

The waiter came to ask if we would be having dinner and I said yes, and no argument, the dinner was mine. She accepted without fuss, and we read the menus.

The fare was chiefly Italian, the decor cosmopolitan, the ambience faintly European tamed by London. A lot of dark red, lamps with glass shades, no wallpaper music. A comfortable place, nothing dynamic. Few diners yet, as the hour was early.

It was not, I was interested to note, a habitual rendezvous place for Clarissa and Greville: none of the waiters treated her as a regular. I asked her about it and, startled, she said they had been there only two or three times, always for lunch.

'We never went to the same place often,' she said. 'It wouldn't have been wise.'

'No.'

She gave me a slightly embarrassed look. 'Do you disapprove of me and Greville?'

'No,' I said again. 'You gave him joy.'

'Oh.' She was comforted and pleased. She said with a certain shyness, 'It was the first time I'd fallen in love. I suppose you'll think that silly. But it was the first time for him too, he said. It was ... truly *wonderful*. We were like ... as if twenty years younger ... I don't know if I can explain. Laughing. Lit up.'

'As far as I can see,' I said, 'the thunderbolt strikes at any age. You don't have to be teenagers.'

'Has it ... struck you?'

'Not since I was seventeen and fell like a ton of bricks for a trainer's daughter.'

'What happened?'

'Nothing much. We laughed a lot. Slept together, a bit clumsily at first. She married an old man of twenty-eight. I went to college.'

'I met Henry when I was eighteen. He fell in love with me ... pursued me ... I was flattered ... and he was so very good looking ... and kind.'

'He still is,' I said.

'He'd already inherited his title. My mother was ecstatic ... she said the age difference didn't matter ... so I married him.'

She paused. 'We had a son and a daughter, both grown up

now. It hasn't been a bad life, but before Greville, incomplete.'

'A better life than most.' I said, aiming to comfort.

'You're very like Greville,' she said unexpectedly. 'You look at things straight, in the same way. You've his sense of proportion.'

'We had realistic parents.'

'He didn't speak about them much, only that he became interested in gemstones because of the museums his mother took him to. But he lived in the present and he looked outward, not inward, and I loved him to distraction and in a way I didn't know him ...' She stopped and swallowed and seemed determined not to let emotion intrude further.

'He was like that with me too,' I said. 'With everyone, I think. It didn't occur to him to give running commentaries on his actions and feelings. He found everything else more interesting.'

'I do miss him,' she said.

'What will you eat?' I asked.

She gave me a flick of a look and read the menu without seeing it for quite a long time. In the end she said with a sigh, You decide.'

'Did Greville?'

'Yes.'

'If I order fried zucchini as a starter, then fillet steak in pepper sauce with linguine tossed in olive oil with garlic, will that do?'

'I don't like garlic. I like everything else. Unusual. Nice.'

'OK. No garlic.'

We transferred to the dining room before seven-thirty and ate the proposed programme, and I asked if she were returning to York that night: if she had a train to catch, if that was why we were eating early.

'No, I'm down here for two nights. Tomorrow I'm going to an old friend's wedding, then back to York on Thursday morning.' She concentrated on twirling linguine onto her fork. 'When Henry and I come to London together we always stay at the Selfridge Hotel, and when I come alone I stay there also. They know us well there. When I'm there alone they don't present me with an account, they send it to Henry.' She ate the forkful of linguine. 'I tell him I go to the cinema and eat in snack bars

... and he knows I'm always back in the hotel before midnight.'

There was a good long stretch of time between this dinner and midnight.

I said, 'Every five weeks or so, when you came down to London alone, Greville met you at King's Cross, isn't that right, and took you to lunch?'

She said in surprise, 'Did he tell you?'

'Not face to face. Did you ever see that gadget of his, the Wizard?'

'Yes, but ...' She was horrified. 'He surely didn't put me in it?'

'Not by name, and only under a secret password. You're quite safe.'

She twiddled some more with the pasta, her eyes down, her thoughts somewhere else.

'After lunch,' she said, with pauses, 'if I had appointments, I'd keep them, or do some shopping ... something to take home. I'd register at the hotel and change, and go to Greville's house. He used to have the flat, of course, but the house was much better. When he came, we'd have drinks ... talk ... maybe make love. We'd go to dinner early, then back to his house.' Her voice stopped. She still didn't look up.

I said, 'Do you want to go to his house now, before midnight?'

After a while, she said, 'I don't know.'

'Well ... would you like coffee?'

She nodded, still not meeting my eyes, and pushed the linguine away. We sat in silence while waiters took away the plates and poured into cups, and if she couldn't make up her mind, nor could I.

In the end I said, 'If you like, come to Greville's house now. I'm sleeping there tonight, but that's not a factor. Come if you like, just to be near him, to be with him as much as you can for maybe the last time. Lie on his bed. Weep for him. I'll wait for you downstairs ... and take you safely to your hotel before the fairy coach changes back to a pumpkin.'

Oh!' She turned what had been going to be a sob into almost a laugh. 'Can I really?'

'Whenever you like.'

'Thank you, then. Yes.'

'I'd better warn you,' I said, 'it's not exactly tidy.' I told her what she would find, but she was inconsolable at the sight of the reality.

'He would have hated this,' she said. 'I'm so glad he didn't see it.'

We were in the small sitting room, and she went round picking up the pink and brown stone bears, restoring them to their tray.

'I gave him these,' she said. 'He loved them. They're rhodonite, he said.'

'Take them to remember him by. And there's a gold watch you gave him, if you'd like that too.'

She paused with the last bear in her hand and said, 'You're very kind to me.'

'It's not difficult. And he'd have been furious with me if I weren't.'

'I'd love the bears. You'd better keep the watch, because of the engraving.'

'OK,' I said.

'I think,' she said with diffidence, 'I'll go upstairs now.'

I nodded.

'Come with me,' she said.

'I looked at her. Her eyes were wide and troubled, but not committed, not hungry. Undecided. Like myself.

'All right,' I said.

'Is there chaos up there too?'

'I picked some of it up.'

She went up the stairs ahead of me at about four times my speed, and I heard her small moan of distress at the desecration of the bedroom. When I joined her, she was standing forlornly looking around, and with naturalness she turned to me and put her arms loosely round my waist, laying her head on my shoulder. I shed the confounded crutches and hugged her tight in grief for her and for Greville and we stood there for a long minute in mutual and much needed comfort.

She let her arms fall away and went over to sit on the bed, smoothing a hand over the black and white chequerboard counterpane.

'He was going to change this room,' she said. 'All this drama ...' She waved a hand at the white furniture, the black carpet,

237

one black wall ... 'It came with the house. He wanted me to choose something softer, that I would like. But this is how I'll always remember it.'

She lay down flat, her head on the pillows, her legs towards the foot of the bed, ankles crossed. I half-hopped, half-limped across the room and sat on the edge beside her.

She watched me with big eyes. I put my hand flat on her stomach and felt the sharp internal contraction of muscles.

'Should we do this?' she said.

'I'm not Greville.'

'No ... Would he mind?'

'I shouldn't think so.' I moved my hand, rubbing a little. 'Do you want to go on?'

'Do you?'

'Yes,' I said.

She sat up fast and put her arms round my neck in a sort of released compulsion.

'I do want this,' she said. 'I've wanted it all day. I've been pretending to myself, telling myself I shouldn't, but yes, I do want this passionately, and I know you're not Greville, I know it will be different, but this is the only way I can love him ... and can you bear it, can you understand it, if it's him I love?'

I understood it well, and I minded not at all.

'I said, smiling, 'Just don't *call* me Greville. It would be the turn-off of the century.'

She took her face away from the proximity of my ear and looked me in the eyes, and her lips too, after a moment, were smiling.

'Derek,' she said deliberately, 'make love to me. Please.'

'Don't beg,' I said.

I put my mouth on hers and took my brother's place.

As a memorial service it was a great success. I lay in the dark laughing in my mind at that disgraceful pun, wondering whether or not to share it with Clarissa.

The catharsis was over, and her tears. She lay with her head on my chest, lightly asleep, contented, as far as I could tell, with the substitute loving. Women said men were not all the same in the dark, and I knew both where I'd surprised her and failed her, known what I'd done like Greville and not done like Greville from the instinctive releases and tensions of her reactions.

Greville, I now knew, had been a lucky man, though whether he had himself taught her how to give exquisite pleasure was something I couldn't quite ask. She knew, though, and she'd done it, and the feeling of her featherlight tattooing fingers on the base of my spine at the moment of climax had been a revelation. Knowledge marched on, I thought. Next time, with anyone else, I'd know what to suggest.

Clarissa stirred and I turned my wrist over, seeing the fluorescent hands of my watch.

'Wake up,' I said affectionately. 'It's Cinderella time.'

'Ohh ...'

I stretched out a hand and turned on a bedside light. She smiled at me sleepily, no doubts remaining.

'That was all right,' she said.

'Mm. Very.'

'How's the ankle:'

'What ankle?'

She propped herself on one elbow, unashamed of nakedness, and laughed at me. She looked younger and sweeter, and I was seeing, I knew, what Greville had seen, what Greville had loved.

'Tomorrow,' she said, 'my friend's wedding will be over by six or so. Can I come here again?' She put her fingers lightly on my mouth to stop me answering at once. 'This time was for him,' she said. 'Tomorrow for us. Then I'll go home.'

'For ever?'

'Yes, I think so. What I had with Greville was unforgettable and unrepeatable. I decided on the train coming down here that whatever happened with you, or didn't happen, I would live with Henry, and do my best there.'

'I could easily love you,' I said.

'Yes, but don't.'

I knew she was right. I kissed her lightly.

'Tomorrow for us,' I agreed. 'Then goodbye.'

When I went into the office in the morning, Annette told me

crossly that Jason hadn't turned up for work, nor had he telephoned to say he was ill.

Jason had been prudent, I thought. I'd have tossed him down the lift shaft, insolence, orange hair and all, given half an ounce of provocation.

'He won't be coming back,' I said, 'so we'll need a replacement.'

She was astonished. 'You can't sack him for not turning up. You can't sack him for anything without paying compensation.'

'Stop worrying,' I said, but she couldn't take that advice.

June came zooming into Greville's office waving a tabloid newspaper and looking at me with wide incredulous eyes.

'Did you know you're in the paper? Lucky to be alive, it says here. You didn't say anything about it!'

'Let's see,' I said, and she laid the *Daily Sensation* open on the black desk.

There was a picture of the smash in which one could more or less see my head inside the Daimler, but not recognisably. The headline read: 'Driver shot, jockey lives', and the piece underneath listed the lucky-to-be-alive passengers as Mr and Mrs Ostermeyer of Pittsburgh, America, and ex-champion steeplechase jockey Derek Franklin. The police were reported to be interested in a grey Volvo seen accelerating from the scene, and also to have recovered two bullets from the bodywork of the Daimler. After that titbit came a rehash of the Hungerford massacre and a query, 'Is this a copycat killing?' and finally a picture of Simms looking happy: 'Survived by wife and two daughters who were last night being comforted by relatives'.

Poor Simms. Poor family. Poor every shot victim in Hungerford.

'It happened on Sunday,' June exclaimed, 'and you came here on Monday and yesterday as if nothing was wrong. No wonder you looked knackered.'

'June!' Annette disapproved of the word.

'Well, he did. Still does.' She gave me a critical, kindly, motherly-sister inspection. 'He could have been killed, and then what would we all have done here?'

The dismay in Annette's face was a measure, I supposed, of the degree to which I had taken over. The place no longer felt like a quicksand to me either and I was beginning by necessity to get a feel of its pulse.

But there was racing at Cheltenham that day. I turned the pages of the newspaper and came to the runners and riders. That was where my name belonged, not on Saxony Franklin cheques. June looked over my shoulder and understood at least something of my sense of exile.

'When you go back to your own world,' she said, rephrasing her thought and asking it seriously, 'what will we do here?'

'We have a month,' I said. 'It'll take me that time to get fit.' I paused. 'I've been thinking about that problem, and, er, you might as well know, both of you, what I've decided.'

They both looked apprehensive, but I smiled to reassure them.

'What we'll do,' I said, 'is this. Annette will have a new title, which will be Office Manager. She'll run things generally and keep the keys.'

She didn't look displeased. She repeated 'Office Manager' as if trying it for size.

I nodded. 'Then I'll start looking from now on for a business expert, someone to oversee the cash flow and do the accounts and try to keep us afloat. Because it's going to be a struggle, we can't avoid that.'

They both looked shocked and disbelieving. Cash flow seemed never to have been a problem before.

'Greville did buy diamonds,' I said regretfully, 'and so far we are only in possession of a quarter of them. I can't find out what happened to the rest. They cost the firm altogether one and a half million dollars, and we'll still owe the bank getting on for three-quarters of that sum when we've sold the quarter we have.'

Their mouths opened in unhappy unison.

'Unless and until the other diamonds turn up,' I said, 'we have to pay interest on the loan and persuade the bank that somehow or other we'll climb out of the hole. So we'll want someone we'll call the Finance Manager, and we'll pay him out of part of what used to be Greville's own salary.'

They began to understand the mechanics, and nodded.

'Then,' I said, 'we need a gemmologist who has a feeling for stones and understands what the customers like and need. There's no good hoping for another Greville, but we will create

241

the post of Merchandise Manager, and that,' I looked at her, 'will be June.'

She blushed a fiery red. 'But I can't ... I don't know enough.'

'You'll go on courses,' I said. 'You'll go to trade fairs. You'll travel. You'll do the buying.'

I watched her expand her horizons abruptly and saw the sparkle appear in her eyes.

'She's too young,' Annette objected.

'We'll see,' I said, and to June I added, 'You know what sells. You and the Finance Manager will work together to make us the best possible profit. You'll still work the computer, and teach Lily or Tina how to use it for when you're away.'

'Tina,' she said, 'she's quicker.'

'Tina, then.'

'What about you?' she asked.

'I'll be General Manager. I'll come when I can, at least twice a week for a couple of hours. Everyone will tell me what's going on and we will all decide what is best to be done, though if there's a disagreement I'll have the casting vote. Right or wrong will be my responsibility, not yours.'

Annette, nevertheless troubled, said, 'Surely you yourself will need Mr Franklin's salary.'

I shook my head. 'I earn enough riding horses. Until we're solvent here, we need to save every penny.'

'It's an adventure!' June said, enraptured.

I thought it might be a very long haul and even in the end impossible, but I couldn't square it with the consciousness of Greville all around me not to try.

'Well,' I said, putting a hand in a pocket and bringing out a twist of gauze, 'we have here five uncut diamonds which cost about seventy-five thousand dollars altogether.'

They more or less gasped.

'How do we sell them?' I said.

After a pause, Annette said, 'Interest a diamantaire.'

'Do you know how to do that?'

After a moment's hesitation, she nodded.

'We can give provenance,' I said. 'Copies of the records of the original sale are on their way here from Guy Servi in Antwerp. They might be here tomorrow. Sight-box number and so on. We'll put these stones in the vault until the papers arrive, then you can get cracking.'

She nodded, but fearfully.

'Cheer up,' I said. 'It's clear from the ledgers that Saxony Franklin is normally a highly successful and profitable business. We'll have to cut costs where we can, that's all.'

'We could cut out Jason's salary,' Annette said unexpectedly. 'Half the time Tina's been carrying the heavy boxes, anyway, and I can do the hoovering myself.'

'Great,' I said with gratitude. 'If you feel like that, we'll succeed.'

The telephone rang and Annette answered it briefly.

'A messenger has left a packet for you down at the front desk,' she said.

'I'll go for it,' June said, and was out of the door on the words, returning in her usual short time with a brown padded jiffy bag, not very large, addressed simply to Derek Franklin in neat handwriting, which she laid before me with a flourish.

'Mind it's not a bomb,' she said facetiously as I picked it up, and I thought with an amount of horror that it was a possibility I hadn't thought of.

'I didn't mean it,' she said teasingly, seeing me hesitate. 'Do you want me to open it?'

'And get your hands blown off instead?'

'Of course it's not a bomb,' Annette said uneasily.

'Tell you what,' June said, 'I'll fetch the shears from the packing room.' She was gone for a few seconds. 'Alfie says,' she remarked, returning, 'we ought to put it in a bucket of water.'

She gave me the shears, which were oversized scissors that Alfie used for cutting cardboard, and for all her disbelief she and Annette backed away across the room while I sliced the end off the bag.

There was no explosion. Complete anti-climax. I shook out the contents which proved to be two objects and one envelope.

One of the objects was the microcassette recorder that I'd left on Prospero Jenks's workbench in my haste to be gone.

The other was a long black leather wallet almost the size of the Wizard, with gold initials G.S.F. in one corner and an ordinary brown rubber band holding it shut.

'That's Mr Franklin's,' Annette said blankly, and June, coming to inspect it, nodded.

I peeled off the rubber band and laid the wallet open on the desk. There was a business card lying loose inside it with Prospero Jenks's name and shops on the front, and on the reverse the single word, 'Sorry.'

'Where did he get Mr Franklin's wallet from?' Annette asked, puzzled, looking at the card.

'He found it,' I said.

'He took his time sending it back,' June said tartly.

'Mm.'

The wallet contained a Saxony Franklin chequebook, four credit cards, several business cards and a small pack of banknotes, which I guessed were fewer in number than when Greville set out.

The small excitement over, Annette and June went off to tell the others the present and future state of the nation, and I was alone when I opened the envelope.

CHAPTER 18

Pross had sent me a letter and certified bank draft: instantly cashable money.

I blinked at the numbers on the cheque and reread them very carefully. Then I read the letter.

It said:

Derek,

    This is a plea for a bargain, as you more or less said. The cheque is for the sum I agreed with Grev for the twelve tear drops and eight stars. I know you need the money, and I need those stones.

    Jason won't be troubling you again. I'm giving him a job in one of my workrooms.

    Grev wouldn't have forgiven the brick, though he might the wallet. For you it's the other way round. You're very like him. I wish he hadn't died.

Pross.

What a mess, I thought. I did need the money, yet if I accepted it I was implicitly agreeing not to take any action against him. The trouble about taking action against him was that however much I might want to I didn't know that I could. Apart from difficulties of evidence, I had more or less made a bargain that for information he would get inaction, but that had been before the wallet. It was perceptive of him, I thought, to

245

see that it was betrayal and attacks on our *brother* that would anger both Greville and me most.

Would Greville want me to extend, if not forgiveness, then at least suspended revenge? Would Greville want me to confirm his forgiveness or to rise up in wrath and tear up the cheque …

In the midst of these sombre squirrelling thoughts the telephone rang and I answered it.

'Elliot Trelawney here,' the voice said.

'Oh, hello.'

He asked me how things were going and I said life was full of dilemmas. Ever so, he said with a chuckle.

'Give me some advice,' I said on impulse, 'as a magistrate.'

'If I can, certainly.'

'Well. Listen to a story, then say what you think.'

'Fire away.'

'Someone knocked me out with a brick …' Elliot made protesting noises on my behalf, but I went on, 'I know now who it was, but I didn't then, and I didn't see his face because he was masked. He wanted to steal a particular thing from me, but although he made a mess in the house searching, he didn't find it, and so didn't rob me of anything except consciousness. I guessed later who it was, and I challenged another man with having sent him to attack me. That man didn't deny it to me, but he said he would deny it to anyone else. So … what do I do?'

'Whew.' He pondered. 'What do you want to do?'

'I don't know. That's why I need the advice.'

'Did you report the attack to the police at the time?'

'Yes.'

'Have you suffered serious after-effects?'

'No.'

'Did you see a doctor?'

'No.'

He pondered some more. 'On a practical level you'd find it difficult to get a conviction, even if the prosecution service would bring charges of actual bodily harm. You couldn't swear to the identity of your assailant if you didn't see him at the time, and as for the other man, conspiracy to commit a crime is one of the most difficult charges to make stick. As you didn't consult a doctor, you're on tricky ground. So, hard as it may seem, my advice would be that the case wouldn't get to court.'

I signed. 'Thank you,' I said.

'Sorry not to have been more positive.'

'It's all right. You confirmed what I rather feared.'

'Fine then,' he said. 'I rang to thank you for sending the Vaccaro notes. We held the committee meeting and turned down Vaccaro's application, and now we find we needn't have bothered because on Saturday night he was arrested and charged with attempting to import illegal substances. He's still in custody, and America is asking for him to be extradited to Florida where he faces murder charges and perhaps execution. And we nearly gave him a gambling licence! Funny old world.'

'Hilarious.'

'How about our drink in The Rook and Castle?' he suggested. 'Perhaps one evening next week?'

'OK.'

'Fine,' he said. 'I'll ring you.'

I put the phone down thinking that if Vaccaro had been arrested on Saturday evening and held in custody, it was unlikely he'd shot Simms from a moving car in Berkshire on Sunday afternoon. But then, I'd never really thought he had.

Copycat. Copycat, that's what it had been.

Pross hadn't shot Simms either. Had never tried to kill me. The Peter-Pan face upon which so many emotions could be read had shown a total blank when I'd asked him what he was doing on Sunday afternoon.

The shooting of Simms, I concluded, had been random violence like the other murders in Hungerford. Pointless and vicious; malignant, lunatic and impossible to explain.

I picked up the huge cheque and looked at it. It would solve all immediate problems: pay the interest already due, the cost of cutting the diamonds and more than a fifth of the capital debt. If I didn't take it, we would no doubt sell the diamonds later to someone else, but they had been cut especially for Prospero Jenks's fantasies and might not easily fit necklaces and rings.

A plea. A bargain. A chance that the remorse was at least half real. Or was he taking me again for a sucker?

I did some sums with a calculator and when Annette came in with the day's letters I showed her my figures and the cheque and asked her what she thought.

'That's the cost price,' I pointed. 'That's the cost of cutting and polishing. That's for delivery charges. That's for loan interest and VAT. If you add those together and subtract them from the figure on this cheque, is that the sort of profit margin Greville would have asked?'

Setting prices was something she well understood, and she repeated my steps on the calculator.

'Yes,' she said finally, 'it looks about right. Not over-generous, but Mr Franklin would have seen this as a service for commission, I think. Not like the rock crystal, which he bought on spec, which had to help pay for his journeys.' She looked at me anxiously. 'You understand the difference?'

'Yes,' I said. 'Prospero Jenks says this is what he and Greville agreed on.'

'Well then,' she said, relieved, 'he wouldn't cheat you.'

I smiled with irony at her faith. 'We'd better bank this cheque, I suppose,' I said, 'before it evaporates.'

'I'll do it at once,' she declared. 'With a loan as big as you said, every minute costs us money.'

She put on her coat and took an umbrella to go out with, as the day had started off raining and showed no signs of relenting.

It had been raining the previous night when Clarissa had been ready to leave, and I'd had to ring three times for a taxi, a problem Cinderella didn't seem to have encountered. Midnight had come and gone when the wheels had finally arrived, and I'd suggested meanwhile that I lend her Brad and my car for going to her wedding.

I didn't need to, she said. When she and Henry were in London, they were driven about by a hired car firm. The car was already ordered to take her to the wedding which was in Surrey. The driver would wait for her and return her to the hotel, and she'd better stick to the plan, she said, because the bill for it would be sent to her husband.

'I always do what Henry expects,' she said, 'then there are no questions.'

'Suppose Brad picks you up from the Selfridge after you get back?' I said, packing the little stone bears and giving them to her in a carrier. 'The forecast is lousy and if it's raining you'll have a terrible job getting a taxi at that time of day.'

She liked the idea except for Brad's knowing her name. I assured her he never spoke unless he couldn't avoid it, but I told her I would ask Brad to park somewhere near the hotel. Then she could call the car phone's number when she was ready to leave, and Brad would beetle up at the right moment and not need to know her name or ask for her at the desk.

As that pleased her, I wrote down the phone number and the car's number plate so that she would recognise the right pumpkin, and described Brad to her; going bald, a bit morose, an open-necked shirt, a very good driver.

I couldn't tell Brad's own opinion of the arrangement. When I'd suggested it in the morning on the rainy way to the office, he had merely grunted which I'd taken as preliminary assent.

When he'd brought Clarissa, I thought as I looked through the letters Annette had given me, he could go on home, to Hungerford, and Clarissa and I might walk along to the restaurant at the end of Greville's street where he could have been known but I was not, and after an early dinner we would return to Greville's bed, this time for us, and we'd order the taxi in better time ... perhaps.

I was awoken from this pleasant daydream by the ever-demanding telephone, this time with Nicholas Loder on the other end spluttering with rage.

'Milo says you had the confounded cheek,' he said, 'to have Dozen Roses dope-tested.'

'For barbiturates, yes. He seemed very sleepy. Our vet said he'd be happier to know the horse hadn't been tranquillised for the journey before he gave him an all-clear certificate.'

'I'd never give a horse tranquillisers,' he declared.

'No, none of us really thought so,' I said pacifyingly, 'but we decided to make sure.'

'It's shabby of you. Offensive. I expect an apology.'

'I apologise,' I said sincerely enough, and thought guiltily of the further checks going on at that moment.

'That's not good enough,' Nicholas Loder said huffily.

'I was selling the horse to good owners of Milo, people I ride for,' I said reasonably. 'We all know you disapproved. In the same circumstances, confronted by a sleepy horse, you'd have done the same, wouldn't you? You'd want to be sure what you were selling.'

Weigh the merchandise, I thought. Cubic zirconia, size for size, was one point seven times heavier than diamond. Greville had carried jeweller's scales in his car on his way to Harwich, presumably to check what the *Koningin Beatrix* was bringing.

'You've behaved disgustingly,' Nicholas Loder said. 'When did you see the horse last? And when next?'

"Monday evening, last. Don't know when next. As I told you, I'm tied up a bit with Greville's affairs.'

'Milo's secretary said I'd find you in Greville's office,' he grumbled. 'You're never at home. I've got a buyer for Gemstones, I think, though you don't deserve it. Where will you be this evening, if he makes a definite offer?'

'In Greville's house, perhaps.'

'Right, I have the number. And I want a written apology from you about those dope tests. I'm so angry I can hardly be civil to you.'

He hardly was, I thought, but I was pleased enough about Gemstones. The money would go into the firm's coffers and hold off bankruptcy a little while longer. I still held the Ostermeyers' cheque for Dozen Roses, waiting for Phil Urquhart's final clearance before cashing it. The horses would make up for a few of the missing diamonds. Looking at it optimistically, saying it quickly, the millstone had been reduced to near one million dollars.

June out of habit brought me a sandwich for lunch. She was walking with an extra bounce, with unashamed excitement. Way down the line, I thought, if we made it through the crisis, what then? Would I simply sell the whole of Saxony Franklin as I'd meant or keep it and borrow against it to finance a stable, as Greville had financed the diamonds? I wouldn't hide the stable! Perhaps I would know enough by then to manage both businesses on a sound basis: I'd learned a good deal in ten days. I had also, though I found it surprising, grown fond of Greville's firm. If we saved it, I wouldn't want to let go.

If I went on riding until solvency dawned I might be the oldest jump jockey in history ...

Again the telephone interrupted the daydreams, and I'd barely made a start on the letters.

It was a man with a long order for cabochons and beads. I hopped to the door and yelled for June to pick up the phone and to put the order on the computer, and Alfie came along to complain we were running out of heavy duty binding tape and to ask why we'd ever needed Jason. Tina did his work in half the time without the swear words.

Annette almost with gaiety hoovered everywhere, though I thought I would soon ask Tina to do it instead. Lily came with downcast eyes to ask meekly if she could have a title also. Stockroom Manager? she suggested.

'Done!' I said with sincere pleasure; and before the day was out we had a Shipment Manager (Alfie) and an Enabling Manager (Tina), and it seemed to me that such a spirit had been released there that the enterprise was now flying. Whether the euphoria would last or not was next week's problem.

I telephoned Maarten-Pagnier in Antwerp and discussed the transit of twelve tear drops, eight stars and five fakes.

'Our customer has paid us for the diamonds,' I said. 'I'd like to be able to tell him when we could get them to him.'

'Do you want them sent direct to him, monsieur?'

'No. Here to us. We'll pass them on.' I asked if he would insure them for the journey and send them by Euro-Securo; no need to trouble his partner again personally as we did not dispute that five of the stones sent to him had been cubic zirconia. The real stones had been returned to us, I said.

'I rejoice for you, monsieur. And shall we expect a further consignment for cutting? Monsieur Franklin intended it.'

'Not at the moment, I regret.'

'Very well, monsieur. At any time, we are at your service.'

After that I asked Annette if she could find Prospero Jenks to tell him his diamonds would be coming. She ran him to earth in one of his workrooms and appeared in my doorway saying he wanted to speak to me personally.

With inner reluctance I picked up the receiver. 'Hello, Pross,' I said.

'Truce, then?' he asked.

'We've banked the cheque. You'll get the diamonds.'

'When?'

'When they get here from Antwerp. Friday, maybe.'

'Thanks.' He sounded fervently pleased. Then he said with hesitation, 'You've got some light blue topaz, each fifteen carats or more, emerald cut, glittering like water ... can I have it? Five or six big stones, Grev said. I'll take them all.'

'Give it time,' I said, and God, I thought, what unholy nerve.

'Yes, well, but you and I need each other,' he protested.

'Symbiosis?' I said.

'What? Yes.'

It had done Greville no harm in the trade, I'd gathered, to be known as the chief supplier of Prospero Jenks. His firm still needed the cachet as much as the cash. I'd taken the money once. Could I afford pride?'

'If you try to steal from me one more time,' I said, 'I not only stop trading with you, I make sure everyone knows why. Everyone from Hatton Garden to Pelikanstraat.'

'Derek!' He sounded hurt, but the threat was a dire one.

'You can have the topaz,' I said. 'We have a new gemmologist who's not Greville, I grant you, but who knows what you buy. We'll still tell you what special stones we've imported. You can tell us what you need. We'll take it step by step.'

'I thought you wouldn't!' He sounded extremely relieved. 'I thought you'd never forgive me the wallet. Your face ...'

'I don't forgive it. Or forget. But after wars, enemies trade.'

It always happened, I thought, though cynics might mock. Mutual benefit was the most powerful of bridge-builders, even if the heart remained bitter. 'We'll see how we go,' I said again.

'If you find the other diamonds,' he said hopefully, 'I still want them.' Like a little boy in trouble, I thought, trying to charm his way out.

Disconnecting, I ruefully smiled. I'd made the same inner compromise that Greville had, to do business with the treacherous child, but not to trust him. To supply the genius in him, and look to my back.

June came winging in and I asked her to go along to the vault to look at the light blue large-stone topaz which I well remembered. 'Get to know it while it's still here. I've sold it to Prospero Jenks.'

'But I don't go into the vault,' she said.

'You do now. You'll go in there every day from now on at spare moments to learn the look and feel of the facetted stones, like I have. Topaz is slippery, for instance. Learn the chemical formulas, learn the cuts and the weights, get to know them so that if you're offered unusual facetted stones anywhere in the world, you can check them against your knowledge for probability.'

Her mouth opened.

'You're going to buy the raw materials for Prospero Jenks's museum pieces,' I said. 'You've got to learn fast.'

Her eyes stretched wide as well, and she vanished.

With Annette I finished the letters.

At four o'clock I answered the telephone yet again, and found myself talking to Phil Urquhart, whose voice sounded strained.

'I've just phoned the lab for the results of Dozen Roses's tests.' He paused. 'I don't think I believe this.'

'What's the matter?' I asked.

'Do you know what a metabolite is?'

'Only vaguely.'

'What then?' he said.

'The result of metabolism, isn't it?'

'It is,' he said. 'It's what's left after some substance or other has broken down in the body.'

'So what?'

'So,' he said reasonably, 'if you find a particular metabolite in the urine, it means a particular substance was earlier present in the body. Is that clear?'

'Like viruses produce special antibodies, so the presence of the antibodies proves the existence of the viruses?'

'Exactly,' he said, apparently relieved I understood. 'Well, the lab found a metabolite in Dozen Roses's urine. A metabolite known as benzyl ecognine.'

'Go on,' I urged, as he paused. 'What is it the metabolite *of*?'

'Cocaine,' he said.

I sat in stunned disbelieving silence.

'Derek?' he said.

'Yes.'

Racehorses aren't routinely tested for cocaine because it isn't a stimulant. Normally a racehorse could be full of cocaine and no one would know.'

'If it isn't a stimulant,' I said, loosening my tongue, 'why give it to them?'

'If you *believed* it was a stimulant, you might. Knowing it wouldn't be tested for.'

'How could you believe it?'

'It's one of the drugs that potentiates adrenalin. I particularly asked the lab to test for all drugs like that because of what you said about adrenalin yourself. What happens with a normal adrenalin surge is that after a while an enzyme comes along to disperse some of it while much gets stored for the future use. Cocaine blocks the storage uptake, so the adrenalin goes roaring round the body for much longer. When the cocaine decays, its chief metabolic product is benzyl ecognine which is what the lab found in its gas chromatograph analyser this afternoon.'

'There were some cases in America ...' I said vaguely.

'It's still not part of a regulation dope test even there.'

'But my God,' I said blankly, 'Nicholas Loder must have known.'

'Almost certainly, I should think. You'd have to administer the cocaine very soon before the race, because its effect is short lived. One hour, an hour and a half at most. It's difficult to tell, with a horse. There's no data. And although the metabolite would appear in the blood and the urine soon after that, the metabolite itself would be detectable for probably not much longer than forty-eight hours, but with a horse, that's still a guess. We took the sample from Dozen Roses on Monday evening about fifty-two hours after he'd raced. The lab said the metabolite was definitely present, but they could make no estimate of how much cocaine had been assimilated. They told me all this very very carefully. They have much more experience with humans. They say in humans the rush from cocaine is fast, lasts about forty minutes and brings little post-exhilaration depression.'

'Nice,' I said.

'In horses,' he went on, 'they think it would probably induce skittishness at once.'

I thought back to Dozen Roses's behaviour both at York and on the TV tapes. He'd certainly woken up dramatically between saddling box and starting gate.

'But,' Phil added, 'they say that at the most it might give more stamina, but not more speed. It wouldn't make the horse

254

go faster, but just make the adrenalin push last longer.'

That might be enough sometimes, I thought. Sometimes you could feel horses 'die' under you near the finish, not from lack of ability, but from lack of perseverance, of fight. Some horses were content to be second. In them, uninhibited adrenalin might perhaps tip the balance.

Caffeine, which had the same potentiating effect, was a prohibited substance in racing.

'Why don't they test for cocaine?' I asked.

'Heaven knows,' Phil said. 'Perhaps because enough to wind up a horse would cost the doper too much to be practicable. I mean ... more than one could be sure of winning back on a bet. But cocaine's getting cheaper, I'm told. There's more and more of it around.'

'I don't know much about drugs,' I said.

'Where have you been?'

'Not my scene.'

'Do you know what they'd call you in America?'

'Straight,' he said.

'I thought that meant heterosexual.'

He laughed. 'That too. You're straight through and through.'

'Phil,' I said, 'what do I do?'

He sobered abruptly. 'God knows. My job ends with passing on the facts. The moral decisions are yours. All I can tell you is that some time before Monday evening Dozen Roses took cocaine into his bloodstream.'

'Via a baster?' I said.

After a short silence he said, 'We can't be sure of that.'

'We can't be sure he didn't.'

'Did I understand right, that Harley Ostermeyer picked up the tube of the baster and gave it to you?'

'That's right,' I said. 'I still have it, but like I told you, it's clean.'

'It might look clean,' he said slowly, 'but if cocaine was blown up it in powder form, there may be particles clinging.'

I thought back to before the race at York.

'When Martha Ostermeyer picked up the blue bulb end and gave it back to Rollway,' I said, 'she was brushing her fingers together afterwards ... she seemed to be getting rid of dust from her gloves.'

'Oh glory,' Phil said.

I sighed and said, 'If I give the tube to you, can you get it tested without anyone knowing where it came from?'

'Sure. Like the urine, it'll be anonymous. I'll get the lab to do another rush job, if you want. It costs a bit more, though.'

'Get it done, Phil,' I said. 'I can't really decide anything unless I know for sure.'

'Right. Are you coming back here soon?'

'Greville's business takes so much time. I'll be back at the weekend, but I think I'll send the tube to you by carrier, to be quicker. You should get it tomorrow morning.'

'Right,' he said. 'We might get a result late tomorrow. Friday at the latest.'

'Good, and er ... don't mention it to Milo'

'No, but why not?'

'He told Nicholas Loder we tested Dozen Roses for tranquillisers and Nicholas Loder was on my phone hitting the roof.'

'Oh God.'

'I don't want him knowing about the tests for cocaine. I mean, neither Milo nor Nicholas Loder.'

'You may be sure,' Phil said seriously, 'they won't learn it from me.'

I was the worst dilemma of all, I thought, replacing the receiver.

Was cocaine a stimulant or was it not? The racing authorities didn't think so: didn't test for it. If I believed it didn't effect speed then it was all right to sell Dozen Roses to the Ostermeyers. If I thought he wouldn't have got the race at York without help, then it wasn't all right.

Saxony Franklin needed the Ostermeyers' money.

The worst result would be that, if I banked the money and Dozen Roses never won again and Martha and Harley ever found out I knew the horse had been given cocaine, I could say goodbye to any future Gold Cups or Grand Nationals on Datepalm. They wouldn't forgive the unforgivable.

Dozen Roses had seemed to me to run gamely at York and to battle to the end. I was no longer sure. I wondered now if he'd won all his four races spaced out, as the orthopod would have described it; as high as a kite.

At the best, if I simply kept quiet, banked the money and rode Dozen Roses to a couple of respectable victories, no one would ever know. Or I could inform the Ostermeyers privately, which would upset them.

There would be precious little point in proving to the world that Dozen Roses had been given cocaine (and of course I could do it by calling for a further analysis of the urine sample taken by the officials at York) because if cocaine weren't a specifically banned substance, neither was it a normal nutrient. Nothing that was not a normal nutrient was supposed to be given to thoroughbreds racing in Britain.

If I disclosed the cocaine, would Dozen Roses be disqualified for his win at York? If he were, would Nicholas Loder lose his licence to train?

If I caused so much trouble, I would be finished in racing. Whistleblowers were regularly fired from their jobs.

My advice to myself seemed to be, take the money, keep quiet, hope for the best.

Coward, I thought. Maybe stupid as well.

My thoughts made me sweat.

CHAPTER 19

June, her hands full of pretty pink beads from the stockroom said, 'What do we do about more rhodocrosite? We're running out and the suppliers in Hong Kong aren't reliable any more. I was reading in a trade magazine that a man in Germany has some of good quality. What do you think?'

'What would Greville have done?' I asked.

Annette said regretfully, 'He'd have gone to Germany to see. He'd never start buying from a new source without knowing who he was trading with.'

I said to June, 'Make an appointment, say who we are, and book an air ticket.'

They both simultaneously said, 'But ...' and stopped.

I said mildly, 'You never know whether a horse is going to be a winner until you race it. June's going down to the starting gate.'

June blushed and went away. Annette shook her head doubtfully.

'I wouldn't know rhodocrosite from granite,' I said. 'June does. She knows its price, knows what sells. I'll trust that knowledge until she proves me wrong.'

'She's too young to make decisions,' Annette objected.

'Decisions are easier when you're young.'

Isn't that the truth, I thought wryly, rehearing my own words. At June's age I'd been full of certainties. At June's age, what would I have done about cocaine-positive urine tests? I didn't know. Impossible to go back.

I said I would be off for the day and would see them all in the morning. Dilemmas could be shelved, I thought. The evening was Clarissa's.

Brad, I saw, down in the yard, had been reading the *Racing Post* which had the same photograph as the *Daily Sensation*. He pointed to the picture when I eased in beside him, and I nodded.

'That's your head,' he said.

'Mm.'

'Bloody hell,' he said.

I smiled. 'It seems a long time ago.'

He drove to Greville's house and came in with me while I went upstairs and put the baster tube into an envelope and then into a jiffy bag brought from the office for the purpose and addressed it to Phil Urquhart.

To Brad, downstairs again, I said. 'The Euro-Securo couriers' main office is in Oxford Street not very far from the Selfridge Hotel. This is the actual address ...' I gave it to him. 'Do you think you can find it?'

'Yerss.' He was again affronted.

'I phoned them from the office. They're expecting this. You don't need to pay, they're sending the bill. Just get a receipt. OK?'

'Yerss.'

'Then pick up my friend from the Selfridge Hotel and bring her here. She'll phone for you, so leave it switched on.'

'Yerss.'

'Then go on home, if you like.'

He gave me a glowering look but all he said was, 'Same time tomorrow?'

'If you're not bored.'

He gave me a totally unexpected grin. Unnerving, almost, to see that gloom-ridden face break up.

'Best time o' my life,' he said, and departed, leaving me literally gasping.

In bemusement, I went along to the little sitting room and tidied up a bit more of the mess. If Brad enjoyed waiting for hours reading improbable magazines it was all right by me, but I no longer felt in imminent danger of assault or death, and I could drive my car myself if I cared to, and Brad's days as bodyguard/chauffeur were numbered. He must realise it, I thought: he'd clung on to the job several times.

259

By that Wednesday evening there was a rapid improvement also in the ankle. Bones, as I understood it, always grew new soft tissue at the site of a fracture, as if to stick the pieces together with glue. After eight or nine days, the soft tissue began to harden, the bone getting progressively stronger from then on, and it was in that phase that I'd by then arrived. I laid one of the crutches aside in the sitting room and used the other like a walking stick, and put my left toe down to the carpet for balance if not to bear my full weight.

Distalgesic, I decided, was a thing of the past. I'd drink wine for dinner with Clarissa.

The front door bell rang, which surprised me. It was too early to be Clarissa: Brad couldn't have done the errand and got to the Selfridge and back in the time he'd been gone.

I hopped along to the door and looked through the peep-hole and was astounded to see Nicholas Loder on the doorstep. Behind him, on the path, stood his friend Rollo Rollway, looking boredly around at the small garden.

In some dismay I opened the door and Nicholas Loder immediately said, 'Oh, good. You're in. We happened to be dining in London so as we'd time to spare I thought we'd come round on the off-chance to discuss Gemstones, rather than negotiate on the telephone.'

'But I haven't named a price,' I said.

'Never mind. We can discuss that. Can we come in?'

I shifted backwards reluctantly.

'Well, yes,' I said, looking at my watch. 'But not for long. I have another appointment pretty soon.'

'So have we,' he assured me. He turned round and waved a beckoning arm to his friend. 'Come on, Rollo, he has time to see us.'

Rollway, looking as if the enterprise were not to his liking, came up the steps and into the house. I turned to lead the way along the passage, ostentatiously not closing the front door behind them as a big hint to them not to stay long.

'The room's in a mess,' I warned them over my shoulder, 'we had a burglar.'

'We?' Nicholas Loder said.

'Greville and I.'

'Oh.'

He said 'Oh' again when he saw the chrysanthemum pot wedged in the television, but Rollway blinked around in an uninterested fashion as if he saw houses in chaos every day of the week.

Rollway at close quarters wasn't any more attractive than Rollway at a distance: a dull dark lump of a man, thickset, middle-aged and humourless. One could only explain his friendship with the charismatic Loder, I thought, in terms of trainer-owner relationship.

'This is Thomas Rollway,' Nicholas Loder said to me, making belated introductions. 'One of my owners. He's very interested in buying Gemstones.'

Rollway didn't look very interested in anything.

'I'd offer you a drink,' I said, 'but the burglar broke all the bottles.'

Nicholas Loder looked vaguely at the chunks of glass on the carpet. There had been no diamonds in the bottles. Waste of booze.

'Perhaps we could sit down,' he said.

'Sure.'

He sat in Greville's armchair and Rollway perched on the arm of the second armchair which effectively left me the one upright hard one. I sat on the edge of it, wanting them to hurry, laying the second crutch aside.

I looked at Loder, big, light-haired with brownish eyes, full of ability and not angry with me as he had been in the recent past. It was almost with guilt that I thought of the cocaine analyses going on behind his back when his manner towards me was more normal than at any time since Greville's death. If he'd been like that from the beginning, I'd have seen no reason to have had the tests done.'

'Gemstones,' he said, 'what do you want for him?'

I'd seen in the Saxony Franklin ledgers what Gemstones had cost as a yearling, but that had little bearing on his worth two years later. He'd won one race. He was no bright star. I doubled his cost and asked for that.

Nicholas Loder laughed with irony. 'Come on, Derek. Half.'

'Half is what he cost Greville originally,' I said.

His eyes narrowed momentarily and then opened innocently. 'So we've been doing our homework!' He actually smiled. 'I've promised Rollo a reasonable horse at a reasonable price. We all know Gemstones is no world-beater, but there are more races in him. His cost price is perfectly fair. More than fair.'

I thought it quite likely was indeed fair, but Saxony Franklin needed every possible penny.

'Meet me half way,' I said, 'and he's yours.'

Nicholas raised his eyebrows at his friend for a decision. 'Rollo?'

Rollo's attention seemed to be focused more on the crutch I'd earlier propped unused against a wall rather than on the matter in hand.

'Gemstones is worth that,' Nicholas Loder said to him judiciously, and I thought in amusement that he would get me as much as he could in order to earn himself a larger commission. Trade with the enemy, I thought: build mutual-benefit bridges.

'I don't want Gemstones at any price,' Rollo said, and they were the first words he'd uttered since arriving. His voice was harsh and curiously flat, without inflection. Without emotion, I thought.

Nicholas Loder protested. 'But that's why you wanted to some here! It was your idea to come here.'

Thomas Rollway, as if absentmindedly, stood and picked up the abandoned crutch, turning it upside down and holding it by the end normally near the floor. Then, as if the thought had at that second occurred to him, he bent his knees and swung the crutch round forcefully in a scything movement a bare four inches above the carpet.

It was so totally unexpected that I wasn't quick enough to avoid it. The elbow-rest and cuff crashed into my left ankle and Rollway came after it like a bull, kicking, punching, over-balancing me, knocking me down.

I was flabbergasted more than frightened, and then furious. It seemed senseless, without reason, unprovoked, out of any sane proportion. Over Rollway's shoulder I glimpsed Nicholas Loder looking dumbfounded, his mouth and eyes stretched open, uncomprehending.

As I struggled to get up, Thomas Rollway reached inside his jacket and produced a handgun; twelve inches of it at least, with the thickened shape of a silencer on the business end.

'Keep still,' he said to me, pointing the barrel at my chest.

A gun ... Simms ... I began dimly to understand and to despair pretty deeply.

Nicholas Loder was shoving himself out of his armchair. 'What are you doing?' His voice was high with alarm, with rising panic.

'Sit down, Nick,' his friend said. 'Don't get up.' And such was the grindingly heavy tone of his unemotional voice that Nicholas Loder subsided, looking overthrown, not believing what was happening.

'But you came to buy his horse,' he said weakly.

'I came to kill him.'

Rollway said it dispassionately, as if it were nothing. But then, he'd tried to before.

Loder's consternation became as deep as my own.

Rollway moved his gun and pointed it at my ankle. I immediately shifted it, trying desperately to get up, and he brought the spitting end back fast into alignment with my heart.

'Keep still,' he said again. His eyes coldly considered me as I half-sat, half-lay on the floor, propped on my elbow and without any weapon within reach, not even the one crutch I'd been using. Then, with as little warning as for his first attack, he stamped hard on my ankle and for good measure ground away with his heel as if putting out a cigarette butt. After that he left his shoe where it was, pressing down on it with his considerable weight.

I swore at him and couldn't move, and thought idiotically, feeling things give way inside there, that it would take me a lot longer now to get fit, and that took my mind momentarily off a bullet that I would feel a lot less, anyway.

'But *why*?' Nicholas Loder asked, wailing. 'Why are you doing this?'

Good question

Rollway answered it.

'The only successful murders,' he said, 'are those for which there appears to be no motive.'

It sounded like something he'd learned on a course. Something surrealistic. Monstrous.

Nicholas Loder, sitting rigidly to my right in Greville's chair, said with an uneasy attempt at a laugh, 'You're kidding, Rollo,

263

aren't you? This is some sort of joke?'

Rollo was not kidding. Rollo, standing determinedly on my ankle between me and the door, said to me, 'You picked up a piece of my property at York races. When I found it was missing I went back to look for it. An official told me you'd put it in your pocket. I want it back.'

I said nothing.

Damn the official, I thought. So helpful. So deadly. I hadn't even noticed one watching.

Nicholas Loder, bewildered, said, 'What piece of property?'

'The tube part of the nebuliser,' Rollway told him.

'But that woman, Mrs Ostermeyer, gave it back to you.'

'Only the bulb. I didn't notice the tube had dropped as well. Not until after the race. After the Stewards' enquiry.'

'But what does it matter?'

Rollway pointed his gun unwaveringly at where it would do me fatal damage and answered the question without taking his gaze from my face.

'You yourself, Nick,' he informed him, 'told me you were worried about Franklin, he was observant and too bright.'

'But that was because I gelded Dozen Roses.'

'So when I found he had the nebuliser, I asked one or two other people their opinion of Derek Franklin as a person, not a jockey, and they all said the same. Brainy. Intelligent. Bright.' He paused. 'I don't like that.'

I was thinking that through the door, down the passage and in the street there was sanity and Wednesday and rain and rush hour all going on as usual. Saturn was just as accessible.

'I don't believe in waiting for trouble,' Rollway said. 'And dead men can't make accusations.' He stared at me. 'Where's the tube?'

I didn't answer for various reasons. If he took murder so easily in his stride and I told him I'd sent the tube to Phil Urquhart I could be sentencing Phil to death too, and besides, if I opened my mouth for any reason, what might come out wasn't words at all but something between a yell and a groan, a noise I could hear loudly in my head but which wasn't important either, or not as important as getting out of the sickening prospect of the next few minutes.

'But he would never have suspected ...' Loder feebly said.

'Of course he did. Anyone would. Why do you think he's had that bodyguard glued to him? Why do you think he's been dodging about so I can't find him and not going home? And he had the horse's urine taken in Lambourn for testing, and there's the official sample too at York. I tell you, I'm not waiting for him to make trouble. I'm not going to jail, I'll tell you.'

'But you wouldn't.'

'Be your age, Nick,' Rollway said caustically, 'I import the stuff. I take the risks. And I get rid of trouble as soon as I see it. If you wait too long, trouble can destroy you.'

Nicholas Loder said in a wailing protest, 'I told you it wasn't necessary to give it to horses. It doesn't make them go faster.'

'Rubbish. You can't tell, because it isn't much done. No one can afford it except people like me. I'm swamped with the stuff at the moment, it's coming in in bulk from the Medellín cartel in Madrid ... *Where's the tube?*' he finished, bouncing his weight up and down.

If not telling him would keep me alive a bit longer, I wasn't going to try telling him I'd thrown it away.

'You can't just shoot him,' Nicholas Loder said despairingly. 'Not with me watching.'

'You're no danger to me, Nick,' Rollway said flatly. 'Where would you go for your little habit? One squeak from you would mean your own ruin. I'd see you went down for possession. For conniving with me to drug horses. They'd take your licence away for that. Nicholas Loder, trainer of Classic winners, down in the gutter.' He paused. 'You'll keep quiet, we both know it.'

The threats were none the lighter for being uttered in a measured unexcited monotone. He made my hair bristle. Heaven knew what effect he had on Loder.

He wouldn't wait much longer, I thought, for me to tell him where the tube was: and maybe the tube would in the end be his downfall because Phil knew whose it was, and that the Ostermeyers had been witnesses, and if I were found shot perhaps he would light a long fuse ... but it wasn't of much comfort at that moment.

With the strength of desperation I rolled my body and with my right foot kicked hard at Rollway's leg. He grunted and took his weight off my ankle and I pulled away from him, shuffling backwards, trying to reach the chair I'd been sitting on to use it

265

as a weapon against him, or at least not to lie there supinely waiting to be slaughtered, and I saw him recover his rocked balance and begin to straighten his arm, aiming and looking along the barrel so as not to miss.

That unmistakable stance was going to be the last thing I would see: and the last emotion I would feel would be the blazing fury of dying for so pointless a cause.

Nicholas Loder, also seeing that it was the moment of irretrievable crisis, sprang with horror from the armchair and shouted urgently, 'No, no, Rollo. No, don't do it!'

It might have been the droning of a gnat for all the notice Rollo paid him.

Nicholas Loder took a few paces forward and grabbed at Rollway and at his aiming arm.

I took the last opportunity to get my hands on something ... anything ... got my fingers on a crutch.

'I won't let you,' Nicholas Loder frantically persisted. 'You mustn't!'

Rollo shook him off and swung his gun back to me.

'No.' Loder was terribly disturbed. Shocked. Almost frenzied.

'It's wrong. I won't let you.' He put his body against Rollway's, trying to push him away.

Rollway shrugged him off, all bull-muscle and undeterrable. Then, very fast, he pointed the gun straight at Nicholas Loder's chest and without pausing pulled the trigger. Pulled it twice.

I heard the rapid phut, phut. Saw Nicholas Loder fall, saw the blankness on his face, the absolute astonishment.

There was no time to waste on terror, though I felt it. I gripped the crutch I'd reached and swung the heavier end of it at Rollway's right hand, and landed a blow fierce enough to make him drop the gun.

It fell out of my reach.

I stretched for it and rolled and scrambled but he was upright and much faster, and he bent down and took it into his hand again with a tight look of fury as hot as my own.

He began to lift his arm again in my direction and again I whipped at him with the crutch and again hit him. He didn't drop the gun that time but transferred it to his left hand and shook out the fingers of his right hand as if they hurt, which I hoped to God they did.

I slashed at his legs. Another hit. He retreated a couple of paces and with his left hand began to take aim. I slashed at him. The gun barrel wavered. When he pulled the trigger, the flame spat out and the bullet missed me.

He was still between me and the door.

Ankle or not, I thought, once I was on my feet I'd smash him down and out of the way and run, run ... run into the street ...

I had to get up. Got as far as my knees. Stood up on my right foot. Put down the left. It wasn't a matter of pain. I didn't feel it. It just buckled. It needed the crutch's help ... and I needed the crutch to fight against his gun, to hop and shuffle forward and hack at him, to put off the inevitable moment, to fight until I was dead.

A figure appeared abruptly in the doorway, seen peripherally in my vision.

Clarissa.

I'd forgotten she was coming.

'Run,' I shouted agonisedly. 'Run. Get away.'

It startled Rollway. I'd made so little noise. He seemed to think the instructions were for himself. He sneered. I kept my eyes on his gun and lunged at it, making his aim swing wide again at a crucial second. He pulled the trigger. Flame. Phut. The bullet zipped over my shoulder and hit the wall.

'Run,' I yelled again with fearful urgency. 'Quick. Oh, be quick.'

Why didn't she run? He'd see her if he turned.

He would kill her.

Clarissa didn't run. She brought her hand out of her raincoat pocket holding a thing like a black cigar and she swung her arm in a powerful arc like an avenging fury. Out of the black tube sprang the fearsome telescopic silvery springs with a knob on the end, and the kiyoga smashed against the side of Rollway's skull.

He fell without a sound. Fell forward, cannoning into me, knocking me backwards. I ended on the floor, sitting, his inert form stomach-down over my shins.

Clarissa came down on her knees beside me, trembling violently, very close to passing out. I was breathless, shattered, trembling like her. It seemed ages before either of us was able to speak. When she could, it was a whisper, low and distressed.

'Derek ...'

'Thanks,' I said jerkily, 'for saving my life.'

'Is he dead?' She was looking with fear at Rollway's head, strain in her eyes, in her neck, in her voice.

'I don't care if he is,' I said truthfully.

'But I ... I hit him.'

'I'll say I did it. Don't worry. I'll say I hit him with the crutch.'

She said waveringly, 'You can't.'

'Of course I can. I meant to, if I could.'

I glanced over at Nicholas Loder, and Clarissa seemed to see him for the first time. He was on his back unmoving.

'Dear God,' she said faintly, her face even paler. 'Who's that?'

I introduced her posthumously to Nicholas Loder, racehorse trainer, and then to Thomas Rollway, drug baron. They'd squirted cocaine into Dozen Roses, I said, struggling for lightness. I'd found them out. Rollway wanted me dead rather than giving evidence against him. He'd said so.

Neither of the men contested the charges, though Rollway at least was alive, I thought. I could feel his breathing on my legs. A pity, on the whole. I told Clarissa which made her feel a shade happier.

Clarissa still held the kiyoga. I touched her hand, brushing my fingers over hers, grateful beyond expression for her courage. Greville had given her the kiyoga. He couldn't have known it would keep me alive. I took it gently out of her grasp and let it lie on the carpet.

'Phone my car,' I said. 'If Brad hasn't gone too far, he'll come back.'

'But ...'

'He'll take you safely back to the Selfridge. Phone quickly.'

'I can't just ... leave you.'

'How would you explain being here, to the police?'

She looked at me in dismay and obstinacy. 'I can't ...'

'You must,' I said. 'What do you think Greville would want?'

'Oh ...' It was a long sigh of grief, both for my brother and, I thought, for the evening together that she and I were not now going to have.

'Do you remember the number?' I said.

'Derek ...'

'Go and do it, my dear love.'

She got blindly to her feet and went over to the telephone. I told her the number, which she'd forgotten. When the impersonal voice of the radio-phone operator said as usual after six or seven rings that there was no reply, I asked her to dial the number again, and yet again. With luck, Brad would reckon three calls spelled emergency.

'When we got here,' Clarissa said, sounding stronger, 'Brad told me there was a grey Volvo parked not far from your gate. He was worried, I think. He asked me to tell you. Is it important?'

God in heaven ...

'Will that phone stretch over here?' I said. See if it will. Push the table over. Pull the phone over here. If I ring the police from here, and they find me here, they'll take the scene for granted.'

She tipped the table on its side, letting the answering machine fall to the floor, and pulled the phone to the end of its cord. I still couldn't quite reach it, and edged round a little in order to do so, and it hurt, which she saw.

'Derek!'

'Never mind.' I smiled at her, twistedly, making a joke of it. 'It's better than death.'

'I can't leave you.' Her eyes were still strained and she was still visibly trembling, but her composure was on the way back.

'You damned well can,' I said. 'You have to. Go out to the gate. If Brad comes, get him to toot the horn, then I'll know you're away and I'll phone the police. If he doesn't come ... give him five minutes, then walk ... walk and get a taxi ... Promise?'

I picked up the kiyoga and fumbled with it, trying to concertina it shut. She took it out of my hands, twisted it, banged the knob on the carpet and expertly returned it closed to her pocket.

'I'll think of you, and thank you,' I said, 'every day that I live.'

'At four-twenty,' she said as if automatically, and then paused and looked at me searchingly. 'It was the time I met

269

Greville.'

'Four-twenty,' I said, and nodded. 'Every day.'

She knelt down again beside me and kissed me, but it wasn't passion. More like farewell.

'Go on,' I said. 'Time to go.'

She rose reluctantly and went to the doorway, pausing there and looking back. Lady Knightwood, I thought, a valiant deliverer with not a hair out of place.

'Phone me,' I said, 'one day soon?'

'Yes.'

She went quietly down the passage but wasn't gone long. Brad himself came bursting into the room with Clarissa behind him like a shadow.

Brad almost skidded to a halt, the prospect before him enough to shock even the garrulous to silence.

'Strewth,' he said economically.

'As you say,' I replied.

Rollway had dropped his gun when he fell but it still lay not far from his left hand. I asked Brad to move it further away in case the drug man woke up.

'Don't touch it,' I said sharply as he automatically reached out a hand, bending down. 'Your prints would be an embarrassment.'

He made a small grunt of acknowledgment and Clarissa wordlessly held out a tissue with which Brad gingerly took hold of the silencer and slid the gun across the room to the window.

'What if he does wake up?' he said, pointing to Rollway.

'I give him another clout with the crutch.'

He nodded as if that were normal behaviour.

'Thanks for coming back,' I said.

'Didn't go far. You've got a Volvo ...'

I nodded.

'Is it the one?'

'Sure to be,' I said.

'Strewth.'

'Take my friend back to the Selfridge,' I said. 'Forget she was here. Forget you were here. Go home.'

'Can't leave you,' he said. 'I'll come back.'

'The police will be here.'

As ever, the thought of policemen made him uneasy.

'Go on home,' I said. 'The dangers are over.'

He considered it. Then he said hopefully, 'Same time tomorrow?'

I moved my head in amused assent and said wryly, 'Why not?'

He seemed satisfied in a profound way, and he and Clarissa went over to the doorway, pausing there and looking back, as she had before. I gave them a brief wave, and they waved back before going. They were both, incredibly, smiling.

'Brad!' I yelled after him.

He came back fast, full of instant alarm.

'Everything's fine,' I said. 'Just fine. But don't shut the front door behind you. I don't want to have to get up to let the police in. I don't want them smashing the locks. I want them to walk in here nice and easy.'

CHAPTER 20

It was a long dreary evening, but not without humour.

I sat quietly apart most of the time in Greville's chair, largely ignored while relays of people came and efficiently measured, photographed, took fingerprints and dug bullets out of walls.

There had been a barrage of preliminary questions in my direction which had ended with Rollway groaning his way back to consciousness. Although the police didn't like advice from a civilian, they did, at my mild suggestion, handcuff him before he was fully awake, which was just as well, as the bullish violence was the first part of his personality to surface. He was on his feet, threshing about, mumbling, before he knew where he was.

While a policeman on each side of him held his arms, he stared at me, his eyes slowly focusing. I was still at that time on the floor, thankful to have his weight off me. He looked as if he couldn't believe what was happening, and in the same flat uninflected voice as before, called me a bastard, among other things not as innocuous.

'I knew you were trouble,' he said. He was still too groggy to keep a rein on his tongue. 'You won't live to give evidence, I'll see to that.'

The police phlegmatically arrested him formally, told him his rights and said he would get medical attention at the police station. I watched him stumble away, thinking of the irony of the decision I'd made earlier not to accuse him of anything at all, much less, as now, of shooting people. I hadn't known he'd shot Simms. I hadn't feared him at all. It didn't seem to have occurred to him that I might not act against him on the matter of cocaine. He'd been ready to kill to prevent it. Yet I hadn't suspected him even of being a large-scale dealer until he'd boasted of it.

While the investigating activity went on around me, I wondered if it were because drug runners cared so little for the lives of others that they came so easily to murder.

Like Vaccaro, I thought, gunning down his renegade pilots from a moving car. Perhaps that was an habitual mode of clean-up among drug kings. Copycat murder, everyone had thought about Simms, and everyone had been right.

People like Rollway and Vaccaro held other peoples' lives cheap because they aimed anyway at destroying them. They made addicition and corruption their business, wilfully intended to profit from the collapse and unhappiness of countless lives, deliberately enticed young people onto a one-way misery trail. I'd read that people could snort cocaine for two or three years before the physical damage hit.The drug growers, shippers, wholesalers knew that. It gave them time for steady selling. Their greed had filthy feet.

The underlying immorality, the aggressive callousness had themselves to be corrupting; addictive. Rollway had self destructed, like his victims.

I wondered how people grew to be like him. I might condemn them, but I didn't understand them. They weren't happy-go-lucky dishonest, like Pross. They were uncaring and cold. As Elliot Trelawney had said, the logic of criminals tended to be weird. If I ever added to Greville's notebook, I thought, it would be something like 'The ways of the crooked are mysterious to the straight', or even 'What makes the crooked crooked and the straight straight?' One couldn't trust the sociologists' easy answers.

I remembered an old story I'd heard sometime. A scorpion asked a horse for a ride across a raging torrent. Why not? said the horse, and obligingly started to swim with the scorpion on his back. Half way across, the scorpion stung the horse. The horse, fatally poisoned, said, 'We will both drown now. Why did you do that?' And the scorpion said, 'Because it's my nature.'

273

Nicholas Loder wasn't going to worry or wonder about anything any more; and his morality, under stress, had risen up unblemished and caused his death. Injustice and irony everywhere, I thought, and felt regret for the man who couldn't acquiesce in my murder.

He had taken cocaine himself, that much was clear. He'd become perhaps dependent on Rollway, had perhaps been more or less blackmailed by him into allowing his horses to be tampered with. He'd been frightened I would find him out: but in the end he hadn't been evil, and Rollway had seen it, had seen he couldn't trust him to keep his mouth shut after all.

Through Loder, Rollway had known where to find me on Sunday afternoon, and through him he'd known where to find me this Wednesday evening. Yet Nicholas Loder hadn't knowingly set me up. He'd been used by his supposed friend; and I hadn't seen any danger in reporting on Sunday morning that I'd be lunching with Milo and the Ostermeyers or saying I would be in Greville's house ready for Gemstones bids.

I hadn't specifically been keeping myself safe from Rollway, whatever he might believe, but from an unidentified enemy, someone *there* and dangerous, but unrecognised.

Irony everywhere ...

I thought about Martha and Harley and the cocaine in Dozen Roses. I would ask them to keep the horse and race him, and I'd promise that if he never did any good I would give them their money back and send him to auction. What the Jockey Club and racing press would have to say about the whole mess boggled the mind. We might still lose the York race: would have to, I guessed.

I thought of Clarissa in the Selfridge Hotel struggling to behave normally with a mind filled with visions of violence. I hoped she would ring up her Henry, reach back to solid ground, mourn Greville peacefully, be glad she'd saved his brother. I would leave the Wizard's alarm set for four-twenty pm, and remember them both when I heard it: and one could say it was sentimental, that their whole affair had been packed with sentimental behaviour, but who cared, they'd enjoyed it, and I would endorse it.

At some point in the evening's proceedings, a highly senior plain-clothes policeman arrived whom everyone else deferred to and called sir.

He introduced himself as Superintendent Ingold and invited a detailed statement from me, which a minion wrote down. The superintendent was short, piercing, businesslike, and considered what I said with pauses before his next question, as if internally computing my answers. He was also, usefully, a man who like racing: who sorrowed over Nicholas Loder and knew of my existence.

I told him pretty plainly most of what had happened, omitting only a few things: the precise way Rollway had asked for his tube, and Clarissa's presence, and the dire desperation of the minutes before she'd arrived. I made that hopeless fight a lot shorter, a lot easier, a rapid knock-out.

'The crutches?' he enquired. 'What are they for?'

'A spot of trouble with an ankle at Cheltenham.'

'When was that?'

'Nearly two weeks ago.'

He merely nodded. The crutch handles were quite heavy enough for clobbering villains, and he sought no other explanation.

It all took a fair while, with the pauses and the writing. I told him about the car crash near Hungerford. I said I thought it possible that it had been Rollway who shot Simms. I said that of course they would compare the bullets the Hungerford police had taken from the Daimler with those just now dug out of Greville's walls, and those no doubt to be retrieved from Nicholas Loder's silent form. I wondered innocently what sort of car Rollway drove. The Hungerford police, I told the superintendent, were looking for a grey Volvo.

After a pause a policeman was despatched to search the street. He came back wide-eyed with his news and was told to put a cordon round the car and keep the public off.

It was by then well past dark. Every time the police or officials came into the house, the mechanical dog started barking and the lights repeatedly blazed on. I thought it amusing which says something for my lightheaded state of mind but it wore the police nerves to irritation.

'The switches are beside the front door,' I said to one of them eventually. 'Why don't you flip them all up?'

They did, and got peace.

275

'Who threw the flower-pot into the television?' the superintendent wanted to know.

'Burglars. Last Saturday. Two of your men came round.'

'Are you ill?' he said abruptly.

'No. Shaken.'

He nodded. Anyone would be, I thought.

One of the policemen mentioned Rollway's threat that I wouldn't live to give evidence. To be taken seriously perhaps.

Ingold looked at me speculatively. 'Does it worry you?'

'I'll try to be careful.'

He smiled faintly. 'Like on a horse?' The smile disappeared. 'You could do worse than hire someone to mind your back for a while.'

I nodded my thanks. Brad, I thought dryly, would be ecstatic.

They took poor Nicholas Loder away. I would emphasize his bravery, I thought, and save what could be saved of his reputation. He had given me, after all, a chance of life.

Eventually the police wanted to seal the sitting room, although the superintendent said it was a precaution only: the events of the evening seemed crystal clear.

He handed me the crutches and asked where I would be going.

'Upstairs to bed,' I said.

'Here?' He was surprised. 'In this house?'

'This house,' I said, 'is a fortress. Until one lowers the drawbridge, that is.'

They sealed the sitting room, let themselves out, and left me alone in the newly quiet hallway.

I sat on the stairs and felt awful. Cold. Shivery. Old and grey. What I needed was a hot drink to get warm from inside, and there was no way I was going down to the kitchen. Hot water from the bathroom tap upstairs would do fine, I thought.

As happened in many sorts of battle, it wasn't the moment of injury that was worst, but the time a couple of hours later when the body's immediate natural anaesthetic properties subsided and let pain take over: nature's marvellous system for allowing a wild animal to flee to safety before hiding to lick its wounds with healing saliva. The human animal was no different. One needed the time to escape, and one needed the pain afterwards to say something was wrong.

At the moment of maximum adrenalin, fight-or-flight, I'd believed I could run on that ankle. It had been mechanics that had defeated me, not instinct, not willingness. Two hours later, the idea of even standing on it was impossible. Movement alone became breathtaking. I'd sat in Greville's chair for another two long hours after that, concentrating on policemen, blanking out feeling.

With them gone, there was no more pretending. However much I might protest in my mind, however much rage I might feel, I knew the damage to bones and ligaments was about as bad as before. Rollway had cracked them apart again. Back to square one ... and the Hennessy only four and a half weeks away ... and I was bloody well going to ride Datepalm in it, and I wasn't going to tell anyone about tonight's little stamping-ground, no one knew except Rollway and he wouldn't boast about that.

If I stayed away from Lambourn for two weeks, Milo wouldn't find out; not that he would care all that much.If he didn't know, though, he couldn't mention it to anyone else. No one expected me to be racing again for another four weeks. If I simply stayed in London for two of those and ran Greville's business, no one would comment. Then once I could walk I'd go down to Lambourn and ride every day ... get physiotherapy, borrow the Electrovet ... it could be done ... piece of cake.

Meanwhile there were the stairs.

Up in Greville's bathroom, in a zipped bag with my washing things, I would find the envelope the orthopaedic surgeon had given me, which I'd tucked into a waterproof pocket and travelled around with ever since. In the envelope, three small white tablets not as big as aspirins, more or less with my initials on: DF 1-1-8s. Only as a last resort, the orthopod had said.

Wednesday evening, I reckoned, qualified.

I went up the stairs slowly, backwards, sitting down, hooking the crutches up with me. If I dropped them, I thought, they would slither down to the bottom again. I wouldn't drop them.

It was pretty fair hell. I reminded myself astringently that people had been known to crawl down mountains with much worse broken bones: they wouldn't have made a fuss over one little flight upwards. Anyway, there had to be an end to everything, and eventually I sat on the top step, with the crutches beside me, and thought that the DF 1-1-8s weren't going to fly along magically to my tongue. I had still got to get them.

I shut my eyes and put both hands round my ankle on top of the bandage. I could feel the heat and it was swelling again already, and there was a pulse hammering somewhere.

Damn it, I thought. God bloody damn it. I was used to this sort of pain, but it never made it any better. I hope Rollway's head was banging like crazy.

I made it to the bathroom, ran the hot water, opened the door of the capacious medicine cabinet, pulled out and unzipped my bag.

One tablet, no pain, I thought. Two tablets, spaced out. Three tablets, unconscious.

Three tablets had definte attractions but I feared I might wake in the morning needing them again and wishing I'd been wiser. I swallowed one with a glassful of hot water and waited for miracles.

The miracle that actually happened was extraordinary but had nothing to do with the pills.

I stared at my grey face in the looking glass over the basin. Improvement, I thought after a while, was a long time coming. Perhaps the damned things didn't work.

Be patient.

Take another ...

No. Be patient.

I looked vaguely at the objects in the medicine cupboard. Talc. Deodorant. Shaving cream. Shaving cream. Most of one can of shaving cream had been squirted all over the mirror by Jason. A pale blue and grey can: 'Unscented', it said.

Greville had an electric razor as well, I thought inconsequentially. It was on the dressing chest. I'd borrowed it that morning. Quicker than a wet shave, though not so long lasting.

The damn pill wasn't working.

I looked at the second one longingly.

Wait a bit.

Think about something else.

I picked up the second can of shaving cream which was scarlet and orange and said: 'Regular Fragrance'. I shook the can and took off the cover and tried to squirt foam onto the mirror.

Nothing happened. I shook it. Tried again. Nothing at all.

Guile and misdirection, I thought. Hollow books and green stone boxes with keyholes but no keys. Safes in concrete, secret drawers in desks ... Take nothing at face value. Greville's mind was a maze ... *and he wouldn't have used scented shaving cream*.

I twisted the shaving cream can this way and that and the bottom ring moved and began to turn in my hand. I caught my breath. Didn't really believe it. I went on turning ... unscrewing.

It would be another empty hiding place, I told myself. Get a grip on hope. I unscrewed the whole bottom off the can, and from a nest of cottonwool a chamois leather pouch fell out into my hand.

Well, all right, I thought, but it wouldn't be diamonds.

With the help of the crutches I took the pouch into the bedroom and sat on Greville's bed, and poured onto the counterpane a little stream of dullish-looking pea-sized lumps of carbon.

I almost stopped breathing. Time stood still. I couldn't believe it. Not after everything ...

With shaking fingers I counted them, setting them in small clumps of five.

Ten ... fifteen ... twenty ... twenty-five.

Twenty-five meant I'd got fifty per cent. Half of what Greville had bought. With half, Saxony Franklin would be safe. I offered heartbursting thanks to the fates. I came dangerously near to crying.

Then, with a sense of revelation, I knew where the rest were. Where they had to be. Greville really had taken them with him to Ipswich, as he'd told Pross. I guessed he'd taken them thinking he might give them to the Maarten-Pagnier partner to take back to Antwerp for cutting.

I'd searched through the things in his car and had found nothing, and I'd held his diamonds in my hand and not known it.

They were ... they had to be ... in that other scarlet and orange can, in the apparent can of shaving cream in his overnight bag, safe as Fort Knox now under the stairs of Brad's mum's house in Hungerford. She'd taken all Greville's things in off the street out of my car to keep them safe in a dodgy neighbourhood. In memory, I could hear Brad's pride in her.

'Smart, our Mum ...'

The DF 1-1-8 was at last taking the edge off the worst.

I rolled the twenty-five precious pebbles around under my fingers with indescribable joy and thought how relieved Greville would have been. Sleep easy, pal, I told him, uncontrollably smiling. I've finally found them.

He'd left me his business, his desk, his gadgets, his enemies, his horses, his mistress. Left me Saxony Franklin, the Wizard, the shaving cream cans, Prospero Jenks and Nicholas Loder, Dozen Roses, Clarissa.

I'd inherited his life and lain him to rest; and at that moment, though I might hurt and I might throb, I didn't think I had ever been happier.

Banker

My sincere thanks for the
generous help of

JEREMY H. THOMPSON MD FRCPI
Professor of Pharmacology
University of California
Los Angeles

and of
MICHAEL MELLUISH
and
JOHN COOPER

CONTENTS

The First Year

MAY

Gordon Michaels stood in the fountain with all his clothes on.

'My God,' Alec said.'What is he doing?'

'Who?'

'Your boss,' Alec said. 'Standing in the fountain.'

I crossed to the window and stared downwards: down two floors to the ornamental fountain in the forecourt of the Paul Ekaterin merchant bank. Down to where three entwining plumes of water rose gracefully into the air and fell in a glittering circular curtain. To where, in the bowl, calf-deep, stood Gordon in his navy pin-striped suit ... in his white shirt and sober silk tie ... in his charcoal socks and black shoes ... in his gold cufflinks and onyx ring ... in his polished City persona ... soaking wet.

It was his immobility, I thought, which principally alarmed. Impossible to interpret this profoundly uncharacteristic behaviour as in any way an expression of lightheartedness, of celebration or of joy.

I whisked straight out of the deep-carpeted office, through the fire doors, down the flights of gritty stone staircase and across the marbled expanse of entrance hall. The uniformed man at the security desk was staring towards the wide glass front doors with his fillings showing and two arriving visitors were looking stunned. I went past them at a rush into the open air and slowed only in the last few strides before the fountain.

'Gordon!' I said.

His eyes were open. Beads of water ran down his forehead from his dripping black hair and caught here and there on his lashes. The main fall of water slid in a crystal sheet just behind his shoulders with scatterings of drops spraying forwards onto him like rain. Gordon's eyes looked at me unblinkingly with earnest vagueness as if he were not at all sure who I was.

'Get into the fountain,' he said.

'Er ... why, exactly?'

'They don't like water.'

'Who don't?'

'All those people. Those people with white faces. They don't like water. They won't follow you into the fountain. You'll be all right if you're wet.'

His voice sounded rational enough for me to wonder wildly whether this was not after all a joke: but Gordon's jokes were normally small, civilised, glinting commentaries on the stupidities of mankind, not whooping, gusty, practical affairs smacking of the surreal.

'Come out of there, Gordon,' I said uneasily.

'No, no. They're waiting for me. Send for the police. Ring them up. Tell them to come and take them all away.'

'But *who*, Gordon?'

'All those people, of course. Those people with white faces.'

His head slowly turned from side to side, his eyes focussed as if at a throng closely surrounding the whole fountain. Instinctively I too looked from side to side, but all I could see were the more distant stone and glass walls of Ekaterin's, with, now, a growing chorus of heads appearing disbelievingly at the windows.

I clung still to a hope of normality. 'They work here,' I said. Those people work here.'

'No, no. They came with me. In the car. Only two or three of them, I thought. But all the others, they were here, you know. They want me to go with them, but they can't reach me here, they don't like the water.'

He had spoken fairly loudly throughout so that I should hear him above the noise of the fountain, and the last of these remarks reached the chairman of the bank who came striding briskly across from the building.

'Now, Gordon, my dear chap,' the chairman said authoritatively, coming to a purposeful halt at my side, 'what's all this about, for God's sake?'

'He's having hallucination,' I said.

The chairman's gaze flicked to my face, and back to Gordon and Gordon seriously advised him to get into the fountain because the people with white faces couldn't reach him there, on account of disliking water.

'Do something, Tim,' the chairman said, so I stepped into the fountain and took Gordon's arm.

'Come on,' I said. 'If we're wet they won't touch us. We don't have to stay in the water. Being wet is enough.'

'Is it?' Gordon said. 'Did they tell you?'

'Yes, they did. They won't touch anyone who's wet.'

'Oh. All right. If you're sure.'

'Yes, I'm sure.'

He nodded understandingly and with only slight pressure from my arm took two sensible-seeming paces through the water and stepped over the knee-high coping onto the paving slabs of the forecourt. I held onto him firmly and hoped to heaven that the people with white faces would keep their distance; and although Gordon looked around apprehensively it appeared that they were not so far trying to abduct him.

The chairman's expression of concern was deep and genuine, as he and Gordon were firm and long-time friends. Except in appearance they were much alike; essentially clever, intuitive, and with creative imaginations. Each in normal circumstances had a manner of speaking which expressed even the toughest commands in gentle politeness and both had a visible appetite for their occupation. They were both in their fifties, both at the top of their powers, both comfortably rich.

Gordon dripped onto the paving stones.

'I think,' the chairman said, casting a glance at the inhabited windows, 'that we should go indoors. Into the boardroom, perhaps. Come along, Gordon.'

He took Gordon Michaels by his other sodden sleeve, and between us one of the steadiest banking brains in London walked obediently in its disturbing fog.

'The people with white faces,' I said as we steered a calm course across the marble entrance hall between clearly human open-mouthed watchers, 'are they coming with us?'

'Of course,' Gordon said.

It was obvious also that some of them came up in the lift with us. Gordon watched them dubiously all the time. The others, as we gathered from his reluctance to step out into the top-floor hallway, were waiting for our arrival.

'It's all right,' I said to Gordon encouragingly. 'Don't forget, we're still wet.'

'Henry isn't,' he said, anxiously eyeing the chairman.

'We're all together,' I said. 'It will be all right.'

Gordon looked doubtful, but finally allowed himself to be drawn from the lift between his supporters. The white faces apparently parted before us, to let us through.

The chairman's personal assistant came hurrying along the corridor but the chairman waved him conclusively to a stop and said not to let anyone disturb us in the boardroom until he rang the bell; and Gordon and I in our wet shoes sloshed across the deep-piled green carpet to the long glossy mahogany board-room table. Gordon consented to sit in one of the comfortable leather arm-chairs which surrounded it with me and the chairman alongside, and this time it was the chairman who asked if the people with white faces were still there.

'Of course,' Gordon said, looking around. 'They're sitting in all the chairs round the table. And standing behind them. Dozens of them. Surely you can see them?'

'What are they wearing?' the chairman asked.

Gordon looked at him in puzzlement, but answered simply enough. 'White suits of course. With black buttons. Down the front, three big black buttons.'

'All of them?' the chairman asked. 'All the same?'

'Oh yes, of course.'

'Clowns,' I exclaimed.

'What?'

'White-faced clowns.'

'Oh no,' Gordon said. 'They're not clowns. They're not funny.'

'White-faced clowns are sad.'

Gordon looked troubled and wary, and kept a good eye on his visitations.

'What's best to do?' wondered the chairman; but he was talking principally to himself. To me directly, after a pause, he

288

said, 'I think we should take him home. He's clearly not violent, and I see no benefit in calling in a doctor here, whom we don't know. I'll ring Judith and warn her, poor girl. I'll drive him in my car as I'm perhaps the only one who knows exactly where he lives. And I'd appreciate it, Tim, if you'd come along, sit with Gordon on the back seat, keep him reassured.'

'Certainly,' I agreed 'And incidentally his own car's here. He said that when he drove in he thought there were two or three of the white faces with him. The rest were waiting here.'

'Did he?' The chairman pondered. 'He can't have been hallucinating when he actually left home. Surely Judith would have noticed.'

'But he seemed all right in the office when he came in,' I said. 'Quiet, but, all right. He sat at his desk for nearly an hour before he went out and stood in the fountain.

'Didn't you talk with him?'

'He doesn't like people to talk when he's thinking.'

The chairman nodded. 'First thing, then,' he said, 'see if you can find a blanket. Ask Peter to find one. And ... er ... how wet are you, yourself?'

'Not soaked, except for my legs. No problem, honestly. It's not cold.'

He nodded, and I went on the errand. Peter, the assistant, produced a red blanket with Fire written across one corner for no good reason that I could think of, and with this wrapped snugly round his by now naked chest Gordon allowed himself to be conveyed discreetly to the chairman's car. The chairman himself slid behind his wheel and with the direct effectiveness which shaped his whole life drove his still half-damp passengers southwards through the fair May morning.

Henry Shipton, chairman of Paul Ekaterin Ltd, was physically a big-framed man whose natural bulk was kept short of obesity by raw carrots, mineral water and will power. Half visionary, half gambler, he habitually subjected every soaring idea to rigorous analytic test: a man whose powerful instinctive urges were everywhere harnessed and put to work.

I admired him. One had to. During his twenty-year stint (including ten as chairman) Paul Ekaterin Ltd had grown from a moderately successful banking house into one of the senior league, accepted world-wide with respect. I could measure

289

almost exactly the spread of public recognition of the bank's name, since it was mine also: Timothy Ekaterin, great-grandson of Paul the founder. In my schooldays people always said 'Timothy *who*? E-*kat*-erin? How do you spell it?' Quite often now they simply nodded — and expected me to have the fortune to match, which I hadn't.

'They're very peaceful, you know,' Gordon said after a while.

'They white faces?' I asked.

He nodded. 'They don't say anything. They're just waiting.'

'Here in the car?'

He looked at me uncertainly. 'They come and go.'

At least they weren't pink elephants, I thought irreverently: but Gordon, like the chairman, was abstemious beyond doubt. He looked pathetic in his red blanket, the sharp mind confused with dreams, the well-groomed businessman a pre-fountain memory, the patina stripped away. This was the warrior who dealt confidently every day in millions, this huddled mass of delusions going home in wet trousers. The dignity of man was everywhere tissue-paper thin.

He lived, it transpired, in leafy splendour by Clapham Common, in a late Victorian family pile surrounded by head-high garden walls. There were high cream-painted wooden gates which were shut, and which I opened, and a short gravelled driveway between tidy lawns.

Judith Michaels erupted from her opening front door to meet the chairman's car as it rolled to a stop, and the first thing she said, aiming it variously between Henry Shipton and myself, was 'I'll throttle that bloody doctor.'

After that she said, 'How is he?' and after that, in compassion, 'Come along, love, it's all right, come along in, darling, we'll get you warm and tucked into bed in no time.'

She put sheltering arms round the red blanket as her child of a husband stumbled out of the car, and to me and to Henry Shipton she said again in fury 'I'll kill him. He ought to be struck off.'

'They're very bad these days about house calls,' the chairman said doubtfully, 'But surely ... he's coming?'

'No, he's not. Now you lambs go into the kitchen — there's some coffee in the pot — and I'll be down in a sec. Come on Gordon, my dear love, up those stairs ...' She helped him through the front door, across a Persian-rugged hall and towards a panelled wood staircase, with me and the chairman following and doing as we were told.

Judith Michaels, somewhere in the later thirties, was a brown-haired woman in whom the life-force flowed strongly and with whom I could easily have fallen in love. I'd met her several times before that morning (at the bank's various social gatherings) and had been conscious freshly each time of the warmth and glamour which were as normal to her as breathing. Whether I in return held the slightest attraction for her I didn't know and hadn't tried to find out, as entangling oneself emotionally with one's boss's wife was hardly best for one's prospects. All the same I felt the same old tug, and wouldn't have minded taking Gordon's place on the staircase.

With these thoughts, I hoped, decently hidden, I went with Henry Shipton into the friendly kitchen and drank the offered coffee.

'A great girl, Judith,' the chairman said with feeling, and I looked at him in rueful surprise and agreed.

She came to join us after a while, still more annoyed than worried. 'Gordon says there are people with white faces sitting all round the room and they won't go away. It's really too bad. It's infuriating. I'm so angry I could *spit*.'

The chairman and I looked bewildered.

'Didn't I tell you?' she said, observing us. 'Oh no, I suppose I didn't. Gordon hates anyone to know about his illness. It isn't very bad, you see. Not bad enough for him to have to stop working, or anything like that.'

'Er ...' said the chairman. 'What illness?'

'Oh, I suppose I'll have to tell you, now this has happened. I could kill that doctor, I really could.' She took a deep breath and said, 'Gordon's got mild Parkinson's disease. His left hand shakes a bit now and then. I don't expect you've noticed. He tries not to let people see.'

We blankly shook our heads.

'Our normal doctor's just retired, and this new man, he's one of those frightfully bumptious people who think they know better than everyone else. So he's taken Gordon off the old pills, which were fine as far as I could see, and put him on some new ones. As of the day before yesterday. So when I rang him

291

just now in an absolute *panic* thinking Gordon had suddenly gone raving mad or something and I'd be spending the rest of my life visiting metal hospitals he says light-heartedly not to worry, this new drug quite often causes hallucinations, and it's just a matter of getting the dosage right. I tell you, if he hadn't been at the other end of a telephone wire, I'd have *strangled* him.'

Both Henry Shipton and I, however, were feeling markedly relieved.

'You mean,' the chairman asked, 'that this will all just ... wear off?'

She nodded. 'That bloody doctor said to stop taking the pills and Gordon would be perfectly normal in thirty-six hours. I *ask* you! And after that he's got to start taking them again, but only half the amount, and to see what happens. And if we were *worried*, he said pityingly, as if we'd no right to be, Gordon could toddle along to the surgery in a couple of days and discuss it with him, though as Gordon would be perfectly all right by tomorrow night we might think there was no need.'

She herself was shaking slightly with what still looked like anger but was more probably a release of tension, because she suddenly sobbed, twice, and said 'Oh God,' and wiped crossly at her eyes.

'I was so frightened, when you told me,' she said, half apologetically. 'And when I rang the surgery I got that damned obstructive receptionist and had to argue for ten minutes before she let me even *talk* to the doctor.'

After a brief sympathetic pause the chairman, going as usual to the heart of things, said, 'Did the doctor say how long it would take to get the dosage right?'

She looked at him with a defeated grimace. 'He said that as Gordon had reacted so strongly to an average dose it might take as much as six weeks to get him thoroughly stabilised. He said each patient was different, but that if we would persevere it would be much the best drug for Gordon in the long run.'

Henry Shipton drove me pensively back to the City.

'I think,' he said, 'that we'll say — in the office — that Gordon felt 'flu' coming on and took some pills which proved hallucinatory. We might say simply that he imagined that he was on holiday, and felt the need for a dip in a pool. Is that agreeable?'

'Sure,' I said mildly.

'Hallucinatory drugs are, after all, exceedingly common these days.'

'Yes.'

'No need, then, Tim, to mention white-faced clowns.'

'No,' I agreed.

'Nor Parkinson's disease, if Gordon doesn't wish it.'

'I'll say nothing,' I assured him.

The chairman grunted and lapsed into silence; and perhaps we both thought the same thoughts along the well-worn lines of drug-induced side effects being more disturbing than the disease.

It wasn't until we were a mile from the bank that Henry Shipton spoke again, and then he said, 'You've been in Gordon's confidence for two years now, haven't you?'

'Nearly three,' I murmured, nodding.

'Can you hold the fort until he returns?'

It would be dishonest to say that the possibility of this offer hadn't been in my mind since approximately ten-fifteen, so I accepted it with less excitement than relief.

There was no rigid hierarchy in Ekaterin's. Few explicit ranks: to be 'in so and so's confidence', as house jargon put it, meant one would normally be on course for more responsibility, but unlike the other various thirty-two-year olds who crowded the building with their hopes and expectations I lived under the severe disadvantage of my name. The whole board of directors, consistently afraid of accusations of nepotism, made me double-earn every step.

'Thank you,' I said neutrally.

He smiled a shade. 'Consult,' he said, 'whenever you need help.'

I nodded. His words weren't meant as disparagement. Everyone consulted, in Ekaterin's, all the time. Communication between people and between departments was an absolute priority in Henry Shipton's book, and it was he who had swept away a host of small-room offices to form opened-up expanses. He himself sat always at one (fairly opulent) desk in a room that contained eight similar, his own flanked on one side by the vice-chairmans and on the other by that of the head of

293

Corporate Finance. Further senior directors from other departments occupied a row of like desks opposite, all of them within easy talking earshot of each other.

As with all merchant banks, the business carried on by Ekaterin's was different and separate from that conducted by the High Street chains of clearing banks. At Ekaterin's one never actually saw any money. There were no tellers, no clerks, no counters, no paying-ins, no withdrawals and hardly any cheque books.

There were three main departments, each with its separate function and each on its own floor of the building. Corporate Finance acted for major clients on mergers, takeovers and the raising of capital. Banking, which was where I worked with Gordon, lent money to enterprise and industry. And Investment Management, the oldest and largest department, aimed at producing the best possible returns from the vast investment funds of charities, companies, pensions, trusts and trade unions.

There were several small sections like Administration, which did everyone's paperwork; like Property, which bought, sold, developed and leased; like Research, which dug around; like Overseas Investments, growing fast, and like Foreign Exchange, where about ten frenetic young wizards bought and sold world currencies by the minute, risking millions on decimal point margins and burning themselves out by forty.

The lives of all the three hundred and fifty people who worked for Ekaterin's were devoted to making money work. To the manufacture, in the main, of business, trade, industry, pensions and jobs. It wasn't a bad thing to be convinced of the worth of what one did, and certainly there was a tough basic harmony in the place which persisted unruffled by the surface tensions and jealousies and territorial defences of everyday office life.

Events had already moved on by the time the chairman and I returned to the hive. The chairman was pounced upon immediately in the entrance hall by a worriedly waiting figure from Corporate Finance, and upstairs in Banking Alec was giggling into his blotter.

Alec, my own age, suffered, professionally speaking, from an uncontrollable bent for frivolity. It brightened up the office no end, but as court jesters seldom made it to the throne his career path was already observably sideways and erratic. The rest of us were probably hopelessly stuffy. Thank God, I often thought, for Alec.

He had a well-shaped face of scattered freckles on cream-pale skin; a high forehead, a mat of tight tow-coloured curls. Stiff blond eyelashes blinked over alert blue eyes behind gold-framed spectacles, and his mouth twitched easily as he saw the funny side. He was liked on sight by almost everybody, and it was only gradually that one came to wonder whether the examiner who had awarded him a First in law at Oxford had been suffering from critical blindness.

'What's up?' I said, instinctively smiling to match the giggles.

'We've been leaked.' He lifted his head but tapped the paper which lay on his desk. 'My *dear*,' he said with mischievous pleasure, 'this came an hour ago and it seems we're leaking all over the place like a punctured bladder. Like a baby. Like the *Welsh*.'

Leeking like the Welsh ... ah well.

He lifted up the paper, and all, or at least a great deal, was explained. There had recently appeared a slim bi-monthly publication called *What's Going On Where It Shouldn't*, which had fast caught the attention of most of the country and was reportedly read avidly by the police. Descendant of the flood of investigative journalism spawned by the tidal wave of Water-gate, *What's Going On* ... was said to be positively bombarded by informers telling *precisely* what was going on, and all the investigating the paper had to do was into the truth of the information: which task it had been known to perform less than thoroughly.

'What does it say?' I asked; as who wouldn't.

'Cutting out the larky innuendo,' he said, 'it says that someone at Ekaterin's has been selling inside information.'

Selling ...'

'Quite so.'

'About a takeover?'

'How did you guess?'

I thought of the man from Corporate Finance hopping from leg to leg with impatience while he waited for the chairman to return and knew that nothing but extreme urgency would have brought him down to the doorstep.

'Let's see,' I said, and took the paper from Alec.'

The piece headed merely 'Tut tut' was only four paragraphs long, and the first three of those were taken up with explaining with seductive authority that in merchant banks it was possible for the managers of investment funds to learn at an early stage about a takeover being organised by their colleagues. It was strictly illegal, however, for an investment manager to act on this private knowledge, even though by doing so he might make a fortune for his clients.

The shares of a company about to be taken over were likely to rise in value.If one could buy them at a low price before even a rumour of takeover started, the gain could be huge.

Such unprofessional behaviour by a merchant bank would be instantly recognised simply *because of* the profits made, and no investment manager would invite personal disaster in that way.

However, [asked the article] *What's Going On in the merchant bank of Paul Ekaterin Ltd? Three times in the past year takovers managed by this prestigious firm have been* 'scooped' *by vigorous buying beforehand of the shares concerned. The buying itself cannot be traced to Ekaterin's investment managers, but we are informed that the information did come from within Ekaterin's, and that someone there has been selling the golden news, either for staight cash or a slice of the action.*

'It's a guess,' I said flatly, giving Alec back the paper. 'There are absolutely no facts.'

'A bucket of cold water,' he complained, 'is a sunny day compared to you.'

'Do you *want* it to be true?' I asked curiously.

'Livens the place up a bit.'

And there, I thought, was the difference between Alec and me. For me the place was alive all the time, even though when I'd first gone there eight years earlier it had been unwillingly; a matter of being forced into it by my uncle. My mother had been bankrupt at that point, her flat stripped to the walls by the bailiffs of everything except a telephone (property of the Post Office) and a bed. My mother's bankrupcy, as both my uncle

296

and I well knew, was without doubt her own fault, but it didn't stop him applying his blackmailing pressure.

'I'll clear her debts and arrange an allowance for her if you come and work in the bank.'

'But I don't want to.'

'I know that. And I know you're stupid enough to try to support her yourself. But if you do that she'll ruin you like she ruined your father. Just give the bank a chance, and if you hate it after three months I'll let you go.'

So I'd gone with mulish rebellion to tread the path of my great-grandfather, my grandfather and my uncle, and within three months you'd have had to prise me loose with a crowbar. I suppose it was in my blood. All the snooty teenage scorn I'd felt for 'money-grubbing', all the supercilious disapproval of my student days, all the negative attitudes bequeathed by my failure of a father, all had melted into comprehension, interest and finally delight. The art of money-management now held me as addicted as any junkie, and my working life was as fulfilling as any mortal could expect.

'Who do you think did it?' Alec said.

'If anyone did.'

'It must have happened,' he said positively. 'Three times in the last year ... that's more than a coincidence.'

'And I'll bet that that coincidence is all the paper's working on. They're dangling a line. Baiting a hook. They don't even say which takeovers they mean, let alone give figures.'

True or not, though, the story itself was bad for the bank. Clients would back away fast if they couldn't trust, and *What's Going On* ... was right often enough to instil disquiet. Henry Shipton spent most of the afternoon in the boardroom conducting an emergency meeting of the directors, with ripples of unease spreading outwards from there through all departments. By going home time that evening practically everyone in the building had read the bombshell, and although some took it as lightheartedly as Alec it had the effect of almost totally deflecting speculation from Gordon Michaels.

I explained only twice about 'flu' and pills: only two people asked. When the very reputation of the bank was being rocked, who cared about a dip in the ornamental fountain, even if the bather had had all his clothes on and was a director in Banking.

On the following day I found that filling Gordon's job was no lighthearted matter. Until then he had gradually given me power of decision over loans up to certain amounts, but anything larger was in his own domain entirely. Within my bracket, it meant that I could arrange any loan if I believed the client was sound and could repay principal and interest at an orderly rate: but if I judged wrong and the client went bust, the lenders lost both their money and their belief in my common sense. As the lenders were quite often the bank itself, I couldn't afford for it to happen too often.

With Gordon there, the ceiling of my possible disasters had at least been limited. For him, though, the ceiling hardly existed, except that with loans incurring millions it was normal for him to consult with others on the board.

These consultations, already easy and informal because of the open-plan lay-out, also tended to stretch over lunch, which the directors mostly ate together in their own private dining room. It was Gordon's habit to look with a pleased expression at his watch at five to one and take himself amiably off in the direction of a tomato juice and roast lamb; and he would return an hour later with his mind clarified and made up.

I'd been lent Gordon's job but not his seat on the board, so I was without the benefit of the lunches; and as he himself had been the most senior in our own green pasture of office expanse, there was no one else of his stature immediately at hand. Alec's advice tended to swing between the brilliantly perceptive and the maniacally reckless, but one was never quite sure which was which at the time. All high-risk Cinderellas would have gone to the ball under Alec's wand: the trick was in choosing only those who would keep an eye on the clock and deliver the crystal goods.

Gordon tended therefore to allocate only cast-iron certainties to Alec's care and most of the Cinderella-type to me, and he'd said once with a smile that in this job one's nerve either toughened or broke, which I'd thought faintly extravagant at the time. I understood, though, what he meant when I faced without him a task which lay untouched on his desk: a request for financial backing for a series of animated cartoon films.

It was too easy to turn things down ... and perhaps miss Peanuts or Mickey Mouse. A large slice of the bank's profits came from the interest paid by borrowers. If we didn't lend, we didn't earn. A toss-up. I picked up the telephone and invited the hopeful cartoonist to bring his proposals to the bank.

Most of Gordon's projects were half-way through, his biggest at the moment being three point four million for an extension to a cake factory. I had heard him working on this for a week, so I merely took on where he had left off, telephoning people who sometimes had funds to lend and asking if they'd be interested in underwriting a chunk of Home-made Heaven. The bank itself, according to Gordon's list, was lending three hundred thousand only, which made me wonder whether he privately expected the populace to go back to eating bread.

There was also, tucked discreetly in a folder, a glossy-prospectus invitation to participate in a multi-million project in Brazil, whereon Gordon had doodled in pencil an army of question marks and a couple of queries? Do *we or don't we? Remember Brasilia! Is coffee enough??* On the top of the front page, written in red, was a jump-to-it memo: *Preliminary answer by Friday.*

It was already Thursday. I picked up the prospectus and went along to the other and larger office at the end of the passage, where Gordon's almost-equal sat at one of the seven desks. Along there the carpet was still lush and the furniture still befitting the sums dealt with on its tops, but the view from the windows was different. No fountain, but the sunlit dome of St Paul's Cathedral rising like a Fabergé egg from the white stone lattice of the City.

'Problem?' asked Gordon's almost-equal. 'Can I help?'

'Do you know if Gordon meant to go any further with this?' I asked. 'Did he say?'

Gordon's colleague looked the prospectus over and shook his head. 'Who's along there with you today?'

'Only Alec. I asked him. He doesn't know.'

'Where's John?'

'On holiday. And Rupert is away because of his wife.'

The colleague nodded. Rupert's wife was imminently dying: cruel at twenty-six.

'I'd take it around,' he said. 'See if Gordon's put out feelers in Research Overseas, anywhere. Form a view yourself. Then if you think it's worth pursuing you can take it to Val and Henry.'

299

Val was head of Banking and Henry was Henry Shipton. I saw that to be Gordon was a big step up indeed, and was unsure whether to be glad or sorry that the elevation would be temporary.

I spent all afternoon drifting round with the prospectus and in the process learned less about Brazil than about the tizzy over the report in *What's Going On* ... Soul-searching appeared to be fashionable. Long faces enquired anxiously, 'Could one possibly ... without knowing ... have mentioned a takeover to an interested party?' And the short answer to that, it seemed to me, was No, one couldn't. Secrecy was everywhere second nature to bankers.

If the article in the paper were true there had to be three people involved; the seller, the buyer and the informant; and certainly neither the buyer nor the informant could have acted in ignorance or by chance. Greed and malice moved like worms in the dark. If one were infested by them, one knew.

Gordon seemed to have asked no one about Brazil, and for me it was make-up-you-mind time. It would have been helpful to know what the other merchant banks thought, the sixteen British accepting houses like Schroders, Hambro's, Morgan Grenfell, Kleinwort Benson, Hill Samuel, Warburg's, Robert Fleming, Singer and Friedlander ... all permitted, like Paul Ekaterin's, to assume that the Bank of England would come to their aid in a crisis.

Gordon's opposite numbers in those banks would all be pursing mouths over the same prospectus, committing millions to a fruitful enterprise, pouring millions down the drain, deciding not to risk it either way.

Which?

One could hardly directly ask, and finding out via the grapevine took a little time.

I carried the prospectus finally to Val Fisher, head of Banking, who usually sat at one of the desks facing Henry Shipton, two floors up.

'Well, Tim, what's your own view?' he said. A short man, very smooth, very charming, with nerves like toughened ice.

'Gordon had reservations, obviously,' I said. 'I don't know enough, and no one else here seems to. I suppose we could either make a preliminary answer of cautious interest and then find out a bit more, or just trust to Gordon's instinct.'

He smiled faintly. 'Which?'

Ah, which?

'Trust to Gordon's instinct, I think,' I said.

'Right.'

He nodded and I went away and wrote a polite letter to the Brazil people expressing regret. And I wouldn't know for six or seven years, probably, whether that decision was right or wrong.

The gambles were all long term. You cast your bread on the waters and hoped it would float back in the future with butter and jam.

Mildew ... too bad.

The First Year

JUNE

Gordon telephoned three weeks later sounding thoroughly fit and well. I glanced across to where his desk stood mute and tidy, with all the paper action now transferred to my own.

'Judith and I wanted to thank you ...' he was saying.

'Really no need,' I said. 'How are you?'

'Wasting time. It's ridiculous. Anyway, we've been offered a half-share in a box at Ascot next Thursday. We thought it might be fun ... We've six places. Would you like to come? As our guest, of course. As a thank-you.'

'I'd love it,' I said. 'But ...'

'No buts,' he interrupted. 'If you'd like to, Henry will fix it. He's coming himself. He agreed you'd earned a day off, so all you have to do is decide.'

'Then I'd like to, very much.'

'Good. If you haven't a morning coat, don't worry. We're not in the Royal Enclosure.'

'If you're wearing one ... I inherited my father's.'

'Ah. Good. Yes, then. One o'clock Thursday, for lunch. I'll send the entrance tickets to you in the office. Both Judith and I are very pleased you can come. We're very grateful. Very.' He sounded suddenly half-embarrassed, and disconnected with a click.

I wondered how much he remembered about the white faces, but with Alec and Rupert and John all in earshot it had been impossible to ask. Maybe at the races he would tell me. Maybe not.

Going racing wasn't something I did very often nowadays, although as a child I'd spent countless afternoons waiting around the Tote queues while my mother in pleasurable agony backed her dozens of hunches and bankers and third strings and savers and lost money by the ton.

'I've won!' she would announce radiantly to all about her, waving an indisputably winning ticket: and the bunch of losses on the same race would be thrust into a pocket and later thrown away.

My father at the same time would be standing drinks in the bar, an amiable open-fisted lush with more good nature than sense. They would take me home at the end of the day giggling happily together in a hired chauffeur-driven Rolls, and until I was quite old I never questioned but that this contented affluence was built on rock.

I had been their only child and they'd given me a very good childhood to the extent that when I thought of holidays it was of yachts on warm seas or Christmas in the Alps. The villain of those days was my uncle who descended on us occasionally to utter Dire Warnings about the need for his brother (my father) to find a job.

My father however couldn't shape up to 'money-grubbing' and in any case had no real ability in any direction; and with no habit of working he had quietly scorned people who had. He never tired of his life of aimless ease, and if he earned no one's respect, few detested him either. A weak, friendly, unintelligent man. Not bad as a father. Not good at much else.

He dropped dead of a heart attack when I was nineteen and it was then that the point of the Dire Warnings became apparent. He and mother had lived on the capital inherited from grandfather, and there wasn't a great deal left. Enough just to see me through college; enough, with care, to bring mother a small income for life.

Not enough to finance her manner of betting, which she wouldn't or couldn't give up. A lot more of the Dire Warnings went unheeded, and finally, while I was trying to stem a hopeless tide by working (of all things) for a bookmaker, the bailiffs knocked on the door.

In twenty-five years, it seemed, my mother had gambled away the best part of half a million pounds; all gone on horses, fast and slow. It might well have sickened me altogether against racing, but in a curious way it hadn't. I remembered how much she and father had enjoyed themselves: and who was to say that it was a fortune ill spent?

'Good news?' Alec said, eyeing my no doubt ambivalent expression.

'Gordon's feeling better.'

'Hm,' he said judiciously, 'So he should be. Three weeks off for 'flu' ...' He grinned. 'Stretching it a bit.'

I made a non-committal grunt.

'Be glad, shall we, when he comes back?'

I glanced at his amused, quizzical face and saw that he knew as well as I did that when Gordon reappeared to repossess his kingdom, I wouldn't be glad at all. Doing Gordon's job, after the first breath-shortening initial plunge, had injected me with great feelings of vigour and good health; had found me running up stairs and singing in the bath and showing all the symptoms of a love affair; and like many a love affair it couldn't survive the return of the husband. I wondered how long I'd have to wait for such a chance again, and whether next time I'd feel as high.

'Don't think I haven't noticed,' Alec said, the eyes electric blue behind the gold-rimmed specs.

'Noticed what?' Rupert asked, raising his head above papers he'd been staring blindly at for ninety minutes.

Back from his pretty wife's death and burial poor Rupert still wore a glazed otherwhere look and tended too late to catch up with passing conversations. In the two days since his return he had written no letters, made no telephone call, reached no decisions. Out of compassion one had had to give him time, and Alec and I continued to do his work surreptitiously without him realising.

'Nothing,' I said.

Rupert nodded vaguely and looked down again, an automaton in his living grief. I'd never loved anyone, I thought, as painfully as that. I think I hoped that I never would.

John, freshly returned also, but from his holidays, glowed with a still-red sunburn and had difficulty in fitting the full lurid details of his sexual adventures into Rupert's brief absences to the washroom. Neither Alec nor I ever believed John's sagas, but at least Alec found them funny, which I didn't. There was an element lurking there of a hatred of women, as if every boasted possession (real or not) was a statement of spite. He didn't actually use the word possession. He said 'made' and 'screwed' and 'had it off with the little cow'. I didn't like him much and he thought me a prig: we were polite in the office and never went together to lunch. And it was he alone of all of us who actively looked forward to Gordon's return, he who couldn't disguise his dismay that it was I who was filling the empty shoes instead of himself.

'Of course, if I'd been here ...' he said at least once a day; and Alec reported that John had been heard telling Gordon's almost-equal along the passage, that now he, John, was back, Gordon's work should be transferred from me to him.

'Did you hear him?' I asked, surprised.

'Sure. And he was told in no uncertain terms that it was the Old Man himself who gave you the green light, and there was nothing John could do about it. Proper miffed was our Lothario. Says it's all because you are who you are, and all that.'

'Sod him.'

'Rather you than me.' He laughed gently into his blotter and picked up the telephone to find backers for a sewage and water purification plant in Norfolk.

'Did you know,' he said conversationally, busy dialling a number, 'that there are so few sewage farms in West Berlin that they pay the East Berliners to get rid of the extra?'

'No, I didn't.' I didn't especially want to know, either, but as usual Alec was full of useless information and possessed by the urge to pass it on.

'The East Berliners take the money and dump the stuff out in the open fields. Untreated, mind you.'

'Do shut up,' I said.

'I saw it,' he said. 'And smelled it. Absolutely disgusting.'

'It was probably fertilizer,' I said, 'and what were you doing in East Berlin?'

'Calling on Nefertiti.'

'She of the one eye?'

'My God, yes, isn't it a shock? Oh ... hello ...' He got through to his prospective money-source and for far too long and with a certain relish explained the need for extra facilities to reverse

305

the swamp of effluent which had been killing off the Broads. 'No risk involved, of course, with a water authority.' He listened. 'I'll put you in, then, shall I? Right.' He scribbled busily and in due course disconnected. 'Dead easy, this one. Ecology and all that. Good emotional stuff.'

I shuffled together a bunch of papers of my own that were very far from dead easy and went up to see Val Fisher, who happened to be almost alone in the big office. Henry Shipton, it seemed, was out on one of his frequent walkabouts through the other departments.

'It's a cartoonist,' I said. 'Can I consult?'

'Pull up a chair.' Vall nodded and waved hospitably, and I sat beside him, spread out the papers, and explained about the wholly level-headed artist I had spent three hours with two weeks earlier.

'He's been turned down by his own local bank, and so far by three other firms like ourselves.' I said. 'He's got no realisable assets, no security. He rents a flat and is buying a car on HP. If we financed him, it would be out of faith.'

'Background?' he asked. 'Covenant?'

'Pretty solid. Son of a Sales Manager. Respected at art school as an original talent: I talked to the Principal. His bank manager gave him a clean bill but said that his head office wouldn't grant what he's asking. For the past two years he's worked for a studio making animated commercials.They say he's good at the job; understands it thoroughly. They know he wants to go it alone, they think he's capable and they don't want to lose him.'

'How old?'

'Twenty-four.'

Val gave me an 'Oh ho ho' look, knowing, as I did, that it was the cartoonist's age above all which had invited negative responses from the other banks.

'What's he asking?' Val said, but he too looked as if he were already deciding against.

'A studio, properly equipped. Funds to employ ten copying artists, with the expectation that it will be a year before any films are completed and can expect to make money. Funds for promotion. Funds for himself to live on. These sheets set out the probable figures.'

Val made a face over the pages, momentarily re-arranging the small neat features, slanting the tidy dark moustache, raising the arched eyebrows towards the black cap of hair.

'Why haven't you already turned him down?' he asked finally.'

'Um,' I said. 'Look at his drawings.' I opened another file and spread out the riotously coloured progression of pages which established two characters and told a funny story. I watched Val's sophisticated world-weary face as he leafed through them: saw the awakening interest, heard the laugh.

'Exactly,' I said.

'Hmph.' He leaned back in his chair and gave me an assessing stare. 'You're not saying you think we should take him on?'

'It's an unsecured risk, of course. But yes, I am. With a string or two, of course, like a cost accountant to keep tabs on things and a first option to finance future expansion.'

'Hm.' He pondered for several minutes, looking again at the drawings which still seemed funny to me even after a fortnight's close acquaintance. 'Well, I don't know. It's too like aiming at the moon with a bow and arrow.'

'They might watch those films one day on space shuttles,' I said mildly, and he gave me a fast amused glance while he squared up the drawings and returned them to their folder.

'Leave these all here, then, will you?' he said. 'I'll have a word with Henry over lunch.' And I guessed in a swift uncomfortable moment of insight that what they would discuss would be not primarily the cartoonist but the reliabilty or otherwise of my judgement. If they thought me a fool I'd be back behind John in the promotion queue in no time.

At four-thirty, however, when my inter-office telephone rang, it was Val at the other end.

'Come up and collect your papers,' he said. 'Henry says this decision is to be yours alone. So sink or swim, Tim, it's up to you.'

One's first exposure to the Royal Ascot meeting was, according to one's basic outlook, either a matter of surprised delight or of puritanical disapproval. Either the spirits lifted to the sight of emerald grass, massed flowers, bright dresses, fluffy hats and men elegant in grey formality, or one despised the expenditure, the frivolity, the shame of champagne and strawberries while some in the world starved.

I belonged, without doubt, to the hedonists, both by upbringing and inclination. The Royal meeting at Ascot was, as it happened, the one racing event from which my parents had perennially excluded me, children in any case being barred from the Royal Enclosure for three of the four days, and mother more interested on this occasion in socialising than betting. School, she had said firmly every year, must come first: though on other days it hadn't, necessarily. So it was with an extra sense of pleasure that I walked through the gates in my father's resurrected finery and made my way through the smiling throng to the appointed, high-up box.

'Welcome to the charade,' Gordon said cheerfully, handing me a bubbling glass, and 'Isn't this *fun*?' Judith exclaimed, humming with excitement in yellow silk.

'It's great,' I said, and meant it; and Gordon, looking sunburned and healthy, introduced me to the owner of the box.

'Dissdale, this is Tim Ekaterin. Works in the bank. Tim — Dissdale Smith.'

We shook hands. His was plump and warm, like his body, like his face. 'Delighted,' he said. 'Got a drink? Good. Met my wife? No? Bettina, darling, say hello to Tim.' He put an arm round the thin waist of a girl less than half his age whose clinging white black-dotted dress was cut low and bare at neck and armholes. There was also a wide black hat, beautiful skin and a sweet and practised smile.

'Hello, Tim,' she said. 'So glad you could come.' Her voice, I thought, was like the rest of her: manufactured, processed, not natural top drawer but a long way from gutter.

The box itself was approximately five yards by three, most of the space being filled by a dining table laid with twelve places for lunch. The far end wall was of windows looking out over the green course, with a glass door opening to steps going down to the viewing balcony. The walls of the box were covered as if in a house with pale blue hessian, and a soft blue carpet, pink flowers and pictures lent an air of opulence far greater than the actual expense. Most of the walls of the boxes into which I'd peered on the way along to this one were of builders' universal margarine colour, and I wondered fleetingly whether it was

Dissdale or Bettina who had the prettying mind.

Henry Shipton and his wife were standing in the doorway to the balcony, alternately facing out and in, like a couple of Januses. Henry across the room lifted his glass to me in a gesture of acknowledgement, and Lorna as ever looked as if faults were being found.

Lorna Shipton, tall, over-assured, and dressed that frilly day in repressive tailored grey, was a woman from whom disdain flowed outward like a tide, a woman who seemed not to know that words could wound and saw no reason not to air each ungenerous thought. I had met her about the same number of times as I'd met Judith Michaels and mostly upon the same occasions, and if I smothered love for one it was irritation I had to hide for the other. It was, I suppose, inevitable, that of the two it was Lorna Shipton I was placed next to at lunch.

More guests arrived behind me, Dissdale and Bettina greeting them with whoops and kisses and making the sort of indistinct introductions that one instantly forgets. Dissdale decided there would be less crush if everyone sat down and so took his place at the top of the table with Gordon, his back to the windows, at the foot. When each had arranged their guests around them there were two empty places, one next to Gordon, one up Dissdale's end.

Gordon had Lorna Shipton on his right, with me beside her: the space on his left, then Henry, then Judith. The girl on my right spent most of her time leaning forward to speak to her host Dissdale, so that although I grew to know quite well the blue chiffon back of her shoulder, I never actually learned her name.

Laughter, chatter, the study of race cards, the refilling of glasses: Judith with yellow silk roses on her hat and Lorna telling me that my morning coat looked a size too small.

'It was my father's,' I said.

'Such a stupid man.'

I glanced at her face, but she was merely expressing her thoughts, not positively trying to offend.

'A beautiful day for racing,' I said.

'You should be working. Your Uncle Freddie won't like it, you know. I'm certain that when he bailed you out he made it a condition that you and your mother should both stay away from

309

racecourses. And now look at you. It's really too bad. I'll have to tell him, of course.'

I wondered how Henry put up with it. Wondered, as one does, why he'd married her. He, however, his ear attuned across the table in a husbandly way, said to her pleasantly, 'Freddie knows that Tim is her, my dear. Gordon and I obtained dispensation, so to speak.' He gave me a glimmer of a smile. 'The wrath of God has been averted.'

'Oh.' Lorna Shipton looked disappointed and I noticed Judith trying not to laugh.

Uncle Freddie, ex-vice chairman, now retired, still owned enough of the bank to make his unseen presence felt, and I knew he was in the habit of telephoning Henry two or three times a week to find out what was going on. Out of interest, one gathered, not from desire to meddle; as certainly, once he had set his terms, he never meddled with mother and me.

Dissdale's last guest arrived at that point with an unseen flourish of trumpets, a man making an entrance as if well aware of newsworthiness. Dissdale leapt to his feet to greet him and pumped him warmly by hand.

'Calder, this is great. Calder Jackson, everybody.'

There were yelps of delight from Dissdale's end and polite smiles round Gordon's. 'Calder Jackson,' Dissdale said down the table, 'You know, the miracle-worker. Brings dying horses back to life. You must have seen him on television.'

'Ah yes,' Gordon responded. 'Of course.'

Dissdale beamed and returned to his guest who was lapping up adulation with a show of modesty.

'Who did he say?' Lorna Shipton asked.

'Calder Jackson,' Gordon said.

'Who?'

Gordon shook his head, his ignorance showing. He raised his eyebrows in a question to me, but I fractionally shook my head also. We listened, however, and we learned.

Calder Jackson was a shortish man with a head of hair designed to be noticed. Designed literally, I guessed. He had a lot of dark curls going attractively grey, cut short towards the neck but free and fluffy on top of his head and over his forehead; and he had let his beard grow in a narrow fringe from in front of his ears round the line of his jaw, the hairs of this being also bushy and curly but grey to white. From in front his weathered face was thus circled with curls: from the side he looked as if he were wearing a helmet. Or a coal-scuttle, I thought unflatteringly. Once seen, in any case, never forgotten.

'It's just a gift,' he was saying deprecatingly in a voice that had an edge to it more compelling than loudness: an accent very slightly of the country but of no particular region; a confidence born of acclaim.

The girl sitting next to me was ecstatic. 'How *divine* to meet you. One has heard so *much* ... Do tell us, now do tell us your secret.'

Calder Jackson eyed her blandly, his gaze sliding for a second beyond her to me and then back again. Myself he quite openly discarded as being of no interest, but to the girl he obligingly said, 'There's no secret, my dear. None at all. Just good food, good care and a few age-old herbal remedies. And, of course ... well ... the laying on of hands.'

'But *how*,' asked the girl, 'how do you do that to horses?'

'I just ... touch them.' He smiled disarmingly. 'And then sometimes I feel them quiver, and I know the healing force is going from me into them.'

'Can you do it infallibly?' Henry asked politely, and I noted with interest that he'd let no implication of doubt sound in his voice: Henry whose gullibility could be measured in micrograms, if at all.

Calder Jackson took his seriousness for granted and slowly shook his head. 'If I have the horse in my care for long enough, it usually happens in the end. But not always. No, sadly, not always.'

'How fascinating,' Judith said, and earned another of those kind bland smiles. Charlatan or not, I thought, Calder Jackson had the mix just right: an arresting appearance, a modest demeanour, no promise of success. And for all I knew, he really could do what he said. Healers were an age−old phenomenon, so why not a healer of horses?

'Can you heal people too?' I asked in a mirror−image of Henry's tone. No doubts. Just enquiry.

The curly head turned my way with more civility than interest and he patiently answered the question he must have been asked a thousand times before. Answered in a sequence of

311

words he had perhaps used almost as often. 'Whatever gift it is that I have is especially for horses. I have no feeling that I can heal humans, and I prefer not to try. I ask people not to ask me, because I don't like to disappoint them.'

I nodded my thanks, watched his head turn away and listened to him willingly answering the next question, from Bettina, as if it too had never before been asked. 'No, the healing very seldom happens instantaneously. I need to be near the horse for a while. Sometimes for only a few days. Sometimes for a few weeks. On can never tell.'

Dissdale basked in the success of having hooked his celebrity and told us all that two of Calder's ex-patients were running that very afternoon. 'Isn't that right, Calder?'

The curly head nodded. 'Cretonne, in the first race, she used to break blood vessels, and Molyneaux, in the fifth, he came to me with infected wounds. I feel they are my friends now. I feel I know them.'

'And shall we back them, Calder?' Dissdale asked roguishly. 'Are they going to win?'

The healer smiled forgivingly. 'If they're fast enough, Dissdale.'

Everyone laughed. Gordon refilled his own guests' glasses. Lorna Shipton said apropos of not much that she had occasionally considered becoming a Christian Scientist and Judith wondered what colour the Queen would be wearing. Dissdale's party talked animatedly among themselves, and the door from the corridor tentatively opened.

Any hopes I might have had that Gordon's sixth place was destined for a Bettina-equivalent for my especial benefit were immediately dashed. The lady who appeared and whom Judith greeted with a kiss on the cheek was nearer forty than twenty-five and more solid than lissom. She wore a brownish pink linen suit and a small white straw hat circled with a brownish pink ribbon. The suit, I diagnosed, was an old friend: the hat, new in honour of the occasion.

Judith in her turn introduced the newcomer: Penelope Warner – Pen – a good friend of hers and Gordon's. Pen Warner sat where invited, next to Gordon and made small-talk with Henry and Lorna. I half listened, and took in a few desultory details like no rings on the fingers, no polish on the nails, no grey in the short brown hair, no artifice in the voice. Worthy, I thought. Well-intentioned; slightly boring. Probably runs the church.

A waitress appeared with an excellent lunch, during which Calder could from time to time be heard extolling the virtues of watercress for its iron content and garlic for the treatment of fever and diarrhoea.

'And of course in humans,' he was saying, 'garlic is literally a life saver in whooping-cough. You make a poultice and bind it onto the bottom of the feet of the child every night, in a bandage and a sock, and in the morning you'll smell the garlic on the breath of the child, and the cough will abate. Garlic, in fact, cures almost anything. A truly marvellous life-giving plant.'

I saw Pen Warner lift her head to listen and I thought that I'd been wrong about the church. I had missed the worldliness of the eyes, the long sad knowledge of human frailty. A magistrate, perhaps? Yes, perhaps.

Judith leaned across the table and said teasingly, 'Tim, can't you forget you're a banker even at the races?'

'What?' I said.

'You look at everyone as if you're working out just how much you can lend them without risk.'

'I'd lend you my soul,' I said.

'For me to pay back with interest?'

'Pay in love and kisses.'

Harmless stuff, as frivolous as her hat. Henry, sitting next to her, said in the same vein, 'You're second in the queue, Tim. I've first option, eh, Judith? Count on me, dear girl, for the last drop of blood.'

She patted his hand affectionately and glowed a little from the deep truth of our idle protestations: and Calder Jackson's voice came through with 'Comfrey heals tissues with amazing speed and will cause chronic ulcers to disappear in a matter of days, and of course it mends fractures in half the time considered normal. Comfrey is miraculous.'

There was a good deal of speculation after that all round the table about a horse called Sandcastle that had won the 2,000 Guineas six weeks earlier and was hot favourite for the King Edward VII Stakes, the top Ascot race for three-year-old colts, due to be run that afternoon.

Dissdale had actually seen the Guineas at Newmarket and was enthusiastic. 'Daisy-cutter action. Positively eats up the ground.' He sprayed his opinions good naturedly to the furthest ear. 'Big rangy colt, full of courage.'

'Beaten in the Derby, though,' Henry said, judiciously responding.

'Well, yes,' Dissdale allowed. 'But fourth, you know. Not a total disgrace, would you say?'

'He was good as a two-year-old,' Henry said, nodding.

'Glory, yes,' said Dissdale fervently. 'And you can't fault his breeding. By Castle out of an Ampersand mare. You can't get much better than that.'

Several heads nodded respectfully in ignorance.

'He's my banker,' Dissdale said and then spread his arms wide and half laughed. 'OK, we've got a roomful of bankers. But Sandcastle is where I'm putting my money today. Doubling him with my bets in every other race. Trebles. Accumulators. The lot. You all listen to your Uncle Dissdale. Sandcastle is the soundest banker at Ascot.' His voice positively shook with evangelical belief. 'He simply can't be beaten.'

'Betting is out for you, Tim,' Lorna Shipton said severely in my ear.

'I'm not my mother,' I said mildly.

'Heredity' Lorna said darkly. 'And your father drank.'

I smothered a bursting laugh and ate my strawberries in good humour. Whatever I'd inherited from my parents it wasn't an addiction to their more expensive pleasures; rather a firm intention never again to lose my record collection to the bailiffs. The stolid men had taken even the rocking horse on which at the age of six I'd ridden my fantasy Grand Nationals. They'd taken my books, my skis and my camera. Mother had fluttered around in tears saying those things were mine, not hers, and they should leave them, and the men had gone on marching out with all our stuff as if they were deaf. About her own disappearing treasures she had been distraught, her distress and grief hopelessly mixed with guilt.

I had been old enough at twenty-four to shrug off our actual losses and more or less replace them (except for the rocking horse) but the fury of that day had affected my whole life since:

and I had been silent when it happened, white and dumb with rage.

Lorna Shipton removed her disapproval from me long enough to tell Henry not to have cream and sugar on his strawberries or she would have no sympathy if he put on weight, had a heart attack, or developed pimples. Henry looked resignedly at the forbidden delights which he wouldn't have eaten anyway. God preserve me, I thought, from marrying a Lorna Shipton.

By the coffee-brandy-cigar stage the tranquil seating pattern had broken up into people dashing out to back their hopes in the first race and I, not much of a gambler whatever Mrs Shipton might think, had wandered out onto the balcony to watch the Queen's procession of sleek horses, open carriages, gold, glitter and fluttering feathers trotting like a fairy tale up the green course.

'Isn't it *splendid*,' said Judith's voice at my shoulder, and I glanced at the characterful face and met the straight smiling eyes. Damn it to hell, I thought, I'd like to live with Gordon's wife.

'Gordon's gone to bet,' she said, 'so I thought I'd take the opportunity … He's appalled at what happened … and we're really grateful to you, you know, for what you did that dreadful day.'

I shook my head. 'I did nothing, believe me.'

'Well, that's half the point. You *said* nothing. In the bank, I mean. Henry says there hasn't been a whisper.'

'But … I wouldn't.'

'A lot of people *would*,' she said. 'Suppose you have been that Alec.'

'I smiled involuntarily. 'Alec isn't unkind. He wouldn't have told.'

'Gordon says he's as discreet as a town-crier.'

'Do you want to go down and see the horses?' I asked.

'Yes. It's lovely up here, but too far from life.'

We went down to the paddock, saw the horses walk at close quarters round the ring and watched the jockeys mount ready to ride out onto the course. Judith smelled nice. Stop it, I told myself. Stop it.

'That horse over there,' I said, pointing, 'is the one Calder

315

Jackson said he cured. Cretonne. The jockey in bright pink.'

'Are you going to back it?' she asked.

'If you like.'

She nodded the yellow silk roses and we queued up in good humour to make the wager. All around us in grey toppers and frothy dresses the Ascot crowd swirled, a feast to the eye in the sunshine, a ritual in make-believe, a suppression of gritty truth. My father's whole life had been a pursuit of the spirit I saw in these Royal Ascot faces; the pursuit and entrapment of happiness.

'What are you thinking,' Judith said, 'so solemnly?'

'That lotus-eaters do no harm. Let terrorists eat lotus.'

'As a steady diet,' she said, 'it would be sickening.'

'On a day like this one could fall in love.'

'Yes, one could.' She was reading her race-card over-intently. 'But should one?'

After a pause I said, 'No, I don't think so.'

'Nor do I.' She looked up with seriousness and understanding and with a smile in her mind. 'I've known you six years.'

'I haven't been faithful,' I said.

She laughed and the moment passed, but the declaration had quite plainly been made and in a way accepted. She showed no awkwardness in my continued presence but rather an increase of warmth, and in mutual contentment we agreed to stay in the paddock for the first short race rather than climb all the way up and find it was over by the time we'd reached the box.

The backs of the jockeys disappeared down the course as they cantered to the start, and I said, as a way of conversation, 'Who is Dissdale Smith?'

'Oh.' She looked amused. 'He's in the motor trade. He loves to make a splash, as no doubt you saw, but I don't think he's doing as well as he pretends. Anyway, he told Gordon he was looking for someone to share the expense of this box here and asked if Gordon would be interested in buying half of the box for today. He's sold halves for the other days as well. I don't think he's supposed to, actually, so better say nothing to anyone else.'

'No.'

'Bettina's his third wife,' she said. 'She's a model.'

'Very pretty.'

'And not as dumb as she looks.'

I heard the dryness in her voice and acknowledged that I had myself sounded condescending.

'Mind you,' Judith said forgivingly, 'his second wife was the most gorgeous thing on earth, but without two thoughts to rub together. Even Dissdale got tired of the total vacancy behind the sensational violet eyes. It's all very well to get a buzz when all men light up on meeting your wife, but it rather kicks the stilts away when the same men diagnose total dimness within five minutes and start pitying you instead.'

'I can see that. What became of her?'

'Dissdale introduced her to a boy who'd inherited millions and had an IQ on a par with hers. The last I heard they were in a fog of bliss.'

From where we stood we couldn't see much of the race, only a head-on view of the horses as they came up to the winning post. In no way did I mind that, and when one of the leaders proved to carry bright pink Judith caught hold of my arm and shook it.

'That's Cretonne, isn't it?' She listened to the announcement of the winner's number. 'Do you realise, Tim, that we've damned well won?' She was laughing with pleasure, her face full of sunshine and wonder.

'Bully for Calder Jackson.'

'You don't trust him,' she said. 'I could see it in all your faces, yours and Henry's and Gordon's. You all have the same way of peering into people's souls: you too, though you're so young. You were all being incredibly polite so that he shouldn't see your reservations.'

I smiled. 'That sounds disgusting.'

'I've been married to Gordon for nine years,' she said.

There was again a sudden moment of stillness in which we looked at each other in wordless question and answer. Then she shook her head slightly, and after a pause I nodded acquiescence: and I thought that with a woman so straightforwardly intelligent I could have been content for ever.

'Do we collect our winnings now or later?' she asked.'

'Now, if we wait awhile.'

Waiting together for the jockeys to weigh-in and the all-clear to be given for the pay-out seemed as little hardship for her as

317

for me. We talked about nothing much and the time passed in a flash; and eventually we made our way back to the box to find that everyone there too had backed Cretonne and was high with the same success. Calder Jackson beamed and looked modest, and Dissdale expansively opened more bottles of excellent Krug, champagne of Kings.

Escorting one's host's wife to the paddock was not merely acceptable but an expected civility, so that it was with a benign eye that Gordon greeted our return. I was both glad and sorry, looking at his unsuspecting friendliness, that he had nothing to worry about. The jewel in his house would stay there and be his alone. Unattached bachelors could lump it.

The whole party, by now markedly carefree, crowded the box's balcony for the big race. Dissdale said he had staked his all on his banker, Sandcastle; and although he said it with a laugh I saw the tremor in his hands which fidgetted with the raceglasses. He's in too deep, I thought. A bad way to bet.

Most of the others, fired by Dissdale's certainty, happily clutched tickets doubling Sandcastle every which-way. Even Lorna Shipton, with a pink glow on each bony cheekbone, confessed to Henry that just for once, as it was a special day, she had staked five pounds in forecasts.

'And you, Tim?' Henry teased. 'Your shirt?'

Lorna looked confused. I smiled. 'Buttons and all,' I said cheerfully.

'No, but ...' Lorna said.

'Yes, but,' I said, 'I've dozens more shirts at home.'

Henry laughed and steered Lorna gently away, and I found myself standing next to Calder Jackson.

'Do you gamble?' I asked, for something to say.

'Only on certainties.' He smiled blandly in the way that scarcely warmed his eyes. 'Though on certainties it's hardly a gamble.'

'And is Sandcastle a certainty?'

He shook his curly head. 'A probability. No racing bet's a certainty. The horse might feel ill. Might be kicked at the start.'

I glanced across at Dissdale who was faintly sweating, and hoped for his sake that the horse would feel well and come sweetly out of the stalls.

'Can you tell if a horse is sick just by looking at him?' I

318

enquired. 'I mean, if you just watched him walk round the parade ring, could you tell?'

Calder answerd in the way that revealed it was again an often-asked question. 'Of course sometimes you can see at once, but mostly a horse as ill as that wouldn't have been brought to the races. I prefer to look at a horse closely. To examine for instance the colour inside the eyelid and inside the nostril. In a sick horse, what should be a healthy pink may be pallid.' He stopped with apparent finality, as if that were the appointed end of that answer, but after a few seconds, during which the whole huge crowd watched Sandcastle stretch out in the sun in the canter to the post, he said almost with awe, 'That's a superb horse. Superb.' It sounded to me like his first spontaneous remark of the day and it vibrated with genuine enthusiasm.

'He looks great,' I agreed.

Calder Jackson smiled as if with indulgence at the shallowness of my judgement compared with the weight of his inside knowledge. 'He should have won the Derby,' he said. 'He got shut in on the rails, couldn't get out in time.'

My place at the great man's side was taken by Bettina, who threaded her arm through his and said, 'Dear Calder, come down to the front, you can see better than here at the back.' She gave me a photogenic little smile and pulled her captive after her down the steps.

In a buzz that rose to a roar the runners covered their mile and a half journey; longer than the 2,000 Guineas, the same length as the Derby. Sandcastle in scarlet and white was making no show at all to universal groans and lay only fifth as the field swept round the last bend, and Dissdale looked as if he might have a heart attack.

Alas for my shirt, I thought. Alas for Lorna's forecasts. Bang goes the banker that can't lose.

Dissdale, unable to watch, collapsed weakly onto one of the small chairs which dotted the balcony, and in the next-door boxes people were standing on top of theirs and jumping up and down and screaming.

'Sandcastle making his move ...' the commentator's voice warbled over the loudspeakers, but the yells of the crowd drowned the rest.

The scarlet and white colours had moved to the outside. The daisy-cutter action was there for the world to see. The superb horse, the big rangy colt full of courage was eating up his ground.

Our box in the grandstand was almost a furlong down the course from the winning post, and when he reached up Sandcastle still had three horses ahead. He was flying, though, like a streak, and I found the sight of this fluid valour, this all-out striving, most immensely moving and exciting. I grabbed Dissdale by his despairing shoulder and hauled him forcefully to his feet.

'Look,' I shouted in his ear. 'Watch. Your banker's going to win. He's a marvel. He's a dream.'

He turned with a gaping mouth to stare in the direction of the winning post and he saw ... he saw Sandcastle among the tumult going like a javelin, free now of all the others, aiming straight for the prize.

'He's won,' Dissdale's mouth said slackly, though amid the noise I could hardly hear him. 'He's bloody won.'

I helped him up the steps into the box. His skin was grey and damp and he was stumbling.

'Sit down,' I said, pulling out the first chair I came to, but he shook his head weakly and made his shaky way to his own place at the head of the table. He almost fell into it, heavily, and stretched out a trembling hand to his champagne.

'My God,' he said, 'I'll never do that again. Never on God's earth.'

'Do what?'

He gave me a flickering glance over his glass and said, 'All on one throw.'

All. He'd said it before. 'All on the banker ...' He surely couldn't, I thought, have meant literally *all*; but yet not much else could have produced such physical symptoms.

Everyone else piled back into the room with ballooning jollity. Everyone without exception had backed Sandcastle, thanks to Dissdale. Even Calder Jackson, when pressed by Bettina, admitted to 'a small something on the Tote. I don't usually, but just this once.' And if he'd lost, I thought, he wouldn't have confessed.

Dissdale, from near fainting, climbed rapidly to pulse-throbbing high, the colour coming back to his plump cheeks in a hectic red. No one seemed to have noticed his near-collapse, certainly not his wife, who flirted prettily with the healer and got less than her due response. More wine easily made its way down every throat, and there was no doubt that for the now commingled party the whole day was a riotous success.

In a while Henry offered to take Judith to the paddock. Gordon to my relief invited Lorna, which left me with the mystery lady, Pen Warner, with whom I'd so far exchanged only the thrilling words 'How do you do.'

'Would you like to go down?' I asked.

'Yes, indeed. But you don't need to stay with me if it's too much bother.'

'Are you so insecure?'

There was a quick widening of the eyes and a visible mental shift. 'You're damned rude,' she said. 'And Judith said you were nice.'

I let her go past me out onto the landing and smiled as she went. 'I should like to stay with you,' I said, 'if it's not too much bother.'

She gave me a dry look, but as we more or less had to walk in single file along the narrow passageway owing to people going in the opposite direction she said little more until we had negotiated the lifts, the escalators and the pedestrian tunnel and had emerged into the daylight of the paddock.

It was her first time at Ascot, she said. Her first time, in fact, at the races.

'What do you think of it?'

'Very beautiful. Very brave. Quite mad.'

'Does sanity lie in ugliness and cowardice?' I asked.

'Life does, pretty often,' she said. 'Haven't you noticed?'

'And some aren't happy unless they're desperate.'

She quietly laughed. 'Tragedy inspires, so they say.'

'They can stick it,' I said. 'I'd rather lie in the sun.'

We stood on the raised tiers of steps to watch the horses walk round the ring, and she told me that she lived along the road from Judith in another house fronting the common. 'I've lived there all my life, long before Judith came. We met casually, as one does, in the local shops, and just walked home together one day several years ago. Been friends ever since.'

'Lucky,' I said.

'Yes.'

'Do you live alone?' I asked conversationally.

Her eyes slid my way with inner amusement. 'Yes, I do. Do you?'

I nodded.

'I prefer it,' she said.

'So do I.'

Her skin was clear and still girlish, the thickened figure alone giving an impression of years passing. That and the look in the eyes, the 'I've seen the lot' sadness.

'Are you a magistrate?' I asked.

She looked startled. 'No, I'm not. What an odd thing to ask.'

I made an apologetic gesture. 'You just look as if you might be.'

She shook her head. 'Wouldn't have time, even if I had the urge.'

'But you do do good in the world.'

She was puzzled. 'What makes you say so?'

'I don't know. The way you look.' I smiled to take away any seriousness and said, 'Which horse do you like? Shall we choose one and bet?'

'What about Burnt Marshmallow?'

She like the name, she said, so we queued briefly at a Tote window and invested some of the winnings from Cretonne and Sandcastle.

During our slow traverse of the paddock crowds on our way back towards the box we came towards Calder Jackson, who was surrounded by respectful listeners and didn't see us.

'Garlic is as good as penicillin,' he was saying. 'If you scatter grated garlic onto a septic wound it will kill all the bacteria ...'

We slowed a little to hear.

' ... and comfrey is miraculous,' Calder said. 'It knits bones and cures intractable skin ulcers in half the time you'd expect.'

'He said all that upstairs,' I said.

Pen Warner nodded, faintly smiling. 'Good sound herbal medicine,' she said. 'You can't fault him. Comfrey contains allantoin, a well-known cell proliferant.'

'Does it? I mean ... do you know about it?'

'Mm.' We walked on, but she said nothing more until we

were high up again in the passageway to the box. 'I don't know whether you'd think I do good in the world ... but basically I dole out pills.'

'Er ...?' I said.

She smiled. 'I'm a lady in a white coat. A pharmacist.'

I suppose I was in a way disappointed, and she sensed it.

'Well,' she sighed, 'we can't all be glamorous. I told you life was ugly and frightening, and from my point of view that's often what it is for my customers. I see fear every day ... and I know its face.'

'Pen,' I said, 'forgive my frivolity. I'm duly chastened.'

We reached the box to find Judith alone there, Henry having loitered to place a bet.

'I told Tim I'm a pharmacist,' Pen said. 'He thinks it's boring.'

I got no further than the first words of protestation when Judith interrupted.

'She's not just "a" pharmacist,' she said. 'She owns her own place. Half the medics in London recommend her. You're talking to a walking gold-mine with a heart like a wet sponge.'

She put her arm round Pen's waist and the two of them together looked at me, their eyes shining with what perhaps looked like liking, but also with the mischievous feminine superiority of being five or six years older.

'Judith!' I said compulsively. 'I ... I ...' I stopped. 'Oh *damn* it.' I said. 'Have some Krug.'

Dissdale's friends returned giggling to disrupt the incautious minute and shortly Gordon, Henry and Lorna crowded in. The whole party pressed out onto the balcony to watch the race, and because it was a time out of reality Burnt Marshmallow romped home by three lengths.

The rest of the afternoon slid fast away. Henry at some point found himself alone out on the balcony beside me while inside the box the table was being spread with a tea that was beyond my stretched stomach entirely and a temptation from which the ever-hungry Henry had bodily removed himself.

'How's your cartoonist?' he said genially. 'Are we staking him, or are we not?'

'You're sure ... I have to decide ... all alone?'

'I said so. Yes.'

'Well ... I got him to bring some more drawings to the bank. And his paints.'

'His *paints*?'

'Yes. I thought if I could see him at work, I'd know ...' I shrugged 'Anyway, I took him into the private interview room and asked him to paint the outline of a cartoon film while I watched; and he did it, there and then, in acrylics. Twenty-five outline sketches in bright colour, all within an hour. Same characters, different story, and terrifically funny. That was on Monday. I've been ... well ... dreaming about those cartoons. It sounds absurd. Maybe they're too much on my mind.'

'But you've decided?'

After a pause I said, 'Yes.'

'And?'

With a sense of burning bridges I said, 'To go ahead.'

'All right.' Henry seemed unalarmed. 'Keep me informed.'

'Yes, of course.'

He nodded and smoothly changed the subject. 'Lorna and I have won quite a bit today. How about you?'

'Enough to give Uncle Freddie fits about the effect on my unstable personality.'

Henry laughed aloud. 'Your Uncle Freddie,' he said, 'knows you better than you may think.'

At the end of that splendid afternoon the whole party descended together to ground level and made its way to the exit; to the gate which opened onto the main road, and across that to the car park and to the covered walk which led to the station.

Calder just ahead of me walked in front, the helmet of curls bent kindly over Bettina, the strong voice thanking her and Dissdale for 'a most enjoyable time.' Dissdale himself, not only fully recovered but incoherent with joy as most of his doubles, trebles and accumulators had come up, patted Calder plumply on the shoulder and invited him over to 'my place' for the weekend.

Henry and Gordon, undoubtedly the most sober of the party, were fiddling in their pockets for car keys and throwing their racecards into wastebins. Judith and Pen were talking to each other and Lorna was graciously unbending to Dissdale's friends. It seemed to be only I, with unoccupied eyes, who saw at all what was about to happen.

We were out on the pavement, still in a group, half-waiting for a chance to cross the road, soon to break up and scatter. All talking, laughing, busy; except me.

A boy stood there on the pavement, watchful and still. I noticed first the fixed, burning intent in the dark eyes, and quickly after that the jeans and faded shirt which contrasted sharply with our Ascot clothes, and then finally with incredulity the knife in his hand.

I had almost to guess at whom he was staring with such deadly purpose, and no time even to shout a warning. He moved across the pavement with stunning speed, the stab already on its upward travel.

I jumped almost without thinking; certainly without assessing the consequences or chances. Most unbankerlike behaviour.

The steel was almost in Calder's stomach when I deflected it. I hit the boy's arm with my body in a sort of flying tackle and in a flashing view saw the weave of Calder's trousers, the polish on his shoes, the litter on the pavement. The boy fell beneath me and I thought in horror that somewhere between our bodies he still held that wicked blade.

He writhed under me, all muscle and fury, and tried to heave me off. He was lying on his back, his face just under mine, his eyes like slits and his teeth showing between drawn-back lips. I had an impression of dark eyebrows and white skin and I could hear the breath hissing between his teeth in a tempest of effort.

Both of his hands were under my chest and I could feel him trying to get space enough to up-end the knife. I pressed down onto him solidly with all my weight and in my mind I was saying 'Don't do it, don't do it, you bloody fool'; and I was saying it *for his sake*, which seemed crazy to me at the time and even crazier in retrospect. He was trying to do me great harm and all I thought about was the trouble he'd be in if he succeeded.

We were both panting but I was taller and stronger and I could have held him there for a good while longer but for the two policemen who had been out on the road directing traffic. They had seen the melee; seen as they supposed a man in morning dress attacking a pedestrian, seen us struggling on the ground. In any case the first I knew of their presence was the

325

feel of vice-like hands fastening onto my arms and pulling me backwards.

I resisted with all my might. I didn't know they were policemen. I had eyes only for the boy: his eyes, his hands, his knife.

With peremptory strength they hauled me off, one of them anchoring my upper arms to my sides by encircling me from behind. I kicked furiously backwards and turned my head, and only then realised that the new assailants wore navy blue.

The boy comprehended the situation in a flash. He rolled over onto his feet, crouched for a split second like an athlete at the blocks and without lifting his head above waist-height slithered through the flow of the crowds still pouring out of the gates and disappeared out of sight inside the racecourse. Through there they would never find him. Through there he would escape to the cheaper rings and simply walk out of the lower gate.

I stopped struggling but the policemen didn't let go. They had no thought of chasing the boy. They were incongruously calling me 'sir' while treating me with contempt, which if I'd been calm enough for reflection I would have considered fairly normal.

'For God's sake,' I said finally to one of them, 'what do you think the knife's doing on the pavement?'

They looked down to where it lay; to where it had fallen when the boy ran. Eight inches of sharp steel kitchen knife with a black handle.

'He was trying to stab Calder Jackson,' I said. 'All I did was stop him. Why do you think he's gone?'

By this time Henry, Gordon, Laura, Judith and Pen were standing round in an anxious circle continually assuring the law that never in a million years would their friend attack anyone except out of direst need, and Calder was looking dazed and fingering a slit in the waistband of his trousers.

The farce slowly resolved itself into duller bureaucratic order. The policemen relinquished their hold and I brushed the dirt off the knees of my father's suit and straightened my tangled tie. Someone picked up my tumbled top hat and gave it to me. I grinned at Judith. It all seemed such a ridiculous mixture of death and bathos.

The aftermath took half of the evening and was boring in the extreme: police station, hard chairs, polystyrene cups of coffee.

No, I'd never seen the boy before.

Yes, I was sure the boy had been aiming at Calder specifically.

Yes, I was sure he was only a boy. About sixteen, probably.

Yes, I would know him again. Yes, I would help with an Identikit picture.

No. My fingerprints were positively not on the knife. The boy had held onto it until he ran.

Yes, of course they could take my prints, in case.

Calder, wholly mystified, repeated over and over that he had no idea who could want to kill him. He seemed scandalised, indeed, at the very idea. The police persisted: most people knew their murderers, they said, particularly when as seemed possible in this case the prospective killer had been purposefully waiting for his victim. According to Mr Ekaterin the boy had known Calder. That was quite possible, Calder said, because of his television appearances, but Calder had *not* known *him*.

Among some of the police there was a muted quality, among others a sort of defiant aggression, but it was only Calder who rather acidly pointed out that if they hadn't done such a good job of hauling me off, they would now have the boy in custody and wouldn't need to be looking for him.

'You could have asked first,' Calder said, but even I shook my head.

If I had indeed been the aggressor I could have killed the boy while the police were asking the onlookers just who was fighting whom. Act first, ask questions after was a policy full of danger, but getting it the wrong way round could be worse.

Eventually we both left the building, Calder on the way out trying his best with unrehearsed words. 'Er ... Tim ... Thanks are in order.... If it hadn't been for you ... I don't know what to say.'

'Say nothing,' I said. 'I did it without thinking. Glad you're OK.'

I had taken it for granted that everyone else would be long gone, but Dissdale and Bettina had waited for Calder, and Gordon, Judith and Pen for me, all of them standing in a group by some cars and talking to three or four strangers.

'We know you and Calder both came by train,' Gordon said,

walking towards us, 'but we decided we'd drive you home.'

'You're extraordinarily kind,' I said.

'My dear Dissdale ...' Calder said, seeming still at a loss for words. 'So grateful, really.'

They made a fuss of him; the endangered one, the lion delivered. The strangers round the cars turned out to be gentlemen of the press, to whom Calder Jackson was always news, alive or dead. To my horror they announced themselves, producing notebooks and a camera, and wrote down everything anyone said, except they got nothing from me because all I wanted to do was shut them up.

As well try to stop an avalanche with an outstretched palm. Dissdale and Bettina and Gordon and Judith and Pen did a diabolical job, which was why for a short time afterwards I suffered from public notoriety as the man who had saved Calder Jackson's life.

No one seemed to speculate about his assailant setting out for a second try.

I looked at my photograph in the papers and wondered if the boy would see it, and know my name.

The First Year

OCTOBER

Gordon was back at work with his faintly trembling left hand usually out of sight and unnoticeable.

During periods of activity, as on the day at Ascot, he seemed to forget to camouflage, but at other times he had taken to sitting forwards in a hunched way over his desk with his hand anchored down between his thighs. I thought it a pity. I thought the tremor so slight that none of the others would have remarked on it, either aloud or to themselves, but to Gordon it was clearly a burden.

Not that it seemed to have affected his work. He had come back in July with determination, thanked me briskly in the presence of the others for my stop-gapping and taken all major decisions off my desk a..d back to his.

John asked him also in the hearing of Alec, Rupert and myself, to make it clear to us that it was he, John, who was the official next-in-line to Gordon, if the need should occur again. He pointed out that he was older and had worked much longer in the bank than I had. Tim, he said, shouldn't be jumping the queue.

Gordon eyed him blandly and said that if the need arose no doubt the chairman would take every factor into consideration. John made bitter and audible remarks under his breath about favouritism and unfair privilege, and Alec told him ironically to find a merchant bank where there *wasn't* a nephew or some such on the force.

'Be your age,' he said. 'Of *course* they want the next generation to join the family business. Why shouldn't they? It's natural.' But John was unplacated, and didn't see that his acid grudge against me was wasting a lot of his time. I seemed to be continually in his thoughts. He gave me truly vicious looks across the room and took every opportunity to sneer and denigrate. Messages never got passed on, and clients were given the impression that I was incompetent and only employed out of family charity. Occasionally on the telephone people refused to do business with me, saying they wanted John, and once a caller said straight out, 'Are you that playboy they're shoving ahead over better men's heads?'

John's gripe was basically understandable: in his place I'd have been cynical myself. Gordon did nothing to curb the escalating hate campaign and Alec found it funny. I thought long and hard about what to do and decided simply to work harder. I'd see it was very difficult for John to make his allegations stick.

His aggression showed in his body, which was roundedly muscular and looked the wrong shape for a city suit. Of moderate height, he wore his wiry brown hair very short so that it bristled above his collar, and his voice was loud, as if he thought volume equated authority: and so it might have done in schoolroom or on barrack square, instead of on a civilised patch of carpet.

He had come into banking via business school with high ambitions and good persuasive skills. I sometimes thought he would have made an excellent export salesman, but that wasn't the life he wanted. Alec said that John got his kicks from saying 'I am a merchant banker' to pretty girls and preening himself in their admiration.

Alec was a wicked fellow, really, and a shooter of perceptive arrows.

There came a day in October when three whirlwind things happened more or less simultaneously. The cartoonist telephoned; *What's Going On Where It Shouldn't* landed with a thud throughout the City; and Uncle Freddie descended on Ekaterin's for a tour of inspection.

To begin with the three events were unconnected, but by the end of the day, entwined.

330

I heard the cartoonist's rapid opening remarks with a sinking heart. 'I've engaged three extra animators and I need five more,' he said. 'Ten isn't nearly enough. I've worked out the amount of increased loan needed to pay them all.'

'Wait,' I said.

He went right on. 'I also need more space, of course, but luckily that's no problem, as there's an empty warehouse next to this place. I've signed a lease for it and told them you'll be advancing the money, and of course more furniture, more materials ...'

'*Stop*.' I said distractedly. 'You *can't*.'

'What? I can't what?' He sounded, of all things, bewildered.

'You can't just keep on borrowing. You've a limit. You can't go beyond it. Look for heaven's sake come over here quickly and we'll see what can be undone.'

'But you said,' his voice said plaintively, 'that you'd want to finance later expansion. That's what I'm doing. Expanding.'

I thought wildly that I'd be licking stamps for a living as soon as Henry heard. Dear *God* ...

'*Listen*,' the cartoonist was saying, 'we all worked like hell and finished one whole film. Twelve minutes long, dubbed with music and sound effects, everything, titles, the lot. And we did some rough-cuts of three others, no music, no frills, but enough ... and I've sold them.'

'You've what?'

'Sold them.' He laughed with excitement. 'It's solid, I promise you. That agent you sent me to, he's fixed the sale and the contract. All I have to do is sign. It's a major firm that's handling them, and I get a big perpetual royalty. World-wide distribution, that's what they're talking about, and the BBC are taking them. But we've got to make twenty films in a year from now, not seven like I meant. Twenty! And if the public like them, that's just the start. Oh heck, I can't believe it. But to do twenty in the time I need a lot more money. Is it all right? I mean ... I was so sure ...'

'Yes,' I said weakly. 'It's all right. Bring the contract when you've signed it, and new figures, and we'll work things out.'

'Thanks,' he said. 'Thanks, Tim Ekaterin, God bless your darling bank.'

I put the receiver down feebly and ran a hand over my head

and down the back of my neck.

'Trouble?' Gordon asked, watching.

'Well no, not exactly ...' A laugh like the cartoonist's rose in my throat. 'I backed a winner. I think perhaps I backed a bloody geyser.' The laugh broke out aloud. 'Did you ever do that?'

'Ah yes,' Gordon nodded, 'Of course.'

I told him about the cartoonist and showed him the original set of drawings, which were still stowed in my desk: and when he looked through them, he laughed.

'Wasn't that application on my desk,' he said, wrinkling his forehead in an effort to remember, 'just before I was away?'

I thought back. 'Yes, it probably was.'

He nodded. 'I'd decided to turn it down.'

'Had you?'

'Mm. Isn't he too young, or something?'

'That sort of talent strikes at birth.'

He gave me a brief assessing look and handed the drawings back. 'Well,' he said. 'Good luck to him.'

The news that Uncle Freddie had been spotted in the building rippled through every department and stiffened a good many slouching backbones. Uncle Freddie was given to growling out devastatingly accurate judgements of people in their hearing and it was not only I who'd found the bank more peaceful (if perhaps also more complacent) when he retired.

He was known as 'Mr Fred' as opposed to 'Mr Mark' (grandfather) and 'Mr Paul', the founder. No one ever called me 'Mr Tim'; sign of the changing times. If true to form Uncle Freddie would spend the morning in Investment Management, where he himself had worked all his office life, and after lunch in the boardroom would put at least his head into Corporate Finance, to be civil, and end with a march through Banking. On the way, by some telepathic process of his own, he would learn what moved in the bank's collective mind; sniff, as he had put it, the prevailing scent on the wind.

He had already arrived when the copies of *What's Going on* hit the fan.

Alec as usual slipped out to the local paper shop at about the time they were delivered there and returned with the six copies which the bank officially sanctioned. No one in the City could afford not to know about What Was Going On on their own doorstep.

Alec shunted around delivering one copy to each floor and keeping ours to himself to read first, a perk he said he deserved.

'You uncle,' he reported on his return, 'is beating the shit out of poor Ted Lorrimer in Investments for failing to sell Wrinkler Consolidated when even a squint-eyed baboon could see it was overstretched in its Central American operation, and a neck sticking out asking for the comprehensive chop.'

Gordon chuckled mildly at the verbatim reporting, and Alec sat at his desk and opened the paper. Normal office life continued for perhaps five more minutes before Alec shot to his feet as if he'd been stung.'

'Jes-us *Christ*,' he said.

'What is it?'

'Our leaker is at it again.'

'What?' Gordon said.

'You'd better read it.' He took the paper across to Gordon whose preliminary face of foreboding turned slowly to anger.

'It's disgraceful,' Gordon said. He made as if to pass the paper to me, but John, on his feet, as good as snatched it out of his hand.

'I should come first,' he said forcefully, and took the paper over to his own desk, sitting down methodically and spreading the paper open on the flat surface to read. Gordon watched him impassively and I said nothing to provoke. When John at his leisure had finished, showing little reaction but a tightened mouth, it was to Rupert he gave the paper, and Rupert, who read it with small gasps and widening eyes, who brought it eventually to me.

'It's bad,' Gordon said.

'So I gather.' I lolled back in my chair and lifted the offending column to eye level. Under a heading of 'Dinky Dirty Doings' it said:

It is perhaps not well known to readers that in many a merchant bank two thirds of the annual profits come from interest on loans. Investment and Trust management and Corporate Finance departments are the public faces and glamour

333

machines of these very private banks. Their investments (of other people's money) in the Stock market and their entrepreneurial role in mergers and takeovers earn the spotlight year by year in the City Pages.

Below stairs, so to speak, lies the tail that wags the dog, the secretive Banking department which quietly lends from its own deep coffers and rakes in vast profits in the shape of interest at rates they can set to suit themselves.

These rates are not necessarily high.

Who in Paul Ekaterin Ltd has been effectively lending to himself small fortunes from these coffers at FIVE per cent? Who in Paul Ekaterin Ltd has set up private companies which are NOT carrying on the business for which the money has ostensibly been lent? Who has not declared that these companies are his?

The man-in-the-street (poor slob) would be delighted to get unlimited cash from Paul Ekaterin Ltd at five per cent so that he could invest it in something else for more.

Don't Bankers have a fun time?

I looked up from the damaging page and across at Alec, and he was, predictably, grinning.

'I wonder who'd had his hand in the cookie jar,' he said.

'And who caught it there,' I asked.

'Wow, yes.'

Gordon said bleakly, 'This is very serious.'

'If you believe it,' I said.

'But this paper ...' he began.

'Yeah,' I interrupted. 'It had a dig at us before, remember? Way back in May. Remember the flap everyone got into?'

'I was at home ... with 'flu'.'

'Oh, yes. Well, the furore went on here for ages and no one came up with any answers. This column today is just as unspecific. So ... supposing all it's designed to do is stir up trouble for the bank? Who's got it in for us? To what raving nut have we for instance refused a loan?'

Alec was regarding me with exaggerated wonder. 'Here we have Sherlock Holmes to the rescue,' he said admiringly.'Now we can all go out to lunch.'

Gordon however said thoughtfully, 'It's perfectly possible,

though, to set up a company and lend it money. All it would take would be paperwork. I could do it myself. So could anyone here, I suppose, up to his authorised ceiling, if he thought he could get away with it.'

John nodded. 'It's ridiculous of Tim and Alec to make a joke of this,' he said importantly. 'The very reputation of the bank is at stake.'

Gordon frowned, stood up, took the paper off my desk, and went along to see his almost-equal in the room facing St Paul's. Spreading consternation, I thought; bringing out cold sweats from palpitating banking hearts.

I ran a mental eye over everyone in the whole department who could possibly have had enough power along with the opportunity, from Val Fisher all the way down to myself; and there were twelve, perhaps, who could theoretically have done it.

But ... not Rupert, with his sad mind still grieving, because he wouldn't have had the appetite or energy for fraud.

Not Alec, surely; because I liked him.

Not John: too self-regarding.

Not Val, not Gordon, unthinkable. Not myself.

That left the people along in the other pasture, and I didn't know them well enough to judge. Maybe one of them did believe that a strong fiddle on the side was worth the ruin of discovery, but all of us were already generously paid, perhaps for the very reason that temptations would be more likely to be resisted if we weren't scratching around for money for the gas.

Gordon didn't return. The morning limped down to lunch time, when John bustled off announcing he was seeing a client, and Alec encouraged Rupert to go out with him for a pie and pint. I'd taken to working through lunch because of the quietness, and I was still there alone at two o'clock when Peter, Henry's assistant, came and asked me to go up to the top floor, because I was wanted.

Uncle Freddie, I thought. Uncle Freddie's read the rag and will be exploding like a warhead. In some way he'll make it out to be my fault. With a gusty sigh I left my desk and took the lift to face the old warrior with whom I had never in my life felt easy.

He was waiting in the top floor hallway, talking to Henry.

335

Both of them at six foot three over-topped me by three inches. Life would never have been as ominous, I thought, if Uncle Freddie had been small.

'Tim,' Henry said when he saw me, 'Go along to the small conference room, will you?'

I nodded and made my way to the room next to the boardroom where four or five chairs surrounded a square polished table. A copy of *'What's Going On'* lay there, already dog-eared from many thumbs.

'Now Tim', said my uncle, coming into the room behind me, 'do you know what all this is about?'

I shook my head and said 'No.'

My uncle growled in his throat and sat down, waving Henry and myself to seats. Henry might be chairman, might indeed in office terms have been Uncle Freddie's boss, but the white-haired old tyrant still personally owned the leasehold of the building itself and from long habit treated everyone in it as guests.

Henry absently fingered the newspaper. 'What do you think?' he said to me. '*Who* ... do you think?'

'It might not be anyone.'

He half smiled. 'A stirrer?'

'Mm. Not a single concrete detail. Same as last time.'

'Last time,' Henry said, 'I asked the paper's editor where he got his information from. Never reveal sources, he said. Useless asking again.'

'Undisclosed sources,' Uncle Freddie said, 'never trust them.'

Henry said, 'Gordon says you can find out, Tim, how many concerns, if any, are borrowing from us at five per cent. There can't be many. A few from when interest rates were low. The few who got us in the past to agree to a long-term fixed rate.' The few, though he didn't say so, from before his time, before he put an end to such unprofitable straitjackets. 'If there are more recent ones among them, could you spot them?'

'I'll look,' I said.

We both knew it would take days rather than hours and might produce no results. The fraud, if it existed, could have been going on for a decade. For half a century. Successful frauds tended to go on and on unnoticed, until some one tripped over them by accident. It might almost be easier to find out who had done the tripping, and why he'd told the paper instead of the bank.

'Anyway,' Henry said, 'that isn't primarily why we asked you up here.'

'No,' said my uncle, grunting. 'Time you were a director.'

I thought: I didn't hear that right.

'Er ... what?' I said.

'A director. A director,' he said impatiently. 'Fellow who sits on the board. Never heard of them, I suppose.'

I looked at Henry, who was smiling and nodding.

'But,' I said, 'so soon ...'

'Don't you want to, then?' demanded my uncle.

'Yes, I do.'

'Good. Don't let me down. I've had my eye on you since you were eight.'

I must have looked as surprised as I felt.

'You told me then,' he said, 'how much you had saved, and how much you would have if you went on saving a pound a month at four per cent compound interest for forty years, by which time you would be very old. I wrote down your figures and worked them out, and you were right.'

'It's only a formula,' I said.

'Oh sure. You could do it now in a drugged sleep. But at *eight*? You'd inherited the gift, all right. You were just robbed of the inclination.' He nodded heavily. 'Look at your father. My little brother. Got drunk nicely, never a mean thought, but hardly there when the brains were handed out. Look at the way he indulged your mother, letting her gamble like that. Look at the life he gave you. All pleasure, regardless of cost. I despaired of you at times. Thought you'd been ruined. But I knew the gift was there somewhere, might still be dormant, might grow if forced. So there you are, I was right.'

I was pretty well speechless.

'We all agree,' Henry said. 'The whole board was unanimous at our meeting this morning that it's time another Ekaterin took his proper place.'

I thought of John, and of the intensity of rage my promotion would bring forth.

'Would you,' I said slowly, 'have given me a directorship if my name had been Joe Bloggs?'

Henry levelly said, 'Probably not this very day. But soon, I promise you, yes. You're almost thirty-three, after all, and I was on the board here at thirty-four.'

'Thank you,' I said.

'Rest assured,' Henry said. 'You've earned it.' He stood up and formally shook hands. 'Your appointment officially starts as of the first of November, a week today. We will welcome you then to a short meeting in the boardroom, and afterwards to lunch.'

They must both have seen the depth of my pleasure, and they themselves looked satisfied. Hallelujah, I thought, I've made it. I've got there ... I've barely started.

Gordon went down with me in the lift, also smiling.

'They've all been dithering about it on and off for months,' he said. 'Ever since you took over from me when I was ill, and did OK. Anyway I told them this morning about your news from the cartoonist. Some of them said it was just lucky. I told them you'd now been lucky too often for it to be a coincidence. So there you are.'

'I can't thank you ...'

'It's your own doing.'

'John will have a fit.'

'You've coped all right so far with his envy.'

'I don't like it, though,' I said.

'Who would? Silly man, he's doing his career no good.'

Gordon straightaway told everyone in the office, and John went white and walked rigidly out of the room.

I went diffidently a week later to the induction and to the first lunch with the board, and then in a few days, as one does, I got used to the change of company and to the higher level of information. In the departments one heard about the decisions that had been made: in the dining room one heard the decisions being reached. 'Our daily board meeting,' Henry said. 'So much easier this way when everyone can simply say what they think without anyone taking notes.'

There were usually from ten to fifteen directors at lunch, although at a pinch the elongated oval table could accommodate the full complement of twenty-three. People would vanish at any moment to answer telephone calls, and to deal. Dealing, and buying and selling of stocks, took urgent precedence over food.

The food itself was no great feast, though perfectly presented. 'Always lamb on Wednesdays,' Gordon said at the buffet table as he took a couple from a row of trimmed lean cutlets. 'Some sort of chicken on Tuesdays, beef wellington most Thursdays. Henry never eats the crust.' Each day there was a clear soup before and fruit and cheese after. Alcohol if one chose, but most of them didn't. No one shoud deal in millions whose brain wanted to sleep, Henry said, drinking Malvern water steadily. Quite a change, all of it, from a rough-hewn sandwich at my desk.

They were all polite about my failure to discover 'paper' companies to whom the bank had been lending at five per cent, although Val and Henry, I knew, shared my own view that the report originated from malice and not from fact.

I had spent several days in the extra-wide office at the back of our floor, where the more mechanical parts of the banking operation were carried on. There in the huge expanse (grey carpet, this time) were row upon row of long desks whose tops were packed with telephones, adding machines and above all computers.

From there went out our own interest cheques to the depositors who had lent us money for us to lend to things like 'Home-made Heaven cakes' and 'Water Purification' plants in Norfolk. Into there came the interest paid *to* us by cakes and water and cartoonists and ten thousand such. Machines clattered, phone bells rang, people hurried about.

Many of the people working there were girls, and it had often puzzled me why there were so few women among the managers. Gordon said it was because few women wanted to commit their whole lives to making money and John (in the days when he was speaking to me) said with typical contempt that it was because they preferred to spend it. In any case, there were no female managers in Banking, and none at all on the Board.

Despite that, my best helper in the fraud search proved to be a curvy redhead called Patty who had taken the *What's Going On* article as a personal affront, as had many of her colleagues.

'No one could do that under our noses,' she protested.

'I'm afraid they could. You know they could. No one could

blame any of you for not spotting it.'

'Well ... where do we start?'

'With all the borrowers paying a fixed rate of five per cent. Or perhaps four per cent, or five point seven five, or six or seven. Who knows if five is right?'

She looked at me frustratedly with wide amber eyes. 'But we haven't got them sorted like that.'

Sorted, she meant, on the computer. Each loan transaction would have its own agreement, which in itself could originally range from one slip of paper to a contract of fifty pages, and each agreement should say at what rate the loan interest was to be levied, such as two above the current accepted base. There were thousands of such agreements typed onto and stored on computer discs. One could retrieve any one transaction by its identifying number, or alphabetically, or by the dates of commencement, or full term, or by the date when the next interest payment was due, but if you asked the computer who was paying at what per cent you'd get a blank screen and the microchip version of a raspberry.

'You can't sort them out by rates,' she said. 'The rates go up and down like see-saws.'

'But there must still be some loans being charged interest at a fixed rate.'

'Well, yes.'

'So when you punch in the new interest rate the computer adjusts the interest due on almost all the loans but doesn't touch those with a fixed rate.'

'I suppose that's right.'

'So somewhere in the computer there must be a code which tells it when not to adjust the rates.'

She smiled sweetly and told me to be patient, and half a day later produced a cheerful-looking computer-programmer to whom the problem was explained.

'Yeah, there's a code,' he said. 'I put it there myself. What you want, then, is a programme that will print out all the loans which have the code attached. That right:'

We nodded. He worked on paper for half an hour with a much-chewed pencil and then typed rapidly onto the computer, pressing buttons and being pleased with the results.

'You leave this programme on here,' he said, 'then feed in

the discs, and you'll get the results on that line-printer over there. And I've written it all out for you tidily in pencil, in case someone switches off your machine. Then just type it all in again, and you're back in business.'

We thanked him and he went away whistling, the aristocrat among ants.

The line-printer clattered away on and off for hours as we fed through the whole library of discs, and it finally produced a list of about a hundred of the ten-digit numbers used to identify an account.

'Now,' Patty said undaunted, 'do you want a complete print-out of all the original agreements for those loans?'

'I'm afraid so, yes.'

'Hang around.'

It took two days even with her help to check through all the resulting paper and by the end I couldn't spot any companies there that had no known physical existence, though short of actually tramping to all the addresses and making an on-the-spot enquiry, one couldn't be sure.

Henry, however, was against the expenditure of time. 'We'll just be more vigilant,' he said. 'Design some more safeguards, more tracking devices. Could you do that, Tim?'

'I could, with that programmer's help.'

'Right Get on with it. Let us know.'

I wondered aloud to Patty whether someone in her own department, not one of the managers, could set up such a fraud, but once she'd got over her instinctive indignation she shook her head.

'Who would bother? It would be much simpler — in fact it's almost dead easy — to feed in a mythical firm who has lent *us* money, and to whom we are paying interest. Then the computer goes on sending out interest cheques for ever, and all the crook has to do is cash them.'

Henry, however, said we had already taken advice on that one, and the 'easy' route had been plugged by systematic checks by the auditors.

The paper-induced rumpus again gradually died down and became undiscussed if not forgotten. Life in our plot went on much as before with Rupert slowly recovering, Alec making jokes and Gordon stuffing his left hand anywhere out of sight.

341

John continued to suffer from his obsession, not speaking to me, not looking at me if he could help it, and apparently telling clients outright that my promotion was a sham.

'Cosmetic of course,' Alec reported him of saying on the telephone. 'Makes the notepaper heading look impressive. Means nothing in real terms, you know. Get through to me, I'll see you right.'

'He said all that?' I asked.

'Word for word.' Alec grinned. 'Go and bop him on the nose.'

I shook my head however and wondered if I should get myself transferred along to the St Paul's-facing office. I didn't want to go, but it looked as if John wouldn't recover his balance unless I did. If I tried to get John himself transferred, would it make things that much worse?

I was gradually aware that Gordon, and behind him Henry were not going to help, their thought being that I was a big boy now and should be able to resolve it myself. It was a freedom which brought responsibility, as all freedoms do, and I had to consider that for the bank's sake John needed to be a sensible member of the team.

I thought he should see a psychiatrist. I got Alec to say it to him lightly as a joke, out of my hearing ('what you need, old pal, is a friendly shrink') but to John his own anger appeared rational, not a matter for treatment.

I tried saying to him straight, 'Look, John, I know how you feel. I know you think my promotion isn't fair. Well, maybe it is, maybe it isn't, but either way I can't help it. You'll be a lot better off if you just face things and forget it. You're good at your job, we all know it, but you're doing yourself no favours with all this bellyaching. So shut up, accept that life's bloody, and let's lend some money.'

It was a homily that fell on a closed mind, and in the end it was some redecorating which came to the rescue. For a week while painters re-whitened our walls the five of us in the fountain-faced office squeezed into the other one, desks jammed together in every corner, 'phone calls made with palms pressed to ears against the noise and even normally placid tempers itching to snap. Overcrowd the human race, I thought, and you always got a fight. In distance lay peace.

342

Anyway, I used the time to do some surreptitious persuasion and shuffling, so that when we returned to our own patch both John and Rupert stayed behind. The two oldest men from the St Paul's office came with Gordon, Alec and myself, and Gordon's almost-equal obligingly told John that it was great to be working again with a younger team of bright energetic brains.

The First Year

NOVEMBER

Val Fisher said at lunch one day, 'I've received a fairly odd request.' (It was a Friday: grilled fish.)

'Something new?' Henry asked.

'Yes. Chap wants to borrow five million pounds to buy a racehorse.'

Everyone at the table laughed except Val himself.

'I thought I'd toss it at you,' he said. 'Kick it around some. See what you think.'

'What horse?' Henry said.

'Something called Sandcastle.'

Henry, Gordon and I all looked at Val with sharpened attention; almost perhaps with eagerness.

'Mean something to you three, does it?' he said, turning his head from one to the other of us.

Henry nodded. 'That day we all went to Ascot. Sandcastle ran there, and won. A stunning performance. Beautiful.'

Gordon said reminiscently, 'The man whose box we were in saved his whole business on that race. Do you remember Dissdale, Tim?'

'Certainly do.'

'I saw him a few weeks ago. On top of the world. God knows how much he won.'

'Or how much he staked,' I said.

'Yes, well,' Val said. 'Sandcastle. He won the 2,000 Guineas, as I understand, and the King Edward VII Stakes at Royal

Ascot. Also the "Diamond" Stakes in July, and the Champion Stakes at Newmarket last month. This is, I believe, a record second only to winning the Derby or the Arc de Triomphe. He finished fourth, incidently, in the Derby. He could race next year as a four-year-old, but if he flopped his value would be less than it is at the moment. Our prospective client wants to buy him now and put him to stud.'

The rest of the directors got on with their fillets of sole while listening interestedly with eyes and ears. A stallion made a change, I suppose, from chemicals, electronics and oil.

'Who is our client?' Gordon asked. Gordon liked fish. He could eat it right handed with his fork, in no danger of shaking it off between plate and mouth.

'A man called Oliver Knowles,' Val said. 'He owns a stud farm. He got passed along to me by the horse's trainer, whom I know slightly because of our wives being distantly related. Oliver Knowles wants to buy, the present owner is willing to sell. All they need is the cash.' He smiled. 'Same old story.'

'What's your view?' Henry said.

'Val shrugged his well-tailored shoulders.'Too soon to have one of any consequence. But I thought, if it interested you at all, we could ask Tim to do a preliminary look-see. He has a background, after all, a lengthy acquaintance, shall we say, with racing.'

There was a murmur of dry amusement round the table.

'What do you think?' Henry asked me.

'I'll certainly do it if you like.'

Someone down the far end complained that it would be a waste of time and that merchant banks of our stature should not be associated with the Turf.

'Our own dear Queen,' someone said ironically, 'is associated with the Turf. And knows the Stud Book backwards, so they say.'

Henry smiled. 'I don't see why we shouldn't at least look into it.' He nodded in my direction. 'Go ahead, Tim. Let us know.'

I spent the next few working days alternately chewing pencils with the computer programmer and joining us to a syndicate with three other banks to lend twelve point four million pounds short term at high interest to an international construction company with a gap in its cash-flow. In between those I telephoned around for information and opinions about Oliver Knowles, in the normal investigative preliminaries to any loan for anything, not only for a hair-raising price for a stallion.

Establishing a covenant, it was called. Only if the covenant was sound would any loan be further considered.

Oliver Knowles, I was told, was a sane, sober man of forty-one with a stud farm in Hertfordshire. There were three stallions standing there with ample provision for visiting mares, and he owned the one hundred and fifty acres outright, having inherited them on his father's death.

When talking to local bank managers one listened attentively for what they left out, but Oliver Knowles' bank manager left out not much. Without in the least discussing his client's affairs in detail he said that occasional fair-sized loans had so far been paid off as scheduled and that Mr Knowles' business sense could be commended. A rave notice from such a source.

'Oliver Knowles?' a racing acquaintance from the past said. 'Don't know him myself. I'll ask around,' and an hour later called back with the news. 'He seems to be a good guy but his wife's just buggered off with a Canadian. He might be a secret wife-beater, who can tell? Otherwise the gen is that he's as honest as any horse-breeder, which you can take as you find it, and how's your mother?'

'She's fine, thanks. She remarried last year. Lives in Jersy.'

'Good. Lovely lady. Always buying us icecreams. I adored her.'

I put the receiver down with a smile and tried a credit rating agency. No black marks, they said: the Knowles credit was good.

I told Gordon across the room that I seemed to be getting nothing but green lights, and at lunch that day repeated the news to Henry. He looked around the table, collecting a few nods, a few frowns and a great deal of indecison.

'We couldn't carry it all ourselves, of course,' Val said. 'And it isn't exactly something we could go to our regular sources with. They'd think us crackers.'

Henry nodded. 'We'd have to canvas friends for private money. I know a few people here or there who might come in.

Two million, I think, is all we should consider ourselves. Two and a half at the outside.'

'I don't approve,' a dissenting director said. 'It's madness. Suppose the damn thing broke its leg?'

'Insurance,' Henry said mildly.

Into a small silence I said, 'If you felt like going into it further I could get some expert views on Sandcastle's breeding, and then arrange blood and fertility tests. And I know it's not usual with loans, but I do think someone like Val should go and personally meet Oliver Knowles and look at his place. It's too much of a risk to lend such a sum for a horse without going into it extremely carefully.'

'Just listen to who's talking,' said the dissenter, but without ill-will.

'Mm,' Henry said, considering. 'What do you think, Val?'

Val Fisher smoothed a hand over his always smooth face. 'Tim should go,' he said. 'He's done the groundwork, and all I know about horses is that they eat grass.'

The dissenting director almost rose to his feet with the urgency of his feelings.

'Look,' he said, 'all this is ridiculous. How can we possibly finance a *horse*?'

'Well, now,' Henry answered. 'The breeding of thorough-breds is big business, tens of thousands of people round the world make their living from it. Look upon it as an industry like any other. We gamble here on shipbuilders, motors, textiles, you name it, and all of those can go bust. And none of them,' he finished with a near-grin, 'can pro-create in their own image.'

The dissenter heavily shook his head. 'Madness. Utter madness.'

'Go and see Oliver Knowles, Tim,' Henry said.

Actually I thought it prudent to bone up on the finances of breeding in general before listening to Oliver Knowles himself, on the basis that I would then have a better idea of whether what he was proposing was sensible or not.

I didn't myself know anyone who knew much on the subject, but one of the beauties of merchant banking was the ramifica-tion of people who knew people who knew people who could find someone with the information that was wanted. I sent out the question-mark smoke signal and from distant out-of-sight mountain tops the answer puff-puffed back.

Ursula Young, I was told, would put me right.'She's a bloodstock agent. Very sharp, very talkative, knows her stuff. She used to work on a stud farm, so you've got it every whichway. She says she'll tell you anything you want, only if you want to see her in person this week it will have to be at Doncaster races on Saturday, she's too busy to spend the time else.'

I went north to Doncaster by train and met the lady at the racecourse, where the last Flat meeting of the year was being held. She was waiting as arranged by the entrance to the Member's Club and wearing an identifying red velvet beret, and she swept me off to a secluded table in a bar where we wouldn't be interrupted.

She was fifty, tough, good-looking, dogmatic and inclined to treat me as a child. She also gave me a patient and invaluable lecture on the economics of owning a stallion.

'Stop me,' she said to begin with, 'if I say something you don't understand.'

I nodded.

'All right. Say you own a horse that's won the Derby and you want to capitalise on your goldmine. You judge what you think you can get for the horse, then you divide that by forty and try to sell each of the forty shares at that price. Maybe you can, maybe you can't. It depends on the horse. With Troy, now, they were queuing up. But if your winner isn't frightfully well bred or if it made little show *except* in the Derby you'll get a cool response and have to bring the price down. OK so far?'

'Um,' I said. 'Why only forty shares?'

She looked at me in amazement. 'You don't know a *thing*, do you?'

'That's why I'm here.'

'Well, a stallion covers forty mares in a season, and the season incidentally, lasts roughly from February to June. The mares come to *him*, of course. He doesn't travel, he stays put at home. Forty is just about average; physically I mean. Some can do more, but others get exhausted. So forty is the accepted number. Now, say you have a mare and you've worked out that if you mate her with a certain stallion you might get a top-class foal, you try to get one of those forty places. The places are

called nominations. You apply for a nomination either directly
to the stud where the stallion is standing, or through an agent
like me, or even by advertising in a breeders' newspaper.
Follow?'

'Gasping,' I nodded.

She smiled briefly. 'People who invest in stallion shares
sometimes have broodmares of their own they want to breed
from.' She paused 'Perhaps I should have explained more
clearly that everyone who owns a share automatically has a
nomination to the stallion every year.'

'Ah,' I said.

'Yes. So say you've got your share and consequently your
nomination but you haven't a mare to send to the stallion, then
you sell your nomination to someone who *has* a mare, in the
ways I already described.'

'I'm with you.'

After the first three years the nominations may vary in price
and in fact are often auctioned, but of course for the first three
years the price is fixed.'

'Why of course?'

She sighed and took a deep breath. 'For three years no one
knows whether the progeny on the whole are going to be
winners or not. The gestation period is eleven months, and the
first crop of foals don't race until they're two. If you work it out,
that means that the stallion has stood for three seasons, and
therefore covered a hundred and twenty mares, before the
crunch.'

'Right.'

'So to fix the stallion fee for the first three years you divide
the price of the stallion by one hundred and twenty, and that's
it. That's the fee charged for the stallion to cover a mare. That's
the sum you receive if you sell your nomination.'

I blinked.

'That means,' I said, 'that if you sell your nomination for
three years you have recovered the total amount of your
original investment?'

'That's right.'

'And after that ... every time, every year you sell your
nomination, it's clear profit?'

'Yes. But taxed, of course.'

'And how long does that go on?'

She shrugged 'Ten to fifteen years. Depends on the stallion's potency.'

'But that's ...'

'Yes,' she said. 'One of the best investments on earth.'

The bar had filled up behind us with people crowding in, talking loudly, and breathing on their fingers against the chill of the raw day outside. Ursula Young accepted a warmer in the shape of whisky and ginger wine, while I had coffee.

'Don't you drink? she asked with mild disapproval.

'Not often in the daytime.'

She nodded vaguely, her eyes scanning the company, her mind already on her normal job. 'And more questions?' she asked.

'I'm bound to think of some the minute we part.'

She nodded. 'I'll be here until the end of racing. If you want me, you'll see me near the weighing room after each race.'

We were on the point of standing up to leave when a man whose head one could never forget came into the bar.

'Calder Jackson!' I exclaimed.

Ursula casually looked. 'So it is.'

'Do you know him?' I asked.

'Everyone does.' There was almost a conscious neutrality in her voice as she didn't want to be caught with her thoughts showing. The same response, I reflected, that he had drawn from Henry and Gordon and me.

'You don't like him?' I suggested.

'I feel nothing either way.' She shrugged. 'He's part of the scene. From what people say, he's achieved some remarkable cures.' She glanced at me briefly. 'I suppose you've seen him on television, extolling the value of herbs?'

'I met him,' I said 'at Ascot, back in June.'

'One tends to.' She got to her feet, and I with her, thanking her sincerely for her help.

'Think nothing of it,' she said. 'Any time.' She paused. 'I suppose it's no use asking what stallion prompted this chat?'

'Sorry, no. It's on behalf of a client.'

She smiled slightly. 'I'm here if he needs an agent.'

We made our way towards the door, a path, I saw, which

would take us close to Calder. I wondered fleetingly whether he would know me, remember me after several months. I was after all not as memorable as himself, just a standard issue six foot with eyes, nose and mouth in roughly the right places, dark hair on top.

'Hello Ursula,' he said, his voice carrying easily through the general din. 'Bitter cold day.'

'Calder.' She nodded acknowledgement.

His gaze slid to my face, dismissed it, focussed again on my companion. Then he did a classic double-take, his eyes widening with recognition.

'Tim,' he said incredulously. 'Tim ...' he flicked his fingers to bring the difficult name to mind, ' ... Tim Ekaterin!'

I nodded.

He said to Ursula, 'Tim, here, saved my life.'

She was surprised until he explained, and then still surprised I hadn't told her. 'I read about it, of course,' she said. 'And congratulated you, Calder, on your escape.'

'Did you ever hear any more,' I asked him. 'From the police, or anyone?'

He shook his curly head. 'No, I didn't.'

'The boy didn't try again?'

'No.'

'Did you really have no idea where he came from?' I said. 'I know you told the police you didn't know, but ... well ... you just might have done.'

He shook his head very positively however and said, 'If I could help to catch the little bastard I'd do it at once. But I don't know who he was. I hardly saw him properly, just enought to know I didn't know him from Satan.'

'How's the healing?' I said. 'The tingling touch.'

There was a brief flash in his eyes as if he had found the question flippant and in bad taste, but perhaps mindful that he owed me his present existence he answered civilly. 'Rewarding,' he said. 'Heartwarming.'

Standard responses, I thought. As before.

'Is your yard full, Calder?' Ursula asked.

'Always a vacancy if needed,' he replied hopefully. 'Have you a horse to send me?'

'One of my clients has a two-year-old which looks ill and half

dead all the time, to the despair of the trainer, who can't get it
fit. She — my client — was mentioning you.'

'I've had great success with that sort of general debility.'

Ursula wrinkled her forehead in indecision. 'She feels Ian
Pargetter would think her disloyal if she sent you her colt. He's
been treating him for weeks, I think, without success.'

Calder smiled reassuringly. 'Ian Pargetter and I are on good
terms, I promise you. He's even persuaded owners himself
sometimes to send me their horses. Very good of him. We talk
each case over, you know, and act in agreement. After all, we
both have the recovery of the patient as our prime objective.'
Again the swift impression of a statement often needed.

'Is Ian Pargetter a vet?' I asked incuriously.

They both looked at me.'

'Er ... yes,' Calder said.

'One of a group practice in Newmarket,' Ursula added. 'Very
forward-looking. Tries new things. Dozens of trainers swear by
him.'

'Just ask him, Ursula,' Calder said. 'Ian will tell you he
doesn't mind owners sending me their horses. Even if he's a bit
open-minded about the laying on of hands, at least he trusts me
not to make the patient worse.' It was said as a self-deprecating
joke, and we all smiled. Ursula Young and I in a moment or
two walked on and out of the bar, and behind us we could hear
Calder politely answering another of the everlasting questions.

'Yes,' he was saying, 'one of my favourite remedies for a
prolonged cough in horses is liquorice root boiled in water with
some figs. You strain the mixture and stir it into the horse's
normal feed ...'

The door closed behind us and shut him off.

'You'd think he'd get tired of explaining his methods,' I said.
'I wonder he never snaps.'

The lady said judiciously, 'Calder depends on television
fame, good public relations and medical success, roughly in that
order. He owns a yard with about thirty boxes on the outskirts
of Newmarket — it used to be a regular training stables before
he bought it — and the yard's almost always full. Short-term
and long-term crocks, all sent to him either from true belief or
as a last resort. I don't pretend to know anything about
herbalism, and as for supernatural healing powers ...' She

shook her head. 'But there's no doubt that whatever his methods, horses do usually seem to leave his yard in a lot better health than when they went in.'

'Someone at Ascot said he'd brought dying horses back to life.'

'Hmph.'

'You don't believe it?'

She gave me a straight look, a canny businesswoman with a lifetime's devotion to thoroughbreds.

'Dying,' she said, 'Is a relative term when it doesn't end in death.'

I made a nod into a slight bow of appreciation.

'But to be fair,' she said, 'I know for certain that he totally and permanently cured a ten-year-old broodmare of colitis X, which has a habit of being fatal.'

'They're not all horses in training, then, that he treats?'

'Oh no, he'll take anybody's pet from a pony to an event horse. Showjumpers, the lot. But the horse has to be worth it, to the owner, I mean. I don't think Calder's hospital is terribly cheap.'

'Exorbitant?'

'Not that I've heard. Fair, I suppose, if you consider the results.'

I seemed to have heard almost more about Calder Jackson than I had about stallion shares, but I did after all have a sort of vested interest. One tended to want a life one had saved to be of positive use in the world. Illogical, I dare say, but there it was. I was pleased that it was true that Calder cured horses, albeit in his own mysterious unorthodox ways: and if I wished that I could warm to him more as a person, that was unrealistic and sentimental.

Ursula Young went off about her business, and although I caught sight of both her and Calder during the afternoon, I didn't see them again to speak to. I went back to London on the train, spent two hours of Sunday morning on the telephone, and early Sunday afternoon drove off to Hertfordshire in search of Oliver Knowles.

He lived in a square hundred-year-old stark red brick house which to my taste would have been friendlier if softened by trailing creeper. Blurred outlines, however, were not in Oliver Knowles' soul: a crisp bare tidyness was apparent in every corner of his spread.

His land was divided into a good number of paddocks of various sizes, each bordered by an immaculate fence of white rails; and the upkeep of those, I judged, as I pulled up on the weedless gravel before the front door, must alone cost a fortune. There was a scattering of mares and foals in the distance in the paddocks, mostly heads down to the grass, sniffing out the last tender shoots of the dying year. The day itself was cold with a muted sun dipping already towards distant hills, the sky quiet with the greyness of coming winter, the damp air smelling of mustiness, wood smoke and dead leaves.

There were no dead leaves as such to be seen. No flower beds, no ornamental hedges, no nearby trees. A barren mind, I thought, behind a business whose aim was fertility and the creation of life.

Oliver Knowles himself opened his front door to my knock, proving to be a pleasant lean man with an efficient, cultured manner of authority and politeness. Accustomed to command, I diagnosed. Feels easy with it; second nature. Positive straightforward, self-controlled. Charming also, in an understated way.

'Mr Ekaterin?' he shook hands, smiling. 'I must confess I expected someone ... older.'

There were several answers to that, such as 'time will take care of it' and 'I'll be older tomorrow', but nothing seemed appropriate. Instead I said 'I report back' to reassure him, which it did, and he invited me into his house.

Preductably the interior was also painfully tidy, such papers and magazines as were to be seen being squared up with the surface they rested on. The furniture was antique, well polished, brass handles shining, and the carpets venerably from Persia. He led me into a sitting room which was also office, the walls thickly covered with framed photographs of horses, mares and foals, and the window giving on to a view of, across a further expanse of gravel, an archway leading into an extensive stable yard.

'Boxes for mares,' he said, following my eyes. 'Beyond them, the foaling boxes. Beyond those, the breeding pen, with the stallion boxes on the far side of that again. My stud groom's bungalow and the lads' hostel, those roofs you can see in the hollow, they're just beyond the stallions.' He paused. 'Would you care perhaps to look round?'

'Very much,' I said.

'Come along, then.' He led the way to a door at the back of the house, collecting an overcoat and a black retriever from a mud room on the way. 'Go on then, Squibs, old fellow,' he said, fondly watching his dog squeeze ecstatically through the opening outside the door. 'Breath of fresh air won't hurt you.'

We walked across to the stable arch with Squibs circling and zig-zagging nose-down to the gravel.

'It's our quietest time of year, of course,' Oliver Knowles said. 'We have our own mares here, of course, and quite a few at livery.' He looked at my face to see if I understood and decided to explain anyway. 'They belong to people who own broodmares but have nowhere of their own to keep them. They pay us to board them.'

I nodded.

'Than we have the foals born to the mares this past spring, and of course the three stallions. Total of seventy-eight at the moment.'

'And next spring,' I said, 'the mares coming to your stallions will arrive?'

'That's right.' He nodded. 'They come here a month or five weeks before they're due to give birth to the foals they are already carrying, so as to be near the stallion within the month following. They have to foal here, because the foals would be too delicate straight after birth to travel.'

'And ... how long do they stay here?'

'About three months altogether, by which time we hope the mare is safely in foal again.'

'There isn't much pause then,' I said. 'Between ... er ... pregnancies?'

He glanced at me with civil amusement. 'Mares come into use nine days after foaling, but normally we would think this a bit too soon for breeding. The oestrus — heat you would call it — lasts six days, then there's an interval of fifteen days, then the mare comes into use again for six days, and this time we breed her. Mind you,' he added, 'Nature being what it is, this cycle

355

doesn't work to the minute. In some mares the oestrus will last only two days, in some as much as eleven. We try to have the mare covered two or three times while she's in heat, for the best chance of getting her in foal. A great deal depends on the stud groom's judgement, and I've a great chap just now, he has a great feel for mares, a sixth sense, you might say.'

He led me briskly across the first big oblong yard where long dark equine heads peered inquisitively from over half-open stable doors, and through a passage on the far side which led to a second yard of almost the same size but whose doors were fully shut.

'None of these boxes is occupied at the moment,' he said, waving a hand around. 'We have to have the capacity, though, for when the mares come.'

Beyond the second yard lay a third, a good deal smaller and again with closed doors.

'Foaling boxes,' Oliver Knowles explained. 'All empty now, of course.'

The black dog trotted ahead of us, knowing the way. Beyond the foaling boxes lay a wide path between two small paddocks of about half an acre each, and at the end of the path, to the left, rose a fair sized barn with a row of windows just below its roof.

'Breeding shed,' Oliver Knowles said economically, producing a heavy key ring from his trouser pocket and unlocking a door set into a large roll-aside entrance. He gestured to me to go in, and I found myself in a bare concrete-floored expanse surrounded by white walls topped with the high windows, through which the dying sun wanly shone.

'During the season of course the floor in here is covered with peat,' he said.

I nodded vaguely and thought of life being generated purposefully in that quiet place, and we returned prosaically to the outer world with Oliver Knowles locking the door again behind us.

Along another short path between two more small paddocks we came to another small stable yard, this time of only six boxes, with feed room, tack room, hay and peat storage alongside.

'Stallions,' Oliver Knowles said.

356

Three heads almost immediately appeared over the half-doors, three sets of dark liquid eyes turning inquisitively our way.

'Rotaboy,' my host said, walking to the first head and producing a carrot unexpectedly. The black mobile lips whiffled over the outstretched palm and sucked the goodie in: strong teeth crunched a few times and Rotaboy nudged Oliver Knowles for a second helping. Oliver Knowles produced another carrot, held it out as before, and briefly patted the horse's neck.

'He'll be twenty next year,' he said. 'Getting old, eh, old fella?'

He walked along to the next box and repeated the carrot routine.'This one is Diarist, rising sixteen.'

By the third box he said, 'This is Parakeet,' and delivered the treats and the pat. 'Parakeet turns twelve on January 1st.'

He stood a little away from the horse so that he could see all three heads at once and said, 'Rotaboy has been an outstanding stallion and still is, but one can't realistically expect more than another one or two seasons. Diarist is successful, with large numbers of winners among his progeny, but none of them absolutely top rank like those of Rotaboy. Parakeet hasn't proved as successful as I'd hoped. He turns out to breed better stayers than sprinters, and the world is mad nowadays for very fast two-year-olds. Parakeet's progeny tend to be better at three, four, five and six. Some of his first crops are now steeplechasing and jumping pretty well.'

'Isn't that good?' I asked, frowning, since he spoke with no great joy.

'I've had to reduce his fee,' he said. 'People won't send their top flat-racing mares to a stallion who breeds jumpers.'

'Oh.'

After a pause he said. 'You can see why I need new blood here. Rotaboy is old, Diarist is middle rank, Parakeet is unfashionable. I will soon have to replace Rotaboy, and I must be sure to replace him with something of at least equal quality. The *prestige* of a stud farm, quite apart from its income, depends on the drawing-power of its stallions.'

'Yes,' I said. 'I see.'

Rotaboy, Diarist and Parakeet lost interest in the conversa-

357

tion and hope in the matter of carrots, and one by one withdrew into the boxes. The black retriever trotted around smelling unimaginable scents and Oliver Knowles began to walk me back towards the house.

'On the bigger stud farms,' he said, 'you'll find stallions which are owned by syndicates.'

'Forty shares?' I suggested.

He gave me a brief smile. 'That's right. Stallions are owned by any number of people between one and forty. When I first acquired Rotaboy it was in partnership with five others. I bought two of them out — they needed the money — so now I own half. That means I have twenty nominations each year, and I have no trouble in selling all of them, which is most satifactory.' He looked at me enquiringly to make sure I understood, which, thanks to Ursula Young, I did.

'I own Diarist outright. He was as expensive in the first place as Rotaboy, and as he's middle rank, so is the fee I can get for him. I don't always succeed in filling his forty places, and when that occurs I breed him to my own mares, and sell the resulting foals as yearlings.'

Fascinated, I nodded again.

'With Parakeet it's much the same. For the last three years I haven't been able to charge the fee I did to begin with, and if I fill his last places these days it's with mares from people who *prefer* steeplechasing, and this is increasingly destructive of his flat-racing image.'

We retraced our steps past the breeding shed and across the foaling yard.

'This place is expensive to run,' he said objectively. 'It makes a profit and I live comfortably, but I'm not getting any further. I have the capacity here for another stallion — enough accommodation, that is to say, for the extra forty mares. I have a good business sense and excellent health, and I feel underextended. If I am ever to achieve more I must have more capital ... and capital in the shape of a world-class stallion.'

'Which brings us,' I said, 'to Sandcastle.'

He nodded. 'If I acquired a horse like Sandcastle this stud would immediately be more widely known and more highly regarded.'

Understatement, I thought. The effect would be galvanic. 'A

358

sort of overnight stardom?' I said.

'Well, yes,' he agreed with a satisfied smile. 'I'd say you might be right.'

The big yard nearest the house had come moderately to life, with two or three lads moving about carrying feed scoops, hay nets, buckets of water and sacks of muck. Squibs with madly wagging tail went in a straight line towards a stocky man who bent to fondle his black ears.

'That's Nigel, my stud groom,' Oliver Knowles said. 'Come and meet him.' And as we walked across he added, 'If I can expand this place I'll up-rate him to stud manager; give him more standing with the customers.'

We reached Nigel, who was of about my own age with crinkly light-brown hair and noticeably bushy eyebrows. Oliver Knowles introduced me merely as 'a friend' and Nigel treated me with casual courtesy but not as the possible source of future fortune. He had a Gloucestershire accent but not pronounced, and I would have placed him as a farmer's son, if I'd had to.

'Any problems?' Oliver Knowles asked him, and Nigel shook his head.

'Nothing except that Floating mare with the discharge.'

His manner to his employer was confident and without anxiety but at the same time diffident, and I had a strong impression that it was Nigel's personality which suited Oliver Knowles as much as any skill he might have with mares. Oliver Knowles was not a man, I judged, to surround himself with awkward, unpredictable characters: the behaviour of everyone around him had to be as tidy as his place.

I wondered idly about the wife who had 'just buggered off with a Canadian', and at that moment a horse trotted into the yard with a young woman aboard. A girl, I amended, as she kicked her feet from the stirrups and slid to the ground. A noticeably curved young girl in jeans and heavy sweater with her dark hair tied in a pony tail. She led her horse into one of the boxes and presently emerged carrying the saddle and bridle, which she dumped on the ground outside the box before closing the bottom half of the door and crossing the yard to join us.

'My daughter,' Oliver Knowles said.

'Ginnie,' added the girl, holding out a polite brown hand. 'Are you the reason we didn't go out to lunch?'

Her father gave an instinctive repressing movement and Nigel looked only fairly interested.

'I don't know,' I said. 'I wouldn't think so.'

'Oh, I would,' she said. 'Pa really doesn't like parties. He uses any old excuse to get out of them, don't you Pa?'

He gave her an indulgent smile while looking as if his thoughts were elsewhere.

'I didn't mind missing it,' Ginnie said to me, anxious not to embarrass. 'Twelve miles away and people all Pa's age ... but they do have frightfully good canapés, and also a lemon tree growing in their greenhouse. Did you know that a lemon tree has everything all at once — buds, flowers, little green knobbly fruit and big fat lemons, all going on all the time?'

'My daughter,' Oliver Knowles said unnecessarily, 'talks a lot.'

'No,' I said, 'I didn't know about lemon trees.'

She gave me an impish smile and I wondered if she was even younger than I'd first thought: and as if by telepathy she said, 'I'm fifteen.'

'Everyone has to go through it,' I said.

Her eyes widened. 'Did you hate it?'

I nodded. 'Spots, insecurity, a new body you're not yet confortable in, self-consciousness ... terrible.'

Oliver Knowles looked surprised. 'Ginnie isn't self-conscious, are you, Ginnie?'

She looked from him to me and back again and didn't answer. Oliver Knowles dismissed the subject as of no importance anyway and said he ought to walk along and see the mare with the discharge. Would I care to go with him?

I agreed without reservation and we all set off along one of the paths between the white-railed paddocks, Oliver Knowles and myself in front, Nigel and Ginnie following, Squibs sniffing at every fencing post and marking his territory. In between Oliver Knowles explaining that some mares preferred living out of doors permanently, others would go inside if it snowed, others went in at nights, others lived mostly in the boxes, I could hear Ginnie telling Nigel that school this term was a dreadful drag owing to the new headmistress being a health fiend and making them all do jogging.

'How do you know what mares prefer?' I asked.

Oliver Knowles looked for the first time nonplussed. 'Er ...' he said. 'I suppose ... by the way they stand. If they feel cold and miserable they put their tails to the wind and look hunched. Some horses never do that, even in a blizzard. If they're obviously unhappy we bring them in. Otherwise they stay out. Same with the foals.' He paused. 'A lot of mares are miserable if you keep them inside. It's just ... how they are.'

He seemed dissatisfied with the loose ends of his answer, but I found them reassuring. The one thing he had seemed to me to lack had been any emotional contact with the creatures he bred: even the carrots for the stallions had been slightly mechanical.

The mare with the discharge proved to be in one of the paddocks at the boundary of the farm, and while Oliver Knowles and Nigel peered at her rump end and made obscure remarks like 'With any luck she won't slip,' and 'It's clear enough, nothing yellow or bloody,' I spent my time looking past the last set of white rails to the hedge and fields beyond.

The contrast from the Knowles land was dramatic. Instead of extreme tidiness, a haphazard disorder. Instead of short green grass in well-tended rectangles, long unkempt brownish stalks straggling through an army of drying thistles. Instead of rectangular brick-built stable yards, a ramshackle collection of wooden boxes, light grey from old creosote and with tarpaulins tied over patches of roof.

Ginnie followed my gaze. 'That's the Watcherleys' place,' she said. 'I used to go over there a lot but they're so grimy and gloomy these days, not a laugh in sight. And all the patients have gone, practically, and they don't even have the chimpanzees any more, they say they can't afford them.'

'What patients?' I said.

'Horse patients. It's the Watcherleys' hospital for sick horses. Haven't you ever heard of it?'

I shook my head.

'It's pretty well known,' Ginnie said. 'Or at least it was until that razzamatazz man Calder Jackson stole the show. Mind you, the Watcherleys were no great shakes, I suppose, with Bob off to the boozer at all hours and Maggie sweating her guts out carrying muck sacks, but at least they used to be fun. The place was *cosy*, you know, even if bits of the boxes were falling off their hinges and weeds were growing everywhere, and all the

361

horses went home blooming, or most of them, even if Maggie
had her knees through her jeans and wore the same jersey for
weeks and weeks on end. But Calder Jackson, you see, is the *in*
thing, with all those chat shows on television and the publicity
and such, and the Watcherleys have sort of got elbowed out.'

Her father, listening to the last of these remarks, added his
own view. 'They're disorganised,' he said. 'No business sense.
People liked their gypsy style for a while, but, as Ginnie says,
they've no answer to Calder Jackson.'

'How old are they?' I asked, frowning.

Oliver Knowles shrugged. 'Thirties. Going on forty. Hard to
say.'

'I suppose they don't have a son of about sixteen, thin and
intense, who hates Calder Jackson obsessively for ruining his
parents' business?'

'What an extraordinary question,' said Oliver Knowles, and
Ginnie shook her head. 'They've never had any children,' she
said. 'Maggie can't. She told me. They just lavish all that love
on animals. It's really grotty, what's happening to them.'

It would have been so neat, I thought, if Calder Jackson's
would-be assassin had been a Watcherley son. Too neat,
perhaps. But perhaps also there were others like the Watcherleys whose star had descended as Calder Jackson's rose. I
said, 'Do you know of any other places, apart from this one and
Calder Jackson's, where people send their sick horses?'

'I expect there *are* some,' Ginnie said. 'Bound to be.'

'Sure to be,' said Oliver Knowles, nodding. 'But of course we
don't send away any horse which falls ill here. I have an
excellent vet, great with mares, comes day or night in
emergencies.'

We made the return journey, Oliver Knowles pointing out to
me various mares and foals of interest and destributing carrots
to any head within armshot. Foals at foot, foals in utero; the
fertility cycle swelling again to fruition through the quiet winter,
life growing steadily in the dark.

Ginnie went off to see to the horse she'd been riding and
Nigel to finish his inspections in the main yard, leaving Oliver
Knowles, the dog and myself to go into the house. Squibs, poor
fellow, got no further than his basket in the mud room, but
Knowles and I returned to the sitting room-office from which

we'd started.

Thanks to my telephone calls of the morning I knew what the acquisition and management of Sandcastle would mean in the matter of taxation, and I'd also gone armed with sets of figures to cover the interest payable should the loan be approved. I found that I needed my knowledge not to instruct but to converse: Oliver Knowles was there before me.

'I've done this often, of course,' he said. 'I've had to arrange finance for buildings, for fencing, for buying the three stallions you saw, and for another two before them. I'm used to repaying fairly substantial bank loans. This new venture is of course huge by comparison, but if I didn't feel it was within my scope I assure you I shouldn't be contemplating it.' He gave me a brief charming smile. 'I'm not a nut case, you know. I really do know my business.'

'Yes,' I said. 'One can see.'

I told him that the maximum length of an Ekaterin loan (if one was forthcoming at all) would be five years, to which he merely nodded.

'That basically means,' I insisted, 'That you'd have to receive getting on for eight million in that five years, even allowing for paying off some of the loan every year with consequently diminishing interest. It's a great deal of money .... Are you sure you understand how much is involved?'

'Of course I understand,' he said. 'Even allowing for interest payments and the ridiculously high insurance premiums on a horse like Sandcastle, I'd be able to repay the loan in five years. That's the period I've used in planning.'

He spread out his sheets of neatly written calculations on his desk, pointing to each figure as he explained to me how he'd reached it. 'A stallion fee of forty thousand pounds will cover it. His racing record justifies that figure, and I've been most carefully into the breeding of Sandcastle himself, as you can imagine. There is absolutely nothing in the family to alarm. No trace of hereditary illness or undesirable tendencies. He comes from a healthy blue-blooded line of winners, and there's no reason why he shouldn't breed true.' He gave me a photocopied genealogical table. 'I wouldn't expect you to advance a loan without getting an expert opinion on this. Please do take it with you.'

He gave me also some copies of his figures, and I packed them all into the brief case I'd taken with me.

'Why don't you consider halving your risk to twenty-one shares?' I asked. 'Sell nineteen. You'd still outvote the other owners — there'd be no chance of them whisking Sandcastle off somewhere else — and you'd be less stretched.'

With a smile he shook his head. 'If I found for any reason that the repayments were causing me acute difficulty, I'd sell some shares as necessary. But I hope in five years time to own Sandcastle outright, and also as I told you to have attracted other stallions of that calibre, and to be numbered among the world's top-ranking stud farms.'

His pleasant manner took away any suggestion of megalomania, and I could see nothing of that nature in him.

Ginnie came into the office carrying two mugs with slightly anxious diffidence.

'I made some tea. Do you want some Dad?'

'Yes, please,' I said immediately, before he could answer, and she looked almost painfully relieved. Oliver Knowles turned what had seemed like an incipient shake of the head into a nod, and Ginnie, handing over the mugs, said that if I wanted sugar she would go and fetch some. 'And a spoon, I guess.'

'My wife's away,' Oliver Knowles said abruptly.

'No sugar,' I said. 'This is great.'

'You won't forget, Dad, will you, about me going back to school?'

'Nigel will take you.'

'He's got visitors.'

'Oh ... all right.' He looked at his watch. 'In half an hour, then.'

Ginnie looked even more relieved, particularly as I could clearly sense the the irritation he was suppressing. 'The school run,' he said as the door closed behind his daughter, 'was one of the things my wife always did. Does ...' He shrugged. 'She's away indefinetely. You might as well know.'

'I'm sorry,' I said.

'Can't be helped.' He looked at the tea-mug in my hand. 'I was going to offer you something stronger.'

'This is fine.'

'Ginnie comes home on four Sundays a term. She's a

364

boarder, of course.' He paused. 'She's not yet used to her mother not being here. It's bad for her, but there you are, life's like that.'

'She's a nice girl,' I said.

He gave me a glance in which I read both love for his daughter and a blindness to her needs. 'I don't suppose,' he said thoughtfully, 'That you go anywhere near High Wycombe on your way home?'

'Well,' I said obligingly, 'I could do.'

I consequently drove Ginnie back to her school, listening on the way to her views on the new headmistress's compulsory jogging programme ('all our bosoms flopping up and down, bloody uncomfortable and absolutely *disgusting* to look at') and to her opinion of Nigel ('Dad thinks the sun shines out of his you-know-what and I dare say he is pretty good with the mares, they all seem to flourish, but what the lads get up to behind his back is nobody's business. They smoke in the feed sheds, I ask you! All that hay around ... Nigel never notices. He'd made a rotten school prefect') and to her outlook on life in general ('I can't wait to get out of school uniform and out of dormitories and being bossed around, and I'm no good at lessons; the whole thing's a *mess*. Why has everything *changed*? I used to be happy, or at least I wasn't *unhappy*, which I mostly seem to be nowadays, and no, it isn't because of Mum going away, or not especially, as she was never as a lovey-dovey sort of mother, always telling me to eat with my mouth shut and so on ... and you must be bored silly hearing all this.')

'No.' I said truthfully. 'I'm not bored.'

'I'm not even *beautiful*, she said despairingly. 'I can suck in my cheeks until I faint but I'll never look pale and bony and interesting.'

I glanced at the still rounded child-woman face, at the peach-bloom skin and the worried eyes.

'Practically no one is beautiful at fifteen,' I said. 'It's too soon.'

'How do you mean — too soon?'

'Well,' I said, 'say at twelve you're a child and flat and undeveloped and so on, and at maybe seventeen or eighteen you're a full-grown adult, just think of the terrific changes your body goes through in that time. Appearance, desires, mental outlook, everything. So at fifteen, which isn't much more than halfway, it's still too soon to know exactly what the end product will be like. And if it's of any comfort to you, you do now look as you may be beautiful in a year or two, or at least not unbearably ugly.'

She sat in uncharacteristic silence for quite a distance, and then she said, 'Why did you come today? I mean, who are you? If it's all right to ask?'

'It's all right. I'm a sort of financial adviser. I work in a bank.'

'Oh.' She sounded slightly disappointed but made no further comment, and soon after that gave me prosaic and accurate directions to the school.

'Thanks for the lift,' she said, politely shaking hands as we stood beside the car.

'A pleasure.'

'And thanks ...' she hesitated. 'Thanks anyway.'

I nodded, and she half-walked, half-ran to join a group of other girls going into the buildings. Looking briefly back she gave me a sketchy wave, which I acknowledged. Nice child, I thought, pointing the car homewards. Mixed up, as who wasn't at that age. Middling brains, not quite pretty, her future a clean stretch of sand waiting for footprints.

The First Year

DECEMBER

It made the headlines in the *Sporting Life* (OLIVER KNOWLES, KING OF THE SANDCASTLE) and turned up as the lead story under less fanciful banners on the racing pages of all the other dailies.

SANDCASTLE TO GO TO STUD, SANDCASTLE TO STAY IN BRITAIN, SANDCASTLE SHARES NOT FOR SALE, SANDCASTLE BOUGHT PRIVATELY FOR HUGE SUM. The story in every case was short and simple. One of the year's top stallions had been acquired by the owner of a heretofore moderately-ranked stud farm. 'I am very happy,' Oliver Knowles was universally reported as saying. 'Sandcastle is a prize for British bloodstock.'

The buying price, all the papers said, was 'not unadjacent to five million pounds,' and a few of them added 'the financing was private.'

'Well,' Henry said at lunch, tapping the *Sporting Life*, 'not many of our loans make so much splash.'

'It's a belly-flop,' muttered the obstinate dissenter, who on that day happened to be sitting at my elbow.

Henry didn't hear and was anyway in good spirits. 'If one of the foals run in the Derby we'll take a party from the office. What do you say, Gordon? Fifty people on open-topped buses?'

Gordon agreed with the sort of smile which hoped he wouldn't actually be called upon to fulfil his promise.

367

'Forty mares,' Henry said musingly. 'Forty foals, surely one of them might be Derby material.'

'Er,' I said, from new-found knowledge. 'Forty foals is stretching it. Thirty-five would be pretty good. Some mares won't "take", so to speak.'

Henry showed mild alarm. 'Does that mean that five or six fees will have to be returned? Doesn't that effect Knowles' programme of repayment?'

I shook my head. 'For a horse of Sandcastle's stature the fee is all up in front. Payable for services rendered, regardless of results. That's in Britain, of course, and Europe. In America they have the system of no foal, no fee, even for the top stallions. A live foal, that is. Alive, on its feet and suckling.'

Henry relaxed, leaning back in his chair and smiling. 'You've certainly learnt a lot, Tim, since this all started.'

'It's absorbing.'

He nodded. 'I know it isn't usual, but how do you feel about keeping an eye on the bank's money at close quarters? Would Knowles object to you dropping in from time to time?'

'I shouldn't think so. Not out of general interest.'

'Good. Do that, then. Bring us progress reports. I must say I've never been as impressed with any horse as I was that day with Sandcastle.'

Henry's direct admiration of the colt had led in the end to Ekaterin's advancing three of the five million to Oliver Knowles, with private individuals subscribing the other two. The fertility tests had been excellent, the owner had been paid, and Sandcastle already stood in the stallion yard in Hertfordshire alongside Rotaboy, Diarist and Parakeet.

December was marching along towards Christmas, with trees twinkling all over London and sleet falling bleakly in the afternoons. On an impulse I sent a card embossed with tasteful robins to Calder Jackson, wishing him well, and almost by return of post received (in the office) a missive (Stubbs reproduction) thanking me sincerely and asking if I would be interested some time in looking round his place. If so, he finished, would I telephone — number supplied.

I telephoned. He was affable and far more spontaneous than usual. 'Do come,' he said, and we made a date for the following Sunday.

I told Gordon I was going. We were working on an inter-bank loan of nine and a half million for five days to a competitor, a matter of little more than a few telephone calls and a promise. My hair had almost ceased to rise at the size and speed of such deals, and with only verbal agreement from Val and Henry I had recently on my own lent seven million for forty-eight hours. The trick was never to lend for a longer time than we ourselves were able to borrow the necessary funds: if we did, we ran the risk of having to pay a higher rate of interest than we were receiving on the loan, a process which physically hurt Val Fisher. There had been a time in the past when owing to a client repaying late he had had to borrow several million for eighteen days at twenty-five per cent, and he'd never got over it.

Most of our dealings weren't on such a heavy scale, and next on my agenda was a request for us to lend fifty-five thousand pounds to a man who had invented a waste-paper basket for use in cars and needed funds for development. I read the letter out to Gordon, who made a fast thumbs-down gesture.

'Pity,' I said. 'It's a sorely needed object.'

'He's asking too little.' He put his left hand hard between his knees and clamped it there. 'And there are far better inventions dying the death.'

I agreed with him and wrote a brief note of regret. Gordon looked up from his pages shortly after, and asked me what I'd be doing at Christmas.

'Nothing much,' I said.

'Not going to your mother in Jersey?'

'They're cruising in the Caribbean.'

'Judith and I wondered ...' he cleared his throat, ' ... if you'd care to stay with us. Come on Christmas Eve, stay three or four days? Just as you like, of course. I daresay you wouldn't find us too exciting ... but the offer's there, anyway.'

Was it wise, I wondered, to spend three or four days with Judith when three to four *hours* at Ascot had tempted acutely? Was it wise, when the sight of her aroused so many natural urges, to sleep so long — and so near — under her roof?

Most unwise.

'I'd like to,' I said, 'very much'; and I thought you're a bloody stupid fool, Tim Ekaterin, and if you ache it'll be your own

369

ridiculous fault.

'Good,' Gordon said, looking as if he meant it. 'Judith will be pleased. She was afraid you might have younger friends to go to.'

'Nothing fixed.'

He nodded contentedly and went back to his work, and I thought about Judith wanting me to stay, because if she hadn't wanted it I wouldn't have been asked.

If I had any sense I wouldn't go: but I knew I would.

Calder Jackson's place at Newmarket, seen that next Sunday morning, was a gem of public relations, where everything had been done to please those visiting the sick. The yard itself, a three-sided quadrangle, had been cosmetically planted with central grass and a graceful tree, and brightly painted tubs, bare now of flowers, stood at frequent intervals outside the boxes. There were park-bench type seats here and there, and ornamental gates and railings in black iron scroll-work, and a welcoming archway labelled 'Comfort Room This Way.'

Outside the main yard, and to one side, stood a small separate building painted glossy white. There was a large prominent red cross on the door, with, underneath it, the single word 'Surgery'.

The yard and the surgery were what the visitor first saw: beyond and screened by trees stood Calder Jackson's own house, more private from prying eyes than his business. I parked beside several other cars on a stretch of asphalt, and walked over to ring the bell. The front door was opened to me by a manservant in a white coat. Butler or nurse?

'This way, sir,' he said deferentially, when I announced my name. 'Mr Jackson is expecting you.'

Butler.

Interesting to see the dramatic hair-cut in its home setting, which was olde-worlde cottage on a grand scale. I had an impression of a huge room, oak rafters, stone flagged floor, rugs, dark oak furniture, great brick fireplace with burning logs ... and Calder advancing with a broad smile and outstretched arm.

'Tim!' he exclaimed, shaking hands vigorously. 'This is a pleasure, indeed it is.'

'Been looking forward to it,' I said.

'Come along to the fire. Come and warm yourself. How about a drink? And ... oh ... this is a friend of mine ...' he waved towards a second man already standing by the fireplace, ' ... Ian Pargetter.'

The friend and I nodded to each other and made the usual strangers-meeting signals, and the name tumbled over in my mind as something I'd heard somewhere before but couldn't quite recall.

Calder Jackson clinked bottles and glasses and upon consultation gave me a Scotch of noble proportions.

'And for you, Ian,' he said. 'A further tincture?'

Oh yes, I thought. The vet. Ian Pargetter, the vet who didn't mind consorting with unlicensed practitioners.

Ian Pargetter hesitated but shrugged and held out his glass as one succumbing to pleasurable temptation.

'A small one, then, Calder,' he said. 'I must be off.'

He was about forty, I judged; large and reliable-looking, with sandy greying hair, a heavy moustache and an air of being completely in charge of his life. Calder explained that it was I who had deflected the knife aimed at him at Ascot, and Ian Pargetter made predictable responses about luck, fast reactions and who could have wanted to kill Calder?

'That was altogether a memorable day,' Calder said. 'Pity he's going to stud so soon.'

I smiled. 'Maybe we'll win on his sons.'

There was no particular secret, as far as I knew, about where the finance for Sandcastle had come from, but it was up to Oliver Knowles to reveal it, not me. I thought Calder would have been interested, but bankers' ethics as usual kept me quiet.

'A superb horse,' Calder said, with all the enthusiasm he'd shown in Dissdale's box. 'One of the greats.'

Ian Pargetter nodded agreement, then finished his drink at a gulp and said he'd be going. 'Let me know how that pony fares, Calder.'

'Yes, of course.' Calder moved with his departing guest towards the door and slapped him on the shoulder. 'Thanks for dropping in, Ian. Appreciate it.'

There were sounds of Pargetter leaving by the front door,

and Calder returned rubbing his hands together and saying that although it was cold outside, I might care to look round before his other guests arrived for lunch. Accordingly we walked across to the open-sided quadrangle, where Calder moved from box to box giving me a brief resumé of the illness and prospects of each patient.

'This pony only came yesterday ... it's a prize show pony supposedly, and look at it. Dull eyes, rough coat, altogether droopy. They say it's had diarrhoea on and off for weeks. I'm their last resort, they say.' He smiled philosophically. 'Can't think why they don't send me sick horses as a *first* resort. But there you are, they always try regular vets first. Can't blame them, I suppose.'

We moved along the line. 'This mare was coughing blood when she came three weeks ago. I was her owner's last resort.' He smiled again. 'She's doing fine now. The cough's almost gone. She's eating well, putting on condition.' The mare blinked at us lazily as we stolled away.

'This is a two-year-old filly,' Calder said, peering over a half-door. 'She'd had an infected ulcer on her withers for six weeks before she came here. Antibiotics had proved useless. Now the ulcer's dry and healing. Most satisfactory.'

We went on down the row.

'This is someone's favourite hunter, came all the way from Gloucestershire. I don't know what I can do for him, though of course I'll try. His trouble, truthfully, is just age.'

Further on: 'Here's a star three-day-eventer. Came to me with intermittent bleeding in the urine, intractable to antibiotics. He was clearly in great pain, and almost dangerous to deal with on account of it. But now he's fine. He'll be staying here for a while longer but I'm sure the trouble is cured.'

'This is a three-year-old colt who won a race back in July but then started breaking blood vessels and went on doing it despite treatment. He's been here a fortnight. Last resort, of course!'

By the next box he said, 'Don't look at this one if you're squeamish. Poor wretched little filly, she's so weak she can't hold her head up and all her bones are sharp under the skin. Some sort of wasting sickness. Blood tests haven't shown what it is. I don't know if I can heal her. I've laid my hands on her twice so far, but there's been nothing. No ... feeling. Sometimes it takes a long time. But I'm not giving up with her, and there's always hope.'

He turned his curly head and pointed to another box further ahead. 'There's a colt along there who's been here two months and is only just responding. His owners were is despair, and so was I, privately, but then just three days ago when I was in his box I could feel the force flowing down my arms and into him, and the next day he was mending.'

He spoke with a far more natural fluency on his home ground and less as if reciting from a script, but all the same I felt the same reservations about the healing touch as I had at Ascot. I was a doubter, I supposed. I would never in my life have put my trust in a seventh son of a seventh son, probably because the only direct knowledge I had of any human seeking out 'the touch' had been a close friend of mine at college who'd had hopeless cancer and had gone to a woman healer as a last resort, only to be told that he was dying because he wanted to. I could vividly remember his anger, and mine on his behalf: and standing in Calder's yard I wondered if that same woman would also think that *horses* got sick to death because they wanted to.

'Is there anything you can't treat?' I asked. 'Anything you turn away?'

'I'm afraid so, yes.' He smiled ruefully. 'There are some things, like advanced laminitis, with which I feel hopeless, and as for coryne ...' he shook his head, ' ... it's a killer.'

'You've lost me,' I said.

'So sorry. Well, laminitis is a condition of the feet where the bone eventually begins to crumble, and the horses in the end can't bear the pain of standing up. They lie down, and horses can't live for more than a few days lying down.' He spoke with regret. 'And coryne,' he went on, 'is a frightful bacterial infection which is deadly to foals. It induces a sort of pneumonia with abcesses in the lungs. Terribly contagious. I know of one stud farm in America which lost seventy foals in one day.'

I listened in horror. 'Do we have it in England?' I asked.

'Sometimes, in pockets, but not widespread. It doesn't affect older horses. Foals of three months or over are safe.' He paused. 'Some very young foals do survive, of course, but they're likely to have scar tissue in the lungs which may impair their breathing for racing purposes.'

373

'Isn't there a vaccine?' I said.

He smiled indulgently. 'Very little research is done into equine diseases, chiefly because of the cost but also because horses are so large, and can't be kept in a laboratory for any controlled series of tests.'

I again had the impression that he had said all this many times before, but it was understandable and I was getting used to it. We proceeded on the hospital round (four-year-old with general debility, show-jumper with festering leg) and came at length to a box with an open door.

'We're giving this one sun treatment,' Calder said, indicating that I should look; and inside the box a thin youth was adjusting the angle of an ultra-violet lamp set on a head-high wall-mounted bracket. It wasn't at the dappled grey that I looked, however, but at the lad, because in the first brief glimpse I thought he was the boy who had tried to attack Calder.

I opened my mouth ... and shut it again.

He wasn't the boy. He was of the same height, same build, same litheness, same general colouring, but not with the same eyes or jawline or narrow nose.

Calder saw my reaction and smiled. 'For a split second, when I saw that boy move at Ascot, I thought it was Jason here. But it wasn't, of course.'

I shook my head. 'Alike but different.'

Calder nodded. 'And Jason wouldn't want to kill me, would you, Jason?' He spoke with a jocularity to which Jason didn't respond.

'No, sir,' he said stolidly.

'Jason is my right-hand man,' said Calder heartily. 'Indispensable.'

The right-hand man showed no satisfaction at the flattery and maintained an impassive countenance throughout. He touched the grey horse and told it to shift over a bit in the manner of one equal talking to another, and the horse obediently shifted.

'Mind you eyes with that lamp,' Calder said. 'Where are your glasses?'

Jason fished into the breast pocket of his shirt and produced some ultra-dark sun-shades. Calder nodded. 'Put them on,' he said, Jasons complied. Where before there had already been a lack of mobility of expression, there was now, with the

374

obscured eyes, no way at all of guessing Jason's thoughts.

'I'll be finished with this one in ten minutes,' he said. 'Is there anything else after that, sir?'

Calder briefly pondered and shook his head. 'Just the evening rounds at four.'

'Your invalids get every care,' I said, complimenting them.

Jason's blacked-out eyes turned my way, but it was Calder who said 'Hard work gets results.' And you've said that a thousand times, I thought.

We reached the last box in the yard, the first one which was empty.

'Emergency bed,' Calder said, jokingly, and I smiled and asked how much he charged for his patients.

He replied easily and without explanation or apology. 'Twice the training fees currently charged for horses in the top Newmarket stables. When their rates go up, so do mine.'

'*Twice* …?'

He nodded. 'I could charge more, you know. But if I charged less I'd be totally swamped by all those "last resort" people, and I simply haven't the room or the time or the spiritual resources to take more cases than I do.'

I wondered how one would ever get to the essence of the man behind the temperate, considerate public face, or indeed if the public face was not a façade at all but the essence itself. I looked at the physical strength of the shoulders below the helmet head and listened to the plain words describing a mystical force, considered the dominating voice and the mild manner, and still found him a man to admire rather than like. 'The surgery,' he said, gesturing towards it as we walked that way. 'My drug store!' He smiled at the joke (how often, I wondered, had he said it?) and produced a key to unlock the door. 'Ther's nothing dangerous or illegal in here, of course, but one has to protect against vandals. So sad, don't you think?'

The surgery, which had no windows, was basically a large brick-built hut. The internal walls, like the outer, were painted white, and the floor was tiled red. There were antiseptic-looking glass-fronted cabinets along the two end walls and a wide bench with drawers underneath along the wall facing the door. On the bench, a delicate-looking set of scales, a pestle and mortar and a pair of fine rubber gloves: behind the glass of the cabinets, rows of bottles and boxes. Everything very business-like and tidy: and along the wall which contained the door stood three kitchen appliances, refrigerator, cooker and sink.

Calder pointed vaguely towards the cabinets. 'In there I keep the herbs in pill and powder form. Comfrey, myrrh, sarsaparilla, golden seal, fo-ti-tieng, things like that.'

'Er ... ' I said. 'What do they do?'

He ran through them obligingly. 'Comfrey knits bones, and heals wounds, myrrh is antiseptic and good for diarrhoea and rheumatism, sarsaparilla contains male hormones and increases physical strength, golden seal cures eczema, improves appetite and digestion, fo-ti-tieng is a revitalising tonic second to none. Then there's liquorice for coughs and papaya enzymes for digesting proteins and passiflora to use as a general pacifier and tranquilliser.' He paused. 'There's ginseng also, of course, which is a marvellous rejuvenator and invigorator, but it's really too expensive in the quantities needed to do a horse significant good. It has to be taken continuously, for ever.' He sighed. 'Excellent for humans, though.'

The air in the windowless room was fresh and smelled very faintly fragrant, and as if to account for it Calder started showing me the contents of the drawers.

'I keep seeds in here,' he said. 'My patients eat them by the handful each day.' Three or four of the drawers contained large opaque plastic bags fastened by bull-dog clips. 'Sunflower seeds for vitamins, phosphorus and calcium, good for bones and teeth. Pumpkin seeds for vigour — they contain male hormones — and also for phosphorus and iron. Carrot seeds for calming nervous horses. Sesame seeds for general health.'

He walked along a yard or two and pulled open an extra-large deep drawer which contained larger bags; more like sacks. 'These are hops left after beer-making. They're packed full of all good things. A great tonic, and cheap enough to use in quantity. We have bagfuls of them over in the feed shed to grind up as chaff but I use these here as one ingredient of my special deccction, my concentrated tonic.'

'Do you make it ... on the stove?' I asked.

He smiled. 'Like a chef.' He opened the refrigerator door. 'I store it in here. Want to see?'

I looked inside. Nearly the whole space was taken with gallon-sized plastic containers full of brownish liquid. 'We mix it in a bran mash, warmed of course, and the horses thrive.'

I knew nothing about the efficiency of his remedies, but I was definitely impressed.

'How do you get the horses to take pills?' I said.

'In an apple, usually. We scoop out half the core, put in the tablet or capsule, or indeed just powder, and replace the plug.'

So simple.

'And incidentally, I make most of my own pills and capsules. Some, like comfrey, are commercially available, but I prefer to buy the dried herbs in their pure form and make my own recipes.' He pulled open one of the lower drawers under the work-bench and lifted out a heavy wooden box. 'This,' he said, laying it on the work surface and opening the lid, 'contains the makings.'

I looked down at a whole array of brass dies, each a small square with a pill-sized cavity in its centre. The cavities varied from tiny to extra large, and from round to oblong.

'It's an antique,' he said with a touch of pride. 'Early Victorian. Dates from when pills were always made by hand — and it's still viable, of course. You put the required drug in powder form into whatever sized cavity you want, and compress it with the rod which exactly fits.' He lifted one of a series of short brass rods from its rack and fitted its end into one of the cavities, tamping it up and down; then picked the whole die out of the box and tipped it right over. 'Hey presto,' he said genially, catching the imaginary contents, 'a pill!'

'Neat,' I said, with positive pleasure.

He nodded. 'Capsules are quicker and more modern.' He pulled open another drawer and briefly showed me the empty tops and bottoms of a host of gelatin capsules, again of varying sizes, though mostly a little larger than those swallowed easily by humans. 'Veterinary size,' he explained.

He closed his gem of a pill-making box and returned it to its drawer, straightening up afterwards and casting a caring eye around the place to make sure everything was tidy. With a nod of private satisfaction he opened the door for us to return to the outside world, switching off the fluorescent lights and locking the door behind us.

A car was just rolling to a stop on the asphalt, and presently two recognised figures emerged from it: Dissdale Smith and his delectable Bettina.

'Hello, hello,' said Dissdale, striding across with ready hand. 'Calder said you were coming. Good to see you. Calder's been showing you all his treasures, eh? The conducted tour, eh, Calder?' I shook the hand. 'Calder's proud of his achievements here, aren't you Calder?'

'With good reason,' I said civilly, and Calder gave me a swift glance and a genuine-looking smile.

Bettina drifted more slowly up to join us, a delight in high heeled boots and cuddling fur, a white silk scarf round her throat and smooth dark hair falling glossily to her shoulders. Her scent travelled sweetly across the quiet cold air and she laid a decorative hand on my arm in an intimate touch.

'Tim the saviour,' she said. 'Calder's hero.'

The over-packaged charm unaccountably brought the contrasting image of Ginnie sharply to mind, and I briefly thought that the promise was more beckoning than the performance, that child more interesting than that woman.

Calder took us all soon into his maxi-cottage sitting-room and distributed more drinks. Dissdale told me that Sandcastle had almost literally saved his business and metaphorically his life, and we all drank a toast to the wonder horse. Four further guests arrived — a married couple with their two twentyish daughters — and the occasion became an ordinarily enjoyable lunch party, undemanding, unmemorable, good food handed round by the manservant, cigars offered with the coffee.

Calder at some point said he was off to America in the New Year on a short lecture tour.

'Unfortunately,' he said, 'I'll be talking to health clubs, not horse people. American racehorse trainers aren't receptive to me. Or not yet. But then, it took a few years for Newmarket to decide I could make a contribution.'

Everyone smiled at the scepticism of America and Newmarket.

Calder said, 'January is often a quiet month here. We don't take any new admissions if I'm away, and of course my head lad just keeps the established routines going until I return. It works pretty well.' He smiled. 'If I'm lucky I'll get some ski-ing; and to be honest, I'm looking forward to the ski-ing much more than the talks.'

Everyone left soon after three, and I drove back to London through the short darkening afternoon wondering if the herbs of antiquity held secrets we'd almost wilfully lost.

'Caffeine,' Calder had been saying towards the end, 'is a get-up-and-go stimulant, tremendously useful. Found in coffee beans of course, and in tea and cocoa and in cola drinks. Good for asthma. Vigorous marvellous tonic. A life-saver after shock. And now in America, I ask you, they're casting caffeine as a villain and are busy taking it out of everything it's naturally *in*. You might as well take the alcohol out of bread.'

'But Calder dear,' Bettina said, 'There's no alcohol in bread.'

He looked at her kindly as she sat on his right.'Bread that is made with yeast definitely does contain alcohol before it's cooked. If you mix yeast with water and sugar you get alcohol and carbon-dioxide, which is the gas which makes the dough rise. The air in a bakery smells of wine ... simple chemistry, my dear girl, no magic in it. Bread is the staff of life and alcohol is good for you.'

There had been jokes and lifted glasses, and I could have listened to Calder for hours.

The Christmas party at Gordon Michael's home was in a way an echo, because Judith's apothecary friend Pen Warner was in attendance most of the time, I got to know her quite well and to like her very much, which Judith may or may not have intended. In any case, it was again the fairy-tale day at Ascot which had led on to friendly relations.

'Do you remember Burnt Marshmallow?' Pen said. 'I bought a painting with my winnings.'

'I spent mine on riotous living.'

'Oh yes?' She looked me up and down and shook her head. 'You haven't the air.'

'What do I have the air of?' I asked curiously, and she answered in amusement, 'Of intelligent laziness and boring virtue.'

'All wrong,' I said.

'Ho hum.'

She seemed to me to be slightly less physically solid than at

Ascot, but it might have been only the change of clothes; there were still the sad eyes and the ingrained worthiness and the unexpected cast of humour. She had apparently spent twelve hours that day — it was Christmas Eve — doling out remedies to people whose illnesses showed no sense of timing, and proposed to go back at six in the morning. Meanwhile she appeared at the Michaels' house in a long festive caftan with mood to match, and during the evening the four of us ate quails with our fingers, and roasted chestnuts, and played a board game with childish gusto.

Judith wore rose pink pearls and looked about twenty-five. Gordon in advance had instructed me 'Bring whatever you like as long as it's informal' and himself was resplendent in a plum velvet jacket and bow tie. My own newly bought cream wool shirt which in the shop had looked fairly theatrical seemed in the event to be right, so that on all levels the evening proved harmonious and fun, much more rounded and easy that I'd expected.

Judith's housekeeping throughout my stay proved a poem of invisibility. Food appeared from freezer and cupboard, remnants returned to dishwasher and dustbin. Jobs were distributed when essential but sitting and talking had priority: and nothing so smooth, I reflected, ever got done without hard work beforehand.

'Pen will be back soon after one tomorrow,' Judith said at midnight on that first evening. 'We'll have a drink then and open some presents, and have our Christmas feast at half past three. There will be breakfast in the morning, and Gordon and I will go to church.' She left an invitation lingering in the air, but I marginally shook my head. 'You can look after yourself, then, while we're gone.'

She kissed me goodnight, with affection and on the cheek. Gordon gave me a smile and a wave, and I went to bed across the hall from them and spent an hour before sleep deliberately not thinking at all about Judith in or out of her nightgown — or not much.

Breakfast was taken in dressing gowns. Judith's was red, quilted and unrevealing.

They changed and went to church. Pray for me, I said, and set out for a walk on the common.

380

There were brightly-wrapped gifts waiting around the base of the silver-starred Christmas tree in Michaels' drawing room, and a surreptitious inspection had revealed one from Pen addressed to me. I walked across the windy grass, shoulders hunched, hands in pockets, wondering what to do about one for her, and as quite often happens came by chance to a solution.

A small boy was out there with his father, flying a kite, and I stopped to watch.

'That's fun,' I said.

The boy took no notice but the father said, 'There's no satisfying the little bleeder. I give him this and he says he wants roller skates.'

The kite was a brilliant phosphorescent Chinese dragon with butterfly wings and a big frilly tail, soaring and circling like a joyful tethered spirit in the Christmas sky.

'Will you sell it to me?' I asked. 'Buy the roller skates instead?' I explained the problem, the need for an instant present.

Parent and child consulted and the deal was done. I wound up the string carefully and bore the trophy home, wondering what on earth the sober pharmacist would think of such a thing: but when she unwrapped it from the gold paper (cadged from Judith for the purpose) she pronounced herself enchanted, and back we all went onto the common to watch her fly it.

The whole day was happy. I hadn't had so good a Christmas since I was a child. I told them so, and kissed Judith uninhibitedly under some mistletoe, which Gordon didn't seem to mind.

'You were born sunny,' Judith said, briefly stroking my cheek, and Gordon, nodding said, 'A man without sorrows, unacquainted with grief.'

'Grief and sorrow come with time,' Pen said, but not as if she meant it imminently. 'They come to us all.'

On the morning after Christmas Day I drove Judith across London to Hampstead to put flowers on her mother's grave.

'I know you'll think me silly, but I always go. She died on Boxing Day when I was twelve. It's the only way I have of remembering her ... of feeling I had a mother at all. I usually go by myself. Gordon thinks I'm sentimental and doesn't like

381

coming.'

'Nothing wrong with sentiment,' I said.

Hampstead was where I lived in the upstairs half of a friend's house. I wasn't sure whether or not Judith knew it and said nothing until she'd deliverd the pink chrysanthemums to the square marble tablet let in flush with the grass and communed for a while with the memories floating there.

It was as we walked slowly back towards the iron gates that I neutrally said, 'My flat's only half a mile from here. This part of London is home ground.'

'Is it?'

'Mm.'

After a few steps she said, 'I knew you lived somewhere here. If you remember, you wouldn't let us drive you all the way home from Ascot. You said Hampstead was too far.'

'So it was.'

'Not for Sir Galahad that starry night.'

We reached the gates and paused for her to look back. I was infinitely conscious of her nearness and of my own stiffled desire; and she looked abruptly into my eyes and said, 'Gordon knows you live here, also.'

'And does he know how I feel?' I asked.

'I don't know. He hasn't said.'

I wanted very much to go that last half mile: that short distance on wheels, that far journey in commitment. My body tingled ... rippled ... from hunger, and I found myself physically clenching my back teeth.

'What are you thinking?' she said.

'For God's sake ... you know damn well what I'm thinking ... and we're going back to Clapham right this minute.'

She sighed. 'Yes, I suppose we must.'

'What do you mean ... you suppose?'

'Well, I ...' she paused. 'I mean, yes we must. I'm sorry ... it was just that ... for a moment ... I was tempted.'

'As at Ascot?' I said.

She nodded. 'As at Ascot.'

'Only here and now,' I said, 'we have the place and the time and the opportunity to do something about it.'

'Yes'.

'And what we're going to do ... is ... nothing.' It came out as half a question, half a statement: wholly an impossibility.

'Why do we *care*?' she said explosively. 'Why don't we just get into your bed and have a happy time? Why is the whole thing so tangled up with bloody concepts like honour?'

We walked down the road to where I'd parked the car and I drove southwards with careful observance at every red light; stop signals making round eyes at me all the way to Clapham.

'I'd have liked it,' Judith said as we pulled up outside her house.

'So would I.'

We went indoors in a sort of deprived companionship, and I realised only when I saw Gordon's smiling unsuspicious face that I couldn't have returned there if it had been in any other way.

It was at lunch that day, when Pen had again resurfaced from her stint among the pills that I told them about my visit to Calder. Pen, predictably, was acutely interested and said she'd dearly like to know what was in the decoction in the refrigerator.

'What's a decoction?' Judith asked.

'A preparation boiled with water. If you dissolve things in alcohol, that's a tincture.'

'One lives and bloody well learns!'

Pen laughed. 'How about carminative, anodyne and vermifuge ... effects of drugs. They simply roll off the tongue with grandeur.'

'And what do they mean?' Gordon asked.

'Getting rid of gas, getting rid of pain, getting rid of worms.'

Gordon too was laughing, 'Have some anodyne tincture of grape.' He poured wine into our glasses. 'Do you honestly believe, Tim, that Calder cures horses by touch?'

'I'm sure *he* believes it.' I reflected. 'I don't know if he will let anyone watch. And if he did, what would one see? I don't suppose with a horse it's a case of "take up you bed and walk."'

Judith said in surprise. 'You sound as if you'd like it to be true. You, that Gordon and Harry have trained to doubt!'

'Calder's impressive,' I admitted. 'So is his place. So are the fees he charges. He wouldn't be able to set his prices so high if he didn't get real results.'

383

'Do the herbs come extra?' Pen said.

'I didn't ask.'

'Would you expect them to?' Gordon said.

'Well ...' Pen considered. 'Some of those that Tim mentioned are fairly exotic. Golden seal — that's hydrastis — said in the past to cure practically anything you can mention, but mostly used nowadays in tiny amounts in eye-drops. Has to be imported from America. And fo-ti-tieng — which is *Hydrocotyle asiatica minor*, also called the source of the elixir of long life — that only grows as far as I know in the tropical jungles of the far east. I mean, I would have thought that giving things like that to horses would be wildly expensive.'

If I'd been impressed with Calder I was probably more so with Pen. 'I didn't know pharmacists were so clued up on herbs,' I said.

'I was just interested so I learned their properties,' she exclaimed. 'The age-old remedies are hardly even hinted at on the official pharmacy courses, though considering digitalis and penicillin one can't exactly see why. A lot of chemists shops don't sell non-prescription herbal remedies, but I do, and honestly for a stack of people they seem to work.'

'And do you advocate garlic poultices for the feet of babies with whooping-cough?' Gordon asked.

Pen didn't. There was more laughter. If one believed in Calder, Judith said firmly, one believed in him, garlic poultices and all.

The four of us spent a comfortable afternoon and evening together, and when Judith and Gordon went to bed I walked along with Pen to her house, where she'd been staying each night, filling my lungs with the fresh air off the common.

'You're going home tomorrow, aren't you?' she said, fishing out her keys.

I nodded. 'In the morning.'

'It's been great fun.' She found the keys and fitted one in the lock. 'Would you like to come in?'

'No ... I'll just walk for a bit.'

She opened the door and paused there. 'Thank you for the kite ... it was brilliant. And goodbye for this time, though I guess if Judith can stand it I'll be seeing you again.'

'Stand what?' I asked.

She kissed me on the cheek. 'Goodnight,' she said. 'And believe it or not, the herb known as passion flower is good for insomnia.'

Her grin shone out like the Cheshire Cat's as she stepped inside her house and closed the door, and I stood hopelessly on her pathway wanting to call her back.

The Second Year

FEBRUARY

Ian Pargetter was murdered at about one in the morning on February 1st.

I learned about his death from Calder when I telephoned that evening on impulse to thank him belatedly for the lunch party, invite him for a reciprocal dinner in London and hear whether or not he had enjoyed his American tour.

'Who?' he said vaguely when I announced myself. 'Who? Oh ... Tim ... Look, I can't talk now, I'm simply distracted, a friend of mine's been killed and I can't think of anything else.'

'I'm so sorry,' I said inadequately.

'Yes ... Ian Pargetter ... but I don't suppose you know ...'

This time I remembered at once. The vet; big, reliable, sandy moustache.

'I met him,' I said 'in your house.'

'Did you? Oh yes. I'm so upset I can't concentrate. Look, Tim, ring some other time, will you?'

'Yes, of course.'

'It's not just that he's been a friend for years,' he said, 'But I don't know ... I really don't know how my business will fare without him. He sent so many horses my way ... such a good friend ... I'm totally distraught ... Look, ring me another time ... Tim, so sorry.' He put his receiver down with the rattle of a shaking hand.

I thought at the time that he meant Ian Pargetter had been killed in some sort of accident, and it was only the next day when my eye was caught by a paragraph in a newspaper that I realised the difference.

Ian Pargetter, well known, much respected Newmarket veterinary surgeon, was yesterday morning found dead in his home. Police suspect foul play. They state that Pargetter suffered head injuries and that certain supplies of drugs appear to be missing. Pargetter's body was discovered by Mrs Jane Halson, a daily cleaner. The vet is survived by his wife and three young daughters, all of whom were away from home at the time of the attack. Mrs Pargetter was reported last night to be very distressed and under sedation.

A lot of succinct bad news, I thought, for a lot of sad bereft people. He was the first person I'd known who'd been murdered, and in spite of our very brief meeting I found his death most disturbing: and if I felt so unsettled about a near-stranger, how, I wondered, did anyone ever recover from the murder of someone one knew well and loved. How did one deal with the anger? Come to terms with the urge to revenge?

I'd of course read reports of husbands and wives who pronounced themselves 'not bitter' over the slaughter of a spouse, and I'd never understood it. I felt furious on Ian Pargetter's behalf that anyone should have had the arrogance to wipe him out.

Because of Ascot and Sandcastle my long-dormant interest in racecourses seemed thoroughly to have reawakened, and on three or four Saturday afternoons that winter I'd trecked to Kempton or Sandown or Newbury to watch the jumpers. Ursula Young had become a familiar face, and it was from this brisk well-informed lady bloodstock agent that I learnt most about Ian Pargetter and his death.

'Drink?' I suggested at Kempton, pulling up my coat collar against a bitter wind.

She looked at her watch (I'd never see her do anything without checking the time) and agreed on a quick one. Whisky-mac for her, coffee for me, as at Doncaster.

'Now tell me,' she said, hugging her glass and yelling in my ear over the general din of a bar packed with other cold customers seeking inner warmth, 'when you asked all those questions about stallion shares, was it for Sandcastle?'

I smiled without actually answering, shielding my coffee inadequately from adjacent nudging elbows.

'Thought so,' she said. 'Look — there's a table. Grab it.'

We sat down in a corner with the racket going on over our heads and the closed-circuit television playing re-runs of the last race fortissimo. Ursula bent her head towards mine. 'A wow-sized coup for Oliver Knowles.'

'You approve?' I asked.

She nodded. 'He'll be among the greats in one throw. Smart move. Clever man.'

'Do you know him?'

'Yes. Meet him often at the sales. He had a snooty wife who left him for some Canadian millionaire or other, and maybe that's why he's aiming for the big-time; just to show her.' She smiled fiendishly. 'She was a real pain and I hope he makes it.'

She drank half her whisky and I said it was a shame about Ian Pargetter, and that I'd met him once at Calder's house.

She grimaced with a stronger echo of the anger I had myself felt. 'He'd been out all evening saving the life of a classic-class colt with colic. It's so beastly. He went home well after midnight, and they reckon whoever killed him was already in the house stealing whatever he could lay his hands on. Ian's wife and family were away visiting her mother, you see, and the police think the killer thought the house would be empty for the night.' She swallowed. 'He was hit on the back of the head with a brass lamp off one of the tables in the sitting room. Just casual. Unpremeditated. Just ... *stupid*.' She looked moved, as I guessed everyone must have been who had known him. 'Such a waste. He was a really nice man, a good vet, everyone like him. And all for practically nothing.... The police found a lot of silver and jewellery lying on a blanket ready to be carried away, but they think the thief just panicked and left it when Ian came home ... all that anyone can think of that's missing is his case of instruments and a few drugs that he'd had with him that evening ... nothing worth killing for ... not even for an addict. Nothing in it like that.' She fell silent and looked down into her nearly empty glass, and I offered her a refill.

'No, thanks all the same, one's enough. I feel pretty maudlin as it is. I liked Ian. He was a good sort. I'd like to *throttle* the little beast who killed him.'

'I think Calder Jackson feels much as you do,' I said.

She glanced up, her good-looking fifty-ish face full of genuine concern. 'Calder will miss Ian terribly. There aren't that number of vets around who'd not only put up with a faith-healer on their doorstep but actually treat him as a colleague. Ian had no professional jealously. Very rare. Very good man. Makes it all the worse.'

We went out again into the raw air and I lost five pounds on the afternoon, which would have sent Lorna Shipton swooning to Uncle Freddie, if she'd known.

Two weeks later with Oliver Knowles' warm approval I paid another visit to his farm in Hertfordshire, and although it was again a Sunday and still winter, the atmosphere of the place had fundamentally changed. Where there had been quiet sleepy near-hibernation there was now a wakeful bustle and eagerness, where a scattering of dams and foals across the paddocks, now a crowd of mares moving alone and slowly with big bellies.

The crop had come to the harvest. Life was ripening into the daylight, and into the darkness the new seed would be sown.

I had not been truly a country child (ten acres of wooded hill in Surrey) and to me the birth of animals still seemed a wonder and joy: to Oliver Knowles, he said, it meant constant worry and profit and loss. His grasp of essentials still rang out strong and clear, but there were lines on his forehead from the details.

'I suppose,' he said frankly, walking me into the first of the big yards, 'that the one thing I hadn't mentally prepared myself for was the value of the foals now being born here. I mean ...' he gestured around at the patient heads looking over the rows of half-doors, ' ... these mares have been to the top stallions. They're carrying fabulous blood-lines. They're history.' His awe could be felt. 'I didn't realise, you know, what anxiety they would bring me. We've always done our best for the foals, of course we have, but if one died it wasn't a tragedy, but with this lot.... ' He smiled ruefully. 'It's not enough just owning Sandcastle. I have to make sure that our reputation for handling top broodmares is good and sound.'

We walked along beside one row of boxes with him telling me

in detail the breeding of each mare we came to and of the foal she carried, and even to my ignorant ears it sounded as if every Derby and Oaks winner for the past half century had had a hand in the coming generation.

'I had no trouble selling Sandcastle's nominations,' he said. 'Not even at forty thousand pounds a throw. I could even choose, to some extent, which mares to accept. It's been utterly amazing to be able to turn away mares that I considered wouldn't do him justice.'

'Is there a temptation,' I asked mildly, 'to sell more than forty places? To ... er ... accept an extra fee ... in untaxed cash ... on the quiet?'

He was more amused than offended. 'I wouldn't say it hasn't been done on every farm that ever existed. But I wouldn't do it with Sandcastle ... or at any rate not this year. He's still young. And untested, of course. Some stallions won't look at as many as forty mares ... though shy breeders do tend to run in families, and there's nothing in his pedigree to suggest he'll be anything but energetic and fertile. I wouldn't have embarked on all this if there had been any doubts.'

It seemed that he was trying to reassure himself as much as me; as if the size and responsibility of his undertaking had only just penetrated, and in penetrating, frightened.

I felt a faint tremor of dismay but stifled it with the reassurance that come hell or high water Sandcastle was worth his buying price and could be sold again even at this late date for not much less. The bank's money was safe on his hoof.

It was earlier in the day than my last visit — eleven in the morning — and more lads than before were to be seen mucking out the boxes and carrying feed and water.

'I've had to take on extra hands,' Oliver Knowles said matter-of-factly. 'Temporarily, for the season.'

'Has recruitment been difficult?' I asked.

'Not really. I do it every spring. I keep the good ones on for the whole year, if they'll stay, of course: these lads come and go as the whim takes them, the unmarried ones, that is. I keep the nucleus on and put them painting fences and such in the autumn and winter.'

We strolled into the second yard, where the butty figure of Nigel could be seen peering over a half-door into a box.

'You remember Nigel?' Oliver said. 'My stud manager?'

Nigel, I noted, had duly been promoted.

'And Ginnie,' I asked, as we walked over, 'is she home today?'

'Yes, she's somewhere about.' He looked around as if expecting her to materialise at the sound of her name, but nothing happened.

'How's it going, Nigel?' he asked.

Nigel's hairy eyebrows withdrew from the box and aimed themselves in our direction. 'Floradora's eating again,' he said, indicating the inspected lady and sounding relieved. 'And Pattacake is still in labour. I'm just going back there.'

'We'll come,' Oliver said. 'If you'd like to? he added, looking at me questioningly.

I nodded and walked on with them along the path into the third, smaller quadrangle, the foaling yard.

Here too, in this place that had been empty, there was purposeful life, and the box to which Nigel led us was larger than normal and thickly laid with straw.

'Foals usually drop at night,' Oliver said, and Nigel nodded. 'She started about midnight. She's just lazy, eh girl?' He patted the brown rump. 'Very slow. Same thing every year.'

'She's not come for Sandcastle, then?' I said.

'No. She's one of mine,' Oliver said. 'The foal's by Diarist.'

We hovered for a few minutes but there was no change in Pattacake. Nigel, running delicately knowledgeable hands over the shape under her ribs, said she'd be another hour, perhaps, and that he would stay with her for a while. Oliver and I walked onwards, past the still closed breeding shed and down the path between the two small paddocks towards the stallion yard. Everything, as before, meticulously tidy.

There was one four-legged figure in one of the paddocks, head down and placid. 'Parakeet,' Oliver said. 'Getting more air than grass, actually. It isn't warm enough yet for the new grass to grow.'

We came finally to the last yard, and there he was, the gilt-edged Sandcastle, looking over his door like any other horse.

One couldn't tell, I thought. True there was a poise to the well-shaped head, and an interested eye and alertly pricked ears, but nothing to announce that this was the marvellous creature I'd seen at Ascot. No one ever again, I reflected, would see that arrow-like raking gallop, that sublime throat-catching valour: and it seemed a shame that he should be denied his ability in the hope that he would pass it on.

A lad, broom in hand, was sweeping scatterings of peat off the concrete apron in front of the six stallion boxes, watched by Sandcastle, Rotaboy and Diarist with the same depth of interest as a bus queue would extend to a busker.

'Lenny,' Oliver said, 'you can take Sandcastle down to the small paddock opposite to the one with Parakeet.' He looked up at the sky as if to sniff the coming weather. 'Put him back in his box when you return for evening stables.'

'Yes, sir.'

Lenny was well into middle age, small, leathery and of obviously long experience. He propped the broom against one of the empty boxes and disappeared into a doorway to reappear presently carrying a length of rope.

'Lenny is one of my most trusted helpers,' Oliver Knowles said. 'Been with me several years. He's good with stallions and much stronger than he looks. Stallions can be quite difficult to handle, but Lenny gets on with them better than with mares. Don't know why.'

Lenny clipped the rope onto the headcollar which Sandcastle, along with every other equine resident, wore at all times. Upon the headcollar was stapled a metal plate bearing the horse's name, an absolute essential for identification. Shuffle all those mares together without their headcollars, I thought, and no one would ever sort them. I suggested the problem mildly to Oliver, who positively blenched. 'God forbid! Don't suggest such things. We're very careful. Have to be. Otherwise, as you say, we could breed the wrong mare to the wrong stallion and never know it.'

I wondered, but privately, how often that in fact had happened, or whether indeed it was possible for two mares or two foals to be permanently swapped. The opportunities for mistakes, if not for outright fraud, put computer manipulation in the shade.

Nigel arrived in the yard, and with his scarcely necessary help Lenny opened Sandcastle's door and led the colt out; and one

392

could see in all their strength the sleek muscles, the tugging sinews, the spring-like joints. The body that was worth its weight in gold pranced and scrunched on the hard apron, wheeling round impatiently and tossing its uncomprehending head.

'Full of himself,' Oliver explained. 'We have to feed him well and keep him fairly fit, but of course he doesn't get the exercise he used to.'

We stepped to one side with undignified haste to avoid Sandcastle's restless hindquarters. 'Has he ... er ... started work yet?' I asked.

'Not yet,' Oliver said. 'Only one of his mares has foaled so far. She's almost through her foal-heat, so when she comes into use in fifteen or sixteen days time, she'll be his first. After that there will be a pause - give him time to think! — then he'll be busy until into June.'

'How often ...?' I murmured delicately.

Oliver fielded the question as if he, like Calder, had had to give the same answer countless times over.

'It depends on the stallion,' he said. 'Some can cover one mare in the morning and another in the afternoon and go on like that for days. Others haven't that much stamina or that much desire. Occasionally you get very shy and choosy stallions. Some of them won't go near some mares but will mate all right with others. Some will cover only one mare a fortnight, if that. Stallions aren't machines, you know, they're individual like everyone else.'

With Nigel in attendance Lenny led Sandcastle out of the yard, the long bag legs stalking in powerful strides beside the almost trotting little man.

'Sandcastle will be all right with mares,' Oliver said again firmly. 'Most stallions are.'

We stopped for Oliver to give two carrots and a pat each to Rotaboy and Diarist, so that we didn't ourselves see the calamity. We heard a distant clatter and a yell and the thud of fast hooves, and Oliver went white as he turned to run to the diaster.

I followed him, also sprinting.

Lenny lay against one of the white painted posts of the small paddock's rails, dazedly trying to pull himself up. Sandcastle,

393

loose and excited, had found his way into one of the paths between the larger paddocks and from his bolting speed must have taken the rails to be those of a racecourse.

Nigel stood by the open gate of the small paddock, his mouth wide as if arrested there by shock. He was still almost speechless when Oliver and I reached him, but had at least begun to unstick.

'For Christ's sake,' Oliver shouted. 'Get going. Get the Land Rover. He can get out onto the road that way through the Watcherleys'. He ran off in the direction of his own house leaving a partially resurrected Nigel to stumble off towards the bungalow, half in sight beyond the stallion yard.

Lenny raised himself and began his excuses, but I didn't wait to listen. Unused to the problem and ignorant of how best to catch fleeing horses, I simply set off in Sandcastle's wake, following his path between the paddocks and seeing him disappear ahead of me behind a distant hedge.

I ran fast along the grassy path between the rails, past the groups of incurious mares in the paddocks, thinking that my brief January holiday ski-ing down the pistes at Gstaad might have its practical uses after all; there was currently a lot more muscle in my legs than was ever to be found by July.

Whereas on my last visit the hedge between Oliver Knowles' farm and the Watcherleys' run-down hospital for sick horses had been a thorny unbroken boundary, there were now two or three wide gaps, so that passing from one side to the other was easy. I pounded through the gap which lay straight ahead and noticed almost unconsciously that the Watcherleys' dilapidation had been not only halted but partially reversed, with new fencing going up and repairs in hand on the roofs.

I ran towards the stable buildings across a thistly field in which there was no sign of Sandcastle, and through an as yet unmended gate which hung open on broken hinges on the far side. Beyond there between piles of rubble and rusting iron I reached the yard itself, to find Ginnie looking around her with unfocussed anxiety and a man and a girl walking towards her enquiringly.

Ginnie saw me running, and her first instinctively cheerful greeting turned almost at once to alarm.

'What is it?' she said. 'Is one of the mares out?'

'Sandcastle.'

'Oh no ...' It was a wail of despair. 'He can get on the road.' She turned away, already running, and I ran after her; out of the Watcherleys' yard, round their ramshackle house and down the short weedy gateless drive to the dangerous outside world where a car could kill a horse without even trying.

'We'll never catch him,' Ginnie said as we reached the road. 'It's no use running. We don't know which way he went.' She was in great distress: her eyes flooding, tears on her cheeks. 'Where's Dad?'

'I should think he's out in his car, looking. And Nigel's in a Land Rover.'

'I heard a horse gallop through the Watcherleys',' she said. 'I was in one of the boxes with a foal. I never thought ... I mean, I thought it might be a mare ...'

A speeding car passed in front of us, followed closely by two others doing at least sixty miles an hour, one of them dicily passing a heavy articulated lorry which should have been home in its nest on a Sunday. The thought of Sandcastle loose in that battlefield was literally goose-pimpling and I began for the first time to believe in his imminent destruction. One of those charging monsters would be sure to hit him. He would waver across the road into their path, swerving, rudderless, hopelessly vulnerable ... a five million pound traffic accident in the making.

'Let's go this way,' I said, pointing to the left. A motorcyclist roared from that direction, head down in a black visor, going too fast to stop.

Ginnie shook her head sharply. 'Dad and Nigel will be on the road. But there's a track over there ...' She pointed slantwise across the road. 'He might just have found it. And there's a bit of a hill and even if he isn't up there at least we might see him from there ... you can see the road in places ... I often ride up there.' She was off again, running while she talked, and I fell in beside her. Her face was screwed up with the intensity of her feelings and I felt as much sympathy for her as dismay about the horse. Sandcastle was insured — I'd vetted the policy myself — but Oliver Knowles' prestige wasn't. The escape and death of the first great stallion in his care would hardly attract future business.

The track was muddy and rutted and slippery from recent rain. There were also a great many hoofprints, some looking new, some overtrodden and old. I pointed to them as we ran and asked Ginnie pantingly if she knew if any of those were Sancastle's

'Oh.' She stopped running suddenly. 'Yes. Of course. He hasn't got shoes on. The blacksmith came yesterday, Dad said ...' She peered at the ground dubiously, ' ... he left Sandcastle without new shoes because he was going to make leather pads for under them ... I wasn't really listening.' She pointed. 'I think that might be him. Those new marks ... they could be, they really could.' She began running again up the track, impelled by hope now as well as horror, fit in her jeans and sweater and jodhpur boots after all that compulsory jogging.

I ran beside her thinking that mud anyway washed easily from shoes, socks and trouser legs. The ground began to rise sharply and to narrow between bare-branched scratchy bushes; and the jumble of hoof marks inexorably led on and on.

Please be up here,' Ginnie was say. 'Please, Sandcastle, please be up here.' Her urgency pumped in her legs and ran in misery down her cheeks. 'Oh please ... *please* ...'

The agony of adolescence, I thought. So real, so overpowering ... so remembered.

The track curved through the bushes and opened suddenly into a wider place where grass grew in patches beside the rutted mud; and there stood Sandcastle, head high, nostrils twitching to the wind, a brown and black creature of power and beauty and majesty.

Ginnie stopped running in one stride and caught my arm fiercely.

'Don't move,' she said. 'I'll do it. You stay here. Keep still. Please keep still.'

I nodded obediently, respecting her experience. The colt looked ready to run again at the slightest untimely movement, his sides quivering, his legs stiff with tension, his tail sweeping up and down restlessly.

He's frightened, I thought suddenly. He's out here, lost, not knowing where to go. He's never been free before, but his instinct is still wild, still against being caught. Horses were never truly tamed, only accustomed to captivity.

Ginnie walked towards him making crooning noises and holding out her hand palm upwards, an offering hand with nothing to offer. 'Come on, boy,' she said. 'Come on boy, there's a good boy, it's all right, come on now.'

The horse watched her as if he'd never seen a human before, his alarm proclaimed in a general volatile trembling. The rope hung down from his headcollar, its free end curling on the ground; and I wondered whether Ginnie would be able to control the colt if she caught him, where Lenny with all his strength had let him go.

Ginnie came to within a foot of the horse's nose, offering her open left hand upwards and bringing her right hand up slowly under his chin, reaching for the headcollar itself, not the rope: her voice made soothing, murmuring sounds and my own tensed muscles began to relax.

At the last second Sandcastle would have none of it. He wheeled away with a squeal, knocking Ginnie to her knees; took two rocketing strides towards a dense patch of bushes, wheeled again, laid back his ears and accelerated in my direction. Past me lay the open track, down hill again to the slaughtering main road.

Ginnie, seen in peripheral vision, was struggling to her feet in desperation. Without thinking of anything much except perhaps what that horse meant to her family, I jumped not out of his way but at his flying head, my fingers curling for the headcollar and missing that and fastening round the rope.

He nearly tore my arms out of their sockets and all the skin off my palms. He yanked me off my feet, pulled me through the mud and trampled on my legs. I clung all the same with both hands to the rope and bumped against his shoulder and knee, and shortly more by weight than skill hauled him to the side of the track and into the bushes.

The bushes, indeed, acted as an anchor. He couldn't drag my heaviness through them, not if I kept hold of the rope; and I wound the rope clumsily round a stump of branch for leverage, and that was roughly that. Sandcastle stood the width of the bush away, crossly accepting the inevitable, tossing his head and quivering but no longer trying for full stampede.

Ginnie appeared round the curve in the track, running and if possible looking more than ever distraught. When she saw me

397

she stumbled and half fell and came up to me uninhibitedly crying.

'Oh, I'm so glad, so glad, and you should never do that, you can be killed, you should never do it, and I'm so grateful, so glad ... oh dear.' She leant against me weakly and like a child wiped her eyes and nose on my sleeve.

'Well,' I said pragmatically, 'what do we do with him now?'

What we dicided, upon consideration, was that I and Sandcastle should stay where we were, and that Ginnie should go and find Nigel or her father, neither she nor I being confident of leading our prize home without reinforcements.

While she was gone I made an inventory of the damage, but so far as my clothes went there was nothing the cleaners couldn't see to, and as for the skin, it would grow again pretty soon. My legs though bruised were functioning, and there was nothing broken or frightful. I made a ball of my handkerchief in my right palm which was bleeding slightly and thought that one of these days a habit of launching oneself at things like fleeing stallions and boys with knives mght prove to be unwise.

Oliver, Ginnie, Nigel and Lenny all appeared in the Land Rover, gears grinding and wheels spinning in the mud. Sandcastle, to their obvious relief, was upon inspection pronounced sound, and Oliver told me forcefully that *no one*, should *ever*, repeat *ever*, try to stop a bolting horse in that way.

'I'm sorry,' I said.

'You could have been killed.'

'So Ginnie said.'

'Didn't it occur to you?' He sounded almost angry; the aftermath of fright. 'Didn't you *think*?'

'No,' I said truthfully. 'I just did it.'

'Never do it again,' he said, 'And thanks,' he paused and swallowed and tried to make light of his own shattered state. 'Thanks for taking care of my investment.'

Lenny and Nigel had brought a different sort of headcollar which involved a bit in the mouth and a fierce looking curb chain, and with these in place the captive (if not chastened) fugitive was led away. There seemed to me to be a protest in the stalking hindquarters, a statement of disgust at the injustices of life. I smiled at that fanciful thought; the pathetic fallacy, the ascribing to animals of emotions one felt only oneself.

Oliver drove Ginnie and me back in the Land Rover, travelling slowly behind the horse and telling how Nigel and Lenny had allowed him to go free.

'Sheer bloody carelessness,' he said forthrightly. 'Both of them should know better. They could see the horse was fresh and jumping out of his skin yet Lenny was apparently holding the rope with only one hand and stretching to swing the gate open with the other. He took his eyes off Sandcastle so he wasn't ready when Nigel made some sharp movement or other and the horse reared and ran backwards. I ask you! Lenny! Nigel! How can they be so bloody stupid after all these years?'

There seemed to be no answer to that so we just let him curse away, and he was still rumbling like distant thunder when the journey ended. Once home he hurried off to the stallion yard and Ginnie trenchantly said that if Nigel was as sloppy with discipline for animals as he was with the lads, it was no wonder any horse with spirit would take advantage.

'Accidents happen,' I said mildly.

'Huh.' She was scornful. 'Dad's right. That accident *shouldn't* have happened. It was an absolute miracle that Sandcastle came to no harm at all. Even if he hadn't got out on the road he could have tried to jump the paddock rails — loose horses often do — and broken his leg or something.' She sounded as angry as her father, and for the same reason; the flooding release after fear. I put my arm round her shoulders and gave her a quick hug, which seemed to disconcert her horribly. 'Oh dear, you must think me so silly ... and crying like that ... and everything.'

'I think you're a nice deal girl who's had a rotten morning,' I said. 'But all's well now, you know; it really is.'

I naturally believed what I said, but I was wrong.

The Second Year

APRIL

Calder Jackson finally came to dinner with me while he was staying in London to attend a world conference of herbalists. He would be glad, he said, to spend one of the evenings away from his colleagues, and I met him in a restaurant on the grounds that although my flat was civilised my cooking was not.

I sensed immediately a difference in him, though it was hard to define; rather as if he had become a figure still larger than life. Heads turned and voices whispered when we walked through the crowded place to our table, but because of television this would have happened anyway. Yet now, I thought, Calder really enjoyed it. There was still no overt arrogance, still a becoming modesty of manner, but something within him had intensified, crystallised, become a governing factor. He was now, I thought, even to himself, the Great Man.

I wondered what, if anything, had specifically altered him, and it turned out to be the one thing I would have least expected: Ian Pargetter's death.

Over a plateful of succulent smoked salmon Calder apologised for the abrupt way he'd brushed me off on the telephone on that disturbing night, and I said it was most understandable.

'Fact is,' Calder said, squeezing lemon juice, 'I was afraid my whole business would collapse. Ian's partners, you know, never approved of me. I was afraid they would influence everyone against me, once Ian had gone.'

'And it hasn't worked out that way?'

He shook his head, assembling a pink forkful. 'remarkably not. Amazing.' He put the smoke salmon in his mouth and made appreciative noises, munching.I was aware, and I guessed he was, too, that the ears of the people at the tables on either side were almost visibly attuned to the distinctive voice, to the clear loud diction with its country edge. 'My yard's still full. People have faith, you know. I may not get quite so many racehorses, that's to be expected, but still a few.'

'And have you heard any more about Ian Pargetter's death? Did they ever find out who killed him?'

He looked regretful. 'I'm sure they haven't. I asked one of his partners the other day, and he said no one seemed to be asking questions any more. He was quite upset. And so am I. I suppose finding his murderer won't bring Ian back, but all the same one wants to *know*.'

'Tell me some of your recent success,' I said, nodding, changing the subject and taking a slice of paper-thin brown bread and butter. ''I find your work tremendously interesting.' I also found it about the only thing else to talk about, as we seemed to have few other points of contact. Regret it as I might, there was still no drift towards an easy personal friendship.

Calder ate some more smoked salmon while he thought. 'I had a colt,' he said at last, 'a two-year-old in training. Ian had been treating him, and he'd seemed to be doing well. Then about three weeks after Ian died the colt started bleeding into his mouth and down his nose and went on and on doing it, and as Ian's partner couldn't find out the trouble the trainer persuaded the owner to send the horse to me.'

'And did you discover what was wrong?' I asked.

'Oh no.' He shook his head. 'It wasn't necessary.I laid my hands on him on three succeeding days, and the bleeding stopped immediately. I kept him at my place for two weeks altogether, and returned him on his way back to full good health.'

The adjacent tables were facinated, as indeed I was myself.

'Did you give him herbs?' I asked.

'Certainly. Of course. And alfalfa in his hay. Excellent for many ills, alfalfa.'

I had only the haziest idea of what alfalfa looked like, beyond it being some sort of grass.

'The one thing you can't do with herbs,' he said confidently, 'is *harm*.'

I raised my eyebrows with my mouth full.

He gave the nearest thing to a grin. 'With ordinary medicines one has to be so careful because of their power and their side effects, but if I'm not certain what's wrong with a horse I can give it all the herbal remedies I can think of all at once in the hope that one of them will hit the target, and it quite often does. It may be hopelessly unscientific, but if a trained vet can't tell exactly what's wrong with a horse, how can I?'

I smiled with undiluted pleasure. 'Have some wine,' I said.

He nodded the helmet of curls, and the movement I made towards the bottle in its ice-bucket was instantly forestalled by a watchful waiter who poured almost reverently into the healer's glass.

'How was the American trip,' I asked, 'way back in January?'

'Mm.' He sipped his wine. 'Interesting.' He frowned a little and went back to finishing the salmon, leaving me wondering whether that was his total answer. When he'd laid down his knife and fork however he sat back in his chair and told me that the most enjoyable part of his American journey had been, as he'd expected, his few days on the ski slopes; and we discussed ski-ing venues throughout the roast beef and burgundy which followed.

With the crepes suzette I asked after Dissdale and Bettina and heard that Dissdale had been to New York on a business trip and that Bettina had been acting a small part in a British movie, which Dissdale hadn't known whether to be pleased about or not. 'Too many gorgeous young studs around,' Calder said, smiling. 'Dissdale gets worried anyway, and he was away for ten days.'

I pondered briefly about Calder's own seemingly non-existent sex-life: but he'd never seen me with a girl either, and certainly there was no hint in him of the homosexual.

Over coffee, running out of subjects, I asked about his yard in general, and how was the right-hand-man Jason in particular.

Calder shrugged. 'He's left. They come and go, you know. No loyalty these days.'

'And you don't fear ... well, that he'd take your knowledge with him?'

He looked amused. 'He didn't know much. I mean, I'd hand out a pill and tell Jason which horse to give it to. That sort of thing.'

We finished amably enough with a glass of brandy for each and a cigar for him, and I tried not to wince over the bill.

'A very pleasant evening,' Calder said. 'you must come out to lunch again one day.'

'I'd like to.'

We sat for a final few minutes opposite each other in a pause of mutual appraisal: two people utterly different but bonded by one-tenth of a second on a pavement in Ascot. Saved and saver, inextricably interested each in the other; a continuing curiosity which would never quite lose touch. I smiled at him slowly and got a smile in return, but all surface, no depth, a mirror exactly of my own feelings.

In the office things were slowly changing. John had boasted too often of his sexual conquests and complained too often about my directorship, and Gordon's almost-equal had tired of such waste of time. I'd heard from Val Fisher in a perhaps edited version that at a small and special seniors meeting (held in my absence and without my knowledge) Gordon's almost-equal had said he would like to boot John vigorously over St Paul's. His opinion was respected. I heard from Alec one day merely that the mosquito which had stung me for so long had been squashed, and on going along the passage to investigate had found John's desk empty and his bull-like presence but a quiver in the past.

'He's gone to sell air-conditioning to Eskimos,' Alec said, and Gordon's almost-equal, smiling affably, corrected it more probably to a partnership with some brokers on the Stock Exchange.

Alec himself seemed restless, as if his own job no longer held him enthralled.

'It's all right for you,' he said once. 'you've the gift. You've the *sight*. I can't tell a gold mine from a pomegranate at five paces, and it's taken me all these years to know it.'

'But you're a conjuror,' I said. 'You can rattle up outside money faster than anyone.'

'Gift of the old gab, you mean.' He looked uncharacteristically gloomy. 'Syrup with a chisel in it.' He waved his hand towards the desks of our new older colleagues, who had both gone out to lunch. 'I'll end up like them, still here, still smooth-talking, part of the furniture, coming up to *sixty*.' His voice held disbelief that such an age could be achieved. 'That isn't life, is it? That's not *all*?'

I said that I supposed it might be.

'Yes, but for you it's exciting,' he said. 'I mean, you love it. Your eyes *gleam*. You get your kicks right here in this room. But I'll never be made a director, let's face it, and I have this grotty feeling that time's slipping away, and soon it will be too late to start anything else.'

'Like what?'

'Like being an actor. Or a doctor. Or an acrobat.'

'It's been too late for that since you were six.'

'Yeah,' he said. 'Lousy, isn't it?' He put his heart and soul ten minutes later, however, into tracking down a source of a hundred thousand for several years and lending it to a businessman at a profitable rate, knitting together such loan packages all afternoon with diligence and success.

I hope he would stay. He was the yeast of the office: my bubles in the dough. As for myself, I had grown accustomed to being on the board and had slowly found I'd reached a new level of confidence. Gordon seemed to treat me unreservedly as an equal, though it was not until he had been doing it for some time that I looked back and realised.

Gordon's hitherto uniformly black hair had grown a streak or two of grey. His right hand now trembled also, and his handwriting had grown smaller through his efforts to control his fingers. I watched his valiant struggles to appear normal and respected his privacy by never making even a visual comment: it had become second nature to look anywhere but directly at his hands. In the brain department he remained energetic, but physically over all he was slowing down.

I had only seen Judith once since Christmas, and that had been in the office at a retirement party given for the head of Corporate Finance, a golden-handshake affair to which all managers' wives had been invited.

'How are you?' she said amid the throng, holding a glass of wine and an unidentifiable canapé and smelling of violets.

'Fine. And you?'

'Fine.'

She was wearing blue, with diamonds in her ears. I looked at her with absolute and unhappy love and saw the strain it put into her face.

'I'm sorry,' I said.

She shook her head and swallowed. 'I thought ... it might be different ... here in the bank.'

'No.'

She looked down at the canapé, which was squashy and yellow. 'If I don't eat this damned thing soon it'll drop down my dress.'

I took it out of her fingers and deposited it in an ashtray. 'Invest in a salami cornet. They stay rock-hard for hours.'

'What's Tim telling you to invest in?' demanded Henry Shipton, turning to us a beaming face.

'Salami,' Judith said.

'Typical. He lent money to a seaweed processor last week. Judith, my darling, let me freshen your glass.'

He took the glass away to the bottles and left us again looking at each other with a hundred ears around.

'I was thinking,' I said, 'When it's warmer, could I take you and Gordon, and Pen if she'd like it, out somewhere one Sunday? Somewhere not ordinary. All day.'

She took longer than normal politeness to answer, and I understood all the unspoken things, but finally, as Henry could be seen returning, she said, 'Yes. We'd all like it. I'd like it ... very much.'

'Here you are,' Henry said. 'Tim, you go and fight for your own refill, and leave me to talk to this gorgeous girl.' He put his arm round her shoulders and swept her off, and although I was vividly aware all evening of her presence, we had no more moments alone.

From day to day when she wasn't around I didn't precisely suffer: her absence was more of a faint background ache. When I saw Gordon daily in the office I felt no constant envy, nor hated him, nor even thought much of where he slept. I liked him for the good clever man he was, and our office relationship continued unruffled and secure. Loving Judith was both pleasure and pain, delight and deprivation, wishes withdrawn,

405

dreams denied. It might have been easier and more sensible to have met and fallen heavily for some young glamorous unattached stranger, but the one thing love never did have was logic.

'Easter,' I said to Gordon one day in the office. 'Are you and Judith going away?'

'We had plans — they fell through.'

'Did Judith mention that I'd like to take you both somewhere — and Pen Warner — as a thank you for Christmas?'

'Yes, I believe she did.'

'Easter Monday, then?'

He seemed pleased at the idea and reported the next day that Judith had asked Pen, and everyone was poised. 'Pen's bringing her kite,' he said. 'Unless it's a day trip to Manchester.'

'I'll think of something,' I said, laughing. 'Tell her it won't be raining.'

What I did eventually think of seemed to please them all splendidly and also to be acceptable to others concerned, and I consequently collected Gordon and Judith and Pen (but not the kite) from Clapham at eight-thirty on Easter Bank Holiday morning. Judith and Pen were in frizzing high spirits, though Gordon seemed already tired. I suggested abandoning what was bound to be a fairly taxing day for him, but he wouldn't hear of it.

'I want to go,' he said. 'Been looking forward to it all week. But I'll just sit in the back of the car and rest and sleep some of the way. 'So Judith sat beside me while I drove and touched my hand now and then, not talking much but contenting me deeply by just being there. The journey to Newmarket lasted two and a half hours and I would as soon it had gone on for ever.

I was taking them to Calder's yard, to the utter fascination of Pen. 'But don't tell him I'm a pharmacist,' she said. 'He might clam up if he knew he had an informed audience.'

'We won't tell,' Judith assured her. 'It would absolutely spoil the fun.'

Poor Calder, I thought: but I wouldn't tell him either.

He greeted us expansively (making me feel guilty) and gave us coffee in the huge oak-beamed sitting room where the memory of Ian Pargetter hovered peripherally by the fireplace.

'Delighted to see you again,' Calder said, peering at Gordon, Judith and Pen as if trying to conjure a memory to fit their faces. He knew of course who they were by name, but Ascot was ten months since, and although it had been an especially memorable day for him he had met a great many new people between then and now. 'Ah *yes*,' he said with relief, his brow clearing. 'Yellow hat with roses.'

Judith laughed. 'Well done.'

'Can't forget anyone so pretty.'

She took it as it was meant, but indeed he hadn't forgotten: as one tended never to forget people whose vitality brought out the sun.

'I see Dissdale and Bettina quite often,' he said, making conversation, and Gordon agreed that he and Judith, also, sometimes saw Dissdale, though infrequently. As a topic it was hardly rivetting, but served as an acceptable unwinding interval between the long car journey and the Grand Tour.

The patients in the boxes were all different but their ailments seemed the same; and I supposed surgeons could be excused their impersonal talk of 'the appendix in bed 14', when the occupants changed week by week but the operation didn't.

'This is a star three-day-eventer who came here five weeks ago with severe muscular weakness and no appetite. Wouldn't eat. Couldn't be ridden.He goes home tomorrow, strong and thriving. Looks well, eh?' Calder patted the glossy brown neck over the half-stable door. 'His owner thought he was dying, poor girl. She was weeping when she brought him here. It's really satisfying, you know, to be able to help.'

Gordon said civilly that it must be.

'This is a two-year-old not long in training. Came with an intractably infected wound on his fetlock. He's been here a week, and he's healing. It was most gratifying that the trainer sent him without delay, since I'd treated several of his horses in the past.'

'This mare,' Calder went on, moving us all along, 'came two or three days ago in great discomfort with blood in her urine. She's responding well, I'm glad to say.' He patted this one too, as he did them all.

'What was causing the bleeding?' Pen asked, but with only an uninformed-member-of-the-public intonation.

407

Calder shook his head. 'I don't know. His vet diagnosed a kidney infection complicated by crystalluria, which means crystals in the urine, but he didn't know the type of germ and, every antibiotic he gave failed to work. So the mare came here. Last resort.' He gave me a wink. 'I'm thinking of simply re-naming this whole place "Last Resort".'

'And you're treating her,' Gordon asked, 'with herbs?'

'With everything I can think of,' Calder said. 'And of course ... with hands.'

'I suppose,' Judith said diffidently, 'that you'd never let anyone watch ...?'

'My dear lady, for you, anything,' Calder said. 'But you'd see nothing. You might stand for half an hour, and nothing would happen. It would be terribly boring. And I might, perhaps, be *unable*, you know, if someone was waiting and standing there.'

Judith smiled understandingly and the tour continued, ending as before in the surgery.

Pen stood looking about her with sociable blankness and then wandered over to the glass-fronted cabinets to peer myopically at the contents.

Calder, happily ignoring her in favour of Judith, was pulling out his antique tablet-maker and demonstrating it with pride.

'It's beautiful,' Judith said sincerely. 'Do you use it much?'

'All the time,' he said. 'Any herbalist worth the name makes his own pills and potions.'

'Tim said you had a universal magic potion in the fridge.'

Calder smiled and obligingly opened the refrigerator door, revealing the brown-filled plastic containers, as before.

'What's in it?' Judith asked.

'Trade secret,' he said, smiling. 'Decoction of hops and other things.'

'Like beer?' Judith said.

'Yes, perhaps.'

'Horses do drink beer,' Gordon said. 'Or so I've heard.'

Pen bent down to pick up a small peach-coloured pill which was lying unobtrusively on the floor in the angle of one of the cupboards, and put it without comment on the bench.

'It's all so *absorbing*,' Judith said. 'So tremendously kind of you to show us everything. I'll watch all your programmes with more fervour than ever.'

Calder responded to her warmly as all men did and asked us into the house again for a drink before we left. Gordon however was still showing signs of fatigue and now also hiding both hands in his pockets which meant he felt they were trembling badly, so the rest of us thanked Calder enthusiastically for his welcome and made admiring remarks about his hospital and climbed into the car, into the same places as before.

'Come back any time you like, Tim,' he said; and I said thank you and perhaps I would. We shook hands, and we smiled, caught in our odd relationship and unable to take it further. He waved, and I waved back as I drove away.

'Isn't he amazing?' Judith said. 'I must say, Tim, I do understand why you're impressed.'

Gordon grunted and said that theatrical surgeons weren't necessarily the best; but yes, Calder was impressive.

It was only Pen, after several miles, who expressed her reservations.

'I'm not saying he doesn't do a great deal of good for the horses. Of course he must do, to have amassed such a reputation. But I don't honestly think he does it all with herbs.'

'How do you mean?' Judith asked, twisting round so as to see her better.

Pen leaned forward. 'I found a pill on the floor. I don't suppose you noticed.'

'I did,' I said. 'You put it on the bench.'

'That's right. Well, that was no herb, it was plain straightforward warfarin.'

'It may be plain straightforward war-whatever to you,' Judith said. 'But not to me.'

Pen's voice was smiling. 'Warfarin is a drug used in humans, and I dare say in horses, after things like heart attacks. It's a coumarin — an anticoagulant. Makes the blood less likely to clot and block up the veins and arteries. Widely used all over the place.'

We digested the information in silence for a mile or two, and finally Gordon said 'How did you know it was warfarin? I mean, how can you tell?'

'I handle it every day,' she said. 'I know the dosages, the sizes, the colours, the manufacturers' marks. You see all those things so often, you get to know them at a glance.'

409

'Do you mean,' I said interestedly, 'that if you saw fifty different pills laid out in a row you could identify the lot?'

'Probably. If they all came from major drug companies and weren't completely new, certainly, yes.'

'Like a wine-taster,' Judith said.

'Clever girl,' Gordon said, meaning Pen.

'It's just habit.' She thought. 'And something else in those cupboards wasn't strictly herbal, I suppose. He had one or two bags of potassium sulphate, bought from Goodison's Garden Centre, wherever that is.

'Whatever for?' Judith asked. 'Isn't potassium sulphate a fertiliser?'

'Potassium's just as essential to animals as to plants,' Pen said. 'I wouldn't be surprised if it isn't one of the ingredients in that secret brew.'

'What else would you put in it, if you were making it?' I asked curiously.

'Oh heavens.' She pondered. 'Any sort of tonic. Perhaps liquorice root, which he once mentioned. Maybe caffeine. All sorts of vitamins. Just a pepping-up mish-mash.'

The hardest part of the day had been to find somewhere decent to have lunch, and the place I'd chosen via the various gourmet guides turned out, as so often happens, to have changed hands and chefs since the books were written. The resulting repast was slow to arrive and disappointing to eat, but the mood of my guests forgave all.

'You remember,' Gordon said thoughtfully over the coffee, 'that you told us on the way to Newmarket that Calder was worried about his business when that vet was killed?'

'Yes,' I said. 'He was, at the time.'

'Isn't it possible,' Gordon said, 'that the vet was letting Calder have regular official medicines, like warfarin, and Calder thought his supplies would dry up, when the vet died?'

'Gordon!' Judith said. 'How devious you are, darling.'

We all thought about it however, and Pen nodded. 'He must have found another willing source, I should think.'

'But,' I protested, 'would vets really do that?'

'They're not particularly brilliantly paid,' Pen said. 'Not badly by my standards, but they're never *rich*.'

'But Ian Pargetter was very much liked,' I said.

'What's that got to do with it?' Pen said. 'Nothing to stop him passing on a few pills and advice to Calder in return for a fat untaxed fee.'

'To their mutual benefit.' Gordon murmured.

'The healer's feet of clay,' Judith said. 'What a shame.'

The supposition seemed slightly to deflate the remembered pleasure of the morning, but the afternoon's visit put the rest of the day up high.

We went this time to Oliver Knowles' stud farm and found the whole place flooded with foals and mares and activity.

'How *beautiful*,' Judith said, looking away over the stretches of white railed paddocks with their colonies of mothers and babies. 'How speechlessly *great*.'

Oliver Knowles, introduced, was as welcoming as Calder and told Gordon several times that he would never, ever, be out of his debt of gratitude to Paul Ekaterin's, however soon he had paid off his loan.

The anxiety and misgivings to be seen in him on my February visit had all disappeared: Oliver was again, and more so the capable and decisive executive I had met first. The foals had done well, I gathered. Not one from the mares coming to Sandcastle had been lost, and none of those mares had had any infection, a triumph of care. He told me all this within the first ten minutes, and also that Sandcastle had proved thoroughly potent and fertile and was a dream of a stallion. 'He's tireless,' he said. 'Forty mares will be easy.'

'I'm so glad,' I said, and meant it from the bottom of my banking heart.'

With his dog Squibs at his heels he showed us all again through the succession of yards, where since it was approximately four o'clock the evening ritual of mucking out and feeding was in full swing.

'A stud farm is not like a racing stable, of course,' Oliver was explaining to Gordon. 'One lad here can look after far more than three horses, because they don't have to be ridden. And here we have a more flexible system because the mares are sometimes in, sometimes out in the paddocks, and it would be impossible to assign particular mares to particular lads. So here a lad does a particular section of boxes, regardless of which

411

animals are in them.'

Gordon nodded, genially interested.

'Why are some foals in the boxes and some out in the paddocks?' Judith asked, and Oliver without hesitation told her it was because the foals had to stay with their dams, and the mares with foals in the boxes were due to come into heat, or were already in heat, and would go from their boxes to visit the stallion. When their heat was over they would go out into the paddocks, with their foals.

'Oh,' Judith said, blinking slightly at this factory aspect. 'Yes, I see.'

In the foaling yard we came across Nigel and also Ginnie, who ran across to me when she saw me and gave me a great hug and a smacking kiss somewhere to the left of the mouth. Quite an advance in confidence, I thought, and hugged her back, lifting her off her feet and whirling her round in a circle. She was laughing when I put her down, and Oliver watched in some surprise.

'I've never known her so demonstrative,' he said.

Ginnie looked at him apprehensively and held onto my sleeve. 'You didn't mind did you?' she asked me worriedly.

'I'm flattered,' I said, meaning it and also thinking that her father would kill off her spontaneity altogether if she wasn't careful.

Ginnie, reassured, tucked her arm into mine and said 'Come and look at the newest foal. It was born only about twenty minutes ago. It's a colt. A darling.' She tugged me off, and I caught a fleeting glance of Judith's face which was showing a mixture of all sorts of unreadable thoughts.

'Oliver's daughter,' I said in explanation over my shoulder, and heard Oliver belatedly introducing Nigel.

They all came to look at the foal over the half-door; a glistening little creature half-lying, half-sitting on the thick straw, all long nose, huge eyes and folded legs, new life already making an effort to balance and stand up. The dam, on her feet, alternatively bent her head to the foal and looked up at us warily.

'It was an easy one,' Ginnie said. 'Nigel and I just watched.'

'Have you seen many foals born?' Pen asked her.

'Oh, hundreds. All my life. Most often at night.'

412

Pen looked at her as if she, as I did, felt the imagination stirred by such an unusual childhood: as if she, like myself, had never seen one single birth of any sort, let alone a whole procession by the age of fifteen.

'This mare has come to Sandcastle,' Oliver said.

'And will that foal win the Derby?' Gordon asked, smiling.

Oliver smiled in return. 'You never know. He has the breeding.' He breathed deeply, expanding his chest. 'I've never been able to say anything like that before this year. No foal born or conceived here has in the past won a classic, but now ...' he gestured widely with his arm, ' ... one day, from these ...' he paused. 'It's a whole new world. It's ... tremendous'

'As good as you hoped?' I asked.

'Better.'

He had a soul after all, I thought, under all that tidy martial efficiency. A vision of the peaks, which he was reaching in reality. And how soon, I wondered, before the glossy became commonplace, the Classic winners a routine, the aristocrats the common herd. It would be what he'd aimed for; but in a way it would be blunting.

We left the foal and went on down the path past the breeding shed, where the main door was today wide open, showing the floor thickly covered with soft brown crumbly peat. Beyond succinctly explaining what went on there when it was inhabited. Oliver made no comment, and we all walked on without stopping to the heart of the place, to the stallions.

Lenny was there, walking one of the horses round the small yard and plodding with his head down as if he'd been doing it for some time. The horse was dripping with sweat, and from the position of the one open empty box I guessed he would be Rotaboy.

'He's just covered a mare,' Oliver said matter-of-factly. 'He's always like that afterwards.'

Judith and Gordona and Pen all looked as if the overt sex of the place was earthier than they'd expected, even without hearing, as I had at one moment, Oliver quietly discussing a vaginal disinfectant process with Nigel. They rallied valiantly however and gazed with proper awe at the head of Sandcastle which swam into view from the inside-box shadows.

He held himself almost imperiously, as if his new role had

413

basically changed his character; and perhaps it had. I had myself seen during my renewed interest in racing how constant success endowed some horses with definite 'presence', and Sandcastle, even lost and frightened up on top of the hill, had perceptibly had it; but now, only two months later, there was a new quality one might almost call arrogance, a fresh certainty of his own supremacy.

'He's splendid,' Gordon exclaimed. 'What a treat to see him again after that great day at Ascot.'

Oliver gave Sandcastle the usual two carrots and a couple of pats, treating the King with familiarity. Neither Judith nor Pen, nor indeed Gordon or myself, tried even to touch the sensitive nose: afraid of getting our fingers bitten off at the wrist, no doubt. It was all right to admire, but distance had virtue.

Lenny put the calming-down Rotaboy back in his box and started mucking out Diarist next door.

'We have two lads looking after the stallions full time,' Oliver said. 'Lenny, here, and another much trusted man, Don. And Nigel feeds them.'

Pen caught the underlying thought behind his words and asked, 'Do you need much security?'

'Some,' he said, nodding. 'We have the yard wired for sound, so either Nigel or I, when we're in our houses, can hear if there are any irregular noises.'

'Like hooves taking a walk?' Judith suggested.

'Exactly.' He smiled at her. 'We also have smoke alarms and massive extinguishers.'

And brick-built boxes and combination locks on these door bolts at night and lockable gates on all the ways out to the roads,' Ginnie said, chattily. 'Dad's really gone to town on security.'

'Glad to hear it,' Gordon said.

I smiled to myself at the classic example of bolting the stable door after the horse had done likewise, but indeed one could see that Oliver had learned a dire lesson and knew he'd been lucky to be given a second chance.

We began after a while to walk back towards the house, stopping again in the foaling yard to look at the new baby colt, who was now shakily on his feet and searching round for his supper.

Oliver drew me to one side and asked if I would like to see Sandcastle cover a mare, an event apparently scheduled for a short time hence.

'Yes, I would,' I said.

'I can't ask them all — there isn't room,' he said. 'I'll get Ginnie to show them the mares and foals in the paddocks and then take them indoors for tea.'

No one demurred at this suggested programme, especailly as Oliver didn't actually mention where he and I were going. Judith, I was sure, would have preferred to join us. Ginnie took them and Squibs off, and I could hear her saying 'Over there, next door, there's another yard. We could walk over that way if you like.'

Oliver, eying them amble along the path that Sandcastle had taken at a headlong gallop and I at a sprint, said, 'The Watcherleys look after any delicate foals or any mares with infections. It's all worked out most satisfactorily. I rent their place and they work for me, and their expertise with sick animals comes in very useful.'

'And you were mending their fences for them, I guess, when I came in February.'

'That's right.' He sighed ruefully. 'Another week and the gates would have been up in the hedge and across their driveway, and Sandcastle would never have got out.'

'No harm done,' I said.

'Thanks to you, no.''

We went slowly back towards the breeding shed. 'Have you seen a stallion at work before?' he asked.

'No, I haven't.'

After a pause he said, 'It may seem strong to you. Even violent. But it's normal to them. Remember that. And he'll probably bite her neck, but it's as much to keep himself in position as an expression of passion.'

'All right,' I said.

'This mare, the one we're breeding, is receptive, so there won't be any trouble. Some mares are shy, some are slow to arouse, some are irritable, just like humans.' He smiled faintly. 'This little lady is a born one-nighter.'

It was the first time I'd heard him make anything like a joke about his profession and I was almost startled. As if himself surprised at his own words he said more soberly, 'We put her to Sandcastle yesterday morning, and all went well.'

'The mares go more than once then, to the stallion?' I asked.

'He nodded. 'It depends of course on the stud farm, but I'm very anxious as you can guess that all the mares here shall have the best possible chance of conceiving.I bring them all at least twice to the stallion during their heat, then we put them out in the paddocks and wait, and if they come into heat again it means they haven't conceived, so we repeat the breeding process.'

'And how long do you go on trying?'

'Until the end of July. That means the foal won't be born until well on in June, which is late in the year for racehorses. Puts them at a disadvantage as two-year-olds, racing against March and April foals which have had more growing time.' He smiled. 'With any luck Sandcastle won't have any late June foals. It's too early to be complacent, but none of the mares he covered three weeks or more ago has come back into use.'

We reached and entered the breeding shed where the mare already stood, held at the head in a loose twitch by one lad and being washed and attended to by another.

'She can't wait, sir,' that lad said, indicating her tail, which she was holding high, and Oliver replied rather repressively, 'Good.'

Nigel and Lenny came with Sandcastle, who looked eagerly aware of where he was and what for. Nigel closed the door to keep the ritual private; and the mating which followed was swift and sure and utterly primaeval. A copulation of thrust and grandeur, of vigour and pleasure, not without tenderness: remarkably touching.

'They're not all like that,' Oliver remarked prosaically, as Sandcastle slid out and backwards and brought his forelegs to earth with a jolt. 'You've seen a good one.'

I thanked him for letting me be there, and in truth I felt I understood more about horses then than I'd ever imagined I would.

We walked back to the house with Oliver telling me that with the four stallions there were currently six, seven or eight matings a day in the breeding shed, Sundays included. The mind stuttered a bit at the thought of all that rampaging

416

fertility, but that, after all, was what the bank's five million pounds was all about. Rarely, I thought, had anyone seen Ekaterin's money so fundamentally at work.

We set off homewards fortified by tea, scones and whisky, with Oliver and Gordon at the end competing over who thanked whom most warmly. Ginnie gave me another but more composed hug and begged me to come again, and Judith kissed her and offered female succour if ever needed.

'Nice child,' she said as we drove away. 'Growing up fast.'

'Fifteen,' I said.

'Sixteen. She had a birthday last week.'

'You got on well with her,' I said.

'Yes,' She looked round at Pen and Gordon, who were again sitting in the back. 'She told us about your little escapade here two months ago.'

'She didn't!'

'She sure did,' Pen said, smiling. 'Why ever didn't you say?'

'I know why,' Gordon said dryly. 'He didn't want it to be known in the office that the loan he'd recommended had very nearly fallen under a lorry.'

'Is that right?' Judith asked.

'Very much so,' I admitted wryly. 'Some of the board were against the whole thing anyway, and I'd have never heard the end of the horse getting out.'

'What a coward,' Pen said, chuckling.

We pottered slowly back to Clapham through the stop-go end-of-Bank-Holiday traffic, and Judith and Pen voted it the best day they'd had since Ascot. Gordon dozed, I drove with relaxation and so we finally reached the tall gates by the common.

I went in wth them for supper as already arranged, but all of them, not only Gordon, were tired from the long day, and I didn't stay late. Judith came out to the car to see me off and to shut the gates after I'd gone.

We didn't really talk. I held her in my arms, her head on my shoulder, my head on hers, close in the dark night, as far apart as planets.

We stood away and I took her hand, lingering, not wanting all contact lost.

417

'A great day,' she said, and I said 'Mm', and kissed her very briefly.

Got into the car and drove away.

The Second Year

OCTOBER

Summer had come, summer had gone, sodden, cold and unloved. It had been overcast and windy during Royal Ascot week and Gordon and I, clamped to our telephones and pondering our options, had looked at the sullen sky and hardly minded that this year Dissdale hadn't needed to sell half-shares in his box.

Only with the autumn, far too late, had days of sunshine returned, and it was on a bright golden Saturday that I took the race train to Newbury to see the mixed meeting of two jump races and four flat.

Ursula Young was there, standing near the weighing room when I walked in from the station and earnestly reading her racecard.

'Hello,' she said when I greeted her. 'Haven't seen you for ages. How's the money-lending?'

'Profitable,' I said.

She laughed. 'Are you here for anything special'

'No. Just fresh air and a flutter.'

'I'm supposed to meet a client.' She looked at her watch. 'Time for a quick sandwich, though. Are you on?'

I was on, and bought her and myself a thin pallid slice of tasteless white meat between two thick pallid tasteless slices of soggy-crusted bread, the whole wrapped up in cardboard and celophane and costing a fortune.

Ursula ate it in disgust. 'They used to serve proper luscious sandwiches, thick, juicy handmade affairs which came in a

419

whole stack. I can't stand all this repulsive hygiene.' The rubbish from the sandwiches indeed littered most of the tables around us ... 'Every so-called advance is a retreat from excellence,' she said, dogmatic as ever.

I totally agreed with her and we chewed in joyless accord.

'How's trade with you?' I said.

She shrugged. 'Fair. The cream of the yearlings are going for huge prices. They've all got high reserves on them because they've cost so much to produce — stallion fees and the cost of keeping the mare and foal to start with, let alone vet's fees and all the incidentals. My sort of clients on the whole settle for a second, third or fourth rank, and many a good horse, mind you, has come from the bargain counter.'

I smiled at the automatic sales pitch. 'Talking of vets,' I said, 'is the Pargetter murder still unsolved?'

She nodded regretfully. 'I was talking to his poor wife in Newmarket last week. We met in the street. She's only half the girl she was, poor thing, no life in her. She said she asked the police recently if they were still even trying, and they assured here they were, but she doesn't believe it. It's been so long, nine months, and if they hadn't any leads to start with, how can they possibly have any now? She's very depressed, it's dreadful.'

I made sympathetic murmurs, and Ursula went on, 'The only good thing you could say is that he'd taken out decent life insurance and paid off the mortgage on their house, so at least she and the children aren't penniless as well. She was telling me how he'd been very careful in those ways, and she burst into tears, poor girl.'

Ursula looked as if the encounter had distressed her also.

'Have another whisky-mac,' I suggested. 'To cheer you up.'

'She looked at her watch. 'All right. You get it, but I'll pay. My turn.'

Over the second drink, in a voice of philosophical irritation, she told me about the client she was presently due to meet, a small-time trainer of steeplechasers. 'He's such a fool to himself,' she said. 'He makes hasty decisions, acts on impulse, and then when things go wrong he feels victimised and cheated and gets angry. Yet he can be perfectly nice when he likes.'

I wasn't especially interested in the touchy trainer, but when I went outside again with Ursula he spotted her from a short distance away and practically pounced on her arm.

'There you are,' he said, as if she'd had no right to be anywhere but at his side. 'I've been looking all over.'

'It's only just time,' she said mildly.

He brushed that aside, a short wiry intense man of about forty with a pork-pie hat above a weatherbeaten face.

'I wanted you to see him before he's saddled,' he said. 'Do come on, Ursula. Come and look at his conformation.'

She opened her mouth to say something to me but he almost forcefully dragged her off, holding her sleeve and talking rapidly into her ear. She gave me an apologetic look of long-suffering and departed in the direction of the pre-parade ring, where the horses for the first race were being led round by their lads before going off to the saddling boxes.

I didn't follow but climbed onto the steps of the main parade ring, round which walked several of the runners already saddled. The last of the field to appear some time later was accompanied by the pork-pie hat, and also Ursula, and for something to do I looked the horse up in the racecard.

Zoomalong, five-year-old gelding, trained by F. Barnet.

F. Barnet continued his dissertation into Ursula's ear, aiming his words from approximately six inches away, which I would have found irritating but which she bore without flinching. According to the flickering numbers on the Tote board Zoomalong had a medium chance in th opinion of the public, so for interest I put a medium stake on him to finish in the first three.

I didn't see Ursula or F. Barnet during the race, but Zoomalong zoomed along quite nicely to finish third, and I walked down from the stands towards the unsaddling enclosure to watch the patting-on-the-back post-race routine.

F. Barnet was there, still talking to Ursula and pointing out parts of his now sweating and stamping charge. Ursula nodded non-committally, her own eyes knowledgeably raking the gelding from stem to stern, a neat competent good looking fifty in a rust-coloured coat and brown velvet beret.

Eventually the horses were led away and the whole cycle of excitement began slowly to regenerate towards the second race.

Without in the least meaning to I again found myself standing

421

near Ursula, and this time she introduced me to the pork-pie hat, who had temporarily stopped talking.

'This is Fred Barnet,' she said. 'And his wife Susan.' A rounded motherly person in blue. 'And their son, Ricky.' A boy taller than his father, dark-haired, pleasant-faced.

I shook hands with all three, and it was while I was still touching the son that Ursula in her clear voice said my name, 'Tim Ekaterin.'

The boy's hand jumped in mine as if my flesh had burned him. I was astonished, and then I looked at his whitening skin, at the suddenly frightened dark eyes, at the stiffening of the body, at the rising panic: and I wouldn't have known him if he hadn't reacted in that way.

'What's the matter, Ricky?' his mother said, puzzled.

He said 'Nothing' hoarsely and looked around for escape, but all too clearly he knew I knew exactly who he was now and could always find him however far he ran.

'What do you think, then, Ursula?' Fred Barnet demanded, returning to the business in hand. 'Will you buy him? Can I count on you?'

Ursula said she would have to consult her client.

'But he was third,' Fred Barnet insisted. 'A good third.... In that company, a pretty good showing. And he'll win, I'm telling you. He'll win.'

'I'll tell my client all about him. I can't say fairer than that.'

'But you do like him, don't you? Look, Ursula, he's a good sort, easy to handle, just right for an amateur ...' He went on for a while in this vein while his wife listened with a sort of aimless beam meaning nothing at all.

To the son, under cover of his father's hard sell, I quietly said, 'I want to talk to you, and if you run away from me now I'll be telephoning the police.'

He gave me a sick look and stood still.

'We'll walk down the course together to watch the next race,' I said. 'We won't be interrupted there. And you can tell me *why*. And then we'll see.'

It was easy enough for him to drop back unnoticed from his parents, who were still concentrating on Ursula, and he came with me through the gate and out across the track itself to the centre of the racecourse, stumbling slightly as if not in

422

command of his feet. We walked down towards the last fence, and he told me why he'd tried to kill Calder Jackson.

'It doesn't seem real, not now, it doesn't really,' he said first. A young voice, slightly sloppy accent, full of strain.

'How old are you?' I asked.

'Seventeen.'

I hadn't been so far out, I thought, fifteen months ago.

'I never thought I'd see you again,' he said explosively, sounding faintly aggrieved at the twist of fate. 'I mean, the papers said you worked in a bank.'

'So I do. And I go racing.' I paused. 'You remembered my name.'

'Yeah. Could hardly forget it, could I? All over the papers.'

We went a few yards in silence. 'Go on.' I said.

He made a convulsive gesture of frustrated despair. 'All right. But if I tell you, you won't tell *them*, will you, not Mum and Dad?'

I glanced at him, but from his troubled face it was clear that he meant exactly what he'd said: it wasn't my telling the police he minded most, but my telling his parents.

'Just get on with it,' I said.

He sighed. 'Well, we had this horse. Dad did. He'd bought it as a yearling and ran it as a two-year-old and at three, but it was a jumper really, and it turned out to be good.' He paused. 'Indian Silk, that's what it was called.'

I frowned. 'But Indian Silk ... didn't that win at Cheltenham this year, in March?'

He nodded. 'The Gold Cup. The very top. He's only seven now and he's bound to be brilliant for years.' The voice was bitter with a sort of resigned, stifled anger.

'But he doesn't any longer belong to your father?'

'No, he doesn't.' More bitterness, very sharp.

'Go on, then,' I said.

He swallowed and took his time, but eventually he said. 'Two years ago this month, when Indian Silk was five, like, he won the Hermitage 'Chase very easily here at Newbury, and everyone was tipping him for the Gold Cup *last* year, though Dad was saying he was still on the young side and to give him time. See, Dad was that proud of that horse. The best he'd ever trained, and it was his own, not someone else's. Don't know if you can understand that.'

'I do understand it.' I said.

He gave a split-second glance at my face. 'Well, Indian Silk got sick,' he said. 'I mean, there was nothing you could put your finger on. He just lost his speed. He couldn't even gallop properly at home, couldn't beat other horses in Dad's yard that he'd been running rings round all year. Dad couldn't run him in races. He could hardly train him. And the vet couldn't find out what was wrong with him. They took blood tests and all sorts, and they gave him antibiotics and purges, and they thought it might be worms or something, but it wasn't.'

We had reached the last fence, and stood there on the rough grass beside it while in twos and threes other enthusiasts straggled down from the grandstand towards us to watch the horses in action at close quarters.

'I was at school a lot of the time, see,' Ricky said. 'I was home every night of course but I was taking exams and had a lot of homework and I didn't really want to take much notice of Indian Silk getting so bad or anything. I mean, Dad does go on a bit, and I suppose I thought the horse just had a virus or something and would get better. But he just got slowly worse and one day Mum was crying.' He stopped suddenly, as if that part was the worst. 'I hadn't seen a grown up cry before,' he said. 'Suppose you'll think it funny, but it upset me something awful.'

'I don't think it funny,' I said.

'Anyway,' he went on, seeming to gather confidence, 'It got so that Indian Silk was so weak he could barely walk down the road and he wasn't eating, and Dad was in real despair because there wasn't nothing anyone could do, and Mum couldn't bear the thought of him going to the knackers, and then some guy telephoned and offered to buy him.'

'To buy a sick horse?' I said, surprised.

'I don't think Dad was going to tell him just how bad he was. Well, I mean, at that point Indian Silk was worth just what the knackers would pay for his carcass, which wasn't much, and this man was offering nearly twice that. But the man said he knew Indian Silk couldn't race any more but he'd like to give him a good home in a nice field for as long as necessary, and it meant that Dad didn't have the expense of any more vets' bills and he and Mum didn't have to watch Indian Silk getting worse and worse, and Mum wouldn't have to think of him going to the knackers for dog meat, so they let him go.'

The horses for the second race came out onto the course and galloped down past us, the jockeys' colours bright in the sun.

'And then what?' I said.

'Then nothing happened for weeks and we were getting over it, like, and then someone told Dad that Indian Silk was back in training and looking fine, and he couldn't believe it.'

'When was that?' I asked.

'It was last year, just before ... before Ascot.'

A small crowd gathered on the landing side of the fence, and I drew him away down the course a bit further, to where the horses would set themselves right to take off.

'Go on,' I said.

'My exams were coming up,' he said. 'And I mean, they were important, they were going to affect my whole life, see?'

I nodded

'Then Dad found that the man who'd bought Indian Silk hadn't put him in any field, he'd sent him straight down the road to Calder Jackson.'

'Ah,' I said.

'And there was this man saying Calder Jackson had the gift of healing, some sort of magic, and had simply touched Indian Silk and made him well. I ask you ... And Dad was in a frightful state because someone had suggested he should send the horse there, to Calder Jackson, while he was so bad, of course, and Dad had said don't be so ridiculous it was all a lot of rubbish. And then Mum was saying he should have listened to her, because she'd said why not try it, it couldn't do any harm, and he wouldn't do it, and they were having rows, and she was crying ...' He gulped for air, the story now pouring out faster almost than he could speak. 'And I wasn't getting any work done with it all going on, they weren't ever talking about anything else, and I took the first exam and just sat there and couldn't do it, and I knew I'd failed and I was going to fail them all because I couldn't concentrate ... and then there was Calder Jackson one evening talking on television, saying he'd got a friend of his to buy a dying horse, because the people who owned it would just of let it die because they didn't believe in

425

healers, like a lot of people, and he hoped the horse would be great again some day, like before, thanks to him, and I knew he was talking about Indian Silk. And he said he was going to Ascot on that Thursday ... and there was Dad screaming that Calder Jackson had stolen thehorse away, it was all a filthy swindle, which of course it wasn't, but at the time I believed him ... and it all got so that I hated Calder Jackson so much that I couldn't think straight. I mean, I thought *he* was the reason Mum was crying and I was failing my exams and Dad had lost the only really top horse he'd have in his whole life, and I just wanted to *kill* him.'

The bed-rock words were out, and the flood suddenly stopped, leaving the echo of them on the October air.

'And did you fail your exams?' I asked, after a moment.

'Yeah. Most of them. But I took them again at Christmas and got good passes.' He shook his head, speaking more slowly, more quietly. 'I was glad even that night that you'd stopped me stabbing him. I mean ... I'd have thrown my whole life away, I could see it afterwards, and all for nothing, because Dad wasn't going to get the horse back whatever I did, because it was a legal sale, like.'

I thought over what he'd told me while in the distance the horses lined up and set off on their three mile steeplechase.

'I was sort of mad,' he said. 'I can't really understand it now. I mean. I wouldn't go around trying to kill people. I really wouldn't. It seems like a different person.'

Adolescence, I thought and not for the first time, could be hell.

'I took Mum's knife out of the kitchen,' he said, 'She never could think where it had gone.'

I wondered if the police still had it; with Ricky's fingerprints on file.

'I didn't know there would be so many people at Ascot,' he said. 'And so many gates into the course. Much more than Newmarket. I was getting frantic because I thought I wouldn't find him. I meant to do it earlier, see, when he arrived. I was out on the road, running up and down the pavement, mad, you know, really, looking for him and feeling the knife kind of burning in my sleeve, like I was burning in my mind ... and I saw his head, all those curls, crossing the road, and I ran, but I

426

was too late, he'd gone inside, through the gate.'

'And then,' I suggested. 'You simply waited for him to come out?'

He nodded. 'There were lots of people around. No one took any notice. I reckoned he'd come up that path from the station, and that was the way he would go back. It didn't seem long, the waiting. Went in a flash.'

The horses came over the next fence down the course like a multi-coloured wave and thundered towards the one where we were standing. The ground trembled from the thud of the hooves, the air rang with the curses of jockeys, the half-ton equine bodies brushed through the birch, the sweat and the effort and the speed filled eyes and ears and mind with pounding wonder and then were gone, flying away, leaving the silence. I had walked down several times before to watch from fences, both there and on other tracks, and the fierce fast excitement had never grown stale.

'Who is it who owns Indian Silk now?' I asked.

'A Mr Chacksworth, comes from Birmingham,' Ricky answered. 'You see him at the races sometimes, slobbering all over Indian Silk. But it wasn't him that bought him from Dad. He bought him later, when he was all right again. Paid a proper price for him, so we heard. Made it all the worse.'

A sad and miserable tale, all of it.

'Who bought the horse from your father?' I said.

'I never met him ... his name was Smith. Some funny first name. Can't remember.'

Smith. Friend of Calder's.

'Could it,' I asked, surprised, 'have been *Dissdale* Smith?'

'Yeah. That sounds like it. How do you know?'

'He was there that day at Ascot,' I said. 'There on the pavement, right beside Calder Jackson.'

'Was he?' Ricky looked disconcerted. 'He was a dead liar, you know, all that talk about nice fields.'

'Who tells the truth,' I said, 'when buying or selling horses?'

The runners were round again on the far side of the track, racing hard now on the second circuit.

'What are you going to do?' Ricky said. 'About me, like? You won't tell Mum and Dad. You won't, will you?'

I looked directly at the boy-man, seeing the continuing

427

anxiety but no longer the first panic-stricken fear. He seemed to sense now that I would very likely not drag him into court, but he wasn't sure of much else.

'Perhaps they should know,' I said.

'No!' His agitation rose quickly. 'They've had so much trouble and I would have made it so much worse if you hadn't stopped me, and afterwards I used to wake up sweating at what it would have done to them; and the only good thing was that I did learn that you can't put things right by killing people, you can only make things terrible for your family.'

After a long pause I said. 'All right. I won't tell them.' And heaven help me, I thought, if he ever attacked anyone again because he thought he could always get away with it.

The relief seemed to affect him almost as much as the anxiety. He blinked several times and turned his head away to where the race was again coming round into the straight with this time an all-out effort to the winning post. There was again the rise and fall of the field over the distant fences but now the one wave had split into separate components, the runners coming home not in a bunch but a procession.

I watched again the fierce surprising speed of horse and jockey jumping at close quarters and wished with some regret that I could have ridden like that: but like Alec I was wishing too late, even strong and healthy and thirty-three.

The horses galloped off towards the cheers on the grandstand and Ricky and I began a slow walk in their wake. He seemed quiet and composed in the aftermath of confession, the soul's evacuation giving him ease.

'What do you feel nowadays about Calder Jackson?' I asked.

He produced a lop-sided smile. 'Nothing much. That's what's so crazy. I mean, it wasn't his fault Dad was so stubborn.'

I digested this. 'You mean,' I said. 'That you think your father should have sent him the horse himself?'

'Yes, I reckon he should've, like Mum wanted. But he said it was rubbish and too expensive, and you don't know my Dad but when he makes his mind up he just gets fighting angry if anyone tries to argue, and he shouts at her, and it isn't fair.'

'If your father had sent the horse to Calder Jackson, I suppose he would still own it,' I said thoughtfully.

'Yes, he would, and don't think he doesn't know it, of course he does, but it's as much as anyone's life's worth to say it.'

We trudged back over the thick grass, and I asked him how Calder or Dissdale had known that Indian Silk was ill.

He shrugged. 'It was in the papers. He'd been favourite for the King George VI on Boxing Day, but of course he didn't run, and the press found out why.'

We came again to the gate into the grandstand enclosure and went through it, and I asked where he lived.

'Exning,' he said.

'Where's that?'

'Near Newmarket. Just outside.' He looked at me with slightly renewed apprehension. 'You meant it, didn't you about not telling?'

'I meant it,' I said. 'Only ...' I frowned a little, thinking of the hot-house effect of his living with his parents.

'Only what?' he asked.

I tried a different tack. 'What are you doing now? Are you still at school?'

'No, I left once I'd passed those exams. I really needed them, like. You can't get a half-way decent job without those bits of paper these days.'

'You're not working for your father, then?'

He must have heard the faint relief in my voice because for the first time he fully smiled. 'No, I reckon it wouldn't be good for his temper, and anyway I don't want to be a trainer, one long worry, if you ask me.'

'What do you do, then?' I asked.

'I'm learning electrical engineering in a firm near Cambridge. An apprentice, like.' He smiled again. 'But not with horses, not me.' He shook his head ruefully and delivered his young-solomon judgement of life. 'Break your heart, horses do.'

The Second Year

NOVEMBER

To my great delight the cartoonist came up trumps, his twenty animated films being shown on television every weeknight for a month in the best time-slot for that sort of humour, seven in the evening, when older children were still up and the parents home from work. The nation sat up and giggled, and the cartoonist telephoned breathlessly to ask for a bigger loan.

'I do need a proper studio, not this converted warehouse. And more animators, and designers, and recordists, and equipment.'

'All right,' I said into the first gap. 'Draw up your requirements and come and see me.'

'Do you *realise*,' he said, as if he himself had difficulty, 'That they'll take as many films as I can make? No limit. They said just go on making them for years and years ... they said *please* go on making them.'

'I'm very glad,' I said sincerely.

'You gave me faith in myself,' he said. 'You'll never believe it, but you did. I'd been turned down so often, and I was getting depressed, but when you lent me the money to start it was like being uncorked. The ideas just rushed out.'

'And are they still rushing?'

'Oh sure. I've got the next twenty films roughed out in drawings already and we're working on those, and now I'm starting on the batch after that.'

'It's terrific,' I said.

'It sure is. Brother, life's amazing.' He put down his receiver and left me smiling into space.

'The cartoonist?' Gordon said.

430

I nodded. 'Going up like a rocket.'

'Congratulations.' There was warmth and genuine pleasure in his voice.Such a generous man, I thought: so impossible to do him harm.

'He looks like turning into a major industry,' I said.

'Disney, Hanna Barbera, eat your hearts out,' Alec said from across the room.

'Good business for the bank.' Gordon beamed. 'Henry will be pleased.'

Pleasing Henry, indeed, was the aim of us all.

'You must admit, Tim,' Alec said, 'That you're a fairish rocket yourself ... so what's the secret?'

'Light the blue paper and retire immediately,' I said good humouredly, and he balled a page of jottings to throw at me, and missed.

At mid-morning he went out as customary for the six copies of *What's Going on Where It Shouldn't* and having distributed five was presently sitting back in his chair reading our own with relish.

Ekaterin's had been thankfully absent from the probing columns ever since the five-per-cent business, but it appeared that some of our colleagues along the road weren't so fortunate.

'Did you know,' Alec said conversationally, 'That some of our investment manager chums down on the corner have set up a nice little fiddle on the side, accepting pay-offs from brokers in return for steering business their way?'

'How do you know?' Gordon asked, looking up from a ledger.

Alec lifted the paper. 'The gospel according to this dicky bird.'

'Gospel meaning good news,' I said.

'Don't be so damned erudite.' He grinned at me with mischief and went back to reading aloud,' *'Contrary to popular belief the general run of so-called managers in merchant banks are not in the princely bracket.'* He looked up briefly. 'You can say that again.' He went on, *'We hear that four of the investment managers in this establishment have been cosily supplementing their middle-incomes by steering fund money to three stockbrokers in particular. Names will be revealed in our next issue. Watch this space.'*

431

'It's happened before,' Gordon said philosophically. 'And will happen again. The temptation is always there.' He frowned. 'All the same, I'm surprised their senior managers and the directors haven't spotted it.'

'They'll have spotted it *now*,' Alec said.

'So they will.'

'It would be pretty easy,' I said musingly, 'To set up a computer programme to do the spotting for Ekaterin's, in case we should ever find the pestilence cropping up here.'

'Would it?' Gordon asked.

'Mm. Just a central programme to record every deal in the Investment Department with each stockbroker, with running totals, easy to see. Anything hugely unexpected could be investigated.'

'But that's a vast job, surely,' Gordon said.

I shook my head. 'I doubt it. I could get our tame programmer to have a go, if you like.'

'We'll put it to the others. See what they say.'

'There will be screeches from Investment Management,' Alec said. 'Cries of outraged virtue.'

'Guards them against innuendo like this, though,' Gordon said, pointing to *What's Going On Where* ...

The board agreed, and in consequence I spent another two days with the programmer, building dykes against future leaks.

Gordon these days seemed no worse, his illness not having progressed in any visible way. There was no means of knowing how he felt, as he never said and hated to be asked, but on the few times I'd seen Judith since the day at Easter, she had said he was as well as could be hoped for.

The best of those times had been a Sunday in July when Pen had given a lunch party in her house in Clapham; it was supposed to have been a lunch-in-the-garden party, but like so much that summer was frustrated by chilly winds. Inside was to me much better, as Pen had written place-cards for her long refectory table and put me next to Judith, with Gordon on her right hand.

The other guests remained a blur, most of them being doctors of some sort or another, or pharmacists like herself. Judith and I made polite noises to the faces on either side of us but spent most of the time talking to each other, carrying on two

432

conversations at once, one with voice, one with eyes; both satisfactory.

When the main party had broken up and gone, Gordon and Judith and I stayed to supper, first helping Pen clear up from what she described as 'repaying so many dinners at one go'.

It had been a day when natural opportunities for touching people abounded, when kisses and hugs of greeting had been appropriate and could be warm, when all the world could watch and see nothing between Judith and me but an enduring and peaceful friendship: a day when I longed to have her for myself worse than ever.

Since then I'd seen her only twice, and both times when she'd come to the bank to collect Gordon before they went on to other events. On each of these times I'd managed at least five minutes with her, stiffly circumspect, Gordon's colleague being polite until Gordon himself was ready to leave.

It wasn't usual for wives to come to the bank: husbands normally joined them at wherever they were going. Judith said, the second time, 'I won't do this often. I just wanted to see you, if you were around.'

'Always here,' I said.

She nodded. She was looking as fresh and poised as ever, wearing a neat blue coat with pearls showing. The brown hair was glossy, the eyes bright, the soft mouth half smiling, the glamour born in her and unconscious.

'I get ... well ... thirsty, sometimes,' she said.

'Permanent state with me,' I said lightly.

She swallowed. 'Just for a moment or two ...'

We were standing in the entrance hall, not touching, waiting for Gordon.

'Just to see you ...' She seemed uncertain that I understood, but I did.

'It's the same for me.' I assured here. 'I sometimes think of going to Clapham and waiting around just to see you walk down the street to the bakers. Just to see you, even for seconds.'

'Do you really?'

'I don't go, though. You might send Gordon to buy the bread.'

She laughed a small laugh, a fitting size for the bank; and he came, hurrying, struggling into his overcoat. I sprang to help

433

him and he said to her, 'Sorry, darling, got held up on the telephone, you know how it is.'

'I've been perfectly happy,' she said, kissing him, 'talking to Tim.'

'Splendid. Splendid. Are we ready then?'

They went off to their evening smiling and waving and leaving me to hunger futilely for this and that.

In the office one day in November Gordon said. 'How about you coming over to lunch on Sunday? Judith was saying it's ages since she saw you properly.'

'I'd love to.'

'Pen's coming, Judith said.'

Pen, my friend; the chaperone.

'Great,' I said positively. 'Lovely.'

Gordon nodded contentedly and said it was a shame we couldn't all have a repeat of last Christmas, he and Judith had enjoyed it so much. They were going this year to his son and daughter-in-law in Edinburgh, a visit long promised; to his son by his first long-dead wife, and his grandchildren, twin boys of seven.

'You'll have fun,' I said regretfully.

'They're noisy little brutes.'

His telephone rang, and mine also, and moneylending proceeded. I would be dutiful, I thought, and spend Christmas with my mother in Jersey, as she wanted, and we would laugh and play backgammon, and I would sadden her as usual by bringing no girl-friend, no prospective producer of litte brutes.

'*Why*, my love,' she said to me once a few years earlier in near despair, 'do you take out these perfectly presentable girls and never marry them?'

'There's always something I don't want to spend my life with.'

'But you do *sleep* with them?'

'Yes, darling, I do.'

'You're too choosy.'

'I expect so,' I said.

'You haven't had a single one that's lasted,' she complained. 'Everyone else's sons manage to have live-in girl friends, sometimes going on for years even if they don't marry, so why can't you?'

I'd smiled at the encouragement to what would once have been called sin, and kissed her, and told her I preferd living alone, but that one day I'd find the perfect girl to love for ever; and it hadn't even fleetingly occured to me that when I found her she would be married to someone else.

Sunday came and I went to Clapham: bitter-sweet hours, as ever.

Over lunch I told them tentatively that I'd seen the boy who had tried to kill Calder, and they reacted as strongly as I'd expected, Gordon saying, 'You've told the police, of course,' and Judith adding 'He's dangerous, Tim.'

I shook my head. 'No. I don't think so. I hope not.' I smiled wryly and told them all about Ricky Barnet and Indian Silk, and the pressure which had led to the try at stabbing. 'I don't think he'll do anything like that again. He's grown so far away from it already that he feels a different person.'

'I hope you're right,' Gordon said.

'Fancy it being Dissdale who bought Indian Silk,' Pen said. 'Isn't it amazing?'

'Especially as he was saying he was short of cash and wanting to sell box-space at Ascot,' Judith added.

'Mm,' I said. 'But after Calder had cured the horse Dissdale sold it again pretty soon, and made a handsome profit, by what I gather.'

'Typical Dissdale behaviour,' Gordon said without criticism. 'Face the risk, stake all you can afford, take the loot if you're lucky, and get out fast.' He smiled. 'By Ascot I guess he'd blown the Indian Silk profit and was back to basics. It doesn't take someone like Dissdale any longer to lose thousands than it does to make them.'

'He must have colossal faith in Calder,' Pen said musingly.

'Not colossal, Pen,' Gordon said. 'Just twice what a knacker would pay for a carcass.'

'Would *you* buy a sick-to-death horse?' Judith asked. 'I mean, if Calder said buy it and I'll cure him, would you believe it?'

Gordon looked at her fondly. 'I'm not Dissdale, darling, and I don't think I'd buy it.'

435

'And that is precisely,' I pointed out, 'why Fred Barnes lost Indian Silk. He thought Calder's powers were all rubbish and he wouldn't lash out good money to put them to the test. But Dissdale *did*. Bought the horse and presumably also paid Calder ... who boasted about his success on television and nearly got himself killed for it.'

'Ironic, the whole thing,' Pen said, and we went on discussing it desultorily over coffee.

I stayed until six, when Pen went off to her shop for a Sunday-evening, stint and Gordon began to look tired, and I drove back to Hampstead in the usual post-Judith state; half-fulfilled, half-starved.

Towards the end of November, and at Oliver Knowles' invitation, I travelled to another Sunday lunch, this time at the stud farm in Hertfordshire.

It turned out, not surprisingly, to be one of Ginnie's days home from school, and it was she, whistling to Squibs, who set off with me through the yards.

'Did you know we had a hundred and fifty-two mares here all at the same time, back in May?' she said.

'That's a lot,' I said, impressed.

'They had a hundred and fourteen foals between them, and only one of the mares and three of the foals died. That's a terrifically good record, you know.'

'Your father's very skilled.'

'So is Nigel.' she said grudgingly. 'You have to give him his due.

I smiled at the expression

'He isn't here just now,' she said. 'He went off to Miami yesterday to lie in the sun.'

'Nigel?'

She nodded. 'He goes about this time every year. Sets him up for the winter, he say.'

'Always Miami?'

'Yes, he likes it.'

The whole atmosphere of the place was back to where I'd known it first, to the slow chill months of gestation. Ginnie, snuggling inside her padded jacket, gave carrots from her pocket to some of the mares in the first yard and walked me without stopping through the empty places, the second yard, the foaling yard, and past the breeding shed.

We came finally as always to the stallion yard where the curiosity of the residents brought their heads out the moment they heard our footsteps. Ginnie distributed carrots and pats with the aplomb of her father, and Sandcastle graciously allowed her to stroke his nose.

'He's quiet now.' she said. 'He's on a much lower diet at this time of year.'

I listened to the bulk of knowledge behind the calm words and I said, 'What are you going to do when you leave school?'

'This, of course,' She patted Sandcastle's neck. 'Help Dad. Be his assistant.'

'Nothing else?'

She shook her head. 'I love the foals. Seeing them born and watching them grow. I don't want to do anything else, ever.'

We left the stallions and walked between the paddocks with their foals and dams, along the path to Watcherleys', Squibs trotting on ahead and marking his fence posts. The neighbouring place, whose ramshakle state I'd only glimpsed on my pursuit of the loose five million, proved now to be almost as neat as the parent spread, with much fresh paint in evidence and weeds markedly absent.

'Dad can't bear mess,' Ginnie said when I remarked on the spit-and-polish. 'The Watcherleys are pretty lucky, really, with Dad paying them rent *and* doing up their place *and* employing them to look after the animals in this yard. Bob may still gripe a bit at not being on his own, but Maggie was telling me just last week that she would be everlastingly thankful that Calder Jackson stole their business.'

'He hardly stole it,' I said mildly.

'Well, you know what I mean. Did better at it, if you want to be pedantic.' She grinned. 'Anyway, Maggie's bought some new clothes at last, and I'm glad for her.'

We opened and went into a few of the boxes where she handed out the last of the carrots and fondled the inmates, both mares and growing foals, talking to them, and all of them responded amiably to her touch, nuzzling her gently. She looked at peace and where she belonged, all growing pains suspended.

437

The Third Year

APRIL

Alec had bought a bunch of yellow tulips when he went out for *What's Going on*, and they stood on his desk in a beer mug, catching a shaft of spring sunshine and standing straight like guardsmen.

Gordon was making notes in a handwriting growing even smaller, and the two older colleagues were counting the weeks to their retirement. Office life: an ordinary day.

My telephone rang, and with eyes still bent on a letter from a tomato grower asking for more time to repay his original loan because of needing a new greenhouse (half an acre) right this minute, I slowly picked up the receiver.

'Oliver Knowles,' the voice said. 'is that you, Tim?'

'Hello,' I replied warmly. 'Everything going well?'

'No.' The word was sickeningly abrupt,and both mentally and physically I sat up straighter.

'What's the matter?'

'Can you come down here?' he asked, not directly answering. 'I'm rather worried. I want to talk to you.'

'Well ... I could come on Sunday,' I said.

'Could you come today?' Or tomorrow?'

I reviewed my work load and a few appointments. 'Tomorrow afternoon, if you like,' I said. 'If it's bank business.'

'Yes, it is.' the anxiety in his voice was quite plain, and communicated itself with much ease to me.

'Can't you tell me what's the trouble?' I asked. 'Is Sandcastle all right?'

'I don't know,' he said. 'I'll tell you when you come.'

'But Oliver ...'

'Listen,' he said. 'Sandcastle is in good health and he hasn't escaped again or anything like that. It's too difficult to explain on the telephone. I want your advice, that's all.'

He wouldn't say any more and left me with the dead receiver in my hand and some horrid suspenseful question marks in my mind.

'Sandcastle? Gordon asked.

'Oliver says he's in good health.'

'That horse is insured against everything — those enormous premiums — so don't worry too much,' Gordon said. 'It's probably something minor.'

It hadn't sounded like anything minor, and when I reached the stud farm the next day I found that it certainly wasn't. Oliver came out to meet me as I braked to a standstill by his front door, and there were new deep lines on his face that hadn't been there before.

'Come in,' he said, clasping my hand. 'I'm seriously worried. I don't know what to do.'

He led the way through the house to the office-sitting room and gestured me to a chair. 'Sit down and read this,' he said, and gave me a letter.

There had been no time for 'nice day' or 'how is Ginnie?' introductory noises, just this stark command. I sat down, and I read, as directed.

The letter dated April 21st, said:

Dear Oliver,

I'm not complaining, because of course one pays one's fee and take's one's chances, but I'm sorry to tell you that the Sandcastle foal out of my mare Spiral Binding has been born with a half of one ear missing. It's a filly, by the way, and I dare say it won't affect her speed, but her looks are ruined.

So sad.

I expect I'll see you one day at the sales.

Yours,

Jane.

439

'Is that very bad?' I asked, frowning.

In reply he wordlessly handed me another letter. This one said:

Dear Mr Knowles,

You asked me to let you know how my mare Girandette, whom you liked so much, fared on foaling. She gave birth safely to a nice colt foal, but unfortunately he died at six days. We had a post mortem, and it was found that he had malformed heart-valves, like hole-in-heart-babies.

This is a great blow to me, financially as well as all else, but that's life I suppose.

Yours sincerely,

George Page.

'And now this,' Oliver said, and handed me a third.

The heading was that of a highly regarded and well-known stud farm, the letter briefly impersonal.

Dear Sir,

Filly foal born March 31st to Poppingcorn.

Sire: Sandcastle.

Deformed foot, near fore.

Put down.

I gave him back the letters and with growing misgiving asked, 'How common are thse malformations?'

Oliver said intensely, 'They happen. They happen occasionally. But those letters aren't all. I've had two telephone calls — one last night. Two other foals have died of holes in the heart. Two more! That's five with something wrong with them.' He stared at me, his eyes like dark pits. 'That's far too many.' He swallowed. 'And what about the others, the other thirty-five? Suppose ... suppose there are more ...'

'If you haven't heard, they're surely all right.'

He shook his head hopelessly.'The mares are scattered all over the place, dropping Sandcastle's foals where they are due to be bred next. There's no automatic reason for those stud managers to tell me when a foal's born, or what it's like. I mean, some do it out of courtesy but they just don't usually bother, and nor do I. I tell the owner of the mare, not the manager of the stallion.'

'Yes, I see.'

'So there may be other foals with deformities ... that I haven't heard about.'

There was a long fraught pause in which the enormity of the position sank coldly into my banking consciousness. Oliver developed sweat on his forehead and a tic beside his mouth, as if sharing his anxiety had doubled it rather than halved.

The telephone rang suddenly, making us both jump.

'You answer it,' he said. 'Please.'

I opened my mouth to protest that it would be only some routine call about anything else on earth, but then merely picked up the receiver.

'Is that Oliver Knowles?' a voice said.

'No .. I'm his assistant.'

'Oh, Then will you give him a message?'

'Yes, I will.'

'Tell him that Patrick O'Marr rang him from Limballow, Ireland. Have you got that?'

'Yes,' I said. 'Go ahead.'

'It's about a foal we had born here three or four weeks ago. I thought I'd better let Mr Knowles know that we've had to put it down, though I'm sorry to give him bad news. Are you listening?'

'Yes,' I said. feeling hollow.

'The poor little fellow was born with a sort of curled-in hoof. The vet said it might straighten out in a week or two, but it didn't, so we had it X-rayed, and the lower pastern bone and the coffin bone were fused and tiny. The vet said there was no chance of them developing properly, and the little colt would never be able to walk, let alone race. A beautiful little fella too, in all other ways. Anyway, I'm telling Mr Knowles because of course he'll be looking out for Sandcastle's first crop to win for him, and I'm explaining why this one won't be there. Pink Roses, that's the mare's name. Tell him, will you? Pink Roses. She's come here to be bred to Dallaton. Nice mare. She's fine herself, tell Mr Knowles.'

'Yes,' I said. 'I'm very sorry.'

'One of those things.' The cultured Irish accent sounded not too despairing. 'The owner of Pink Roses is cut up about it, of course, but I believe he'd insured against a dead or deformed foal, so it's a case of wait another year and better luck next time.'

'I'll tell Mr Knowles,' I said. 'And thank you for letting us know.'

'Sorry and all,' he said. 'But there it is.'

I put the receiver down slowly and Oliver said dully, 'Another one? Not another one.'

I nodded and told him what Patrick O'Marr had said.

'That's six,' Oliver said starkly. 'And Pink Roses ... that's the mare you saw Sandcastle cover, this time last year.'

'Was it?' I thought back to that majestic mating, that moment of such promise. Poor little colt, conceived in splendour and born with a club foot.

'What am I going to do?' Oliver said.

'Get out Sandcastle's insurance policy.'

He looked blank. 'No, I mean, about the mares. We have all the mares here who've come this year to Sandcastle. They've all foaled except one and nearly all of them have already been covered. I mean ... there's another crop already growing, and suppose those ... suppose all of those ...' He stopped as if he simply couldn't make his tongue say the words. 'I was awake all night,' he said.

'The first thing,' I said again, 'is to look at that policy.'

He went unerringly to a neat row of files in a cupboard and pulled out the needed document, a many-paged affair, partly printed, partly typed. I spread it open and said to Oliver, 'How about some coffee? This is going to take ages.'

'Oh, All right.' He looked around him vaguely. 'There'll be some put ready for me for dinner. I'll go and plug it in.' He paused. 'Percolator,' he explained.

I knew all the symptoms of a mouth saying one thing while the mind was locked on to another. 'Yes,' I said. 'That would be fine.' He nodded with the same unmeshed mental gears, and I guessed that when he got to the kitchen he'd have trouble remembering what for.

The insurance policy had been written for the trade and not the customer, a matter of jargon-ridden sentences full of words that made plain sense only to people who used them for a living.

442

I read it very carefully for that reason; slowly and thoroughly from start to finish.

There were many definitions of the word 'accident', with stipulations about the number of veterinary surgeons who should be consulted and should give their signed opinions before Sandcastle (hereinafter called the horse) could be humanely destroyed for any reason whatsoever. There were stipulations about fractures, naming those bones which should commonly be held to be repairable, and about common muscle, nerve and tendon troubles which would not be considered grounds for destruction, unless of such severity that the horse couldn't actually stand up.

Aside from these restrictions the horse was to be considered to be insured against death from any natural causes whatsoever, to be insured against accidental death occurring while the horse was free (such a contingency to be guarded against with diligence, gross negligence being a disqualifying condition) to be insured against death by fire should the stable be consumed, and against death caused maliciously by human hand. He was insured fully against malicious or accidental castration and against such accidental damage being caused by veterinarians acting in good faith to treat the horse. He was insured against infertility on a sliding scale, his full worth being in question only if he proved one hundred per cent infertile (which laboratory test had shown was not the case).

He was insured against accidental or malicious poisoning and against impotence resulting from non-fatal illness, and against incapacitating or fatal injuries inflicted upon him by any other horse.

He was insured against death caused by the weather (storm, flood, lightning, etc.) and also, surprisingly, against death or incapacity caused by war, riot or civil commotion, causes usually specifically excluded from insurance.

He was insured against objects dropped from the sky and against being driven into by mechanical objects ont he ground and against trees falling on him and against hidden wells opening under his feet.

He was insured against every foreseeable disaster except one. He was not insured against being put out of business because of congenital abnormalities among his progeny.

443

Oliver came back carrying a tray on which sat two kitchen mugs containing tea, not coffee. He put the tray on the desk and looked at my face, which seemed only very slightly to deepen his despair.

'I'm not insured, am I,' he said, 'against possessing a healthy potent stallion to whom no one will send their mares.'

I don't know.'

'Yes ... I see you do.' He was shaking slightly. 'When the policy was drawn up about six people, including myself and two vets, besides the insurers themselves, tried to think of every possible contingency, and to guard against it. We threw in everything we could think of.' He swallowed. 'No one ... no one thought of a whole crop of deformed foals.'

'No,' I said.

'I mean, breeders usually insure their own mares, if they want to, and the foal, to protect the stallion fee, but many don't because of the premiums being high. And I ... I'm paying this enormous premium ... and the one thing ... the one thing that happens is something we never ... no one ever imagined ... could happen.'

The policy, I thought, had been too specific. They should have been content with something like 'any factor resulting in the horse not being considered fit for stud pruposes'; but perhaps the insurers themselves couldn't find underwriters for anything so open to interpretation and opinion. In any case, the damage was done. All-risk policies all too often were not what they said; and insurance companies never paid out if they could avoid it.

My own skin felt clammy. Three million pounds of the bank's money and two million subscribed by private people were tied up in the horse, and if Oliver couldn't repay, it was we who would lose.

I had recommended the loan. Henry had wanted the adventure and Val and Gordon had been willing, but it was my own report which had carried the day. I couldn't have foreseen the consequences any more than Oliver, but I felt most horribly and personally responsible for the mess.

'What shall I do?' he said again.

'About the mares?'

'And everything else.'

I stared into space. The disaster that for the bank would mean a loss of face and a sharp dip in profits and to the private subscribers just a painful financial set-back meant in effect total ruin for Oliver Knowles.

If Sandcastle couldn't generate income, Oliver would be bankrupt. His business was not a limited company, which meant that he would lose his farm, his horses, his house; everything he possessed. To him too, as to my mother, the bailiffs would come, carrying off his furniture and his treasures and Ginnie's books and toys....

I shook myself mentally and physically and said, 'The first thing to do is nothing. Keep quiet and don't tell anyone what you've told me. Wait to hear if any more of the foals are ... wrong. I will consult with the other directors at Ekaterin's and see what can be done in the way of providing time. I mean ...I'm not promising ... but we might consider suspending repayments while we look into other possibilties.'

He looked bewildered. 'What possibilities?'

'Well ... of having Sandcastle tested. If the original tests of his fertility weren't thorough enough, for instance, it might be possible to show that his sperm had always been defective in some way, and then the insurance policy would protect you. Or at least it's a very good chance.'

The insurers, I thought, might in that case sue the laboratory that had originally given the fertility all-clear, but that wasn't Oliver's problem, nor mine. What did matter was that all of a sudden he looked a fraction more cheerful, and drank his tea absentmindedly.

'And the mares?' he said

I shook my head. 'In fairness to their owners you'll have to say that Sandcastle's off colour.'

'And repay their fees,' he said gloomily.

'Mm.'

'He'll have covered two today,' he said. 'I haven't mentioned any of this to Nigel. I mean. It's his job to organise the breeding sessions. He has a great eye for those mares, he knows when they are feeling receptive. I leave it to his judgement a good deal, and he told me this morning that two were ready for Sandcastle. I just nodded. I felt sick. I didn't tell him.'

'So how many does that leave, er, uncovered?'

445

He consulted a list, fumbling slightly. 'The one that hasn't foaled, and ... four others.'

Thirty-five more mares, I thought numbly, could be carrying that seed.

'The mare that hasn't yet foaled,' Oliver said flatly, 'Was bred to Sandcastle last year.'

I stared. 'You mean ... one of his foals will be born *here*?'

'Yes.' He rubbed his hand over his face. 'Any day.'

There were footsteps outside the door and Ginnie came in, saying on a rising, enquiring inflection, 'Dad?'

She saw me immediately and her face lit up. 'Hello! How lovely. I didn't know you were coming.'

I stood up to give her a customarily enthusiastic greeting, but she sensed at once that the action didn't match the climate. 'What's the matter?' she looked into my eyes and then at her father. 'What's happened?'

'Nothing,' he said.

'Dad, you're lying.' She turned to me. 'Tell me. I can see something bad has happened.I'm not a child any more. I'm seventeen.'

'I thought you'd be at school,' I said.

'I've left. At the end of last term. There wasn't any point in me going back for the summer when all I'm interested in is here.'

She looked far more assured, as if the schooldays had been a crysallis and she were now the imago, flying free.The beauty she had longed for hadn't quite arrived, but her face was full of character and far from plain, and she would be very much liked, I thought, throughout her life.

'What is it?' she said. 'What's happened?'

Oliver made a small gesture of despair and capitulatioin. 'You'll have to know sometime.' He swallowed. 'Some of Sandcastle's foals ... aren't perfect.'

'How do you mean, not perfect?'

He told her about all six and showed her the letters, and she went slowly, swaying, pale. 'Oh Dad, no. No. It can't be. Not Sandcastle. Not that beautiful boy.'

'Sit down,' I said, but she turned to me instead, burying her face against my chest and holding on to me tightly. I put my arms round her and kissed her hair and comforted her for an

446

age as best I could.

I went to the office on the following morning, Friday, and with a slight gritting of teeth told Gordon the outcome of my visit to Oliver.

He said 'My God,' several times, and Alec came over from his desk to listen also, his blue eyes for once solemn behind the gold-rimmed spectacles, the blond eyelashes blinking slowly and the laughing mouth grimly shut.

'What will you do?' he said finally, when I stopped.

'I don't really know.'

Gorden stirred, his hands trembling unnoticed on his blotter in his overriding concern. 'The first thing, I suppose,' he said, 'is to tell Val and Henry. Though what any of us can do is a puzzle. As you said, Tim, we'll have to wait to assess quite how irretrievable the situation is, but I can't imagine anyone with a top-class broodmare having the confidence to send her to Sandcastle in the future. Can you, really, Tim? Would *you*?'

I shook my head. 'No.'

'Well, there you are,' Gordon said. 'No one would.'

Henry and Val received the news with undisguised dismay and told the rest of the directors at lunch. The man who had been against the project from the beginning reacted with genuine anger and gave me a furious dressing-down over the grilled sole.

'No one could foresee this,' Henry protested, defending me.

'Anyone could foresee,' said the dissenting director caustically, 'that such a scatterbrained scheme would blow up in our faces. Tim has been given too much power too soon, and it's his judgement that's at fault here, his alone. If he'd had the common nous to recognise the dangers, you would have listened to him and turned the proposal down. It's certainly because of his stupidity and immaturity that the bank is facing this loss, and I shall put my views on record at the next board meeting.'

There were a few uncomfortable murmurs round the table and Henry with unruffled geniality said, 'We are all to blame, if blame there is, and it is unfair to call Tim stupid for not foreseeing something that escaped the imaginations of all the various experts who drew up the insurance policy.'

The dissenter however repeated his 'I told you so' remarks endlessly through the cheese and coffee, and I sat there depressedly enduring his digs because I wouldn't give him the satisfaction of seeing me leave before he did.

'What will you do next?' Henry asked me, when at long last everyone rather silently stood up to drift back to their desks. 'What do you propose?'

I was grateful that by implication he was leaving me in the position I'd reached and not taking the decisions out of my hands. 'I'm going down to the farm tomorrow,' I said, 'to go through the financial situation. Add up the figures. They're bound to be frightful.'

He nodded with regret. 'Such a marvellous horse. And no one, Tim, whatever anyone says, could have dreamt he'd have such a flaw.'

I signed. 'Oliver has asked me to stay tomorrow night and Sunday night. I don't really want to, but they do need support.'

'They?'

'Ginnie, his daughter, is with him. She's only just seventeen. It's very hard on them both. Shattering, in fact.'

Henry patted my arm and walked with me to the lift. 'Do what you can,' he said. 'Let me know the full state of affairs on Monday.'

Before I left home that Saturday morning I had a telephone call from Judith.

'Gordon's told me about Sandcastle. Tim, it's so terrible. Those poor, poor people.'

'Wretched,' I said.

'Tim, tell Ginnie how sorry I am. Sorry ... how hopeless words are, you say sorry if you bump someone in the supermarket. That dear child ... she wrote to me a couple of times from school, just asking for feminine information, like I'd told her to.'

'Did she?'

'Yes. She's such a nice girl. So sensible. But this ... this is too much. Gordon says they're in danger of losing *everything*.'

'I'm going down there today to see where he stands.'

'Gordon, told me. Do please give them my love.'

'I will.' I paused fractionally. 'My love to you, too.'

'Tim ...'

'I just wanted to tell you. It's still the same.'

'We haven't seen you for weeks. I mean ... I haven't.'

'Is Gordon in the room with you?' I asked.

'Yes, that's right.'

I smiled twistedly. 'I do hear about you, you know,' I said. 'He mentions you quite often, and I ask after you ... it makes you feel closer.'

'Yes,' she said in a perfectly neutral voice. 'I know exactly what you mean. I feel the same about it exactly.'

'Judith ...' I took a breath and made my own voice calm to match hers. 'Tell Gordon I'll phone him at home, if he'd like, if there is anything that needs consultation before Monday.'

'I'll tell him. Hang on.' I heard her repeating the question and Gordon's distant rumble of an answer, and then she said, 'Yes, he says please do, we'll be at home this evening and most of tomorrow.'

'Perhaps you'll answer when the telephone rings.'

'Perhaps.'

After a brief silence I said, 'I'd better go.'

'Goodbye then, Tim,' she said. 'And do let us know. We'll both be thinking of you all day, I know we will.'

'I'll call,' I said. 'You can count on it.'

The afternoon was on the whole as miserable as I'd expected and in some respects worse. Oliver and Ginnie walked about like pale automatons making disconnected remarks and forgetting where they'd put things, and lunch, Ginnie version, had consisted of eggs boiled too hard and packets of potato crisps.

'We haven't told Nigel or the lads what's happening,' Oliver said. 'Fortunately there is a lull in Sandcastle's programme. He's been very busy because nearly all his mares foaled in mid-March, close together, except for four and the one who's still carrying.' He swallowed. 'And the other stallions, of course, their mares are all here too, and we have their foals to deliver and their matings to be seen to. I mean ... we have to go on. We have to.'

Towards four o'clock they both went out into the yards for evening stables, visibly squaring their shoulders to face the

449

stable hands in a normal manner, and I began adding the columns of figures I'd drawn up from Oliver's records.

The tally when I'd finished was appalling and meant that Oliver could be an undischarged bankrupt for the rest of his life. I put the results away in my briefcase and tried to think of something more constructive; and Oliver's telephone rang.

'Oliver?' a voice, sounding vaguely familiar.

'He's out,' I said. 'Can I take a message?'

'Get him to ring me. Ursular Young. I'll give you the number.'

'Ursula!' I said in surprise. 'This is Tim Ekaterin.'

'Really?' For her it was equally unexpected. 'What are *you* doing there?'

'Just staying the weekend. Can I help?'

She hesitated slightly but then said, 'Yes, I suppose you can. I'm afraid it's bad news for him, though. Disappointing, you might say.' She paused. 'I've a friend who has a small stud farm, just one stallion, but quite a good one, and she's been so excited this year because one of the mares booked to him was in foal to Sandcastle. She was thrilled, you see, to be having a foal of that calibre born on her place.'

'Yes,' I said.'

'Well, she rang me this morning, and she was crying.' Ursula herself gulped: she might appear tough but other people's tears always moved her. 'She said the mare had dropped the Sandcastle foal during the night and she hadn't been there. She said the mare gave no sign yesterday evening, and the birth must have been quick and easy, and the mare was all right, but ...'

'But what?' I said, scarcely breathing.

'She said the foal — a filly — was on her feet and suckling when she went to the mare's box this morning, and at first she was overjoyed, but then ... but then ...'

'Go on,' I said hopelessly.

'Then she saw. She says it's dreadful.'

'Ursula ...'

'The foal has only one eye.'

Oh my god, I thought: dear *God*.

'She says there's nothing on the other side,' Ursula said, 'No proper socket.' She gulped again. 'Will you tell Oliver? I

450

thought he'd better know. He'll be most disappointed. I'm so sorry.'

'I'll tell him.'

'These things happen, I suppose,' she said. 'But it's so upsetting when they happen to your friends.'

'You're very right.'

'Goodbye then, Tim. See you soon, I hope, at the races.'

I put down the receiver and wondered how I would ever tell them, and in fact I didn't tell Ginnie, only Oliver, who sat with his head in his hands, despair in every line of his body.

'It's hopeless,' he said.

'Not yet,' I said encouragingly, though I wasn't as certain as I sounded. 'There are still the tests to be done on Sandcastle.'

He merely slumped lower. 'I'll get them done, but they won't help. The genes which are wrong will be minute. No one will see them, however powerful the microscope.'

'You can't tell. If they can see DNA, why not a horse's chromosomes?'

He raised his head slowly. 'Even then ... it's such a long shot.' He sighed deeply. 'I think I'll ask the Equine Research Establishment at Newmarket to have him there, to see what they can find. I'll ring them on Monday.'

'I suppose,' I said tentatively, 'Well, I know it sounds silly, but I suppose it couldn't be anything as simple as something he'd *eaten*? Last year, of course.'

He shook his head. 'I thought of that. I've thought of bloody well everything, believe me. All the stallions had the same food, and none of the others' foals are affected ... or at least we haven't heard of any. Nigel feeds the stallions himself out of the feed room in that yard, and we're always careful what we give them because of keeping them fit.'

Carrot?' I said.

'I give carrots to every horse on the place. Everyone here does. Carrots are good food. I buy them by the hundredweight and keep them in the first big yard where the main feed room is. I put handfuls in my pockets each day. You've seen me. Rotaboy, Diarist and Parakeet all had them. It can't possibly be anything to do with carrots.'

'Paint: something like that? Something new in the boxes,

451

when you put in all the security? Something he could chew?'

He again shook his head. 'I've been over it and over it. We did all the boxes exactly the same as each other. There's nothing in Sandcastle's box that wasn't in the others. They're all exactly alike.' He moved restlessly. 'I've been down there to make sure there's nothing Sandcastle could reach to lick if he put his head right over the half-door as far as he could get. There's nothing, nothing at all.'

'Drinking pails?'

'No. They don't always have the same pails. I mean, when Lenny fills them he doesn't necessarily take them back to the particular boxes they come from. The pails don't have the stallions' names on, if that's what you mean.'

I didn't mean anything much: just grabbing at straws.

'Straw ...' I said. 'How about an allergy? An allergy to something around him: Could an allergy have such an effect?'

'I've never heard of anything like that. I'll ask the Research people, though, on Monday.'

He got up to pour us both a drink. 'It's good to have you here,' he said. 'A sort of net over the bottomless pit.' He gave me the glass with a faint half-smile, and I had a definite impression that he would not in the end go to pieces.

I telephoned then to the Michaels' house and Gordon answered at the first ring as if he'd been passing nearby. Nothing good to report, I said, except that Ginnie sent Judith her love. Gordon said Judith was in the garden picking parsley for supper, and he would tell her. 'Call tomorrow,' he said, 'if we can help.'

Our own supper, left ready in the refrigerator by Oliver's part-time housekeeper, filled the hollows left by lunch, and Ginnie went to bed straight afterwards, saying she would be up at two o'clock and out with Nigel in the foal yard.

'She goes most nights,' Oliver said. 'She and Nigel make a good team. He says she's a great help, particularly if three or four mares are foaling at the same time. I'm often out there myself, but with all the decisions and paperwork as well I get very tired if I do it too much. Fall asleep over meals, that sort of thing.'

We ourselves went to bed fairly early, and I awoke in the large high-ceilinged guest room while it was still blackly dark. It was one of those fast awakenings which mean that sleep won't come back easily, and I got out of bed and went to the window, which looked out over the yard.

I could see only roofs and security lights and a small section of the first yard. There was no visible activity, and my watch showed four-thirty.

I wondered if Ginnie would mind if I joined her in the foaling yard; and got dressed and went.

They were all there, Nigel and Oliver as well as Ginnie, all in one open-doored box where a mare lay on her side on the straw. They all turned their heads as I approached but seemed unsurprised to see me and gave no particular greeting.

'This is Plus Factor,' Oliver said. 'In foal to Sandcastle.'

His voice was calm and so was Ginnie's manner, and I guessed that they still hadn't told Nigel about the deformities. There was hope, too, in their faces, as if they were sure this one, after all, would be perfect.

'She's coming,' Nigel said quietly. 'Here we go.'

The mare gave a grunt and her swelling sides heaved. The rest of us stood silent, watching, taking no part. A glistening half-transparent membrane with a hoof showing within it appeared, followed by the long slim shape of the head, followed very rapidly by the whole foal, flopping out onto the straw, steaming, the membrane breaking open, the fresh air reaching the head, new life beginning with the first fluttering gasp of the lungs.

'Amazing, I thought.

'Is he all right?' Oliver said, bending down, the anxiety raw, unstifled.

'Sure,' Nigel said. 'Fine little colt. Just his foreleg's doubled over ..'

He knelt beside the foal who was already making the first feeble efforts to move his head, and he stretched out both hands gently to free the bent leg fully from the membrane, and to straighten it. He picked it up ... and froze.

We could all see.

The leg wasn't bent. It ended in a stump at the knee. No cannon bone, no fetlock, no hoof.

Ginnie beside me gave a choking sob and turned abruptly towards the open door, towards the dark. She took one rocky pace and then another, and then was running: running nowhere, running away from the present, the future, the unimaginable. From the hopeless little creature on the straw.

I went after her, listening to her footsteps, hearing them on gravel and then losing them, guessing she had reached the grass. I went more slowly in her wake down the path to the breeding pen, not seeing her, but sure she was out somewhere in the paths round the paddocks. With eyes slowly acclimatising I went that way and found her not far off, on her knees beside one of the posts, sobbing with the deep sound of wholly adult desperation

'Ginnie,' I said.

She stood up as if to turn to me was natural and clung to me fiercely, her body shaking from the sobs, her face pressed hard against my shoulder, my arms tightly round her. We stood like that until the paroxysm passed; until, dragging a handkerchief from her jeans, she could speak.

'It's one thing knowing it in theory,' she said, her voice full of tears and her body still shaking spasmodically from aftersobs. 'I read those letters. I did know. But *seeing* it ... that's different.'

'Yes,' I said.

'And it means ...' She took gulps of air, trying hard for control. 'It means, doesn't it, that we'll lose our farm. Lose everything?'

'I don't know yet. Too soon to say that.'

'Poor Dad.' The tears were sliding down her cheeks, but like harmless rain after a hurricane. 'I don't see how we can bear it.'

'Don't despair yet. If there's a way to save you, we'll find it.'

'Do you mean ... your bank?'

'I mean everybody.'

She wiped her eyes and blew her nose, and finally moved away a pace, out of my arms, strong enough to leave shelter. We went slowly back to the foaling yard and found nobody there except horses. I undid the closed top half of Plus Factor's box and looked inside; looked at the mare standing there patiently without her foal and wondered if she felt any fretting sense of loss.

'Dad and Nigel have taken him, haven't they?' Ginnie said.

'Yes.'

She nodded, accepting that bit easily. Death to her was part

of life, as to every child brought up close to animals. I closed
Plus Factor's door and Ginnie and I went back to the house
while the sky lightened in the east to the new day, Sunday.

The work of the place went on.

Oliver telephoned to various owners of the mares who had
come to the other three stallions, reporting the birth of foals
alive and well and one dead before foaling, very sorry. His
voice sounded strong, civilised, controlled, the competent
captain at the helm, and one could almost see the steel creeping
back, hour by hour, into his battered spirit. I admired him for
it; and I would fight to give him time, I thought, to come to
some compromise to avert permanent ruin.

Ginnie, showered, breakfasted, tidy in sweater and shirt,
went off to spend the morning at the Watcherleys' and came
back smiling; the resilience of youth.

'Both of those mares are better from their infections,' she
reported, 'and Maggie says she's heard Calder Jackson's not
doing so well lately, his yard's half empty. Cheers Maggie up no
end, she says.'

For the Watcherleys too, I thought briefly, the fall of Oliver's
business could mean a return to rust and weeds, but I said, 'Not
enough sick horses just now, perhaps.'

'Not enough sick horses with rich owners, Maggie says.'

In the afternoon Ginnie slept on the sofa looking very
childlike and peaceful, and only with the awakening did the
night's pain roll back.

'Oh dear ...' The slow tears came. 'I was dreaming it was all
right. That that foal was a dream, only a dream ...'

'You and your father,' I said. 'Are brave people.'

She sniffed a little, pressing against her nose with the back of
her hand. 'Do you mean,' she said slowly, 'that whatever
happens, we musn't be defeated?'

'Mm.'

She looked at me, and after a while nodded. 'If we have to,
we'll start again. We'll work. He did it all before, you know.'

'You both have the skills,' I said.

'I'm glad you came.' She brushed the drying tears from her
cheeks. 'God knows what it would have been like without you.

I went with her out into the yards for evening stables, where

455

the muck-carrying and feeding went on as always. Ginnie fetched the usual pocketful of carrots from the feed room and gave them here and there to the mares, talking cheerfully to the lads while they bent to their chores. No one, watching and listening, could ever have imagined that she feared the sky was falling.

'Evening, Chris, how's her hoof today?'

'Hi, Danny. Did you bring this one in this morning?'

'Hello, Pete. She looks as if she'll foal any day now.'

'Evening, Shane. How's she doing?'

'Hi, Sammy, is she eating now OK?'

The lads answered her much as they spoke to Oliver himself, straightforwardly and with respect, and in most cases without stopping what they were doing. I looked back as we left the first big yard for the second, and for a moment took one of the lads to be Ricky Barnet.

'Who's that?' I said to Ginnie

She followed my gaze to where the lad walked across to the yard tap, swinging an empty bucket with one hand and eating an apple with the other.

'Shane. Why?'

'He reminded me of someone I knew.'

She shrugged 'He's all right. They all are, when Nigel's looking, which he doesn't do often enough.'

'He works all night,' I said mildly.

'I suppose so.'

The mares in the second yard had mostly given birth already and Ginnie that evening had special eyes for the foals. The lads hadn't yet reached those boxes and Ginnie didn't go in to any of them, warning me that mares with young foals could be protective and snappy.

'You never know if they'll bite or kick you. Dad doesn't like me going in with them alone.' She smiled. 'He still thinks I'm a baby.

We went on to the foaling yard, where a lad greeted as Dave was installing a heavy slow-walking mare into one of the boxes.

'Nigel says she'll foal tonight.' he told Ginnie.

'He's usually right.'

We went on past the breeding pen and came to the stallions, where Larry and Ron were washing down Diarist (who appeared to have been working) in the centre of the yard, using a lot of water, energy and oaths.

'Mind his feet,' Larry said. 'He's in one of his moods.'

Ginnie gave carrots to Parakeet and Rotaboy, and we came finally to Sandcastle. He looked as great, as charismatic as ever, but Ginnie gave him his tit-bit with her own lips compressed.

'He can't help it all, I suppose,' she said sighing. 'But I do wish he'd never won any races.

'Or that we'd let him die that day on the main road?'

'Oh no!' She was shocked. 'We couldn't have done that, even if we'd known ...'

Dear girl, I thought; many people would personally have mown him down with a truck.

We went back to the house via the paddocks, where she fondled any heads that came to the railings and parted with the last of the crunchy orange goodies. 'I can't believe that this will all end.' she said, looking over the horse-dotted acres. 'I just *can't* believe it.'

I tentatively suggested to both her and Oliver that they might prefer it if I went home that evening, but they both declared themselves against.

'Not yet,' Ginnie said anxiously and Oliver nodded forcefully. 'Please do stay, Tim, if you can.'

I nodded, and rang the Michaels', and this time got Judith.

'Do let me speak to her,' Ginnie said, taking the receiver out of my hand. 'I do so want to.'

And I, I thought wryly, I too want so much to talk to her, to hear her voice, to renew my own soul through her: I'm no one's universal pillar of strength, I need my comfort too.

I had my crumbs, after Ginnie, Ordinary words, all else implied; as always.

'Take care of yourself,' she said finally.

'You, too,' I said.

'Yes.' The word was a sigh, faint and receding, as if she'd said it with the receiver already away from her mouth. There was the click of disconnection, and Oliver was announcing briskly that it was time for whisky, time for supper; time for anything perhaps but thinking.

Ginnie decided that she felt too restless after supper to go to bed early, and would go for a walk instead.

'Do you want me to come?' I said.

'No. I'm all right. I just thought I'd go out. Look at the stars.' She kissed her father's forehead, pulling on a thick cardigan for warmth. 'I won't go off the farm. You'll probably find me in the foal yard, if you want me.'

He nodded to her fondly but absentmindedly, and with a small wave to me she went away. Oliver asked me gloomily, as if he'd been waiting for us to be alone, how soon I thought the bank would decide on his fate, and we talked in snatches about his daunting prospects, and hour or two sliding by on possibilities.

Shortly before ten, when we had probably twice repeated all there was to say, there came a heavy hammering at the back door.

'Whoever's that?' Oliver frowned, rose to his feet and went to find out.

I didn't hear the opening words, but only the goose-pimpling urgency in the rising voice.

'She's where?' Oliver said loudly, plainly, in alarm. 'Where?'

I went quickly into the hallway. One of the lads stood in the open doorway, panting for breath, wide-eyed and looking very scared.

Oliver glanced at me over his shoulder, already on the move. 'He says Ginnie's lying on the ground unconscious.'

The lad turned and ran off, with Oliver following and myself close behind: and the lad's breathlessness, I soon found, was owing to Ginnie's being on the far side of the farm, away down beyond Nigel's bungalow and the lads' hostel, right down on the far drive, near the gate to the lower road.

We arrived there still running, the lad now doubling over in his fight for breath, and found Ginnie lying on her side on the hard asphalt surface with another of the lads on his knees beside her, dim figures in weak moonlight, blurred outlines of shadow.

Oliver and I too knelt there and Oliver was saying to the lads, 'What happened, what happened? Did she fall?'

'We just found her.' the kneeling lad said. 'We were on our way back from the pub. She's coming round, though, sir, she's been saying things.'

Ginnie in fact moved slightly, and said 'Dad.'

'Yes, Ginnie, I'm here.' He picked up her hand and patted it.

'We'll soon get you right.' There was relief in his voice, but short-lived.

'Dad,' Ginnie said, mumbling. 'Dad.'

'Yes, I'm here.'

'Dad ...'

'She isn't hearing you,' I said worriedly.

He turned his head to me, his eyes liquid in the dark of his face. 'Get an ambulance. There's a telephone in Nigel's house. Tell him to get an ambulance here quickly. I don't think we'll move her.... Get an ambulance.'

I stood up to go on the errand but the breathless lad said, 'Nigel's out. I tried there.There's no one. It's all locked.'

'I'll go back to the house.'

I ran as fast on the way back and had to fight to control my own gulping breaths there to make my words intelligible. 'Tell them to take the lower road from the village ... the smaller right fork ... where the road divides. Nearly a mile from there ...wide metal farm gate, on the left.'

'Understood,' a man said impersonally. 'They'll be on their way.'

I fetched the padded quilt off my bed and ran back across the farm and found everything much as I'd left it. 'They're coming,'I said. 'How is she?'

Oliver tucked the quilt round his daughter as best he could.

'She keeps saying things. Just sounds, not words.'

'Da—' Ginnie said.

Her eyelids trembled and slightly opened.

'Ginnie,' Oliver said urgently. 'This is Dad.'

Her lips moved in a mumbling unformed murmur.The eyes looked at nothing, unfocussed, the gleam just reflected moon-light, not an awakening.

'Oh God,' Oliver said. 'What's happened to her? What can have happened?'

The two lads stood there, awkward and silent, not knowing the answer.

'Go and open the gate,' Oliver told them. 'Stand on the road. Signal to the ambulance when it comes.'

They went as if relieved; and the ambulance did come, lights flashing, with two brisk men in uniform who lifted Ginnie without much disturbing her onto a stretcher. Oliver asked

459

them to wait while he fetched the Land Rover from Nigel's garage, and in a short time the ambulance set off to the hospital with Oliver and me following.

'Lucky you had the key,' I said, indicating it in the ignition. Just something to say: anything.

'We always keep it in that tin on the shelf.'

The tin said 'Blackcurrant Coughdrops. Take as required.'

Oliver drove automatically, following the rear lights ahead. 'Why don't they go faster?' he said, though their speed was quite normal.

'Don't want to jolt her, perhaps.'

'Do you think it's a stroke?' he said.

'She's too young.'

'No. I had a cousin ... an aneurysm burst when he was sixteen.'

I glanced at his face: lined, grim, intent on the road.

The journey seemed endless, but ended at a huge bright hospital in a sprawling town. The men in uniform opened the rear doors of the ambulance while Oliver parked the Land Rover and we followed them into the brightly lit emergency reception area, seeing them wheel Ginnie into a curtained cubicle, watching them come out again with their stretcher, thanking them as they left.

A nurse told us to sit on some nearby chairs while she fetched a doctor. The place was empty, quiet, all readiness but no bustle. Ten o'clock on Sunday night.

A doctor came in a white coat, stethoscope dangling. An Indian, young, black-haired, rubbing his eyes with forefinger and thumb. He went behind the curtains with the nurse for about a mintute. Oliver clasped and unclasped his fingers, unable to contain his anxiety.

The doctor's voice reached us clearly, the Indian accent making no difference.

'They shouldn't have brought her here,' he said. 'She's dead.'

Oliver was on his feet, bounding across the shining floor, pulling back the curtains with a frantic sweep of the arm.

'She's not dead. She was talking. Moving. She's not dead.'

In dread I followed him. She couldn't be dead, not like that, not so fast, not without the hospital fighting long to save her. She *couldn't* be.

The doctor straightened up from bending over her, withdrawing his hand from under Ginnie's head, looking at us across the small space.

'She's my daughter,' Oliver said. 'She's not dead.'

A sort of weary compassion drooped in the doctor's shoulders. 'I am sorry,' he aaid. 'Very sorry. She is gone.'

'No!' The word burst out of Oliver in an agony. 'You're wrong. Get someone else.'

The nurse made a shocked gesture but the young doctor said gently, 'There is no pulse. No heartbeat. No contraction of the pupils. She has been gone for perhaps ten minutes, perhaps twenty. I could get someone else, but there is nothing to be done.'

'But *why*?' Oliver said. 'She was talking.'

The dark doctor looked down to where Ginnie was lying on her back, eyes closed, brown hair falling about her head, face very pale. Her jerseys had both been unbuttoned for the stethoscope, the white bra showing, and the nurse had also undone the waistband of the skirt, pulling it loose. Ginnie looked very young, very defenceless, lying there so quiet and still, I stood numbly, not believing it, unable, like Oliver, to accept such a monstrous change.

'Her skull is fractured,' the doctor said. 'If she was talking, she died on the way here, in the ambulance. With head injuries it can be like that. I am sorry.'

There was a sound of an ambulance's siren wailing outside, and sudden noise and rushing people by the doors where we had come in, voices raised in a jumble of instructions.

'Traffic accident,' someone shouted, and the doctor's eyes moved beyond us to the new need, to the future, not the past.

'I must go,' he said, and the nurse, nodding handed me a flat white plastic bottle which she had been holding.

'You may as well take this,' she said. 'It was tucked into the waistband of her skirt, against the stomach.'

She made as if to cover Ginnie with a sheet, but Oliver stopped her.

'I'll do it,' he said. 'I want to be with her.'

The young doctor nodded, and he and I and the nurse stepped outside the cubicle, drawing the curtains behind us. The doctor looked in a brief pause of stillness towards the three

461

or four stretchers arriving at the entrance, taking a breath, seeming to summon up energy from deep reserves.

'I've been on duty for thirty hours,' he said to me. 'And now the pubs are out. Ten o'clock, Sundays. Drunk drivers, drunk pedestrians. Always the same.'

He walked away to his alive and bleeding patients and the nurse pinned a 'Do Not Enter' sign onto the curtains of Ginnie's cubicle, saying she would be taken care of later.

I sat drearily on a chair, waiting for Oliver. The white plastic bottle had a label stuck onto one side saying 'Shampoo'. I put it into my jacket pocket and wondered if it was just through overwork that the doctor hadn't asked how Ginnie's skull had been fractured, asked whether she'd fallen onto a rock or a kerb … or been hit.

The rest of the night and all the next day were in their own way worse, a truly awful series of questions, answers, forms and officialdom, with the police slowly taking over from the hospital and Oliver trying to fight against a haze of grief.

It seemed to me wicked that no one would leave him alone. To them he was just one more in a long line of bereaved persons, and although they treated him with perfunctory sympathy, it was for their own paperwork and not for his benefit that they wanted signatures, information and guesses.

Large numbers of policemen descended on the farm early in the morning and it gradually appeared that that area of the country was being plagued by a stalker of young girls who jumped out of bushes, knocked them unconscious and sexually assaulted them.

'Not Ginnie …' Oliver protested in deepening horror.

The most senior of the policemen shook his head. 'It would appear not. She was still wearing her clothing. We can't discount, though, that it was the same man, and that he was disturbed by your grooms. When young girls are knocked unconscious at night, it's most often a sexual attack.'

'But she was on my own land,' he said, disbelieving.

The policeman shrugged. 'It's been known in surburban front gardens.'

He was a fair-haired man with a manner that was not exactly brutal but spoke of long years of acclimatisation to dreadful experiences. Detective Chief Inspector Wyfold, he'd said, introducing himself. Forty-fivish, I guessed, sensing the hardness within him at sight and judging him through that day more dogged than intuitive, looking for results from procedure, not hunches.

He was certain in his own mind that the attack on Ginnie had been sexual in intent and he scarcely considered anything else, particularly since she'd been carrying no money and had expressly said she wouldn't leave the farm.

'She could have talked to someone over the gate,' he said, having himself spent some time on the lower drive. 'Someone walking along the road. And there are all your grooms that we'll need detailed statements from, though from their preliminary answers it seems they weren't in the hostel but down at the village, in the pubs.'

He came and went and reappeared again with more questions at intervals through the day and I lost track altogether of the hours. I tried, in his presence and out, and in Oliver's the same, not to think much about Ginnie herself. I thought I would probably have wept if I had, of no use to anyone. I thrust her away into a defensive compartment knowing that later, alone, I would let her out.

Some time in the morning one of the lads came to the house and asked what they should do about one of the mares who was having difficulty foaling, and Lenny also arrived wanting to know when he should take Rotaboy to the breeding pen. Each of them stood awkwardly, not knowing where to put their hands, saying they were so shocked, so sorry, about Ginnie.

'Where's Nigel?' Oliver said.

They hadn't seen him, they said. He hadn't been out in the yards that morning.

'Didn't you try his house?' Oliver was annoyed rather than alarmed: another burden on a breaking back.

'He isn't there. The door's locked and he didn't answer.'

Oliver frowned, picked up the telephone and pressed the buttons: listened: no reply.

He said to me, 'There's a key to his bungalow over there on the board, third hook from the left. Would you go and look ... would you mind?'

'Sure.'

463

I walked down there with Lenny who told me repeatedly how broken up the lads were over what had happened, particularly Dave and Sammy, who'd found her. They'd all liked her, he said. All the lads who lived in the hostel were saying that perhaps if they'd come back sooner, she wouldn't have been attacked.

'You don't live in the hostel, then?' I said.

'No. Down in tthe village. Got a house. Only the ones who come just for the season, they're the ones in the hostel. It's shut up, see, all winter.'

We eventually reached Nigel's bungalow where I rang the doorbell and banged on the knocker without result. Shaking my head slightly I fitted the key in the lock, opened the door, went in.

Curtains were drawn across the windows, shutting out a good deal of daylight. I switched on a couple of lights and walked into the sitting room, where papers, clothes and dirty cups and plates were strewn haphazardly and the air smelled faintly of horse.

There was no sign of Nigel. I looked into the equally untidy kitchen and opened a door which proved to be that of a bathroom and another which revealed a room with bare-mattressed twin beds. The last door in the small inner hall led into Nigel's own bedroom ... and there he was, face down, fully clothed, lying across the counterpane.

Lenny, still behind me, took two paces back.

I went over to the bed and felt Nigel's neck behind the ear. Felt the pulse going like a steam-hammer. Heard the rasp of air in the throat. His breath would have anaesthetised a crocodile, and on the floor beside him lay an empty bottle of gin. I shook his shoulder unsympathetically with a complete lack of result.

'He's drunk,' I said to Lenny. 'Just drunk.'

Lenny looked all the same as if he was about to vomit. 'I thought ... I thought.'

'I know,' I said: and I'd feared it also, instictively, the one because of the other.

'What will we do, then, out in the yard?' Lenny asked.

'I'll find out.'

We went back into the sitting room where I used Nigel's telephone to call Oliver and report.

'He's flat out,' I said. 'I can't wake him. Lenny wants instructions.'

After a brief silence Oliver said dully, 'Tell him to take Rotaboy to the breeding shed in half an hour. I'll see to things in the yards. And Tim?'

'Yes?'

'Can I ask you ... would you mind ... helping me here in the office?'

'Coming straight back.'

The disjointed, terrible day wore on. I telephoned to Gordon in the bank explaining my absence and to Judith also, at Gordon's suggestion, to pass on the heartbreak, and I took countless incoming messages as the news spread. Outside on the farm nearly two hundred horses got fed and watered, and birth and procreation went inexorably on.

Oliver came back stumbling from fatigue at about two o'clock, and we ate some eggs, not tasting them, in the kitchen. He looked repeatedly at his watch and said finally, 'What's eight hours back from now? I can't even *think*.'

'Six in the morning,' I said.

'Oh.' He rubbed a hand over his face. 'I suppose I should have told Ginnie's mother last night.' His face twisted. 'My wife ... in Canada ...' He swallowed. 'Never mind, let her sleep. In two hours I'll tell her.'

I left him alone to that wretched task and took myself upstairs to wash and shave and lie for a while on the bed. It was in taking my jacket off for those purposes that I came across the plastic bottle in my pocket, and I took it out and stood it on the shelf in the bathroom while I shaved.

An odd sort of thing, I thought, for Ginnie to have tucked into her waistband. A plastic bottle of shampoo; about six inches high, four across, one deep, with a screw cap on one of the narrow ends. The white label saying 'Shampoo' had been handwritten and stuck on top of the bottle's original dark brown, white-printed label, of which quite a bit still showed around the edges.

'*Instructions*,' part of the underneath label said. '*Shake well. Be careful not to get the shampoo in the dog's eyes. Rub well into the coat and leave for ten or fifteen minutes before rinsing.*'

At the bottom, below the stuck-on label, were the words, in

465

much smaller print, '*Manufactured by Eagle Inc., Michigan, U.S.A. List number 29931.*

When I'd finished shaving I unscrewed the cap and tilted the bottle gently over the basin.

A thick greenish liquid appeared, smelling powerfully of soap.

Shampoo: what else.

The bottle was to all intents full. I screwed on the cap again and put it on the shelf, and thought about it while I lay on the bed with my hands behind my head.

Shampoo for dogs.

After a while I got up and went down to the kitchen, and in a high cupboard found a small collection of empty, washed, screw-top glass jars, the sort of thing my mother had always saved for herbs and picnics. I took one which would hold perhaps a cupful of liquid and returned upstairs, and over the washbasin I shook the bottle well, unscrewed the cap and carefully poured more than half of the shampoo into the jar.

I screwed the caps onto both the bottle and the jar, copied what could be seen on the original label into the small engagement diary I carried with me everywhere, and stowed the now half full round glass container from Oliver's kitchen inside my own sponge-bag: and when I went downstairs again I took the plastic bottle with me.

'Ginnie had it?' Oliver said dully, picking it up and squinting at it. 'Whatever for?'

'The nurse at the hospital said it was tucked into the waistband of her skirt.'

A smile flickered.'She always did that when she was little. Plimsols, books, bits of string, anything. To keep her hands free, she said. They all used to slip down into her little knickers, and there would be a whole shower of things sometimes when we undressed her.' His face went hopelessly bleak at this memory. 'I can't believe it, you know,' he said. 'I keep thinking she'll walk through the door.' He paused. 'My wife is flying over. She says she'll be here tomorrow morning.' His voice gave no indication as to whether that was good news or bad.

'Stay tonight, will you?'

'If you want.'

'Yes.'

466

Chief Inspector Wyfold turned up again at that point and we gave him the shampoo bottle, Oliver explaining about Ginnie's habit of carrying things in her clothes.

'Why didn't you give this to me earlier?' he asked me.

'I forgot I had it. It seemed so paltry at the time, compared with Ginnie dying.'

The Chief Inspector picked up the bottle by its serrated cap and read what one could see of the label, and to Oliver he said, 'Do you have a dog?'

'Yes.'

'Would this be what you usually use, to wash him?'

'I really don't know. I don't wash him myself. One of the lads does.'

'The lads being the grooms?'

'That's right.'

'Which lad washed your dog?' Wyfold asked.

'Um ... any. Whoever I ask.'

The Chief Inspector produced a thin white folded paper bag from one of his pockets and put the bottle inside it. 'Who to your knowledge has handled this, besides yourselves?' he asked.

'I suppose,' I said, "the nurse at the hospital ... and Ginnie.'

'And it spent from last night until now in your pocket?' He shrugged. 'Hopeless for prints, I should think, but we'll try.' He fastened the bag shut and wrote on a section of it with a ball pen. To Oliver, almost as an aside, he said, 'I came to ask you about your daughter's relationship with men.'

Oliver said wearily, 'She didn't have any. She's only just left school.'

Wyfold made small negative movements with head and hands as if amazed at the naiveté of fathers. 'No sexual relationship to your knowledge?'

'And you sir?' he turned to me. 'What were your relations with Virginia Knowles?'

'Friendship.'

'Including sexual intercourse?'

'No.'

Wyfold looked at Oliver who said tiredly, 'Tim is a business friend of mine. A financial adviser, staying here for the weekend, that's all.'

467

The policeman frowned at me with disillusion as if he didn't believe it. I gave him no amplified answer because I simply couldn't be bothered, and what could I have said? That with much affection I'd watched a child grow into an attractive young woman and yet not wanted to sleep with her? His mind ran on carnal rails, all else discounted.

He went away in the end taking the shampoo with him, and Oliver with immense fortitude said he had better go out into the yards to catch the tail end of evening stables. 'Those mares,' he said. 'Those foals ... they still need the best of care.'

'I wish I could help,' I said, feeling useless.

'You do.'

I went with him on his rounds, and when we reached the foaling yard, Nigel, resurrected, was there.

His stocky figure leaned against the doorpost of an open box as if without its support he would collapse, and the face he slowly turned towards us had aged ten years. The bushy eyebrows stood out starkly over charcoal shadowed eyes, puffiness in his skin swelling in the eyelids and sagging in deep bags on his cheeks. He was also unshaven, unkempt and feeling ill.

'Sorry,' he said. 'Heard about Ginnie. Very sorry.' I wasn't sure whether he was sympathising with Oliver or apologising for the drunkenness. 'A big noise of a policeman came asking if I'd killed her. As if I would.' He put a shaky hand on his head, almost as if physically to support it on his shoulders. 'I feel rotten. My own fault. Deserve it. This mare's likely to foal tonight. That shit of a policeman wanted to know if I was sleeping with Ginnie. Thought I'd tell you ... I wasn't.'

Wyfold, I reflected, would ask each of the lads individually the same question. A matter of time, perhaps, before he asked Oliver himself; though Oliver and I, he had had to concede, gave each other a rock-solid alibi.

We walked on towards the stallions and I asked Oliver if Nigel often got drunk, since Oliver hadn't shown much surprise.

'Very seldom,' Oliver said. 'He's once or twice turned out in that state but we've never lost a foal because of it. I don't like it but he's so good with the mares.' He shrugged. 'I overlook it.'

He gave carrots to all four stallions but scarcely glanced at

Sandcastle, as if he could no longer bear the sight.

'I'll try the Research people tomorrow,' he said. 'Forget about it, today.'

From the stallions he went, unusually, in the direction of the lower gate, past Nigel's bungalow and the hostel, to stand for a while at the place where Ginnie had lain in the dark on the night before.

The asphalt driveway showed no mark. Oliver looked to where the closed gate sixty feet away led to the road and in a drained voice said, 'Do you think she could have talked to someone out there?'

'She might have, I suppose.'

'Yes.' He turned to go back. 'It's all so *senseless*. And unreal. Nothing feels real.'

Exhaustion of mind and body finally overtook him after dinner and he went grey-faced to bed, but I in the first quiet of the long day went out again for restoration: for a look at the stars, as Ginnie had said.

Thinking only of her I walked slowly along some of the paths between the paddocks, the way lit by a half-moon with small clouds drifting, and stopped eventually at the place where on the previous morning Id held her tight in her racking distress. The birth of the deformed foal seemed so long ago, yet it was only yesterday: the morning of the last day of Ginnie's life.

I thought about that day, about the despair in its dawn and the resolution of its afternoon. I thought of her tears and her courage, and of the waste of so much goodness. The engulfing, stupefying sense of loss which had hovered all day swamped into my brain until my body felt inadequate, as if it wanted to burst, as if it couldn't hold in so much feeling.

When Ian Pargetter had been murdered I had been angry on his behalf and had supposed that the more one loved the dead person the greater one's fury against the killer. But now I understood that anger could simply be crowded out by something altogether more overwhelming. As for Oliver, he had displayed shock, daze, desolation and disbelief in endless quantities all day, but of anger, barely a flicker.

It was too soon to care who had killed her. The fact of her death was too much. Anger was irrelevant, and no vengeance could give her life.

I had loved her more than I'd known, but not as I loved Judith, not with desire and pain and longing. I'd loved Ginnie as a friend; as a brother. I'd loved her, I thought, right back from the day when I'd returned her to school and listened to her fears. I'd loved her up on the hill, trying to catch Sandcastle, and I'd loved her for her expertise and for her growing adult certainty that here, in these fields, was where her future lay.

I'd thought of her young life once as being a clear stretch of sand waiting for footprints, and now there would be none, now only a blank, chopping end to all she could have been and done, to all the bright love she had scattered around her.

'Oh ... *Ginnie*,' I said, aloud, calling to her hopelessly in tearing body-shaking grief. 'Ginnie ... little Ginnie ... come back.'

But she was gone from there. My voice fled away into darkness, and there was no answer.

The Third Year

MAY

On and off for the next two weeks I worked on Oliver's financial chaos at my desk in the bank, and at a special board meeting argued the case for giving him time before we foreclosed and made him sell all he had.

I asked for three months, which was considered scandalously out of the question, but got him two, Gordon chuckling over it quietly as we went down together afterwards in the lift.

'I suppose two months was what you wanted?' he said.

'Er ... yes.'

'I know you,' he said. 'They were talking of twenty-one days maximum before the meeting, and some wanted to bring in liquidators at once.'

I telephoned Oliver and told him. 'For two months you don't have to pay any interest or capital repayments, but this is only temporary, and it is a special, fairly unusual concession. I'm afraid, though, that if we can't find a solution to Sandcastle's problem or come up with a cast-iron reason for the insurance company to pay out, the prognosis is not good.'

'I understand,' he said, his voice sounding calm. 'I haven't much hope, but thank you, all the same, for the respite — I will at least be able to finish the programmes for the other stallions, and keep all the foals here until they're old enough to travel safely.'

'Have you heard anything about Sandcastle?'

'He's been at the Research Establishment for a week, but so

471

far they can't find anything wrong with him. They don't hold out much hope, I'd better tell you, of being able to prove anything one way or another about his sperm, even though they're sending specimens to another laboratory, they say.'

'They'll do their best.'

'Yes, I know. But ... I walk around here as if this place no longer belongs to me. As if it isn't mine. I know, inside, that I'm losing it. Don't feel too badly, Tim. When it comes, I'll be prepared.'

I put the receiver down not knowing whether such resignation was good because he would face whatever came without disintegration, or bad because he might be surrendering too soon. A great host of other troubles still lay ahead, mostly in the shape of breeders demanding the return of their stallion fees, and he needed energy to say that in most cases he couldn't return them. The money had already been lodged with us, and the whole situation would have to be sorted out by lawyers.

The news of Sandcastle's disgrace was so far only a doubtful murmur here and there, but when it broke open with a screech it was, I suppose predictably, in *What's Going On Where It Shouldn't*.

The bank's six copies were read to rags before lunch on the day Alec fetched them, eyes lifting from the page with anything from fury to a wry smile.

Three short paragraphs headed 'House on Sand,' said:

Build not your house on sand. Stake not your banking house on a Sandcastle.

The five million pounds advanced by a certain prestigious merchant bank for the purchase of the stallion Sandcastle now look like being washed away by the tide. Sadly, the investment has produced faulty stock, or in plain language, several deformed foals.

Speculation now abounds as to what the bank can do to minimise its losses, since Sandcastle himself must be considered as half a ton of highly priced dog-meat.

'That's done it,' Gordon said, and I nodded: and the dailies, who always read *What's Going On* as a prime news source, came up in the racing columns the next day with a more cautious approach, asking 'Sandcastle's progeny Flawed?' and saying things like 'rumours have reached us' and 'we are reliably informed.'

Since our own home-grown leaker for once hadn't mentioned the bank by name, none of the dailies did either, and for them of course the bank itself was unimportant compared with the implications of the news.

Oliver, in the next weekday issues, was reported as having been asked how many, precisely, of Sandcastle's foals were deformed, and as having answered that he didn't know. He had heard of some, certainly, yes. He had no further comment.

A day later still the papers began printing reports telephoned into them by the stud farms where Sandcastle's scattered progeny had been foaled, and the tally of disasters mounted. Oliver was reported this time as having said the horse was at the Equine Research Establishment at Newmarket, and everything possible was being done.

'It's a mess,' Henry said gloomily at lunch, and even the dissenting director had run out of insults, beyond saying four times that we were the laughing-stock of the City and it was all my fault.

'Have they found out who killed Knowles' daughter?' Val Fisher asked.

'No.' I shook my head. 'He says the police no longer come to the house.'

Val looked regretful. 'Such sadness for him, on top of the other.'

There were murmurs of sympathy and I didn't think I'd spoil it by telling them what the police thought of Oliver's lads.

'That man Wyfold,' Oliver had said on the telephone during one of our almost daily conversations, 'he more or less said I was asking for trouble, having a young girl on the place with all those lads. What's more, it seems many of them were half-way drunk that night, and with three pubs in the village they weren't even all together and have no idea of who was where at what time, so one of Wyfold's theories is that one of them jumped her and Dave and Sammy interrupted him. Alternatively Nigel did it. Alternatively some stranger walking down the road did it. Wyfold's manner is downright abrasive but I'm past caring. He despises my discipline. He says I shouldn't let my lads get drunk — as if anyone could stop them. They're free men. It's their business, not mine, what they do with their money and time on Sunday nights. I can only take action if they don't turn up on Monday morning. And as for Nigel being paralytic!' Words momentarily failed him. 'How can Nigel possibly expect the lads to stay more or less sober if he gets like that? And he says he can't remember anything that happened the night Ginnie died. Nothing at all. Total alcoholic black-out. He's been very subdued since.'

The directors, I felt, would not be any more impressed than the Detective Chief Inspector with the general level of insobriety, and I wondered whether Nigel's slackness with the lads in general had always stemmed from a knowledge of his own occasional weakness.

The police had found no weapon, Oliver said on another day. Wyfold had told him that there was no way of knowing what had been used to cause the depressed fracture at the base of her brain. Her hair over the fracture bore no traces of anything unexpected. The forensic surgeon was of the opinion that there had been a single very heavy blow. She would have been knocked unconscious instantly. She wouldn't even have known. The period of apparent semi-consciousness had been illusory: parts of her brain would have functioned but she would not have been aware of anything at all.

'I suppose it's a mercy,' Oliver said. 'With some girls you hear of ... how do their parents bear it?'

His wife, he said, had gone back to Canada. Ginnie's death seemed not to have brought mother and father together, but to have made the separation complete.

'The dog shampoo?' Oliver repeated, when I asked. 'Wyfold says that's just what it was, they checked it. He asked Nigel and all the lads if it was theirs, if they'd used it for washing Squibs, but none of them had. He seems to think Ginnie may have seen it lying in the road and picked it up, or that she got into conversation over the gate with a man who gave her the shampoo for Squibs as a come-on and then killed her afterwards.'

'No,' I said

'Why not?'

'Because he'd have taken the shampoo away again with him.'

474

'Wyfold says not if he couldn't find it, because of its being dark and her having hidden it to all intents and purposes under her skirt and two jumpers, and not if Dave and Sammy arrived at that point.'

'I suppose it's possible,' I said doubtfully.

'Wyfold says that particular shampoo isn't on sale at all in England, It's American, and there's absolutely no way at all of tracing how it got here. There weren't any fingerprints of any use; all a blur except a few of yours and mine.'

Another day he said, 'Wyfold told me the hardest murders to solve were single blows on the head. He said the case would remain open, but they are busy again with another girl who was killed walking home from a dance, and this time she definitely is one of that dreadful series, poor child … I was lucky, Tim, you know, that Dave and Sammy came back when they did.'

There came a fine May day in the office when Alec, deciding we needed some fresh air, opened one of the windows which looked down to the fountain. The fresh air duly entered but like a lion, not a lamb, and blew papers off all the desks.

'That's a hurricane,' I said 'For God's sake shut it.'

Alec closed off the gale and turned round with a grin. 'Sorry and all that,' he said.

We all left our chairs and bent down like gleaners to retrieve our scattered work, and during my search for page 3 of a long assessment of a proposed sports complex I came across a severe and unwelcome shock in the shape of a small pale blue sheet off a memo pad.

There were words pencilled on it and crossed out with a wavy line, with other words underneath.

Build your castle not on Sand was crossed out, and so was *Sandcastle gone with the tide*, and underneath was written *Build not your house on Sand, Build not your banking house on a Sandcastle*.

'What's that?' Alec said quickly, seeing it in my hand and stretching out his own. 'Let's see.'

I shook my head and kept it in my own hand while I finished picking up the sportsdrome, and when order was restored throughout the office I said, 'Come along to the interview room.'

'Right now?'

'Right now.'

We went into the only room on our floor where any real privacy was possible and I said without shilly-shallying, 'This is your handwriting. Did you write the article in *What's Going On?*'

He gave me a theatrical sigh and a tentative smile and a large shrug of the shoulders.

'That's just doodling,' he said. 'It means nothing.'

'It means, for a start,' I said, 'that you shouldn't have left it round the office.'

'Didn't know I had.'

'Did you write the article?'

The blue eyes unrepentantly gleamed at me from behind the gold rims. 'It's a fair cop, I suppose.'

'But *Alec* ...' I protested.

'Yeah.'

'And the others,' I said, 'Those other leaks, was that you?'

He sighed again, his mouth twisting.

'Was it?' I repeated, wanting above all things to hear him deny it.

'Look,' he said, 'What harm did it do? Yes, all right, the stories did come from me. I wrote them myself, actually, like that one.' He pointed to the memo paper in my hand. 'And don't give me any lectures on disloyalty because none of them did us any harm. Did us good, if anything.'

'Alec ...'

'Yes,' he said, 'but just think, Tim, what did those pieces really do? They stirred everyone up, sure, and it was a laugh a minute to see all their faces, but what else? I've been thinking about it, I assure you. It wasn't why I did it in the first place, that was just wanting to stir things, I'll admit, but *because* of what I wrote we've now got much better security checks than we had before.'

I listened to him open-mouthed.

'All that work you did with the computer, making us safer against frauds, that was because of what I wrote. And the Corporate Finance boys, they now go around with their mouths zipped up like suitcases so as not to spill the beans to the investment managers. I did *good*, do you see, not harm.'

476

I stood and looked at him, at the tight tow-coloured curls, the cream coloured freckled skin, the eyes that had laughed with me for eight years. I don't want to lose you, I thought: I wish you hadn't done it.

'And what about this piece about Sandcastle? What good has that done?' I said.

He half grinned. 'Too soon to say.'

I looked at the damaging scrap in my hands and almost automatically shook my head.

'You're going to say,' Alec said, 'that I'll have to leave.'

I looked up. His face was wholly calm.

'I knew I'd have to leave if any of you ever found out.'

'But don't you *care*?' I said frustratedly.

He smiled. 'I don't know. I'll miss *you*, and that's a fact. But as for the job … well, I told you, it's not my whole life, like it is yours. I loved it, I grant you, when I came here. All I wanted was to be a merchant banker, it sounded great. But to be honest it was the glamour I suppose I wanted, and glamour never lasts once you've got used to something. I'm not a dedicated money-man at heart … and there's honesty for you, I never thought I'd admit that, even to myself.'

'But you do it well.'

'Up to a point. We discussed all that.'

'I'm sorry,' I said helplessly.

'Yeah, well, so am I in a way, and in a way I'm not. I've been dithering for ages, and now that it isn't my choice I'm as much relieved as anything.'

'But … what will you do?'

He gave a full cherubic smile. 'I don't suppose you'll approve.'

'What, then?'

'*What's Going On*,' he said, 'have offered me a whole-time job.' He looked at my shattered expression. 'I've written quite a bit for them, actually. About other things, of course, not us. But in most editions there's something of mine, a paragraph or two or a whole column. They've asked me several times to go, so now I will.'

I thought back to all those days when Alec had bounded out for the six copies and spent his next hour chuckling. Alec, the gatherer of news, who knew all the gossip.

'They get masses of information in,' Alec said, 'but they need someone to evaluate it properly, and there aren't so many merchant bankers looking for that sort of job.'

'No,' I said dryly. 'I can imagine. For a start, won't your salary be much less?'

'A bit,' he admitted, cheerfully. 'But my iconoclastic spirit will survive.'

I moved restlessly, wishing things had been different.

'I'll resign from here,' he said. 'Make it easier.'

Rather gloomily I nodded. 'And will you say why?'

He looked at me thoughtfully. 'If you really want me to, yes,' he said finally. 'Otherwise not. You can tell them yourself, though, after I've gone, if you want to.'

'You're a damned fool,' I said explosively, feeling the loss of him acutely. 'The office will be bloody dull without you.'

He grinned, my long-time colleague, and pointed to the piece of memo paper. 'I'll send you pin-pricks now and then. You won't forget me. Not a chance.'

Gordon, three days later, said to me in surprise, 'Alec's leaving, did you know?'

'I knew he was thinking of it.'

'But why? He's good at his job, and he always seemed happy here.'

I explained that Alec had been unsettled for some time and felt he needed to change direction.

'Amazing,' Gordon said. 'I tried to dissuade him, but he's adamant. He's going in four weeks.'

Alec, ndeed, addressed his normal work with the bounce and zealousness of one about to be liberated, and for the rest of his stay in the office was better company than ever. Chains visibly dropped from his spirits, and I caught him several times scribbling speculatively on his memo pad with an anything but angelic grin.

Oliver had sent me at my request a list of all the breeders who had sent their mares to Sandcastle the previous year, and I spent two or three evenings on the telephone asking after those foals we didn't know about. Oliver himself, when I'd asked him, said he frankly couldn't face the task, and I didn't in the least blame him: my enquiries brought forth an ear-burning amount of blasphemy.

478

The final count came to:

Five foals born outwardly perfect but dead within two weeks because of internal abnormalities.
One foal born with one eye. (Put down.)
Five foals born with deformed legs, deformation varying from a malformed hoof to the absent half-leg of Plus Factor's colt. (All put down.)
Three foals born with part of one or both ears missing. (All still living.)
One foal born with no tail. (Still living.)
Two foals born with malformed mouths, the equivalent of human hare lip. (Both put down.)
One foal born with a grossly deformed head. (Foaled with heart-beat but couldn't breathe; died at once.)

Apart from this horrifying tally, four mares who had been sent home as in foal had subsequently 'slipped' and were barren: one mare had failed to conceive at all; three mares had not yet foaled (breeders' comments incendiary); and fourteen mares had produced live healthy foals with no defects of any sort.

I showed the list to Gordon and Henry, who went shockedly silent for a while as if in mourning for the superb racer they had so admired.

'There may be more to come,' I said, not liking it. 'Oliver says thirty mares covered by Sandcastle this year are definitely in foal. Some of those will be all right ... and some may not.'

'Isn't there a test you can do to see if a baby is abnormal?' Henry said. 'Can't they do that with the mares, and abort the deformed foals now, before they grow?'

I shook my head. 'I asked Oliver that. He says amniocentesis — that's what that process is called — isn't possible with mares. Something to do with not being able to reach the target with a terile needle because of all the intestines in the way.'

Henry listened with the distaste of the non-medical to these clinical realities. 'What it means, I suppose,' he said, 'is that the owners of all of those thirty-one mares will have the foals aborted and demand their money back.'

'I'd think so, yes.'

479

He shook his head regretfully. 'So sad, isn't it. Such a shame. Quite apart from the financial loss, a tragedy in racing terms.'

Oliver said on the telephone one morning, 'Tim, I need to talk to you. Something's happened.'

'What?' I said, with misgivings.

'Someone has offered to buy Sandcastle.'

I sat in a mild state of shock, looking at Alec across the room sucking his pencil while he wrote his future.

'Are you there?' Oliver said.

'Yes. What for and for how much?'

'Well, he says to put back in training. I suppose it's possible. Sandcastle's only five. I suppose he could be got fit to race by August or September, and he might still win next year at six.'

'Good heavens.'

'He's offering twenty-five thousand pounds.'

'Um,' I said. 'Is that good or bad?:'

'Realistically, it's as much as he's worth.'

'I'll consult with my seniors here,' I said. 'It's too soon, this minute, to say yes or no.'

'I did tell him that my bankers would have to agree, but he wants an answer fairly soon, because the longer the delay the less time there is for training and racing this season.'

'Yes,' I said, understanding. 'Where is he? Sandcastle, I mean.'

'Still in Newmarket. But it's pointless him staying there any longer. They haven't found any answers. They say they just don't know what's wrong with him, and I think they want me to take him away.'

'Well,' I pondered briefly. 'You may as well fetch him, I should think.'

'I'll arrange it,' he said.

'Before we go any further,' I said. 'Are you sure it's a bona-fide offer and not just some crank?'

'I had a letter from him and I've talked to him on the telephone, and to me he sounds genuine,' Oliver answered. 'Would you like to meet him?'

'Perhaps, yes.'

We fixed a provisional date for the following Saturday morning, and almost as an afterthought I asked the potential buyer's name.

'Smith,' Oliver said. 'A Mr Dissdale Smith.'

I went to Hertfordshire on that Saturday with a whole host of question marks raising their eyebrows in my mind, but it was Dissdale, as it so happened, who had the deeper astonishment.

He drove up while I was still outside Oliver's house, still clasping hands in greeting and talking of Ginnie. Dissdale had come without Bettina, and the first thing he said, emerging from his car, was 'Hello, Tim, what a surprise, didn't know you knew Oliver Knowles.'

He walked across, announced himself, shook hands with Oliver, and patted me chubbily on the shoulder. 'How's things, then? How are you doing, Tim?'

'Fine,' I said mildly.

Oliver looked from one of us to the other. 'You know each other already?'

Dissdale said, 'How do you mean, already?'

'Tim's my banker,' Oliver said in puzzlement. 'It was his bank, Ekaterin's, which put up the money for Sandcastle.'

Dissdale stared at me in stunned amazement and looked bereft of speech.

'Didn't you know?' Oliver said. 'Didn't I mention it?'

Dissdale blankly shook his head and finally found his voice. 'You just said your banker was coming.... I never for a moment thought ...'

'It doesn't make much odds,' Oliver said. 'If you know each other it may simply save some time. Let's go indoors. There's some coffee ready.' He led the way through his immaculate house to the sitting room-office, where a tray stood on the desk with coffee hot in a pot.

Oliver himself had had four weeks by then in that house without Ginnie, but to me, on my first visit back, she seemed still more sharply alive. It was I, this time, who kept expecting her to walk into the room; to give me a hug, to say hello with her eyes crinkling with welcome. I felt her presence vividly, to an extent that to start with I listened to Dissdale with only surface attention.

'It might be better to geld him,' he was saying. 'There are some good prizes, particularly overseas, for geldings.'

481

Oliver's instinctive response of horror subsided droopingly to defeat.

'It's too soon,' I said, 'to talk of that.'

'Tim, face facts,' Dissdale said expansively. 'At this moment in time that horse is a walking bomb. I'm making an offer for him because I'm a bit of a gambler, you know that, and I've a soft spot for him, whatever his faults, because of him winning so much for me that day the year before last, when we were all in my box at Ascot. You remember that, don't you?'

'I do indeed.'

'He saved my life, Sandcastle did.'

'It was partly because of that day,' I said, nodding. 'That Ekaterin's lent the money for him. When the request came in from Oliver, it was because Henry Shipton — our chairman, if you remember — and Gordon and I had all seen the horse in action that we seriously considered the proposition.'

Dissdale nodded his comprehension. 'A great surprise though,' he said. 'I'm sorry it's you and Gordon. Sorry it's your bank, I mean, that's been hit so hard. I read about the deformed foals in the papers, of course, and that's what gave me the idea of buying Sandcastle in the first place, but it didn't say which bank...'

I wondered fleetingly if Alec could claim that omission as a virtue along with everything else.

Oliver offered Dissdale more coffee which he accepted with cream and sugar, drinking almost absentmindedly while he worked through the possible alterations he would need in approach now he'd found he was dealing with semi-friends. Having had time myself over several days to do it, I could guess at the speed he was needing for reassessment.

'Dissdale,' I said neutrally, deciding to disrupt him, 'Did the idea of buying Sandcastle come from your profitable caper with Indian Silk?'

His rounded features fell again into shock. 'How ... er ... did you know about that?'

I said vaguely, 'Heard it on the racecourse, I suppose. But didn't you buy Indian Silk for a pittance because he seemed to be dying, and then sent him to Calder?'

'Well ...'

'And didn't Calder cure him? And then you sold him again,

but well this time, no doubt needing the money, as don't we all, since when Indian Silk's won the Cheltenham Gold Cup? Isn't that right?'

Dissdale raised a plump hand palm upwards in a gesture of mock defeat. 'Don't know where you heard it, but yes, there's no secret, that's what happened.'

'Mm.' I smiled at him benignly. 'Calder said on television, didn't he, that buying Indian Silk was his idea originally, so I wondered … I'm wondering if this is his idea too. I mean, did he by any chance suggest a repeat of the gamble that came off so happily last time?'

Dissdale looked at me doubtfully.

'There's nothing wrong in it,' I said. 'Is it Calder's idea?'

'Well, yes,' he said, deciding to confide. 'But it's my money, of course.'

'And, um, if you do buy Sandcastle, will you send him too along to Calder, like Indian Silk?'

Dissdale seemed not to know whether to answer or not, but appearing to be reassured by my friendly interest said finally, 'Calder said he could give him a quick pepping-up to get him fit quickly for racing, yes'

Oliver, having listened restlessly up to this point, said, 'Calder Jackson can't do anything for Sandcastle that I can't.'

Both Dissdale and I looked at Oliver in the same way, hearing the orthodox view ringing out with conviction and knowing that it was very likely untrue.

'I've been thinking these past few days,' I said to Dissdale, 'First about Indian Silk. Didn't you tell Fred Barnet, when you offered him a rock-bottom price, that all you were doing was providing a dying horse with a nice quiet end in some gentle field?'

'Well, Tim,' he said knowingly. 'You know how it is. You buy for the best price you can. Fred Barnet, I know he goes round grousing that I cheated him, but I didn't, he could have sent his horse to Calder the same as I did.'

I nodded. 'So now, be honest, Dissdale, are you planning again to buy for the best price you can? I mean, does twenty-five thousand pounds for Sandcastle represent the same sort of bargain?'

'Tim,' Dissdale said, half affronted, half in sorrow, 'What a

483

naughty suspicious mind. That's not friendly, not at all.'

I smiled. 'I don't think I'd be wise, though, do you, to recommend to my board of directors that we should accept your offer without thinking it over very carefully?'

For the first time there was a shade of dismay in the chubby face. 'Tim, it's a fair offer, anyone will tell you.'

'I think my board may invite other bids,' I said. 'If Sandcastle is to be sold, we must recoup the most we can.'

The dismay faded: man-of-the-world returned. 'That's fair,' he said. 'As long as you'll come back to me, if anyone tops me.'

'Sure,' I said. 'An auction, by telephone. When we're ready, I'll let you know.'

With a touch of anxiety he said, 'Don't wait too long. Time's money, you know.'

'I'll put your offer to the board tomorrow.'

He made a show of bluff contentment, but the anxiety was still there underneath. Oliver took the empty coffee cup which Dissdale still held and asked if he would like to see the horse he wanted to buy.

'But isn't he in Newmarket? Dissdale said, again looking disconcerted.

'No, he's here. Came back yesterday.'

'Oh. Then yes, of course, yes, I'd like to see him.'

He's out of his depth, I thought abruptly: for some reason Dissdale is very very unsettled.

We went on the old familiar walk through the yards, with Oliver explaining the lay-out to the new visitor. To me there was now a visible thinning out of numbers, and Oliver, with hardly a quiver in his voice, said that he was sending the mares home with their foals in an orderly progression as usual, with in consequence lower feed bills, fewer lads to pay wages to, smaller expenses all round: he would play fair with the bank, he said, matter-of-factly, making sure to charge what he could and also to conserve what he could towards his debt. Dissdale gave him a glance of amused incredulity as if such a sense of honour belonged to a bygone age, and we came in the end to the stallion yard, where the four heads appeared in curiosity.

The stay in Newmarket hadn't done Sandcastle much good, I thought. He looked tired and dull, barely arching his neck to life his nose over the half-door, and it was he, of the four, who turned away first and retreated into the gloom of his box.

'Is that Sandcastle?' Dissdale said, sounding disappointed. 'I expected something more, somehow.'

'He's had a taxing three weeks,' Oliver said. 'All he needs is some good food and fresh air.'

'And Calder's touch,' Dissdale said with conviction. 'That magic touch most of all.'

When Dissdale had driven away Oliver asked me what I thought, and I said, 'If Dissdale's offering twenty-five thousand he's certainly reckoning to make much more than that. He's right, he is a gambler, and I'll bet he has some scheme in mind. What we need to do is guess what the scheme is, and decide what we'll do on that basis, such as doubling or trebling the ante.'

Oliver was perplexed. 'How can we possibly guess?'

'Hm,' I said. 'Did you know about Indian Silk?'

'Not before today.'

'Well, suppose Dissdale acts to a pattern, which people so often do. He told Fred Barnet he was putting Indian Silk out to grass, which was diametrically untrue; he intended to send him to Calder and with luck put him back in training. He told *you* he was planning to put Sandcastle back into training, so suppose that's just what he *doesn't* plan to do. And he suggested gelding, didn't he?'

Oliver nodded.

'Then I'd expect gelding to be furthest from his mind,' I said. 'He just wants us to believe that's his intention.' I reflected 'Do you know what I might do if I wanted to have a real gamble with Sandcastle?'

'What?'

'It sounds pretty crazy,' I said. 'But with Calder's reputation it might just work.'

'What are you talking about?' Oliver said in some bewilderment. 'What gamble?'

'Suppose,' I said, 'that you could buy for a pittance a stallion whose perfect foals would be likely to win races.'

'But no one would risk ...'

'Suppose,' I interrupted. 'There was nearly a fifty per cent chance, going on this year's figures, that you'd get a perfect foal. Suppose Dissdale offered Sandcastle as a sire at say a thousand pounds, the fee only payable if the foal was born perfect and lived a month.'

Oliver simply stared.

'Say Sandcastle's perfect progeny do win, as indeed they should. There are fourteen of them so far this year, don't forget. Say that in the passage of time his good foals proved to be worth the fifty per cent risk. Say Sandcastle stands in Calder's yard, with Calder's skill on the line. Isn't there a chance that over the years Dissdale's twenty-five thousand pound investment would provide a nice steady return for them both?'

'It's impossible,' he said weakly.

'No, not impossible. A gamble.' I paused. 'You wouldn't get people sending the top mares, of course, but you might get enough dreamers among the breeders who'd chance it.'

'Tim ...'

'Just think of it,' I said. 'A perfect foal by Sandcastle for peanuts. And if you got a malformed foal, well, some years your mare might slip or be barren anyway.'

He looked at his feet for a while, and then into the middle distance, and then he said, 'Come with me. I've something to show you. Something you'd better know.'

He set off towards the Watcherleys', and would say nothing more on the way. I walked beside him down the familiar paths and thought about Ginnie because I couldn't help it, and we arrived in the next-door yard that was now of a neatness to be compared with all the others.

'Over here,' Oliver said, going across to one of the boxes. 'Look at that.'

I looked where directed: at a mare with a colt foal suckling, not unexpected in that place.

'He was born three days ago,' Oliver said. 'I do so wish Ginnie had seen him.'

'Why that one, especially?'

'The mare is one of my own,' he said. 'And the foal is Sandcastle's.'

It was my turn to stare. I looked from Oliver to the foal and back again. 'There's nothing wrong with him,' I said.

'No.'

'But ...'

Oliver smiled twistedly. 'I was going to breed her to Diarist. She was along here at the Watcherleys' because the foal she had then was always ailing, but she herself was all right. I was along here looking at her one day when she'd been in season a while, and on impulse I led her along to the breeding pen and told Nigel to fetch Sandcastle, and we mated them there and then. The foal's the result' He shook his head regretfully. 'He'll be sold, of course, with everything else. I wish I could have kept him, but there it is.'

'He should be worth quite a bit,' I said.

'I don't think so,' Oliver said. 'And that's the flaw in your gamble. It's not just the racing potential that raises prices at auction, it's the chance of breeding. And no one could be sure, breeding from Sandcastle's stock, that the genetic trouble wouldn't crop up for evermore. It's not on, I'm afraid. No serious breeder would send him mares, however great the bargain.'

We stood for a while in silence.

'It was a good idea,' I said, 'while it lasted.'

'My dear Tim ... we're clutching at straws.'

'Yes.' I looked at his calm strong face; the captain whose ship was sinking. 'I'd try anything, you know, to save you,' I said.

'And to save the bank's money?'

'That too.'

He smiled faintly. 'I wish you could, but time's running out.'

The date for bringing the receivers had been set, the insurance company had finally ducked, the lawyers were closing in and the respite I'd gained for him was trickling away with no tender plant of hope growing in the ruins.

We walked back towards the house, Oliver patting the mares as usual as they came to the fences.

'I suppose this may all be here next year,' he said, 'looking much the same. Someone will buy it ... it's just I who'll be gone.'

He lifted his head, looking away over his white painted rails to the long line of the roofs of his yards. The enormity of the loss of his life's work settled like a weight on his shoulders and there was a haggard set to his jaw.

'I try not to mind,' he said levelly. 'But I don't quite know how to bear it.'

When I reached home that evening my telephone was ringing. I went across the sitting room expecting it to stop the moment I reached it, but the summons continued, and on the other end was Judith.

'I just came in,' I said.

'We knew you were out. We've tried once or twice.'

'I went to see Oliver.'

'The poor, poor man.' Judith had been very distressed over Ginnie and still felt that Oliver needed more sympathy because of his daughter than because of his bankruptcy, which I wasn't sure was any longer the case. 'Anyway,' she said, 'Pen asked me to call you as she's tied up in her shop all day and you were out when she tried ... She says she's had the reply from America about the shampoo are you still interested?'

'Yes, certainly.'

'Then ... if you're not doing anything else ... Gordon and I wondered if you'd care to come here for the day tomorrow, and Pen will bring the letter to show you.'

'I'll be there,' I said fervently, and she laughed.'

'Good, then. See you.'

I was at Clapham with alacrity before noon, and Pen, over coffee, produced the letter from the drug company.

'I sent them a sample of what you gave me in that little glass jar,' she said. 'And, as you asked, I had some of the rest of it analysed here, but honestly, Tim, don't hope too much from it for finding out who killed Ginnie, it's just shampoo, as it says.'

I took the official-looking letter which was of two pages clipped together, with impressive headings.

Dear Madam,

We have received the enquiry from your pharmacy and also the sample you sent us, and we now reply with this report, which is a copy of that which we recently sent to the Hertfordshire police force on the same subject.

The shampoo in question is our 'Bannitch' which is formulated especially for dogs suffering from various skin troubles, including eczema. It is distributed to shops selling goods to dog owners and offering cosmetic canine services, but would not normally be used except on the advice of a veterinarian.

We enclose the list of active ingredients and excipients, as requested.

'What are excipients?' I asked, looking up.

'The things you put in with the active drug for various reasons,' she said. 'Like for instance chalk for bulk in pills.'

I turned the top page over and read the list on the second.

> BANNITCH
> EXCIPIENTS
> *Bentonite*
> *Ethylene glycol monostearate*
> *Citric acid*
> *Sodium phosphate*
> *Glyceryl monoricinoleate*
> *Perfume*
> ACTIVE INGREDIENTS
> *Captan*
> *Amphoteric*
> *Selenium*

'Terrific,' I said blankly. 'What do they all mean?'

Pen, sitting beside me on the sofa, explained.

'From the top ... Bentonite is a thickening agent so that everything stays together and doesn't separate out. Ethylene glycol monostearate is a sort of wax, probably there to add bulk. Citric acid is to make the whole mixture acid, not alkaline, and the next one, sodium phosphate, is to keep the acidity level more or less constant. Glyceryl monoricinoleate is a soap, to make later, and perfume is there so that the dog smells nice to the owner when she's washing him.'

'How do you know so much?' Gordon asked, marvelling.

'I looked some of them up,' said Pen frankly, with a smile. She turned back to me and pointed to the short lower column of active ingredients. 'Captan and Amphoteric are both drugs for killing fungi on the skin, and Selenium is also anti-fungal and is used in shampoos to cure dandruff.' She stopped and looked at me doubtfully. 'I did tell you not to hope too much. There's nothing there of any consequence.'

'And nothing in the sample that isn't on the manufacturer's

list?'

She shook her head. 'The analysis from the British lab came yesterday, and the shampoo in Ginnie's bottle contained exactly what it should.'

'What did you expect, Tim?' Gordon asked.

'It wasn't so much expect, as hope,' I said regretfully. 'Hardly hope, really. Just a faint outside chance.'

'Of what?'

'Well ... the police thought — think — that the purpose of killing Ginnie was sexual assault, because of those other poor girls in the neighbourhood.'

They all nodded.

'But it doesn't *feel* right, does it? Not when you know she wasn't walking home from anywhere, like the others, and not when she wasn't actually, well, interfered with. And then she had the shampoo ... and the farm was in such trouble, and it seemed to me possible, just slightly possible, that she had somehow discovered that something in that bottle was significant ...' I paused, and then said slowly to Pen, 'I suppose what I was looking for was something that could have been put into Sandcastle's food or water that affected his reproductive organs. I don't know if that's possible. I don't know anything about drugs ... I just *wondered*.'

They sat in silence with round eyes, and then Gordon, stirring, said with an inflection of hope, 'Is that possible, Pen? Could it be something like that?'

'Could it *possibly*?' Judith said.

'My loves,' Pen said. 'I don't know.' She looked also as if whatever she said would disappoint us. 'I've never heard of anything like that, I simply haven't.'

'That's why I took the shampoo and gave it to you,' I said. 'I know it's a wild and horrible idea, but I told Oliver I'd try everything, however unlikely.'

'What you're suggesting,' Judith said plainly, 'Is that someone might *deliberately* have given something to Sandcastle to make him produce deformed foals, and that Ginnie found out ... and was killed for it.'

There was silence.

'I'll go and get a book or two,' Pen said. 'We'll look up the ingredients, just in case. But honestly, don't *hope*.'

She went home leaving the three of us feeling subdued. For me this had been the last possibility, although since I'd heard from Oliver that the police check had revealed only the expected shampoo in the bottle, it had become more and more remote.

Pen came back in half an hour with a thick tome, a piece of paper, and worried creases across her forehead. 'I've been reading,' she said. 'Sorry to be so long. I've been checking up on sperm deformities, and it seems the most likely cause is radiation.'

I said instantly, 'Let's ring Oliver.'

They nodded and I got through to him with Pen's suggestion

'Tim!' he said. 'I'll see if I can get anyone in Newmarket ... even though it's Sunday ... I'll ring you back.'

'Though how a stallion could get anywhere near a radioactive source,' Pen said while we were waiting, 'would be a first-class mystery in itself.' She looked down at the paper she carried. 'This is the analysis report from the British lab, bill attached, I'm afraid. Some ingredients, though written in the opposite order, practically, with selenium put at the top, which means that that's the predominant drug, I should think.'

Oliver telephoned again in a remarkably short time. 'I got the chief researcher at home. He says they did think of radiation but discounted it because it would be more likely to result in total sterility, and there's also the improbability of a horse being near any radio-active isotopes.' He sighed. 'Sandcastle has never even been X-rayed.'

'See if you can check,' I said. 'If he ever was irradiated in any way it would come into the category of accidental or even malicious damage, and we'd be back into the insurance policy.'

'All right,' he said. 'I'll try.'

I put down the receiver to find Pen turning the pages of her large pharmacological book with concentration.

'What's that?' Judith asked, pointing.

'Toxicity of minerals,' Pen answered absentmindedly. 'Ethylene glycol ...' she turned pages, searching. 'Here we are.' She read down the column, shaking her head. 'Not that, anyway.' She again consulted the index, read the columns, shook her head. 'Selenium ... selenium ...' She turned the pages, read the columns, pursed her lips. 'It says that selenium

491

is poisonous if taken internally, though it can be beneficial on the skin.' She read some more. 'It says that if animals eat plants which grow in soil which has much selenium in it, they can die.'

'What is selenium?' Judith asked.

'It's an element,' Pen said. 'Like potassium and sodium.' She read on, 'It says here that it is mostly found in rocks of the Cretaceous Age — such useful information — and that it's among the most poisonous of elements but also an essential nutrient in trace quantities for both animals and plants.' She looked up. 'It says it's useful for flower-growers beause it kills insects, and that it accumulates mostly in plants which flourish where there's a low annual rainfall.'

'Is that all?' Gordon asked, sounding disappointed.

'No, there's pages of it. I'm just translating the gist into understandable English.'

She read on for a while, and then it seemed to me that she totally stopped breathing. She raised her head and looked at me, her eyes wide and dark.

'What is it?' I said.

'Read it,' She gave me the heavy book, pointing to the open page.

I read:

Selenium is absorbed easily from the intestines and affects every part of the body, more lodging in the liver, spleen, and kidneys than in brain and muscle. Selenium is teratogenic.

'What does teratogenic mean?' I asked.

'It means,' Pen said, 'that it produces deformed offspring.'

'*What*? I exclaimed. 'You don't mean ...'

Pen was shaking her head. 'It couldn't affect Sandcastle. It's impossible. It would simply poison his system. Teratogens have nothing to do with males.'

'Then what ...?'

'They act on the developing embryo,' she said. Her face crumpled almost as if the knowledge was too much and would make her cry. 'You could get deformed foals if you fed selenium *to the mares*.'

I went on the following morning to see Detective Chief

Inspector Wyfold, both Gordon and Henry concurring that the errand warranted time off from the bank. The forceful policeman shook my hand, gestured me to a chair and said briskly that he could give me fifteen minutes at the outside, as did I know that yet another young girl had been murdered and sexually assaulted the evening before, which was now a total of six, and that his superiors, the press and the whole flaming country wre baying for an arrest? 'And we are no nearer now,' he added with anger, 'than we were five months ago, when it started.'

He listened all the same to what I said about selenium, but in conclusion shook his head.

'We looked it up ourselves. Did you know it's the main ingredient in an anti-dandruff shampoo sold off open shelves all over America in the drug stores? It used to be on sale here too, or something like it, but it's been discontinued. There's no mystery about it. It's not rare, nor illegal. Just ordinary.'

'But the deformaties ...'

'Look,' he said restively, 'I'll bear it in mind. But it's a big jump to decide from one bottle of ordinary dog shampoo that *that's* what's the matter with those foals. I mean, is there any way of proving it?'

With regret I said, 'No, there isn't.' No animal, Pen's book had inferred, would retain selenium in its system for longer than a day or two if it was eaten only once or twice and in non-fatal amounts.

'And how, anyway,' Wyfold said, 'would you get a whole lot of horses to drink anything as nasty as shampoo?' He shook his head. 'I know you're very anxious to catch Virginia Knowles' killer, and don't think we don't appreciate your coming here, but we've been into the shampoo question thoroughly, I assure you.'

His telephone buzzed and he picked up the receiver, his eyes still turned in my direction but his mind already elsewhere. 'What?' he said. 'Yes, all right. Straightaway.' He put down the receiver. 'I'll have to go.'

'Listen,' I said, 'Isn't it possible that one of the lads was giving selenium to the mares this year also, and that Ginnie somehow found out ...'

He interrupted. 'We tried to fit that killing onto one of those

493

lads, don't think we didn't, but there was no evidence, absolutely none at all.' He stood up and came round from behind his desk, already leaving me in mind as well as body. 'If you think of anything else Mr Ekaterin, by all means let us know. But for now — I'm sorry, but there's a bestial man out there we've got to catch — and I'm still of the opinion he tried for Virginia Knowles too, and was interrupted.'

He gave me a dismissing but not impatient nod, holding open the door and waiting for me to leave his office ahead of him. I obliged him by going, knowing that realistically he couldn't be expected to listen to any further unsubstantiated theories from me while another victim lay more horribly and recently dead.

Before I went back to him, I thought, I had better dig further and come up with connected, believable facts, and also a basis, at least, for proof.

Henry and Gordon heard with gloom in the bank before lunch that at present we were 'insufficient data' in a Wyfold pigeonhole.'

'But you still believe, do you, Tim ...?' Henry said enquiringly.

'We have to,' I answered. 'And yes, I do.'

'Hm.' He pondered. 'If you need more time off from the office, you'd better take it. If there's the slightest chance that there's nothing wrong with Sandcastle after all, we must do our absolute best not only to prove it to our own satisfaction but also to the world in general. Confidence would have to be restored to breeders, otherwise they wouldn't send their mares. It's a tall order altogether.'

'Yes,' I said. 'Well ... I'll do all I can'; and after lunch and some thought I telephoned to Oliver, whose hopes no one had so far raised.

'Sit down,' I said.

'What's the matter?' He sounded immediately anxious. 'What's happened?'

'Do you know what teratogenic means?' I said.

'Yes, of course. With mares one always has to be careful.'

'Mm ... Well, there was a teratogenic drug in the bottle of dog shampoo that Ginnie had.'

What?' His voice rose an octave on the word, vibrating with instinctive unthinking anger.

494

'Yes,' I said. 'Now calm down. The police say it proves nothing either way, but Gordon and Henry, our chairman, agree that it's the only hope we have left.'

'But Tim ...' The realisation hit him, 'That would mean ... that would mean ...'

'Yes,' I said. 'It would mean that Sandcastle was always breeding good and true and could return to gold-mine status.'

I could hear Oliver's heavily disturbed breathing and could only guess at his pulse rate.

'No,' he said. 'No. If shampoo had got into a batch of feed, all the mares who ate it would have been affected, not just those covered by Sandcastle.'

'If the shampoo got into the feed accidentally, yes. If it was given deliberately, no.'

'I can't ... I can't ...'

'I did tell you to sit down,' I said reasonably.

'Yes, so you did.' There was a pause. 'I'm sitting,' he said.

'It's at least possible,' I said, 'That the Equine Research people could find nothing wrong with Sandcastle because there actually *isn't* anything wrong with him.'

'Yes,' he ageed faintly.

'It is possible to give teratogenic substances to mares.'

'Yes.'

'But horses wouldn't drink shampoo.'

'No, thoroughbreds especially are very choosy.'

'So how would you give them shampoo, and when?'

After a pause he said, still breathlessly, 'I don't know how. They'd spit it out. But when is easier, and that could probably be no more than three or four days after conception. That's when the body tube is forming in the embryo ... that's when a small amount of teratogenic substance could do a lot of damage.'

'Do you mean,' I said, 'that giving a mare selenium just *once* would ensure a deformed foal?'

'Giving a mare what?'

'Sorry. Selenium. A drug for treating dandruff.'

'Good ... heavens.' He rallied towards his normal self. 'I suppose it would depend on the strength of the dose, and its timing. Perhaps three or four doses ... No one could really *know*, because no one would have tried ... I mean, there

495

wouldn't have been any research.'

'No,' I agreed. 'But supposing that in this instance someone got the dosage and timing right, and also found a way of making the shampoo palatable, then *who was it*?'

There was a long quietness during which even his breathing abated.

'I don't know,' he said finally. 'Theoretically it could have been me, Ginnie, Nigel, the Watcherleys or any of the lads who wre here last year. No one else was on the place often enough.

'Really no one? How about the vet or the blacksmith or just a visiting friend?'

'But there were *eighteen* deformed foals,' he said. 'I would think it would have to have been someone who could come and go here all the time.'

'And someone who knew which mares to pick,' I said. 'Would that knowledge be easy to come by?'

'Easy!' he said explosively. 'It is positively thrust at everyone on the place. There are lists in all the feed rooms and in the breeding pen itself saying which mares are to be bred to which stallion. Nigel has one, there's one in my office, one at the Watcherleys — all over. Everyone is supposed to double-check the lists all the time, so that mistakes aren't made.'

'And all the horses,' I said slowly, 'Wear head-collars with their names on.'

'Yes, that's right. An essential precaution.'

All made easy, I thought, for someone intending mischief towards particular mares and not to any others.

'Your own Sandcastle foal,' I said, 'he's perfect ... and it may be because on the lists your mare was down for Diarist.'

'Tim!'

'Look after him,' I said. 'And look after Sandcastle.'

'I will,' he said fervently.

'And Oliver ... is that lad called Shane still with you?'

'No, he's gone. So have Dave and Sammy, who found Ginnie.'

'Then could you send me at the bank a list of the names and addresses of all the people who were working for you last year, and also this year? And I mean *everyone*, even your housekeeper and anyone working for Nigel or cleaning the lads' hostel, things like that.'

'Even my part-time secretary girl?'

'Even her.'

'She only comes three mornings a week.'

'That might be enough.'

'All right,' he said. 'I'll do it straight away.'

'I went to see Chief Inspector Wyfold this morning,' I said. 'But he thinks it's just a coincidence that Ginnie had shampoo with a foal-deforming drug in it. We'll have to come up with a whole lot more, to convince him. So anything you can think of ...'

'I'll think of nothing else.'

'If Dissdale Smith should telephone you, pressing for an answer,' I said, 'just say the bank are deliberating and keeping you waiting. Don't tell him anything about this new possibility. It might be best to keep it to ourselves until we can prove whether or not it's true.'

'Dear God,' he said fearfully, 'I hope it is.'

In the evening I talked to Pen, asking her if she knew of any way of getting the selenium out of the shampoo.

'The trouble seems to be,' I said, 'That you simply couldn't get the stuff into a horse as it is.'

'I'll work on it,' she said, 'But of course the manufacturer's chemists will have gone to a great deal of trouble to make sure the selenium stays suspended throughout the mixture and doesn't all fall to the bottom.'

'It did say "Shake Well" on the bottle.'

'Mm, but that might be for the soap content, not for the selenium.'

I thought. 'Well, could you get the soap out, then? It must be the soap the horses wouldn't like.'

'I'll try my hardest,' she promised. 'I'll ask a few friends.' She paused. 'There isn't much of the shampoo left. Only what I kept after sending the sample off to America and the British lab.'

'How much?' I said anxiously.

'Half an egg-cupful. Maybe less.'

'Is that enough?'

'If we work in test-tubes ... perhaps.'

'And Pen ... Could you or your friends make a guess, as well, as to how much shampoo you'd need to provide enough selenium to give a teratogenic dose to a mare?'

'You sure do come up with some difficult questions, dearest Tim, but we'll certainly try.'

Three days later she sent a message with Gordon, saying that by that evening she might have some answers, if I would care to go down to her house after work.

I cared and went, and with a smiling face she opened her front door to let me in.

'Like a drink?' she said.

'Well, yes, but ...'

'First things first.' She poured whisky carefully for me and Cinzano for herself. 'Hungry?'

'Pen ...'

'It's only rolls with ham and lettuce in. I never cook much, as you know.' She disappeared to her seldom-used kitchen and returned with the offerings, which turned out to be nicely squelchy and much what I would have made for myself.

'All right,' she said finally, pushing away the empty plates, 'Now I'll tell you what we've managed.'

'At last.'

She grinned. 'Yes. Well then, we started from the premise that if someone had to use shampoo as the source of selenium then that someone didn't have direct or easy access to poisonous chemicals, which being so he also wouldn't have sophisticated machinery available for separating one ingredient from another — a centrifuge, for instance. OK so far?'

I nodded.

'So what we needed, as we saw it, was a *simple* method that involved only everyday equipment. Something anyone could do anywhere. So the first thing we did was to let the shampoo drip through a paper filter, and we think you could use almost anything for that purpose, like a paper towel, a folded tissue or thin blotting paper. We actually got the best and fastest results from a coffee filter, which is after all specially designed to retain very fine solids while letting liquids through easily.'

'Yes, I said. 'Highly logical.'

Pen smiled. 'So there we were with some filter-papers in which, we hoped , the microscopic particles of selenium were trapped. The filters were stained bright green by the shampoo. I brought one here to show you ... I'll get it.' She whisked off to the kitchen taking the empty supper plates with her, and returned carrying a small tray with two glasses on it.

One glass contained cut pieces of green-stained coffee filter lying in what looked like oil, and the second glass contained only an upright test-tube, closed at the top with a cork and showing a dark half-inch of solution at the bottom.

'One of my friends in the lab knows a lot about horses,' Pen said,' and he reckoned that all race horses are used to the taste of linseed oil, which is given them in their feed quite often as a laxative. So we got some linseed oil and cut up the filter and soaked it.' She pointed to the glass. 'The selenium particles floated out of the paper into the oil.'

'Neat.' I said.

'Yes. So then we poured the result into the test-tube and just waited twenty-four hours or so, and the selenium particles slowly gravitated through the oil to the bottom.' She looked at my face to make sure I understood. 'We transferred the selenium from the wax-soap base in which it would remain suspended into an oil base, in which it *wouldn't* remain suspended.'

'I do understand,' I assured her.'

'So here in the test-tube,' she said with a conjuror's flourish, 'we have concentrated selenium with the surplus of oil poured off.' She picked the tube out of the glass, keeping it upright, and showed me the brownish shadowy liquid lying there, darkest at the bottom, almost clear amber at the top. 'We had such a small sample to start with that this is all we managed to collect. But that dark stuff is definitely selenium sulphide. We checked it on a sort of scanner called a gas chromatograph.' She grinned. 'No point in not using the sophisticated apparatus when it's there right beside you — and we were in a research lab of a teaching hospital, incidentally.'

'You're marvellous.'

'Quite brilliant,' she agreed with comic modesty. 'We also calculated that that particular shampoo was almost ten per cent selenium, which is a very much higher proportion than you'd find in shampoos for humans. We all agree that this much, in the test-tube, is enough to cause deformity in a foal — or in any other species, for that matter. We found many more references in other books — lambs born with deformed feet, for instance, where the sheep had browsed off plants growing on selenium-rich soil. We all agree that it's the *time* when the mare ingests the selenium that's most crucial, and we think that to be sure of getting the desired result you'd have to give the selenium every day for three or four days, starting two or three days after conception.'

I slowly nodded. 'That's the same sort of time-scale that Oliver said.'

'And if you gave too much,' she said, 'Too large a dose, you'd be more likely to get abortions than really gross deformaties. The embryo would only go on growing at all, that is, if the damage done to it by the selenium was relatively minor.'

'There were a lot of *different* deformities,' I said.

'Oh sure. It could have affected any developing cell, regardless.'

I picked up the test-tube and peered closely at its murky contents. 'I suppose all you'd have to do would be stir this into a cupful of oats.'

'That's right.'

Or ... could you enclose it in a capsule?'

'Yes, if you had the makings. We could have done it quite easily in the lab. You'd need to get rid of as much oil as possible, of course, in that case, and just scrape concentrated selenium into the capsules.'

'Mm. Calder could do it, I suppose?'

'Calder Jackson? Why yes, I guess he could if you wanted him to. He had everything there that you'd need.' She lifted her head, remembering something. 'He's on the television tomorrow night, incidentally.'

'Is he?'

'Yes. They were advertising it tonight just after the news, before you came. He's going to be a guest on that chat show ... Mickey Bonwith's show ... Do you ever see it?'

'Sometimes,' I said, thoughtfully. 'It's transmitted live, isn't it?'

'Yes, that's right.' She looked at me with slight puzzlement. 'What's going on in that computer brain?'

'A slight calculation of risk,' I said slowly, 'and of grasping unrepeatable opportunities. And tell me, dearest Pen, if I found myself again in Calder's surgery, what should I look for, to bring out?'

She stared at me literally with her mouth open. Then recovering, she said, 'You can't mean ... *Calder*?'

'Well,' I said soberly. 'What I'd really like to do is to make sure one way or another. Because it does seem to me, sad though it is to admit it, that if you tie in Dissdale's offer for Sandcastle with someone deliberately poisoning the mares, and then add Calder's expertise with herbs — in which selenium-soaked plants might be included — you do at least get a *question mark*. You do want to know for sure, don't you think, whether or not Calder and Dissdale set out deliberately to debase Sandcastle's worth so that they could buy him for peanuts ... So that Calder could perform a well publicised "miracle cure" of some sort on Sandcastle, who would thereafter always sire perfect foals, and gradually climb back into favour. Whose fee might never return to forty thousand pounds, but would over the years add up to a fortune.'

'But they couldn't,' Pen said, aghast. 'I mean ... Calder and Dissdale ... we *know* them.'

'And you in your trade, as I in mine, must have met presentable, confidence-inspiring crooks.'

She fell silent, staring at me in a troubled way, until finally I said. 'There's one other thing. Again nothing I could swear to — but the first time I went to Calder's place he had a lad there who reminded me sharply of the boy with the knife at Ascot.'

'Ricky Barnet,' Pen said, nodding.

'Yes. I can't remember Calder's lad's name, and I couldn't identify him at all now after all this time, but at Oliver's I saw another lad, called Shane, who *also* reminded me of Ricky Barnet. I've no idea whether Shane and Calder's lad are one and the same person, though maybe not, because I don't think Calder's lad was called Shane, or I *would* have remembered, if you see what I mean.'

'Got you.' she said.

'But *if* — and it's a big if — if Shane did once work for Calder, he might *still* be working for him ... feeding selenium to mares.'

Pen took her time with gravity in the experienced eyes, and at last said,' *Someone* would have had to be there on the spot to do the feeding, and it certainly couldn't have been Calder or

501

Dissdale. But couldn't it have been that manager, Nigel? It would have been easy for him. Suppose Dissdale and Calder paid him ...? Suppose they promised to employ him, or even give him a share in Sandcastle, once they'd got hold of the horse.'

I shook my head. 'I did wonder. I did think of Nigel. There's one good reason why it probably isn't him, though, and that's because he and only he besides Oliver knew that one of the mares down for Diarist was covered by Sandcastle,' I explained about Oliver's impulse mating. 'The foal is perfect, but might very likely not have been if it was Nigel who was doing the feeding.'

'Not conclusive,' Pen said, slowly.

'No.'

She stirred. 'Did you tell the police all this?'

'I meant to,' I said, 'But when I was there with Wyfold on Monday it seemed impossible. It was all so insubstantial. Such a lot of guesses. Maybe wrong conclusions. Dissdale's offer could be genuine. And a lad I'd seen for half a minute eighteen months ago ... it's difficult to remember a strange face for half an hour, let alone all that time. I have only an impression of blankness and of sunglasses ... and I don't have the same impression of Oliver's lad Shane. Wyfold isn't the sort of man to be vague to. I thought I'd better come up with something more definite before I went back to him.'

She bit her thumb. 'Can't you take another good look at this Shane?'

I shook my hed. 'Oliver's gradually letting lads go, as he does every year at this time, and Shane is one who has already left. Oliver doesn't know where he went and has no other address for him, which he doesn't think very unusual. It seems that lads can drift from stable to stable for ever with their papers always showing only the address of their last or current employer. But I think we *might* find Shane, if we're lucky.

'How?'

'By photographing Ricky Barnet, side view, and asking around on racetracks.'

She smiled. 'It might work. It just might.'

'Worth a try.'

My mind drifted back to something else worth a try, and it

seemed that hers followed.

'You don't really mean to break into Calder's surgery, do you?' she said.

'Pick the lock,' I said. 'Yes.'

'But ...'

'Time's running out, and Oliver's future and the bank's money with it, and yes, sure, I'll do what I can.'

She curiously looked into my face. 'You have no real conception of danger, do you?'

'How do you mean?'

'I mean ... I saw you, that day at Ascot, simply hurl yourself at that boy, at that knife. You could have been badly stabbed, very easily. And Ginnie told us that you frightened her to tears jumping at Sandcastle the way you did, to catch him. She said it was suicidal ... and yet you yourself seemed to think nothing of it. And at Ascot, that evening, I remember you being *bored* with the police questions, not stirred up high by a brush with death ...'

Her words petered away. I considered them and found in myself a reason and an answer.

'Nothing that has happened so far in my life,' I said seriously, 'has made me fear I might die. I think ... I know it sounds silly ... I am unconvinced of my own mortality.'

The Third Year

JUNE

On the following day, Friday, June 1st, I took up a long-offered invitation and went to lunch with the board of a security firm to whom we had lent money for launching a new burglar alarm on the market. Not greatly to their surprise I was there to ask a favour, and after a repast of five times the calories of Ekaterin's they gave me with some amusement three keys which would unlock almost anything but the crown jewels, and also a concentrated course on how to use them.

'Those pickers are strictly for opening doors in emergencies,' the locksmiths said, smiling. 'If you end up in jail, we don't know you.'

'If I end up in jail, send me another set in a fruit cake.'

I thanked them and left, and practised discreetly on the office doors in the bank, with remarkable results. Going home I let myself in through my own front door with them, and locked and unlocked every cupboard and drawer which had a keyhole. Then I put on a dark roll-neck jersy over my shirt and tie and with scant trepidation drove to Newmarket.

I left my car at the side of the road some distance from Calder's house and finished the journey on foot, walking quietly into his yard in the last of the lingering summer dusk, checking against my watch that it was almost ten o'clock, the hour when Micky Bonwith led his guests to peacock chairs and dug publicly into their psyches.

Calder would give a great performance, I thought: and the

regrets I felt about my suspicions of him redoubled as I looked at the outline of his house against the sky and remembered his uncomplicated hospitality.

The reserve which had always at bottom lain between us I now acknowledged as my own instinctive and stifled doubt. Wanting to see worth, I had seen it: and the process of now trying to prove myself wrong gave me more sadness than satisfaction.

His yard was dark and peaceful, all lads long gone. Within the hall of the house a single light burned, a dim point of yellow glimpsed through the bushes fluttering in a gentle breeze. Behind the closed doors of the boxes the patients would be snoozing, those patients with festering sores and bleeding guts and all manner of woes awaiting the touch.

Sandcastle, if I was right, had been destined to stand there, while Calder performed his 'miracle' without having to explain how he'd done it. He never had explained: he'd always broadcast publicly that he didn't know *how* his power worked, he just knew it did. Thousands, perhaps millions, believed in his power. Perhaps even breeders, those dreamers of dreams, would have believed, in the end.

I came to the surgery, a greyish block in the advancing night, and fitted one of the lock-pickers into the keyhole. The internal tumblers turned without protest, much oiled and used, and I pushed the door open and went in.

There were no windows to worry about. I closed the door behind me, and switched on the light, and immediately began to search for which I'd come: to find selenium in home-made capsules, or in a filtering device, or in bottles of shampoo.

Pen had had doubts that anyone would have risked giving selenium a second year if the first year's work had proved so effective, but I'd reminded her that Sandcastle had already covered many new mares that year before the deformed foals had been reported.

'Whoever did it couldn't have known at that point that he'd been successful. So to make sure, I'd guess he'd go on, and maybe with an increased dose ... and if no selenium was being given this year, *why did Ginnie have it?*'

Pen had reluctantly given in. 'I suppose I'm just trying to find reasons for you not to go to Calder's.'

'If I find anything, Chief Inspector Wyfold can go there later with a search warrant. Don't worry so.'

'No,' she'd said, and gone straight on looking anxious.

The locked cabinets at both ends of Calder's surgery proved a doddle for the picks, but the contents were a puzzle, as so few of the jars and boxes were properly labelled. Some indeed had come from commercial suppliers, but these seemed mostly to be the herbs Calder talked of: hydrastis, comfrey, fo-ti-tieng, myrrh, sarsaparilla, liquorice, passiflora, papaya, garlic; a good quantity of each.

Nothing was obligingly labelled selenium.

I had taken with me a thickist polythene bag which had a zip across one end and had formerly enclosed a silk tie and handkerchief, a present from my mother at Christmas. Into that I systematically put two or three capsules from each bottle, and two or three pills of each sort, and small sachets of herbs: and Pen, I thought, was going to have a fine old time sorting them all out.

With the bag almost half full of samples I carefully locked the cabinets again and turned to the refrigerator, which was of an ordinary domestic make with only a magnetic door fastening.

Inside there were no bottles of shampoo. No coffee filters. No linseed oil. There were simply the large plastic containers of Calder's cure-all tonic.

I thought I might as well take some to satisfy Pen's curiosity, and rooted around for a small container, finding some empty medicine bottles in a cupboard below the work bench. Over the sink I poured some of the tonic into a medicine bottle, screwed on the cap, and returned the plastic container carefully to its place in the 'fridge. I stood the medicine bottle on the workbench ready to take away, and turned finally to the drawers where Calder kept things like hops and also his antique pill-making equipment.

Everything was clean and tidy, as before. If he had made capsules containing selenium there, I could see no trace.

With mounting disappointment I went briefly through every drawer. Bags of seeds: sesame, pumpkin, sunflower. Bags of dried herbs, raspberry leaves, alfalfa. Boxes of the empty halves of gelatine capsules, waiting for contents. Empty unused pill bottles. All as before: nothing I hadn't already seen.

The larger bottom drawer still contained the plastic sacks of hops. I pulled open the neck of one of them and found only the expected strong-smelling crop: closed the neck again, moving the bag slightly to settle it back into its place, and saw that under the bags of hops lay a brown leather briefcase, ordinary size, six inches deep.

With a feeling of wasting time I hauled it out onto the working surface on top of the drawers, and tried to open it.

Both catches were locked. I fished for the keys in my trousers pocket and with the smallest of the picks delicately twisted until the mechanisms clicked.

Opened the lid. Found no bottles of dog shampoo, but other things that turned me slowly to a state of stone.

The contents looked at first sight as if the case belonged to a doctor: stethoscope, pen torch, metal instruments, all in fitted compartments. A cardboard box without its lid held four or five small tubes of antibiotic ointment. A large bottle contained only a few small white pills, the bottle labelled with a long name I could scarcely read, let alone remember, with 'diuretic' in brackets underneath. A pad of prescription forms, blank, ready for use.

It was the name and address rubber-stamped onto the prescription forms and the initials heavily embossed in gold into the leather beneath the case's handle which stunned me totally.

I.A.P. on the case.

Ian A. Pargetter on the prescriptions.

Ian Pargetter, veterinary surgeon, address in Newmarket.

His case had vanished the night he died.

This case ...

With fingers beginning to shake I took one of the tubes of antibiotics and some of the diuretic pills and three of the prescription forms and added them to my other spoils, and then with a heart at least beating at about twice normal speed checked that everything was in its place before closing the case.

I felt as much as heard the surgery door open, the current of air reaching me at the same instant as the night sounds. I turned thinking that one of Calder's lads had come on some late hospital rounds and wondering how I could ever explain my presence; and I saw that no explanation at all would do.

It was Calder himself crossing the threshold. Calder with the

507

light on his curly halo, Calder who should have been a hundred miles away talking to the nation on the tube.

His first expression of surprise turned immediately to grim assessment, his gaze travelling from the medicine bottle of tonic mixture on the workbench to the veterinary case lying open. Shock, disbelief and fury rose in an instantly violent reaction,and he acted with such speed that even if I'd guessed what he would do I could hardly have dodged.

His right arm swung in an arc, coming down against the wall beside the door and pulling from the bracket which held it a slim scarlet fire extinguisher. The swing seemed to me continuous. The red bulbous end of the fire extinguisher in a split second filled my vision and connected with a crash against my forehead, and consciousness ceased within a blink.

The world came back with the same sort of on-off switch: one second I was unaware, the next, awake. No grey area of daze, no shooting stars, simply on-off, off-on.

I was lying on my back on some smelly straw in an electrically lit horse box with a brown horse peering at me suspiciously from six feet above.

I couldn't remember for a minute how I'd got there; it seemed such an improbable position to be in. then I had a recollection of a red ball crashing above my eyes, and then, in a snap, total recall of the evening.

Calder

I was in a box in Calder's yard. I was there because presumably, Calder had put me there.

Pending? I wondered.

Pending what?

With no reassuring thoughts I made the moves to stand up, but found that though consciousness was total, recovery was not. A whirling dizziness set the walls tilting, the grey concrete blocks seeming to want to lean in and fall on me. Cursing slightly I tried again more slowly and made it to one elbow with eyes balancing precariously in their sockets

The top half of the stable door abruptly opened with the sound of an unlatching bolt. Calder's head appeared in the doorway, his face showing shock and dismay as he saw me awake.

'I thought,' he said, 'that you'd be unconscious ... that you wouldn't know. I hit you so hard ... you're supposed to be out.' His voice saying these bizzare words sounded nothing but normal.

'Calder ...' I said.

He was looking at me no longer with anger but almost with apology. 'I'm sorry, Tim,' he said. 'I'm sorry you came.'

The walls seemed to be slowing down.

'Ian Pargetter ...' I said. 'Did *you* ... kill him? Not you?'

Calder produced an apple and fed it almost absentmindedly to the horse. 'I'm sorry, Tim. He was so stubborn. He refused ...' He patted the horse's neck. 'He wouldn't do what I wanted. Said it was over, he'd had enough. Said he'd stop me, you know.' He looked for a moment at the horse and then down to me. 'Why did you come? I've liked you. I wish you hadn't.'

I tried again to stand up and the whirling returned as before. Calder took a step backwards, but only one, stopping when he saw my inability to arise and charge.

'Ginnie,' I said. 'Not Ginnie ... Say it wasn't you who hit Ginnie ...'

He simply looked at me, and didn't say it. In the end he said merely, and with clear regret, 'I wish I'd hit you harder ... but ... it seemed ... enough.' He moved another step backwards so that I could see only the helmet of curls under the light and dark shadows where his eyes were; and then while I was still struggling to my knees he closed the half door and bolted it, and from outside switched off the light.

Night-blindness made it even harder to stand up but at least I couldn't *see* the walls whirl, only feel they were spinning. I found myself leaning aginst one of them and ended more or less upright, spine supported, brain at last settling into equilibrium.

The grey oblong of window gradually detached itself from the blackness, and when my equine companion moved his head I saw the liquid reflection of an eye.

Window ... way out.

I slithered round the walls to the window and found it barred on the inside, not so much to keep horses in, I supposed, but to prevent them breaking the glass. Five strong bars, in any case, were set in concrete top and bottom, as secure as any prison cell, and I shook them impotently with two hands in proving them immovable.

Through the dusty window panes I had a sideways view across the yard towards the surgery, and while I stood there and held onto the bars and watched, Calder went busily in and out of the open lighted doorway, carrying things from the surgery to his car. I saw what I was sure was Ian Pargetter's case go into the boot, and remembered with discomfiture that I'd left the bunch of picks in one of its locks. I saw him carry also an armful of the jars which contained unlabelled capsules and several boxes of unguessable contents, stowing them in the boot carefully and closing them in.

Calder was busy obliterating his tracks.

I yelled to him, calling his name, but he didn't even hear or turn his head. The only result was startled movement in the horse behind me, a stamping of hooves and a restless swinging round the box.

'All right,' I said soothingly. 'Steady down. All right. Don't be frightened.'

The big animal's alarm abated, and through the window I watched Calder switch off the surgery light, lock the door, get into his car and drive away.

He drove away out of his driveway, towards the main road, not towards his house. The lights of his car passed briefly over the trees as he turned out through the gates, and then were gone: and I seemed suddenly very alone, imprisoned in that dingy place for heaven knew how long.

Vision slowly expanded so that from the dim light of the sky I could see again th outlines within the box: walls, manger ... horse. The big dark creature didn't like me being there and wouldn't settle, but I could think of no way to relieve him of my presence.

The ceiling was solid, not as in some stbles open through the rafters to the roof. In many it would have been possible for an agile man to climb the partition from one box to the next, but not here, and in any case there was no promise of being better off next door.One would be in a different box but probably just as simply and securely bolted in.

There was nothing in my trousers pockets but a handkerchief. Penknife, money and house keys were all in my jacket in the boot of my own unlocked car out on the road. The dark jersey which had seemed good for speed, quiet and concealment had left me without even a coin for a screwdriver.

I thought concentratedly of what a man could do with his fingers that a horse couldn't do with superior strength, but found nothing in the darkness of the door to unwind or unhinge; nothing anywhere to pick loose. It looked most annoyingly as if that was where I was going to stay until Calder came back.

And then ... what?

If he'd intended to kill me, why hadn't he already made sure of it? Another swipe or two with the fire extinguisher would have done ... and I would have known nothing about it.

I thought of Ginnie, positive now that that was how it had been for her, that in one instant she had been thinking, and in the next ... not.

Thought of Ian Pargetter, dead from one blow of his own brass lamp. Thought of Calder's shock and grief at the event, probably none the less real despite his having killed the man he mourned. Calder shattered over the loss of a business friend ... the friend he himself struck down.

He must have killed him, I thought, on a moment's ungovernable impulse, for not ... what had he said? ... for not wanting to go on, for wanting to stop Calder doing ... what Calder planned.

Calder had struck at me with the same sort of speed: without pause for consideration, without time to think of consequences. And he had lashed at me as a friend too, without hesitation, while saying shortly after that he liked me.

Calder, swinging the fire extinguisher, had ruthlessly aimed at killing the man who had saved his life.

Saved Calder's life ... Oh God, I thought, why ever did I do it?

The man in whom I had wanted to see only goodness had after that day killed Ian Pargetter, killed Ginnie: and if I hadn't saved him they would both have lived.

The despair of that thought filled me utterly, swelling with enormity, making me feel, as the simpler grief for Ginnie had done, that one's body couldn't hold so much emotion. Remorse and guilt could rise like dragon's teeth from good intentions, and there were in truth unexpected paths to hell.

I thought back to that distant moment that had affected so many lives: to that instinctive reflex, faster than thought, which had launched me at Ricky's knife. If I could have called it back I would have been looking away, not seeing, letting Calder die ... letting Ricky take his chances, letting him blast his young life to fragments, destroy his caring parents.

One couldn't help what came after.

A fireman or a lifeboatman or a surgeon might fight to the utmost stretch of skill to save a baby and find he had let loose a Hitler, a Nero, Jack the Ripper. It couldn't always be Beethoven or Pasteur whose life one extended. All one asked was an ordinary, moderately sinful, normally well-intentioned, fairly harmless human. And if he cured horses ... all the better.

Before that day at Ascot Calder couldn't even have thought of owning Sandcastle, because Sandcastle at that moment was in mid-career with his stud value uncertain. But Calder had seen, as we all had, the majesty of that horse, and I had myself listened to the admiration in his voice.

At some time after that he must have thought of selenium, and from there the wickedness had grown to encompass us all: the wickedness which would have been extinguished before birth if I'd been looking another way.

I knew logically that I couldn't have not done what I did; but in heart and spirit that didn't matter. It didn't stop the engulfing misery or allow me any ease.

Grief and sorrow came to us all, Pen had said: and she was right.

The horse became more restive and began to paw the ground. I looked at my watch, the digital figures bright in the darkness: twenty minutes or thereabouts since Calder had left. Twenty minutes that already seemed like twenty hours.

The horse swung round suddenly in the gloom with unwelcome vigour, bumping against me with his rump.

'Calm down now, boy,' I said soothingly. 'We're stuck with each other. Go to sleep.'

The horse's reply was the equivalent of unprintable: the crash of a steel-clad hoof against a wall.

Perhaps he didn't like me talking, I thought, or indeed even moving about. His head swung round towards the window, his bulk stamping restlessly from one side of the box to the other, and I saw that he, unlike Oliver's horses, wore no head-collar: nothing with which to hold him, while I calmed him, patting his neck.

His head reared up suddenly, tossing violently, and with a foreleg he lashed forward at the wall.

Not funny, I thought. Horrific to have been in the firing-line of that slashing hoof. For heaven's sake, I said to him mentally, I'll do you no harm. Just stay quiet. Go to sleep

I was standing at that time with my back to the door, so that to the horse I must have been totally in shadow: but he would know I was there. He could smell my presence, hear my breathing. If he could see me as well, would it be better?

I took a tentative step towards the dim oblong of window, and had a clear, sharp and swiftly terrifying view of one of his eyes.

No peace. No sleep. No prospect of anything like that. The horse's eye was stretched wide with white showing all round the usual darkness, staring not at me but as if blind, glaring wildly at nothing at all.

The black nostrils looked huge. The lips as I watched were drawing back from the teeth. The ears had gone flat to the head and there was froth forming in the mouth. It was the face, I thought incredulously, not of unrest or alarm ... but of madness.

The horse backed suddenly away, crashing his hindquarters into the rear wall and rocking again forwards, but this time advancing with both forelegs off the ground, the gleams from thrashing hooves curving in silvery streaks in the gloom, the feet hitting the wall below the window with sickening intent.

I pressed in undoubted panic into the corner made by wall and door, but it gave no real protection. The box was roughly ten feet square by eight feet high, a space even at the best of times half filled by horse. For that horse at the moment it was a strait-jacket confinement out of which he seemed intent of physically smashing his way.

The manger, I thought. Get in the manger.

The manger was built at about waist height diagonally across one of the box's rear corners; a smallish metal trough set into a sturdy wooden support. As a shelter it was pathetic, but at least

513

I would be off the ground....

The horse turned and stood on his forelegs and let fly backwards with an almighty double kick that thudded into the concrete wall six inches from my head, and it was then, at that moment, that I began to fear that the crazed animal might not just hurt but kill me.

He wasn't purposely trying to attack; most of his kicks were in other directions. He wasn't trying to bite, though his now open mouth looked savage. He was uncontrollably wild, but not with me ... though that, in so small a space, made little difference.

He seemed in the next very few seconds to go utterly berserk. With speeds I could only guess at in the scurrying shadows he whirled and kicked and hurled his bulk aginst the walls and I, still attempting to jump through the tempest into the manger, was finally knocked over by one of his flailing feet.

I didn't realise at that point that he'd actually broken one of my arms because the whole thing felt numb. I made it to the manger, tried to scramble up, got my foot in ... sat on the edge ... tried to raise my other, now dangling foot ... and couldn't do it fast enough. Another direct hit crunched on my ankle and I knew, that time, that there was damage.

The air about my head seemed to hiss with hooves and the horse was beginning a high bubbling whinny. Surely someone, I thought desperately, someone would hear the crashing and banging and come ...

I could see him in flashes against the window, a rearing, bucking, kicking, rocketting nightmare. He came wheeling round, half seen, walking on his hind legs, head hard against the ceiling, the forelegs thrashing as if trying to climb invisible walls ... and he knocked me off my precarious perch with a swiping punch in the chest that had half a ton of weight behind it and no particular aim.

I fell twisting onto the straw and tried to curl my head away from those lethal feet, to save instinctively one's face and gut ... and leave backbone and kidney to their fate. Another crashing thud landed on the back of my shoulder and jarred like a hammer through every bone, andI could feel a scream forming somewhere inside me, a wrenching cry for mercy, for escape, for an end to battering, for release from terror.

His mania if anything grew worse, and it was he who was finally screaming, not me. The noise filled my ears, bounced off the walls, stunning, mind-blowing, the roaring of furies.

He somehow got one hoof inside my rolled body and tumbled me fast over, and I could see him arching above me, the tendons like strings, the torment in him too, the rage of the gods bursting from his stretched throat, his forelegs so high that he was hitting the ceiling.

This is death, I thought. This is dreadful, pulverising extinction. Only for this second would I see and feel ... and one of his feet would land on my head and I'd go ... I'd go ...

Before I'd even finished the thought his forelegs came crashing down with a hoof so close it brushed my hair; and then again, as if driven beyond endurance, he reared dementedly on his hind legs, the head going up like a reverse thunderbolt towards the sky, the skull meeting the ceiling with the force of a ram. The whole building shook with the impact, and the horse, his voice cut off, fell in a huge collapsing mass across my legs, spasms shuddering through his body, muscles jerking in stiff kicks, the air still ringing with the echoes of extremity.

He was dying in stages, unconscious, reluctant, the brain finished, the nerve messages still passing to convulsing muscles, turmoil churning without direction in stomach and gut, the head already inert on the straw.

An age passed before it was done. Then the heavy body fell flaccid, all systems spent, and lay in perpetual astonishing silence, pinning me beneath.

The relief of finding him dead and myself alive lasted quite a long time, but then, as always happens with the human race, simple gratitude for existence progressed to discontent that things weren't better.

He had fallen with his spine towards me, his bulk lying across my legs from my knees down; and getting out from under him was proving an impossibility.

The left ankle, which felt broken, protested screechingly at any attempted movement. I couldn't lift my arm for the same reason. There was acute soreness in my chest, making breathing itself painful and coughing frightful; and the only good thing I could think of was that I was lying on my back and not face down in the straw.

515

A very long time passed very slowly. The crushing weight of the horse slowly numbed my legs altogether and transferred the chief area of agony to thw whole of my left arm, which I might have thought totally mangled if I hadn't been able to see it dimly lying there looking the same as usual, covered in blue sweater, white cuff slightly showing, hand with clean nails, gold watch on wrist.

Physical discomfort for a while shut out much in the way of thought, but eventually I began to add up memories and ask questions, and the biggest, most immediate question was what would Calder do when he came back and found me alive.

He wouldn't expect it. No one could really expect anyone to survive being locked in with a mad horse, and the fact that I had was a trick of fate.

I remembered him giving the horse an apple while I'd struggled within the spinning walls to stand up. Giving his apple so routinely, and patting the horse's neck.

I remember Calder saying on my first visit that he gave his remedies to horses in hollowed-out apples. But this time it had been no remedy, this time something opposite, this time a drug to make crazy, to turn a normal steel-shod horse into a killing machine.

What had he said when he'd first found me conscious? Those bizarre words ... 'I thought you'd be out. I thought you wouldn't know ...' And something else ... 'I wish I'd hit you harder, but it seemed enough.'

He had said also that he was sorry, that he wished I hadn't come ... He hadn't meant, I thought, that I should be aware of it when the horse killed me. At the very least, he hadn't meant me to see and hear and suffer that death. But also, when he found me awake, it hadn't prevented him from *then* giving the apple, although he knew that I *would* see, *would* hear, would ... suffer.

The horse hadn't completed the task. When Calder returned, he would make good the deficit. It was certain.

I tried, on that thought, again to slide my legs out, though how much it would have helped if I had succeeded was debateable. It was as excrutiating as before, since the numbness proved temporary. I concluded somewhat sadly that dragging a broken ankle from beneath a dead horse was no jolly entertainment, and in fact, given the state of the rest of me couldn't be done.

I had never broken any bones before, not even ski-ing. I'd never been injured beyond the transient bumps of childhood. Never been to hospital, never troubled a surgeon, never slept from anaesthetic. For thirty-four years I'd been thoroughly healthy and, apart from chicken-pox and such, never ill. I even had good teeth.

I was unprepared in a way for the onslaught of so much pain all at once, and also not quite sure how to deal with it. All I knew was that when I tried to pull out my ankle the protests throughout my body brought actual tears into my eyes and no amount of theoretical resolution could give me the power to continue. I wondered if what I felt was cowardice. I didn't much care if it was. I lay with everything stiffening and getting cold and worse, and I'd have given a good deal to be as oblivious as the horse.

The oblong of window at length began to lighten towards the new day; Saturday, June 2nd. Calder would come back and finish the job, and no reasonable pathologist would swear the last blow had been delivered hours after the first. Calder would say in bewilderment, 'But I had no idea Tim was coming to see me ... I was in London for the television ... I have no idea how he came to shut himself into one of the boxes ... because it's just possible to do that, you know, if you're not careful.... I've no idea why the horse should have kicked him, because he's a placid old boy, as you can see ... the whole thing's a terrible accident, and I'm shattered ... most distressed ...', and anyone would look at the horse from whose bloodstream the crazing drug would have departed and conclude that I'd been pretty unintelligent and also unlucky, and too bad.

Ian Pargetter's veterinary case had gone to a securer hiding place or to destruction, and there would be only a slight chance left of proving Calder a murderer. Whichever way one considered it, the outlook was discouraging.

I couldn't be bothered to roll my wrist over to see the time. The sun rose and shone slantingly through the bars with the pale brilliance of dawn. It had to be five o'clock, or after.

Time drifted. The sun moved away. The horse and I lay in intimate silence, dead and half dead; waiting.

517

A car drove up fast outside and doors slammed.

It will be now, I thought, Now. Very soon.

There were voices in the distance, calling to each other. Female and male. *Strangers*.

Not Calder's distinctive, loud, edgy, public voice. Not his at all.

Hope thumped back with a tremendous surge and I called out myself, saying 'Here ... Come here,' but it was at best a croak, inaudible beyond the door.

Suppose they were looking for Calder, and when they didn't find him, drove away ... I took all possible breath into my lungs and yelled 'Help ... Come here.'

Nothing happened. My voice ricocheted off the walls and mocked me, and I dragged in another grinding lungful and shouted again ... and again ... and again.

The top half of the door swung outward and let in a dazzle of light and a voice yelled incredulously, 'He's *here*. He's in here ...'

The bolt on the lower half-door clattered and the daylight grew to an oblong, and against the light three figures appeared, coming forward, concerned, speaking with anxiety and joy and bringing life.

Judith and Gordon and Pen.

Judith was gulping and so I think was I.

'Thank God,' Gordon said. 'Thank God.'

'You didn't go home,' Pen said. 'We were worried.'

'Are you all right?' Judith said.

'Not really ... but everything's relative. I've never been happier, so who cares.'

'If we put our arms under your shoulders,' Gordon said, surveying the problem, 'We should be able to pull you out.'

'Don't do that,' I said.

'Why not?'

'One shoulder feels broken. Get a knacker.'

'My dear Tim,' he said, puzzled.

'They'll come with a lorry ... and a winch. Their job is dead horses.'

'Yes, I see.'

'And an ambulance,' Pen said. 'I should think.'

I smiled at them with much love, my fairly incompetent

saviours. They asked how I'd got where I was, and to their horror I briefly told them: and I in turn asked why they'd come, and they explained that they'd been worried because Calder's television programme had been cancelled.

'Micky Bonwith was taken ill,' Pen said. 'They just announced it during the evening. There would be no live Micky Bonwith show, just an old recording, very sorry, expect Calder Jackson at a later date.'

'Pen telephoned and told us where you were going, and why,' Judith said.

'And we were worried,' Gordon added.

'You didn't go home ... didn't telephone,' Pen said.

'We've been awake all night,' Gordon said. 'The girls were growing more and more anxious ... so we came.'

They'd come a hundred miles. You couldn't ask for better friends.

Gordon drove away to find a public telephone and Pen asked if I'd found what I'd come for.

'I don't know,' I said. 'Half the things had no labels.'

'Don't talk any more,' Judith said. Enough is enough.'

'I might as well.'

'Take your mind off it,' Pen nodded, understanding.

'What time is it?' I asked.

Judith looked at her watch. 'Ten to eight.'

'Calder will come back ...' And the lads too, I thought. He'd come when the lads turned up for work. About that time. He'd need witnesses to the way he'd found me.

'Tim,' Pen said with decision, 'if he's coming ... Did you take any samples? Did you get a chance?'

I nodded weakly.

'I suppose you can't remember what they were ...'

'I hid them.'

'Wouldn't he have found them?' She was gentle and prepared to be disappointed; careful not to blame.

I smiled at her. 'He didn't find them. They're here.'

She looked blankly round the box and then at my face. 'Didn't he search you?' She said in surprise. 'Pockets ... of course, he would.'

'I don't know ... but he didn't find the pills.'

'Then where *are* they?'

'I learned from Ginnie about keeping your hands free,' I said. 'They're in a plastic bag ... below my waistband ... inside my pants.'

They stared incredulously, and then they laughed, and Judith with tears in her eyes said, 'Do you mean ... all the time ...?'

'All the time,' I agreed. 'And go easy getting them out.'

Some things would be best forgotten but are impossible to forget, and I reckon one could put the next half hour into that category: at the end of it I lay on a table-like stretcher in the open air, and my dead-weight pal was half up the ramp of the knacker's van that Gordon with exceptional persuasiveness had conjured out at that hour of the morning.

The three lads who had at length arrived for work stood around looking helpless, and the two ambulance men, who were not paramedics, were farcically trying to get an answer on a radio with transmission troubles as to where they were supposed to take me.

Gordon was telling the knacker's men that I said it was essential to remove a blood sample from the horse and that the carcass was not to be disposed of until that was done. Judith and Pen both looked tired, and were yawning. I wearily watched some birds wheeling high in the fair blue sky and wished I were up there with them, as light as air; and into this rivetting tableau drove Calder.

Impossible to know what he thought when he saw all the activity, but as he came striding from his car his mouth formed an oval of apprehension and shock.

He seemed first to fasten his attention on Gordon, and then on the knacker's man who was saying loudly, 'If you want a blood sample you'll have to give us a written authorisation, because of calling in a vet and paying him.'

Calder looked from him to the dead horse still halfway up the ramp, and from there towards the horse's normal box, where the door stood wide open.

From there he turned with bewilderment to Judith, and then with horror saw the bag Pen held tightly, the transparent plastic bag with the capsules, pills and other assorted treasures showing clearly inside.

Pen remarkably found her voice and in words that must have

sounded like doom to Calder said, 'I didn't tell you before …
I'm a pharmacist.'

'Where did you get that?' Calder said, staring at the bag as if
his eyes would burn it. 'Where …'

'Tim had it.'

Her gaze went to me and Calder seemed finally to realise that
my undoubted stillness was not that of death. He took two
paces towards the stretcher and looked down at my face and
saw me alive, awake, aware.

Neither of us spoke. His eyes seemed to retreat in the sockets
and the shape of the upper jaw stood out starkly. He saw in me
I dare say the ravages of the night and I saw in him the
realisation become certainty that my survival meant his ruin.

I thought: you certainly should have hit harder; and maybe
he thought it too. He looked at me with a searing intensity that
defied analysis and then turned abruptly away and walked with
jerky steps back to his car.

Gordon took two or three hesitant steps towards perhaps
stopping him, but Calder without looking back started his
engine, put his foot on the accelerator and with protesting tyres
made a tight semi-circular turn and headed for the gate.

'We should get the police,' Gordon said, watching him go.

Judith and Pen showed scant enthusiasm and I none at all. I
supposed we would have to bring in the police in the end, but
the longer the boring rituals could be postponed, from my point
of view, the better. Britain was a small-island, and Calder too
well-known to go far.

Pen looked down at the plastic store-house in her hands and
then without actual comment opened her handbag and put the
whole thing inside. She glanced briefly at me and smiled faintly,
and I nodded with relief that she and her friends would have the
unravelling of the capsules to themselves.

On that same Saturday, at about two-thirty in the afternoon, a
family of picnickers came across a car which had been parked
out of sight of any road behind some clumps of gorse bushes.
The engine of the car was running and the children of the
family, peering through the windows, saw a man slumped on
the back seat with a tube in his mouth.

They knew him because of his curly hair, and his beard.

521

The children were reported to be in a state of hysterical shock and the parents were angry, as if some authority, somewhere or other, should prevent suicides spoiling the countryside.

Tributes to Calder's miracle-working appeared on television that evening, and I thought it ironic that the master who had known so much about drugs should have chosen to gas his way out.

He had driven barely thirty miles from his yard. He had left no note. The people who had been working with him on the postponed Micky Bonwith show said they couldn't understand it, and Dissdale telephoned Oliver to say that in view of Calder's tragic death he would have to withdraw his offer for Sandcastle.

I, by the time I heard all this, was half covered in infinitely irritating plaster of paris, there being more grating edes of bone inside me than I cared to hear about, and horse-shoe-shaped crimson bruises besides.

I had been given rather grudgingly a room to myself, privacy in illness being considered a sinful luxury in the national health service, and on Monday evening Pen came all the way from London again to report on the laboratory findings.

She frowned after she'd kissed me. 'You look exhausted,' she said.

'Tiring place, hospital.'

'I suppose it must be. I'd never thought ...'

She put a bunch of roses in my drinking-water jug and said they were from Gordon and Judith's garden.

'They send their love,' she said chattily, 'and their garden's looking lovely.'

'Pen ...'

'Yes. Well.' She pulled the visitor's chair closer to the bed upon which I half sat, half lay in my plaster and borrowed dressing gown on top of the blankets. 'You have really, as they say, hit the jackpot.'

'Do you mean it?' I exclaimed.

She grinned cheerfully. 'It's no wonder that Calder killed himself, not after seeing you alive and hearing you were going to get the dead horse tested, and knowing that after all you had taken all those things from his surgery. It was either that or years in jail and total disgrace.'

'A lot of people would prefer disgrace.'

'Not Calder, though.'

'No.'

She opened a slim black briefcase on her knees and produced several typewritten pages.

'We worked all yesterday and this morning,' she sid, 'But first I'll tell you that Gordon got the dead horse's blood test done immediately at the Equine Research Establishment and they told him on the telephone this morning that the horse had been given ethyl isobutrazine, which was contrary to normal veterinary practice.'

'You don't say.'

Her eyes gleamed. 'The Research people told Gordon that any horse given ethyl isobutrazine would go utterly berserk and literally try to climb the walls.'

'That's just what he did,' I said soberly.

'It's a drug which is used all the time as a tranquilliser to stop dogs barking or getting car-sick, but it has an absolutely manic effect on horses. One of its brand names if Diquel, in case you're interested. All the veterinary books warn against giving it to horses.'

'But normally ... in a horse ... it would wear off?'

'Yes, in six hours or so, with no trace.'

Six hours, I thought bleakly. *Six hours* ...

'In your bag of goodies,' Pen said, 'guess what we found? Three tablets of Diquel.'

'Really?'

She nodded. 'Really. And now pin back your ears, dearest Tim, because when we found what Calder had been doing, words simply failed us.'

They seemed indeed to fail her again, for she sat looking at the pages with a faraway expression.

'You remember,' she said at last, 'when we went to Calder's yard that time at Easter, we saw a horse that had been bleeding in its urine ... crystalluria was what he called it ... that antibiotics hadn't been able to cure?'

'Yes,' I said. 'Other times too, he cured horses with that.'

'Mm. And those patients had been previously treated by Ian Pargetter before he died, hadn't they?'

I thought back. 'Some of them, certainly.'

'Well ... you know you told me before they carted you off in the ambulance on Saturday that some of the jars of capsules in the cupboards were labelled only with letters like a + w, b + w, and c + s?'

I nodded.

'Three capsules each with one transparent and one blue end, *did* contain c and s. Vitamin C, and sulphanilamide.' She looked at me for a possible reaction, but Vitamin C and sulphanilamide sounded quite harmless, and I said so.

'Yes,' she said, 'seperately they do nothing but good, but *together they can cause crystalluria.*'

I stared at her.

'Calder had made those capsules expressly to *cause the horse's illness* in the first place, so that he could "cure" it afterwards. And then the only miracle he'd have to work would be to stop giving the capsules.'

'My God,' I said.

She nodded. 'We could hardly believe it. It meant, you see, that Ian Pargetter almost certainly *knew*. Because it was he, you see, who could have given the horse's trainer or owner or lad or whatever a bottle of capsules labelled "antibiotic" to dole out every day. And those capsules were precisely what was making the horse ill.'

'*Pen!*'

'I'd better explain just a little, if you can bear it,' she said. 'If you give sulpha drugs to anyone — horse or person — who doesn't need them, you won't do much harm because urine is normally slightly alkaline or only slightly acid and you'll get rid of the sulpha safely. But vitamin C is ascorbic acid and makes the urine *more* acid, and the acid works with sulpha drugs to form crystals, and the crystals cause pain and bleeding ... like powdered glass.'

There was a fairly long silence, and then I said, 'It's diabolical.'

She nodded. 'Once Calder had the horse in his yard he could speed up the cure by giving him bicarbonate of soda, which will make the urine alkaline again and also dissolve the crystals, and with plenty of water to drink the horse would be well in no time. Miraculously fast, in fact.' She paused and smiled, and went on, 'We tested a few more things which were perfectly harmless

524

herbal remedies and then we came to three more homemade capsules, with pale green ends this time, and we reckon that they were your a + w.'

'Go on, then,' I said. 'What's a, and what's w?'

'A is antibiotic, and w is warfarin. And before you ask, warfarin is a drug used in humans for reducing the clotting ability of the blood.'

'That pink pill you found on the surgery floor,' I said. 'That's what you said.'

'Oh yes.' She looked surprised. 'So I did. I'd forgotten. Well ... if you give certain antibiotics *with* warfarin you increase the effect of the warfarin to the extent that blood will hardly clot at all ... and you get severe bleeding from the stomach, from the mouth, from anywhere where a small blood-vessel breaks ... when normally it would clot and mend at once.'

I let out a held breath. 'Every time I went, there was a bleeder.'

She nodded. 'Warfarin acts by drastically reducing the effect of vitamin K, which is needed for normal clotting, so all Calder had to do to reverse things was feed lots of vitamin K ... which is found in large quantities in alfalfa.'

'And b + w?' I asked numbly.

'Barbiturate and warfarin. Different mechanism, but if you used them together and then stopped just the barbiturate, you could cause a sort of delayed bleeding about three weeks later.' She paused. 'We've all been looking up our pharmacology textbooks, and there are warnings there, plain to see if you're looking for them, about prescribing antibiotics or barbiturates or indeed phenylbutazone or anabolic steroids for people on warfarin without carefully adjusting the warfarin dosage. And you see,' she went on, 'putting two drugs together in one capsule was really brilliant, because no one would think they were giving a horse two drugs, but just one ... and we reckon Ian Pargetter could have put Calder's capsules into any regular bottle, and the horse's owner would think that he was giving the horse what it said on the label.'

I blinked. 'It's incredible.'

'It's easy,' she said. 'And it gets easier as it goes on.'

'There's more?'

'Sure there's more.' She grinned. 'How about all those poor

animals with extreme debility who were so weak they could hardly walk?'

I swallowed. 'How about them?'

'You said you found a large bottle in Ian Pargetter's case with only a few pills in it? A bottle labelled "diuretic", or in other words, pills designed to increase the passing of urine?'

I nodded.

'Well, we identified the ones you took, and if you simply gave those particular thiazide diuretic pills over a long period to a horse you would cause *exactly* the sort of general progressive debility shown by those horses.'

I was past speech.

'And to cure the debility,' she said, 'you just stop the diuretics and provide good food and water. And hey presto!' She smiled blissfully. 'Chemically, it's so elegant. The debility is caused by constant excessive excretion of potassium which the body needs for strength, and the cure is to restore potassium as fast as safely possible ... with potassium salts, which you can buy anywhere.'

I gazed at her with awe.

She was enjoying her revelations. 'We come now to the horses with non-healing ulcers and sores.'

Always those, too, in the yard, I thought.

'Ulcers and sores are usually cleared up fairly quickly by applications of antibiotic cream. Well ... by this time we were absolutely bristling with suspicions, so last of all we took the little tube of antibiotic cream you found in Ian Pargetter's case, and we tested it. And lo and behold, it didn't contain antibiotic cream at all.'

'What them?'

'Cortisone cream.'

She looked at my non-comprehension and smiled. 'Cortisone cream is fine for eczema and allergies, but *not* for general healing. In fact, if you scratched a horse and smeared some dirt into the wound to infect it and then religiously applied cortisone cream twice a day you would get a nice little ulcer which would never heal. Until, of course, you sent your horse to Calder, who would lay his hands upon your precious ... and apply antibiotics at once, to let normal healing begin.'

'Dear God in heaven.'

'Never put cortisone cream on a cut,' she said. 'A lot of people do. It's stupid.'

'I never will,' I said fervently.

Pen grinned. 'They always fill toothpaste from the blunt end. We looked very closely and found that the end of the tube had been unwound and then re-sealed. Very neat.'

She seemed to have stopped, so I asked 'Is that the lot?'

'That's the lot.'

We sat for a while and pondered.

'It does answer an awful lot of questions,' I said finally.

'Such as?'

'Such as why Calder killed Ian Pargetter,' I said. 'Ian Pargetter wanted to stop something ... which must have been this illness caper. Said he'd had enough. Said also that he would stop Calder too, which must have been his death warrant.'

Pen said, 'Is that what Calder actually told you?'

'Yes, that's what he said, but at the time I didn't understand what he meant.'

'I wonder,' Pen said, 'why Ian Pargetter wanted to stop altogether? They must have had a nice steady income going between the two of them. Calder must have recruited him years ago.'

'Selenium,' I said.

'What?'

'Selenium was different. Making horses ill in order to cure them wasn't risking much permanent damage, if any at all. But selenium would be forever. The foals would be deformed. I'd guess when Calder suggested it the idea sickened Ian Pargetter. Revolted him, probably, because he was after all a vet.'

'And Calder wanted to go on with it all ... enough to kill.'

I nodded. 'Calder would have had his sights on a fortune as well as an income. And but for Ginnie somehow getting hold of that shampoo, he would very likely have achieved it.'

'I wonder how she did,' Pen said.

'Mm.' I shifted uncomfortably on the bed. 'I've remembered the name of the lad Calder had who looked like Ricky Barnet. It was Jason. I remembered it the other night ... in that yard ... funny the way the mind works.'

'What about him?' Pen said sympathetically.

'I remembered Calder saying he gave the pills to Jason for

527

Jason to give to the horses. The herb pills, he meant. But with Ian Pargetter gone, Calder would have needed someone else to give those double-edged capsules to horses ... because he still had horses in his yard with those same troubles long after Ian Pargetter was dead.'

'So he did,' she said blandkly. 'Except....'

'Except what?'

'Only that when we got to the yard last Saturday, before I heard you calling, we looked into several other boxes, and there weren't many horses there. The place wasn't full, like it had been.'

'I should think,' I said slowly, 'that it was because Jason had been busy working for three months or more at Oliver's farm, feeding selenium in apples.'

A visual memory flashed in my brain. *Apples* ... Shane, the stable lad, walking across the yard, swinging a bucket and eating an apple. Shane, Jason: one and the same.

'What is it?' Pen said.

'Photos of Ricky Barnet.'

'Oh yes.'

'They say I can leave here tomorrow,' I said, 'if I insist.'

She looked at me with mock despair. 'What exactly did you break?'

'They said this top lot was scapula, clavicle, humerus, sternum and ribs. Down there,' I pointed, 'they lost me. I didn't know there *were* so many bones in one ankle.'

'Did they pin it?'

'God knows.'

'How will you look after yourself?'

'In my usual clumsy fashion.'

'Don't be silly,' she said. 'Stay until it stops hurting.'

'That might be weeks ... there's some problem with ligaments or tendons or something.'

'What problem?'

'I didn't really listen.'

'*Tim*.' She was exasperated.

'Well ... it's so boring,' I said.

She gave an eyes-to-heaven laugh. 'I brought you a present from my shop.' She dug into her handbag. 'Here you are, with my love.'

528

I took the small white box she offered, and looked at the label on its side.

Comfrey, it said.

She grinned. 'You might as well try it,' she said. 'Comfrey does contain allantoin, which helps to knit bones. And you never know ... Calder really was an absolute expert with all sorts of drugs.'

* * *

On Tuesday, June 4th, Oliver Knowles collected me from the hospital to drive me on some errands and then take me to his home, not primarily as an act of compassion but mostly to talk business. I had expected him to accept my temporary disabilities in a straightforward and unemotional manner, and so he did, although he did say dryly when he saw me that when I had invited myself over the telephone I had referred to a 'crack or two' and not to half an acre of plaster with clothes strung on in patches.

'Never mind,' I said. 'I can hop and I can sit and my right arm is fine.'

'Yes. So I see.'

The nurse who had wheeled me in a chair to his car said however, 'He can't hop, it jars him,' and handed Oliver a slip of paper. 'There's a place along the road ...' she pointed, '... where you can hire wheel-chairs.' To me she said, 'Get a comfortable one. And one which lets your leg lie straight out, like this one. You'll ache less. All right?'

'All right,' I said.

'Hm. Well ... take care.'

She helped me into the car with friendly competence and went away with the hospital transport, and Oliver and I did as she advised, storing the resulting cushioned and chromium comfort into the boot of his car.

'Right,' I said. 'Then the next thing to do is buy a good instant camera and a stack of films.'

Oliver found a shop and bought the camera while I sat in the front passenger seat as patiently as possible.'

'Where next?' he said, coming back with parcels.

'Cambridge. An engineering works. Here's the address.' I handed him the piece of paper on which I'd written Ricky

Barnet's personal directions. 'We're meeting him when he comes out of work.'

'Who?' Oliver said. 'Who are we meeting?'

'You'll see.'

We parked across the road from the firm's gate and waited, and at four-thirty on the dot the exodus occurred.

Ricky Barnet came out and looked this way and that in searching for us, and beside me I heard Oliver stir and say, 'But that's Shane' in surprise, and then relax and add doubtfully, 'No it isn't.'

'No, it isn't.' I leaned out of the open window and called to him 'Ricky ... over here.'

He crossed the road and stopped beside the car.

'Hop in,' I said.

'You been in an accident?' he said disbelievingly.

'Sort of.'

He climbed into the back of the car. He hadn't been too keen to have his photograph taken for the purpose I'd outlined, but he was in no great position to refuse; and I'd made my blackmailing pressure sound like honey, which I wasn't too bad at, in my way. He still wasn't pleased however, which had its own virtues, as the last thing I wanted was forty prints of him grinning.

Oliver drove off and stopped where I asked at a suitably neutral background — a grey-painted factory wall — and he said he would take the photographs if I explained what I wanted.

'Ricky looks like Shane,' I said. 'So take pictures of Ricky in the way he *most* looks like Shane. Get him to turn his head slowly like he did when he came out of work, and tell him to hold it where it's best.'

'All right.'

Ricky got out of the car and stood in front of the wall, with Oliver focussing at head-and-shoulder distance. He took the first picture and we waited for it to develop.

Oliver looked at it, grunted, adjusted the light meter, and tried again.

'This one's all right,' he said, watching the colours emerge. 'Looks like Shane. Quite amazing.'

With a faint shade of sullenness Ricky held his pose for as

530

long as it took to shoot four boxes of film. Oliver passed each print to me as it came out of the camera, and I laid them in rows along the seat beside me while they developed.

'That's fine,' I said, when the films were finished. 'Thank you, Ricky.'

He came over to the car window and I asked him without any great emphasis, 'Do you remember, when Indian Silk got so ill with debility, which vet was treating him?'

'Yeah, sure, that fellow that was murdered. Him and his partners. The best, Dad said.'

I nodded non-committally. 'Do you want a ride to New-market?'

'Got my motor-bike, thanks.'

We took him back to his engineering works where I finally cheered him up with payment for his time and trouble, and watched while he roared off with a flourish of self-conscious bravado.

'What's now?' Oliver said. 'Did you say Newmarket?'

I nodded. 'I've arranged to meet Ursula Young.'

He gave me a glance of bewilderment and drove without protest, pulling duly into the mid-town car park where Ursula had said to come.

We arrived there first, the photography not having taken as long as I'd expected, and Oliver finally gave voice to a long restrained question.

'Just what,' he sid.' 'Are the photographs *for*?'

'For finding Shane.'

'But why?'

'Don't explode.'

'No.'

'Because I think he gave the selenium to your mares.'

Oliver sat very still. 'You asked about him before,' he said. 'I did wonder ... if you thought ... he killed Ginnie.'

It was my own turn for quiet.

'I don't know if he did,' I said at last. 'I don't know.'

Ursula arrived in her car with a rush, checking her watch and apologising all the same, although she was on time. She, like Oliver and Ricky, looked taken aback at my unorthodox attire, but rallied in her usual no-nonsense fashion and shuffled into the back seat of Oliver's car, leaning forward to bring her face

531

on a level with ours.

I passed her thirty of the forty pictures of Ricky Barnet, who of course she knew immediately.

'Yes, but,' I explained, 'Ricky looks like a lad who worked for Oliver, and it's *that* lad we want to find.'

'Well, all right. How important is it?'

Oliver answered her before I could. 'Ursula, if you find him, we might be able to prove there's nothing wrong with Sandcastle. And don't ask me how, just believe it.'

Her mouth had opened.

'And Ursula,' Oliver said, 'if you find him — Shane, that lad — I'll put business your way for the rest of my life.'

I could see that to her, a middle-rank bloodstock agent, it was no mean promise.

'All right,' she said briskly. 'You're on. I'll start spreading the pictures about at once, tonight, and call you with results.'

'Ursula,' I said. 'If you find where he is now, make sure he isn't frightened off. We don't want to lose him.'

She looked at me shrewdly. 'This is roughly police work?'

I nodded. 'Also, if you find anyone who employed him in the past, ask if by any chance a horse he looked after fell ill. Or any horse in the yard, for that matter. And don't give him a name … he isn't always called Shane.'

'Is he dangerous?' she said straightly.

'We don't want him challenged,' I said. 'Just found.'

'All right. I trust you both, so I'll do my best. And I suppose one day you'll explain what it's all about?'

'If he's done what we think,' I said, 'we'll make sure the whole world knows. You can count on it.'

She smiled briefly and patted my unplastered shoulder. 'You look grey,' she said, and to Oliver, 'Tim told me a horse kicked him and broke his arm. Is that right?'

'He told me that, too.'

'And what else?' she asked me astringently. 'How did you get in this state?'

'The horse didn't know its own strength.' I smiled at her. 'Clumsy brute.'

She knew I was dodging in some way, but she lived in a world where the danger of horse kicks was ever present and always to be avoided, and she made no more demur. Stowing the photographs in her capacious handbag she wriggled her way out of the car, and with assurances of action drove off in her own.

'What now?' Oliver said.

'A bottle of scotch.'

He gave me an austere look which then swept over my general state and softened to understanding.

'Can you wait until we get home?' he said.

That evening, bit by bit, I told Oliver about Pen's analysis of the treasures from Calder's surgery and of Calder's patients' drug-induced illnesses. I told him that Calder had killed Ian Pargetter, and why, and I explained again how the idea of first discrediting, then buying and re-building Sandcastle had followed the pattern of Indian Silk.

'There may be others besides Indian Silk that we haven't heard of,' I said thoughtfully. 'Show jumpers, eventers, even prize ponies. You never know. Dissdale might have gone along more than twice with his offer to buy the no-hoper.'

'He withdrew his offer for Sandcastle the same night Calder died.'

'What exactly did he say?' I asked.

'He was very upset. Said he'd lost his closest friend, and that without Calder to work his miracles there was no point in buying Sandcastle.'

I frowned. 'Do you think it was genuine?'

'His distress? Yes, certainly.'

'And the belief in miracles?'

'He did *sound* as if he believed.'

I wondered if it was in the least possible that Dissdale was an innocent and duped accomplice and hadn't known that his bargains had been first made ill. His pride in knowing the Great Man had been obvious at Ascot, and perhaps he had been flattered and foolish but not wicked after all.

Oliver asked in the end how I'd found out about the drug-induced illnesses and Ian Pargetter's murder,and I told him that too, as flatly as possible.

He sat staring at me, his gaze on the plaster.

'You're very lucky to be in a wheel-chair, and not a coffin.' he said. 'Damn lucky.'

'Yes.'

He poured more of the brandy we had progressed to after dinner. Anaesthesia was coming along nicely.

'I'm almost beginning to believe,' he said, 'That somehow or other I'll still be here next year, even if I do have to sell Sandcastle and whatever else is necessary.'

I drank from my replenished glass. 'Tomorrow we'll make a plan contingent upon Sandcastle's being reinstated in the eyes of the world. Look out the figures, see what the final damage is likely to be, draw up a time scale for recovery. I can't promise because it isn't my final say-so, but if the bank gets all its money in the end, it'll most likely be flexible about when.'

'Good of you,' Oliver said, hiding emotion behind his clipped martial manner.

'Frankly,' I said, 'you're more use to us salvaged than bust.'

He smiled sryly. 'A banker to the last drop of blood.'

Because of stairs being difficult I slept on the sofa where Ginnie had dozed on her last afternoon, and I dreamed of her walking up a path towards me looking happy. Not a significant dream, but an awakening of fresh regret. I spent a good deal of the following day thinking of her instead of concentrating on profit and loss.

In the evening Ursula telephoned with triumph in her strong voice and also a continual undercurrent of amazement.

'You won't believe it,' she said, 'but I've already found three racing stables in Newmarket where he worked last summer and autumn, and in *every case* one of the horses in the yard fell sick!'

I hadn't any trouble at all with belief and asked what sort of sickness.

'They all had crystalluria. That's crystals ...'

'I know what it is,' I said.

'And ... it's absolutely incredible ... but all three were in stables which had in the past sent horses to Calder Jackson, and these were sent as well, and he cured them straight away. Two of the trainers said they would swear by Calder, he had cured horses for them for years.'

'Was the lad called Shane?' I asked.

'No. Bret. Bret Williams. The same in all three places.'

She dictated the addresses of the stables, the names of the trainers, and the dates (approximate) when Shane — Jason —

534

Bret had been in their yards

'These lads just come and go,' she said. 'He didn't work for any of them for as long as a month. Just didn't turn up one morning. It happens all the time.'

'You're marvellous,' I said.

'I have a feeling,' she said with less excitement, 'that what I'm telling you is what you expected to hear.'

'Hoped.'

'The implications are unbelievable.'

'Believe them.'

'But *Calder*,' she protested. 'He couldn't ...'

'Shane worked for Calder,' I said. 'All the time. Permanently. Wherever he went, it was to manufacture patients for Calder.'

She was silent so long that in the end I said 'Ursula?'

'I'm here,' she said. 'Do you want me to go on with the photos?'

'Yes, if you would. To find him.'

'Hanging's too good for him,' she said grimly. 'I'll do what I can.'

She disconnected, and I told Oliver what she'd said.

'Bret Williams? He was Shane Williams here.'

'How did you come to employ him?' I asked.

Oliver frowned, looking back. 'Good lads aren't that easy to find, you know. You can advertise until you're blue in the face and only get third- or fourth-rate applicants. But Nigel said Shane impressed him at the interview and that we should give him a month's trial, and of course after that we kept him on, and took him back gladly this year when he telephoned asking, because he was quick and competent and knew the job backwards, and was polite and a good time-keeper ...'

'A parágon.' I said dryly.

'As lads go, yes.'

I nodded. He would have to have been good; to have taken pride in his deception, with the devotion of all traitors. I considered those fancy names and thought that he must have seen himself as a sort of macho hero, the great foreign agent playing out his fantasies in the day to day tasks, feeling superior to him employers while he tricked them with contempt.

He could have filled the hollowed cores of apples with

capsules, and taken a bit or two round the outside to convince, and fed what looked like remainders to his victims. No one would ever have suspected, because suspicion was impossible.

I slept again on the sofa and the following morning Oliver telephoned to Detective Chief Inspector Wyfold and asked him to come to the farm. Wyfold needed persuading; reluctantly agreed; and nearly walked out in a U-turn when he saw me waiting in Oliver's office.

'No. Look,' he protested, 'Mr Ekaterin's already approached me with his ideas and I simply haven't time ...'

Oliver interrupted. 'We have a great deal more now. Please do listen. We quite understand that you are busy with all those other poor girls, but at the very least we can take Ginnie off that list for you.'

Wyfold finally consented to sit down and accept some coffee and listen to what we had to say: and as we told him in turns and in detail what had been happening his air of impatience dissipated and his natural sharpness took over.

We gave him copies of Pen's analyses, the names of 'Bret's' recent employers and the last ten photographs of Ricky. He glanced at them briefly and said, 'We interviewed this groom, but ...'

'No, you didn't,' Oliver said. 'The photo is of a boy who looks like him if you don't know either of them well.'

Wyfold pursed his lips, but nodded. 'Fair enough.'

'We do think he may have killed Ginnie, even if you couldn't prove it,' Oliver said.

Wyfold began putting together the papers we'd given him. 'We will certainly redirect our enquiries,' he said, and giving me a dour look added, 'If you had left it to the police to search Calder's surgery, sir, Calder Jackson would not have had the opportunity of disposing of Ian Pargetter's case and any other material evidence. These things are always mishandled by amateurs.' He looked pointedly at my plaster jacket. 'Better have left it to the professionals.'

I gave him an amused look but Oliver was gasping. 'Left to you,' he said, 'there would have been no search at all ... or certainly not in time to save my business.'

Wyfold's expression said plainly that saving people's businesses wasn't his prime concern, but beyond mentioning that picking locks and stealing medicinal substances constituted a breach of the law he kept any further disapproval to himself.

He was on his feet ready to go when Ursula rang again, and he could almost hear every word she said because of her enthusiasm.

'I'm in Gloucestershire,' she shouted. 'I thought I'd work from the other end, if you see what I mean. I remembered Calder had miraculously cured Binty Rockingham's utterly brilliant three-day-eventer who was so weak he could hardly totter, so I came here to her house to ask her, and guess what?'

'What?' I asked obligingly.

'That lad worked for her!' The triumph exploded. 'A good lad, she says, would you believe it? He called himself Clint. She can't remember his last name, it was more than two years ago and he was only here a few weeks.'

'Ask her if it was Williams,' I said.

There was some murmuring at the other end and then Ursula's voice back again, 'She thinks so, yes.'

'You're a dear, Ursula,' I said.

She gave an unembarrassed laugh. 'Do you want me to go on down the road to Rube Golby's place? He had a show pony Calder cured a fair time ago of a weeping wound that wouldn't heal.'

'Just one more, then, Ursula. It's pretty conclusive already, I'd say.'

'Best to be sure,' she said cheerfully. 'And I'm enjoying myself, actually, now I'm over the shock.'

I wrote down the details she gave me and when she'd gone off the line I handed the new information to Wyfold.

'Clint,' he said with disillusion. 'Elvis next, I shouldn't wonder.'

I shook my head. 'A man of action, our Shane.'

Perhaps through needing to solve at least one murder while reviled for not catching his rapist, Wyfold put his best muscle into the search. It took him two weeks only to find Shane, who was arrested on leaving a pub in the racing village of Malton, Yorkshire, where he had been heard boasting several times about secret exploits of undisclosed daring.

Wyfold told Oliver, who telephoned me in the office, to

which I'd returned via a newly installed wheel-chair ramp up the front steps.

'He called himself Dean,' Oliver said. 'Dean Williams. It seems the police are transferring him from Yorkshire back here to Hertfordshire, and Wyfold wants you to come to his police headquarters to identify Shane as the man called Jason at Calder's yard.'

I said I would.

I didn't say that with honesty I couldn't.

'Tomorrow,' Oliver added. 'They're in a hurry because of holding him without a good enough charge, or something.'

'I'll be there.'

I went in a chauffeur-driven hired car, a luxury I seemed to have spent half my salary on since leaving Oliver's house.

I was living nearer the office than usual with a friend whose flat was in a block with a lift, not up stairs like my own. The pains in my immobile joints refused obstinately to depart, but owing to a further gift from Pen (via Gordon) were forgettable most of the time. A new pattern of 'normal' life had evolved, and all I dearly wanted was a bath.

I arrived at Wyfold's police station at the same time as Oliver, and together we were shown into an office. Oliver pushing me as if born to it. Two months minimum they'd warned me to expect of life on wheels. Even if my shoulder would be mended before then, it wouldn't stand my weight on crutches. Patience, I'd been told. Be patient. My ankle had been in bits and they'd restored it like a jig-saw puzzle and I couldn't expect miracles, they'd said.

Wyfold arrived, shook hands briskly (an advance) and said that this was not a normal identity parade, as of course Oliver knew Shane very well, and I obviously knew him also, because of Ricky Barnet.

'Just call him Jason,' Wyfold told me, 'If you are sure he's the same man you saw at Calder Jackson's.'

We left the office and went along a fiercely-lit institutional corridor to a large interview room which contained a table, three chairs, a uniformed policeman standing ... and Shane, sitting down.

He looked cocky, not cowed.

When he saw Oliver he tilted his head almost jauntily,

showing not shame but pride, not apology but a sneer. On me he looked with only a flickering glance, neither knowing me from our two brief meetings nor reckoning on trouble from my direction.

Wyfold raised his eyebrows to me to indicate the need for action.

'Hello, Jason,' I said.

His head snapped round immediately and this time he gave me a full stare.

'I met you at Calder Jackson's yard,' I said.

'You never did.'

Although I hadn't expected it. I remembered him clearly. 'You were giving sun-lamp treatment to a horse and Calder Jackson told you to put on your sunglasses.'

He made no more effort to deny it. 'What of it, then?' he said.

'Conclusive evidence of your link with the place, I should think,' I said.

Oliver, seeming as much outraged by Shane's lack of contrition as by his sins, turned with force to Wyfold and in half-controlled bitterness, 'Now prove he killed my daughter.'

'*What !*'

Shane had risen in panic to his feet, knocking his chair over behind him and losing in an instant the smart-alec assurance. 'I never did,' he said.

We all watched him with interest, and his gaze travelled fast from one face to another, seeing only assessment and disbelief and nowhere admiration.

'I didn't kill her,' he said, his voice hoarse and rising. 'I didn't. Straight up, I didn't. It was him. He did it.'

'Who?' I said.

'Calder. Mr Jackson. He did it. It was him, not me.' He looked across us all again with desperation. 'Look, I'm telling you the truth, straight up I am. I never killed her, it was him.'

Wyfold began telling him in a flat voice that he had a right to remain silent and that anything he said might be written down and used in evidence, but Shane wasn't clever and fright had too firm a hold. His fantasy world had vanished in the face of unimaginable reality, and I found myself believing every word he said.

539

'We didn't know she was there, see. She heard us talking, but we didn't know. And when I carried the stuff back to the hostel he saw her moving so he hit her. I didn't see him do it, I didn't but when I went back there he was with Ginnie on the ground and I said she was the boss's daughter, which he didn't even know, see, but he said all the worse if she was the boss's daughter because she must have been standing there in the shadow listening and she would have gone straight off and told everybody.'

The words, explanations, excuses came tumbling out in self-righteous urgency and Wyfold thankfully showed no signs of regulating the flow into the careful officialese of a formal statement. The uniformed policeman, now sitting behind Shane, was writing at speed in a notebook, recording, I imagined, the gist.

'I don't believe you,' Wyfold said impatiently. 'What did he hit her with?'

Shane redoubled his efforts of convince, and from then on I admired Wyfold's slyly effective interrogatory technique.

'With a fire extinguisher,' Shane said. 'He kept it in his car, see, and he had it in his hand. He was real fussy about fire always. Would never let anyone smoke anywhere near the stables. That Nigel ...' the sneer came back temporarily, ' ... the lads all smoked in the feed room, I ask you, behind his back. He'd no idea what went on.'

'Fire extinguisher ...' Wyfold spoke doubtfully, shaking his head.

'Yeah, it was. It was. One of them red things about this long.' Shane anxiously held up his hands about fifteen inches apart. 'With the nozzle, sort of, at the top. He was holding it by that, sort of swinging it. Ginnie was lying flat on the ground, face down, like, and I said, "What have you gone and done?" and he said she'd been listening.'

Wyfold sniffed.

'It was like that, straight up,' Shane said urgently.

'Listening to what?'

'We were talking about the stuff, see.'

'The shampoo ...'

'Yeah.' He seemed only briefly to feel the slightest alarm at the mention of it. 'I told him, see, that the stuff had really

540

worked because there'd been a foal born that morning with half a leg, that Nigel he tried to hush it up but by afternoon he was half cut and he told one of the lads so we all knew. So I told Mr Jackson and he said great, because it was time we'd heard, and there hadn't been a murmur in the papers and he was getting worried he hadn't got the dose right, or something. So anyway when I told him about the foal with the half a leg he laughed, see, he was so pleased, and he said this was probably the last lot I'd have to do, just do the six bottles he'd brought, and then scarper.'

Oliver looked very pale, with sweat along his hair-line and whitely clenched fists. His mouth was rigidly closed with the effort of self control, and he listened throughout without once interrupting or cursing.

'I took the six bottles off to the hostel but when I got there I'd only got five, so I went back to look for the one I'd dropped, but I forgot it, see, when I saw him standing there over Ginnie and him saying she'd heard us talking, and then he said for me to come with him down to the village in his car and he'd drop me at a pub where the other lads were, so as I couldn't have been back home killig the boss's daughter, see? I remembered about the bottle I'd dropped when we were on our way to the village but I didn't think he'd be best pleased and anyway I reckoned I'd find it all right when I went back, but I never did. I didn't think it would matter much, because no one would know what it was for, it was just dog shampoo, and anyway I reckoned I'd skip using the new bottles after all because of the fuss there would be over Ginnie. But if it hadn't been for that bottle I wouldn't have gone out again at all, see, and I wouldn't know it was him that killed her, and it wasn't me, it *wasn't*.'

He came to what appeared in his own mind to be a halt, but as far as Wyfold, Oliver and myself were concerned he had stopped short of enough.

'Are you saying,' Wyfold said, 'That you walked back from the village with the other grooms, knowing what you would find?'

'Well, yeah. Only Dave and Sammy, see, they'd got back first, and when I got back there was an ambulance there and such, and I just kept in the background.'

What did you do with the other five bottles of shampoo?'

Wyfold asked. 'We searched all the rooms in the hotel. We didn't find any shampoo.'

The first overwhelming promptings of fear were beginning to die down in Shane, but he answered with only minimal hesitation, 'I took them down the road a ways and threw them in a ditch. That was after they'd gone off to the hospital.' He nodded in the general direction of Oliver and myself. 'Panicked me a bit, it did, when Dave said she was talking, like. But I was glad I'd got rid of the stuff afterwards, when she was dead after all, with everyone snooping around.'

'You could show me which ditch?' Wyfold said.'

'Yeah, I could.'

'Good.'

'You mean,' Shane said, with relief, 'you believe what I told you ...'

'No, I don't mean that,' Wyfold said repressively. 'I'll need to know what you ordinarily did with the shampoo.'

'What?'

'How you prepared it and gave it to the mares.'

'Oh.' An echo of the cocky cleverness came back: a swagger to the shoulders, a curl to the lip. 'It was dead easy, see. Mr Jackson showed me how. I just had to put a coffee filter in a wash basin and pour the shampoo through it, so's the shampoo all ran down the drain and there was that stuff left on the paper, then I just turned the coffee filter inside out and soaked it in a little jar with some linseed oil from the feed shed, and then I'd stir a quarter of it into the feed it it was for a mare I was looking after anyway, or let the stuff fall to the bottom and scrape up a teaspoonful and put it in an apple for the others. Mr Jackson showed me how. Dead easy, the whole thing.'

'How many mares did you give it to?'

'Don't rightly know. Dozens, counting last year. Some I missed. Mr Jackson said better to miss some than be found out. He liked me to do the oil best. Said too many apples would be noticed.' A certain amount of anxiety returned. 'Look, now I've told you all this, you know I didn't kill her, don't you?'

Wyfold said impassively, 'How often did Mr Jackson bring you bottles of shampoo?'

'He didn't. I mean, I had a case of it under my bed. Brought it with me when I moved in, see, same as last year. But this year

I ran out, like, so I rang up from the village one night for some more. So he said he'd meet me at the back gate at nine on Sunday when all the lads would be down in the pub.'

'That was a risk he wouldn't take,' Wyfold said sceptically.

'Well, he did.'

Wyfold shook his head.

Shane's panic resurfaced completely. 'He was there,' he almost shouted. 'He was. He *was*.'

Wyfold still looked studiedly unconvinced and told Shane that it would be best if he now made a formal statement, which the sergeant would write down for him to sign when he, Shane, was satisfied that it represented what he had already told us: and Shane in slight bewilderment agreed.

Wyfold nodded to the sergeant, opened the door of the room, and gestured to Oliver and me to leave. Oliver in indiluted grimness silently pushed me out. Wyfold, with a satisfied air, said in his plain uncushioning way, 'There you are then, Mr Knowles, that's how your daughter died, and you're luckier than some. That little sod's telling the truth. Proud of himself, like a lot of crooks. Wants the world to know.' He shook hands perfunctorily with Oliver and nodded briefly to me, and walked away to his unsolved horrors where the papers called for his blood and other fathers choked on their tears.

Oliver pushed me back to the outside world but not directly to where my temporary chauffeur had said he would wait. I found myself making an unscheduled turn into a small public garden, where Oliver abruptly left me beside the first seat we came to and walked jerkily away.

I watched his back, ramrod stiff, disappearing behind bushes and trees. In grief, as in all else, he would be tidy.

A boy came along the path on roller skates and wheeled round to a stop in front of me.

'You want pushing?' he said.

'No. But thanks all the same.'

He looked at me judiciously. 'Can you make that chair go straight, using just one arm?'

'No. I go round in a circle and end where I started.'

'Thought so.' He considered me gravely. 'Just like the earth,' he said.

He pushed off with one foot and sailed away straight on the

other and presently, walking firmly, Oliver came back.

He sat on the bench beside me, his eyelids slightly reddened, his manner calm.

'Sorry,' he said, after a while.

'She died happy,' I said. 'It's better than nothing.'

'How do you mean?'

'She heard what they were doing.She picked up the shampoo Shane dropped. She was coming to tell you that everything was all right, there was nothing wrong with Sandcastle and you wouldn't lose the farm. At the moment she died she must have been full of joy.'

Oliver raised his face to the pale summer sky.

'Do you think so?'

'Yes, I do.'

'Then I'll believe it,' he said.

544

The Third Year

OCTOBER

Gordon was coming up to sixty, the age at which everyone retired from Ekaterin's, like it or not. the bustle of young brains, the founder Paul had said, was what kept money moving, and his concept still ruled in the house.

Gordon had his regrets but they were balanced, it seemed to me, by a sense of relief. He had battled for three years now against his palsy and had finished the allotted work span honourably in the face of the enemy within. He began saying he was looking forward to his leisure, and that he and Judith would go on a celebratory journey as soon as possible. Before that, however, he was to be away for a day of medical tests in hospital.

'Such a bore,' he said, 'but they want to make these checks and set me up before we travel.'

'Very sensible,' I said. 'Where will you go?'

He smiled with enthusiasm. 'I've always wanted to see Australia. Never been there, you know.

'Nor have I.'

He nodded and we continued with our normal work in the accord we had felt together for so many years. I would miss him badly for his own sake, I thought, and even more because through him I would no longer have constant news and contact with Judith. The days seemed to gallop towards his birthday and my spirits grew heavy as his lightened.

Oliver's problems were no longer the day-to-day communiqués at lunch. The dissenting director had conceded that even blue-chip certainties weren't always proof against well-planned malice and no longer grumbled about my part in things, particularly since the day that Henry in his mild-steel voice made observations about defending the bank's money beyond the call of duty.

'And beyond the call of common sense,' Val murmured in my ear. 'Thank goodness.'

Oliver's plight had been extensively aired by Alec in *What's Going On Where It Shouldn't*, thanks to comprehensive leaks from one of Ekaterin's directors; to wit, me.

Some of the regular newspapers had danced round the subject, since with Shane still awaiting trial the business of poisoning mares was supposed to be sub judice. Alec's paper with its usual disrespect for secrecy had managed to let everyone in the bloodstock industry know that Sandcastle himself was rock-solid investment, and that any foals already born perfect would not be carrying any damaging genes.

As for the mares covered this year, [the paper continued] there is a lottery as to whether they will produce deformed foals or not. Breeders are advised to let their mares go to term, because there is a roughly fifty per cent chance that the foal will be perfect. Breeders of mares who produce deformed or imperfect foals will, we understand, have their stallion fees refunded and expenses reimbursed.

The bloodstock industry is drawing up its own special guidelines to deal with this exceptional case.

Meanwhile, fear not. Sandcastle is potent, fertile and fully reinstated. Apply without delay for a place in next year's programme.

Alec himself telephoned me in the office two days after the column appeared.

'How do you like it?' he said.

'Absolutely great.'

'The editor says the newsagents in Newmarket have been ringing up like mad for extra copies.'

'Hm,' I said. 'I think perhaps I'll get a list of all breeders and bloodstock agents and personally — I mean anonymously —

send each of them a copy of your column, if your editor would agree.'

'Do it without asking him,' Alec said. 'He would probably prefer it. We won't sue you for infringement of copyright, I'll promise you.'

'Thanks a lot,' I said. 'You've been really great.'

'Wait till you get an eyeful of the next issue. I'm working on it now. *Do-it-yourself-Miracles*, that's the heading. How does it grab you?'

'Fine.'

'The dead can't sue,' he said cheerfully. 'I just hope I spell the drugs right.'

'I sent you the list,' I protested.

'The typesetters,' he said, 'can scramble eggs, let alone sulphanilamide.'

'See you someday,' I said, smiling.

'Yeah. Pie and beer. We'll fix it.'

His miracle-working column in the next issue demolished Calder's reputation entirely and made further progress towards restoring Sandcastle's and after a third bang on the Sandcastle-is-tops going in the issue after that, Oliver thankfully reported that confidence both in his stallion and his stud farm was creeping back. Two thirds of the nominations were filled already, and enquiries were arriving for the rest.

'One of the breeders whose mare is in foal now is threatening to sue me for negligence, but the bloodstock associations are trying to dissuade him. He can't do anything, anyway, until after Shane's trial and after the foal is born, and I just hope to God it's one that's perfect.'

From the bank's point of vew his affairs were no longer in turmoil. The board had agreed to extend the period of the loan for three extra years, and Val, Gordon and I had worked out the rates at which Oliver could repay without crippling himself. All finally rested on Sandcastle, but if his progeny should prove to have inherited his speed, Oliver should in the end reach the prosperity and prestige for which he had aimed.

'But let's not,' Henry said, smiling one day over roast lamb, 'let's not make a habit of going to the races.'

Gordon came to the office one Monday saying he had met Dissdale the day before at lunch in a restaurant which they both liked.

'He was most embarrassed to see me,' Gordon said. 'But I had quite a talk with him. He really didn't know, you know, that Calder was a fake. He says he can hardly believe, even now, that the cures weren't cures, or that Calder actually killed two people. Very subdued, he was, for Dissdale.'

'I suppose,' I said diffidently, 'You didn't ask him if he and Calder had ever bought, cured and sold sick animals before Indian Silk.'

'Yes, I did, actually, because of your thoughts. But he said they hadn't. Indian Silk was the first, and Dissdale rather despondently said he supposed Calder and Ian Pargetter couldn't bear to see all their time and trouble go to waste, so when Ian Pargetter couldn't persuade Fred Barnet to try Calder, Calder sent Dissdale to buy the horse outright.'

'And it worked a treat.'

Gordon nodded. 'Another thing Dissdale said was that Calder was as stunned as he was himself to find it was Ekaterin's who had lent the money for Sandcastle. There had been no mention of it in the papers. Dissdale asked me to tell you that when he told Calder who it was who had actually put up the money, Calder said 'My God' several times and walked up and down all evening and drank far more than usual. Dissdale didn't know why, and Calder wouldn't tell him, but Dissdale says he thinks now it was because Calder was feeling remorse at hammering Ekaterin's after an Ekaterin had saved his life.'

'Dissdale,' I said dryly, 'is still trying to find excuses for his hero.'

'And for his own admiration of him,' Gordon agreed. 'But perhaps its true. Dissdale said Calder had liked you very much.'

Liked me, and apologised, and tried to kill me: that too.

Movement had slowly returned to my shoulder and arm once the body-restricting plaster had come off, and via electrical treatment, exercise and massage normal strength had returned.

In the ankle department things weren't quite so good: I still after more than four months wore a brace, though now of removable aluminium and strapping, not plaster. No one would promise I'd be able to ski on the final outcome and meanwhile all but the shortest journeys required sticks. I had tired of hopping up and down my Hampstead stairs on my return there to the extent of renting a flat of my own with a lift to take me aloft and a garage in the basement, and I reckoned life had basically become reasonable again on the day I drove out of there in my car: automatic gear change, no work for the left foot, perfect.

A day or two before he was due to go into hospital for his check-up Gordon mentioned in passing that Judith was coming to collect him from the bank after work to go with him to the hospital, where he would be spending the night so as to be rested for the whole day of tests on Friday.

She would collect him again on Friday evening and they would go home together, and he would have the weekend to rest in before he returned to the office on Monday.

'I'll be glad when it's over,' he said frankly. 'I hate all the needles and the pulling and pushing about.'

'When Judith has settled you in, would she like me to give her some dinner before she goes home?' I said.

He looked across with interest, the idea taking root. 'I should think she would love it. I'll ask her.'

He returned the next day saying Judith was pleased, and we arranged between us that when she left him in the hospital she would come to join me in a convenient restaurant that we all knew well: and on the following day, Thursday, the plan was duly carried out.

She came with a glowing face, eyes sparkling, white teeth gleaming; wearing a blue full-skirted dress and shoes with high heels.

'Gordon is fine, apart from grumbling about tomorrow,' she reported, 'and they gave him almost no supper, to his disgust. He says to think of him during our fillet steaks.'

I doubt if we did. I don't remember what we ate. The feast was there before me on the other side of the small table, Judith looking beautiful and telling me nonsensical things like what happens to a blasé refrigerator when you pull its plug out.

'What, then?'

'It loses its cool.'

I laughed at the stupidity of it and brimmed over with the intoxication of having her there to myself, and I wished she was

549

my own wife so fiercely that my muscles ached.

'You'll be going to Australia ...' I said.

'Australia?' She hesitated. 'We leave in three weeks.'

'It's so soon.'

'Gordon's sixty the week after next,' hse said. 'You know he is. There's the party.'

Henry, Val and I had clubbed together to give Gordon a small sending-off in the office after his last day's work, an affair to which most of the banking managers and their wives had been invited.

'I hate him going,' I said.

'To Australia?'

'From the bank.'

We drank wine and coffee and told each other much without saying a word. Not until we were nearly leaving did she say tentatively 'We'll be away for months, you know.'

My feelings must have shown. 'Months ... How many?'

'We don't know. We're going to all the places Gordon or I have wanted to see that couldn't be fitted into an ordinary holiday. We're going to potter. Bits of Europe, bits of the Middle East, India, Singapore, Bali, then Australia, New Zealand, Tahiti, Fiji, Hawaii, America.' She fell silent, her eyes not laughing now but full of sadness.

I swallowed. 'Gordon will find it exhausting.'

'He says not. He passionately wants to go, and I know he's always yearned to have the time to see things ... and we're going slowly, with lots of rests.'

The restaurant had emptied around us and the waiters hovered with polite faces willing us to go. Judith put on her blue coat and we went outside onto the cold pavement.

'How do you plan to go home now?' I asked.

'Underground.'

'I'll drive you,' I said.

She gave me a small smile and nodded, and we walked slowly across the road to where I'd left the car. She sat in beside me and I did all the automatic things like switching on the lights and letting off the handbrake, and I drove all the way to Clapham without consciously seeing the road.

Gordon's house behind the big gates lay quiet and dark. Judith looked up at its bulk and then at me, and I leaned across in the car and put my arms round her and kissed her. She came close to me, kissing me back with a feeling and a need that seemed as intense as my own, and for a while we stayed in that way, floating in passion, dreaming in deep unaccustomed touch.

As if of one mind we each at the same time drew back and slowly relaxed against the seat. She put her hand on mine and threaded her fingers through, holding tight.

I looked ahead through the windscreen, seeing trees against the stars: seeing nothing.

A long time passed.

'We can't,' I said eventually.

'No.'

'Especially not,' I said, 'in his own house.'

'No.'

After another long minute she let go of my hand and opened the door beside her, and I too opened mine.

'Don't get out,' she said, 'because of your ankle.'

I stood up however on the driveway and she walked round the car towards me. We hugged each other but without kissing, a long hungry minute of body against body; commitment and farewell.

'I'll see you,' she said, 'at the party'; and we both knew how it would be, with Lorna Shipton talking about watching Henry's weight and Henry flirting roguishly with Judith whenever he could, and everyone talking loudly and clapping Gordon on the back.

She walked over to the front door and unlocked it, and looked back, briefly, once, and then went in, putting the walls between us in final, mutual, painful decison.

The Third Year

DECEMBER

I felt alone and also lonely, which I'd never been before, and I telephoned to Pen one Sunday in December and suggested taking her out to lunch. She said to come early as she had to open her shop at four, and I arrived at eleven thirty to find coffee percolating richly and Pen trying to unravel the string of the Christmas kite.

'I found it when I was looking for some books,' she said. 'It's so pretty. When we've had coffee, let's go out and fly it.'

We took it onto the common, and she let the string out gradually until the dragon was high on the wind, circling and darting and fluttering its frilly tail. It took us slowly after it across the grass, Pen delightedly intent and I simply pleased to be back there in that place.

She glanced at me over her shoulder. 'Are we going too far for your ankle? Or too fast?'

'No and no,' I said.

'Still taking the comfrey?'

'Religiously.'

The bones and other tissue round my shoulder had mended fast, I'd been told, and although the ankle still lagged I was prepared to give comfrey the benefit of the doubt. Anything which would restore decent mobility attracted my enthusiasm: life with brace and walking stick, still boringly necessary, made even buying groceries a pest.

We had reached a spot on a level with Gordon and Judith's

house when a gust of wind took the kite suddenly higher, setting it weaving and diving in bright-coloured arcs and stretching its land-line to tautness. Before anything could be done the string snapped and the dazzling butterfly wings soared away free, rising in a spiral, disappearing to a shape, to a black dot, to nothing.

'What a pity,' Pen said, turning to me with disappointment and then pausing, seeing where my own gaze had travelled downwards to the tall cream gates, firmly shut.

'Let her go,' Pen said soberly, 'like the kite.'

'She'll come back.'

'Take out some other girl,' she urged.

I smiled lop-sidedly. 'I'm out of practice.'

'But you can't spend your whole life ...' she stopped momentarily, and then said, 'Parkinson's disease isn't fatal. Gordon could live to be eighty or more.'

'I wouldn't want him dead,' I protested. 'How could you think it?'

'Then what?'

'Just to go on, I suppose, as we are.'

She took my arm and turned me away from the gates to return to her house.

'Give it time,' she said. 'You've got months. You both have.'

'I glanced at her. 'Both?'

'Gordon and I don't go around with our eyes shut.'

'He's never said anything ...'

'She smiled. 'Gordon likes you better than you like him, if possible. Trusts you, too.' She paused. 'Let her go, Tim, for your own sake.'

We went silently back to her house and I thought of all that had happened since the day Gordon stood in the fountain, and of all I had learned and felt and loved and lost. Thought of Ginnie and Oliver and Calder, and of all the gateways I'd gone though to grief and pain and the knowledge of death. So much — to much — compressed into so small a span.

'You're a child of the light,' Pen said contentedly. 'Both you and Judith. You always take sunshine with you. I don't suppose you know it, but everything brightens when people like you walk in.' She glanced down at my slow foot. 'Sorry. When you limp in. So carry the sunlight to a new young girl who isn't married to Gordon and doesn't break your heart.' She paused. 'That's good pharmacological advice, so take it.'

'Yes, doctor,' I said: and knew I couldn't.

On Christmas Eve when I had packed to go to Jersey and was checking around the flat before leaving, the telephone rang.

'Hello,' I said.

There was a series of clicks and hums and I was about to put the receiver down when a breathless voice said, 'Tim ...'

'Judith?' I said incredulously.

'Yes.'

'Where are you?'

'Listen, just listen. I don't know who else to ask, not at Christmas ... Gordon's ill and I'm alone and I don't know, I don't know ...'

'Where are you?'

'India ... He's in hospital. They're very good, very kind, but he's so ill ... unconscious ... they say cerebral haemorrhage ... I'm so afraid ... I do so love him ...' She was suddenly crying, and trying not to, the words coming out at intervals when control was possible. 'It's so much to ask ... but I need ... help.'

'Tell me where,' I said. 'I'll come at once.'

'Oh ...'

She told me where. I was packed and ready to go, and I went.

Because of the date and the off-track destination there were delays and it took me forty hours to get there. Gordon died before I reached her, on the day after Christmas, like her mother.